P9-CNB-481

"MAGNIFICENT."
—*Publishers Weekly* (starred review)

"Fans of Sharon Kay Penman's writing know what to hungrily anticipate in her massive historical novels; total immersion into the turbulent world of the Middle Ages, intricate plots that chime with the authenticity of meticulous research, and enough noble and nefarious characters to populate a Cecil B. DeMille epic. Penman, a virtuoso storyteller, is well-nigh unmatched at restoring vigorous, passionate life to the people and places of a shadowy, bygone Britain. . . . Her sure sense of history is one hallmark of Penman's writing, but equally important to her success is the depth of respect and admiration she accords all her wealth of characters. As their lives ricochet from the soap opera of bedrooms to the Shakespearean drama of the battlefield, small touches render them human; the grand gesture makes them heroic."

—*The Orlando Sentinel*

"Tirelessly researched . . . Demonstrates a keen understanding of its time and place and renders historical figures in terms of flesh and blood rather than as cardboard cutouts . . . A place to lose oneself for hours on end."

—*Booklist*

"Gorgeously presented . . . Filled with period detail, teeming with scheming men and strong women."

—*San Jose Mercury News*

"Penman's greatest strength in this, as in all her books, is her ability to bring these legendary characters to life. She paints them with an astounding intimacy."

—*Austin American Statesman*

When Christ and His Saints Slept

ALSO BY SHARON KAY PENMAN

The Sunne in Splendour

Here Be Dragons

Falls the Shadow

The Reckoning

SHARON KAY PENMAN

When Christ and His Saints Slept

BALLANTINE BOOKS · NEW YORK

Sale of this book without a front cover may be unauthorized. If this book is coverless, it may have been reported to the publisher as "unsold or destroyed" and neither the author nor the publisher may have received payment for it.

Copyright © 1995 by Sharon Kay Penman

All rights reserved under International and Pan-American Copyright Conventions. Published in the United States by Ballantine Books, a division of Random House, Inc., New York, and distributed in Canada by Random House of Canada Limited, Toronto.

This edition published by arrangement with Henry Holt and Company.

Library of Congress Catalog Card Number: 95-94983

ISBN: 0-345-39668-5

Cover design by Barbara Leff and Min Choi
Cover illustration by Brian Leister

Manufactured in the United States of America

First Ballantine Books Edition: February 1996
10 9 8 7 6

To Valerie Ptak LaMont

King William I m. Matilda
(1066–1087) of Flanders

Stephen m. Adela
Count of Blois

King William Rufus
(1087–1100)

Robert
Duke of Normandy

William Clito

Theobald
Count of Blois

Issue

Henry
Bishop of Winchester

Matilda m. Stephen
de Boulogne
King of England
(1135–1154)

Baldwin

Matilda

William

Mary

Eustace

===== Broken Line Denotes Illegitimacy

©1995 A·Karl/J·Kemp

Issue King Henry I m. Maude
(1100–1135) of Scotland

William Maude m. (2nd) Geoffrey
m. (1st) Count of Anjou
German
Emperor
Heinrich V

Issue

Henry William

Geoffrey

Rainald m. Beatrice
Earl of Cornwall

Issue

Robert m. Amabel Fitz Hamon
Earl of Gloucester

William Roger Maud m. Randolf
de Gernons, Earl of Chester

Philip Issue

Issue

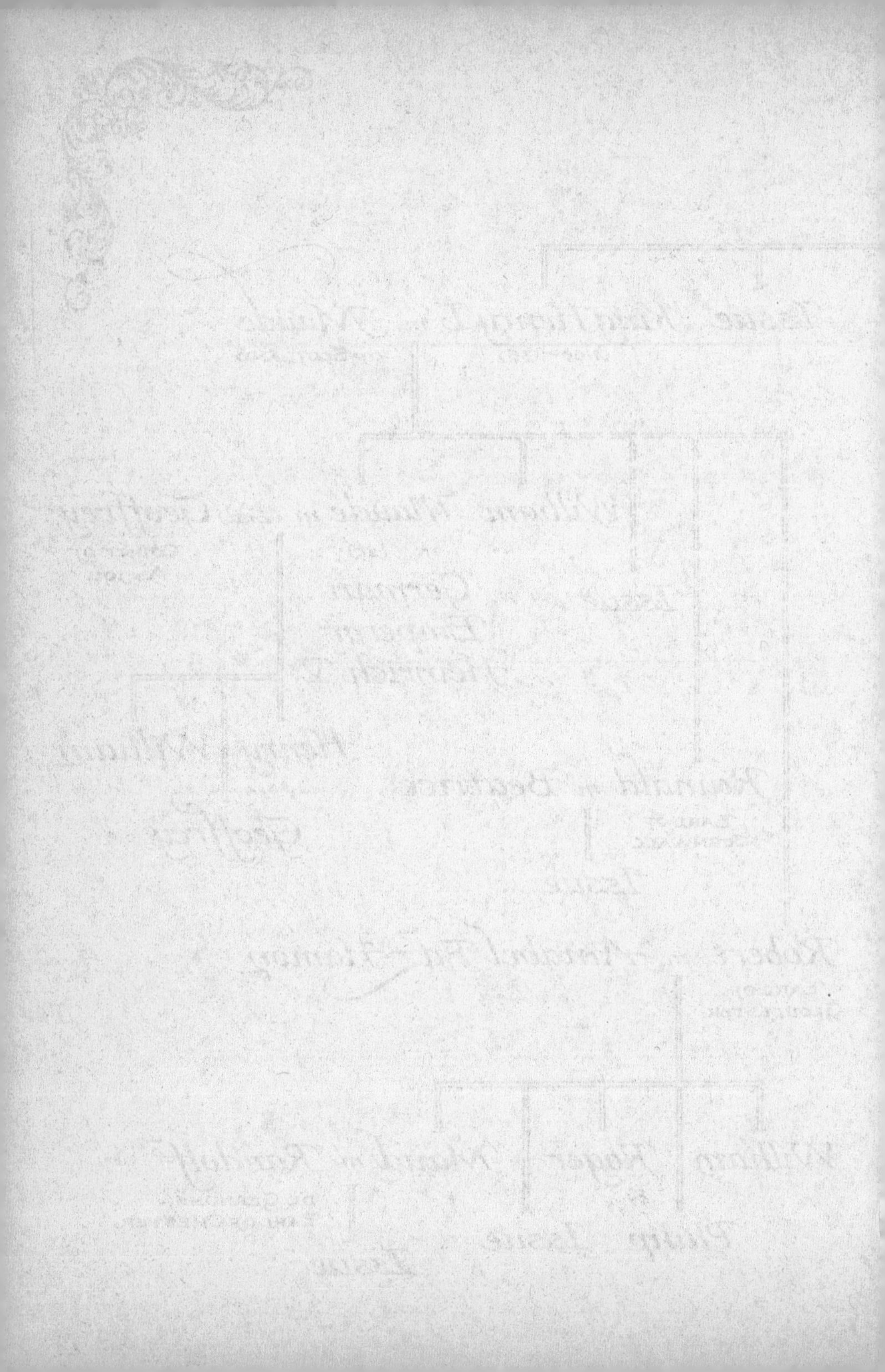

Never before had there been greater wretchedness in the country. . . . And they said openly that Christ and his saints slept.

—THE PETERBOROUGH CHRONICLE

ENGLAND
English Channel
FLANDERS
Barfleur
Rouen
Pacy
Castle
Caen
NORMANDY
Falaise
Argentan
PARIS
Chartres
ÎLE
DE
FRANCE
CHAMPAGNE
BRITTANY
Domfront
Castle
Le Mans
Beaugency
BURGUNDY
Château-
du-Loir
Blois
Angers
Tours
ANJOU
FRANCE
Fontevrault
Abbey
POITOU
Poitiers
Bay
of
Biscay
LA
MARCHE
AQUITAINE
Bordeaux
Miles
0
100
0
100
Kms.
GASCONY
©A·Karl/J·Kemp, 1995

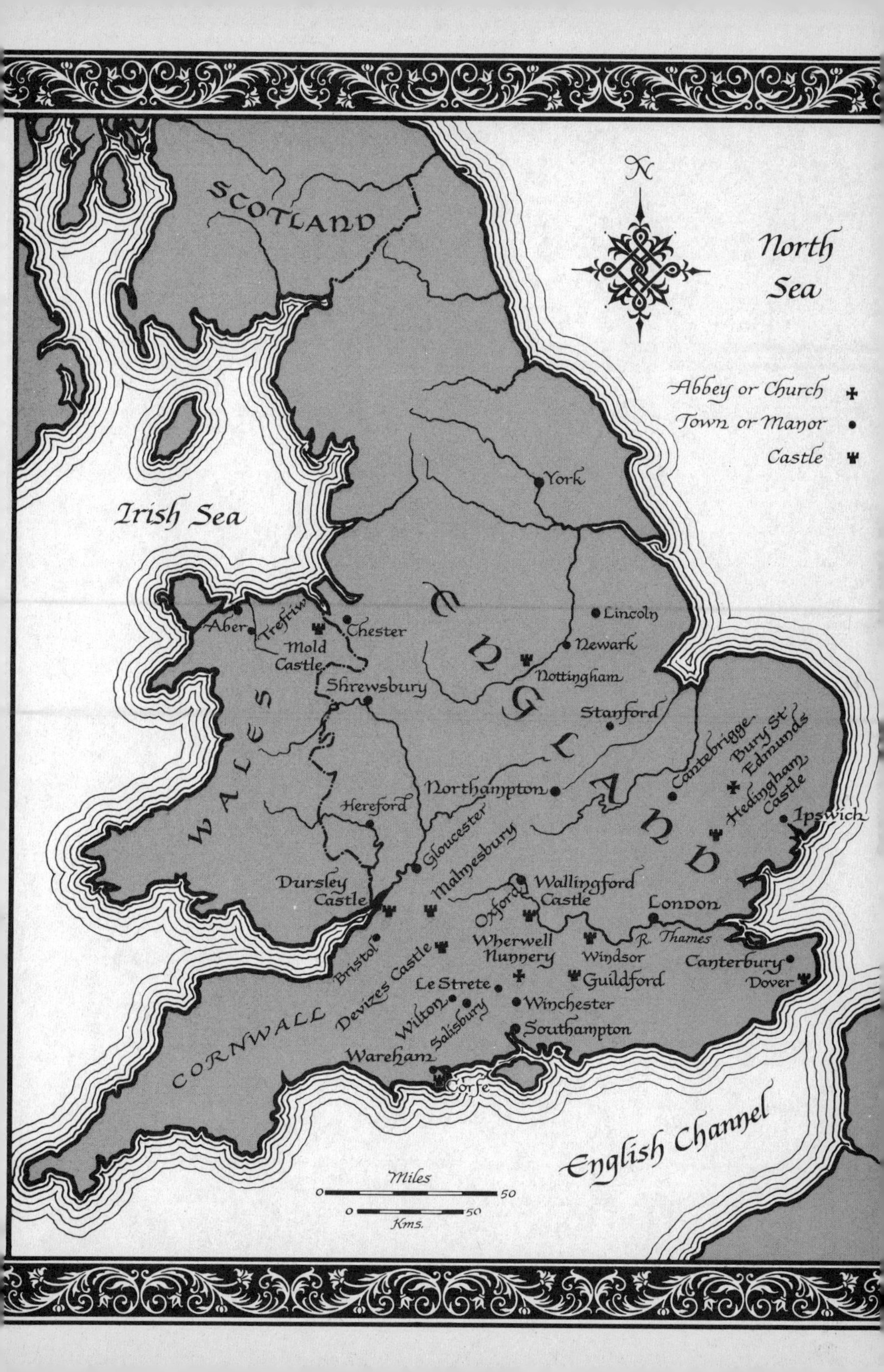
N
North Sea
Abbey or Church
Town or Manor
Castle
SCOTLAND
Irish Sea
ENGLAND
WALES
CORNWALL
York
Lincoln
Newark
Nottingham
Stanford
Chester
Aber
Trefriw
Mold Castle
Shrewsbury
Hereford
Northampton
Cantebrigge
Bury St Edmunds
Hedingham Castle
Ipswich
Gloucester
Malmesbury
Dursley Castle
Wallingford Castle
Oxford
London
R. Thames
Bristol
Devizes Castle
Wherwell Nunnery
Windsor
Canterbury
Dover
Le Strete
Guildford
Wilton
Salisbury
Winchester
Southampton
Wareham
Corfe
English Channel
Miles
0
50
0
50
Kms.

When Christ and His Saints Slept

Prologue

CHARTRES CATHEDRAL, FRANCE

January 1101

STEPHEN was never to forget his fifth birthday, for that was the day he lost his father. In actual fact, that wasn't precisely so. But childhood memories are not woven from facts alone, and that was how he would remember it.

He'd come with his parents and two elder brothers to this great church of the Blessed Mary to hear a bishop preach about the Crusade. He didn't know who the bishop was, but his sermon was a long, dull one, and Stephen had fidgeted and squirmed through most of it, for he was safely out of his mother's reach. She had no patience with childhood mischief, no patience with mischief of any kind. "Remember who you are" was her favorite maternal rebuke, and her older children had soon learned to disregard that warning at their peril.

But it puzzled Stephen; why would he forget? He knew very well who he was: Stephen of Blois, son and namesake of the Count of Blois and the Lady Adela, daughter of William the Bastard, King of England and Duke of Normandy. Stephen had never met his celebrated grandfather, but he knew he'd been a great man. His mother often said so.

Stephen knew about the Crusade, too, for people talked about it all the time. His father had taken the cross, gone off to free the Holy Land from the infidel. Stephen was still in his cradle then, and two when his father came back. There was something shameful about his return. Stephen did not understand why, though, for he was convinced his father could do no wrong, not the man who laughed so often and winked at minor misdeeds and had promised him a white pony for this long-awaited fifth birthday. Stephen had already picked out a name—Snowball—so sure he was that his father would not forget, that the pony would be waiting for them back at the castle.

Stephen had hoped they'd be returning there once the Mass was done, but instead they lingered out in the cloisters with the bishop, discussing the new army of crusaders that was making ready to join its Christian brethren in the Holy Land. Ignored by the adults, bored and restless, Stephen soon slipped back into the cathedral.

Within, all was shadowed and still. With the candles quenched and the parishioners gone, the church seemed unfamiliar to Stephen, like a vast, dark cave. Sun-blinded, he tripped over a prayer cushion and sprawled onto the tiled floor. But he was not daunted by a scraped knee, scrambled up, and groped his way down the nave toward the choir.

He was curious to get a better look at the Sancta Camisia, draped over a reliquary upon the High Altar. Up close, though, it was a disappointment, just a faded chemise, frayed and wrinkled. He'd expected something fancier, mayhap cloth of gold or spangled silk, for this shabby garment was among the most revered relics in Christendom, said to have been worn by the Blessed Lady Mary as she gave birth to the Holy Christ Child. Stephen's eldest brother, Will, had once dared to ask how it could have survived so many centuries and their mother had slapped him across the mouth for such blasphemy. Carefully wiping his hand on his tunic, Stephen was reaching out to touch the Sancta Camisia when the door opened suddenly, spilling sunlight into the nave.

Stephen ducked down behind the High Altar, willing these intruders to go away. Instead, the footsteps came nearer. When he peeped around the altar cloth, he gasped in dismay. It would be bad enough to be caught by a priest, but this was far worse. He feared his mother's wrath more than the anger of priests and bishops, even more than God's, for He was in Heaven and Mama was right here in Chartres.

Adela stopped before she reached the High Altar, but she was still so close that Stephen could almost have touched her skirts. The second set of footsteps was heavier and familiar. Some of Stephen's anxiety began to abate now that his father was here, too. He still hoped to escape detection, though, for discipline was his mother's province.

"I cannot believe you hold my life so cheaply, Adela." Stephen knew his parents had been quarreling for days, but his father did not sound angry now; to Stephen, he sounded tired and even sad.

"I am your wife, Stephen. Of course I value your life. But I value your honour, too . . . more than you do, I fear."

"That is not fair! When the Crusade was first preached, I took the cross, more to please you than God, if truth be told. And now you would have me go back? Are you that eager to be a widow?"

"I am not sending you back to die, Stephen, but to redeem your honour. You owe your sons that, and you owe me that. You must fulfill your crusader's vow. If not, you'll live out all your days haunted by the shame of Antioch."

"Christ Jesus, woman . . . I've told you again and again why I left the siege. I was ailing and disheartened and sickened by all the needless killing—"

"How can you say that? What greater glory could there be than to die for the liberation of Jerusalem?"

"Jerusalem has been liberated, Adela, more than a year ago—"

"Yes, but you were not there to see it, were you? No, you were back at Chartres, taking your ease whilst Christians were being slain by enemies of the True Faith!"

There was silence after that, lasting so long that the little boy risked a covert glance over the top of the High Altar. His parents were standing several feet away, looking at each other. "You've shared my bed for nigh on twenty years, Adela; you know every scar my body bears, battle scars, all of them. You ought to have been the last one to doubt my courage. Instead, you were amongst the first. So be it, then. I will do what you demand of me. I will take the cross again, go back to that accursed land, and make you proud," the count said, so tonelessly that his son shivered.

Stephen did not hear his mother's response, for he'd thrust his fist into his mouth, biting down on his thumb. His vision blurred as he sought to blink back tears. Footsteps were receding, a door clanging shut. Getting to his feet, Stephen left the shelter of the High Altar, only to find himself face-to-face with his father.

The Count of Blois was clearly taken aback. He caught his breath on an oath, was starting to frown when Stephen whispered, "Do not go away, Papa . . ."

"Ah, lad . . ." And then Stephen was swept up in his father's arms, being held in a close embrace as he dried his tears on the count's soft wool mantle.

"Why do you have to go, Papa?" He'd once asked his father what the Holy Land was like, and still remembered the terse reply: "A hellish place." "You do not want to go back," he said, "so stay here, please do not go away . . ."

"I have no choice." His father rarely called Stephen by his given name, preferring "lad" or "sprout" or a playful "imp." He did now, though, saying "Stephen" quietly, sounding sad again. "I'd hoped to wait until you were older . . . When I was in the Holy Land, I made a mistake. It did not seem so at the time. It was, though, the greatest mistake of my life. We'd been besieging Antioch for nigh on eight months. I'd been taken ill with fever, had withdrawn to nearby Alexandretta. The day after I left, our forces captured the city. But then a large Saracen army arrived and trapped them within Antioch. They seemed doomed for certes, and I . . . well, I chose to go home, back to Blois."

He paused, ruffling Stephen's hair, the same tawny shade as his own, before resuming reluctantly. "But the crusaders besieged in Antioch were saved by a miracle. You see, lad, they found an ancient lance in one of Antioch's churches, supposedly revealed in a vision from God. Whether this was truly the Holy Lance that had pierced Our Lord Christ on the Cross or not, what matters is that men believed it to be so. They marched out of Antioch to confront the Saracen army, and against all odds, won a great victory. So Antioch was spared and I . . . I was shamed before all of Christendom, what I saw as common sense seen by others as cowardice . . ."

He paused again, and then set the boy back on his feet. "I know you do not understand what I am telling you, lad, but—"

"Yes, I do!" Stephen insisted, although all he truly understood was that his father was going away and for a long time. "Papa . . . promise me," he said. "Promise me you'll come back soon." And he took comfort when his father readily promised him that he would, for he was too young to be troubled by the softly added words, "God Willing."

STEPHEN convinced himself that his father would come back when his mother's new baby was born, for he knew grown people made much ado about babies. But his brother was born and christened Henry and his father did not come.

That summer Henry was stricken with croup. Stephen was fond of Henry; he'd been delighted to have a brother younger than he was. Although he worried about Henry's cough, it also occurred to him that the baby's illness would likely bring their father home. But it was not to be. Henry got better; their father did not return.

Stephen's faith did not falter, though. It would be Christmas for certes. It was not. His sixth birthday, then. Again he was disappointed. And then at Easter, they got the letter Stephen had been awaiting every day for the past thirteen months, the letter that said his father was finally coming home.

JULY was hot and dry in that year of God's Grace, 1102. August brought no relief; the sky over Chartres was a glazed, brittle blue, and the roads leading into the city were clogged with pilgrims and choked with dust. It was midmorning, almost time for dinner. Stephen had gone down to the stables to see a recently whelped litter of greyhounds. Playing with the puppies raised his spirits somewhat, but he was still perturbed by his mother's revelation, that she meant to send him to England, to live at the court of the king.

Seeing his distress, she'd impatiently assured him that he would not be going for a while yet, not until he was older. But he must set his mind to it, that his future lay in England. His elder two brothers would inherit their father's titles, his little brother, Henry, would be pledged to the Church, and he, Stephen, would go to her brother Henry, the English king.

Stephen did not want to go so far away, to live with strangers. He let a puppy lick his hand, reminding himself that his father would be back soon, surely by summer's end, and Papa would not let him be sent away. He felt better then and dropped to his knees in the straw beside the squirming balls of brindle and fawn fur. He lost all track of time, and was still in the stables when his mother came looking for him later that afternoon.

Stephen jumped to his feet in alarm, for he'd forgotten all about dinner. "I . . . I am sorry, Mama," he stammered, but she did not seem to hear his flustered apology. Even in that dimmed light, he saw how pale she was. Her hands were clasped together, so tightly that her rings were being driven into her flesh, and her mouth was thinned and tautly set, as if to keep secrets from escaping. "Mama?" he said uneasily. "Mama?"

"God's Will is not always to be understood," she said abruptly, "but it must be accepted. So it is now, Stephen. A letter has come from the Holy Land. Your lord father is dead."

Stephen stared at her, his eyes flickering from her face to the coral rosary entwined around her clutching fingers. "But . . . but Papa was coming home," he said, "he promised . . ."

Adela blinked rapidly, looked away. All of her sons had gotten their father's fair coloring, but only Stephen had been blessed—or cursed—with his obliging, generous nature, one utterly lacking in rancor or guile but lacking, too, in the steely self-discipline and single-minded tenacity that had enabled her father to conquer and then rule two turbulent domains, England and Normandy.

"Your father's departure for home was delayed by bad weather," she said, and managed to steady both her voice and her resolve by sheer force of will, for she must not show weakness now, not before the child. "He was still at Jaffa when King Baldwin of Jerusalem sought his aid in laying siege to Ramleh. But they were greatly outnumbered. Baldwin was one of the few to escape. Your father . . . he held fast and was slain."

Stephen's mouth had begun to quiver, his eyes to fill with tears, and Adela reached out swiftly, pulling him toward her. "No, Stephen," she said. "You must not weep. He died a noble, proud death, in the service of Almighty God and a Christian king. Do not grieve for him, lad. Be thankful that he has atoned for his past sins and gained by his crusader's death the surety of salvation, life everlasting in the Kingdom of Heaven."

But it was your fault! Papa did not want to go, and you made him. If not for you, he would not be dead and gone away. The words were struggling to break free, burning Stephen's throat, too hot to hold back. But he must, for those were words he dared not say aloud. To stop himself, he bit down on his tongue until he tasted blood, then stood rigid and mute in his mother's embrace as she talked to him of honour and pride and Christian duty.

After a time, she grazed his cheek with one of her rare kisses and withdrew. Stephen retreated into the shadows, into an empty stall. Flinging himself down into the matted, trampled straw, he wept for his father, who'd died at Ramleh, alone and far from home.

1

BARFLEUR, NORMANDY

November 1120

THE ship strained at its moorings, like a horse eager to run. Berold stopped so abruptly that he almost collided with a passing sailor, for in all of his sixteen years, he'd never seen a sight so entrancing. The esneque seemed huge to him, at least eighty feet long, with a towering mast and a square sail striped in vertical bands of yellow and scarlet. The hull was as sleek as a swan and just as white, and brightly painted shields hung over the gunwales, protecting the oarsmen from flying spray. Above the mast flew several streaming pennants and a silver and red banner of St George. The harbor resembled a floating forest, so many masts were swaying and bobbing on the rising tide. More than twenty ships were taking on cargo and passengers, for the royal fleet of the English King Henry, first of that name since the Conquest, was making ready to sail. But Berold had eyes only for the White Ship.

"Smitten, are you, lad?" Startled, Berold spun around, found himself looking into eyes narrowed and creased from searching out distant horizons and squinting up at the sun. The sailor's smile was toothless but friendly, for he'd recognized a kindred soul in this gangling youngster swaddled in a bedraggled sheepskin cloak. "Not that I blame you, for she's a ripe beauty for certes, a seaworthy siren if ever I saw one."

Berold was quick to return the sailor's smile. "That she is. The talk in the tavern was all of the White Ship. Wait till I tell my brother that I saw the most celebrated ship in the English king's fleet!"

"Did you hear how her master came to the king? His father, he said, had taken the king's father to England when he sailed to claim a crown in God's Year, 1066. He begged for the honour of conveying the king as his father had done. King Henry had already engaged a ship, but he was moved by the man's appeal, and agreed to let his son, Lord William, sail on the White Ship. When word got out, all the other young lordlings clamored to sail on her, too. There—down on the quay—you can see them preening and strutting like so many peacocks. The dark one is the Earl of Chester, and yonder is the Lord Richard, one of the king's bastards, and the youth in the red mantle is said to be a kinsman of the German emperor. The king's favorite nephew, the Lord Stephen, is supposed to sail on her, too, but I do not see him yet . . . he's one who'd be late for his own wake, doubtless snug in some wanton's bed—"

"I've seen the Lord Stephen, almost as near to me as you are now," Berold interrupted, for he did not want the sailor to think he was an ignorant country churl. "I've dwelled in Rouen for nigh on six months, for my uncle has a butcher's shop and is teaching me his trade. Twice did I see the king ride through the city streets, with Lord Stephen at his side. The people liked Stephen well, for he always had an eye for a pretty lass and he was open-handed with his alms-giving."

"All the way from Rouen, eh? You are the well-traveled one," the sailor murmured, and was amused to see that the boy took his good-natured gibe as gospel truth.

"Indeed, it was not a trek for the faint of heart," Berold agreed proudly. "I wore out two pairs of shoes on the road, got lost in the fog, and was nearly run down by a cart in Bayeux! But I had to get to Barfleur, for I must book passage to England. I have a . . . a quest to fulfill."

That caught the sailor's interest; butchers' lads were not likely candidates for pilgrimages or perilous sea voyages. "A quest? Did you swear a holy oath, then?"

Berold nodded solemnly. "My family has long been split asunder, ever since my brother Gerard quarreled with our father, who cursed him for his willfulness and cast him out like Cain. For five winters, we knew not whether he still lived, but then a neighbor's seafaring son came to us at Michaelmas, said he'd seen Gerard in an English town called London. It was the answer to our heartfelt prayers, for my father has been ailing since the summer, suffering from a gnawing pain in his vitals, and he yearns to make peace with his firstborn ere he dies. I swore to my father and to the Father of All that I'd seek out Gerard, fetch him home."

The sailor could not help admiring the boy's pluck, but he suspected that Berold's mission was one doomed to failure. "I wish you well, lad. To tell you true, though, you're not likely to find passage this day. The king's ships are already crowded with his lords, his soldiers, and servants. They'll be taking aboard none but their own."

"I know," Berold admitted. "But God directed me to a tavern where I met Ivo—that's him over there, the one with the eyepatch. We got to talking, and when he learned of my plight, he offered to help. He is cousin to a helmsman on one of the king's ships, and his cousin will get me aboard if I make it worth his while. That must be him coming now, so I'd best be off." With a cheerful wave, he started across the street toward his new-found friends, followed by the sailor's hearty "Go with God, lad!"

"Are you Mauger?" Ivo's cousin ignored Berold's smile, merely grunted as Ivo made the introductions. He was a big-boned man, pock-marked and dour, and Berold was grateful that he had the amiable Ivo to act as go-between.

But Ivo did not seem as affable as he had been in the tavern. "Come on," he said brusquely. Berold had to hasten to keep pace, dodging passersby and mangy, scavenging dogs. A young prostitute plucked at his sleeve, but he kept on going, for she was dirty and very drunk. Although Barfleur was exciting, it was unsettling, too, for it seemed that all he'd heard about the sinfulness of seaports was true. The streets were crowded with quarrelsome, swaggering youths, the taverns were full, and even to Berold's innocent eye, there was a surfeit of whores, beggars, peddlers, and pickpockets. He was indeed fortunate to have found Ivo in this den of thieves and wantons.

They were heading away from the harbor. Berold took one last lingering look at the White Ship, then followed Ivo into the shadows of a narrow, garbage-strewn alley. He'd assumed they were taking a shortcut, but the alley was a dead end. In such close quarters, the stench of urine was overwhelming, and he started to back out, saying politely, "I'll wait whilst you piss." But before he could retreat, a huge hand slammed into the side of his head, and he lurched forward, falling to his knees. His shocked cry was cut off as Mauger slipped a thin noose around his neck, and suddenly the most precious commodity in his world was air. As Berold choked and gasped and tore frantically at the thong, Ivo leaned over him, in his upraised fist an object dark and flat. It was the last thing Berold saw.

He was never to know how long he had been unconscious. At first he was aware only of pain; his head was throbbing, and when he tried to rise, he doubled over, vomiting up his dinner. Groaning, he reached for a broken broom handle, used it for support as he dragged himself upright. Only then did he think of the money he carried in a pouch around his neck, the money meant to pay his passage to England, to bring his brother home. He groped for it with trembling fingers, continued to fumble urgently within his tunic long after he'd realized the pouch was gone. The theft of his father's money was, for Berold, a catastrophe of such magnitude that he was utterly unable to deal with it. What was he to do? Blessed Lady, how could this happen? He'd never be able to go home again, never. How could he face his family after failing so shamefully? Papa would not die at peace, Gerard would never be forgiven, and it was his fault, God curse him, all his fault.

By the time he staggered back into the street, he was so tear-blinded that he never saw the horses—not until he reeled out in front of them. Fortunately, the lead rider was a skilled horseman. He swerved with seconds to spare. So close had Berold come to disaster, though, that the stallion's haunches brushed his shoulder, sent him sprawling into the muddied street.

"You besotted fool! I ought to wring your wretched neck!"

Berold shrank back from this new assault, made mute by his fear. These men who'd almost trampled him were lords. Their fine clothing and swords proclaimed them to be men of rank, men who could strike down a butcher's apprentice as they would a stray dog. The angriest of them was already dismounting, and Berold shuddered, bracing himself for a beating—or worse.

"Use the eyes God gave you, Adam. The lad's not drunk. He's hurt."

The man called Adam was glaring down contemptuously at the cowering boy. "A few more bruises would do him no harm, my lord, might teach him to look where he is going next time." But he'd unclenched his fists, coming to a reluctant halt.

Astounded by the reprieve, Berold scrambled hastily to his feet as his defender dismounted. But he was as wobbly as a newborn colt and would have fallen had the man not grabbed his arm, pulling him toward the shelter of a mounting block.

"You seem bound and determined to get yourself run over, lad. Sit, catch your breath whilst I look at that bloody gash of yours. Ah . . . not so bad. You must have a hard head! Were you set upon by thieves?"

Berold nodded miserably. "They took all my money, and now my father will die—" He got no further; to his shame, he began to sob.

Adam grimaced in disgust. They'd already wasted time enough on this paltry knave. It was truly fortunate that his lord showed such boldness on the battlefield, lest men wonder at his womanlike softheartedness. But now that the dolt had bestirred his lord's curiosity, they'd likely be stuck here till sunset, listening to this fool's tale of woe.

Just as he feared, the boy's cryptic remark was bait his lord could not resist. "You'd best tell me what happened," he said, and as Adam fumed, Berold did so. He was fast losing touch with reality. Why should one so highborn pay any heed to him? That this was a great lord, Berold did not doubt; he had never seen anyone so elegant. Shoulder-length flaxen hair that was so shiny and clean no lice would dare to nest in it. A neatly trimmed beard, and a smile that showed white, healthy teeth, not a one broken off or rotted. A bright-blue mantle that looked softer than any wool ever spun, luxuriously lined with grey fox fur. Cowhide boots dyed to match, laced all the way to the knee. A hat adorned with a dark-red jewel. Worn at his left hip, as lightly as a feather, a sword Berold doubted he could even lift. He could not begin to imagine what life must be like for this handsome young lord, for there was no earthly bridge between their worlds. And yet there was an odd sense of familiarity about his saviour, as if their paths had crossed ere this. Even as Berold explained haltingly about his father and lost brother and Ivo's foul treachery, he found himself straining to remember. When he did, he was so stunned that he forgot all else, blurting out in one great gasp:

"You are the king's nephew! You are the Lord Stephen!"

Stephen acknowledged his identity with a smile, aware of the impatient muttering of his men but feeling a flicker of pity for this luckless butcher's lad, scared and grass-green and far from home. "Now," he said, "what can we do about you, Berold?" The boy was looking up at him like a lost puppy, eyes filled with silent pleading, forlorn hope. Stephen studied him for a moment more, and then shrugged. Why not?

"Tell me," he said, "how would you like to sail to England on the White Ship?"

STEPHEN had no liking for ships, did not know any man of sense who did; who would willingly seek out the triple perils of storms, shipwrecks, and sea monsters? He was fascinated, nonetheless, by the sight that met his eyes: the English king's fleet, riding at anchor in Barfleur Harbor. They were very like the ships that had carried his grandfather William the Bastard on his invasion of England more than fifty years past, but Stephen neither knew nor cared about that; like most people, he lived for the moment, had no interest in any history not his own. But he enjoyed pageantry, was amused by chaos, and relished turmoil—all of which he found in full measure on this Thursday of St Catherine in Barfleur Harbor.

Up and down the beach, small boats were being launched, ferrying passengers out to the waiting ships. Only those fortunate enough to be traveling on the White Ship or the English king's vessel were spared that wet, rough ride and undignified, hazardous boarding. They had just to venture out onto the quay, then cross a gangplank to the safety of their ship.

Stephen was standing now on that same quay, wanting to bid his uncle Godspeed before they sailed. So far he'd looked in vain for the stout, formidable figure of the king. As he was in no hurry, he was content to loiter there on the pier, bantering with acquaintances and passersby. But his nonchalance camouflaged a soldier's sharp eye, and he alone noticed the small boy tottering toward the far end of the quay. Shoving aside the people in his path, he darted forward, snatching up the child just before he reached the wharf's edge.

The little boy let out a yowl of protest. It subsided, though, as soon as he recognized Stephen, for Ranulf was a sunny-natured child, given to mischief but not tantrums. Stephen had concluded that Ranulf must take after his mother, for not even King Henry's greatest admirers ever claimed he had an amiable temperament.

"Well, look what I caught! What sort of queer fish could this be?" Ranulf was too young to comprehend the joke, for he was barely past his second birthday. Nor did he fully understand his kinship to Stephen. He knew only that Stephen was always kind to him, that Stephen was fun, and he squealed happily now as his cousin swung him high up into the air.

"More," he urged, "more!" But Stephen insisted upon lowering him back onto the quay, for he'd seen the women hastening toward them.

"Ranulf!" Angharad reached them first, with the white-faced nurse just a step behind. Catching her son in a close embrace, she held him until he started to squirm, then turned upon Stephen a torrent of gratitude.

Laughing, he held up his hand to stem the tide. "Lady Angharad, you do me too much credit. The lad was in no real danger. Even if he had taken a tumble into the water, we'd have fished him out quick enough." He was not surprised, though, that his assurances counted for naught; he'd never known a more doting mother than his uncle's young Welsh mistress.

Stephen treated all women with courtesy, felt protective toward most of them. But Angharad, in particular, had always stirred his sense of chivalry. He knew little of her past, only that she'd been brought back by his uncle from one of his campaigns in Wales. She couldn't have been much more than fifteen at the time, and he sometimes wondered how she'd felt about being claimed as a prize of war by an enemy more than thirty years her senior. Stephen had been quite young himself then, and had only a few hazy memories of a timid country lass with nary a word to say for herself, downswept lashes and sidelong glances and a shyness that served as her shield. But in the six years that she'd been at Henry's court, she'd learned to speak French, adopted Norman fashions, and borne Henry two children, a stillborn son and Ranulf.

Stephen knew that most people would envy Angharad, not pity her, for her life held comforts undreamed-of in Wales. The king's concubine would never go hungry, never lack for warm clothes or a soft bed. As tight-fisted as Henry was, he looked after his own, freely acknowledging all his bastard-born children. He was said to have sired at least twenty offspring out of wedlock, and had made brilliant marriages for many of them. Stephen did not doubt Ranulf was fortunate, indeed, that his mother had been fair enough to catch a king's eye. Whether that was true or not for Angharad, too, he had no way of knowing.

Hoisting Ranulf up onto his shoulders, Stephen escorted Angharad and the nurse across the gangplank, found for them a space under the canvas tent, and wished them a safe and speedy journey. Returning to the quay, he was hailed by a husky female voice. "Stephen, you fool! My husband will be here any moment, and when he finds you lusting after me like this, he'll slay us both!"

Stephen bit back a grin. "If ever there were a woman worth dying for, it would be you, my dearest . . . dearest . . . no, do not tell me! Clemence? No . . . Rosamund?"

That earned him a sharp poke in the ribs. "Swine!" She laughed, and he reached out, gave her a hug, for they were kin and could take such liberties without giving rise to gossip.

They were not really related, though, not by blood; it was Amabel's husband, Robert, who was Stephen's cousin. While King Henry provided well for his illegitimate children, he preferred not to do so out of his own coffers. For Robert, his firstborn son, he'd found Amabel Fitz Hamon, daughter of the Lord of Creully, a rich heiress who'd brought Robert the lordship of Glamorgan, the vast Honour of Gloucester. Stephen had recently heard that the king meant to bestow upon Robert, too, the earldom of Gloucester. His was not a jealous nature, but he did begrudge Robert so much good fortune. No man so self-righteous, he thought, deserved an earldom and Amabel and a king's favor, too.

"So," Amabel said, linking her arm in his, "what sort of trouble have you been up to? I heard you ran down some poor soul in the street this afternoon?"

Stephen shook his head in mock regret. "Never give credence to rumors, love. As it happens, I was being a Good Samaritan." And he related for her, then, his rescue of Berold, the hapless butcher's lad. When he was done, she clapped her hands and called him "St Stephen," but her brown eyes were alight with admiration, a look Stephen liked very much, indeed.

Not that he expected anything to come of it. Amabel was a flirt, but she was also a devoted wife. Like all marriages, hers had been an arranged union, one that had proved to be surprisingly successful, for they were an odd match, she and Robert, theirs the attraction of utter opposites, Amabel as lively and playful and outgoing as Robert was deliberate and staid and brooding. They'd been wed for thirteen years, were the parents of several sons, and Stephen well knew that for all her teasing and languid looks, Amabel would never stray from Robert's bed. He was content, too, to have it so, for a dalliance with a married woman was no small sin. He saw no reason, though, why he and Amabel should not play the more innocent of lovers' games, and they were laughing together with obvious enjoyment when Robert came upon them.

Stephen knew that many a husband would have resented such familiarity. He knew, too, that Robert would not—and liked him none the better for his lack of jealousy. Such petty emotions were beneath Robert the

Pure, he thought, and then felt a twinge of remorse, for he was not usually so uncharitable. But there was no denying it: Robert had always been a bone in his throat.

Although they were first cousins, the two men were as unlike in appearance as they were in character, Stephen tall and fair, Robert several inches shorter, far less outgoing, with brown hair and eyes, a quick, cool smile. He was the older of the two, thirty years to Stephen's twenty-four, but people often assumed the age gap was greater than that, for Robert's was the dignity of a man settled and sedate, one long past the wayward urges and mad impulses of youth. He was a man of honour—Stephen would concede that—a man of courage, loyal and steadfast. But he was not a boon companion, not one to visit the taverns and bawdy-houses with. Stephen liked to joke that not even God would dare to call him "Rob," and would have been truly amazed had he known that in the intimacy of Robert's marriage bed, he was Amabel's "sweet Robin."

Robert had impeccable manners; he believed all men were deserving of courtesy. He made no attempt, though, to feign warmth as he greeted Stephen, for he drew a clear distinction between civility and hypocrisy. But Stephen did not even notice. He'd forgotten all about Robert as soon as he recognized the girl at Robert's side.

To Stephen, Matilda de Boulogne was living proof that small packages could hold intriguing surprises. For this little slip of a lass, barely coming up to his chest, so slight and fair and fragile she put him in mind of a delicate white violet—one that could be bruised by rough handling or chilled by a cold breath—bore in her veins the royal blood of kings. Her mother was a Scots princess and the sister of King Henry's dead queen. Her father was the Count of Boulogne, two of her uncles successive kings of Jerusalem. She herself was a great heiress. This convent-bred innocent would bring to her husband not only the county and crown of Boulogne but vast estates, as well, in the south of England. She blushed prettily as Stephen kissed her hand, and as he gazed down into iris-blue eyes, he was not thinking only of those fertile fields and prosperous manors in Kent and Boulogne.

Amabel had known for some time that Matilda was smitten with Stephen, and she was not surprised in the least, for few young girls were not susceptible to high spirits, good looks, and gallantry. Robert now saw it, too, although with none of his wife's benevolent approval. He supposed it was only to be expected that a fifteen-year-old virgin maiden would not have the wisdom to tell gilt from true gold. But women worldly enough to know better made the same foolish mistake, and it baffled him that it should be so. It was not that he wished Stephen ill; he did not. Nor did he deny that Stephen had courage, good humor, and a giving heart, admirable qualities for certes. But Robert did not think Stephen was reliable, and for Robert, that was one of the most damning judgments he could pass upon another man.

"Well, I'd best get back to the White Ship." Reaching again for Matilda's hand, Stephen raised it to his mouth. "God keep you, Lady Matilda. Till the morrow at Southampton."

"Oh!" It was an involuntary cry, and a revealing one. "You are not coming with us?" Matilda's disappointment was keen enough to embolden her. "I'd hoped," she confided, "that you would make the journey on our ship. I have ever hated the sea. But I would not be so afraid if you were there to laugh at my fears, to make me laugh, too . . ." Her lashes fluttered up, just long enough to give Stephen one look of intense, heartfelt entreaty, then swept down, shadowing her cheeks like feathery golden fans.

Amabel grinned; coming from such an innocent, that was not badly done at all. Robert glanced at his wife but refrained from commenting. Stephen was momentarily caught off balance, not sure what to say. He really did want to sail on the White Ship, had been laying wagers with friends that it would be the first ship into Southampton Harbor. But he found himself staring at Matilda's long, fair lashes; was that shine behind them the glint of tears?

"White Ship? I never heard of it," he said, and discovered then that any ship was well lost for the sake of her smile.

THOMAS FITZ STEPHEN, the proud master of the White Ship, was not pleased to learn that Stephen had defected to the king's vessel, for the more lords of rank aboard, the greater his prestige. But he had no time to brood about Stephen's change of plans, for the king's son had finally arrived. The Lord William was a prideful, cocky youth of seventeen who'd inherited his father's stocky frame, black hair, and iron-edged will. He did not have Henry's ice-blooded control and vaunted patience, though, and soon grew restless, abandoning the ship for the more convivial pleasures of the nearest quayside tavern. But before he departed, he won over the crew by breaking out three of the casks of cargo wine, ordering them shared between passengers and sailors alike.

Most of the cargo had already been loaded: huge wine casks and heavy, padlocked coffer chests said to contain the king's treasure. They were now secured in the center of the ship, covered with canvas. A large tarpaulin tent was being set up near the bow so the highborn passengers could be sheltered—somewhat—from the cold and flying spray. When Berold had first come aboard, he'd been awed by the spaciousness of the ship. It was filling up fast, though. He'd heard in the tavern that there were fifty oarsmen on the White Ship, but his counting skills were rudimentary at best, and he could only guess at the number of passengers milling about; at least two hundred, he reckoned, mayhap many more.

Berold had been dismayed to learn that Stephen would not be sailing with them. With Stephen aboard, he'd have felt safe, would have feared neither storms nor prowling Channel pirates, not even the disdain of these highborn passengers. With Stephen not there to speak up for him, what if one of the lords ordered him off the ship? He'd found for himself an out-of-the-way corner at the stern, near the steering oar, and drawing his knees up to his chin, he pulled his cloak close, tried to make himself as inconspicuous as possible. He knew, though, that his very appearance marked him out as an intruder in their midst. The drab grey of his home-spun tunic—neither bleached nor dyed—contrasted starkly with the vivid blues and scarlets and greens swirling around him. And while he was grateful for the warmth of his sheepskin cloak, he saw the scornful smiles it attracted, for the wool was on the outside, a style worn only by rustics, the poor, and baseborn. But when his fears finally came to pass, when a knight objected belligerently to the presence of "this meagre whelp," the Lord Richard Fitz Roy waved the man aside with a quip about "one of Lord Stephen's strays."

Berold closed his eyes in thankfulness, then blessed the Lord Stephen again, for still casting a protective shadow. Sliding his hand under his cloak, he squeezed the leather pouch hidden in his tunic, his secret talisman, Stephen's farewell generosity. The coins clinked reassuringly as he touched them. Settling back against the gunwale, he at last felt free to enjoy his astonishing good fortune: sailing to England on the king's newest, fastest ship, amongst these great and powerful lords and their ladies. What stories he would have to tell Gerard!

He began to eavesdrop, seeking to catch snatches of conversation, for he wanted to identify as many as possible of his celebrated shipmates. Richard Fitz Roy looked to be in his early twenties; he was said to be well loved by his father, the king, who'd recently betrothed him to a Norman heiress. Berold wondered if she was one of the women sailing with them, wondered too, if the Lord William's young wife was aboard. He was utterly fascinated by the female passengers, for never had he been in such close proximity to ladies of rank.

He counted at least fifteen of these alluring beings, all of them clean, clad in rich, vibrant colors, and whenever one of them passed nearby, there wafted to him on the damp salt air the fragrances of summer. Their gowns were concealed under long surcotes and wool mantles, but they wore no hoods despite the November chill, just delicate veils held in place by jeweled circlets, their hair swinging down in long braids, often adorned with ribbons. One carried the smallest dog Berold had ever seen, and its ears, too, sported jaunty red ribbons. Berold was bewitched by each and every one of them, these ladies of the White Ship, but above all, by the Lady Mahault, Countess of Perche, and the Lady Lucia, Countess of Chester. They were both handsome young women. Mahault was slim and dark, while Lucia's blonde plaits gleamed like braided sunlight against the emerald of her mantle, reaching almost to her knees. Berold could not take his eyes off them once he learned who they were, for Mahault was one of King Henry's natural daughters and Lucia was his niece, Stephen's sister.

All day the sun had shone fitfully, with a pallid winter warmth. As if to compensate for that, it flamed out in a spectacular fusion of crimson and gold and purple. The last traces of light were fading along the horizon when Berold saw a lantern suddenly flare on the king's ship. As the lamp was hoisted to the masthead, a trumpet fanfare echoed across the dark waters of the bay. The creaking of windlasses sounded, raising anchors, and the cry went up to "unfurl the sails!" The royal fleet of Henry I, King of England and Duke of Normandy, was getting under way.

But the White Ship remained at its moorings, for Lord William and the Earl of Chester and a number of the young lords were still ashore. Sounds of loud laughter floated out from the tavern, sounds so cheerful and beguiling that others were tempted to join the revelries. Few men faced a sea voyage without some trepidation, and as the night sky darkened, more and more of them discovered how easy it was to drown their qualms in a free flow of wine. The crew, having been given access to the royal wine casks, were quite good-humored about the delay. Only the ship's master was vexed by their failure to sail with the tide, but when he ventured ashore to complain, he learned that a ship captain's authority did not carry much clout with a youth who would one day rule all England and Normandy.

By the time the White Ship was finally ready to sail, it was full dark and bitter cold. The waiting had been hard on Berold. He'd not even had the solace of wine as the other passengers did, for he'd not dared to join in the crew's carousing, and he was one of the few people on board who was still sober when the ship's master gave the command to cast off. A small crowd had gathered to watch their departure and was pleasantly scandalized when the young lords leaning precariously over the gunwales jeered and mocked the priests who'd come to offer a blessing for "they that go down to the sea in ships." As the spectators gasped and the priests angrily denounced their impiety, the anchor was raised, the shrouds were tightened, the sails were unfurled, and the White Ship slowly moved away from the quay, out into the blackness of the harbor.

The night was clear, the sky adrift in stars. The moon was on the wane, casting a wavering, silvery gleam upon the cresting waves. The ship rode low in the water, and Berold was unnerved to realize the freeboard was only three feet or so above the surface of the bay. He was already feeling queasy, and whispered a quick plea to St Elmo, who was said to pity those poor souls stricken with seasickness. He'd heard that, depending upon the wind and tides, a crossing from Barfleur to Southampton might take a day. Twelve hours lay ahead then, the longest twelve hours of his life.

Berold might have been comforted had he known that his anxiety was shared by most of the highborn passengers, including the king's son. William had crossed the Channel more times than he could remember, but his body always reacted as if each voyage were his first time on shipboard. He had so many miserable memories of seasick suffering that he had only to look upon a ship to experience a queasy pang. This was one reason why he'd gotten so drunk, in the hope that wine might settle his treacherous stomach, keep him from making a fool of himself, for at seventeen, there are few greater fears than the dread of public humiliation. That others, too, were often stricken with the same undignified malaise consoled him not at all, for he was England's future king and must not give in to the weaknesses of lesser men. His lord father never did, and by God, neither would he.

But as soon as they headed toward open water, William bolted for the ship's bow, then clung to the gunwale as he vomited into the waves splashing over the prow. "Greensick so soon, Will?" The voice was sympathetic, but it also held a hint of amusement, the smug indulgence of a good sailor. William felt too wretched, though, for resentment, and he let his brother help him up, steer him toward the canvas tarpaulin, where he flopped down on a blanket, grabbed a handhold, and held on for dear life. When Richard checked on him again a little later, he'd rolled over onto his back, was snoring softly.

"Richard . . . how fares Will?"

"The wine has done him in. With luck, he'll sleep through the night, poor lad."

Richard reached out then, as the ship pitched, helped to steady his sister and cousin. Mahault could only marvel at his surefootedness; he'd had almost as much wine as Will, but he seemed none the worse for it. Why, she wondered, were men such fools? Lucia was less judgmental. Poor Will, she thought, he'll be shamed as well as dog-sick come the morn. Aloud, she said, "I'll stay with him in case he awakens."

Richard was more interested at that moment in his lost gamble, for he'd wagered a goodly sum that the White Ship would beat the rest of the king's fleet to Southampton. As soon as he could catch Thomas Fitz

Stephen's eye, he beckoned the ship's master over to find out if there was still a chance of victory.

The ship's master shrugged. "We are in God's Hands, my lord. They are well ahead of us, but if we caught a good wind . . ." He shrugged again. "We'll not be able to make up much time till we are out into the Channel and can rely on the sail. I've told the oarsmen and my helmsman to keep close to Barfleur Point as long as we can, so we can avoid the worst of the contrary currents offshore. At least it is a cloudless night, so we'll have the polestar to steer by. I would hope—Jesus God!"

Both men were flung backwards as the ship suddenly shuddered, stopped dead in the water. There was a crunching sound, and then the ship began to list, sending screaming passengers careening into one another, slamming into the casks and treasure chests, into the struggling oarsmen. Thomas Fitz Stephen managed to regain his footing, skidded across the slanting deck. He already knew what had happened. It had all come together for him with horrific clarity in the span of seconds—the tide dropping, the reef that men called Chaterase lurking just beneath the surface, his tipsy oarsmen straining for speed. An ashen-faced sailor lurched against him, clutching at his arm. "We hit a rock and staved in the port side!"

Fitz Stephen swung about, shouting at the stunned helmsman, "Up on the helm!" The ship shifted again, provoking more screams. He had to clamber over prostrate, thrashing bodies to reach the port side. "Fetch boat hooks! Mayhap we can push her off!"

He thought he'd been braced for the worst. But he hadn't, not for the sight of that gaping hole in the hull, his ship's death wound. As his crew pushed against the rock with boat hooks and oars, he stood frozen for a moment. Then he pulled himself together, for there was a trust still to be honoured, one last duty to perform. Grabbing one of his sailors, he gave the man a terse, urgent order, then searched among the frightened passengers for the captain of William's guard. "Get your lord over to the starboard side. We're going to launch the spare boat, and it must be done quick—whilst the passengers still think themselves safer aboard ship."

The man gaped at him. "Jesú, is it as bad as that?"

The ship's master gave him a hard, quailing stare. "You're less than two miles from Barfleur, close enough to make it safe to shore. But go now. You understand? Save the king's son."

William had never experienced a nightmare so vivid, so intense, so endless. Groggy, dazed, and disoriented, he found himself scrabbling about in darkness, entangled in suffocating folds of collapsed canvas. Then hands were reaching for him, pulling him free. His head spinning, his stomach heaving, he decided he must still be dreaming, for now he was being roughly pushed and shoved, his ears filled with screams and curses. He stumbled and fell forward into a boat; at least he thought it was a boat. Trying to recover his balance, he cracked his head and slumped back, groaning, wanting only to wake up.

Opening his eyes, he gasped as a spray of stinging salt water doused him in the face. He struggled to sit up, and voices at once entreated him to "Keep still, my lord, lest you tip the boat!" And as he looked about him, William sobered up in the time it took to draw icy sea air into his constricted lungs, for he was adrift in a pitching open boat in the middle of a black, surging sea.

"What happened?"

"The White Ship . . . she is sinking, my lord!"

"That cannot be!" William twisted around to look, causing the boat to rock from side to side. "Christ Jesus . . ." For it was indeed so. The White Ship was listing badly, and he could hear the despairing wails of its doomed passengers. Mahault, Richard, Lucia, all his friends, his father's steward. "We've got to help them, cannot let them drown!"

The men continued to row, and to bail, for water was sloshing about in the bottom of the boat. "They'll be in no danger, my lord, once they get off the rock. This was but a safeguard, for you are the king's only lawfully begotten son and your life is precious to the Almighty."

William so wanted to believe him. But it was then that he thought he heard a woman's voice, high-pitched and shrill with fear. "Will, do not leave me to drown!"

"My sister! We must go back for her!"

"My lord, we dare not! We cannot put your life at risk!"

William was deaf to their pleading, to all but Mahault's cry of terror. "I am to be your king and I command you! Obey me or I'll have the lot of you hanged, I swear it!"

They were appalled by the order, but obedience had been bred and beaten into them from the cradle, and even now they dared not defy a royal command. As they strained at the oars, William yelled, "Mahault, we're coming for you! You'll have to jump into the water, but we'll pick you up! We'll send help back for the others!"

As they drew closer to the stricken ship, William half rose and had to be pulled down by one of the sailors before he swamped the boat. Peering through the darkness, he sought in vain for his sister midst the panicked passengers clustered along the starboard side. Shouting until his throat was raw, he began to tremble with cold and fear. None of this seemed real. Surely God would not let the White Ship sink? Mayhap the men were right and the ship in no danger. But then the screaming intensified, taking on a new frenzy, and the sailor closest to William said in awe, "Oh, sweet Jesus, she is breaking up!"

"We're too close, she'll drag us down with her!" Desperately manning the oars, the men struggled to draw away from the sinking ship. It seemed to be splitting in half, water gushing into its smashed hull, washing people overboard. "The mast is coming down!" More screams. The masthead lantern was swinging wildly, then went out. Their boat was wallowing in the swells, water breaking over the bow. They heard splashing in the darkness, the surface churning with flailing bodies. One man managed to reach their boat, pleading for help, too weak to heave himself up over the side. A sailor grabbed his arm, sought to pull him in. But then others were floundering toward them, clutching at their oars, clinging to the sides. Realizing their danger, they tried to repel these drowning, plucking hands, to save themselves. But it was too late. Their frail craft was being buffeted by the surging waves, caught in the undertow of the dying ship, and then it was going under, and William was flung into the water, opening his mouth to scream and swallowing salt water, with no one to answer his choking cry for help, for they were all drowning, the passengers and crew of the White Ship.

Berold's lungs were bursting, aching for air. It was too late now for prayer. He'd been too petrified when there'd still been time, huddling in the stern, whimpering each time the ship lurched, paralyzed by fear. And then the deck seemed to fall away, water was flooding in, and he was swept over the side, sure that he would die unshriven, lost to God's Grace. But he continued to fight instinctively for life, kicking and clawing his way back to the surface.

All around him people were struggling, splashing, snatching at floating debris. Not far away, a wine cask was bobbing, and Berold plunged toward it, managed by sheer luck to catch one of its trailing ropes. Nearby, he could hear a woman sobbing to the Blessed Lady for deliverance, but the sea was pitching and rolling as the White Ship went under, and he could see nothing but waves rising against the sky. The hugh cask was unwieldy; try as he might, he could not get a secure grip. Clinging to its rope, he was waging a losing battle to stay afloat; swells were breaking over his head, and he sputtered and gasped for air between submersions. And then the cask thudded into something solid. There was a jarring thump, and he mustered his dwindling strength, grabbed for this new lifeline. For a time, he just concentrated upon holding on, upon breathing. Gradually his numbed brain began to function again. Shredded canvas and crossed wooden beams—the White Ship's yardarm and mast. That realization gave him his first flicker of hope. Clenching his fists in the rigging ropes, he slowly dragged himself up onto the spar.

He was not alone. Other men were straddling the mast, clutching at the sail, hanging on to the yardarm, and these fortunate few were the only ones to survive the sinking of the White Ship. They clung to their precarious refuge and listened as their shipmates drowned. It did not take long, for the water was very cold. Soon the screaming stopped, and an ominous silence settled over the bay. Berold saw one of the men securing himself with the rigging rope, and he, too, groped for the halyard, fumbled until he'd knotted it around his waist. No one talked; they were saving their strength for staying alive. But the boy took comfort in knowing they were there, sharing his fate. Shivering, he squeezed his eyes shut and began to pray.

Never had Berold been so cold. But his heavy sheepskin cloak shielded him from the worst of the wind. As wet and wretched as he was, he was still better off than the other men, and as the hours passed, the cold began to claim victims. One by one, their grips loosened, their wits started to wander, and they slipped silently off the mast, disappeared into the dark, icy sea.

At last there were but two, Berold and the young man who'd lashed himself to the yardarm. Berold watched him sag lower in the water and pleaded with him to hold on, not to die. He got no answer, for the youth had no breath for talking. When he did speak, his teeth were chattering so violently that Berold could hardly understand him. "I am Geoffrey Fitz Gilbert de l'Aigle. Tell my family, tell them . . ." After that, he said no more, and Berold began to cry, silently and hopelessly, for he was alone now on this tossing spar with a dead man, and there would be none to know when death came for him, too.

During the night, fog swept in from the west, patches of ghostly grey lying low along the horizon. Sometimes he slept. Or did he? His thoughts were rambling, confused. He could not always remember where he was, or why he was suffering so. Why could he not recall the patron saint for sailors, for those in peril on the sea? Why was the Almighty taking so long to bring him home?

When he heard the voices, muffled and distorted in the fog, he felt a weary wonderment that his ordeal was over, that God's good angels were coming for him at last. But they came not in winged chariots, as the priests had taught. Instead, they glided out of the fog in a small fishing craft, its hull painted yellow and black, its single sail as bright as blood.

Berold tried to yell; it emerged as a hoarse croak. But they'd already seen him, were dipping their oars into the sea. And then they were alongside, and one of the men had nimbly scrambled out onto the mast, was cutting him loose, and Berold realized that for him, salvation had come in the unlikely guise of three Breton fishermen. He had been spared to bear witness, to tell the world that the White Ship had gone down off Barfleur Point, with the loss of the English king's son and all aboard, save only a butcher's lad from Rouen.

IT was two days before they dared to tell the English king. Henry was shattered by the loss of his children, his dreams of a dynasty. Within two months, he'd taken a new wife, the daughter of the Duke of Lower Lorraine. Adeliza was just eighteen and beautiful, but the marriage proved barren; she could give him no son for the one he had lost.

Men thought it God's inexplicable joke that Henry should have sired twenty-three children, and of them all only two born in wedlock—William and his sister Maude, who'd been sent off to Germany as a child of eight, wed to the Emperor Heinrich V. When Henry's lords debated the succession in the aftermath of the Barfleur tragedy, none thought of Maude, for there were worthy male candidates: the king's two nephews, sons of his sister, Adela: Theobald, Count of Blois, and his younger brother Stephen, Count of Mortain. There was also Robert Fitz Roy, for as some pointed out, Henry's great father had been bastard-born, too, and still claimed a crown.

One man alone saw Maude as Henry's successor. When, five years after the sinking of the White Ship, Maude was suddenly a young widow, Henry called her home. Maude, he announced, would be his heir. This was a notion so alien to their world—that a woman should rule in her own right—that his barons and council fought him on it. But age had not weakened his will, and he would not be thwarted. As he had forced Maude to return from Germany, so did he force the lords of his realm to swear fealty to her. When he died, Maude would be queen.

2

CITY OF ANGERS, PROVINCE OF ANJOU, FRANCE

August 1129

BARBE knew that her sister, Marthe, was a whore. When Marthe had returned to the village three months ago for the funeral of their mother, their stepfather had turned her away, saying she had shamed them all with her evil, ungodly life. As young as Barbe was—just thirteen—she understood what a whore did, that she sold her body to men for money. She understood, too, that it was a grievous sin. Nonetheless, she loved her wanton sister and detested her pious, righteous stepfather. She loathed his new wife, too, for he'd married again with indecent haste, claiming he needed a woman to mind his young sons. There was no room in his new family circle for Barbe, the unwanted, the child not his. She found herself facing a dismal future, treated as a servant, likely to be married off to the first elderly widower willing to accept her youth in lieu of a marriage portion. Barbe wept softly at night, nursing her bruises and muffling her sobs in her straw mattress, praying for the courage to run away. But it was not the Almighty who came to her rescue, it was her sinful sister.

When Marthe came back for her, Barbe never hesitated. Stuffing her meagre belongings into a hemp sack, she walked away from her home and village without a backward look. It was only as their cart neared the city walls of Angers that Barbe began to have qualms about what she'd done. It was plain that her sister did not lack for money, not if she could afford to hire a cart and driver. But what lay ahead in Angers? What would life be like for her here?

A week had passed since then, a week of continual surprises for Barbe. She had been vastly relieved to find that her sister did not live in a brothel. Indeed, Marthe's residence was the most luxurious dwelling she'd ever seen; it had a kitchen and a hall, with a bedchamber and a loft above, and a garden view of the river. Barbe was astounded, but she was too shy to probe, and Marthe offered no explanation, only a sly smile and a jest about having an accommodating landlord. Marthe had a coffer chest full of clothes, plump hens scratching about in her garden, even a servant, a widow who came in every day to cook and clean. What she did not seem to have was a means of support. Where were the men come to buy what her sister was selling? Since Barbe had been there, nary a one had shown up. Who was paying for Marthe's fine house and food and jasmine perfume?

Barbe got her answer—and the greatest surprise of all—at week's end. He rode up at twilight, pounded on the door, and when she pulled back the latch, he brushed past her as if she did not exist, shouting for her sister, using Marthe's new name, the one Barbe could not get accustomed to: Mirabelle. "You'll not believe what that bitch did, Mirabelle! I swear to Christ that I'd have throttled her if I'd stayed—" But by now he and Mirabelle were on their way up the stairs, and the closing door cut off the rest of his rage.

Barbe stared open-mouthed after them, for as brief as her glimpse had been, it was enough. She'd seen this handsome, angry youth once before, had watched in awe as he and several hunting companions stopped in her village for wine, while word of his identity spread from house to house, emptying the entire population out into the dusty street. Barbe's knees had begun to tremble and she sat down abruptly on the closest stool, overwhelmed by the realization that her sister's mystery lover was the Count of Anjou.

Barbe slept fitfully that night in the loft, and when she awoke the next morning, her sister was already up, gossiping in the kitchen with her neighbor, the red-haired, bawdy Brigette. Barbe started down the stairs, only to stop at sight of the bedchamber door, invitingly ajar. Before she could think better of it, she crept forward.

One of the shutters had been unlatched, and half of the chamber was filled with hot, hazy sunlight, half still deep in night shadows. The floor was littered with discarded clothing and several empty wine flagons, and a scabbard was buried in the rushes, almost at Barbe's feet. The Count of Anjou was sprawled, naked, upon Mirabelle's bed, his legs entangled in the sheets, an arm flung across his eyes. His skin was fair and seemed remarkably clean and smooth, tanned wherever he'd been exposed to the sun, white where he had not. His hair was shoulder length and curly, the color of copper, as was the hair between his legs. He was clean-shaven, in the fashion for youths, and when he stirred sleepily, his arm dropping away from his face, Barbe caught her breath, for never had she seen any man so beautiful as this young drunken lord.

When a hand suddenly grasped Barbe's shoulder, she cried out in fright, spinning around so fast that she tripped over her own skirts. Mirabelle signaled for silence, then pushed her toward the door. Her face flaming, Barbe scurried down the stairs. She began to stammer an apology once they reached the hall, not wanting a witness to her sister's scolding. But Mirabelle waved her on into the kitchen, where Brigette was drinking cider left over from the Lammas Day celebration. "You'll not believe where I found the little lass, Brigette—by the bed, lusting after my young lordling!"

Barbe's face went even redder. "I was not!" she gasped, sounding so horrified that both women burst out laughing. Some of Barbe's discomfort began to fade as she realized her sister was not angry with her. "I ought not to have gone into the bedchamber," she admitted, "but . . . but I could not help myself. Is he really your lover, Mart—Mirabelle? For how long? And who was he so angry with? Not . . . not his wife, surely?"

"Oh, so you know about the wife, do you?" Mirabelle asked, but she did not sound annoyed, and Barbe nodded shyly.

"Oh, yes, for that was all we talked about last year, that Lord Geoffrey was to wed the King of England's daughter. We heard that they had a splendid wedding, that she was a beautiful bride. Is . . . is that not so?"

"Yes, she is a handsome wench, is the Lady Maude. But I'd not say she made so fair a bride, not when she went to the altar like one going to the gallows!"

Barbe was astonished. "Why ever would she not want to wed the Lord Geoffrey? I do not understand, for he is so handsome," she sighed, and then blushed again when the women laughed.

"Geoffrey could not understand it, either! But it seems the lady felt she was marrying beneath her. She had been the wife of the Holy Roman Emperor, after all, and Geoffrey was merely the son of a count. And then he was just a lad, only fourteen, and she was a woman grown and worldly-wise of twenty-five. It may be, too, that she did not want to make a marriage so sure to displease her future subjects, who loathed the Angevins. Her objections were for naught, though. The English king was set upon the marriage, for he saw it as a means of thwarting William Clito's claim to the crown."

"Who is he?"

"He was another of the English king's nephews, his elder brother Robert's son. When Clito allied himself with the French king, Maude's father feared that Count Fulk of our Anjou would join forces with them against England. Are you following this so far?"

Barbe nodded, wide-eyed. "How do you know all this?" she asked admiringly, and Mirabelle pointed ceilingward, to the bedchamber above their heads.

"Men talk in bed, too," she said dryly. "So . . . to win over Count Fulk, the English king proposed a marriage between the Lady Maude and the count's eldest son, Geoffrey. The count agreed, but the Norman barons liked it little, and the Lady Maude not at all. She balked, refused to make the marriage."

Barbe was amazed; she'd never heard of a woman's daring to defy male authority. "Could she do that?"

"Well, she surely tried. But the king was no man to cross, and he had his way in the end. She yielded, and plans went forward for the wedding."

"Maude's father did make one concession in her favor," Brigette interjected, and Mirabelle nodded.

"I was just getting to that. You see, Barbe, the King of Jerusalem faced the same predicament as the English king: no son to succeed him. His eldest daughter was to be queen, and was in need of a husband. And so it was arranged for Count Fulk to take her to wife. As King of Jerusalem, he could well afford to cede Anjou to Geoffrey, so the Lady Maude would at least be marrying a count. And indeed, it all came to pass as the English king would have it. Geoffrey and Maude were wed last year, two months before his fifteenth birthday, in a magnificent ceremony at Le Mans. Count Fulk later departed for the Holy Land and his new destiny, the English king returned contentedly to his own domains, and the war began."

"War? With that . . . that William Clito?"

"No, William Clito's claim came to an abrupt and unexpected end, thanks to a mortal spear thrust. He was wounded whilst putting down a rebellion in Flanders and died soon afterward, little more than a month after Geoffrey and Maude's wedding! Geoffrey called that 'ironic,' a word I know not, but I suspect it is just a fancy way of saying his marriage need not have been. No, when I talked of war, I meant the one between Geoffrey and Maude. It began on their wedding night, and I see no truce in sight. Indeed, their fighting has gotten worse in past weeks. In truth, I've never seen Geoffrey as wroth as he was last night. It was no easy task, calming him down, took every drop of wine in the house!"

Barbe felt an odd sense of disappointment, for she'd always assumed that the highborn led blessed and blissful lives. "Why do they not get along?" she asked, and Mirabelle shrugged.

"Geoffrey has complaints beyond counting. To hear him tell it, Maude has no virtues, only vices. He says she is arrogant and sharp-tongued and quick-tempered, utterly lacking in womanly softness or warmth. But if I were seeking to understand why he hates her so, I'd look no further than their marriage bed. Keep this in mind, child, if you remember nothing else I teach you. There is no insult that wounds a man more than one aimed at his manhood."

"I . . . I do not understand."

"I mean that Geoffrey's wife finds no pleasure in his bed and lets him know it," Mirabelle said bluntly, and Barbe blushed anew.

"Well . . . why does he not shun her bed, then?" she suggested timidly. "If he has you, Mirabelle, why does he need Maude?"

"Alas, it is not so simple, Barbe. Geoffrey does need Maude—to give him an heir. And then, too, he is just sixteen. If he were older, her coldness would not matter so much to him. But he has never had an unwilling bedmate, not until now. Why would he, with a face like a wayward angel and all Anjou his for the taking? Women have been chasing after him since he was fourteen or thereabouts, and more often than not, he'd let them catch him. It was a great blow to his pride to discover that his beautiful wife does not want him. He is hurting and angry and baffled, and each time she rejects him, it gets worse. So he punishes her in bed, the one place where he is in control. That only makes her scorn him all the more, of course. Her scorn then goads him into maltreating her again, which . . . well, just think of a dog chasing his tail if you want to understand this accursed marriage of theirs! They must—Barbe? Lass, are you weeping?"

Barbe ducked her head, trying to hide the tears welling in her eyes. "It is just so sad," she said, "that they are so unhappy . . ."

"Save your pity for those who truly need it, for mothers with hungry babes to feed, for that one-legged beggar we saw in the marketplace, for lepers or women with no men to protect them. Geoffrey and Maude may be miserable, but misery is much easier to bear in a castle, child."

"Amen," Brigette said fervently, and she and Mirabelle laughed. Barbe was quiet after that, startled by her sister's unsentimental assessment of her royal lover's plight.

"Do you think Maude will truly rule England and Normandy one day?" she asked, for she found it incomprehensible that a woman could wield power like a man. "How would she know what to do?"

"Oh, she is clever enough to match wits with most men. Even Geoffrey admits as much. She knows how to read and write, she is fluent in French and German, and Geoffrey says she understands a little Latin. If you ask me, though, I think she is one of God's great fools. That lad up there in my bed is not a bad sort. But there is no forgiveness in him, none at all. Once he decides that Maude owes him a debt, she will be paying it off for the rest of their marriage. She—"

"Mirabelle, where are you? Get a basin up here fast, for I'm going to be sick!"

The voice was young, imperious, and urgent. Mirabelle grinned and got to her feet. "Coming, my love!" Gathering up a basin, a pitcher of water, and several towels, she started for the stairs, pausing to wink and say softly, "Time to earn the rent."

Brigette raised her cup and Barbe leaned over, politely poured more cider. "Brigette . . . what will happen to them, the Lord Geoffrey and the Lady Maude?"

"Who knows?" After a moment, though, Brigette grinned. "If you're one for gambling, Lucas the Fleming is taking wagers that they'll kill each other ere the year is out!"

"OPEN the shutters, Minna. I would know the worst," Maude said tautly. The older woman hesitated, then did as she was bade. Summer sunlight flooded the room, warming and indolent and unsparingly bright. Maude drew a deep breath, then raised the mirror. It had been a gift from her first husband, the German Emperor Heinrich, the work of a master craftsman, carved ivory and polished brass, sheeted in thin glass. The metallic reflection was distorted, somewhat blurred, but not enough to hide her swollen, split lip and the mottled, darkening bruises on her cheek. Maude closed her eyes for a moment, then sank down in the window seat.

"What am I to do, Minna? The abbot will be here from St Aubin's within the hour, and he'll have only to look at me to know. They all will, anyone with eyes to see . . ."

Minna's and Maude's lives had first intersected at Utrecht, where the young widow had been chosen to attend the even younger empress. After

Maude was widowed in her turn, Minna had forsaken her German homeland and accompanied her mistress back to England. They'd been together now for more than ten years, but never had Minna heard Maude sound like this, so utterly despairing. "Mayhap we can cover the bruises with powder, madame."

"There would not be enough powder in Christendom for that." Rising from the window seat, Maude began to pace. "Damn him," she cried suddenly, "damn him to Hellfire Everlasting!"

Minna wondered which one she meant, husband or father. "My lady, my fear for you bids me be bold, bids me speak my mind. You cannot go on like this. Something must be done."

"What would you have me do, Minna? Cut his throat whilst he sleeps?" Maude's mouth twisted. "I've thought about it, you may be sure!"

"My lady . . . please hear me out. You'll not like what I am about to say, but I cannot keep silent, not when I see him hurting you like this. So far he has not lost all control. He may have been angry enough to strike you, but he stopped at that. What happens when he does not? Madame, slaps lead to beatings, sooner or later. You cannot let it reach that point, for there will be no going back then. You must save yourself whilst there is still time."

"How?" Maude asked, but if the question itself was dispassionate, the tone was not, so defensive that Minna knew it was hopeless, that Maude would not heed her.

"My lady, your husband the emperor was not an easy man to live with, either. He was prey to dark moods and melancholy and sudden fits of temper, and yet . . . yet you were able to make your marriage tolerable. You learned to deal with his demons, to defer to him when need be. Lady Maude, can you not do the same with Lord Geoffrey? It might well mean your life!"

But Maude was already shaking her head. "No, Minna," she said, "I cannot do what you ask of me. It is true that I deferred to Heinrich, I do not dispute that. But I was only eight years old when I first met him, and he was a man of stature and significance, crowned by Our Holy Father the Pope. It did not diminish me to acknowledge his authority. And whilst it is true that he was a solitary, secretive man, aloof even in . . . intimate moments, he never begrudged me his respect. He treated me as his empress, and there was dignity in our marriage."

She paused, and her hand strayed to her face, her fingers brushing against her throbbing, discolored cheek. "How can you compare them, Heinrich and Geoffrey?" She all but spat the second name. "Heinrich was King of the Germans, the Holy Roman Emperor. But Geoffrey . . . he is a callow, willful boy, a selfish, boastful whelp who thinks a wife is just one more possession, another mare to ride at his pleasure! You cannot imagine how demeaning it is, Minna, to be subject to a stripling's whims, to have no rights at all, not even over my own body. You know how I fought against this marriage, but it has been even worse than I'd feared, more than fourteen months of pain and humiliation and misery. I cannot compel Geoffrey to show me the respect a wife deserves. I cannot even deny him my bed. But I will not let him strip away the last shreds of my dignity. I will not beg or grovel before him. I will never give him that satisfaction!"

"My lady, I would never ask that of you. But there must be some ground between defiance and submission. Can you not try to find it? Pride is admirable for certes, but it can also be dangerous, and if you—"

"You do not understand, Minna, not at all. Pride is the only defense I have," Maude said, and turned away so abruptly that Minna realized she was struggling to hold back tears. She was not a woman who wept easily or often, and knowing that, Minna said no more. Maude had moved to the window. Picking up the mirror again, she stared at her reflection for a long moment. And then she said, "Help me braid my hair, Minna. The abbot will soon be here."

"My lady, you do not have to do this. I can tell him you are ailing—"

"No!" Maude was very pale, and that ugly blotch of a bruise stood out like a brand, but her dark eyes glittered with a glazed, feverish intensity. "I will not cower up here in my chamber. I am no coward, and I will not hide away like one. I cannot stop people from gossiping behind my back, but I can damned well dare them to do it to my face!"

IT was dusk by the time Geoffrey returned to his formidable stone fortress above the River Maine. He felt wretched, his head pounding, his stomach still queasy, for he was not accustomed to drinking so much. Dismounting in the stable, he surprised the grooms by insisting upon unsaddling his mount himself. He lingered in the stable for almost an hour, rubbing his stallion down, feeding and watering it as the grooms looked on in bafflement. But he finally ran out of chores, and with a leaden step, he crossed the bailey, entered the great hall. To his relief, Maude was not there. He was acutely conscious, though, of the stares, the speculative glances, the eyes averted whenever he turned around. They knew, all of them. So did the townspeople. Most likely every last one of his vassals did, too. Had they begun to wonder how he could govern Anjou, a man unable to rule his own wife? Stalking from the hall, he rapidly mounted the stairs to Maude's bedchamber.

They were ready for him, having heard the jangling of his spurs on the narrow stone steps. He wasted no time on preliminary skirmishing, saying curtly, "Minna, leave us," vexed but not surprised when she looked to Maude for confirmation of his command. But he knew how to pay her back, and as soon as she'd reluctantly withdrawn, he slammed the bolt into place, knowing she'd be hovering on the other side of the door, listening.

Leaning back against the door, he said, "Alone at last," more for the eavesdropping Minna's benefit than for Maude's. His wife had yet to say a word. She knew more ways to unsettle a man than any woman he'd ever met, silence being only one of them. She was standing in the shadows behind the table, but he was sure she'd not stay there for long. However much she might fear him, he knew she'd fear showing it even more.

As he expected, she soon circled around the table. But he drew a sharp breath as she moved into the lamp's light. Jesú, her face was swollen up like a melon! He had not realized he'd hit her that hard. Not that he was sorry. She deserved it, by God she did.

He found, though, that he did not like to look at her bruises, for they were uncomfortable reminders of his own failure. He had his share of the notorious Angevin temper. His father had always claimed it was Lucifer's legacy, passed down from the Devil's daughter, said to have beguiled a long-dead Count of Anjou into taking her to wife. But Geoffrey had never given that accursed anger free rein, not as his father had, for it was very important to him—being in control at all times. That was why he'd suffered through so few drunken dawns like today's, why he'd learned at such an early age that words could be crafted into weapons, giving him power over others. Yet not over Maude, never over her. No matter how often he vowed not to let her goad him again into a heedless, fool's rage, it always came to that: someone he did not even know shouting and raving at her like a madman, losing more than his temper.

Maude watched warily as he moved about the chamber, slanting toward her an occasional sideways glance that gave away nothing of his thoughts. He guarded his secrets well. In that, he was a worthy opponent, for she rarely knew what he was thinking. What was he doing here? Not to offer an apology, for certes! What did he want of her? To share her bed? God, no . . . not after last night's ugliness. Surely he could not expect her to . . . not so soon? But of course he would, if that was what he wanted. Had he not proved that often enough?

"We need to talk, Maude," Geoffrey said abruptly. "Things must change between us. This constant quarreling must stop. I am bone-weary of entering this bedchamber and having it become a battlefield."

"I assure you it gives me no joy, either, Geoffrey."

"Then you ought to be willing to do your part. Are you?"

Maude hesitated, searching his face intently. Was he sincere about making a new beginning? Or was this some sort of trap? "What do you want of me?"

"It is very simple. I want you to start acting like a wife."

She should have known better. "You mean obey you in all particulars?"

He ignored her sarcasm. "Why not? You alone would think to question that, for the rest of Christendom recognizes it as a natural right, that a wife owes her husband obedience."

"And does the husband owe nothing? Is that all marriage is to you, a lifelong debt incurred by the woman?"

She saw the muscles tighten along his jawline, but he surprised her, then, by saying coolly, "So tell me what I owe. I cannot very well satisfy a debt unless I know what it is."

"I want you to treat me with courtesy. If I balk at obeying you, it is because you shame me in front of others. In truth, you speak more kindly to your dogs than you do to me. It would not unman you to ask instead of order, and you'd get better results."

Geoffrey could feel heat rising resentfully in his face. "I was willing to treat you well. You were the one who—" No, not again. This time he would not be provoked—by Corpus, he would not. "Fair enough," he said brusquely. "I show you courtesy and you show me respect. Anything else?"

"You truly need to ask? Look at my face!"

"That was as much your doing as mine!"

"What are you saying—that I wanted to be hit?"

"I am saying it would not have happened if not for your shrew's temper and poison tongue. You do not want it to happen again? That is fine with me. Just do not give me cause, as easy as that."

Maude clenched her fists in the folds of her skirt. Her breathing had quickened, but she couldn't seem to get enough air into her lungs and she felt as if she were going to suffocate on her choked-back rage. She said nothing, but gave Geoffrey a look of utter loathing, a look that was not lost upon him.

"We are agreed, then," he said, "that we stop entertaining all of Anjou with our feuding. From now on, we do our squabbling behind closed doors. Is that understood?"

"Yes, I understand. All your talk of change was just that—talk. You do not want to make peace between us. You do not even want a truce, merely a public pretense."

"A 'public pretense' is the best I can hope for—dear wife. If you were to tell me otherwise, I'd know you lied. You can no more sheathe your claws than a wildcat can, and as for your bed thawing out . . . well, we'll see the Second Coming first."

Maude flushed. "If my bed is cold, the blame is yours."

"The Devil it is!"

"If you treated your yellow-haired harlot the way you do me, you'd have to pay her a lot more money than you do now! You never ask, you just take. You force yourself upon me whenever you choose, and you do not care if I am ailing or tired. It is not unreasonable to want to say no sometimes. But then, you'd never hear me, would you?"

Geoffrey was incredulous. "Christ Jesus, woman, you make it sound as if I rape you!"

"You do," she said flatly, and his disbelief exploded into outrage.

"Have you gone mad?" When he strode toward her, she took an involuntary backward step, for although she was tall for a woman, he still towered above her. "I have every right to lay with you, for you are my wife! Need I remind you of that?"

"As if I could forget!"

His eyes were of a changeable color, blue or grey depending upon his mood or the light. They were dark now, like slate. He'd made no move to touch her, but as soon as she could retreat without seeming to, she put some space between them.

"I would to God I knew what ails you, woman. Mayhap you're not just bad-tempered and perverse, mayhap you're truly crazy! I do not know how else to explain half of what you say. Unless you are mocking me? Is that it, Maude?"

"No!" she protested. "Why is it honesty when a man speaks his mind and madness when a woman does?"

He shook his head in disgust. "God help the English if ever you do become queen. But until then, you are going to do what I say. I am not offering you a choice, Maude. I can compel your obedience if need be, and we both know that."

Maude swallowed. "I am not afraid of you, Geoffrey."

"Then you are truly a fool," he said coldly, "for you've given me no reason to think fondly of you. You've proven yourself to be a disagreeable companion, an indifferent bedmate, and a barren wife . . . Have I left any of your failings out?"

Maude gasped. "That is not so! I bore the emperor a son!"

"Dead," he shot back. "What good does it do a man to have a stillborn heir?"

"My son lived . . ." she began, but she got no further; to her horror, her voice was no longer steady.

"Not long enough. How old were you when you started to share the imperial bed . . . thirteen? Fourteen? So you had nigh on ten years to conceive another child, and you could not do it. Your husband needed a healthy, living heir, and you failed him. So why should I think you could do any better for me?"

"God will give me a son," she said huskily, "a son who will be king. My only regret is that the child must be yours, for I would rather lay with any man but you! Even a leper's touch could not be more loathsome than yours—"

It was then that he lunged at her. But as fast as he was, she was even faster, and his hand just brushed her sleeve. She spun around and he thought she meant to dart behind the table. Instead, she snatched something from an open casket and whirled back to face him. "You will not hit me again," she warned, "I swear by the Rood that you will not!"

He took a quick step toward her and then froze, shocked into immobility not by her defiance but by the sight of that jeweled dagger glinting in her fist. His eyes narrowed, flicking from the knife to her white face, back to the dagger again. She was holding it too high, too far out from her body. She'd not had his training with weapons. Nor did she have his greater reach. Measuring the risk, he decided he could probably get the blade away from her without too much trouble. He made no attempt to do so, though. Her breathing was uneven and shallow; he could see how rapidly her breasts rose and fell. Perspiration had begun to trickle down her neck, into her cleavage, and a pulse was throbbing in her throat. She'd never looked so desirable, or so desperate. But it was as if he were watching her from a distance. Even his anger had suddenly iced over. And he knew then what he would do.

"I have had enough," he said. "The throne of England is not worth this. The Throne of Heaven itself would not be worth it. Our marriage is over." And he turned away, strode toward the door.

Maude was stunned. "What are you saying?"

Sliding the bolt free, he looked back over his shoulder. "I no longer want you as my wife. Tell your women to start packing, for I'd have you gone by first light."

Before she could respond, the door closed, quietly, and that was somehow more ominous than if he'd slammed it shut. Reaction set in and she began to tremble. The dagger slid from her fingers, dropped into the floor rushes.

"My lady? What happened? You look white as chalk! He did not hurt you?"

"No, Minna." The other woman shoved a brimming wine cup into her hand, and Maude drank gratefully, entwining her fingers around the stem to steady her grip. "He says . . . says the marriage is over."

Minna was dumbfounded. "He cannot mean that, madame . . . can he?"

"No," Maude said, as emphatically as she could. "Of course he does not mean it! There is too much at stake—the succession of Anjou, England,

and Normandy. The scandal would be beyond belief. All of my father's plans would be set at naught." She paused, turning then, to meet Minna's troubled gaze. "My father," she said softly, "would never forgive me . . ."

MAUDE spent the evening's remaining hours seeking to convince herself that Geoffrey could not possibly have been serious. But she still slept badly and awakened at dawn, so tense and edgy that she decided she had but one course of action: to confront Geoffrey straightaway.

Her husband's squire could not hide his surprise, for she'd never before made an early-morning appearance in Geoffrey's bedchamber. Geoffrey was already up and dressed; his high boots and dark-green tunic indicated he had a day's hunting in mind. He gave Maude a cool, mocking glance. "Into the lion's den? How brave of you, darling."

Now it was Maude's turn to say, "We need to talk. Will you send Raimund away?" Forcing herself to add "please" through gritted teeth.

He shrugged, dismissing his squire with a casual gesture. "Have you come, then, to bid me farewell?"

Maude stared at him. "You cannot do this, Geoffrey. You could not be so irresponsible, so reckless!"

"You think not? Go to the window, then. Your escort is waiting below, ready to see you safe into Normandy or Hell or wherever else you care to go."

"For God's sake, Geoffrey, this is madness! You've not thought this through. The Church will not annul our marriage; we have no grounds. You'll not be able to wed again. Neither one of us will. What will you do for an heir?"

Moving to the table, he poured himself a breakfast beverage of watered-down wine. "If it comes to that, I suppose I can wait for you to die, dear heart. The only benefit of having such an older wife is that you're not likely to outlive me, are you?"

"This is nothing to joke about! What of your father? He'll be enraged if you commit this folly and well you know it!"

"I expect so," he acknowledged airily. "But Jerusalem is a long, long way from Angers. It'll be months ere he even hears."

"*My* father is not in Jerusalem," she snapped. "What of *his* rage?"

"That is your problem, dear heart, not mine," he said, and smiled at her.

It was like looking at a stranger. He even sounded different; there was malice in his tone but no anger. Maude was at a loss, not knowing how to deal with this new Geoffrey, defeated by this odd mixture of boyish flippancy and adult resolve. "So be it," she said at last. "I'll not beg."

"A pity," he said, "for that would have been one memory of our marriage I might have cherished." The smile he gave her was lighthearted, quite genuine. Moving past her to the door, he said, "Well, I'm off to the hunt. It would be sporting of you to wish me luck. I wish you Godspeed and a safe journey. But Maude . . . do be gone by the time I get back tonight."

He didn't bother to close the door; she could hear him whistling as he started down the stairs. Maude stood very still, listening to the sounds of his receding footsteps in the stairwell, the fading echoes of his jaunty tune. God in Heaven, what now?

IN early September, Maude arrived at her father's royal manor at Quevilly, in the parish of Saint-Sever on the outskirts of Rouen. The king was no longer in Normandy, though, having returned to England in July. Writing to her father was one of the most difficult tasks Maude had ever faced. It left her pride in tatters, lacerated and raw. But she had no choice. Her father had to know how Geoffrey had abused her, how miserable he'd made her. If he understood that, he might not blame her for the breakup of her marriage.

After dispatching a letter to her father at Windsor, Maude then had a confidential, candid, and disheartening discussion with Hugh d'Amiens, the new Archbishop of Rouen. He confirmed what she already knew: that the Church recognized but three grounds for dissolving a marriage—a previous plight troth, a blood kinship within the seventh degree, or a spiritual kinship such as godparent and godchild—and that Geoffrey and Maude could satisfy none of them. Which meant, Maude later confided bitterly to Minna, that she was chained to Geoffrey as surely as if he'd cast her into an Angevin dungeon and clapped her in irons. As wretched as their life together had been, all she could hope for was that he might relent and take her back. If he did not, her father's dynastic dreams would be destroyed, and so would her own dreams of queenship, for Henry would not keep her as his heir if she could not give him a grandson.

She'd always liked Rouen, but now she hated it. Heads turned and whispers began each time she ventured into the city's streets. She found it intensely humiliating, knowing that she was the object of so much gossip, much of it salacious, her broken marriage the butt of alehouse jokes and crude tavern humor. But worst of all was the suspense, the silence from England as the weeks passed. She wrote again, and after that, all she could do was wait for her father's response.

It came at last on a rain-chilled October eve. Maude and Minna were seated before the solar hearth, playing a game of chess. Maude glanced up as the door opened, expecting a servant, and found herself gazing at her eldest brother and his wife.

"Robert, thank God!" Maude was not demonstrative by nature, but now she flung herself into Robert's arms and even embraced Amabel, although the two women had nothing in common except Robert. "Why did you not let me know you were coming? How the sight of you gladdens me! You . . . you do know about Geoffrey?"

"Yes," he said, "that is why I am here." There was a brief delay while Robert and Amabel exchanged pleasantries with Minna and wine was served. But as soon as they were alone, Robert took a sealed parchment from a pouch at his belt and silently held it out to her.

He watched sadly as Maude read their father's letter, saw the color fade from her face, only to flood back as she continued to read, and then ebb away again. Raising wide, stricken eyes to his, she said, "Papa blames me, Robert. He says it is all my fault."

"I know."

"This is so unjust! Did he not get my letters? Did he read them?"

When he nodded reluctantly, she reached out and caught his arm. "Then he knows how Geoffrey maltreated me! What did he say to that?"

"I do not remember, lass," he said, no longer meeting her eyes.

"Robert, tell me!"

Still he said nothing. It was Amabel who finally told Maude what her husband would not. "He said, Maude, that you'd likely brought it upon yourself."

Maude stared at her sister-in-law, then swung back toward her brother. "He truly said that?"

"He was in a rage, Maude. When men are angry, they are careless, ofttimes say what they do not mean—"

"No," Maude said, "not Papa. He never says what he does not mean." She was badly shaken, and it showed. "How can he be so uncaring? How can he take Geoffrey's side over mine?"

"Maude, he is not doing that."

"No? It certainly sounds that way to me! But I am not the one who murdered our marriage. It is Geoffrey's dagger buried in the body, for it was Geoffrey who cast me out. What would Papa have me do? Beg him to take me back? This was not my fault, Robert. Why could you not make Papa see that?"

"Ah, Maude . . ." He glanced at her, then looked away, and it was then that Maude saw the truth.

"My God," she whispered. "You, too? You think I am to blame?"

"Maude, it is not a matter of blame. I am not defending Geoffrey, in truth I am not. But I would to God it had never happened, that you—"

He broke off, but not in time. "Go on," Maude challenged. "Finish the thought, Robert! What ought I to have done? Suffered in silence? Let him beat me black and blue without complaint?"

"You know better than that," he said quietly. "This serves for naught. We can talk in the morning when you are not so distraught. But for now, I think it is best that we bid you goodnight." Stepping forward, he kissed her upon the cheek and then paused, as if waiting for her to speak. She did not, and he turned toward the door. Amabel followed.

Maude moved to the hearth. She was suddenly so cold that she'd actually begun to shiver. When the door opened, she did not turn, assuming it was Minna. But it was Amabel.

"There is something I would say to you, Maude. You must not blame Robert. This was not a mission of his choosing. His father commanded him to come. He would never willingly hurt you, and you ought to know that by now."

"All I know is that I was the one wronged. I am here because Geoffrey banished me from Anjou. So how is it that I am at fault? Suppose you tell me, Amabel. You've never been at a loss for words!"

"Indeed, I do speak my mind. And I will now, woman to woman. I do agree that you have been wronged. If your marriage was a ship, Geoffrey was the one who ran it upon the rocks. But you ought to have seen this coming. A ship does not sink with no warning. Why were you not aware that it was taking on water? In all honesty, I do not understand how you botched this so badly. You are a beautiful woman, Maude. Why you could not bedazzle or bewitch a lad of fifteen—"

"How dare you pass judgment on me! Does Robert ever hit you? Does he boast openly of his bedmates? Take pleasure in your pain? Unless you can answer those questions with a yes, you cannot know what my marriage was like, and you have no right to criticize me!"

"There is truth in what you say," Amabel admitted. "But there is truth in what I said, too, and for your sake, I hope you can see that in time. Sooner or later, Geoffrey will take you back. Surely you know that? Your father is not about to let a headstrong cub thwart his will or undo his carefully crafted plans for the succession. Geoffrey will come to his senses; the king will see to that. And when he does, I hope you'll remember what I said this night."

"Go away, Amabel," Maude said, and although her sister-in-law looked aggrieved, she did. Maude still clutched her father's letter, crumpled within her fist. She smoothed it out now, but did not reread it. Instead, she thrust it into the hearth. A scorching smell filled the room as the parchment caught fire, began to smolder. She watched it burn, not moving until it was engulfed in flames.

3

CHARTRES CASTLE, FRANCE

February 1133

"To know Scriptures is to know God's Will," the Bishop of Winchester declared, with utter certainty. "And Scriptures say: 'Permit not a woman to teach, nor to usurp authority over the man, but to be in silence. For Adam was first formed, then Eve.' How much more clearly can it be put than that? A female king is not only a contradiction in terms, it is an abomination unto the Lord, and it must not come to pass."

In appearance, the bishop was unprepossessing, but he had a rich, resonant voice, and had justly gained himself a reputation for stirring oratory. His latest effort was wasted, though, upon this particular audience. To the rest of Christendom, Henry of Blois was a respected prince of the Church, one of England's youngest bishops, clever and cultivated and a likely candidate to wear one day the mitre of Canterbury's archbishop, for he was known to stand high in the favor of his uncle the English king. But to Theobald, Count of Blois and Champagne, and Stephen, Count of Boulogne and Mortain, he was still their younger brother, and his impressive adult successes would always be competing with memories of the child he'd once been, awkward and precocious and obstinate, a lonely little figure chasing after them down the byways of their boyhood, never quite catching up.

No one hearing Henry could doubt the sincerity of his convictions, but Theobald had no great interest in the succession to the English throne. For some years now, he had quite competently ruled the prosperous domains he'd inherited, first from his father and then from his uncle—Blois, Chartres, Sancerre, Châteaudun, Meaux, and Champagne—and he was pragmatic enough to be satisfied with what God had given him. Stephen, too, was content with his lot in life; his marriage to Matilda de Boulogne had brought him both wealth and happiness. Unlike Theobald, though, he could not afford to be indifferent to English politics, for he held vast English estates. But he was not comfortable with Henry's harangues about their cousin Maude; they stirred up too many doubts, too much unease.

When a servant entered the solar with word of a guest's unexpected arrival, Theobald was quick to make his escape, hastening down to the great hall to welcome their cousin the Earl of Gloucester. Stephen developed a sudden, unlikely desire to greet Robert, too, but Henry would have none of it, insisting that he remain, and Stephen sank down in his chair again, trapped by his reluctance to be rude.

Henry was not troubled by Theobald's defection, for his argument had been aimed at Stephen. Seeing that he was about to resume his homily upon Maude's unholy queenship, Stephen sought to head him off with humor.

"What I cannot understand," he said, "is how you can be so convinced that women are such inept, frail, hapless creatures. What of our lady mother? Until Theobald came of age, she governed Blois for him, did she not? And for all that she humbly signs her letters these days as 'Adela, the nun of Marcigny,' we both know she has that poor prioress utterly cowed, rules the nunnery as surely as ever she did Blois. Moreover, I'd wager that once she gets to Heaven, she'll not be there a week ere she has the Almighty Himself on a tight rein!"

Henry was not amused. "Do not blaspheme, Stephen. Our mother is unlike other women, and well you know that. But even she would not dare to claim a kingdom as Maude does."

Stephen doubted that exceedingly, saw no point in saying so, though. During his boyhood, Adela had often remarked, "How like your father you are," and he'd known even then that she'd not meant it as a compliment. But there was no question as to which of their parents Henry took after, he thought, for nothing less than an Act of God could deflect him from his purpose. He was already drawing breath to continue his sermon, and Stephen had no liking for sermons.

"What of our oaths?" he interrupted. "I swore to accept Maude as queen when our uncle dies. So did you, Henry. So did we all. Or has that somehow slipped your mind?"

"How could you have refused?" Henry demanded, had his answer in Stephen's silence. "None of us could, for our uncle is not a man to be defied. Need I remind you that an oath given under duress is not binding in the eyes of Holy Church?"

They'd had this discussion before, more times than Stephen could count. "Do you remember that embroidered wall-hanging in our mother's bedchamber? The one that depicted her father's conquest of England? It faced the bed, so it would be the first thing she saw every morn, the last thing at night. I've wondered at times if our father was ever tempted to set it afire . . ."

His brother was frowning. "For God's sake, Stephen, why are we speaking of a wall-hanging in our mother's bedchamber? How is that relevant?"

"I just hope she bequeathes it to you, Henry, for no one could cherish it more. Can we call a halt to the invasion plans . . . at least for tonight? In truth, I do not feel comfortable with this conversation. I'm fond of Maude and I—"

"You are?" The bishop sounded astonished. "Why?"

"Is it truly so surprising? Maude has candor and courage and"—Stephen grinned—"it does not hurt that she is so easy on the eyes! Moreover, I cannot help pitying her plight, shackled for life to a husband she loathes."

"So her marriage is less than perfect," Henry said impatiently. "All marriages have rough patches."

"'Less than perfect'? Try 'hellish.' She is miserable with the man, and who can blame her? First Geoffrey shames her before all of Christendom by packing her off to her father as if she were defective goods. Then he changes his mind two years later and decides that mayhap he can put up with her after all—no great surprise there, for how many wives bring along a crown as their marriage portion? So he writes to her father, who calls a council to discuss Geoffrey's demand, and they all agree that she must go back to Anjou. But one voice seems to have been missing from this great debate: Maude's. Does it not strike you as odd, Henry, that our uncle would make her queen, and yet give her no say whatsoever in the matter of her own marriage?"

The only thing odd to the bishop was his brother's peculiar way of thinking. Stephen always seemed to be wandering off the road onto paths he alone could see. Henry was fond of Stephen, but he did not understand him at all, constantly baffled and frustrated by what he saw as Stephen's overly sentimental and impractical approach to life. Theobald would have been his first choice, but Theobald had so far shown even less enthusiasm than Stephen. Oh, he'd likely take the crown if it were dropped into his lap. But the bishop had long ago learned that a man must fight for what he wanted in this life. His uncle could not be allowed to carry out this mad gamble of his. For a gamble it was, one that put both England and Normandy at risk, that might even imperil the Church itself. And he was not going to let that happen, by the Rood, he was not. He would see Stephen crowned in spite of himself if need be, and as his reward for saving England from Maude's disastrous queenship, he would claim the Church's most influential see, that of Canterbury. A crown for Stephen, an archbishop's mitre for himself: a fair trade for thwarting an old man's unforgivable folly.

"Of course Maude ought to have gone back to Geoffrey," he said, marveling that he must waste time in pointing out the obvious. "A wife must obey her husband. And that is but another reason why Maude must never be allowed to claim the English throne. Who amongst us would want to be ruled by Geoffrey of Anjou?"

To Henry's intense annoyance, Stephen laughed. "I know Maude better than that!"

"Our lady mother agrees with me," Henry said, and Stephen's laughter stopped abruptly. "I have visited her at the nunnery in Marcigny, and she sees matters as I do. By claiming the crown, you would be serving God and the English people, whilst bringing glory to your family's name. A crown, she said, will do honour to our father's memory, rid it of a lingering blotch, the shame he suffered at Antioch—"

"I should think," Stephen said, "that he expiated any and all sins by dying as he did at Ramleh."

There was a surprising edge to Stephen's voice, for it was a longstanding family joke that his anger was like a bear denned up for the winter, all but impossible to bestir. He'd gotten to his feet, and the bishop said hastily:

"Those were our mother's words, not mine. For all her virtues, she is overly prideful, and I'll not deny it. I respect your doubts, for this is not an undertaking to be entered into lightly. Take the time you need to consider what I've said. But I would ask you one question, and I want you to answer me honestly, without jesting or evasions. Can you truly tell me, Stephen, that you believe Maude could rule England and Normandy as well as a man could . . . as you could?"

Stephen did not want to answer, but his brother was implacable, appeared willing to wait as long as necessary. "No," he said at last, "I do not."

"Nor do I," Henry said, not firing the most formidable weapon in his arsenal until Stephen reached the door. "Do you think often of the White Ship?"

Stephen stopped, his hand on the door latch. "Our sister drowned in that wreck. Of course I think of it."

"You almost drowned, too, Stephen. Few men come as close to death as you did that November night . . . and walk away. Have you never wondered why you were spared? Was it truly happenchance? Or did the Almighty spare you for a purpose of His own?"

"What purpose, Henry? To save England from Maude? Would it not have been simpler then, just to let the White Ship miss that rock? If Will had not drowned, Maude would still be in Germany, our uncle would have a son to succeed him, and you and I would not be having this conversation."

That was not the response Bishop Henry had been hoping for, but he still felt confident that he had planted a seed in fertile soil, for what man did not ponder his own place in the mysterious workings of the Almighty? He let Stephen go, content to wait.

GOING down into the great hall, Stephen found Theobald sharing a hospitable wine flagon with their cousin. He and Robert greeted each other with a marked and mutual lack of enthusiasm, but he had a much warmer welcome for Robert's young squire. Ranulf had passed several years in Stephen's household serving as a page, for that was the approved method of educating youths of good birth. That past November he'd turned fourteen, and Robert had then assumed responsibility for the next stage of his schooling, in which he would learn about horses and weapons and the art of war. Stephen was quite fond of the boy, an affection Ranulf returned in full measure, and their reunion was highly pleasing to them both. But night had fallen some time ago, and Matilda had long since gone up to bed. Stephen soon excused himself and did likewise.

Matilda was already asleep, but when Stephen drew her into his arms, she snuggled drowsily into his embrace. He kissed the corner of her mouth, then the pulse in her throat, and her lashes quivered. "I've been told," he murmured, "that there is a good-hearted lady here who never turns a needy stranger away from her door. What are my chances of getting what I need?"

"I'd say just fair to middling." But he felt Matilda smiling against his neck, and when he caught hold of her blonde braid, she took it back, then tickled his nose with the tip.

"My cousin Robert arrived after you went above-stairs." He bent over, licking the soft hollow of her elbow. "He is on his way to visit Maude at Le Mans. Her father wants to know how she is faring, for Robert says she has been ailing, that her pregnancy has not been an easy one."

Matilda was wide awake by now. "You and Henry were in the solar for a long time. Once or twice I thought about coming to your rescue, but I could not think of an excuse he'd find credible."

"Next time, love, claim the castle is on fire," Stephen suggested, and she laughed softly, entwining her fingers in his chest hair and tugging gently. There were few secrets between them, for theirs was that most fortunate of unions, a marriage of state that was also a genuine love match. But he'd yet to tell her of past "crown conversations" with Henry, and he did not tell her of this latest one, either, although he could not have explained—even to his own satisfaction—why he kept silent.

Matilda was still smiling, her lips invitingly parted, and he lowered his mouth to hers. The kiss was a long one, no longer playful. But he surprised her, then, by saying, "I think we ought to ride along with Robert.

He says Maude's time is almost nigh, and I doubt she is getting much comfort from Geoffrey."

Matilda doubted it, too, and was sorry that Maude's marriage was so unhappy. But she still did not want to go to Le Mans. She and Maude were first cousins, for their mothers had been sisters; their uncle David was the current King of Scotland. They were linked as well by Matilda's marriage to Stephen. But there was no friendship between them; they were too unlike for that. Moreover, Matilda was eager to return to Boulogne, where their young sons awaited them. "If you truly want to go, Stephen . . ."

"But you would rather not," he said, not fooled by her dutiful denial. "I do think I ought to go, love." He hesitated, unable to explain why he felt this urgent need to offer Maude support. "But you are not obliged to go with me. You could await me here at Chartres, or . . . or you could ride south to Marcigny and pass a few days with my mother."

Matilda could not hide her dismay; she was thoroughly intimidated by her formidable mother-in-law. "If that is truly your wish . . . ," she began gamely, but then the deferential wife gave way to the suspicious one, and she raised up to look sharply into his face. "That," she cried, "was a cruel joke," and she yanked his pillow away, hit him with it.

Stephen was laughing too hard to offer an effective defense, and Matilda soon pummeled him into submission. Flushed and triumphant, she rolled over into his arms again. "I will go with you to visit Maude if it means that much to you. I will go wherever you desire, my lord husband," she said, and heaved a mock martyr's sigh before adding, "except to the nunnery at Marcigny!"

Stephen laughed again, then reached up and drew the bed-hangings snug around their bed, shutting out the world.

MAUDE was delighted to have company in these last weeks of her pregnancy. She was always glad to see Robert, who'd done his best to mend her rift with their father. She was quite fond of Ranulf. And Stephen was not just her cousin; he was one of the few men with whom she could let down her guard. She was even pleased for once to see Matilda, for Matilda had borne Stephen two children, knew what to expect in the birthing chamber.

Maude believed in being well prepared for any eventuality, but her own memories of childbirth were clouded as much by grief as by the passage of time. All she remembered with clarity was the pain afterward, once she'd been told that her son's life had been measured in but a few feeble breaths, a fading heartbeat. Minna was no help, for her marriage had been barren. And when Maude had asked other women, all too often they had assumed an indulgent tone that she found infuriating: the battle-seasoned soldier spinning war stories to awe the raw recruit. While Maude had never liked her shy, soft-spoken cousin, she felt confident that condescension was not one of Matilda's character flaws.

Robert had brought Maude a letter from their father, the warmest letter she'd gotten in some time. He was not a man to forgive easily, but it seemed that he was willing to let bygones be bygones now that Maude was back with Geoffrey where she belonged, and about to give birth to his grandchild. Maude was very resentful of his judgmental attitude; the letter pleased her, though, in spite of herself. After supper, she played chess with Robert, persuaded Stephen to teach her a popular dice game, and had a quiet talk with Matilda, who was able to reassure her that the pains she'd been having in recent days were quite normal and no cause for concern. It was one of the most pleasant evenings Maude had passed in months, and she even unbent enough to let her young brother Ranulf feel her baby's kicking. There was only one shadow cast over their gathering: Geoffrey's conspicuous absence.

The irony of it did not escape her—that for once she found herself listening intently for the sound of his footsteps, wanting to hear them. But as little as she enjoyed Geoffrey's company, still less did she enjoy being a figure of pity. She'd already been held up to ridicule and censure as a repudiated wife, and she could not bear to be seen now as a neglected wife, too, pregnant and pathetic, left at home alone while her husband took his pleasure in other beds, with other women.

She slept poorly that night, unable to find a comfortable position, and awoke the next morning feeling as if she'd never been to bed. Her ankles were swollen, her head aching, her legs cramping, and by the time Minna had helped her to dress, she'd begun to get random sharp pains in her lower back. According to Dame Rohese, her midwife, she was not due for another fortnight. But on this cold Lenten Sunday in early March, a fortnight seemed longer to Maude than a twelvemonth.

The Church said childbirth was the Curse of Eve, but she couldn't help wondering why men were spared their fair share of the burden. Granted, it was Eve who'd first let herself be tempted by the serpent, but Adam had tasted that wretched apple, too, had he not?

Minna was accustomed to her mistress's acerbic morning musings, and she continued calmly to braid Maude's long, dark hair, pointing out that the babe might well be born on Palm Sunday—an auspicious beginning, indeed, for a future king.

Maude went to Geoffrey's bedchamber as soon as she was dressed, and was angered and disconcerted to discover that his bed had not been slept in. If he did not return from his nocturnal hunting within the next few hours, his continued absence would become known to all in the castle, for there could be no other explanation for his failure to appear at dinner.

Her guests were soon up and stirring, too polite to ask about Geoffrey's whereabouts. But the dinner hour was rapidly drawing nigh; it was already past ten. Snatching up her mantle, Maude left the hall; mayhap if she consulted with the cooks about the menu, it would take her mind off her missing husband. And it was then, as she crossed the bailey toward the kitchen, that she saw Geoffrey ride in through the gatehouse.

For one who'd been out all night, he looked remarkably debonair and dapper. At the time of their wedding, he'd been a good-looking boy. Now, in his twentieth year, he'd matured into a man to turn female heads and claim female hearts, able to seduce with a smile and the age-old allure of fire and ice, the sudden glint of flames in the depths of a cool blue-grey gaze. Only one woman was indifferent to his swagger and sly, wayward charm—the wife who was now staring at him with intense, impotent fury.

Geoffrey acknowledged her presence with a cheerful wave on his way to the stables. Feeling awkward and ungainly, trapped in a stranger's heavy, bloated body, Maude trudged after him. He was already dismounting, handing over his stallion to a groom by the time she reached the stable doorway. "Where were you last night, Geoffrey?"

Although she kept her voice low-pitched, it throbbed with angry accusation. Geoffrey gave her a surprised look, a faintly mocking smile. "I think she said her name was Annette . . . why? I find it hard to believe you were lying awake all night, dear heart, craving my caresses."

"My brothers and cousins are here," she said through clenched teeth, "and I'll not have you shaming me before them." Even as she spoke, she knew she was going about this the wrong way, for Geoffrey balked at the merest prick of the spurs. But she could not bring herself to beg for the respect that ought to have been hers by right.

Although Geoffrey was scowling, the taunt she was expecting died on his lips. That imperious tone was all too familiar to him. But this was not his enemy the empress, the reluctant wife who'd wanted neither his title nor his embraces, prideful and stubborn and damnably desirable. This was a tired, tense woman with a swollen belly and slumped shoulders, much too pale, great with his child. "Fair enough," he said grudgingly. "You need not fret, Maude. I'll give you no reason to complain whilst your kin are here."

Maude was momentarily at a loss, wondering if she was supposed to thank him. She settled upon a sardonic echo of his own terse "Fair enough" and rejected his offer to escort her into the hall. Almost at once, she regretted it, for their confrontation had sapped the last of her dwindling energy, and the kitchen now seemed miles away. She opened her mouth to call Geoffrey back, but pride prevailed over exhaustion. She just needed to catch her breath, she decided. She'd only taken a few steps, though, before she was jolted by a sharp pain, and for a frightening moment, the earth lurched beneath her feet. She gasped, but she did not fall, for Geoffrey had suddenly materialized at her side, his arm around her shoulders, holding her upright until her world stopped spinning.

Maude's dizziness soon passed. But when her vision cleared, she gasped again, this time in astonishment. "Stephen!"

"Do you think you can walk now? Or would you rather wait a while?" Stephen asked, and when she nodded, he guided her into the stables, toward a nearby bale of hay.

Maude sank down on it thankfully, but as their eyes met, she flushed, for by now she'd solved the mystery of his providential appearance. To have reached her so fast, he must have come from the stables, and that meant he had overheard her conversation with Geoffrey.

"I . . . I would rather you say nothing of this," she said, and although the words seemed to refer to her dizzy spell, she was asking more than that, and they both knew it.

"I'd gone out to the stables to check upon my roan's foreleg. He gashed it on the road yesterday. But I cannot imagine that being of interest to anyone else."

"No, not likely," Maude agreed, and some of the color began to fade from her face. This was not the first time she'd had reason to be grateful for his gallantry, and as she beckoned him to sit beside her on the bale, she found herself remembering those unhappy months after her marriage foundered.

It had not been an easy time, for all knew her father was furious with her, and theirs was a society in which cues were taken from the king. What scant sympathy she'd gotten had been surreptitiously offered—Adeliza, her father's young queen—or left unsaid—Brien Fitz Count, his foster son. It was true that her little brother Ranulf had spoken up for her, asking with an eleven-year-old's forthrightness, "If Geoffrey told her to go, why are people not blaming him?" But only one man had dared to make a public defense; only Stephen had pointed out—as Ranulf had—that she'd not been the one to end the marriage. She'd been heartened by his loyalty, and comforted by his private comment, that "Geoffrey was a fool to let you go." A harmless bit of flattery—Stephen was always one for flirting—but her bruised and lacerated pride had needed such balm. She'd not forgotten his kindness, meant to reward it well once she was England's queen.

Stephen was worried by her pallor. "Shall I summon Minna?" he asked, not at all surprised when she stubbornly shook her head. "Maude . . . do you want me to talk to Geoffrey? You ought not to be under stress now, not with your time so near."

"Thank you, Stephen, but no. Actually, Geoffrey and I have been getting along better of late. He was truly pleased when I got with child, has his heart set upon a son, of course. But then, so do I," she said, and smiled.

They were quiet after that, but it was a companionable quiet. Maude slid her hand under her mantle, pressing it against her abdomen. Once she'd become pregnant, she'd envisioned her womb as a placid pool, with her baby swimming in its depths like a tiny tadpole. He was almost ready now to break the surface, to come up for air. "Stephen . . . I would ask you a question. But I want the truth, not what you think I need to hear."

Stephen stiffened, for he was afraid he knew what she was about to ask: if he thought she'd make a good queen. "Go on," he said warily, all the while wondering what he would say.

"This is likely to sound foolish, but do you think I'll be a good mother?"

His relief was considerable; he had not wanted to lie to her. "That is an odd question," he acknowledged, "not one to occur to most of us. People have babies if it is God's Will, and no one frets much over how they are raised. But yes, I think you will be a very good mother. I've heard it said that no earthly creature is as fearless as a mother lioness, defending her cubs unto the death!"

"I take it there is a compliment in there somewhere," Maude said, and laughed. "I barely remember my own mother. Of course I was so young when they sent me to Germany—just eight—and she was dead by the time I set foot again on English soil. But . . . but I never felt her presence, Stephen. There was always a distance, and it had naught to do with miles. I do not want that for my children. I want to matter more to them, to give them all that I can and make of them all they can be, to teach them to strive for excellence, to obey God's Commandments, and—for my eldest son—to be a good king."

"There is one more lesson I hope you teach them, Maude—that it is not sinful to fail," Stephen said, and she stared at him in surprise.

Surely he could not be speaking of himself? Maude knew her aunt was a demanding woman, but she thought any parent would be proud of a son like Stephen. He showed courage on the battlefield, courtesy in the hall; he had earned a king's favor, made an advantageous marriage, and sired sons of his own. Moreover—and it was this talent that Maude secretly envied, for she knew it was one she lacked herself—he had a knack for putting others at ease, had more friends and fewer enemies than any man she knew.

"If Aunt Adela is truly disappointed in you," she said, "then she must be beyond satisfying. What more could she ask for in a son?"

"One with more flint in his soul," he said with a wry smile. "My lady mother, bless her, sets standards that the Holy Christ Child could not have met. You know nothing then, of her feud with my eldest brother?"

Maude shook her head. "I thought she and Theobald were on good terms."

"They are, but Theobald is not the firstborn. I meant my brother Will. He and my mother were always at cross purposes. They fought through most of his boyhood. I do not know the whole of it, for I was too young, but I've been told Will swore a public oath that he would kill the Bishop of Chartres. He was just a lad, talking crazed, most likely drunk at the time, but my mother never forgave him. She and the bishop acted to deny Will his birthright, vesting my father's titles in Theobald, the second son. I am not surprised that you knew none of this, for you were but a babe, and it was skillfully and discreetly done. There was no scandal. Will did not fight her, and lives quietly upon the lands of his wife, at Sully, seemingly content . . . but not the Count of Blois."

Maude was silent for a time. "I could not disinherit my son," she said. "It would be like cutting out my own flesh."

"Is it wise to be so set upon a son? It could be a girl, after all."

"I want no daughters," she said, "not ever."

Stephen was puzzled by her vehemence. "Matilda recently confided that she may be with child again, and if so, we both hope for a lass this time. Why would you want to deny yourself the pleasure a daughter would bring?"

"Because," Maude said, "daughters are but pawns, utterly powerless—"

She broke off so abruptly that Stephen knew she'd had another pang. "Is it common to have these pains?"

"The midwife assured me that they come and go in the days before the birthing begins. But the ones I've had today have been different, in my back, and I—" Maude's mouth contorted, and then an alarmed expression crossed her face. "Jesú!" she cried. "My water has broken!"

Stephen jumped to his feet. "We'd best get you inside straightaway."

"No . . . you go in and tell them." Maude was looking everywhere but at Stephen's face. "I . . . I will follow in a moment or so."

"Maude, that makes no sense!" He stared at her in utter bafflement and had his answer, then, in her crimson cheeks, averted eyes, and sodden skirts. God save the lass, she was embarrassed! "Sweet cousin, listen. You must come with me. You cannot have your baby in a stable. This is Le Mans, not Bethlehem."

As he hoped, that won him a flicker of a smile, and she held out her hands, let him help her to her feet. "Take me in, Stephen," she said. "I doubt you'd make a good midwife . . ."

GEOFFREY and Stephen were dicing to pass the time. Robert had found a whetstone and was occupying himself productively in sharpening his sword. And Ranulf roamed the hall like a lost soul, edgy and impatient, generally making a nuisance of himself.

"How much longer will it be?" he asked yet again. "It has been hours already."

"That is only to be expected, lad," Robert said calmly. "It has even been known to take days."

"Days?" Ranulf and Geoffrey echoed in unison, sounding equally appalled.

"You are indeed a comfort, Cousin," Stephen said dryly. "Matilda will let us know if the birthing goes wrong. It is foolhardy to borrow trouble needlessly."

"You are right," Geoffrey agreed, reaching again for the dice. "Who wants to wager on the sport above-stairs? What say you, Stephen? I'll put up a garnet ring that Maude births a son."

Stephen shook his head in a good-natured refusal. "A man would be a fool to wager against Maude. She says it'll be a lad, and that is enough for me."

Soon after, Matilda came downstairs, bearing the same message as on earlier trips, that all was going well. The babe seemed in a hurry, too, so it would not be much longer.

This time she did not go back upstairs, instead sat down wearily in one of the recessed window seats. Stephen soon joined her. "Are you not going up again, Tilda?"

"No," she said, "I think not." Seeing his surprise, she said quietly, "In truth, love, I doubt that Maude wants me there. A woman is never so helpless, so vulnerable as when she gives birth. Her will counts for naught; it is her body that has the mastery of her. It is a frightening feeling, Stephen, knowing you must deliver your babe or die. It strips a woman down to her soul, and my cousin Maude finds that a harsher penance than the pain. She wants few witnesses to her travail, and most assuredly, I am not one of them."

"You read people like monks read books," Stephen said admiringly, and agreed readily when she suggested they go to the castle chapel to pray for Maude and her child. Once there, though, he found himself assailed by conflicting urges. Maude's claim to the crown would be strengthened if she gave birth to a son. For England's sake, it might well be best if she birthed a lass. But as he approached the altar, he seemed to hear again Maude's voice, "I want no daughters," and after a brief struggle with his conscience, he knelt and offered up a prayer for Maude, that she should be blessed with a son.

WHEN the pains got too bad, Minna and the midwife urged her to scream, but Maude would not do it. Instead, she stifled her cries by biting down on the corner of a towel. It made no sense to her that she could be shivering and sweating at the same time. The midwife insisted, however, that nothing was amiss. She'd been worried, she confessed, about Lady Maude's water breaking so soon, for that might well have prolonged the birthing. But the pains were coming sharp and strong, and the mouth of her womb was opening as it ought. It would not be much longer.

Maude tilted her head so Minna could spoon honey into her mouth, fighting back her queasiness. "You said . . . ," she panted, "said it would take about twelve hours . . ."

"Most often that is so, my lady," the midwife said, and then grinned. "But this babe of yours is not willing to wait!"

When Minna briefly opened the shutters, Maude caught a glimpse of the darkening sky. Night was coming on. The women did what they could to ease her suffering, gave her feverfew in wine, fed her more honey to keep her strength up, brought a chamber pot when she had need of it, blotted away her sweat, cleaned up her bloody discharge, prepared a yarrow poultice in case she began to bleed heavily, and prayed to St Margaret and the Blessed Virgin for mother and child.

In the distance, a church bell was pealing. Was it a "passing bell" tolling the death of a parishioner? A bell to welcome into the world a new Christian soul? Or was it the sound of Compline being rung? Maude had lost all track of time. And then the midwife gave a triumphant cry, "I see the head!"

Hastily pouring thyme oil into the palms of her hands, she knelt in the floor rushes at Maude's feet, gently massaging the baby's crown. Maude braced herself upon the birthing stool, groaning. The contractions no longer came in waves; she was caught up in a flood tide, unable to catch her breath or reach the shore. A voice was warning her not to bear down anymore. Hands were gripping hers, and she clung tightly, scoring Minna's flesh with her nails. Her eyes were squeezed shut. When she opened them again, she saw her child, wet head and shoulders already free, squirming between her thighs into the midwife's waiting hands.

"Almost there, my lady, almost . . ." Maude shuddered and jerked, then sagged back on the birthing stool. "Glory to God!" The jubilant midwife held up the baby, red and wrinkled and still bound to Maude's body by a pulsing, blood-filled cord. "A son," she laughed, "my lady, you have a son!"

IT was over. The afterbirth had been expelled. Maude had been cleaned up and put to bed. The women had bathed her son, swaddled him in soft linen, and called in the wet nurse to suckle him. Maude struggled not to fall asleep, for they'd warned her it was dangerous so soon after the birth. But she must have dozed, for when she opened her eyes again, Geoffrey was standing by the bed.

He was smiling, and after a moment's hesitation, leaned over and kissed her on the cheek. "You have given me a fine, robust son," he said. "You ought to be proud."

"I am," she said. "Where is he? I want to see him."

Minna emerged from the shadows, beaming, and laid a swaddled bundle in Maude's arms. "Lord Geoffrey is right, my lady. He is a fine little lad."

The baby was bigger than Maude had expected, and seemed to be a sound sleeper. His skin was not as red now, or as puckered. Maude touched his cheek with her finger, and it was like stroking silk. She was intrigued to see how much hair he had. Even by candlelight, it held unmistakably coppery glints.

"He looks like you," she said, and Geoffrey peered intently into his son's small face.

"You think so?" he asked, sounding pleased. "Maude, the priest says he ought to be christened as soon as possible. I think we'd best have it done on the morrow."

Maude nodded. She was finding it harder and harder to stay awake, but she was not yet ready to relinquish her son, even for a few hours. "I suppose you still want to name him Fulk, after your father," she said drowsily.

Geoffrey looked at her, then at the baby. "Well . . . no," he said, and Maude's lashes fluttered upward in surprise. "I know we've been quarreling over names, but I've changed my mind. You can name him, Maude. I think you've earned the right."

Maude did, too. "Thank you," she said, and smiled sleepily at her husband and son. The baby chose that moment to open his eyes, and startled them both by letting out a loud, piercing wail. They looked so nonplussed that the midwife and wet nurse started to laugh. And it was then that Minna opened the door and ushered Robert, Ranulf, Stephen, and Matilda into the bedchamber.

Maude was not a woman to find humor in chaos. But for once she did not care about decorum or dignity. Cradling her screaming little son, she said happily, "Come closer so you can hear over his shrieks. I want to present Henry, England's future king."

4

LONDON, ENGLAND

April 1135

IT had been a day of chill winds and random rain showers, a day that had offered but one wan glimpse of the sun and not even a hint of coming spring. An oppressive, damp early dusk had settled over the city, and by the time Sybil neared the river, she was cursing herself for having mislaid her lantern, for the night sky was starless and the narrow, twisting streets were deep in shadow. Ahead lay the bridge. As she approached it, church bells began to toll; off to the west, St Martin Le Grand was chiming the curfew. Sybil swore under her breath, quickening her step, for the city gates would now be closing.

Fortunately, the guards were young, and she won their sympathy with a pretty smile, a lie about seeking a leech for her fevered child. She was the last one allowed through the gate, out onto the bridge.

The wind was gusting, the river surging against the wooden pilings, and Sybil was thankful when she reached the far shore. Turning west along the priory wall of St Mary Overy, she headed toward the Bankside. Londoners took pride in their city's ancient past, stretching back a thousand years to Londinium, capital of Roman Britain. Southwark's history was more obscure, but Sybil suspected that it, too, had existed then, luring Roman soldiers across the river to drink, gamble, and sin. Long before Norman-French adventurers followed William the Bastard into his newly conquered kingdom, Southwark was notorious, a haven for fugitives and felons and those seeking whores, ale, or trouble.

Southwark, be it Roman, Saxon, or Norman, was no safe place for a woman alone, even in broad daylight, and now, with the curfew bells still echoing across the river and every alleyway black as pitch, every door bolted against thieves and drunken knaves, Sybil hastened along the Bankside, keeping to the center of the street, for she knew the shadows hid watching eyes.

Had it been daylight, the Bankside would have been teeming with raucous, ribald life—with peddlers, beggars, sailors from the quays, pick-pockets on the prowl, prostitutes too old or ailing for the bawdy-houses, foraging dogs, hissing geese, even a stray pig or two. Now the street was deserted, mired in mud and strewn with rotting garbage. Detecting movement from the corner of her eye, Sybil whirled as a scrawny grey cat scuttled under a broken wagon wheel. "Fiend take me," she said ruefully, "if my nerves are not on the raw this night! How is it that you're so stout-hearted, Emma, whilst I'm so skittish?"

She got no answer, but did not expect one, for her daughter's cheerful babble had yet to translate into recognizable words. Shifting the baby to her other hip, she swerved to avoid a deep, muddy rut in the road, and it was then that the men stepped from the shadows, barring her way.

"What is your hurry, sweeting?" The smile may have been meant to be ingratiating, but it emerged as a leer, and as he lurched toward her, Sybil caught the reek of cheap wine. She had already marked out the other man as the more dangerous of the two, and when he grabbed for her, she sidestepped, spun out of his grasp, and backed up against the closest wall.

He smirked. "Nowhere to run now, wench," he gloated, and lunged, only to halt abruptly, blinking at sight of the slender blade that had suddenly materialized from under her cloak.

"I do not give away free samples!" she spat. "Put your stinking hands on me again and you'll bleed like a stuck pig!"

"Bitch!" he snarled. But he kept his eyes on her knife, kept his distance.

His partner was peering at Sybil in bleary-eyed confusion, which slowly gave way to sheepish recognition. "Sybil . . . ? A pox on us, Wat, she's one of the doxies from the Cock!" The leer came back. "Sorry, lass, we just meant to have a bit of fun . . ."

"You still can," she said coldly, "as long as you pay for it," thinking all the while, Not in this life or the next, for they stank of sweat and grease and spilled wine, and her gorge rose at the thought of their dirty hands and foul breath in her bed. She knew better than to trust to the honour of thieves, and kept her knife out and at the ready as she circled around them. Her heart was thudding and her face flushed, but she moved at a deliberate pace, seeking to appear unafraid, for defiance had often proved to be as effective a weapon as her dagger in fending off rape. They shouted after her, making lewd offers and then obscene threats, all of which she ignored. But she did not sheathe her knife, not until she saw ahead the whitewashed wooden houses of the Southwark stews.

She'd heard it said that the brothels were whitewashed so they'd be easily visible to would-be customers on the other side of the river, and it was true that they stood out, even on a moonless night like this one. There were more than a dozen of these Bankside bordellos; unlike the protruding ale-stakes that hung over alehouses and taverns, the brothel names were painted right on the buildings, a crudely drawn crane or bell or crown. Passing the first three by, Sybil headed for the sign of the cock, slipping in a side door.

The kitchen was a contraband chamber, for bawdy-houses were prohibited from serving food or drinks. But like most of the laws intended to regulate Southwark's sin industry, this one was sporadically enforced, and tonight the cook was stirring a savory beef-marrow broth in a large cauldron. Dragging her makeshift cradle toward the hearth, Sybil put her daughter to bed. After tucking in the blankets, she lingered, fishing out a freshly plucked goose feather for Emma to suck upon, loath as always to leave her child. But then Berta strode in. "You're late, my girl—Jesú, not again! This is no fitting place for a babe, Sybil! How often do you have to hear it?"

Sybil was unimpressed by the bawd's tirade; they both knew that she was the Cock's star attraction. "A neighbor's lass usually looks after Emma whilst I'm at work, but she was stricken with toothache. What would you have me do, Berta . . . leave a babe of seven months to fend for herself?"

Berta continued to grumble, but without any real heat. Sybil knew there were stew-holders who ran roughshod over their whores, but neither Berta nor her taciturn, morose husband, Godfrey, had a talent for tyranny. Sybil accorded them a casual sort of deference because it was politic to do so, but she never doubted that in any clash of wills, the stronger one would prevail—hers. Giving Emma one last quick kiss, she shed her cloak and sauntered into the common room.

She did not like what she found there: a surfeit of working women, a dearth of paying customers. It was, she saw, going to be a long night. There were a few foreign sailors, a drunken dockworker, a nervous youth whom she dismissed as a serious prospect; lads that young had the itch but rarely the money to scratch it. The sailors were already snared, sitting at a table with Loveday, sharing ale and bawdy laughter, apparently not handicapped by their lack of a common language, for they knew only Norwegian, and Loveday, like most of the Southwark harlots, was of Saxon birth, which meant that English—not Norman French—was her native tongue.

As Sybil entered, Loveday gave her a wave. Between them, they had the pick of the Cock's clientele, but their rivalry was a friendly one, for they were rarely in direct competition; they appealed to very different male needs. Loveday was a big-boned, good-natured country girl, crude and blunt-spoken, with thick masses of untidy curly hair, dyed yellow or gold or red as the whim took her. She always looked somewhat disheveled, breasts spilling out of her low-cut bodice, so well-rouged that she seemed sunburned, perfumed and powdered but none too clean. There were many men, though, drawn by her brazen earthiness, reassured by her easygoing approachability. And for the others, there was Sybil: tall and slender, with small wrists and feet, high breasts and unblemished skin, so prideful and poised that a man could easily indulge in fantasy, could pretend he was bedding a lady.

Sybil poured herself some wine, sat down at one of the trestle tables. She felt no surprise when Eve soon drifted over. She'd vowed not to take the younger girl under her wing; she had enough on her plate as it was. But Eve, a timid, frail fourteen-year-old newcomer to the stews, needed no more encouragement than a lost, scared puppy would, and as she took a seat with a shy smile, Sybil grudgingly admitted to herself that she was stuck with yet another stray. She was frowning over an ugly greenish bruise that was only partially hidden by the sleeve of Eve's gown when Avelina pulled up a stool, helped herself to Sybil's wine, and announced glumly that she had missed her flux again.

Time was never a friend to women in their precarious profession, and tonight it was the enemy. Loveday went off with her sailors. Sybil suggested some herbs—tansy and pennyroyal—that Avelina might try. The drunkard in the corner spilled an entire flagon of ale and took it out on the little kitchen maid, who fled in tears. Avelina was cheered by the arrival of a portly goldsmith, one of her regulars. But he was intercepted by Jacquetta the Fleming, who'd been blessed with blue eyes and long blonde hair but no scruples; she had no qualms about stealing another girl's customer, as she proved now, coaxing the goldsmith above-stairs before Avelina could muster up an effective protest. Sybil ordered another wine flagon and they set about drinking in earnest, for there seemed no better way to pass the hours. But it was then that the door banged and their watchdog barked and the young lords swaggered in.

She could tell they were gentry, Sybil explained to Eve, by their swords and fine wool cloaks and bold manner; did Eve not see how Berta and Godfrey were fawning over them? Knights—no, too young, she amended, most likely squires to some lord, for that was how the Norman highborn educated their sons, sending them off to serve in great households, first as pages and then as squires.

Eve was fascinated; Sybil never failed to impress her by how much she knew of the ways of the world. But her admiring glance went unnoticed. Sybil was coolly assessing these new arrivals, as alert as a cat on the scent of prey, for she well knew there was both danger and opportunity in any encounter with the highborn. They would have money, these young lordlings, and they'd need no urging, would be quick to spill their seed, not like some of her customers, who required tiresome coaxing to prime the pump. She was fastidious by nature, much preferred to couple with a body that was young and firm and reasonably clean, and these cocky lads were more to her taste than aging merchants or unwashed sailors. But if the rewards were greater, so, too, were the risks. What did a Southwark whore's wishes matter to a baron's son? Who would object if he chose to maltreat a lowborn harlot? Who would even care?

They were coming her way now, and Sybil sat up straighter, giving her bodice a discreet tug. Avelina and Eve looked hopeful, but the youths had eyes only for Sybil, and the two girls reluctantly withdrew, leaving her in possession of the battlefield.

Up close, they were younger than Sybil first thought. Seventeen or so, she reckoned, and as unlike as chalk and cheese: a red-haired, freckle-faced giant, a swarthy, handsome lad with glittering black eyes, and a wiry youth of middle height whose most striking feature was his uncommon coloring—deep-brown eyes and sun-streaked fair hair. He seemed, at first glance, overshadowed by his comrades, lacking the redhead's impressive stature or the other's smoldering Saracen intensity. But Sybil had noted that when they conferred with Berta, he'd done all the talking, and he was the one she favored with a provocative, slightly wary smile.

"We are seeking," he said, "a lass who speaks French. The stew-master assures us that our hunt is over. Is it?"

"Indeed, I do speak French," she said, "as I've just proved. If you and your friends would like to join me, mayhap we could discuss what else you are seeking this night."

He studied her for a moment more, then he grinned, and Sybil thought, God has been too good to you, lad, for with a smile like yours, you do not need money, too. It transformed his face as if by some erotic alchemy, a smile to cajole and disarm and bewitch and break hearts . . . and she'd wager that he knew it.

"I am Ranulf," he said, "and my companions here are Gilbert and Ancel," gesturing carelessly toward the redhead and the Saracen in turn. "I believe the bawd said you are called Sybil?"

Sybil nodded. "You sound as if that surprises you?"

"It was not what I was expecting."

Ancel gave a snort of laughter. "Why be so tactful? What Ranulf seems loath to say straight out is that your sisters in sin usually prefer to call themselves Petronilla or Mirabelle or Rosamund, fancy whore names. Sybil . . . now that sounds plain as dirt, drab as homespun. Have you no more imagination than that?"

Sybil's smile was so sultry that Ancel saw only the promise, not the mockery. "In a world full of Cassandras and Clarices, a simple, plain Sybil is sure to be remarked upon . . . and remembered."

Ranulf was watching her approvingly, dark eyes agleam with amusement. "I think," he said, "that you are exactly what we are looking for, Sybil plain and simple."

"Ere you say that, my lord Ranulf—you are a lord, I suspect—I think we ought first to reach an understanding. It would be my pleasure to entertain you and your friends, but one at a time. Crowds are fine for fairs and markets, not for beds. And I bruise easily, so I find it best to say this beforehand: no games that involve whips or ropes or bleeding. Other than that, I am amenable to suggestions . . . and can offer up a few of my own."

They seemed taken aback by her candor, and she decided they were even younger than she'd realized—sixteen at most—for their lust was still a simple, uncomplicated urge, not yet shadowed by darker, deviant needs. Ancel guffawed too loudly and Gilbert actually blushed. Ranulf's mouth curved. "You are the one who does not yet understand, Mistress Sybil. We do not want you to play the whore. We want you to play a nun."

Although Sybil was only nineteen, she was sure she'd long ago lost the ability to be surprised. Ranulf had just proved her wrong. "I am likely to regret saying this," she said at last, "but tell me more."

Ranulf relaxed, flashing another of those beguiling grins. "It is quite simple, truly. We have a grudge to settle, and with your help, we can. We are all squires in the household of Robert Fitz Roy, the Earl of Gloucester, and—"

Ancel would have interrupted then, but Ranulf shook his head impatiently. "Nay, no false names, Ancel. Either we trust the lass or we do not, and if not, why are we still sitting here? There is a knave in Earl Robert's service who is badly in need of a lesson. His name is Baldric Fitz Gerald, and I'll not lie to you: he has powerful kin, for he is a cousin to the Earl of Leicester and Leicester's twin brother, Count Waleran. When Baldric was a squire like us, he well nigh drove us mad with his boasting and conniving. Now that he has been knighted, he has become even more insufferable. With Earl Robert, he pretends to be a man of honour, but he amuses himself by playing cruel tricks upon those who cannot defend themselves—kitchen maids and stable lads and the pages in Earl Robert's service."

"He calls me Judas," Gilbert chimed in indignantly, "because of my red hair, and when Ancel got green sick the first time he had too much wine, Baldric made up a song about it, sang it for a hall full of highborn guests. He put a burr under Ranulf's saddle whilst we were at the king's Christmas court in Rouen, and brayed like a jackass when the stallion pitched Ranulf into a mud wallow. I know, Ranulf, we cannot prove it. But I'd wager any sum you name that he was the culprit!"

Ranulf shrugged, clearly not pleased to have that particular memory dredged up again. "Let's keep to what we can prove for certes. I know he was molesting that little kitchen maid back in Caen, for I came upon her weeping afterward. We know, too, that he caused the other servants to shun that stable groom with the red blotch on his face, claiming it was the Devil's sign, the way Satan marked out his own. The lad finally ran off, and no one knows what became of him."

Sybil was not sure how much of this she should believe. She knew the king was still in Normandy, but Earl Robert could be back in London; these Norman lords made frequent trips to check upon their English estates. "From what I've heard of Earl Robert," she said, "he is a decent sort, and truly believes that a lord owes protection to the weak and powerless, to Christ's poor. Why not just go to him, tell him of this Baldric's true nature?"

They looked at her blankly, as if she'd suddenly begun to speak an unknown tongue. There was much about the male mind that she found incomprehensible, and nothing more so than the credo that men—especially young men—must settle their grievances on their own, that it was somehow dishonourable to appeal to higher authority for help. "Whatever was I thinking of? Well, then, tell me what part I am to play in this scheme of yours?"

"Baldric is a hypocrite and a cheat, and I think it time he showed his true colors to the rest of the world, not just to his prey." Ranulf was smiling faintly, but his voice held a sudden, hard edge. "What I want," he said, "is to see him publicly shamed, his sins stripped naked for all to look upon."

"I am beginning to understand," Sybil said, looking at Ranulf with new respect. "You make a bad enemy, love. Few sins are as serious as seducing a nun."

"The best part of this plan," he said, "is that Baldric will be the instrument of his own ruin. He does not have to take the bait . . . but he will. You need only lure him into a compromising position. We'll provide the witnesses. You'll not even have to let him tumble you; that is a pleasure the whoreson does not deserve!" He laughed then, and Sybil could not help herself; she laughed, too. "Well?" he prompted. "What say you—"

The cry was muffled, quickly cut off, but it had carried enough pain to swivel all heads toward the sound. Sybil saw at once what had happened. Berta—damn her grasping soul—had sent Eve over to entice the drunkard above-stairs, and Eve had botched it, for the girl was scared witless of drunks, had yet to learn how to handle a man deep in his cups.

Now she cringed back in her seat, whimpering, as her assailant turned upon her the full blast of his alcoholic rage. Sybil half rose, only to sink back again. They had a hireling to deal with drunks, a huge, clumsy bear of a man, not too bright yet big enough to intimidate all but the most belligerent of troublemakers. He was out sick, though, and Godfrey, as she well knew, was not about to put himself at risk to protect a whore. Fighting back her anger, she reminded herself that there was nothing she could do. But then the drunk struck Eve across the mouth, and she jumped to her feet, shouting for him to stop.

She did not expect the drunk to heed her, nor did he. But Ranulf did. As she watched in amazement, he crossed the chamber in three quick strides, grabbed the man before he could aim another blow, and told him curtly to "Go home, sleep it off." It may have been his tone, the echoes of rank and privilege. It may have been the sword at his hip. But he somehow penetrated the man's wine-sodden haze. Seeing that, Godfrey hurried over to offer some belated support, and Sybil sighed with relief, sure now that the worst was over.

Ancel and Gilbert had kept their seats during the fracas. Now Ancel gave a comical grimace, winking at Sybil. "I swear that lad could find turmoil in a cemetery! Usually he sucks us into it, too, and his heroic impulses have gotten me more bruises and black eyes than I care to count. Not that it's entirely his fault. The two men who've loomed largest in his life are Earl Robert and Count Stephen of Boulogne. Good men, both, but Robert is an earthly saint, and Stephen . . . well, he's quite mad, never happier than when he's rescuing damsels in distress or chasing after dragons to slay. No wonder Ranulf's grasp of the real world is so tenuous!"

"You might do well," Sybil murmured, "to follow in Ranulf's footsteps. You see, women find 'heroic impulses' very alluring, indeed . . . even irresistible."

Ancel's smile flickered. For a fleeting moment he wondered if she could be making fun of him, but almost at once, he dismissed the suspicion as preposterous. Women were invariably charmed by him; the older ones mothered him and the younger ones flirted with him. Why should this Bankside harlot be any different? "Women already find me irresistible," he joked. "So . . . what say you, Sybil, my sweet? Shall we pick a nun's name for you? How about Sister Mary Magdalene?"

Sybil saw no humor in the jest; it was too obvious, too heavy-handed. But Ancel and Gilbert thought it was hilarious. She waited patiently until they were done laughing, and then said blandly, "Alas, I shall have to decline the honour."

They were dumbfounded by her refusal, began to bombard her with perplexed queries and protests. "It is not that I am not tempted," she admitted when they finally gave her a chance to respond, "for I am. But the danger is too great. What if this scheme went awry? How could Ranulf protect me from Baldric's wrath? If he is kin to an earl—"

She stopped, then, for both boys were grinning widely. They exchanged knowing looks and nudges before Ancel said, with just a trace of smugness, "Ranulf's protection would shield you from the malice of a hundred Baldrics. He is much more than a squire to Earl Robert. They are brothers."

Sybil's mouth dropped open, and she twisted around to stare at Ranulf, who was making a gallant attempt to comfort the sobbing Eve. "Ranulf is one of the old king's bastards?"

Ancel nodded proudly. "King Henry has sired so many he needs a tally stick to keep count of them all! Ranulf is the youngest but one, born to a Welsh lass the king fancied. None would deny the king is a hard man, but none would deny, too, that he tends to his own. Ranulf grew up at his court, has wanted for nothing. His mother died when he was just a lad, and after Count Stephen wed the Lady Matilda, Ranulf was sent into his household as a page. Then, when he turned fourteen, Earl Robert took on his training as a squire. The king is right fond of him, would be willing to find him an heiress when he's of an age to wed, but Ranulf and my sister have been mad for each other as far back as I can remember, and Ranulf appears content to settle for whatever marriage portion my father can provide. No one could ever fault his courage, but his judgment leaves much to be desired!"

"Especially in my choice of friends," Ranulf jeered, reclaiming his seat, and Sybil saw that this barbed banter was their normal form of discourse. "Are you done blabbing all my family secrets, Ancel? If so, I'd like to get back to the matter at hand. This is what we had in mind, Sybil. We'll lure Baldric to some secluded spot, mayhap out by Holywell, near the nunnery, where you will be waiting. You entreat his aid—we'll think of a plausible story for you—and then you need only give him a few lingering looks. The privacy and your beauty and his own vile nature will do the rest. Just in time we'll happen by with a few witnesses, possibly a priest or two. Of course we'll have to wait till the weather warms up, for not even Baldric would be keen for futtering out in the mud and rain! How would—what? You see a weakness in our plan?"

Sybil shook her head. "Nay, you have thought of everything . . . or almost everything."

"Ah, of course!" Ranulf smiled at her as if they were old and intimate friends, while spilling coins out onto the table. "This seems a fair sum to me."

Sybil's eyes widened, for he'd casually offered three times what she might expect to earn for a night's work. And in that moment, she no longer doubted, sure that Ranulf had spoken only the truth, for who but a king's son would be so lavish with his money?

"This is most fair," she agreed, returning Ranulf's smile. "That was not what I meant, though. I fear we have a problem that wants solving. I cannot hope to convince Baldric unless I well and truly look the part. But wherever are we going to find a nun's wimple and habit?"

RANULF and his friends left the city through Bishopsgate, headed north along the Ermine Way. It was usually a well-traveled road, the chief route to York. But most wayfarers had already sought a night's lodging, for dusk was encroaching from the west. Just moments before, the sky had been veined with coppery-gold streaks; it was now smudging with smoke-colored shadows. They passed few houses, as most people felt safer dwelling within the city walls. Before the light had faded, the countryside had been pleasant to look upon, the fields and meadows green and lush in the first flowering of spring. But the boys turned a blind eye to the pastoral beauty around them, and welcomed the sun's demise, for theirs was an undertaking that needed darkness. They rode in silence for the most part, not reining in until they saw the priory walls looming up through the deepening twilight. It was cloaked in quiet, stretching from the road back toward the River Walbrook—the Augustinian nunnery of St John the Baptist at Holywell.

Gilbert stared morosely at those moss-green walls. "I cannot believe we are actually going to do this," he muttered, not for the first time that evening, and the other two glared at him. "It is not too late to reconsider," he insisted. "Stealing from a nunnery is—"

"We are not thieves!" Ranulf snapped. "We are merely going to borrow a nun's habit for a few days. We will return it undamaged, and with a goodly sum to aid in their alms-giving. What harm in that?"

"But what if something goes wrong? If—"

"What could go wrong?" Ancel demanded. "Our plan is too simple to miscarry. It is not as if we're tying to sneak into the dorter and snatch a habit from a sleeping nun! We know the priory has spare habits on hand. We need only find where they are kept, most likely in the undercroft below the dorter, where the chambress stores her linens and beddings. The nuns will be asleep; they go to bed as soon as Compline is rung. Now I ask you, Gilbert, what have we to fear from a convent full of sleeping nuns?"

Gilbert grinned reluctantly at that, and Ranulf leaned over, punching him playfully on the arm. "What a comfort you are to us, Gib. If I looked at life the dour way you do, I'd not dare get out of bed in the morn! Why is it that you always expect the worst to happen?"

"Most likely because the two of you keep concocting lunatic schemes like this!" But Gilbert raised no more objections, and once it was fully dark, he hitched their horses in a nearby grove of trees, settled down to keep a wary watch as his friends disappeared into the shadows surrounding the priory.

It proved to be as easy as Ancel had predicted. They had no difficulty in scaling the wall, and detected no signs of life as they crept stealthily toward the church. It was deserted, and they moved swiftly through the nave, out into the silent cloisters. Ancel was to be the lookout, and took up position in one of the sheltered carrels as Ranulf started along the east walkway. He had no warning; suddenly the dorter's door swung open. He froze as a woman appeared in the doorway. What was she doing out here? And then she gave a low whistle and Ranulf swore softly. A dog, sweet Lady Mary, she had a dog! The Church forbade pets, but the prohibition was more ignored than obeyed, and cats and small dogs were common occupants of English convents. Why had he not remembered that? It was too late now, for the nun's dog was shooting through the air, swerving toward him in midstride, barking shrilly.

Ranulf kept his head, spun around and ran for the slype, the narrow passage that offered the cloister's only escape. The dog was at his heels, nipping at his boots, and the nun had begun to scream. He caught a blurred movement off to his left, and spared a second or so to hope it was Ancel, retreating back into the church. Shutters were banging, the dorter windows flung open. But he was almost there—just another few feet and he'd be on his way to safety.

It was then, though, that Ranulf learned one of life's uglier lessons: that when luck starts to sour, anything that can possibly go wrong, does. As he darted past the Chapter House, the door flew open and he collided with the priory chaplain, who should have been abed in his own lodgings at such an hour. The impact sent them both sprawling. Before Ranulf could get his breath back, the nun's lapdog landed on his chest, sinking needle-sharp teeth into his forearm. But he was still sure he could get away, for he was younger and far more fit than the priest. Kicking at the dog, he rolled over and lurched to his feet, just as the priory's porter came plunging through the slype, cudgel raised to strike.

Ranulf's shoulders slumped, and he sagged back against the Chapter House door. He was well and truly caught, by God, might as well accept it with good grace. He looked about at the chaos he'd unleashed upon the cloistered quiet of this small, peaceful priory, looked at the snarling little dog and shrieking mistress, the fearful faces peering down from the dorter windows, the bewildered priest, still scrabbling about on his hands and knees in the grass, the hulking porter, flushed and panting—and he suddenly started to laugh, for this was lunacy beyond even Gilbert's dire expectations.

He saw at once that his laughter had shocked them, and he struggled to contain his imprudent mirth, to sound sober and serious and above all, sincere, that this was merely a vast and outlandish misunderstanding. But then the porter shouted, "You misbegotten, whoreson thief, I'll teach you to steal from God!" and swung his cudgel toward Ranulf's head.

TOWER ROYAL was one of London's most impressive dwellings, as well it should be, for it had been a king's gift, presented to Stephen at the time of his marriage to the Lady Matilda de Boulogne. The neighboring residents of Watling Street and Cheapside were accustomed to noise and torchlight spilling over the manor walls. Stephen was a lavish host, and whenever he was in London, Tower Royal served as a magnet, drawing to its hospitable hearth Norman lords and their ladies, officials of the court, influential churchmen, even some of the city's more prosperous merchants and ward aldermen, for if Stephen liked a man's company, he was indifferent to whether that man was Saxon or Norman, citizen or baron. His good-natured, indiscriminate affability had subjected him, at times, to gossip and the disapproval of his peers, but it had won him the hearts of Londoners; there was no man in the city more popular than he.

On this mild April evening, he had entertained his younger brother, Henry, Bishop of Winchester. After a meal of roast duck and stewed eels, Henry's favorite foods, they settled down to a game of chess, and Stephen's wife politely excused herself from their company so they might talk of politics without constraint; the bishop, like so many of his fellow clerics, felt that women were not meant to have a voice in matters of state. Matilda, who had less malice in her nature than any of her sisters in Christendom, nonetheless found herself wondering occasionally how her brother-in-law would cope once he must answer to a queen—and an imperious one at that, for those who knew Henry's daughter knew, too, that Maude would be no docile, biddable pawn. When God called her father to Heaven's Throne, Maude would never be content merely to reign. She would rule, too; on that, her allies and enemies could all agree.

After leaving the hall, Matilda made a quick detour into the nursery, where she did a loving inventory of the three small sailors adrift in a featherbed boat: Baldwin, Eustace, and William. Their night's voyage was a peaceful one; they were all sound asleep. So, too, was the little girl in the corner cradle, her baby, her namesake. Blowing kisses to her brood, Matilda quietly withdrew.

Back in her own chamber, she dismissed her maid, then sat down amidst the cushions in the window seat and began to unbraid her hair. It floated about her like a veil of woven gold threads; Matilda was very proud of her hair, and tended it with such diligence that her chaplain had chided her for vanity. Matilda had accepted the rebuke meekly enough, as was her way, but continued to brush and burnish her hip-length blonde tresses, for she knew that Scriptures said, "If a woman hath long hair, it is a glory to her," and that secret stubbornness was also her way.

The step was well known to her, but she felt surprise, nonetheless, when she looked up, for she'd not expected her husband until the hearth had burned low. "Stephen? Is the chess game done so soon?"

"I let Henry win," Stephen said, cheerfully ignoring the fact that he was a mediocre player at best and his brother a very good one. "I then begged off from a rematch, explaining that I wanted to get above-stairs in time to watch my wife undress for bed."

Matilda's eyes widened. "Oh, Stephen, you did not—and he a priest!"

"He'd not like to hear you call him that, my love, for Brother Henry is one for holding fast to the least of his honours. A bishop he is, and would aim higher still; have you not noticed how solicitous he is of our ailing archbishop? Mayhap that's why the archbishop always looks so uneasy around Henry, almost as if he were hearing vulture wings hovering overhead!"

Matilda clicked her tongue against her teeth. "Ah, Stephen, do be serious just this once. You did not really say that to Henry, did you?"

Stephen laughed, and dropped down beside her in the window seat, marveling that after ten years of marriage and four children, she still could not tell when he was teasing her. "Mayhap I did, mayhap not."

Matilda gazed calmly into his eyes, and then turned her head aside so he'd not see her smile. "Better I not know," she said, and sighed as he drew back her hair, kissing the curve of her throat. "It gladdens me that you still find pleasure in looking upon my body, even if I'd rather you not boast about it to men of the Church."

"Indeed, I do find pleasure in looking, and in touching and caressing and stroking and fondling . . . what did I leave out?" he asked, and when he laughed this time, she did, too. He'd lifted her onto his lap and she'd gone soft and languid in his arms by the time a repeated rapping sounded on the door.

"We're not here," Stephen said loudly as Matilda sought to muffle her giggles against his shoulder. When the knocking persisted, he got reluctantly to his feet. "I'll get rid of them right quick," he assured her, and she watched as he strode across the chamber and opened the door. After a brief exchange, he turned with an apologetic smile. "It is my cousin Ranulf, and he says it is urgent. I'll have to see him, Tilda, but not for long, that I promise." Returning to the window seat, he began to speculate what Ranulf might want at such an hour. "He is a good lad, but nary a day goes by without him getting into devilment of some sort, most of which he manages to keep from my uncle the king. Did I ever tell you about the time he—"

He got no further, for the servant was back. But the two youths being ushered into the bedchamber were strangers to Stephen. "Who in blazes are you?"

The taller of the two came forward, knelt, and said hastily, "Forgive us, my lord, for lying to you, but we knew no other way to gain admittance. My name is Gilbert Fitz John and this is Ancel de Bernay. We are squires to the Earl of Gloucester, and Ranulf's friends. He needs your help, my lord Stephen, for he has been arrested!"

Stephen was surprised, but not shocked, for youthful sins were both expected and indulged, provided that the sinners were highborn, like Ranulf. "What has he done? An alehouse brawl?"

The boys exchanged glances. Gilbert hesitated, then blurted out, "Nay, it is far more serious than that. Ranulf was caught breaking into the priory of St John at Holywell. I very much fear he'll be charged with attempted theft or even rape. But it is not true, I swear it. He meant only to borrow a nun's habit!"

There was a silence after that. Stephen and Matilda shared the same expression, one of utter astonishment. But then the corner of Stephen's mouth quirked. Turning back to his wife, he said, "I am sorry, my love, but I cannot keep my promise. This is one story I have got to hear!"

RANULF would not have believed it had he ever been told he could be afraid of the dark. But he'd never experienced darkness like this, lacking the faintest glimmer of light, as black as the pits of Hell. He was not alone; an occasional rustling in the straw warned him of that. Mice, he guessed, or rats. He stamped his feet to discourage any undue familiarity, slumping back against the wall. His manacles were rubbing his wrists raw, and his head was throbbing, but a headache was of minor moment when he considered what might have happened. If he'd not ducked in time, he'd have suffered much more than a grazed, bloody scalp; the porter's cudgel would have split his skull like a ripe gourd.

He did not know whether it was a hopeful sign or not that he'd been taken to the Tower and not the gaol of London. It might just be a matter of convenience; the Tower, built by his royal grandsire, was closer to the priory than the city gaol, off to the west by the River Fleet. He was quite familiar with the Tower, for its upper two floors contained his father's London residence and the chapel of St John. But he'd never expected to find himself confined in a small, underground cell near the storage chamber. He'd never, ever expected to be manhandled and shoved and treated like a felon.

His experience in the past few hours had taught him—if the porter's cudgel had not already done so—that his predicament held no humor whatsoever. Theft was a serious offense, and "stealing from God" was a crime he could hang for. He might also be charged with attempted rape, for people would be quick to suspect the worst of a man caught at night in a nunnery. Ranulf tried to recall what he'd heard about rape laws. All he knew for certes was that it was a much more serious crime if a man forced himself upon a virgin, and nuns were all virgins—save an occasional widow—Brides of Christ.

Ranulf knew, of course, that he held the key to his prison. He need only speak up, reveal his identity. They were not likely to believe his story, and who could blame them? Yet it would matter little whether they believed him or not. It would be enough that he was King Henry's son. If he admitted who he was, he'd be freed. But if he did, his brother would have to know, and Ranulf could not bear that Robert find out. Robert would never understand. He'd not even be angry, just baffled and disappointed. Ranulf would not willingly disappoint Robert for the very surety of his soul. But as the hours crept by, he found his common sense—which argued for disclosure—at war with his inbred optimism, his illogical yet intense faith that all would somehow still end well.

He had time, though, to make up his mind, for he did not think they would summon the Tower's castellan until the morrow. He knew the man, with an effort even prodded his memory into disgorging the name—Aschuill. What he did not know was whether Aschuill would remember him. Well, he'd find out come morning, one way or another. Leaning his head on his drawn-up knees, he made a halfhearted attempt to sleep. But he was too tense, too bruised, too busy berating himself for not having heeded Gilbert's warning. At least Gib and Ancel had gotten away. Surely they'd know better than to confess to Robert? Pray God they did! If—He jerked his head up, scarcely breathing as he strained to hear: sounds in the stairwell, the clanking of spurs against stone, growing closer now. And then there was a jangling of keys and the door was swinging open, letting in a sudden spill of lantern light, bright enough to blind.

Ranulf blinked, unable to see beyond its glare, and struggled to his feet. As he did, a familiar voice said, "I've known men who put their lives at peril for gold or for lust, and occasionally even for love. But you, lad, are the very first to risk the gallows for a woman's wool garment—and with the woman not even in it!"

Ranulf burst out laughing. "I do not think," he confessed, "that I've ever been so happy to see anyone in all my born days!"

"It is just me, lad," Stephen said wryly, "not the blessed Angel Gabriel!" He gestured then for the guard to unlock his young cousin's irons, and it took no more than that—the most casual of commands—for Ranulf to gain his freedom.

ALTHOUGH it was long past curfew, the alehouse owner did not mind being roused from sleep. The chance to do a favor for the Count of Boulogne was an opportunity not to be missed, for the count would remember should he ever need a favor in return. And if the City Watch did appear, he knew the count would send them away, well content with a few coins and a bit of friendly banter. So he hastily ordered his sleepy servant to pour ale and wine for the count's men while he himself brought a flagon to the count's table, returning a few moments later with cold chicken from his own larder.

Ranulf fell upon the chicken with gusto, continuing his adventures between huge bites. Stephen interrupted only twice, once to gibe that a full day in gaol would have brought Ranulf to the very brink of starvation, and once to ask how Gilbert and Ancel had gotten back to the city, for the gates had been barred hours ago. When Ranulf explained that they'd bribed a guard at Aldgate to let them in once they had the nun's habit, Stephen shook his head and predicted they would end up on the gallows unless they repented. But his sermon's impact was lessened somewhat by the laughter lurking beneath the rebuke.

Ranulf's hunger was contagious, and Stephen soon helped himself to a drumstick. "Your trouble, lad, is that you have too much imagination. Anyone else with a score to settle would have been content to slip a purgative into Baldric's wine or glue into his boots. And no, those are not suggestions! Now . . . may I assume that I need fear no more deranged plots to enliven Baldric's days?"

Ranulf nodded, summoning up a discomfited smile. "It will take a lifetime to repay you for tonight, Cousin Stephen. Thank the Lord Christ that you happened to be in London!"

"Saintly soul that I am, I can never resist a chance to do good. But I am curious why you did not ask Robert for aid."

"Robert is the last man in Christendom whom I'd want to know! Can you not imagine his shame at being told his brother had been arrested in a nunnery? He'd find no humor in it, no sense at all, and would likely end up blaming himself for my failings!"

"I suppose it is lucky for you, then, that I lack Robert's moral superiority and incorruptible honour."

Ranulf looked at the older man in dismay. "If I have offended you, I am indeed sorry. You and Robert are both men of honour, men I would follow to the very borders of Hell if need be. I meant only that you are . . . less judgmental than Robert, that you find it easier to forgive daft sins like mine."

After a moment, Stephen shrugged. "Doubtless that comes from my own misspent youth." But Ranulf was left with an uneasy impression, that his cousin's flare of jealousy had been no joke.

"You and Robert . . . you have been my family," he said softly, and somewhat awkwardly, for he was no more accustomed than most males to sharing sentiment. "I am not faulting my lord father when I say that, for he has been good to me. But . . . but I've always felt as if I were confined to his outer bailey, not allowed up into the keep itself."

Stephen nodded. "My uncle is not an easy man to know. But then he is a king, lad, and kings cannot be judged like other men."

Ranulf leaned closer, for wine and the night's harrowing events had loosened his tongue, and he suddenly saw a chance to ask Stephen what he'd never dared to ask another living soul, especially Robert. "I know a king is bound to attract gossip, like bees to honey. The stories they tell of my father . . . how do I know which are true, Stephen, and which are wicked lies?"

Stephen studied the boy. "Have you any particular stories in mind, Ranulf?"

Ranulf almost lost his nerve then. He squirmed in his seat, reached for his wine, only to set it down untasted. "Is it true that he blinded his own granddaughters?"

Stephen did not respond at once, seemed to be weighing his words, and Ranulf had never seen him do that before. "Yes," he said slowly, "he did. It happened the year before the White Ship sank. I'll see if I can try to make sense of it for you. Your father had wed his daughter Juliane to a man named Eustace de Pacy, and promised Pacy that he could have the castle of Ivry. But Henry was loath to lose it, and he kept putting Pacy off with promises. To keep the peace, it was agreed that Pacy and Ivry's castellan should exchange their children as hostages for each man's good faith. Unfortunately, Pacy's good faith was not worth spit, and he blinded the castellan's son. Henry was so outraged by this treachery that he allowed the castellan to maim Pacy and Juliane's two young daughters; they were blinded and the tips of their noses cut off."

Ranulf said nothing, shocked into silence, for he'd not expected that tale to be validated as true. Stephen watched him, then said quietly, "It was not that your father lacked pity, lad; they were but little lasses and his own blood kin. But he felt men must be able to rely upon the king's sworn word. He told me once that a king's greatest mistake would be to make a threat and then not carry it out."

Ranulf nodded, struggling to understand, needing to give his father the benefit of any doubt. But he could not help asking, "Could you have done that, Stephen?"

Stephen drained his wine cup, reached for the flagon, and poured again. "No," he said, "no, lad, I could not . . ."

Ranulf's appetite was gone, and he pushed aside the rest of the chicken. "What . . . what of the stories of how he became king? Are they true, too?"

"I do not know what you've heard," Stephen said, adding with a forced smile, "and I am not sure I want to know!" When would he learn to look ere he leapt? But the lad had a need to talk, and it seemed harmless enough to indulge him; so why were they of a sudden hinting at regicide?

"I'll tell you what I know," Stephen said reluctantly. "Your father and others were hunting in the New Forest with his brother the king. William Rufus was shot by mischance—took an arrow in the chest—and died there in the woods. He had no sons, which meant that his crown would be claimed by one of his brothers. Robert was the firstborn, but he was on his way back from the Holy Land, and your father . . . well, he was luckier, for he was within riding distance of Winchester, where the royal treasury was kept. He headed for Winchester at a gallop, and by sunset, he was calling himself England's king. As you know, Robert eventually challenged him, and ended his days confined to the great keep of Cardiff Castle in South Wales. More than that, I cannot say. No man can."

Ranulf looked intently into Stephen's face and then away. Stephen had deliberately drawn no conclusions, offered no opinion of his own about Henry's hunt for a crown, for the words "by mischance" seemed dictated more by prudence than by conviction. Did Stephen believe, as many men did, that William Rufus's death had been too convenient to be a mere hunting accident? But it was a question Ranulf could not bring himself to ask, nor in fairness, expect Stephen to answer.

"Is it true," he asked instead, "that he abandoned William Rufus's body in the woods, rode off and left him?"

"I'll not lie to you, lad, he did. It does not sound very brotherly, I'll admit. But do not make more of it than that. All we can say is that it proves what we already know—that men lust after crowns even more than they lust after women!"

Ranulf joined gratefully in Stephen's laughter, relieved to return to safer ground, for he'd ventured further than he'd intended; better to backtrack, for both their sakes. "Do all men lust after crowns, Stephen? Do you?"

"Ranulf, my lad, if you searched the length and breadth of England, you might eventually find a man with no interest whatsoever in being its king . . . and if you did, you could be sure he lied!"

Ranulf grinned. "You'll probably think me truly demented then, if I confess that I'd not want to be a king. I would not want to be powerless, mind you. I want to be respected, to have lands of my own and friends I can rely upon and Annora de Bernay as my wife. But I'd rather serve the Crown, Stephen, than wear one. I only wish it could have been yours!"

Stephen looked startled. So did Ranulf; he'd not meant to say that, for it was a betrayal of Maude, and he loved his sister. "Maude would not forgive me for this," he said, "and I truly wish I had no qualms about her queenship. Mayhap if she were not wed to that Angevin hellspawn . . . but she is, even if it was not a marriage of her choosing. She has the right to the English throne, though, a blood right, and I will hold to my sworn oath, accept her as England's queen and Normandy's duchess when that time comes. But I will always harbor a secret, reluctant regret: that it could not have been you, Cousin Stephen."

Stephen was gazing into the bottom of his cup, as if it held answers instead of wine. "All is in God's Hands," he said gravely. "We do what we must, lad, and hope that our inner voices speak true, that we are indeed acting in the furtherance of the Almighty's Will. No man can do more than that."

"I suppose not," Ranulf agreed, somewhat hazily, puzzled by the serious turn the conversation had suddenly taken.

Stephen saw that and reached over, clinking his wine cup to Ranulf's. "Let us drink then," he said, "to the sanctity of nunneries, bad luck to rogues, and good fortune to a spirited Southwark harlot named Sybil."

Ranulf laughed. "Aye, and may Sybil and the good nuns and you, my lord Count of Boulogne, all prosper under the reign of Queen Maude," he said, atoning for his earlier disloyalty to his sister, and raised his cup. But Stephen set his own cup down, for he could not in good conscience drink to the queenship of his cousin, a brave and honourable woman, but a woman withal.

5

BERNAY, NORMANDY

November 1135

THE Bernay family took its surname from the town that had sprung up around a Benedictine abbey. The bulk of Raymond de Bernay's lands lay across the Channel, in England, though, for Raymond's father had profited handsomely when Normandy's duke claimed by conquest the English crown. But it had been many months since Raymond had visited his English estates. King Henry had been dwelling in Normandy for the past two years, seemed in no hurry to return to his island kingdom, and Raymond thought it prudent to follow his liege lord's example.

When the dogs began to bark, Raymond's daughter darted out the door into the bailey, heedless of the snow and cold. Ranulf was just swinging down from his saddle when Annora flung herself into his arms. "Fool!" he laughed. "Where is your mantle? Do you want to freeze?"

"Are you saying you cannot keep me warm?" She laughed back at him, and he took the dare, kissing her with enough passion to keep the cold at bay, at least until Edith hastened outside and chased them both into the manor, grumbling about such unseemly behavior.

Annora had no memories of her mother, who'd died while she was still in her cradle. But she could not remember a time when Edith had not been part of her life: nurse, confidante, mainstay. She was quite unfazed, though, by Edith's sermon; she well knew the older woman would forgive her any sin under God's sky.

Ranulf was equally unperturbed by Edith's scolding. For all that she freely sprinkled her conversation with "rascal" and "young rogue," hers was a bark that lacked bite; Edith was utterly delighted that her "darling lass" was to wed the king's son. At least this was what she told Annora, for she'd never admit that she found Ranulf's ready grin and good humor as appealing as his royal bloodlines. Jesú forfend that Annora ever suspect the shameful truth, that she was a secret romantic with a weakness, even now, for a likely lad.

The Bernays' cook also had a fondness for Ranulf, and sent out a heaping platter of hot cheese-filled wafers. As Ranulf divided his attention between Edith and the wafers, Annora fidgeted. When her patience, never in plentiful supply, ran out, she got to her feet so abruptly that she spilled Ranulf's cider, insisting that he accompany her outside to see the stable cat's newborn kittens.

As excuses go, it was pitifully thin; only nuns and an occasional eccentric viewed cats as pets. But Edith waved them on indulgently, for Annora's elder brother Fulk was due back that night, and he'd be far more vigilant about safeguarding his sister's virtue. Let her lamb and the lad have some sweet stolen moments together. Even if they could not be trusted to be prudent—and in her heart she knew that discretion was an utterly alien concept to Annora—at the very worst, they'd just have to hasten the date for the wedding. But she had no problems with that, for her lamb was fifteen now, old enough to be a bride, a wife and mother.

Ranulf and Annora reached the stables in record time. Once they were safely within its sheltering shadows, Ranulf headed for the nearest bale of hay and drew Annora down onto his lap. Pulling off her veil, he reached under her mantle, then began to kiss her upturned face.

By their society's rigid standards, Annora was no beauty, for she bore no resemblance whatsoever to the tall, willowy, golden-haired maidens so admired by their minstrels and poets, fair maidens demure and docile and unfailingly deferential to male authority. No bards would be singing Annora's praises; she was short and dark and stubborn and so volatile that her brothers called her Hellcat.

So did Ranulf, but on his lips, it became an endearment. He wished now that he could have unbraided her hair; when loose, it put him in mind of a hot summer night, so black and sultry-soft was it. But that was out of the question; he could not let her emerge from the stables looking like a wanton, hair unbound and clothes askew. What would be the measure of his love if he cared naught for her honour?

It had not been easy, putting limitations upon their lovemaking. But he meant for Annora to come to their marriage bed a virgin, even if his forbearance half killed him, and at times, he feared it might. It was not that he believed they'd be sinning, for he did not; they'd been plight-trothed since the summer, since Annora's fifteenth birthday, and a plight troth was almost as binding as a church ceremony. It was not his sense of sin that had so far kept Annora chaste; it was his sense of honour. Annora's father trusted him, allowed him to see her often and alone, and Ranulf could not bring himself to betray Raymond's trust by seducing Raymond's daughter, however much he wanted to—however much Annora wanted him to.

Thankfully, their waiting was almost done; her father was talking of a spring wedding.

Ranulf was the one to end their embrace; Annora never made it easy for him. "I suppose," he muttered, "that all this self-control will stand me in good stead should I ever decide to become a monk."

"A monk? I thought you were aiming for sainthood," Annora gibed, and then gave a squeal when he yanked her braid. "How long can you stay?"

"Just till week's end. My father had a sudden urge to go hunting, so Monday off he went to his lodge at Lyons-la-Forêt, with Robert, a handful of earls, and a bishop or two. When I reminded Robert that Bernay was only a day's ride away, he gave me leave to 'pay your respects to your betrothed,'" Ranulf quoted, switching to a passable imitation of his brother's gravely deliberate tones. "I promised, though, to be waiting when they return to Rouen on Friday. But we'll not be apart for long. I'm sure your father plans to attend the king's Christmas court, does he not?"

Annora nodded. "Of course. Who would miss it? Ah . . . but Maude would, it seems. We heard she quarreled with your father, that she then dared to leave Rouen without his permission. Can that be true, Ranulf?"

"Yes," he said reluctantly. "But it was not a quarrel of Maude's making. My father had promised to yield some castles to her husband, and Geoffrey became convinced he was not acting in good faith. So he seized them, which vexed my father sorely. They've been squabbling about it all summer, whilst Maude sought to make peace betwixt them, to no avail. At last she wearied of all the strife, and returned to Geoffrey in Anjou. She ought not to have gone without bidding my father farewell, but I can understand her anger, Annora. My father forced her to marry Geoffrey, and for him now to berate her for Geoffrey's sins is unjust, to say the least."

Annora's mouth curved down. "Sometimes I think you'll be defending that woman with your dying breath. Why you're so fond of her, I'll never understand, for no one else can abide her foul tempers and arrogance—"

"You're not being fair, Annora. People are too quick to find fault with Maude, judge her too harshly. It is true that she has ever been one for speaking her mind, and mayhap such forthrightness is unseemly in a woman, but I rather like it myself. There is no pretense to Maude; she says what she thinks and means what she says. As for her temper, I'll not deny she is quick to anger. But if that be a sin, it is one she shares with most of mankind. And she is very loyal to those she loves. Do you remember me telling you about that remarkable dog I saw in Paris last year? It looked verily like a wolf, but with a jaunty, bushy tail curling over its back. It belonged to a Norwegian merchant, and he said such dogs were common in his homeland, known as dyrehunds, that they were bold hunters, able to track elk, moose, wolves, even bears—"

"I do not care if they can chase down unicorns! What do dyrehunds have to do with Maude?"

"If you'll curb your impatience, you'll find out. I was much taken with the dog, but the man would not sell it. I happened to mention it to Maude, and she sent for the man, secretly arranged for him to bring back two breeding pairs of dyrehunds on his next trip to Oslo, and surprised me with them on my birthday. Handsome beasts, I cannot wait for you to see them. But how many people would have done what Maude did for me? She has a giving heart, and that should count for more than a sharp tongue."

Annora was not convinced. "I'm glad she got you the Norse dogs you fancied. But the world is still filled with people who love that lady not. At the mere thought of her queenship, my father turns the color of moldy cheese!"

"I know how common such qualms are," Ranulf conceded. "We've never had a queen who ruled in her own right, and the novelty of that scares a lot of people. If only Maude were not wed to Geoffrey of Anjou! He may lack for scruples, but not for enemies, and every one of them is now Maude's enemy, too, for they fear that he'd share her throne as he does her bed. Poor Maude, she cannot win, for when men are not berating her for her unwomanly willfulness, they are accusing her of being Geoffrey's pawn! How can she be both a virago and a puppet?"

"Poor Maude, indeed! She was born a king's daughter, wed first to the Holy Roman Emperor and then the Count of Anjou, she's borne Geoffrey two healthy sons, she'll one day be Queen of England and Duchess of Normandy, and the Lord God saw fit to make her a beauty in the bargain. There has probably never been a woman so blessed since Eve woke up in Eden!"

Ranulf grinned. "I'd say you were more blessed than Maude. After all, you're going to marry me!" he said, and stifled her riposte with a kiss. "What you say about Maude is true enough, Annora. But truth, as my cousin Stephen is fond of pointing out, has as many layers as an onion. Peel away a few of them and you get a different truth, a view of Maude's life not quite so 'blessed.' She was sent to Germany at age eight, wed to a man nigh on twenty years her senior, a man of black moods and brooding temper, notorious for having betrayed his own father. She somehow made a success of the marriage, though, and won the hearts of her husband's subjects, too. When she was widowed, they wanted her to stay in Germany. So did she, for she'd learned by then to look upon Germany as her home. But my father insisted that she return to England, and when she did, he named her as his heir."

"Oh, no! To be burdened with a crown—that poor lass."

Ranulf tweaked her braid again. "But the crown had a baited hook in it, for he then forced her to wed Geoffrey of Anjou. When she objected, he confined her within his queen's chambers under guard, kept her there until she yielded."

"I never knew that! The king made Maude a prisoner?" When Ranulf nodded, Annora felt a twinge of grudging pity for Maude; her own upbringing had been one of indulgence and coddling, as the youngest and the only girl in a family of sons. "I'll admit that Maude's marriage does sound like a match made in Hell. But they did in time make their peace, did they not?"

"More like an armed truce. It helped when Maude gave birth to a son two years ago, and then a second lad a year later. Both Maude and Geoffrey dote on the boys, especially young Henry, their firstborn. But for all that they've iced over their differences, a bystander could still get frostbite if he lingered too long in their company. Do you see what I am saying, Annora? Do you remember last summer, when Maude nearly died in childbirth? She was stricken with childbed fever, and for nigh on a week, she suffered the torments of the damned. I was there at Rouen; I saw her agony. We were sure she was dying. So was she, and she told us she wanted to be buried at the abbey of Bec. But my father . . . he said no, that he would have her buried in Rouen. Even on her deathbed, Annora, she was given no say."

Annora reached up, put her fingers to his lips. "I yield. You've convinced me that some of Maude's blessings have been bittersweet. But I still think she brought much of her trouble on herself. If she'd not been so haughty, if she'd been more tactful, more womanly—"

Ranulf laughed rudely. "Like you? Sweetheart, I'd back your claws against Maude's any day!"

Annora pretended to pout. "I suppose you'd prefer a meek little lamb like the Lady Matilda—oh!" Her hand flew to her mouth, as if to catch her heedless words. The gesture was affected, but her remorse was real. "I ought not to have said that," she said contritely. "My heart goes out to Matilda, Ranulf, truly it does. I can think of no greater grief than the loss of a child . . ."

Ranulf nodded somberly, and for a moment, they both were silent, thinking of the sudden death that summer of Stephen and Matilda's son. Theirs was an age in which too many cemeteries held pitifully small graves; one of every three children never even reached the age of five. But Baldwin had been their firstborn, a lively, clever nine-year-old whose death had left a huge, ragged hole in their lives.

"Their grieving was painful to look upon," Ranulf said sadly. "They buried him in London, at Holy Trinity Priory. They're in Boulogne now; I've seen them just once since their return. They'll probably come to Rouen, though, for my father's Christmas court. Indeed, I do hope so.

Mayhap it would cheer them somewhat, being at the revelries," he said, with the well-intentioned, misguided optimism of youth, and sought to banish Death's spectre then, by focusing all his attention upon the girl on his lap.

Annora cooperated so enthusiastically that the shadow of Stephen and Matilda's small son soon receded, unable to compete with the lure of smooth, female flesh, soft curves, and the fragrance of jasmine. After a time, they broke apart by mutual consent, breathing deeply, and smiled at each other. Ranulf had begun to stroke her cheek, and Annora gave a contented sigh; as exciting as it was when the fire burned hot between them, she also took pleasure in quiet moments like this, for Ranulf could be gentle, too.

They talked idly of the upcoming Christmas revelries, and then Annora related the latest Paris scandal. Ranulf was not surprised that she should be so well informed about the bed-roving of the French nobility; Annora adored gossip the way a child craved sweets. But he was momentarily at a loss when she insisted, "Now you owe me some good gossip in return—and it has to make me blush or it does not count."

Ranulf pondered for a moment. "Well . . . Queen Adeliza's confessor is said to be smitten with one of her ladies-in-waiting, following the lass about like a lovesick swain—"

"Ah, Ranulf, Ranulf . . . you'll have to do better than that. The Church can preach chastity for its priests from now till Judgment Day, and that will not change the fact that half the clerics in Christendom have wives or hearthmates. Jesú, what of the Bishop of Salisbury, the old king's justiciar? He's openly kept a concubine for thirty years, even got their bastard son appointed chancellor. No, my lad, you'd best look farther afield for scandal. Catching wayward priests is like spearing fish in a barrel; there is no sport in it."

Ranulf laughed softly, pulling her back into his arms. "We'll just have to make our own scandal then," he said, and began to kiss her again. But the dogs were barking out in the bailey, and they reluctantly drew apart, hurriedly adjusting their clothing.

"I suppose that will be Fulk," Ranulf said glumly, for there would be no dalliance with Annora as long as her elder brother was on hand. But the brother who now burst into the stable wasn't Fulk; it was Ancel, who should have been at Lyons-la-Forêt with Robert and the royal hunting party.

"Ancel? What are you doing here?"

"Your brother sent me to fetch you straightaway. It is your lord father, Ranulf . . . He was taken ill soon after we arrived at the hunting lodge."

"How ill? Ancel . . . how ill?" Ranulf repeated tensely, for it had not escaped him that Ancel had yet to meet his eyes.

"That is for the doctors to say, not me," Ancel said evasively. "But Lord Robert said . . . he said for you to make all haste. He said not to tarry."

Ranulf sucked in his breath, for he understood then what Ancel was so loath to tell him. They thought his father was dying.

WHEN Ranulf had assured Robert that Bernay was just a day's ride from Rouen, he'd stretched the truth somewhat; it was thirty miles, more or less, and indeed a hard-riding traveler could cover the distance in one day—a summer's day. Travel on rutted and icy winter roads was a far riskier and slower venture. Ranulf knew, though, that he was racing Death, and he and Ancel spurred their horses without regard for their safety, making their way by glimmering lantern light as darkness fell. When they halted, it was only to rest their lathered mounts. But their reckless, breakneck dash through the frozen December countryside still took them all night and most of the following day. They reached the hunting lodge at dusk, only to learn that Ranulf's father had died at dawn.

HAVING completed his prayer for his father's soul, Ranulf got stiffly to his feet and stood staring down at his father's body. Henry seemed at peace; Ranulf had been assured that he'd died in God's Grace, shriven of his sins by the Bishop of Rouen. Ranulf fervently hoped it was so, but his treacherous memory refused to cooperate, conjuring up shadows of his father's blinded, maimed granddaughters, the ghost of a king slain mysteriously in the New Forest, a brother's body abandoned in the woods whilst Henry raced for Winchester to claim a crown. Even if his father had sincerely repented all his earthly misdeeds, a lengthy stay in Purgatory seemed a foregone conclusion.

It was odd; he could have been looking upon a stranger. Why was he so calm, so queerly detached? He felt exhausted, numbed, regretful that he'd not been able to bid his father a final farewell. But his sorrowing was muted; his eyes were dry.

The door opened quietly behind him. Robert looked tired and tense, but composed. Ranulf glanced at his elder brother, then back at the dead man, thinking of Adeliza, his father's queen. Would she weep for Henry? Would any eyes? It was a disturbing thought, that a man could wield great power as God's anointed on earth, he could rule an empire, and yet leave none to mourn him when he died.

"People will say they grieve for him," he said softly, "but they will be lying. He'll be forgotten even ere he is buried, for men's thoughts are al-

ready turning to tomorrow, to Maude. It sounds mad to say this, Robert, for I knew he would die one day, and I knew, too, that he'd not change his mind about the succession. So why does it come as such a surprise?"

"That he should die? Or that Maude should be queen?"

Ranulf considered. "Both, I think."

Robert was quiet for a time. "In that, lad, I'd wager you're not alone," he said, and Ranulf turned, gave him a startled, searching look, half fearful of what he might find. If even Robert was so troubled by their sister's coming queenship, it did not bode well for Maude, for England. Men might not mourn his father, but there'd be many who'd dread his death, dread the unsettled times that lay ahead.

"I've been praying for Papa, Robert. But mayhap we ought to be praying, too, for Maude," he said, sounding so uneasy and so earnest that Robert reached out, let his hand rest briefly on the boy's arm, a gesture that Ranulf found both surprising and bracing, for Robert was as reticent as Maude about open displays of affection.

"I think, lad," Robert agreed, "that it would not be amiss to pray for Maude. And whilst you are at it, pray, too, for England."

ANGERS, the ancient capital of Anjou, was bisected by the River Maine. But the heart of the city beat upon the east bank, for there was to be found the abbey of St Aubin, the great cathedral, and the hilltop castle where generations of Angevin counts had dwelled and died. It was toward the castle that Ranulf rode, bringing his sister Robert's letter, bringing the news of their father's death.

Maude already knew. Ranulf saw that as soon as he was ushered into the great hall. She wore the somber shades of mourning, and her demeanor was solemn, as befitting one newly bereaved. But her eyes were as dry as Ranulf's own. She welcomed him with the aloof dignity that public decorum demanded, her pleasure at seeing him revealed only in the slight curve of her mouth, the alacrity with which she suggested that they withdraw to her private chamber.

Once they reached her bedchamber, Maude sent a servant for wine and then turned to Ranulf, taking his hands in hers. "I am so glad that you've come," she said. "Were you with Papa when he died?"

"No," Ranulf said regretfully, "but Robert was," and he handed her their brother's letter. Because he did not know what Robert had written, he told Maude then what he had learned about their father's death. "He was stricken on Monday eve, the 25th of November, after eating a heaping plateful of stewed lamprey eels, and died early the following Sunday."

Maude had begun to read Robert's letter, but at that, she slanted a

sudden glance in his direction. "Lamprey eels," she said, shaking her head. "The doctors warned him time and time again that he ought not to eat them. Of course he paid them no heed."

Neither of them took notice of the opening door, assuming it was a servant with the wine.

"Well, if it is not the little brother."

The voice was low-pitched and would have been very pleasing to the ear if not for the suggestion of smugness, echoes of the mockery that insinuated itself into Geoffrey's every utterance; Ranulf doubted that he could even pray to the Almighty without sounding disrespectful. "The sight of you gladdens me, too, Geoffrey," he said sourly, for he'd long ago learned the futility of squandering courtesy upon Maude's husband.

Geoffrey seemed amused by Ranulf's sarcasm; it vexed Ranulf enormously that his sister's husband never took him seriously enough to quarrel with. He watched sullenly now as Geoffrey sauntered over, grazed Maude's cheek with a careless kiss, while glancing covertly at the letter she held open in her hand.

Maude casually shifted the letter. "Did you want anything in particular, Geoffrey?"

"Why, I was looking for you, dear heart," he said blandly. "I was told your brother had arrived. Alas, I was not told that it was the wrong brother."

"What do you mean by that?"

"I should think my meaning would be obvious. Robert ought to have come himself rather than send this green lad. You are, after all, more than his right beloved sister now. You're to be his queen."

It infuriated Ranulf to hear himself dismissed as a "green lad," for the age difference was not that great; he was seventeen to Geoffrey's twenty-two. Even more did he resent the slur upon Robert, and he said hotly, "Robert still had duties to perform for our father. He had to escort the body back to Rouen, and then go to Falaise, for my father had instructed him to withdraw sixty thousand pounds from the royal treasury to pay the wages of his servants and soldiers and give alms to the poor, that they might pray for his soul."

Geoffrey's mouth quirked. "If he thought to bribe his way past Heaven's Gate, I daresay he found that even sixty thousand pounds would not buy him prayers enough. He'd have been better off spending the money to earn himself some goodwill amongst the Devil's minions."

Ranulf gasped, but Maude put a restraining hand upon his arm. "You would know more about pleasing the Devil than most men. The counts of Anjou trace their descent from Lucifer's daughter, do they not?"

Geoffrey was not offended. "Her name is Melusine." Seeing their

blank looks, he added helpfully, "The Devil's daughter who wed one of my ancestors—her name was Melusine."

"I have the utmost trust in Robert," Maude said, very coolly, and Geoffrey's smile became a smirk.

"You trust the sainted Robert. You trust Cousin Stephen. You trust young Ranulf here, and God knows how many others in that flock of bastard brothers of yours. Dear heart, it pains me to say this, but you're as free with your trust as a whore is with her favors, and you run the same risk that the whore does, for men hold cheaply what comes to them too easily."

"The same can be said for your advice, Geoffrey. I might value it more if you offered it less."

Geoffrey's eyes narrowed, and Ranulf shifted uncomfortably. All his sympathies were with Maude; it still was no fun, though, to be caught in their crossfire. But at that moment a servant entered with the wine, dispelling some of the tension. Geoffrey and Ranulf drank in a less than convivial silence as Maude conferred with the servant. Once the man had withdrawn, she smiled at Ranulf. "Since you missed dinner, I've instructed the cooks to prepare an uncommonly lavish supper this eve in your honour. I told them to serve baked pike stuffed with chestnuts, for that is a favorite of yours, no?"

Ranulf nodded, pleased that she should have remembered. But Geoffrey's brows shot upward. "Shall you be up to it? You must not be alarmed, Ranulf, if your sister bolts the hall in the midst of the meal. Other women suffer from morning sickness when they are breeding, but Maude is, as ever, a law unto herself, and her queasiness comes at night!"

Ranulf swung around to stare at his sister. "You are with child?"

Maude nodded, and Geoffrey moved to her side, striking the playful pose of a proud father-to-be. He might even be sincere, Ranulf allowed grudgingly, for to give the Devil his due, Geoffrey did seem fond of his sons. As he looked at them now, Ranulf could not help admiring the picture they presented, for whatever else might be said of them, they made a very handsome couple.

Handsome was a word often applied to Geoffrey, for not only was he taller than most men, he'd been blessed, too, with an athlete's build and a cat's grace. His hair color was a bronzed reddish-gold, his eyes a compelling shade of blue-grey, fringed with thick, tawny lashes, eyes agleam with sardonic humor, boundless confidence, and a sharp, calculating intelligence, yet not a hint of warmth.

As for Maude, Ranulf had to acknowledge that her youth was gone, for she was thirty-three, past a woman's prime. But her age had not yet impaired her ability to turn male heads. Like Annora, she'd been cursed with unfashionable coloring: she had inherited her father's dark hair and eyes. But she was more fortunate than Annora in that her skin was fair and flawless, and her features so finely sculptured that none could deny her beauty; no man looking upon the high curve of her cheekbones or the red fullness of her mouth was likely to care that her eyes were brown.

Indeed, a handsome couple. But did they think so? Did they find each other as desirable as others found them? For a moment, Ranulf tried to imagine what it would be like, making love to a woman he loathed. It was not an appealing prospect, and he decided that he'd not have traded places with Geoffrey or Maude for all the crowns in Christendom. How lucky he was to have Annora, to— Suddenly becoming aware of the silence, he saw that they were staring at him, and he flushed in embarrassment, looking hastily away lest they somehow read his mind.

"Well? Are you not going to offer your congratulations?" Geoffrey was shaking his head, as if lamenting Ranulf's bad manners, but Ranulf had an uncomfortable suspicion that his brother-in-law knew what he'd been thinking. He stammered an apology, belatedly wished them well, and was greatly relieved when Geoffrey headed for the door.

As soon as they were alone, Ranulf smiled at his sister, eager to make amends. "I am right glad about the babe," he lied. "When is the birth?"

"Not for months yet, not till the summer."

Her smile did not linger, and Ranulf found himself wondering if she feared the coming birth. He did, for certes, remembering that harrowing week in Rouen. That was not something he could ask her, though. A faint frown had settled across her brow; the brown eyes were opaque, inward-looking. But then she said briskly, "The timing could not have been worse, could it? The English are already skittish about being ruled by one who wears skirts. Somehow I suspect the sight of a swelling belly beneath those skirts is not likely to reassure."

As always, Ranulf was impressed by her candor. "Well," he said, "they shall have to get used to it. And I may as well confess that I'm looking forward to watching as certain high-flying lords get their wings clipped!"

So was Maude. "Anyone in particular?"

"The Earl of Chester, amongst others. He's made no secret of his reluctance to take orders from a woman. Think how gladdened he'll be to grovel before one great with child!"

"Chester is not a man to grovel, lad, not even to God. But he will pay me the debt he owes his sovereign, one of obeisance and fealty and homage. They all will."

Ranulf felt a surge of admiration, strong enough to let him forget his own past qualms about her queenship. How many women could face such a formidable challenge with so much fortitude? For that matter, most men would have been daunted, too, by the demands that were about to be made upon his sister. "Your coronation will be but the beginning. Your greatest trials will be still to come. Maude . . . does it not scare you at all, knowing the troubles that lie ahead?"

"Scare me?" she echoed, sounding genuinely surprised. "Ah, no, Ranulf, I do not fear. I know it will not be easy. I know there will be men who'd be content that I merely reign, not rule. But I *will* rule—by God, I will. The Crown of England is a burden and a blessing and my birthright. To me, it means . . ."

She paused, and Ranulf waited, curious to hear how she would complete the sentence: power? duty? opportunity? But then she smiled, a smile he would long remember, for it was the smile of a hopeful, eager young girl, not a woman widowed and disenchanted and wretchedly wed. "It means," she said, "freedom."

SUPPER that evening was as sumptuous as Maude had promised. Her cooks had to confine their menu to fish, for the season of Advent was upon them, but they did themselves proud with Ranulf's pike, gingered carp, white trout in mustard sauce, almond rice, roasted apples, marzipan, and cinnamon wafers, all washed down with ample servings of spiced red wine, hippocras, and malmsey.

Afterward, Maude told Ranulf of her plans. She meant to depart on the morrow for Normandy. The Vicomte Guigan Algason had sent word that he wanted to do homage to her for his holdings in Argentan, Domfront, and Exmes. She would be pleased, she added, to have Ranulf at her side upon her entry into Argentan. Ranulf assured her that he would be honored to witness Algason's submission to his new duchess, and then asked, as tactfully as he could, if Geoffrey would be accompanying them. To his vast relief, Maude said that Geoffrey had agreed—for the present—to remain in Angers.

Ranulf could not say so, of course, but he thought that was a shrewd tactical move; the Norman barons would be much more likely to acknowledge Maude's suzerainty if she was not encumbered by the unwelcome presence of her detested Angevin husband. Thank the Lord Christ that Geoffrey was choosing to be so accommodating, to get Maude's reign off to the best possible beginning. But how long was his cooperation likely to last? And how could they stop him when he decided to take his rightful place at her side as husband, consort, . . . or even, God forbid, king?

"I have been trying to decide which of my lords I can rely upon and which of them will seek to take advantage of me if I let them. Hear me out, Ranulf, and see if you agree with my conclusions."

Ranulf nodded, enormously flattered that Maude should see him as a worthy confidant. "I'm no soothsayer, but I'd wager I can name the chief prop of your throne," he predicted, unable to resist this small jab at Geoffrey. "Robert."

"Robert," Maude echoed, "Robert first and foremost. And then my uncle David; I am indeed blessed that my lady mother was sister to the Scots king. There are others, too, who will do whatever they can to make my throne secure. My cousin Stephen, of course. Stephen's elder brother Theobald has rarely set foot in England; his interests are firmly rooted in his own domains. And the youngest brother, the bishop . . . he is too ambitious to be truly trustworthy. As for our brothers, Rainald is quite able, can be of great help as long as he reins in that runaway temper of his. And then there is Brien Fitz Count. You remember Brien, do you not, Ranulf?"

Ranulf thought he did. "The lord of Wallingford Castle?"

Maude nodded. "He is a good friend of Stephen's, and like Stephen, he is a man of honour. He was utterly loyal to my father, treated almost as a foster son, and I trust he will be just as loyal to me."

Geoffrey had drifted over in time to catch Maude's declaration of faith in Brien Fitz Count. "There is that word again—*trust*. Passing strange, how often it crops up in your conversation, dear heart."

Maude's mouth thinned, but a cease-fire, however precarious, was to be preferred to outright marital warfare; that was a lesson she'd learned the hard way. "Then," she said, "to please you, Geoffrey, we shall now speak of those I do not trust. The Earl of Chester. His half-brother, William de Roumare. That self-seeking constable of the Tower, Geoffrey de Mandeville. Waleran and Robert Beaumont."

"Ah, yes, the Beaumont twins, double trouble." But Geoffrey's humor was wasted on Ranulf, and Maude was turning away to hear a servant's murmur.

"A messenger has just arrived," she said, "from England, from Brien Fitz Count. Did I not tell you that Brien would be amongst the first to declare his allegiance to his queen?"

Left alone with Geoffrey on the dais, Ranulf concentrated upon his wine cup, trying to ignore his brother-in-law's amused gaze. But Geoffrey was impossible to ignore. "So . . . tell me, Ranulf, have you forsworn eating lamprey pie ever again? It is one of my favorite dishes, I confess, but it would have been in bad taste, I suppose, to have served it tonight—so soon after your father's unfortunate eel encounter."

Ranulf gritted his teeth until his jaw ached. Geoffrey was entertained by his silent struggle for control, but he knew it was a losing battle, knew how easy it would be to fire the lad's temper—almost too easy, for it was already smoldering. He was getting ready to fan the flames when Ranulf stiffened, half rose in his seat. "Maude?"

Geoffrey turned, puzzled, and then forgot about badgering the boy at sight of his wife. Maude had spun back toward the dais, all the color gone from her face, a parchment crumpled in her hand.

"Christ Jesus, woman, what ails you?" Geoffrey came down the dais steps in two strides, for in seven turbulent years of marriage, he'd never seen Maude look as she did now: vulnerable.

Ranulf was even faster, reached her first. "Maude, what is it? What did Brien tell you?"

Maude looked blindly at him, her eyes wide, dark, and dazed. "Stephen . . ." She stopped, swallowed. "He has claimed the English throne," she said, with the unnatural calm, the dulled disbelief of one still in shock.

There was a moment of stunned silence. Then Geoffrey spat out an extremely obscene oath, and Ranulf cried, "No, that cannot be! It must be a mistake, for Stephen would never do that, Maude, never!"

Maude's hand clenched into a fist, shredding Brien's letter with fingers that shook. "But he did," she said tautly. "God rot him, Ranulf—he did!" She drew a ragged, betrayed breath. "Stephen has stolen my crown."

6

TOWER ROYAL, LONDON, ENGLAND

December 1135

THE storm raged in from the west, assailing London with stinging rain and sleet. Christmas festivities were muted in consequence, for the city was soon swamped in mud, buffeted by frigid, wet winds. All people of common sense were keeping close to their own hearths, and the streets were deserted as a small band of armed horsemen splashed up Cheapside. The woman they escorted was muffled in a dark, travel-stained mantle and hood, attracting no attention from the few passersby they encountered. They would have been startled, indeed, had they known they were looking upon England's new queen.

Matilda's arrival at Tower Royal caused quite a stir; she was supposed to be in Boulogne. Even in crisis, though, she clung to her good manners, for making a scene was her concept of a cardinal sin. Shedding her wet, muddied mantle, she dealt patiently with the flustered servants, saw to the needs of her weary, rain-soaked escort. And then she squared her small shoulders, bracing herself for whatever lay ahead, for whatever Stephen might tell her of his mad, perilous quest for a crown.

She found her husband in the great hall, surrounded by boisterous, jubilant, joking men. She very much doubted that they were celebrating the birth of the Holy Christ Child, and she drew a sharp, shallow breath, one of relief mingled with unease and a twinge of regret. So Stephen had won! She was suddenly sure of that, for she knew these men—highborn lords all, not ones to link themselves to a losing cause.

Waleran and Robert Beaumont, sprawled by the hearth like two huge, lazy mastiffs, good-natured until they caught the scent of blood. The ever-elegant Geoffrey de Mandeville, sitting aloof in the shadows. Hugh Bigod, boastful and wine-besotted. Simon de Senlis, a man who'd let a family betrayal sour his outlook and his life. He was the stepson of the Scots king, and David had claimed—with the connivance of his wife, Simon's mother—the English earldom that should have been his, that of Huntingdon; by throwing in with Stephen so soon, he no doubt hoped to recoup some of his lost lands at David's expense. And conspicuously close by Stephen's side, the Bishop of Winchester, his brother.

As always, the sight of them together made her think of changelings, of babies switched at birth, so unlike were they. Her Stephen, tawny-haired and long-legged, utterly at ease in his own body, looking at least a decade shy of his thirty-nine years, years he'd somehow shrugged off onto Henry, who was paunchy and stoop-shouldered, pale hair already starting to recede. Henry, who lacked Stephen's grace and easy charm, but whose wits were as sharp as any to be found in Christendom. Henry, whose ambitions soared higher than hawks, far above his brother's earthbound dreams. The Kingmaker.

It was Geoffrey de Mandeville who noticed Matilda first; he was not a man to miss much. "I thought," he said, "that you left your lady wife behind in Boulogne."

"I did," Stephen said. "I could not put Matilda's safety at risk, so we agreed she would wait until I knew if my claim would prevail. Why?" But as he glanced toward Mandeville, he saw his wife standing in the doorway. "Matilda?" Astonishment kept him in his seat for a moment or so, and then he was on his feet, crossing the hall in several strides to sweep Matilda into his arms.

"I could wait no longer," she confessed. "I had to come, Stephen, had to find out for myself what was happening."

Stephen's smile was more expressive than any words could have been, revealing not only his triumph and pride but his sense of wonder, too, that it had been so easy. But he was denied the privilege of telling her himself, for his brother was quicker, saying with a smile, "Your womanly fears were for naught, Matilda, my dear. You are now looking upon God's anointed. Stephen was crowned at Westminster three days ago."

Matilda gasped. "So fast as that?" she blurted out, and then blushed when the men laughed, feeling like a fool. Speed was essential, after all, in a race for a disputed throne. "With your permission, my lord husband," she said softly, taking refuge in a familiar role, "I'd best change these wet clothes."

The men watched approvingly as she departed the hall, for Matilda was their society's embodiment of female perfection, a great heiress who was also pretty, fertile, sweet-tempered, and submissive. But the bishop had no high regard for wives, perfect or not, and his eyes, an odd smoky shade neither blue nor grey, narrowed upon Matilda's slim, fragile figure as she disappeared into the shadows of the stairwell.

"Amazing," he said slowly, "truly amazing. Most men would have balked at a winter Channel crossing. I am astounded, Stephen, that the lass dared to take such a risk, and yes, dismayed, too, for such foolhardiness does not bode well for the future. I think you ought to take her to task—gently, of course—for acting on her own like that. Trust me, that is not a habit you'd want her to cultivate. Women can be headstrong, foolish creatures, especially if they lack a firm male hand on the reins."

He raised a few eyebrows; a man would have used that supercilious tone with the old king but once. Stephen now showed himself to be more tolerant than his royal uncle; he seemed more amused than offended by the lecture. "What astounds me, Brother Henry, is how a man so learned can have such glaring gaps in his education. You speak at least three languages fluently, and yet you can understand women in none of them! Now . . . I'm sure you gentlemen can amuse yourselves quite well without me. As much as I enjoy your company," he said, grinning, "I much prefer the company of the lady awaiting me above-stairs."

Waleran Beaumont waited until Stephen was out of hearing range, then leaned confidentially toward the bishop. "Is it wise, my lord bishop, to apply the spurs so soon? A clever rider lets the horse get accustomed to his weight in the saddle first."

"I'll not deny that I shall be offering my advice freely to my brother the king, and indeed, I trust mine will be a voice he heeds, as I speak for the Holy Church."

"And of course you would not want any rivals for the royal ear, least of all one who shares the king's bed. I daresay you gave her nary a thought until now, but suddenly the timid little wife does not seem quite so timid or so trifling, does she? But then, what would a priest know of pillow talk? And if you do, by all that's holy, you'd best not own up to it!"

Waleran guffawed at his own jest. So did his brother, and the bishop blistered a glance between the two of them. He had long harbored contempt for Waleran and Robert Beaumont, privately dubbing them the "Norsemen," for they were as fair-haired and brash and bold as the Viking raiders of ancient lore, men of loud laughter, coarse humor, and earthy pleasures. But his disdain had led him astray; he saw that now, saw how it had distorted his judgment. Waleran Beaumont was brazen and self-seeking, but he was not stupid—far from it. He would bear watching, he and his churl of a brother. Stephen must be guarded, lest he fall prey to Beaumont snares. "I am sure the queen would never think to meddle in matters of state. I would that I could say as much for you, my lord!"

Waleran's good humor was no pose; his temper was not easily kindled. He found it hard, therefore, to understand men like the bishop, prickly and readily provoked; as puffed up, he thought, as any barnyard cock. A pity the bishop was so greedy, for there were spoils enough for all. But if this conniving priest thought he'd cheat the Beaumonts out of their fair share, he'd soon regret it. Stephen was—thankfully—a different sort of man altogether, not one to forget his friends.

"Meddling," he said cheerfully, "is much like whoring, one of those sins too sweet to forswear!" Waleran and his brother both laughed at that; the bishop did not.

"I will not permit you to take advantage of the king's goodwill, his trusting nature," Henry warned, his voice cutting enough to pierce the Beaumont complacency. Waleran scowled, but before he could retort in kind, Geoffrey de Mandeville began to laugh.

"Just out of idle curiosity, my lord bishop, how do you mean to do that?" he queried, turning upon them glittering dark eyes full of mockery. "We might as well be candid. Our choice was between Maude, who listens to no one, and Stephen, who will listen to anyone. As to which flaw be worse, only time will reveal, but I can tell you now which one is like to be the most profitable," he said and laughed again.

He laughed alone, though. The other men were all glaring at him. A suspicious, tense silence settled over the hall as Stephen's first Christmas as king drew to an uneasy end.

MATILDA had not permitted any of her ladies-in-waiting to accompany her, as she had not known what might await her in England. With no one to help her undress, she had difficulty unfastening the wet lacings of her gown. Finally freeing herself from its sodden folds, she dragged a chair close to the fire, began to unbraid her hair with fingers that shook. She was exhausted, for it had taken almost three days to cover the seventy mud-rutted miles from Dover, but she couldn't go to bed yet, not until Stephen came to her. When he did, she gave him no chance to speak first. "Are you angry with me for not waiting in Boulogne?"

"Angry? My darling, I am delighted!" Taking her hands in his, he smiled down at her with so much pride that she felt tears prick against her eyelids. "I only wish, sweetheart, that you'd gotten here three days ago, in time to be crowned with me. But no matter, you'll have your own coronation, Tilda, as splendid as I can make it, that I promise. What of Easter? Would that please you?"

She'd just been offered a crown, but her dreams had never been of thrones. "Stephen, why did you not tell me?"

"Tilda, there was no time. I had to sail with the tide for England; even a single day's delay could have tipped the scales against me."

She shook her head, unwillingly remembering that dreadful scene in their bedchamber at Boulogne, remembering her disbelief, her scared sense that the world had suddenly gone spinning out of control, listening as Stephen hurriedly explained that his uncle the king was dead and he was departing for England within the hour, that he meant to claim Maude's crown for himself. "I am not talking of that . . . that day. Why did you keep your intent from me? You obviously laid your plans long before the old king's death, yet you said nary a word to me—me, your wife! Why, Stephen, why?"

"We decided it was best that you not know beforehand." He saw her face change and said hastily, "Of course I trusted you, Matilda! But I knew how you'd worry, and I wanted to spare you that if I could."

She could not help thinking that he'd kept silent, too, lest she try to talk him out of it. "'We decided,'" she echoed. "I assume you are not using the royal 'we,' so who, then? Your brother the bishop?"

Stephen stared at her, for that was as close as she'd ever come to sarcasm. "Yes," he acknowledged. "Henry felt from the first that our uncle ought to have named me as his heir. I do not say this to disparage Maude, for I'm sure she would have done her best. But no woman could rule as a man must. My uncle was mad to insist upon Maude. Scriptures tell wives to submit themselves unto their husbands, tell women to keep silent in the churches. So how could it ever be God's Will that a woman should wield royal power?"

The words were Stephen's, but she knew whose voice she was really hearing. "And so you and Henry were ready when the king died . . .? "

He nodded. "Three weeks from my uncle's death to my coronation; that is all it took, just three weeks. Surely that says much, Matilda, about the mood of the realm. No one wanted Maude to rule, sweetheart, you know they did not. There was no great rush into Anjou after my uncle died, was there? A number of lords at once sought out my brother Theobald, though, and I think it is safe to assume they had more in mind than telling him of the king's death. The sainted Robert was with them, by the way, when they got word that they were too late, that I had been recognized as king. Some of them, I heard, had even urged Robert to claim the crown himself!"

He left unsaid that Robert had turned the offer down. Matilda bit her lip, waiting until she was sure she, too, would leave it unsaid. "And . . . and did it all go as planned? When I landed at Dover, I was told there had been trouble at the castle. . . ?"

"Indeed, there was. They refused me entry, and so did the garrison at Canterbury. Not so surprising, I suppose, since they're Robert's castles, but still not the most auspicious beginning to my quest." Stephen's smile was rueful. "Thank God for the Londoners! If not for their heartfelt support, the warmth of their welcome, my hopes might well have withered right on the vine. From London I rode to Winchester, where Henry was waiting with my uncle's justiciar. They recognized the validity of my claim and handed over the royal treasury. That left but one hurdle to overcome: the qualms of the Archbishop of Canterbury, for he, too, had sworn that oath to Maude."

"So you reminded him that the Church does not enforce oaths sworn under duress." It was easy enough to hazard such a guess, for what other argument could he have made? "You pointed out that none of you gave those oaths freely, that the old king would brook no refusal. And obviously you convinced him."

Stephen surprised her then, by shaking his head. "No," he said slowly, "not at first . . ." His reluctance was painfully apparent, but she was prepared to wait as long as necessary. Their eyes met, briefly, before his slid away. Faint patches of color suddenly stood out across his cheekbones. "It was Hugh Bigod who persuaded him," he said at last. "He told the archbishop that he'd been with the king at Lyons-la-Forêt, that the king named me over Maude as he lay dying."

Matilda was shocked. "Was it true?"

The color was more noticeable in his face now. "Why should it not be true? All know how he'd quarreled with Maude ere he died." He gave her one quick, sharp glance, frowned at what he found, and then admitted tautly, "I do not know, did not ask."

"Oh, Stephen . . ." Matilda could not hide her dismay, for perjury was a far greater sin than a disavowed oath. "What have you done?"

She'd not meant to speak the words aloud, but there was no calling them back. He flinched, and then stepped forward, grasping her by the shoulders and compelling her to look up at him.

"What have I done? I have spared England a disastrous reign, one that was likely to end in bloodshed! Can you truly imagine men like Chester and the Beaumonts submitting to a woman's whims, obeying a woman's commands? They'd have defied her with impunity, for what could she do—take the field against them? Can you tell me in all honesty, Matilda, that you wanted to see Maude as England's queen?"

"No," she whispered, "you know I did not . . ." It was an unfinished sentence, but he did not seem to notice. His grip eased on her shoulders, and some of the tension left his face.

"I will be a good king, Tilda," he said, "that I do swear to you upon the life of our son, our son who will be king after me. Tell me you believe that."

She nodded mutely, with no hesitation, for as much as she cherished honour, she cherished Stephen more, and she understood now his need, his own inner doubts about what he'd done. Such doubts could not be left to fester; like proud flesh, they must be cut away. That much she comprehended of power and the conscience of kings.

Sliding her arms up his back, she rested her cheek against his chest. "I love you," she said, not knowing what else to say. But it was what he needed to hear, and his arms tightened around her. She almost told him then of her own news, that she was with child again. She would be conjuring up a ghost if she did, though—Baldwin, their firstborn, who would never know his father had been crowned as England's king. She clung to Stephen, thinking of her dead son and the baby now growing within her body, a secret she chose to keep to herself for a while longer, to keep safe.

Stephen was stroking her hair, smoothing it back from her face. "I bear Maude no ill will," he said. "I understand her disappointment and her anger and blame her not, for the fault lay with my uncle, who ought to have known better. It is my hope, Tilda, that Maude will come to accept my kingship, and when she does, I shall make her most welcome at my court, shall do all in my power to mend the rift between us."

Matilda tried to imagine Maude's humbling herself to Stephen—tried and failed. "Do you truly think Maude will ever accept your kingship, love?" she asked dubiously, and Stephen gave her a quizzical smile.

"What other choice," he asked, "does she have?"

NORMANDY'S lower capital was swathed in a wet February fog. It clogged the narrow, muddied streets, obscured the skyline of soaring church steeples, and muffled the normal noonday sounds, so that Caen seemed like a city asleep, as if night had somehow come hours before its time. From his vantage point in an upper-story window of the castle keep, Ranulf should have had a sweeping view of the town and its twin rivers, but when he jerked back the shutters, all he got was a surge of cold air, a glimpse of grey.

Robert glanced over at his wife and then got slowly to his feet. "I'd hoped I could make you understand, lad, but—"

Ranulf spun away from the window. "Understand? Not in this lifetime! How can you do it, Robert? How can you recognize Stephen as king?"

"How can I not? All have accepted him, Ranulf. Even Maude's uncle the Scots king has come to terms with Stephen. If I alone continue to hold out, my defiance will cost me more than I can afford to lose. Unless I agree to do homage, he will declare all my lands forfeit."

"Let him! At least you'd still have your honour!"

That was too much for Amabel. "Honour is a right tasty dish, too, especially when served with mustard! Is that what you'd have us feed our children, Ranulf?"

Robert shook his head, almost imperceptibly, and Amabel subsided, albeit with poor grace. "Think you that I want to yield to Stephen?" he demanded, and for the first time his voice held echoes of anger. "I am doing what I must. I am indeed sorry that Maude has been cheated of her birthright. But it is my son's birthright I must try to save now. How will it help Maude if I forfeit the earldom of Gloucester?"

Ranulf had no ready answer, and he swung back to the window, looking out blindly at the fog-shrouded sky. "And what do we tell Maude? That it is all over, that Stephen has won? I cannot do that to her, Robert, and by God, I will not!"

"I said I had agreed to submit to Stephen. I did not say he had won."

Ranulf turned around to stare at his brother. "What do you mean?"

"I told Stephen that I would come to his Easter court and swear homage to him as England's king. I specified, though, that my oath would be binding only as long as he kept his promises, kept faith with me. Our father would never have agreed to such terms, not even with a dagger pricked at his throat. But Stephen did."

"I still do not understand. So you swear to Stephen. What then?"

"We wait," Robert said succinctly. "What happens after that will be up to Stephen. If he keeps faith with me, so shall I keep faith with him. But I do not believe he will, lad. He will begin to make mistakes, and then, to make enemies, and when he first feels his throne quaking under him, he will look around for a scapegoat, for someone to blame for all his troubles. As likely as not, he will look to me. But by then, he'll no longer be the dragon-slayer. Men will have come to see his halo for what it truly is—a stolen crown. And they may well conclude that Stephen was not the lesser of evils, after all."

Ranulf was not reassured by this prediction of coming strife. He was too young yet to feel comfortable with ethical ambiguities, and Robert's pragmatic realism seemed somewhat cynical to him and not altogether admirable. Although he could not have expressed his need, in the wake of Stephen's shocking betrayal, Ranulf yearned for moral certainties, for a world with no shadings of grey, no dubious choices, no compromises.

Robert easily read his inner agitation, for Ranulf's was not a face for secrets. Thinking that innocence could be just as dangerous as a broken battle-lance or cracked shield, he urged, "Sail back to England with me, lad. Make your peace with Stephen. If God wills it, Maude's chance shall come."

"No," Ranulf said hoarsely. "I'll never recognize him as king—never!"

Such a dramatic declaration cried out for an equally dramatic departure, and Ranulf now provided one, striding purposefully from the chamber without looking back. Robert made no attempt to stop him, but he winced as the door slammed shut and sat down wearily in the window seat.

Amabel's irritation ebbed, and she crossed quickly to her husband's side, putting a sympathetic hand upon his knee. "How simple the world seems at seventeen. It is easy enough for Ranulf to pledge Maude his undying loyalty, for what does he have to lose?"

"I would that were so, Amabel, but the sad truth is that the lad has a great deal to lose. He may have no lands to forfeit, but his loyalty to Maude may well cost him what he values most—that lass of his. Raymond de Bernay is liegeman to Simon de Senlis, one of Stephen's most fervent supporters. Unless Ranulf comes to his senses and does homage to Stephen soon, Bernay will disavow the plight troth for certes."

"I trust that you pointed this out to Ranulf?"

"Of course I did. But he does not believe me. Ranulf has been cursed with a dangerous defect in his vision: he can see only what he wants to see. He remains convinced that a happy ending is not only possible, it is a certainty, so sure is he that virtue and justice must prevail. He can no more conceive of losing Annora than he can of Stephen triumphing over Maude."

Amabel shivered suddenly. "Close the shutters, love, ere we catch our deaths. That 'dangerous defect' of Ranulf's—you know who else shares it?"

"Stephen," he said promptly, and she gave a satisfied nod.

"Indeed. I've never known anyone who thrives on hope as Stephen does. He never doubts that every storm must have a rainbow, and if he falls into a stream, he fully expects to rise up with a fish in his cap!"

Robert slid the shutter latch into place, closing out the cold but casting the window seat into shadow. "Well, I would wager that the next time our new king stumbles into a stream, he'll find himself in water over his head. The pity of it," he added grimly, "is that he'll not drown alone, but will drag some good men down with him. I just hope Ranulf will not be one of them."

RAYMOND DE BERNAY was a man of uncommon patience, and his fondness for Ranulf was genuine. But he was not willing to wait indefinitely, and on a cool, overcast day in early June, Ranulf at last ran out of time.

"I have been more than fair with you, lad. I've given you every chance to repent your folly and make your peace with the king. I will ask you but once more. Will you come to England, swear homage to Stephen?"

"No," Ranulf said softly, "I cannot."

Raymond had expected no other answer. "So be it, then." Striding to the solar door, he beckoned to his son. "Ancel, you are to watch over your sister whilst she and Ranulf say their farewells," he said, and although his voice held no anger, it held no hope of reprieve, either.

Ancel had not seen Ranulf in several months, for his father had taken him from Robert's household as soon as Robert's loyalty came into question, placing him with a lord whose allegiance was not suspect, Simon de Senlis. Ancel looked acutely uncomfortable; while he had no objections to being cast as the defender of his sister's virtue, that was not a role he'd ever wanted to play with Ranulf. He mustered up a sheepish smile, a shrug, and was relieved when Ranulf smiled back.

"You need not be so discomfited, Ancel, for this came as no surprise. I knew how your father would react. Just as I know what a hard task lies ahead of me, trying to persuade Annora to be patient and—"

The door was thrown open with such force that the closest candle flame flared and then waned. Annora's eyes were swollen and darkly circled, her pallor so pronounced that she looked ill. Wakeful nights and tear-drenched days, bewilderment and betrayal—it all showed so nakedly upon her face that Ranulf's utter assurance faltered for a moment, much like that quavering candle. But Annora's eyes were dry, for she'd vowed that she was done with weeping. She stopped just out of reach, and said bitterly, "So you are still set upon this madness."

"I have no choice, Annora. I cannot do homage to a man who stole my sister's crown and then perjured himself to keep—"

"Oh, you did have a choice! You chose Maude over me!"

Ranulf frowned. "That is not true. You know better, Annora, for we have talked about this, and I've told you my reasons, why I must support Maude's claim over Stephen's—"

"I do not want to hear any more, not another word! You knew that if you balked at swearing homage to Stephen, you'd lose me; you knew that, but still you clung to that haughty, vengeful bitch, still you—"

"Annora, stop it! You are not being fair, to me or to Maude. Yes, I am loyal to my sister. But you are the one I love, the one I mean to wed. We may have to wait awhile, but we will be wed, that I promise you," he vowed, with all the conviction at his command. When he reached for her, though, Annora recoiled abruptly.

"Do not touch me," she warned, "not ever again! You had your chance, made your choice, and I will never forgive you for it—never!" She was perilously close to tears, and she whirled, stumbling from the chamber before Ranulf could see them fall.

Ancel hastily grabbed for the fire tongs, busied himself in scattering stone-cold ashes about the hearth. But he soon felt foolish, gave up the pretense, and turned reluctantly to face his friend. It was not as bad as he'd feared. Ranulf looked unhappy and angry, but not desolate or defeated, not in need of the sort of comfort Ancel did not know how to give.

"With a temper like hers, your father must save a fortune on firewood." It was a wan attempt at humor, but Ancel chuckled long and loud, so grateful was he that Ranulf was jesting, not raving or ranting or, Jesú forfend, expecting him to stanch the bleeding.

Ranulf was fumbling in his tunic. "I've a letter for Annora," he said, "and I want you to give it to her once her anger cools."

"If we live that long," Ancel gibed, but he reached for the letter, and even tried to look as if he truly believed that it was not too late.

THEY were on the road by dawn. The sun quickly burned away the morning mist, and the sky took on that glazed blue unique to early autumn, a color so clear and vivid that it did not seem quite real. In the distance, the trees appeared to be dusted with gold, as the green shades of summer slowly yielded to October's amber and copper and russet. The villages they passed through were shuttered and still, ghost villages bereft of life, for when an army was on the march, people of common sense fled, or cowered behind bolted doors and prayed.

"Guirribecs!" The warning had raced ahead, outrunning horses, spurred on by pure panic. "Guirribecs!" A Norman term of contempt for the ancient enemies of Anjou, now ravaging their lands, burning their churches, plundering their towns. "Guirribecs!" they spat, watching from hiding as this new army rode past, marveling that these men did not stop to torch or loot. They did not understand their reprieve, but they thanked God for it, never suspecting that they should also be thanking the woman who would be their duchess.

Riding at his sister's side, Ranulf caught an occasional glimpse of a creaking shutter, an astonished face staring after them in wonder. An army lived on the land whenever it could, and those who had the bad luck to be in its path were bound to suffer. But Maude was too shrewd to turn her army loose upon the very people she meant to rule. Ranulf wished that Geoffrey had shown the same restraint. This was Geoffrey's second foray into Normandy, and each time his men had pillaged and raped and robbed on such a grand scale that for every castle won, he'd lost Maude hearts beyond counting.

So far Geoffrey's campaign had yielded mixed results; he'd won some impressive victories, but he'd also suffered a few sharp setbacks. He'd taken Carrouges after a three-day siege, only to be repulsed at Montreuil. But he'd then captured Moutiers-Hubert, and as Michaelmas had approached, he'd made ready to besiege a grand prize, indeed, the prosperous city of Lisieux. Maude felt confident that he would prevail. However often she'd damned him to Hell Everlasting over the past eight years, she'd never denied his abilities as a battle commander.

Each time Ranulf glanced over at his sister, he felt a throb of pride, for it was not so long ago that Maude had given birth to her third son, and the delivery had not been an easy one. But she'd responded to Geoffrey's summons with alacrity, gathered two thousand men under her command, and set such a punishing pace that by dusk on this first day of October, they expected to be within sight of the city walls of Lisieux.

Catching Ranulf's eye, Maude smiled. "It gladdens me that you'll be there to witness the fall of Lisieux," she said, and Ranulf knew she was thinking of the brother who would not be there: Robert, who'd been in England since April, at Stephen's court. Nor was he alone, for their brother Rainald had also come to terms with Stephen. But it was Robert's defection that haunted Maude, one more act of betrayal.

A sudden flurry off to the side of the road drew their attention. The thickets rustled, and Ranulf's two dyrehunds went streaking off into the underbrush. "They must have flushed a rabbit," Ranulf said, but he made no attempt to call them back, knowing they'd catch up again once their hunt was over.

Maude decided, then, that this was a good time to rest their horses, and gave the order to halt. "Have you had any word about that lass of yours . . . Anna, was it?"

"Annora . . . and no, I have not. If she were still at Bernay, I know she would have been able to get a letter to me by now. But her father returned to England in July, and he took Annora with him."

Maude had met Annora on several occasions and had been quick to conclude that the girl was quite ordinary, not at all the sort of wife she would have chosen for Ranulf. But now none of that mattered. If Ranulf wanted Annora, she would move Heaven and Earth to see that he got her. She would not forget those who had stood by her when it truly counted . . . or those who had not.

"You and your lass will be well rewarded for your patience," she promised. "I'll give you a wedding so lavish that the festivities will last for days."

"Between the two of us, Annora and I could not scrape up enough patience to fill a thimble," Ranulf said ruefully. "Fortunately, we'll not have to wait much longer. Once you take Normandy away from Stephen, he'll find he's seized control of a sinking ship. Even the rats will start swimming for shore," he predicted with a grin.

Maude gave him an amused look. "The rats must be jumping overboard in droves after what happened at Exeter," she said, and they both laughed, for they'd not expected Stephen to begin blundering so soon. Until Exeter, he'd been making all the right moves, placating the Pope and buying peace with the Scots king. But then Baldwin de Redvers had seized Exeter Castle. Stephen had promptly assaulted the stronghold, and after a three-month siege, victory was his for the taking. It was then that he'd tarnished his triumph with an act of mercy so misguided that men were still marveling at it. He'd heeded the pleas of Baldwin de Redvers's fellow barons, allowed the castle garrison to go free.

"They were in rebellion against him," Maude said, baffled that Stephen had failed to grasp so basic a tenet of kingship. "Those men should have been hanged, or at the least, maimed, so their fate might serve as a lesson for other would-be rebels. Instead, he sets them free! Forgiveness is well and good for saints and holy men and Christian martyrs, but that is not an indulgence any king can afford. This was Stephen's first test of strength, and he failed miserably, for men now know they need not fear the king's wrath."

"Stephen never could resist a gallant gesture," Ranulf jeered, summoning up scorn to keep from remembering those times when Stephen's gallantry had served as his own lifeline. He'd never realized how dangerous memories could be, not until he had a lifetime of them to deny, for if the man himself had proved false, it must follow that the memories, too, were false . . . did it not? These were not thoughts he cared to dwell upon, and he hastily groped for a more innocuous topic. "Tell me about Geoffrey's new ally. I've never met him; what sort of man is he?"

There was no need to be more specific; Maude knew at once whom he meant. "Well . . . William is not one to be overlooked, for he's a vast mountain of a man, with hungers to match his size. Even his titles are weighty: Duke of Aquitaine and Count of Poitou. He has a booming laugh, an eye for a pretty face, a temper hotter than brimstone, and even more enemies than Geoffrey. Have I left anything out?"

"Not that I can think of. Oh . . . have you ever seen his daughter?" Ranulf thought the question sounded quite casual and offhand, but Maude was not taken in.

"Does Annora know you're lusting after Eleanor of Aquitaine?" she teased, and he flushed, then laughed. "No, lad, I have not seen the girl, so I cannot tell you if she is truly as dazzling as men claim. Since she is such a great heiress, it does not seem fair that she should have been favored with great beauty, too, does it?"

"The same could be said for you," Ranulf pointed out, and although she merely shrugged, he knew he'd pleased her; Geoffrey's compliments were always barbed enough to draw blood. "I'll admit I am curious about the Lady Eleanor, would like to judge this beauty of hers for myself. It puzzles me, though, that her father did not marry again after he lost his wife and son. Surely he must have qualms about entrusting Aquitaine to a mere slip of a lass—"

He caught himself, too late. But Maude was not affronted. "You need offer no apologies, Ranulf, for saying what so many think. Nor have I ever claimed that all members of my sex are capable of wielding power. I can only speak for myself, and I have no doubts whatsoever that I can rule as well as any man and better than most, for certes better than my usurping cousin, damn his sly, thieving soul to Hell!"

"And you'll soon be able to prove it, too, that I— Maude? Look over there, through the trees. Smoke!"

Maude was shortsighted, but she soon saw it, too, a distant, dark cloud smudging the purity of that limpid, azure sky. They both said it at once, in dismayed comprehension: "Lisieux!"

MAUDE'S scout reined in a lathered horse, swung from the saddle to give her his bad news. Stephen had entrusted the defense of Normandy to Waleran Beaumont, and Waleran had garrisoned Lisieux with battle-wise Breton soldiers. When it had begun to look as if the capture of the city was inevitable, the Breton commander gave the order to fire the town, choosing to destroy Lisieux rather than surrender it.

Maude turned aside, struggling to mask her disappointment. Ranulf was disappointed, too, but he was also shocked by the ruthlessness of the Breton commander's act. He said nothing, though, for he was still a month shy of his eighteenth birthday, and he knew he had much to learn about how wars were waged. The scout was not done. Thwarted at Lisieux, he said, Count Geoffrey and the Duke of Aquitaine had then fallen back on the town of Le Sap. It was being stoutly defended by Walter de Clare, and a battle was raging even now in the streets.

THE day's last light was fading along the horizon. But the sky was lit by a hundred fires. The church of St Peter was the heart of Le Sap. Now flames were shooting from every window. As Maude and Ranulf watched, the rafters gave way and the roof collapsed with a hellish roar. Embers and sparks and burning brands rained down upon the spectators, spooking several horses and unseating their riders. As the wind shifted, Ranulf found himself choking on dense, swirling smoke. He could hear screaming, and hoped it was not coming from the church, for it was utterly engulfed in surging, wind-lashed flames. The air was hot enough to sear his skin, and when his stallion panicked, he was tempted to let it bolt, for in that moment his desire to put Le Sap's death throes far behind was almost overwhelming. Instead, he calmed the fearful animal, then reined in beside his sister.

Maude had clapped her veil over her nose and mouth. "Well, Le Sap is ours, what is left of it. It looks like the castle has fallen, too. But—"

"Lady Maude!" Striding toward them out of the murky smoke and cinders was an armor-clad giant, his coif pulled back to reveal a tousled head of curly, damp hair, his face streaked with soot, his hauberk liberally splattered with blood. "Thank God you're here, for you've got to talk some sense into that lunatic you married!"

Maude's smile was sour; as if she could! "You give me too much credit, Will. Where is Geoffrey . . . at the castle?"

"No, he is still being treated by the doctor."

"Doctor? Geoffrey has been hurt?" Maude slid from the saddle before the Duke of Aquitaine could offer his assistance. "Is it serious?"

"No, more's the pity," he snapped, and Ranulf barely stifled an involuntary laugh. But the duke, whose tactlessness was legendary, seemed unaware how inappropriate a remark that was to make to a man's wife, even a less than doting one. "It happened about noon," he said, "whilst we were besieging the castle. One of their crossbowmen got off a lucky shot and hit Geoffrey in the foot. I'll not deny it is a nasty wound, for he broke a few bones, and those fool doctors did almost as much damage as the bowman when they cut out the bolt. So there has to be a goodly amount of pain. But Christ on the Cross, Maude, a man cannot give in to it!"

"Geoffrey has never been wounded before, Will, not even so much as a scratch. In fact, he rarely gets sick at all—mayhap a fever or cough, but no more than that since we've been wed. It is not surprising, then, that he'd be such a poor patient, for he's had no practice at it."

"No, Maude, you do not understand . . . not yet. He says the campaign is over, says he is going home to Anjou on the morrow!"

THE doctor was standing in front of Geoffrey's command tent. At sight of Maude, he looked like a man reprieved from the gallows. "Madame, how glad I am to see you! If you could talk to the count, mayhap you could—" But Maude brushed past the man as if he didn't exist, with Ranulf and the Duke of Aquitaine hard on her heels.

Geoffrey had been trying to drown his pain in wine, but he'd succeeded only in making himself queasy, too. His face was grey and beaded with cold sweat; he looked so haggard that even Ranulf felt a flicker of pity. Maude hastened toward the bed, snatching up a candle along the way. "Geoffrey?"

Blinking in the sudden flare of light, Geoffrey focused hazily upon the white, tense face so close to his. "Get me a doctor," he said huskily. "That dolt out there could not heal a blister without holy help from Above . . ."

"Geoffrey, you cannot give up the campaign! If you retreat now, you'll lose all you've gained so far, and your suffering will have been for naught!"

"And my suffering just breaks your heart," he muttered, gesturing toward his wine flagon. After Maude had helped him to drink, he struggled upright with difficulty. He acknowledged neither Ranulf nor the unhappy doctor, hovering nervously in the entrance. But he targeted the Duke of Aquitaine with a bloodshot, accusing glare. "Did you bother to tell her about my wound first, Will? Or did you plunge right in, bemoaning all your lost plunder, your chance to spill some blood?"

The duke glared back, calling Geoffrey an obscene name that was wasted upon Ranulf, for he spoke no langue d'oc, the native tongue of the duke's domains. Maude ignored the acrimonious exchange, keeping her eyes riveted upon her husband's face.

"Geoffrey, this is not a decision to be made in haste. I'm sure you'll see it differently on the morrow—"

"And how would you know that, Maude? Have you ever been wounded in battle?"

No, but I damned near died bearing your son! Maude somehow managed to bite the words back; what would it serve to squabble over who had suffered more? "Geoffrey, I am not making light of your pain. But with so much at stake, you must not lose heart. If you do, we'll lose Normandy!"

"Normandy will wait for me to heal at home. And so will you . . . dear heart," he added, investing the endearment with such lethal sarcasm that Maude's temper took fire.

"'Heal at home,'" she echoed scathingly. "For God's sake, Geoffrey, you were not gut-shot! Since when is a foot wound fatal?"

Geoffrey's hand jerked, spilling his wine onto the bed covers. "You meddlesome bitch, look what you've done! I curse the day my father yoked me to a spiteful, provoking scold like you, and God help me, but you get worse with age! If I say we go back to Anjou, we go, and I'll hear no more on it, not unless you want me to leave you behind to fend for yourself. Now fetch me more wine, and then find me another doctor, a competent one this time."

Maude went hot with humiliation and impotent fury. Her face flaming, she drew back into the tent's shadows until she could trust herself. He'd said worse to her, done worse, too, but not in public. She would never forgive him for shaming her like this before Ranulf and the duke, and it took every shred of her self-control to keep silent. But she must think of her sons, think of her Henry, who would one day rule England after her. She would not let Geoffrey steal her sons as Stephen had stolen her crown. Damn his poisoned tongue and that bowman's wretched aim and Robert's defection, damn all the men who treated their dogs better than their women! Bracing herself, she turned around then, her head high, only to find that Ranulf and the duke had gone, leaving her alone with her husband.

RANULF was sitting upon an overturned bucket within view of Geoffrey's tent. He'd wangled a joint of roast beef from one of the camp cooks, although he'd ended up sharing most of it with his dogs. For the past hour he'd been trying to convince himself that he'd done the right thing, the only thing he could do. He knew Maude's pride, hoped he'd been able to salvage some of it.

It had been hard, though, saying nothing whilst that misbegotten hellspawn humbled his sister as if she were a serving wench. And yet what could he say? Even the duke had held his peace, and he wanting only to throttle Geoffrey there in his bed. But they could not meddle between a man and his wife, however much they wanted to. The female dyrehund seemed to sense his mood, nudging his knee fondly, but keeping an eye peeled on that beef bone. "Here, girl, catch," he said, and watched as she disappeared into the darkness before her mate could claim the bone.

When Maude emerged from the tent, he jumped hastily to his feet. She paused, then came toward him. They walked in silence for a time. Whenever they passed a soldier carrying a torch, Ranulf studied her face, not even sure what he was searching for. He wanted to ask if she was all right; it seemed safer, though, to pretend nothing had happened. But there was something they could not ignore: Geoffrey's threat.

"Do you think he meant it?" he asked, and Maude nodded.

"He meant it," she said tersely. "We depart on the morrow for Anjou."

Ranulf had been half expecting to hear that, but it still had the power to shock. "Our father must have been mad to make you wed that man!" Maude shrugged; he could read nothing in her profile, and he reached out uneasily, touched her arm. "Maude . . . you are not giving up?"

She turned to face him then, giving him a glimpse of narrowed dark eyes, cheekbones burning with feverish heat. "Give up? No, Ranulf," she said, sounding desperate and determined and bitter beyond words. "I will never give up, not until my dying breath, and not even then."

7

FALAISE, NORMANDY

June 1137

AFTER fifteen months as England's king, Stephen felt secure enough upon his throne to turn his efforts toward Normandy. Determined to bring the duchy more firmly under his control, he crossed the Channel in March. At first he met with heartening success; the French king recognized his claim to Normandy. But in May, Geoffrey led an army across the River Sarthe.

Stephen was besieging Mezidon by then, punishing a recalcitrant baron. He wasted no time, though, in dispatching a large armed force to block Geoffrey's invasion. Having ravaged the countryside around Exmes, Geoffrey then pressed northward, leaving behind a trail of charred ruins, skeletal, smoke-blackened silhouettes rising up like ghostly tombstones to mark his army's passing. He'd advanced within ten miles of Robert's stronghold at Caen when he encountered Stephen's army at Argences.

A battle seemed imminent, one that might settle the disputed succession once and for all. But Stephen's army was an uneasy mix of Norman barons and Flemish mercenaries, and they were as wary of one another as they were of Geoffrey's Angevins. Stephen had entrusted command to William de Ypres, a Flemish adventurer with a chequered past, an abundance of courage, and a skeptical streak far wider than the stream separating the two hostile armies. Ypres's suspicions were aimed at Robert, for he was convinced that Maude's brother was a Trojan horse in the Norman camp, awaiting an opportune moment to switch sides. He made no secret of these suspicions, and Robert withdrew angrily to his castle at Caen, amid a flurry of mutual, embittered accusations. Robert's departure demoralized his fellow barons, and Norman-Flemish hostility soon reached such a pitch that Ypres abandoned his campaign, riding off in a rage to join Stephen at the siege of Mezidon.

Geoffrey decided it would not be prudent to force Robert to make a choice just yet, and he withdrew as far as Argentan. Stephen soon followed, though. By June, he'd summoned his army to Lisieux and was preparing to launch an assault upon Argentan. Once more it looked as if England's crown would be won or lost upon the thrust of a blade, bought with blood.

THE tavern was hard to find, tucked away at the end of an alley in one of the more disreputable neighborhoods of Falaise. By the time he finally spotted the protruding ale-pole, Gilbert Fitz John had gotten his boots thoroughly muddied, almost had his money pouch stolen by a nimble-fingered thief, and had been forced to fend off so many beggars and harlots that he doubted he'd reach the Rutting Stag with either his purse or his honour intact. Brushing aside the most persistent of the beggars, he plunged through the open doorway and found himself in a crowded common room that stank of sweat and unwashed bodies and cheap wine. The chamber was meagrely lit by a few reeking tallow candles, and Gilbert backed into a corner until his eyes adjusted to the gloom, all the while trying to appear inconspicuous, no mean feat for a youth with flaming red hair who towered head and shoulders above the other tavern customers.

"Do you know what you look like? A man who's strayed into Hell by mistake, and is politely pretending not to notice the flames, brimstone, and burning flesh."

At sound of that familiar voice, Gilbert sighed with relief, then said grumpily, "Given a choice, I think I'd take Hell over the Rutting Stag. Leave it to you to pick a hovel like this!"

Ranulf grinned. "Say what you will of this sty, it is not a place where I am likely to be recognized."

"You hope," Gilbert said, with fervor. "You have not changed a whit, have you, Ranulf? God save us both, as reckless as ever, with Stephen's army barely a stone's throw away and Falaise aswarm with his spies!" Ranulf shrugged. "If I am crazed for setting up this meeting, what does that make you for agreeing to it?"

"A fool, for certes. But I'm here now, and we may as well make the best of it. You can at least buy me a drink ere some of Stephen's Flemish hirelings drag us off to gaol."

Ranulf laughed. "Wait till you taste the wine they sell here; it puts swill to shame!" Once they'd shoved their way to a corner table, Ranulf leaned forward, resting his elbows upon the warped, greasy wood, and studied his friend. It had been more than fifteen months since they'd seen each other, for Gilbert had continued to serve as one of Robert's squires, following his lord to Stephen's English court. "I'm right glad you came, Gib. Damn me if else, but I've even missed you . . . a little."

"Of course I came," Gilbert muttered, sounding both pleased and embarrassed. "And so will Ancel. He'd never miss a chance to risk his neck." He knew what Ranulf was about to ask, and tried to head it off, saying hastily, "I did not see much of Ancel these months past, for Lord Robert came to the king's court only when summoned. Robert did not even sail for Normandy with Stephen's fleet, preferring to cross the Channel in his own ship."

"You'll not be struck by a lightning bolt if you say her name aloud," Ranulf said, and Gilbert ducked his head, staring down at the table as if he were intent upon memorizing every crack, splinter, and stain.

"Annora de Bernay. See . . . no thunderbolts. I am not loath to talk about Annora. I just hope Ancel had the mother wit to seek her out ere he left England. If he has forgotten to bring her letters, I'll be tempted to prod his memory with a poleax! Keep this betwixt us, but I never thought our separation would last this long, Gib. It would ease my mind greatly if I could reassure Annora that our waiting is almost done. There is no chance of that, though, not unless I learn to walk on water." Ranulf paused, waiting for a response that didn't come, and gave an exaggerated, comic sigh. "Friends are supposed to laugh at each other's jokes, no matter how lame."

Gilbert managed a dutiful, unconvincing chuckle. "So you think, then, that Stephen is riding close to the cliff these days?"

"Any closer and he'd better hope his horse sprouts wings! Robert could earn his living as a soothsayer if needs must, for he predicted it with dead-aim accuracy—that Stephen would begin to make mistakes and then to make enemies. He infuriated the Marcher lords when he balked at putting down that rising in Wales last year. Then that Flemish brigand of his, William de Ypres, caused a breach with Robert, the one man Stephen should be trying to win over. And rumor has it that he has fallen out with his brother, for it's been six months since the Archbishop of Canterbury died and Henry's patience is wearing thin. I can understand why Stephen is wary of nominating him, but if he does not, Henry will never forgive him. No, Gib, Stephen's crown has lost a lot of its luster. Once he loses Normandy, too, his hold upon England will crack beyond mending."

Gilbert did not agree that the loss of Normandy was a foregone conclusion, not with Stephen's army just twenty miles away, poised to launch an assault upon Argentan. But he kept his doubts to himself, instead asked Ranulf if Maude was still at Argentan with Geoffrey.

Ranulf shook his head. "Maude is often at Argentan; she believes that her presence in Normandy helps to strengthen her claim to the duchy." Leaving unsaid the obvious, that Maude's unhappy marriage was another reason why she'd prefer Argentan to her husband's domains. "But when Geoffrey invaded Normandy last month, he forced Maude to withdraw with their sons to Domfront. Supposedly it was done for their safety's sake, but I think Geoffrey just wanted Maude out of the way. He's not one for letting a minor detail—that Maude is the rightful heiress—interfere with his ambitions. Remember, Gib, how we used to worry that Geoffrey might insist upon sharing Maude's throne? Well, that fear was for naught. In truth, Geoffrey would not care if England sank into the sea without a trace. It is Normandy he covets, and you may be sure—"

A large hand clamped down on Ranulf's shoulder. Startled, he spun around to confront a burly stranger, one with heavily muscled arms, a massive chest, and a face twisted askew by several puckered scars. "I know who you are!" the man cried, and Ranulf jerked free, fumbling for his sword hilt. But his blade never cleared the scabbard, for his assailant was already backing away. "I meant no harm! Your friend said it was just a joke!"

Ranulf snatched up his wine, gulping it down in two swallows. Gilbert drained his own cup just as fast. As they watched, Ancel tossed a coin to his baffled accomplice before sauntering toward them. "Well?" he demanded, "have you no greeting for me?" and then pretended to stagger backward, arm upraised to ward off the wave of scalding invective coming his way. When Ranulf and Gilbert had exhausted their supply of obscenities, if not their indignation, Ancel straddled a bench and began to laugh. "I am sorry to say this, Ranulf, but being around Maude has not been good for you; you're becoming as grim and humorless as she is! Now our poor Gib never had a sense of humor to lose, but I did expect better of you."

"When I called you a misbegotten, witless whelp without the brains God gave a flea . . . I was being too kind."

Ancel laughed even harder at that, then waved an arm expansively about the tavern. "A great place you picked for our reunion, Ranulf. What . . . the lepers would not let you use their lazar house?" Catching a serving maid's eye, he pantomimed a drink order. "If I pay for the next round of the local poison, can we agree to a truce? So tell me, why are you not barricaded with Geoffrey behind Argentan's walls? Poor Maude—her luck has soured for certes. What irked her more, being penned up with her loving husband or missing the wedding in Bordeaux?"

Ranulf knew at once what he meant, for there were only two topics of conversation that summer, the war and the wedding. The Duke of Aquitaine had gone off on pilgrimage after his abortive campaign with Geoffrey, and he'd died that past April in Spain, lingering long enough to arrange a marriage between his fifteen-year-old daughter, Eleanor, and Louis, the son of the French king. It was his deathbed hope that he was thus safeguarding Aquitaine for Eleanor, giving her a husband powerful enough to protect her inheritance. The wedding was to take place in July, and had the circumstances been different, Ranulf would have enjoyed attending the revelries, watching Eleanor the Fair take her first step onto the road that led to the throne of France. But he was not amused by Ancel's jest, for he resented its implications, that Maude was a vain, frivolous female, one who'd give equal weight to a crown and a wedding fête. He'd become very protective of his sister in these past eighteen months, had long since forgotten that he'd once harbored the same doubts about feminine resolve or womanly valor, and he said impatiently:

"There is not a soul to be found in all of Christendom who could distract Maude from what truly matters—claiming the throne Stephen stole. And if you think I'd rather talk about Eleanor of Aquitaine than Annora, you're either drunk or demented or both. I've gone a year with no word from your sister, and that was long enough to last a lifetime. So let's strike a deal here and now. You hand over Annora's letters and I'll not inspect her seal to see if you read them on the sly!"

Ranulf grinned and reached across the table for Annora's letters. But Ancel had turned, was glaring accusingly at Gilbert. "You did not tell him?"

"Me? It was not my place to tell him," Gilbert protested. "She is your sister, not mine!"

Ranulf frowned. "Tell me what? Annora is not ailing?"

"No," Ancel said reluctantly, "she is well enough. But you'd best put her out of your mind, Ranulf, for she is married."

Ranulf stared at him, then laughed. "How gullible do you think I am, Ancel? Next you'll be telling me she has decided to become a nun!"

"Ranulf, I am not jesting. She is married, I swear it."

Ranulf half rose from the bench, grabbed Ancel's wrist. "That is a lie!"

"No . . . it is not. She was wed last Michaelmas to Gervase Fitz Clement." Ancel tried unsuccessfully to break Ranulf's grip. "I know you do not want to hear this, but it was for the best. It was a good match, for he is a kinsman of my father's liege lord, Simon de Senlis, and holds manors in Shropshire and Leicestershire and Yorkshire—"

"Why are you lying like this? I know your father, know how he dotes upon Annora. He'd never force her to wed against her will, no matter how many manors the man had!"

"For Christ's sake, lower your voices," Gilbert urged, "for we are starting to attract attention!"

"Annora was not forced! She wanted the marriage!" Ancel was suddenly free. He rubbed his wrist, drew a deep breath, and repeated, "She wanted it, Ranulf, and that is God's Truth."

AS soon as he moved, Ranulf was assailed by pain. Squeezing his eyes shut, he lay very still, waiting for it to pass. It didn't, though, and he forced himself to sit up, fighting back a wave of nausea. He had no idea where he was. It seemed to be a tiny cubicle up under the eaves of a roof, a dingy, sparsely furnished room that reeked of perfume and held only a straw mattress, a chamber pot, and several coffer chests that doubled as seats. The lone window was shuttered, and the air fetid and stale, oppressively hot. His clothes were scattered about in the floor rushes, and by gritting his teeth, he managed to ignore his throbbing head long enough to collect his crumpled tunic, linen shirt, and braies. He had to hunt for his chausses, finally finding the striped hose entangled in the sheets. But a search of the entire room did not turn up his money pouch.

He was slowly pulling on his boots when the door opened and a woman entered. "Awake at last, are you? I was beginning to think I'd have to charge you rent, sweeting!"

The light was so dim that Ranulf could tell only that she was young and plump. "What time is it?" he mumbled, and then, "No! Do not open the window!" But he was too late. Pulling the shutters back, she blinded him with a sudden surge of bright afternoon sunlight.

GROPING his way down a narrow stairway, Ranulf emerged into an inn's common chamber. A few men were seated in the shadows, and one of them now beckoned. As he moved closer, he recognized Ancel.

"Jesus God, you look like somebody pried off the lid of your coffin! Sit down ere you fall down, over here at the table. I do not suppose you want anything to eat yet?" Ranulf was not able to suppress a shudder, and Ancel grinned. "No, I thought not. I'm not surprised you're so greensick, for you damned near drank Falaise dry. Oh . . . ere I forget, here is your money pouch. We thought I'd better hold on to it, since you were in no shape to fend off a mewling kitten, much less any of the cutthroat knaves prowling about this hellhole." He watched as Ranulf slumped onto a stool, then slid a clay goblet across the table. "Have a few swallows of ale."

Ranulf peered into the cup, thirst warring with queasiness. "So you paid the wench above-stairs, then? I owe her no money?"

"I even chaffered her price down, and a good deal I got for you, too. She was worth it, I trust? Ah . . . but you do not remember, do you? I suppose you do not remember the doxy at the Crane on Tuesday, either? A pity, for that one looked hotter than Hades!"

Ranulf took a tentative sip of the ale. "Where is Gib?"

"He'd begun to fret so about letting Lord Robert down that I finally sent him back to Caen. You'll have to help me concoct a plausible excuse for my absence, or Lord Simon will have my hide."

Ranulf blinked. "Tuesday, you said? What day is this?"

"Thursday." Ancel laughed at Ranulf's startled look. "Indeed, you have not drawn a sober breath for nigh on three days! Is that a record, you think?"

Ranulf glanced at Ancel, then away. Three days lost and he could remember none of it—Jesú! "I suppose I ought to thank you and Gib for making sure I did not do anything crazy—like breaking into another nunnery," he said, with a grimace of a smile. "Ancel . . . tell me what happened."

"When we got to England, Annora was hurting and angry and of a mind to listen when my father proposed the match with Gervase Fitz Clement. I know what you're thinking, that she did it to spite you, and mayhap that is so, for Annora always did have a hellcat's temper. But the marriage was the right choice, even if she did make it for the wrong reasons. Gervase is a man of breeding and wealth and influence. As I told you on Monday eve, he is kin to my lord, Simon de Senlis."

"That I remember," Ranulf snapped. "What of it?"

"He'll be able to take good care of Annora, Ranulf. She'll want for nothing. And he seems right fond of her, seems pleased to have such a lively young wife. His first wife died two years ago, leaving him with three children . . . and they took to Annora straightaway. Sometimes a second wife loses out when there are children from an earlier marriage. But Gervase has enough to provide well for his heir, and for any sons Annora gives him—"

Ranulf set the goblet down with a thud, sloshing ale onto the table. Annora naked in another man's bed, bearing his children: the image was so vivid that he gasped. Tears burned his eyes and his throat closed up as he struggled with emotion just as raw and ravaging as physical pain. When he finally won his battle for control, he looked up, shaken, to find Ancel watching him with helpless pity.

"Ranulf, I am truly sorry. But it was for the best, and you'll come to see that in time. You and Annora are too much alike; your marriage bed would have become a battlefield ere the year was out."

Ranulf slammed his fist onto the table, a foolish move that triggered so much pain he feared his head would split wide open. "Damn you, shut your mouth!"

Ancel took no offense; in fact, he even looked contrite. An awkward silence fell between them, until Ranulf forced himself to ask, "Is . . . is she happy?"

Ancel hesitated. "When I saw her at Christmas, three months after her wedding, she seemed content. I'm sorry if that is not what you want to hear . . ."

Ranulf said nothing, for at that moment, he truly did not know what he'd wanted to hear. Ancel went to fetch more ale, was bringing it back to the table when the door was flung open with a resounding crash. Ranulf winced, turning away from the blaze of light, but Ancel stopped abruptly. "Gilbert? Why are you not in Caen?"

Gilbert strode toward them. "You've got to get back to Lisieux, Ancel, and right fast, for your lord is sure to be in a tearing rage. All hell broke loose in Lisieux on Tuesday eve. Stephen's army fought a bloody battle in the city streets, but not with Geoffrey's Angevins—it was Normans against Flemings, and they're still counting the dead!"

"You're not serious, surely?"

"No, Ancel, I'm jesting. I rode all the way from Caen just for the fun of it! I'm telling you the truth, and have the saddle sores to prove it. A squabble started between several Norman and Flemish soldiers over a wine cask, and it soon became a brawl and then a battle. A lot of men died, and some of the Norman lords were so wroth they abandoned the campaign and rode off—without even seeking Stephen's permission! Can you imagine anyone defying the old king like that?"

"Only if they had a death wish," Ranulf said, with his first real smile in three days.

Gilbert reached over, helped himself to Ancel's ale. "It sounds," he said, "as if your sister's luck has finally taken a turn for the better!"

"I AM Ranulf Fitz Roy, and I am here to see my brother, the Earl of Gloucester."

That was all it took to gain Ranulf entry into Caen Castle. As he followed a guard across the inner bailey toward the keep, he tried to shake off his fatigue, to decide what he would say to Robert. That was no easy task, for he was not even sure why he was here. It had not been planned. He'd told Ancel and Gilbert he was joining Maude in Domfront, but after they'd departed, he'd passed several more utterly aimless days in Falaise. And when he'd finally mounted his horse, he'd found himself heading north instead of south. He'd covered almost all of the twenty miles to Caen before he'd even admitted that was his destination. But he'd realized that he needed more comfort than he could get from wine and whores. Now, as he climbed the stairs to Robert's solar, it occurred to him that whenever he'd been hurting in the past, he'd turned to Stephen to stanch the bleeding, and he laughed bitterly, earning a curious look from the guard.

Any qualms he'd harbored about his welcome were vanquished at once, dispelled by the warmth in Robert's surprised smile. Amabel, too, seemed genuinely glad to see him, and he'd not been sure that would be so, for he knew Amabel was less forgiving than Robert. But after one glimpse of his haggard face and bloodshot eyes, she sent a servant down to the kitchen with an order for Ranulf's favorite foods, and steered him firmly toward a cushioned settle.

Amabel's charm was undeniable when she chose to exert it, and uniquely her own, by turns flirtatious and maternal, with a tart tongue leavened by easy, earthy laughter, a free spirit securely anchored to reality. She lavished that charm now upon Ranulf, full force, scolding him playfully for sins of omission, teasing him about losing his razor, for his wine-blurred week in Falaise had given him the beginnings of a blond beard. In their society, youths were clean-shaven; men were not. To Robert and Amabel, the sight then, of Ranulf's new-grown stubble was significant in a symbolic sort of way, proof of passage across that most unsettled of borders, the one dividing boyhood and manhood.

"You're not drinking your wine, Ranulf. Is it not to your liking?"

Ranulf's smile was wry. "In truth, Amabel, I'd sooner quaff blood. I had a very wet week, and I'm still drying out."

Robert nodded sympathetically. "We feared you'd take it hard, lad."

Ranulf could not hide his surprise. "You know, then?"

"Of course we do. How is Maude bearing up?"

"Maude? What does Maude have to do with Annora's marriage?"

"Annora?" Amabel drew a quick, comprehending breath. "Your lass wed another man? Ah, Ranulf, I am indeed sorry!"

By now, Ranulf was thoroughly confused and increasingly uneasy. "If you did not know about Annora, what then, did you mean? Why should Maude be distraught? With Stephen's soldiers spilling their own blood, she has every reason to rejoice. Unless . . . unless it was not true?"

"No," Robert assured him, "it is true enough. The feuding between Normans and Flemings flared into violence, and the Earl of Surrey's son and other Norman lords then withdrew from Lisieux in a rage."

"Well, then, as I said, Maude has reason to rejoice, for the end is now in sight. When Geoffrey marches on Lisieux, how can Stephen hope to hold him off?"

"Stephen saw that, too, lad. Whatever his failings as a king, he is a seasoned battle commander. He realized that his campaign was in shambles and his throne at risk, and so he made Geoffrey an offer—two thousand marks in return for a two-year truce."

Ranulf was stunned. "You cannot be saying that Geoffrey agreed?"

"Yes," Robert said quietly, "he did."

RANULF had spared neither his horse nor himself, and they were both exhausted by the time the city walls of Domfront rose up against the sky, high above the River Varenne. The closer he came to Domfront, the more Ranulf dreaded what lay ahead. How could Maude not be shattered by this latest and cruelest of all her betrayals? To have the English crown at last within her reach, only to be snatched away again, this time by the perfidy of her own husband. He could not blame her if she had no more heart for this unequal, unending struggle. But if she admitted defeat, he'd fought—and lost Annora—all for nothing.

MAUDE was alone in her solar, standing by an open window. The morning light was warm and scented by the gardens below, but it was not kind, accentuating Maude's pallor, her hollow-eyed fatigue. At sight of Ranulf, though, her sudden smile belied the strain and sleepless nights and thwarted hopes. "You're back!"

Ranulf stopped short. "You did not doubt it?"

"Of course I did not, Ranulf!" she protested, sounding so surprised and so sincere that he felt a flicker of comfort; at least he'd been able to do that much for her, to gain her trust.

They looked at each other in silence for a moment, and then Ranulf said abruptly, "If there is any justice under God's sky, that double-dealing Judas will rot in Hell, right alongside Stephen!"

Maude gave him another smile, but this one never reached her eyes. "Give Geoffrey his due, lad. Judas sold his soul for thirty pieces of silver, but Geoffrey turned a much better profit; he extorted two thousand marks from Stephen!"

"What did he say to you, Maude? What justification could he possibly offer?"

"That the price was right, too tempting to refuse. Ah, but he did throw me a few crumbs of comfort. He assured me, you see, that making a truce and honouring it are not necessarily spokes on the same wheel."

Ranulf swore under his breath. "So what now? We wait on his whim, wait until he gets bored enough or restless enough to resume the war?"

"Yes," Maude said, very dryly, "that sums it up rather well."

"And you believe him?"

"I have to, Ranulf," she said, "I have to . . ."

Ranulf felt a rush of relief, realizing in that moment just how much he'd feared hearing her say it was done, that he'd sacrificed his happiness with Annora for an elusive, unattainable dream. "You astound me," he said huskily. "No matter how often these whoresons shove you into the fire, you always rise from the ashes again, just like that mythical bird, the . . . the phoenix."

"This time I singed my wings well and good, and lost a few tail feathers, too," she conceded. "But they'll grow back."

They both turned, then, toward the open window, for the sound of "Mama" floated up, clear as a bell, on the mild summer air. Below them, a groom led a dappled grey pony, and sitting proudly in the saddle was a beaming little boy. As soon as they appeared at the window, he waved. "Mama, look! I'm riding Smoky! Watch me, Uncle Ranulf!"

"We're watching, Henry," Maude called back. "You're doing very well!"

"I know," Henry agreed, with such a cocky grin that Ranulf and Maude both laughed. In coloring, Henry was very much his father's son, and the sun haloed his reddish-gold hair, windblown and copper-bright. As young as he was, he knew his own mind, and they were not surprised to hear him arguing with the groom, insisting he could handle the reins himself. He was not one for whining, though; he was usually a cheerful, high-spirited child whose most common sins were cheekiness and an insatiable curiosity, sins easy enough to forgive. His younger brother Geoffrey was quick to throw tantrums when he was thwarted, but that was not Henry's way, and he sought to persuade the groom now with a precocious mix of childish logic and coaxing charm.

"I thought you'd told Henry he could not have a horse of his own until he turned five. What changed your mind, Maude?"

"Geoffrey very helpfully told Henry that he'd learned to ride when he was four. I'll not deny my heart was in my mouth the first time I saw him lifted into the saddle. But I do Henry no favor by coddling him. I must ever bear that in mind, the hardest lesson a mother has to learn."

Her dark eyes were following her firstborn as he explored the confines of the garden. "When I was pregnant with Henry," she said, "I remember being urged to eat these vast meals. Whenever I balked, there was always some meddlesome but well-meaning soul to remind me that I was eating for two. Well, now I am fighting for two, Ranulf. It was not just my birthright Stephen stole; it was Henry's, too. So . . . I cannot give up. I will not fail my son as so many have failed me."

THAT summer was exceedingly hot, and by September, the crops were shriveling in the fields, rivers running shallow and sluggish, and the roads so cracked and pitted that travelers found themselves choking on clouds of thick red dust. The great hall in Rouen's castle was stifling, windows unshuttered in the vain hope of drawing in a breeze, attracting only flies and swarms of gnats. But most of the people present were indifferent to the heat and the insects, for their attention was riveted upon the confrontation taking place between the English king and the most powerful—and, therefore, most dangerous—of his barons.

Stephen's face was flushed with anger. "My lord Earl of Gloucester, you have kept away from my court all summer, agreeing to come only after the Archbishop of Rouen pledged to vouch for your safety. Your suspicions are as outrageous as they are insulting. You'd best explain yourself, if indeed you can!"

"If you want answers, my lord king," Robert said coldly, "seek them from him." And he turned, drawing all eyes toward the window seat where William de Ypres was sitting.

The Fleming was not a big man, some inches shorter than Stephen. But he was well muscled, sturdy, and robust, a formidable foe on or off the battlefield. His long hair was streaked with silver, but the color was so fair that the grey was not at once noticeable. Much more conspicuous was a crescent-shaped scar that angled from his left eyebrow up into his hairline; his enemies called it the Devil's brand. He and Robert had more in common than either man cared to admit. They were the same age, forty-seven, and both labored under the same disadvantage, for both were born out of wedlock.

Robert had fared better, though, than William de Ypres. The Fleming was a bastard son of a Count of Ypres, grandson of a Count of Flanders, and when his cousin was assassinated, he'd pushed his own claim to Flanders. He might even have prevailed, if not for the widespread suspicion that he'd been privy to his cousin's murder. He'd been forced to flee his homeland, and for the past four years he'd been a trusted member of Stephen's household. But if Stephen trusted him, few others did, and sentiment in the hall was very much with Robert as Ypres got to his feet without haste, approached the dais with a calculated swagger.

"Ask of me what you will," he challenged, and Robert swung back toward Stephen, pointing an accusing finger at the Fleming.

"Whilst we were at Argences in June, waiting to do battle with Count Geoffrey of Anjou, this man—your man—plotted to ambush me. Fortunately, I was warned beforehand, and was able to safeguard myself against his treachery. But a man would be a fool to rely upon such luck a second time . . . would he not, my liege?"

The hall was utterly still. Not a man or woman there failed to hear what Robert left unspoken, the implication that if the deed was Ypres's, the desire was Stephen's. Stephen knew what they were thinking; a muscle twitched in his cheek as he looked from Robert to Ypres. "Will? What say you to this accusation?"

Ypres was not at all flustered to find himself in the storm's center. In fact, he looked as if he relished it. "And was it not convenient, my lord Gloucester, to have an excuse to hole up in Caen, safely above the fray? It would have been awkward, after all, if you'd actually had to fight!"

"Are you questioning my courage?"

"Indeed not, my lord. I am questioning your loyalty."

Robert was white with fury. "Dare you deny that you plotted to ambush me?"

"No," Ypres said, and there was a stir in the audience. Matilda stepped unobtrusively from the shadows, lightly touched Stephen's arm. Her husband did not appear to notice, keeping his eyes locked upon the two men.

The other barons had begun to murmur among themselves. Ypres silenced them with a gesture. "Ere you start building a gallows, I have more to say. I did plot against the Countess of Anjou's brother. But I was not seeking his death. I aimed to flush him out into the open. It was my hope that he would betray himself, and to judge by the unseemly haste with which he abandoned our campaign, I'd say he did!"

"That is sheer drivel!" Few in the hall had ever seen Robert so angry, for his rage was usually iced over. "Had your scheme gone as planned, you'd have been able to bury your guilt in my grave. But you got unlucky—I survived. If you hope to escape punishment, though, you'll have to do better than this. You expect us to take your word that you never meant murder? Christ's Blood, you've left a trail of lies from Flanders to Boulogne that a blind man could follow!"

"What vexes you the most, my lord earl? That I took steps to smoke you out? Or that I reminded men of a fact you would rather we forgot—your blood kinship to a woman who is our king's sworn enemy?"

"Enough!" Stephen got to his feet, striding toward the edge of the dais. "You've both had your say. Hurling insults and accusations at each other serves for naught. My lord of Gloucester, I can understand your anger. Whatever my lord de Ypres's intent, he had not the right to put your loyalty to a test. It was an unfortunate incident, but it is over now, and best forgotten. As I am responsible for what is done in my name, I offer you my apology."

To Robert, that was too little, too late. "I accept your apology," he said, with perfunctory courtesy. "But what of Ypres? What penalty does he pay?"

"That is for me to decide. But you need not fear, for it will never happen again. On that, you have my oath."

Robert's mouth thinned. "I have your oath?" The words themselves were innocuous, but with a rising inflection, they became a sardonic commentary upon the king's credibility.

"Yes, by God, my oath—the oath of a crowned, anointed king!" Stephen stalked down the dais steps, and Matilda held her breath, for a long-smoldering fire seemed about to burst into a hellish conflagration. Her relief knew no bounds when Robert chose not to strike that fatal flint, and she sat down hastily in the closest seat, so disquieted she did not even notice it was Stephen's throne.

Stephen's triumph was so fleeting, though, that he had no chance to savor it. As enraged as he was by Robert's oblique defiance, he would not have let it fester, for if the voice was Robert's, the hostility was Maude's, and was thus easy to shrug off. But when he turned toward their audience, he was jolted by what he saw on so many faces: the same skepticism, the same doubt that his word was good. And standing there in the great hall of Rouen's royal castle, he suddenly realized a very unpalatable truth: that most men might recognize him as England's king, but they no longer saw him as a man of honour.

MATILDA could not sleep unless she was sure that her children slept, too, and cupping her candle, she bent over the bed. They were sprawled in an ungainly tangle, legs and arms protruding at odd angles, as flaxen-haired as their father; Eustace had claimed both pillows, and William had fallen asleep sucking his thumb again. Smiling, she gently tucked the blankets about them, for she had at last banished Baldwin's ghost from the nursery, no longer saw his curly blond head on the pillow beside his brothers'. Not a day passed when she did not think of him, her firstborn, taken too soon. She'd had two years, though, to come to terms with his loss. But her little girl's grave was too newly dug, for they had buried her in ground frozen and snow-encrusted, last winter's grief, too recent and raw for healing. Matilda straightened up slowly, backed quietly away from the bed where her sons slept, while whispering, soft as a breath, as she did every night, "Blessed Mary Ever Virgin, keep my lads safe, spare them hurt or harm, Amen."

Her daughter stirred as soon as she approached the bed, mumbling a sleepy "Mama?" Matilda sat beside her, lifting the child onto her lap. When Mary began to nuzzle her breast, she opened her gown and let the little girl suckle. She had not nursed her older children, for women of rank were expected to hire wet nurses. But she had insisted upon nursing Mary, despite Stephen's objections, prompted by feelings she could not fully explain, a need that was somehow related to her grieving for Baldwin. Whatever her reasons, she had cause to be thankful for her obstinacy, for the intimacy of that physical bonding with her baby when God suddenly took her other daughter, her namesake, just days away from her second birthday.

Mary had been a godsend, solace for her empty, aching arms, balm for her buffeted and bleeding faith. She knew hers was a common grief, knew how often children died in their first fragile years of life. She knew, too, that it was not for her to question the mysterious workings of the Almighty. But God had reclaimed two of her children; what if He wanted the others, too? And so she had decided to give Him one, to give Him Mary.

Stephen had resisted at first, for daughters were a king's political capital; many an alliance had been forged in the heat of the marriage bed. Their little Tilda had been buried with a betrothal ring, having been plight-trothed to Waleran Beaumont a few months before her death. But his wife's entreaties had soon won Stephen over; he'd reluctantly agreed that Mary would be pledged as a nun. And Matilda, mourning her dead daughter, was comforted, for surely Mary would find contentment in the cloistered peace of the convent. As a Bride of Christ, her salvation would be assured, her happiness more certain than as a bartered bride for a Waleran Beaumont or a Geoffrey of Anjou.

Once she'd rocked Mary back to sleep, Matilda headed for the stairwell that led up to her own bedchamber. The room was shuttered and still, and she wondered why it had not been made ready for her. Raising her candle, she moved toward the table, then recoiled at a sudden movement in the shadows. "Stephen? You scared me so! Why are you sitting here in the dark?"

He shrugged, saying nothing. Matilda subjected him to a candlelit scrutiny, and then retraced her steps to the door, where she discreetly dismissed the servant just entering with an oil lamp. She'd not expected this, that he should still be brooding about his clash with Robert of Gloucester; he'd always been one for living utterly in the present, with little patience for sifting through yesterday's mistakes, even less interest in borrowing tomorrow's troubles. Crossing to his chair, she tried to massage away the tension coiled in the muscles of his neck and shoulders.

"Have you decided what you shall do about William de Ypres, Stephen?"

"Nothing," he said wearily. "How can I in good conscience punish him for reading my mind? He was wrong to act upon his suspicions, but they were mine, too. Anytime now I expect to find Brother Robert perched on the foot of my bed, watching to see if I stop breathing in the night. He is worse than a vulture, though, Tilda. At least they do not begin their deathwatch until their prey is down and floundering. Robert—damn his eyes—began his vigil as soon as he set foot in my realm."

Matilda sighed softly. "He will like it not if you refuse to chastise Ypres."

"Even if I did lesson Ypres, Robert would still find fault with it. Nothing I do would satisfy him—short of abdicating my throne in favor of his wretched sister."

Matilda's fingers had stopped moving, lay still against the nape of his neck. It worried her in no small measure, his failure to make peace with Robert. She blamed them both, Robert for being so stiff-necked and self-righteous, Stephen for being so defensive and suspicious, so unwilling to bid for Robert's allegiance. Had the power only been hers, she'd have lavished Robert with royal favor; she'd have done whatever she could to give him compelling reasons for wanting Stephen's kingship to succeed. But try though she might, she'd not been able to mute the echoes of their lifelong rivalry, and could only watch with foreboding as the rift between them widened. If Robert of Gloucester repudiated Stephen's authority and openly declared himself for his sister, would his defection cause a few earth tremors . . . or an earthquake?

She'd rarely heard Stephen sound so disheartened. "I was proud of you today," she said, "proud of the way you took responsibility for Ypres's plotting. That was a forthright and courageous act, love."

He shrugged again, and then surprised her by saying, "The old king would not have apologized."

"Mayhap he would not," she agreed, somewhat hesitantly, for she was not sure where he was going with this. "But it was right, Stephen, and honourable, and what else matters?"

"You are such an innocent," he said, and rose abruptly to his feet. "I tried to do what was 'right and honourable' at the siege of Exeter; you remember, Tilda? Baldwin de Redvers's wife came out to plead for mercy, hair streaming down her back, feet bare like one doing penance, face wet with tears. A man would have had a heart of flint if he were not moved by her pleas. And then Redvers's fellow barons added their voices, arguing for clemency. So I agreed to pardon Redvers, I freed the garrison, and I was glad to do it. Even after Redvers then turned to piracy and fled the country, finding refuge with Maude, I was not sorry I spared them. I thought I'd done the right thing, and that was enough. But not for my barons. They've been laughing at me ever since, mocking me for showing mercy, for showing weakness—and this from the very same men who'd argued on Redvers's behalf!"

"Even if that is so," Matilda said, "you followed your conscience. What more can a man do than that, Stephen?"

"I do not know," he admitted. "That is just the trouble, Matilda, I do not know!"

She was on her feet now, too, reaching out to him. "I've never heard you talk like this. What has happened?"

"I had a rightful claim to the English throne. It was no usurpation, for I was the old king's favorite nephew, grandson of the great William the Bastard of Normandy. None wanted a woman on the throne, you know they did not. And I was urged to it, by men who rejoiced that I'd be sparing them—and England—untold misery. My oath to Maude meant nothing, writ on water, they said. But in breaking that oath, I became less in their eyes. Where is the fairness in that?"

"Ah, Stephen . . ." Matilda got no further, not knowing what to say.

"I looked out across that hall today, and I realized that I could trust none of them. None of them, Matilda!"

"Surely that is not so! What of your brother and the Beaumont twins?"

"Ah, yes, my faithful brother. How faithful do you think he'll be if I do not set that archbishop's mitre upon his head? And the Beaumonts will stay loyal—as long as they benefit from that loyalty. But do not fool yourself, Matilda—they'd go over to Maude without a qualm if she could come up with a big enough bribe. Even William de Ypres is suspect, for when a man's loyalty is for sale to the highest bidder, there is always a risk of being outbid."

He turned at her touch, looked down bleakly into her face. "No one I can trust, Tilda," he repeated, and then pulled her to him, holding her against his chest, so close she could hear the thudding of his heart. "Only you," he said softly, "only you . . ."

8

CAEN, NORMANDY

April 1138

Spring in Caen was cold and damp and disappointing, for April had so far shown itself to be winter's accomplice. Amabel, a restless sleeper, soon kicked the coverlets off. But when she rolled over, drowsily seeking Robert's warmth, she found only the chill of an empty bed. Sitting up, she peered into the lurking night shadows, then groped for her bed-robe.

"Lent is over, Robert. How much longer do you mean to deny yourself sleep?"

"It is not penance, Amabel. If I'm wakeful, it is not by choice. But you need not keep vigil with me. Go back to bed."

"Indeed not! If you broke a leg, I'd fetch a doctor to set it. If you were suffering from a fever, I'd treat it with sage and vervain. So why should I do any less now? You've a conscience in need of mending, and I've a needle and thread at the ready. Shall I start stitching?"

She could always coax a smile from him, however brief. "Are you so sure you'd know where to stitch?"

"Who would know your wounds better than I? This particular wound was inflicted the day you knelt before Stephen and pledged him your fealty. I'd hoped it would heal in time, but it has begun to fester. You'd best cut it out, Robert, ere its poison starts to spread."

He could not hide his surprise. "You urged me from the first to make peace with Stephen. Are you saying now that you were wrong?"

"No . . . but *you* were, for listening to me!"

"Amabel, this is too serious a matter for jesting. If I were to renounce my allegiance to Stephen, you could accept that? You'd not fear the consequences?"

"Of course I'd fear them—not being a fool! But what I fear more is Stephen's fear. For he does fear you: your power, your castles, your vassals, and your kinship to Maude. And all the while, William de Ypres hovers close at hand, awaiting his chance. How long ere that Flemish viper talks Stephen into moving against you? One failed ambush is enough, by God! If war is sure to come, then you may as well follow your heart—and the oath you swore to your father on Maude's behalf."

"You are a constant source of wonderment, Amabel. I know you like Maude not. You never wanted to see her as England's queen, never."

"What of it? Neither did you." Holding up her hand before he could protest. "Admit it, Robert. Your fondness for Maude notwithstanding, you had grave doubts about a woman's wielding a man's power, especially a woman wed to Geoffrey of Anjou. But Maude has a son, a son with the blood-right to Normandy and England, and I'd wager that is what robs you of sleep at night."

Robert was silent for several moments, marveling at how well she knew him, how easily she'd seen into the most private corners of his soul. "You are right," he conceded. "I did have qualms about Maude's queenship. I let her down and I regret that. But it is young Henry who has been haunting my peace. I tried to do what was best for us, for England, and I failed, I failed miserably. Stephen has not the makings of a king, however well-meaning he may be. Nor can I trust him, and if—"

"What more is there to say, then? Why let Stephen choose the time and place for your reckoning? You choose, Robert—here and now."

Robert's relief rendered him speechless. It had taken him months to reach that same conclusion, and with great reluctance, for he was that paradox, a man of courage whose nature was inherently cautious and conservative, and rebellion was as rash and reckless an action as he could envision. It was also inevitable, but even after he'd finally acknowledged that, he'd not known how to break the news to his wife, loath to cause her pain.

"I thank God for your change of heart," he said, "but I'll confess that I did not expect it. I well remember how you argued with me, insisting that I must recognize Stephen as king."

"And I was right—then. You'd have stood alone, without allies. But time has favored Maude, not Stephen. The Scots king has led another army across the border, is burning and pillaging Northumbria even as we speak. Stephen's disgruntled brother grows weary of waiting for that archbishop's mitre, and who can count all the lords who've come to resent the royal favors lavished upon the Beaumonts and their kin? It would have been sheer folly to urge a mutiny when the ship was still in the harbor, sails just catching the wind. But now that same ship is taking on water, those splendid new sails are in tatters, reefs lie ahead . . . and how much more likely it is that the crew shall be willing to heave Stephen overboard!"

Even after three decades of marriage, Robert could be taken aback by his wife's ice-blooded practicality, so at odds with the conventional wisdom that women were sentimental creatures, good-hearted and guileless and charmingly giddy. As much as he'd come to value Amabel's commonsense shrewdness, it troubled him occasionally that honour weighed so lightly on her ethical scales. But not now. Now he was grateful for the stark single-mindedness of her vision, and he said, "It means much to me, that you understand what I must do."

"I always understand, my love," Amabel said fondly. "I just do not always approve! Now I think we'd best end this midnight council. No man ever died of conscience pangs. The same cannot be said, though, for men who court chills in drafty, cold, fireless chambers." And taking his arm, she drew him back to the warmth of their marriage bed.

ON a windy, cool day in June, Geoffrey and Maude rode into the Norman city of Caen. The procession was a colorful one, for they both appreciated the value of pageantry, those "bread and circuses" offered by royalty since time immemorial. They made a striking couple, mounted on matching white palfreys, dressed in rich shades of red silk, Maude's gold-threaded veil a gossamer swirl of sunlight, Geoffrey's scabbard aglitter with studded gemstones. The citizens were impressed by their splendor, but they were not won over. However handsome Geoffrey was, he was still Angevin, of the Devil's Brood, and no Norman could rejoice in his triumph. They were a practical people, though, and now that their liege lord had seen fit to welcome the Angevin and his haughty wife, they turned out in large numbers to watch, if not to cheer.

As the procession wound its way through the narrow, thronged streets, the attention of the crowd shifted from their would-be duchess and her hated husband, focusing instead upon the tawny-haired, dark-eyed youth riding at Maude's side. Ranulf's spirits were soaring higher than Caen's circling, raucous gulls, and his laughing exuberance was so contagious that only the most dour soul could resist smiling at his antics.

He was flirting shamelessly with every pretty girl he passed, fishing out coins for street urchins and beggars, saluting priests and widows, and teasing the small boys who were trying to keep pace. As they neared the castle, a young woman leaned from an upper window, throwing down a long-stemmed rose. Ranulf caught it deftly, casting about him for a favor to give in return. Several streets back, he'd amused the crowd by plucking a flowering sprig from an overhanging tree and presenting it to a giggling redhead. Now, though, he saw no gardens to raid. But then his gaze fell upon a nearby street vendor. Moments later, he triggered a burst of laughter by tossing a spiced wafer to the girl at the window—laughter that spread as he then distributed wafers with comic gallantry to all female spectators within reach.

Of those watching, Maude alone was not entertained. Although she was Norman-French and Scots by blood, her formative years had been spent in Germany, and she still clung to those lessons she'd learned at the august and regal court of her first husband, the Holy Roman Emperor. By the time she'd come home to England, it was an alien land, and she'd yearned for the ceremonial elegance and protective protocol of her husband's world, a world she'd made her own, only to have it taken from her by death and her father's implacable will. Even now she was disconcerted by informality, finding it too closely akin to familiarity, and Ranulf's free and easy manner jarred her sense of decorum. It was not seemly that he should jest with these Norman peddlers and craftsmen and their women, for he was a king's son. She said nothing, though, for this was neither the time nor the place for a reprimand. Geoffrey would overhear and laugh rudely. Nor did she want to spoil the moment for Ranulf. He was entitled to play the fool, as long as he did not make a habit of it.

Ahead lay the castle. The gates were open wide, the walls lined with curious faces, and as they rode across the drawbridge into the bailey, they found Robert and Amabel waiting within, ready to bid them welcome. They were smiling, and Maude smiled back, reining in her palfrey and holding out her hand so Robert could help her dismount. But her pleasure was not as pure and uncomplicated as Ranulf's, for as much as she rejoiced in Robert's return to the True Faith, and as much as she wanted to forget his betrayal, she had never learned how to forgive.

IT had rained for days, a cold, pelting rain that defied the calendar and frustrated Londoners, for they'd yearned for June's warmth during a long, bleak winter, and now June was here, but more like March in disguise. Although a fire had been lit in the royal bedchamber, it had yet to chase away the damp. On nights like this, Matilda missed her cozy chamber at Tower Royal; the palace at Westminster might be a more fitting residence for England's king, but Matilda preferred the manor house that had been her home for most of her marriage.

"When will Papa be back?"

Eustace was straddling a bench by the fire, kicking rushes into the hearth. He sounded quite ingenuous, as if his only concern were with Stephen's whereabouts, but Matilda knew better, for she knew her son. Of all her children, Eustace was the most stubborn, the one most determined to get his own way. It was bedtime he was resisting, for he'd decided that since he was eight now, he should not have to go to sleep at the same time as his younger brother, William. Occasionally he'd hide, but his usual tactic was delay, the strategy he was employing tonight, and he'd been bombarding his mother with earnest queries about how long dragons live and whether elephants truly fear mice and why it never snows in summer. His sudden interest in his father's itinerary didn't fool Matilda in the least, but she was a woman of infinite patience, and she said indulgently:

"Passing strange, for I was sure I'd told you all about your father's capture of Hereford Castle. It had been seized by a wicked man named Talbot, an accomplice of Maude's, but Stephen hastened west with an army and took the castle after a four-week siege. As his last letter said he was about to return to London, we may expect him any day now. So . . . the sooner you go off to bed, the sooner the morrow will arrive—and possibly your papa, too."

It was not that easy, of course. Eustace made use of all the weapons in his arsenal: pleading, whining, sulking, even tears. Stephen would have capitulated early on, but Matilda was made of sterner stuff than her soft-spoken demeanor would indicate, and she prevailed.

Stephen arrived much sooner than Matilda expected, that very night, as she was making ready for bed. She hastily dismissed her ladies, for she shied away from public displays of affection, waiting until the door closed to welcome her husband home. His mantle was dripping, and underneath, his tunic was wet, too. She was not surprised, for he was as indifferent to weather as he was to late hours, often riding by torchlight or in a drenching downpour; he was, she knew, one of the few battle commanders willing to undertake a winter campaign. What did surprise her, though, was his subdued, offhand greeting. By now he'd shed his mantle, and she helped him struggle free of his soggy woolen tunic. His shirt seemed dry, and she steered him toward the hearth, then poured a cupful of hippocras before beginning her gentle interrogation.

"You seem oddly glum for a man who's captured a castle and put his enemies to flight. What is amiss, Stephen?"

"You know me too well, sweet. Lord save me if ever I have a serious secret to keep from you!"

She was not taken in, either by his ready smile or by his rueful jest, and waited. He drank, paused to pull off his boots, and drank again. "My victory lasted about as long as one of our Eustace's promises not to hit his brother. The garrison surrendered when the town caught fire; I suppose they feared it would spread to the castle. I let them go free, for they were but following Geoffrey Talbot's orders."

He shot her a challenging look, was reassured by her obvious approval. "I'd not have been so merciful to that hellspawn Talbot. He was not willing to take his chances with his men, though, and fled as the siege began. But as soon as I rode away from Hereford, he skulked back and torched the houses on the south side of the river."

"The coward!" she said indignantly. "But you must not brood about such a craven sinner, Stephen. He'll answer for his treachery, if not before your throne at Westminster, before the Throne of the Almighty come Judgment Day."

"Talbot is the least of my problems, Tilda. I've got the Scots king ravaging the North, and Geoffrey of Anjou leading an army into Normandy again . . . and on the road to London, I encountered a herald from the Earl of Gloucester. Robert Fitz Roy had renounced his homage, claiming that I'd broken faith by sanctioning William de Ypres's treachery and that I was no true king, having usurped the throne from the rightful heiress, his sister."

"Oh, no . . ." Matilda stared at him in such pained dismay that he reached out swiftly, drew her into his arms. She clung tightly, fearfully, for what she'd most dreaded had come to pass. Behind her closed eyelids, an image formed: Robert of Gloucester, so controlled, so competent, and so dangerous. She'd never doubted that if there was one man in Christendom capable of wresting the crown from Stephen, it was Robert. Why had Stephen not done more to keep Robert content? Too late, though, for recriminations, too late. "So . . . it is to be war?"

"Yes," he said, "and I shall need your help, Tilda."

"Just tell me what you would have me do."

"Besiege Dover Castle."

"Me?" she gasped. "You are jesting, of course?"

"No, sweetheart, I am quite serious. I'd intended to march north and force the Scots king to take the field against me. But Robert's treachery poses a greater threat. I've good men in Yorkshire, men whom I can trust to repel the Scots whilst I strike at the heart of Robert's domains—Bristol Castle. It will not be easy to capture, God knows, but it is much too dangerous to remain a rebel stronghold, not when it can menace the whole of the West Country. Yet I dare not overlook Dover Castle, either. Dover would be Robert's natural choice for a landing. If I can deny Maude a safe port, mayhap I can strand them in Normandy, and then—"

"Stephen, I understand that, I do. But I cannot—"

"Matilda, you can and you must. You are the Countess of Boulogne in your own right, can summon vassals not only from Boulogne but the Honour of Kent, too. Your fleet can blockade Dover's harbor, starve the castle into submission if need be, and patrol the Channel, making it too risky for Maude and Robert to attempt an invasion. You have the power, lass, and now I need you to use it on my behalf."

Matilda shook her head mutely, daunted by the magnitude of what he was asking, and he stepped back, looking down intently into her face.

"You are their liege lady; you have the right." Adding coaxingly, "It is not as if you'd be making command decisions, sweet. You'd have battle captains to direct the siege. No one would expect you to pitch a tent under the castle walls or to launch the mangonels with your own hand!"

But she would be expected to give commands, to deal with unruly vassals, to enter into a man's world and make all believe she belonged there. "Stephen, I do not think I can do this. It is not a woman's place . . ."

"Tell that to Maude!" His smile was wry, but his hands had tightened upon her shoulders. "You must agree, my love. You must do this for me. You are the only one who can."

STEPHEN quickly realized that his siege of Bristol Castle was going to take months, and with no certainty of success. Robert's chief castle was virtually impregnable, ensconced behind two fast-flowing rivers, the Avon and the Frome, encircled by a deep ditch, protected not only by its own bailey walls but by those of the town, too. Patience had never been one of Stephen's virtues, and he soon grew restless, then discouraged, and was not long in deciding that Bristol's downfall could wait. Abandoning the siege, he went looking for easier targets and found them at Castle Cary and Harptree, held by Robert's vassals. But as July ebbed away in a haze of heat, trouble flared in the border town of Shrewsbury.

Shrewsbury's castle had been given by the old king to his young queen Adeliza twelve years earlier. As castellan, she'd appointed the sheriff of Shropshire, William Fitz Alan—a man of influence in the Marches—Lord of Blancminster. But he was also a man with marital ties to the enemy camp: his wife, Christina, was niece to Robert and Amabel Fitz Roy. As soon as Robert renounced his allegiance to Stephen, Fitz Alan did, too, declaring that he held Shrewsbury Castle for his liege lady and rightful queen, the Empress Maude. By the first week of August, he found himself disputing that point with his king.

SHREWSBURY had been blessed with natural defenses; the town lay within a horseshoe curve of the River Severn. Surrounded on three sides by water, Shrewsbury could be approached by land only from the north—site of the castle. For the past four weeks, a royal army had been encamped before the rebel fortress. But so far Stephen's assaults had been driven off, and Fitz Alan remained defiant, scorning all demands for surrender.

The sky was barren of clouds, a bleached blue-white that shimmered with heat, for August had been a month of drought and dust. Stephen's stallion had broken out in a sweat and was pawing the trampled grass. War-horses were bred as much for their fiery tempers as for their strength, and those nearest to Stephen prudently retreated. Stephen himself did not notice his destrier's restiveness, for his attention was utterly focused upon the castle.

It looked deserted, for most of its inhabitants were barricaded within the great keep, and the men posted along the bailey walls were hunkered down out of sight, rising up occasionally to heave a lance or shoot a bow, then hastily ducking behind the stockade as Stephen's archers returned the fire. Large rocks scattered about the bailey, churned-up earth, smashed horse troughs, and collapsed wooden sheds—all testified to the damage done by Stephen's siege machines. As he watched, one of his mangonels went into action again. A creaking windlass slowly hauled the beam back, the men loaded a pile of heavy stones, and then released the triggering cord, causing the beam to snap upright, slamming into the crossbar and catapulting a rock shower over the castle walls. They could hear the thudding as the stones hit, and then a choked-off scream.

That was a familiar sound, though, and they paid it no heed. By now Stephen's companions were watching him as intently as he was studying the castle. The Earl of Leicester was the first to lose patience, for the Beaumonts had as scanty a supply of that particular commodity as Stephen did. "What say you, my liege? Are we going to make another try with the scaling ladders or not?"

"No . . . we've lost enough men that way." Stephen tightened the reins, swinging his mount in a circle. "Meet me in my command tent—all of you."

They did, although it took a good quarter hour to gather them together. Stephen sat cross-legged on his bed, watching them jockey for position in the tent's confining quarters. Robert Beaumont was comfortably seated on a coffer chest, swapping bawdy jokes with Miles Fitz Walter, but his blue eyes were keeping Stephen under an unobtrusive surveillance. Stephen had come to realize that the nonchalant affability of the Beaumonts masked a shrewd sense of their own worth and their own wants. He'd come, too, to rely upon that shrewdness, even if he sometimes fretted that their loyalties were not rooted deep. He did believe they'd keep faith, though, for no family had benefited as much from his kingship as theirs had done.

Geoffrey de Mandeville had profited, too. So had Simon de Senlis, for Stephen had restored to him part of his lost patrimony, granting him the earldom of Northampton to compensate for the earldom claimed by his stepfather, the Scots king. Stephen's gaze rested upon them both for a moment before moving on to Maude's men, for that was how he thought of Miles Fitz Walter and Brien Fitz Count.

Miles was not one to escape notice, for he had a redhead's temper, a soldier's taste for blunt speaking, and a steely-eyed stare that was in itself a formidable weapon. He looked like a man who'd spent most of his life outdoors, with flyaway reddish-brown hair that always appeared windblown and skin deeply freckled by the sun, taut as leather. Bowlegged and barrel-chested, he was a skilled huntsman and an aggressive, able battle commander. He cast a lengthy shadow over the Marches, sheriff of Gloucestershire and Staffordshire, and it was often said of him that he ruled the whole Welsh border, "from the River Severn to the sea." He'd been devoted to the old king; his allegiance to Stephen had yet to be tested. But if he made an uncertain friend, he'd make a more dangerous enemy, and so Stephen was trying hard to convince himself that self-interest would keep Miles loyal.

If what first impressed about Miles was the coiled power, the sheer physical impact of his presence, the initial impression of Brien Fitz Count was of polished, impeccable courtesy, a disarming smile, and distance. The most superficial assessment revealed Miles to be just what he was—a man most at home in the saddle, sword in hand. Brien, attractive, urbane, and unusually well educated, was obviously a courtier, and thus easily dismissed by those scanning the horizon for political rivals. That was too simple, though, for there was nothing at all simple about Brien Fitz Count, a man who kept his own counsel, a cynic who was still saddened whenever his jaundiced view of mankind was confirmed, a man of deliberation and caution who was reckless in the extreme upon the battlefield, a man of noble blood and ignoble birth, tolerant of all failures but his own.

Stephen trusted Brien even less than he did Miles, for Brien was that rarity, a man who seemed willing to admit women into that select circle of those who wielded royal authority. Stephen had long suspected that Brien would defect to Maude within hours of her landing on English soil, and oddly, that hurt, for he had a genuine liking for this illegitimate, honourable son of a Breton count, sensing that they shared an uncommon willingness to forgive human folly. A great pity, he thought, that Brien should be so eager to entangle himself in Maude's web.

They were all here by now, all but one. Stephen was not surprised that it should be the Earl of Chester who'd keep them waiting; nor did he doubt it was deliberate. Randolph de Gernons counted it a day wasted if he did not ruffle a few feathers, and if the feathers were royal, so much the better. He was a man with vast estates, numerous vassals, and equally numerous enemies, for he was as bad-tempered as a badger, as proud as Lucifer, and he collected grudges as if he thought they were coins of the realm. But even if he'd possessed the serene temperament of a saint, he'd have been the object of Stephen's suspicions, for his young wife was Robert Fitz Roy's daughter, not only Maude's namesake but her favorite niece. So far, though, Chester had remained aloof from the political turmoil afflicting England and Normandy, and if he had any interest in making Maude Queen of England, he alone knew it.

Chester seemed to sense just how far he could push his provocations, and he made his entrance mere moments before Stephen's irritation flared into active anger. Swarthy and stocky, with deep-set dark eyes half hidden under lowering brows, lanky ink-black hair that reached below his shoulders, and a harsh, gravelly voice that could rattle shutters when he was in full cry, Chester looked at first glance more like a brigand than a baron of the realm, and since he so often acted as if his only true peer were God, he got no warm welcome now from the other lords. Unfazed by the chill, he elbowed his way toward Stephen. "I assume this summons means we'll be launching another attack, and high time, too!"

Stephen ignored the gibe. "We have no choice but to attack again, for it could take months to starve them out. And they've made it offensively clear that they'll not surrender."

"God's Bones, why should they surrender? They know full well that their defiance will cost them nothing, no more than it did the garrisons at Exeter and Hereford."

Stephen glowered at the outspoken earl. "And of course," he said sarcastically, "men would be so much quicker to surrender if they expected to be hanged!" Satisfied with his riposte, he glanced back at the other men. "We have much to do and little time to spare, for I want the assault to begin at noon."

There were surprised murmurs, for none saw the need for such haste. "Why today?" Miles asked curiously. "Why not wait till the morrow?"

"Because," Stephen said, "we cannot be sure that on the morrow the wind will still be blowing from the north." And he watched, smiling faintly, as he saw them absorb, understand, and approve.

THE final assault upon Shrewsbury Castle began after a priest called upon the Almighty to grant them victory. The castle defenders, warned by the sudden activity in the royal encampment, had taken up position along the bailey walls, watching warily as the battering ram was brought up. They were puzzled, though, by what the king did next, for he dispatched a small armed force toward the castle. Crouching behind large shields, they advanced upon the castle moat. A deep, dry ditch, it had been filled in weeks ago by Stephen's soldiers, heaped with dirt and brushwood and rocks. When the castle garrison realized that the men below them were throwing more brushwood and straw into the ditch, they understood, and arrows and stones began to rain down from the battlements. But they were too late. Torches were already searing through the air, aimed at the sun-dried straw, and within moments, the moat was filled with fire.

The garrison tried frantically to contain the flames, pouring water onto the timbered walls in a vain attempt to keep the blaze from spreading. But in fighting the fire, they exposed themselves to another sort of fire, coming from Stephen's archers and crossbowmen. What drove them off the walls, though, was the smoke. Men were soon coughing and choking, for the wind was blowing dense black clouds over the walls. They retreated, reeling about blindly in the sudden dark smothering the bailey. And by then, the king's battering ram was smashing into the smoldering wooden gates.

The siege of Shrewsbury Castle had lasted more than four weeks. The final assault lasted less than four hours. Once Stephen's men had control of the bailey, they set fire to the door of the keep, forced their way into Fitz Alan's refuge. The fighting was brief and bloody and over by Vespers. As the peaceful pealing of church bells echoed through the town, the fearful citizens bolted their doors, shuttered their windows, and prayed that Shrewsbury would be spared the fallen castle's fate.

But Stephen's triumph was flawed, and his initial elation was soon curdled by disappointment, for a thorough search of the castle revealed a frustrating fact—that William Fitz Alan had somehow managed to escape the trap. He was not among the prisoners taken, nor among the bodies being collected for burial. An interrogation of the survivors revealed nothing of substance, for Fitz Alan's men were loyal and Stephen loath to resort to torture. Fitz Alan's wife was gone, too, but Stephen had expected that, for rumors had circulated for weeks that all the women had been spirited out of the castle before the siege began. Fitz Alan's flight was far more recent, possibly only hours old, and Stephen gave orders for a house-to-house search of Shrewsbury, although without any expectation of success. His men had barricaded both of Shrewsbury's bridges, but he knew Fitz Alan could have gotten a small boat, crossed the river by night, and so there was no surprise when the town's search proved futile.

If Fitz Alan had slipped through the royal nets, his uncle was not so lucky. Arnulf de Hesdin had remained behind, and that night he was escorted into the great hall to confront his king. The hall still bore the visible scars of the day's assault. Broken tables and stools had been piled in a corner, forming a forlorn pyramid of splintered wood. There had been no time to sweep up the bloodied floor rushes, and the smell of smoke still hung heavily upon the air. Arnulf de Hesdin had not emerged unscathed, either, from the siege. His thinning hair was matted and snarled, his eyes smoke-reddened, a rivulet of dried blood smudging his cheek, caking in his beard. But he stode into the hall as if his chains were badges of honour, and faced Stephen defiantly, without a trace of fear or repentance. "I am here, my lord king. Do with me what you will," he said, flinging down his submission as if it were a gauntlet.

"One might think you were the anointed king," Stephen snapped, "instead of a miserable wretch of a rebel, that craven Fitz Alan's scapegoat."

Arnulf flushed angrily. "My nephew is no coward! We insisted he get away whilst he could, for he'd be of no use to the Empress Maude in one of your prisons."

Stephen had reddened, too. "How dare you speak so to me, your king? You come before me in chains, boast of your loyalty to that unworthy woman, and you expect me to do . . . what? Commend you for your candor? No, by God, no—I've had enough!"

Stephen paused for breath, his chest heaving. His rage was surging to the surface, like a river spilling its banks, for his resentment had been rising for months, and there in Shrewsbury Castle's great hall, it at last reached flood tide, breaking loose in a torrent of infuriated, frustrated accusation and reproach.

"I swore to rule by law and God's Holy Word, to do justice to every man, be he beggar or bishop. I sought no bloodshed, forgave betrayals with a good heart, and held out my hand to enemies and rebels and malcontents alike, for Scriptures would have us 'forgive their inequity and remember their sin no more.' And my reward was to be mocked, to be made the butt of jokes, to see my mercy scorned as weakness."

Again, he paused. The hall was utterly silent. All were listening attentively for once. Let them listen, let them learn! "But Scriptures speak of more than forgiveness," he said hoarsely, for his throat had become tight and raw. "They say, too, that 'rebellion is as the sin of witchcraft' and 'the wages of sin is death.' This man, Arnulf de Hesdin, was taken in rebellion against his lawful king. He deserves to hang . . . and hang he will."

Stephen swallowed with an effort. Arnulf de Hesdin's mouth was ajar, his color draining away. There was open surprise on the faces of his barons, and sudden wariness on the faces of the other prisoners, but not outright fear, not yet. They owed him a mortal debt, every man jack of them; did they think him too softhearted to demand payment? He'd show them otherwise. He knew full well what his uncle the old king would have done, and he said harshly:

"Hang the garrison, too. Hang them all."

THE following day dawned in a burst of late-summer sunlight; by midmorning, the great hall was stifling. Stephen's bitter satisfaction had ebbed away during the night; he awoke in an oddly morose mood, not sure why his triumph should have soured while he slept. He picked indifferently at the food on his breakfast trencher, and refused curtly when he was asked if he wished to watch Arnulf de Hesdin die.

The doomed men had been given a night's grace to make their peace with God, but once the sky lightened, the executions began. There were too many for a gallows—ninety-four of them, more than Stephen had realized—and so his Flemish mercenaries were dragging them up onto the castle battlements. Bodies were soon dangling above the moat like grotesque decorations, a sight to strike terror into the hearts of the cowed townspeople, but death was much quicker this way, if less dignified: most of the men died of broken necks rather than the slow strangulation of a gallows execution. Stephen's chosen hangmen went about their task with matter-of-fact efficiency, but the sheer numbers of the condemned slowed them down, and as the morning wore on, Stephen grimly concluded that the hangings were likely to take all day.

Stephen's fraying temper was subjected to still more strain by the unexpected noontime arrival of his brother the Bishop of Winchester. Attended by his usual deferential entourage, the bishop swept into the great hall like an ill wind, made Stephen a perfunctory obeisance, subject to sovereign, and then demanded, brother to brother, to know what was going on.

"That should be obvious," Stephen said tersely. "We are hanging the castle garrison."

The bishop nodded approvingly. "God's Will be done," he said sententiously, and then lowered his voice, revealing he did have a modicum of tact. "I'm glad to hear that you're finally showing some sense. In truth, Stephen, if you'd heeded my advice all along, you'd not be racing about the country like a crazed fire fighter, dousing one blaze only to have another flare up as soon as you move on."

The bishop glanced about the hall then, frowning, for it was filled with men he little liked or trusted. One of those high-flying Beaumont hawks. Waleran? No—the other one, Leicester, for Waleran was in Normandy, trying to chase Geoffrey back into Anjou. The taciturn Earl of Northampton, a man likely to welcome salvation with a scowl. That hellspawn Mandeville, looking much too comfortable at Stephen's side. Maude's spies, Miles Fitz Walter and that Breton count's bastard get. The Earl of Chester, holding court across the hall as if he and Stephen were competing kings. Not men he'd want as an audience. Not men he'd want within a hundred miles of his brother, but Stephen was a sheep stubbornly set upon running with wolves. "I need to speak with you, Stephen . . . in private."

Stephen could guess what was in store for him: another of his brother's lectures about his manifold failings as a king, interspersed with indignant rebukes for taking so unforgivably long to name him Archbishop of Canterbury. Not that Stephen could actually bestow the archbishop's mitre, as that was for an ecclesiastical synod to do. But the king's candidate would clearly have the advantage, and Henry was determined to obtain Stephen's official endorsement, an endorsement Stephen was equally determined to withhold, for both he and Matilda were convinced that his brother could not be trusted with so much power. Yet he was reluctant to be the one to slay Henry's dream, and so he'd been temporizing for months now, hoping that if the problem could be ignored long enough, it might somehow go away. Of course it did not; the bishop only grew more insistent, more aggrieved, and Stephen knew a confrontation was inevitable. But not today, God Willing, not today.

"I would that I could spare the time," he said, "but I've promised to grant an audience to the townspeople and the monks from the abbey."

The citizens of Shrewsbury had dreaded the castle's fall, not because they were so devoted to Maude's cause, or even to their lord, William Fitz Alan. Most of them cared little about who ruled in faraway Westminster, as long as they were left in peace. Instead, they'd found themselves caught up in a rebellion not of their making, spoils of war for Stephen's much-feared Flemings, as it was customary to reward a victorious army with plunder and looting.

They were luckier than they knew, though, for William de Ypres was in Normandy with Waleran Beaumont. Had he been at the siege, the town's fate might have been far different; he'd have insisted that Shrewsbury be turned over to his Flemish mercenaries for their sport. But Stephen had chosen to rein them in, much to their disappointment. There had been enough killing, he said brusquely, and although they'd continued to grumble among themselves, they'd not dared to disobey him. Those bodies already stinking in the sun were a convincing argument, indeed, that this king was not to be trifled with, after all.

The townspeople had selected their provost and a handful of their most prominent citizens to plead their case with the king. Stephen was not interested in their carefully rehearsed pledges of heartfelt support, only half listening to their predictable disavowals of entanglement in Fitz Alan's treachery. But when they were done, he agreed to spare Shrewsbury his royal wrath, provided that they kept faith from now on. The delegation willingly promised loyalty to the grave, so great was their relief at their reprieve, and they then made haste to withdraw, lest Stephen change his mind.

Stephen was not as accommodating to the abbot of the Benedictine monastery of St Peter and St Paul, for he'd been stung by the monks' attempt to remain neutral, as if he and Maude were claimants on equal footing, as if he were not a consecrated king and a good son of the Church. Nor was Abbot Herbert a particularly effective advocate, for he was a well-meaning man of limited vision, and not even ten years at the abbey's helm had done much to expand his horizons. Stephen had already decided to levy punitive fines upon the townspeople and the monks. He was wondering whether or not the abbey might also benefit from a change of command when a courier was ushered into the hall, crying out that he was the bearer of news the king must hear straightaway.

The messenger was disheveled and dusty, his tunic sweat-stained, his fatigue as deeply etched in his face as the dirt of the road. He looked triumphant, though, and as he knelt before Stephen, he broke into a wide, cocky grin. "I come from His Grace, the Archbishop of York, my liege. He would have you know that a great battle was fought against the Scots army on Monday last at Cowton Moor near Northallerton. God was with us, my lord king, for your enemies were utterly routed. The field was strewn with their bodies and the Scots king fled like a hare! So did his son—"

But Stephen was no longer listening; the details could wait. Rising to his feet, he gave a jubilant shout, silencing the hall. "Did you all hear?" he demanded. "We have defeated the Scots king, slaughtered his army, and sent him slinking back across the border where he belongs!"

Stephen was immediately surrounded by men eager to offer their congratulations and share in his joy. Some were motivated by a desire to curry favor with the king. Others—such as Robert Beaumont—had a vested interest in Stephen's survival. The Earl of Northampton rejoiced in David's defeat fully as much as Stephen; he was actually smiling. The Earl of Chester had a rivalry of his own with the Scots king, for he and David had competing claims to the Honour of Carlisle. And many of the men were simply grateful that an alien Scots invasion had been thwarted. Only two exchanged a covert glance of quickly masked dismay—Miles Fitz Walter and Brien Fitz Count—for Maude had gone down to defeat with David at Cowton Moor, and they both knew it.

Wine was soon flowing in abundance. Toasts were drunk to the aged Archbishop of York, and then to Robert de Ferrers and William d'Aumale, Stephen's battle commanders, the heroes of the day. Jokes were made at the Scots king's expense and Maude came in for her share, too. The Scots were damned as a savage, barbaric people; highly partisan accounts of Scots atrocities were related, for which they blamed Maude fully as much as David. She was, after all, the man's niece, they reminded themselves, and only Brien and Miles remembered that David was Matilda's uncle, too.

But in the midst of these revelries, Stephen suddenly grew quiet. Setting down his wine cup, he gazed across the hall toward the unshuttered windows, and then said pensively, "I was wondering if it might not be a Christian act to spare those prisoners who've not yet been hanged. What better way to thank the Almighty for our victory?"

They stared at him, momentarily startled into silence. All but the abbot, who'd been waiting patiently for the king to resume their interrupted audience. There were worldly men of God, and then there were those like Abbot Herbert. Beaming at Stephen, he said warmly, "Bless you, my liege, that would be a deed well done!"

"In a pig's eye!" Robert Beaumont sputtered, half choking on his wine, and Miles reached over, thumping him solicitously on the back.

"You disappoint me, Rob. Where is your sense of charity? I think the king is right, that it would indeed please the Almighty to pardon those poor wretches."

"For certes, it would please the Lady Maude," the bishop said acidly, "as you know right well, my lord!"

By now the hall was in turmoil, each man attempting to voice his opinion, to make himself heard above the din. Only two held their peace, Geoffrey de Mandeville and Brien Fitz Count. The former looked faintly amused by the uproar, the latter pained. It was not that Brien did not want to see the condemned prisoners reprieved, for he did. In Brien's eyes, they were not rebels, and they did not deserve to die for keeping faith with their queen. For Maude was the rightful sovereign, not Stephen, and God forgive him, but he ought never to have disavowed his oath, for in saving his lands, he'd sacrificed his honour.

But still Brien kept silent, unable to encourage Stephen's folly, as Miles was doing with such zest. If Stephen had determined at the outset to spare the Shrewsbury garrison, as he had spared the garrisons at Exeter and Hereford, he'd have done himself no good for certes. However much mercy might be admired in saints, Brien mused, it made men most uneasy when encountered in kings. But to condemn the prisoners and then relent, that would be sheer madness. He might stand aside and watch as Stephen cut his own throat. He could not bring himself to offer Stephen a dagger.

Stephen was under siege, being assailed from all sides by insistent voices. His head had begun to ache. Why did a crown complicate matters so? As Count of Mortain and Boulogne, he'd done what he pleased, and an easier life it had been, too. He glared at his brother the bishop. How dare Henry speak to him like this, as if he were a green stripling without a grain of sense! Well, he'd best learn to content himself with Winchester, for by all that's holy, he'd never get his grasping hands upon Canterbury. If only Tilda were here. But she was at Dover and his only allies a weakling abbot and that crafty tame fox of Maude's. If Miles was urging clemency, it must be wrong. So why, then, did it feel right?

"Enough!" he said angrily, flinging up his hand for silence. "You chatter at me like a flock of hungry magpies, and for naught. I never said I intended for certes to pardon those men. It was idle talk, no more than that."

They subsided, relieved. Eventually conversation resumed, men drifted away from the dais, talk turned again to the humiliation of the Scots king, the likely whereabouts of William Fitz Alan, the need to appoint a new sheriff in his place, and out upon the castle battlements, men continued to die.

A GHOSTLIKE swirling fog had wafted in from the Channel, shrouding the chalky cliffs usually visible for miles. The night air was damp, uncommonly cold for September, and a sea-salted wind chilled victors and vanquished alike as the gates of Dover Castle slowly swung open to admit the Queen of England.

The sight that met Matilda's eyes was an eerie one: a circle of flickering flames, yellow beacons of light stabbing through the fog. As she drew nearer, she realized that she was looking upon the flaring torches of her own guards, for they'd insisted upon entering the castle first, intent upon making sure that there would be no surprises, no eleventh-hour change of heart by the castellan. Her nervousness eased somewhat as she rode toward their beckoning glow, wondering if sailors felt this way upon catching the reassuring glimmer of Dover's light tower.

Blessed Lady Mary, how lucky she had been and how well served! It had been her vassals' duty to respond, of course, once she'd called upon them. But she'd gotten from these men of Kent and Boulogne more than grudging service. Rank seemed not to matter, for she'd found champions in equal numbers among her knights, serjeants, and men-at-arms. She still did not understand how she'd managed to touch their calloused soldiers' hearts, could only be grateful for it.

She was grateful, too, for the man riding at her side. She was convinced that the arrival of Robert de Ferrers, fresh from his triumph over the Scots, had marked a turning point in the siege. How good of Stephen to send her such a stalwart knight. He'd be well rewarded; she and Stephen would see to that.

"There he is, my lady. Walkelin Maminot, who held the castle for Robert Fitz Roy, and waits now to deliver it into your hands." Reining in his stallion, Robert de Ferrers swung to the ground, then reached up to help Matilda dismount.

Approaching her was one of the largest men she'd ever seen, towering over her like a massive oak. To look up into his face, she had to tilt her head back so far that her veil started to slip. She grabbed for it awkwardly, more uneasy than she cared to admit.

"I yield to you, my lady." The giant had a surprisingly gentle voice. His face was grave, but unafraid, for he'd been assured there would be no bloody reprisals taken against his men, as at Shrewsbury. Drawing his sword from its sheath, he held it out to her, hilt first, and as she timidly took it, he sank to his knees before her. "Madame, Dover Castle is yours."

"I accept it in the name of my lord husband, the king," Matilda said as loudly as she could; she well knew that her whispery little-girl's voice did not carry far, and it was important that all should hear. Turning, she handed the sword to Robert de Ferrers, glad to be rid of it, and then motioned Walkelin Maminot to raise. At that, her men raised a cheer, for the siege of Dover Castle was over.

"My lady, may I escort you back to the priory guesthouse?"

She nodded, and took Ferrers's arm, letting him lead her toward her mare. "Sir Robert, thank you. If not for you, Dover Castle would not have surrendered. You may be sure I will not forget."

He shrugged off her praise with a smile. "I talked some sense into Walkelin, no more than that. It would have been foolhardy for him not to listen, in truth, what with him wed to my daughter!"

"This is an evil war," Matilda sighed. "I know that is a woman's belief and not one you'd be likely to share. But this war is more accursed than most, Sir Robert, for it is tearing families asunder."

"God Willing, it shall soon be over now. The loss of Dover Castle is a grievous blow to Maude's hopes. But you give me too much credit and yourself too little, my lady. It was your fleet that blockaded Dover's harbor, was it not? Those were your captains directing the siege, your men vowing to hold fast, through the winter if need be. They were fighting for you, my lady. You came often to the camp, you fetched a priest for the dying, you comforted the wounded. Believe me, madame, this victory was yours, too."

Matilda almost argued with him, so strong was the force of habit. But then she smiled, a smile of sudden realization and startled reassessment. "Yes," she said proudly, "it truly was!"

9

NOTTINGHAM, ENGLAND

April 1139

HIGH white clouds dappled a sapphire-colored sky, and a brisk wind rippled the tall marsh grass, giving an occasional glimpse of sun-silvered water. As days go, this one was well nigh perfect, Stephen thought, with the best yet to come. The creature perched upon his fist was equally expectant, its hooded gaze turning instinctively toward the sky, talons digging into the leather of his gauntlet. The greyhounds and their handlers were in position by now, downriver. It was time, and Stephen signaled for his men to flush their prey. As they moved in, the reeds parted, there was a flash of grey, and a large crane flew upward, powerful, beating wings taking it into the air over their heads.

Stephen removed the hood without haste, and by the time he cast the gerfalcon off, the crane was well on its way toward the River Trent. The gerfalcon rose higher and higher into the sky, white and sleek and silent, as if racing the clouds rather than the crane. But then, with sudden and terrible speed, it was diving, a deadly streak of light swooping down upon its quarry. They collided in midair, the gerfalcon striking with such force that the larger bird could not break free, and they plummeted together to earth in a flurry of bloodied feathers.

Stephen gave an exultant shout, echoed by the other men, for hawking was a universally shared passion, even though the best birds were reserved for those of high birth. The dogs had been set loose, and were racing toward the struggling crane. Greyhounds were favored for heron hunting, as there was always a danger that a falcon might be injured by so large a bird; cranes and herons were not its natural prey. Stephen waited tensely, his view blocked by the high marsh grass. But then one of the dog handlers rose up, gesturing triumphantly, and Stephen turned back to his companions, saying with a relieved grin:

"All is well. Come, let's not keep her waiting for her reward." As he started to dismount, though, his attention was drawn by approaching riders, already within recognition range: the brothers Beaumont, Waleran and Robert and their younger brother Hugh, newly named as Earl of Bedford.

"Were you in time to see the kill? That was Diana, as fine a Greenland falcon as you'll find on English shores. Did you see her stoop? Faster than any arrow ever launched!"

They had indeed witnessed the gerfalcon's strike, and were not stinting in their praise. Waleran was unusually well read for a nobleman—many of his rank scorned reading as a clerk's skill—and he was knowledgeable enough to appreciate the aptness of the gerfalcon's name. But he was curious as to how Stephen had learned of a pagan goddess of the hunt, well aware that the king neither knew nor cared about the religious beliefs of ancient Rome. When Stephen explained that the gerfalcon had been a gift from his brother the Bishop of Winchester, Waleran laughed aloud, pleased to have solved the puzzle with such ease.

"Mind her well," he said jovially, "for you'll be getting no more hawks from that one, not with his hopes as dead as Diana's crane!"

Stephen did not join in the laughter, for his breach with his brother was no joking matter. But neither did he chide Waleran for his plain speaking, as he'd only said what they all knew—that the bishop had been nursing a mortal grudge since December, when a church synod had elected Theobald, Abbot of Bec, as the new Archbishop of Canterbury.

Dismounting, the Beaumonts followed Stephen and William de Ypres toward the river. By now, it was all over; the crane had been killed, the gerfalcon retrieved, and the greyhounds rewarded. The crane's heart had been cut out, saved for Stephen, and he was feeding it to Diana when Geoffrey de Mandeville rode up. He at once urged Stephen to fly the gerfalcon again, complaining that his own falcons were already in moult. Stephen had intended to return to the castle, still visible in the distance, for it had been built upon a towering rock of red sandstone high above the meadows of the Rivers Leen and Trent. It was filling rapidly with highborn guests, summoned to attend his Easter court, and he knew he ought to be getting back. But when the Beaumonts added their voices to Mandeville's, he let himself be persuaded, and they were soon heading downriver in search of fresh prey.

As they rode along, Stephen boasted of the coming festivities. Virtually every peer of the realm would be at Nottingham to witness his ratification of the treaty Matilda had negotiated at Durham with the Scots king's envoys. She was due to arrive any day now, and bringing with her young Harry, David's son and heir. The lad was to be treated as an honoured guest, Stephen said, but with a sly smile, for they all knew he was also a valuable hostage, a pledge of his father's good faith, and when Waleran wondered aloud how Matilda had ever coaxed the Scots king's consent, Stephen laughed.

"My little bird," he said proudly, "has begun to try her wings, to fly farther and farther from the nest. It was her own suggestion that she be the one to meet with the Scots. Maude was not David's only niece, she said, and it was time she reminded him of that. I ask you, Waleran, who could have guessed how much fulfillment she'd get from besieging a castle? Women are truly the most mysterious of the Almighty's creations, and beyond the puny powers of mortal men to comprehend!"

He laughed again, a soaring sound of pure pleasure, the laughter of a man utterly content with his wife, his hawks, and his world on this mild Thursday in Holy Week.

The Beaumonts did not share Stephen's admiration for Matilda's newfound fortitude. They feared few rivals at the king's court, but they well knew the queen could pose a formidable threat should she begin meddling in matters of statecraft. What did it avail them to have the king's ear whilst in the hall or on the hunt? As long as Matilda held sway in the royal marriage bed, the last word would always be hers. They were too canny to criticize her directly, though, contenting themselves now with expressing qualms about the Scots treaty. Was there not a risk that men might think the king had been overly generous in its terms?

Stephen was not troubled by their doubts. "I know men will like it not," he conceded. "The talk in alehouses and taverns would scorch my ears off! And I'll not deny that I paid a high price for peace with the Scots. But I had no choice, not if I was to avoid fighting two wars at once. How could I hope to drive Maude and Robert Fitz Roy into the sea if all the while, I had to keep watching my back? We know what happens to grain when it is caught between two millstones: it is pounded into grist. So if I must buy David's millstone, I will, and not begrudge the cost, for that frees me to repel Maude's invasion, if and when it ever comes."

"Why do you say that, my liege?" Robert Beaumont asked. "Think you that Maude will lose heart now that her appeal to the Pope has come to naught?"

He sounded so dubious that Stephen had to chuckle. "No, Rob, I do not, however much I'd like to. If I've learned nothing else in these past three years, it is that Maude's stubbornness runs wider and deeper than the River Thames. One of God's own angels could appear before her in a blaze of light, tell her that it was the Almighty's Will that she abandon this doomed quest of hers, and she'd not listen. But she is still stranded in Normandy, and that is not likely to change in the foreseeable future. I control all the ports now, save only Bristol, and Robert would never let her attempt a Bristol crossing, for it would be much too dangerous to sail all the way around Cornwall. So let her plot and scheme and lust after my crown to her heart's content, just as long as she does it from a distance!"

The Beaumonts exchanged speculative glances, in which they silently agreed that Stephen was deluding himself if he truly believed Maude was safely "stranded in Normandy." But they agreed, too, that there was no reason to dispute his delusions, not today. Waleran guided his stallion closer to Stephen's handsome roan, saying quietly, "Indeed, I hope you are right, my liege, for we have enemies enough in our midst, scheming not 'from a distance' like Maude, but ofttimes in your very presence."

"You mean the Earl of Chester, I suppose. I'll not deny that he'll be enraged once he learns the terms of the Scots treaty. Nor will I deny that he'll ne'er forgive me for granting the Honour of Carlisle to David's son. We did not trust him anyway, though, so naught has been lost. He's one for blustering and ranting to get his way, but outright rebellion—I think not."

"You know I like Chester not, my lord king. But we face a more dangerous foe than he, one protected by powerful armor, indeed—the trappings of Holy Church."

Stephen reined in his mount, turning to stare at the younger man. "My brother? I'll grant you that I've never seen him so wroth. He blames you, too, since the new archbishop comes from Bec, which has benefited handsomely from Beaumont largesse. But even if he truly believes we're guilty of a sinister conspiracy to deprive him of his just due, I do not think he'd betray me."

"I was not speaking of your brother, the Bishop of Winchester. It is the Bishop of Salisbury whom I fear."

"Why?" Stephen was not surprised, though, for he'd long harbored his own suspicions of his uncle's justiciar.

"No subject of the king should wield the power that Salisbury does. He has more kinsmen at Westminster than a dog has fleas. Just consider how far and wide he has cast his nets. His nephew Nigel is your treasurer and Bishop of Ely. Another nephew, Alexander, is Bishop of Lincoln. His bastard son is your chancellor. And God alone knows how many more cousins and lackeys are underfoot, eager to do his bidding. The Chancery is his and so is the Exchequer. He holds your government in the palm of his hand, and if that were not troubling enough, he controls, as well, some of the best fortified castles in the realm. Sherborne, Devizes, Malmesbury, Newark, Sleaford, and Salisbury. Jesú pity us, my liege, if those strongholds were to fall into Maude's hands!"

"You have reason to fear that they would?"

"Indeed, I do. My informants tell me that Salisbury and his nephews have begun to stock the larders of those castles, to garrison them with Breton and Flemish mercenaries. They never venture out these days without a large armed bodyguard. If they are innocent, why are they preparing for war?"

"You truly believe they are conspiring with Maude?" Stephen asked, and Waleran nodded solemnly. "Have you any proof of their treachery?"

"No . . . not yet. But if we wait till we have the evidence in hand, it may be too late."

By now William de Ypres and Geoffrey de Mandeville had reined in their horses, too, and were listening intently. When Waleran admitted that evidence was lacking, Stephen's disappointment was so obvious that Geoffrey de Mandeville saw his opportunity. "Proofs can always be . . . found," he said significantly.

That was a miscalculation. "No," Stephen said sharply, "I'll have no forgeries foisted upon me!"

Geoffrey de Mandeville was a proud man. For a moment, his courtier's mask slipped, and he came close—dangerously close—to reminding Stephen that his kingship was based upon a lie: Hugh Bigod's convenient claim that he'd heard the old king's deathbed repudiation of Maude. He caught himself just in time, and by then Waleran Beaumont had control of the conversation again.

"No one said anything of forgeries, my liege. There is another way. I understand that Bishop Roger has refused to attend your Easter court . . . a suspicious refusal, in truth. Summon him again to your court, and this time make it a royal command."

Stephen frowned, for he was still irked with Geoffrey de Mandeville, and vexed, too, by his failure to follow Waleran's thinking. "And if I did? What then?"

"Bishop Roger and his nephews will come—reluctantly, but they'll come. We can also be sure that they'll arrive with an armed escort. All know how hot-tempered the Flemings are, how quick to brawl, especially once wine starts to flow. If trouble breaks out at your court, you'd have every right to demand that the bishops yield their castles to the Crown, for it is a serious offense to breach the King's Peace."

Stephen was silent for several moments. "Yes," he said at last, "I would have the right, just as you say. But what if the bishop's men cause no trouble?"

"You may be sure, my lord king," Waleran said blandly, "that there will be trouble."

DURING the first week of July, Normandy was battered with gale-force winds and drenching rains, and it seemed drearily appropriate to Maude that the storm should have swept in from the south, from Geoffrey's Anjou. By Friday, the squall had blown over, but summer had not yet reclaimed its lost territory, and all evening the servants had been stoking a fire in the open hearth. The scene in Argentan Castle's great hall was one of familiar and reassuring domestic tranquillity—deceptively so, for strain and disappointment and splintered hopes were not always visible to the casual eye.

The women were stitching patterns, later to be pieced together into a vast and intricate wall-hanging, an ambitious undertaking that Amabel meant to rival the famous tapestry of Bayeux, depicting William the Bastard's English invasion. Maude alone had declined to contribute to Amabel's creation. She was a very proficient needlewoman, easily Amabel's equal, for she was that most driven of beings, a perfectionist, compelled to excel even at pastimes that gave her no pleasure. But she cared little for female companionship and even less for traditional female pursuits, preferring instead to challenge Robert to a game of chess.

Robert was a skilled player, his game flawed only by an excess of caution, but because he made his moves with the protracted deliberation that men usually reserved for life-or-death decisions, Maude had ample opportunities to observe the other inhabitants of the hall.

Their brother Rainald was dozing in the closest window seat. Maude envied him that ability to catnap at will; he never seemed to let their troubles diminish the zest he took in satisfying hungers of the flesh, be they for food, ale, women, or sleep. He was as rash as Robert was circumspect, headstrong and easily angered, but he did not lack for courage and he could be boisterous, exuberant good company. He'd been quick to follow Robert's lead, and Maude had found it easier to welcome him back into the fold, for she'd never expected as much from him as she had from Robert.

Robert was still contemplating the chessboard, and she turned to check upon her son. Henry should have been abed with his brothers, and the command was forming on her lips. But the scene that met her eyes was so engaging that she smiled, instead.

That spring Ranulf had bred his dyrehunds, resulting in a litter of five furry little whirlwinds. Now that they had reached their eighth week, Ranulf had promised Henry his pick, and the boy was rolling about in the floor rushes, fending off pink tongues and cold noses and nipping milk teeth. Ranulf was sprawled beside him, as if he and Henry were both of an age, keeping an eye upon Cinder, the wary mother. As Maude watched, Henry lost the battle and the puppies swarmed over him like a pack of pocketsized wolves, making him shriek with laughter.

"I can see where this is going," Maude said ruefully. "What do you wager that Henry will want them all?"

Robert looked up blankly, still intent upon the game. And it was then that the castle dogs began to bark, Ranulf's dyrehunds joined in, and a servant hastened into the hall to announce the arrival of Maude's husband.

The temperature in the hall had dropped dramatically by the time Geoffrey strode through the doorway. He paused just long enough to register the sudden chill in the air, and then faced them with the cocksure, beguiling smile his wife had long ago learned to hate. Maude got slowly to her feet. Robert was already rising. But Henry was quicker.

"Papa!" Abandoning the puppies, he raced across the hall and flung himself joyfully at his father. Geoffrey pretended to stagger backward, an old game between them, and then swung the little boy up into the air, high enough to make Henry squeal with delight. Maude's mouth tightened. She'd tried to convince herself that Geoffrey's fondness was feigned, just another of his stratagems—more subtle than most—in their marital warfare. But his playful patience was too convincing; even Geoffrey was not that good an actor. No, as baffling and out of character as it seemed to her, Geoffrey was a genuinely attentive father, a very real rival for the affections of their sons . . . and of all the wrongs he'd done her, that was the greatest wrong of all.

Setting his son back on the ground, Geoffrey started across the hall, and Maude had no choice but to meet him halfway. Their union had been rockier than usual in recent months, for she'd been bitterly disappointed by his Normandy campaign. When Waleran Beaumont and William de Ypres had thwarted his siege of Falaise, that was all the proof Maude had needed to confirm her direst suspicions. Geoffrey wanted Normandy, that she did not doubt, but not enough to bleed for it. And in that aggrieved state of mind, she'd brought their sons to Angers for his Easter court, only to discover one of his concubines in residence.

His adultery came as no surprise. She knew he'd sired at least three children out of wedlock, for he was conscientious about claiming them as his own. But she had neither expected nor desired fidelity. Let him seek his pleasures in any bed but hers—as long as he was discreet about it. At Easter he had not been discreet, and her rage and lacerated pride had fueled one of the most heated quarrels of their marriage. Yet now that he was here at Argentan, once again she found herself compelled to patch up their tattered flag of truce, for pride demanded that they make a public pretense of marital harmony, even before her brothers, who knew better.

"Are you hungry, Geoffrey?" she asked, for a wife was expected to care about her husband's comforts. "I can rouse the cooks if so. And I'd best send servants to make a chamber ready for you. If only you'd sent us word of your coming—"

"I've no need of my own bed, dear heart, not when I can share yours." Smiling, he pulled her into his arms, bringing his mouth down upon hers in a wet, probing kiss, and Maude knew then that his anger had not abated in the weeks since Easter, that it still burned at full flame.

Keeping his arm around his rigid, unresponsive wife, Geoffrey offered jaunty greetings to her brothers. Robert's reply was civil, if unenthusiastic. Ranulf and Rainald didn't even manage that much. But their grudging attempts at courtesy seemed to amuse Geoffrey enormously.

Releasing Maude, he turned then toward the other women, engaging in a round of gallant hand-kissing. Amabel accepted his attentions with aplomb, but several of the women blushed and giggled. One in particular, the youngest and prettiest of her ladies, seemed much too receptive for Amabel's liking, casting Geoffrey a long-lashed sideways glance that did not speak well for her discretion. Or her common sense, Amabel thought, promising herself a long and frank talk with Dame Agnes at the first opportunity. She could not blame the lass for looking, though; Geoffrey of Anjou was a sight to fill any woman's eyes. Of course he was also false and perverse, and had he been her husband, she'd have been sorely tempted to flavor his wine with hemlock. But she knew, too, with just a trace of smugness, that she'd have handled him much better than Maude.

"Papa!" Henry was jerking impatiently at Geoffrey's sleeve. "Come see my puppies!" Geoffrey obliged, was soon teasing his son about "this pack of meagre, mangy whelps." Maude ordered wine, then sat down again at the chessboard, reaching for a chessman, a display of composure that might have been more convincing had the rook not been Robert's.

"Let's leave this till the morrow," he said quietly, and when Geoffrey sauntered back, he spoke out before Maude's silence could become conspicuous. "So . . . tell us, Geoffrey, what news are you bringing from Anjou?"

"I do have news," Geoffrey said, "but from England, not Anjou." Claiming a wine cup, he settled himself in a high-backed chair, turning a vibrant smile upon Dame Agnes when she demurely offered a cushion. "Did you hear about Stephen's heroic feat at Ludlow? Whilst he was besieging the castle, the garrison swung a large grappling hook over the wall and caught a very big fish, indeed—none other than the Scots king's son! They'd begun to reel him in when Stephen galloped up, grabbed the hook, and pulled their fish free!"

"That is already known to us," Rainald said, so brusquely that it bordered upon rudeness.

Geoffrey ignored the interruption. "What with Stephen's saving the lad from capture, mayhap that treaty of Matilda's will last, after all. Your little cousin has had quite a remarkable year, dear heart. First taking Dover Castle and then coaxing David over to Stephen's side. I'd not be surprised if she deserves credit, too, for the Pope's finding in Stephen's favor!"

Maude took the bait, hook and all. "That is not so," she snapped. "The Pope did not decide my appeal on the merits. As for Matilda's meddling, it matters little, for she can do us no harm. Calling a wren a merlin does not make her a hawk, Geoffrey. It merely raises doubts about the soundness of your judgment."

Geoffrey's smile held steady, but his eyes reflected the light like shards of blue ice. "Now who could blame me, Maude, for admiring such a loyal, loving little wife? So few men are lucky enough to wed a Matilda, after all."

Maude fought back a barbed rejoinder, with an effort obvious to them all. Her brothers were struggling with their own indignation, Ranulf and Rainald glaring as balefully as hawks, Robert showing his displeasure with more subtle signals, but easily read by his wife. Amabel would have been hard put to say which one vexed her more, Geoffrey or Maude. They were worse than children, she fumed, for marriage was a serious matter, a Sacrament. Did these fools think contentment was ladled out onto their trenchers just for the asking? But no, they could not make their peace like sensible souls, and she'd say "So be it" if not for the fact that they kept miring Robert down, too, in this matrimonial swamp of theirs. One more exchange of insults and that hothead Rainald would be lunging for Geoffrey's throat, with Ranulf not far behind, and her Robert having to mop up the blood, as always.

"Well," she said abruptly, "unless you have other news to share, Geoffrey, I think it time we bid one another a good night. Of a sudden I am weary beyond words."

"Ah, but I do have more news," Geoffrey said, "news sure to startle." He paused then, deliberately, to ask Dame Agnes if she might pour him another cupful of wine. "There was a great scandal when Stephen's council met last month at Oxford. It began with a brawl at the dinner table, ended with Stephen's chancellor and the Bishops of Salisbury, Lincoln, and Ely in disgrace, arrested as enemies of the Crown."

Geoffrey got the response he was aiming for: exclamations of shock, giving way almost at once to a barrage of sharp questions. But he was in no hurry to relinquish center stage, and he drew out his account in provocative, provoking detail, telling them how the bishops had been summoned to attend Stephen's council, how the Earl of Richmond's men had gotten into a squabble with retainers of Bishop Roger of Salisbury, how swords were drawn, a mêlée breaking out that left one knight dead and several sorely wounded. Stephen had blamed the bishops, demanded that they surrender their castles, as "pledges of their good faith," Geoffrey reported, drawling out the phrase with ironic relish.

"If it was the castles Stephen wanted, why were they then arrested?"

"The Bishop of Ely was loath to 'pledge his faith' and fled Oxford, taking refuge behind the walls of Devizes Castle. When Stephen followed with an army, Bishop Nigel still refused to yield, even when Stephen threatened to hang his cousin Roger . . . so much for family fondness. But the old bishop's concubine could not abide the sight of her son with a hempen rope about his neck, and she prevailed upon the garrison to surrender. Lucky that some women are so tenderhearted, is it not?"

"Stephen must have gone mad," Robert marveled, "for the Church will never forgive him for this. They insist upon the sole right to punish their own."

"That seems to have occurred to Stephen, too," Geoffrey agreed, "for he is claiming that he acted against these men in their capacity as ministers of the Crown, not as shepherds of the Church's flock. I rather doubt whether that particular hawk will fly, but to give credit where due, it's a devilishly clever argument."

"Too clever by half," Maude said caustically, "all of it. Stephen could no more hatch a scheme like this than he could hatch an egg! I'd wager the whole concoction was brewed up elsewhere and then spoon-fed to Stephen, with enough sweetness added to conceal any sour aftertaste."

"You do 'know thine enemy,' dear heart," Geoffrey conceded. "The verdict amongst the English echoes yours—that Stephen is not guileful enough to spring a trap like this on his own. Stephen may have fostered this crafty offspring, but it was most likely sired by a Beaumont."

Geoffrey's guess hit its target dead-on, and there were knowing nods of agreement. Their resentment of Geoffrey was muted for the moment, and they began feverish speculation as to how they could turn the Oxford events to Maude's benefit, for they were all sure that Stephen had blundered badly. It was Ranulf who unwittingly fanned the flames again, for the hostility between Maude and Geoffrey never fully died out, and there were always a few smoldering embers waiting to catch fire. The spark this time was a seemingly innocuous question. "When," Ranulf wondered, "did all of this happen?" And Geoffrey's casual response, "Midsummer's Day," drew murmurs of surprise.

Even Maude was looking at Geoffrey with reluctant respect. "The 24th? And you had word in less than a fortnight? I was not aware, Geoffrey, that you had such reliable English sources of information."

"Unfortunately, I do not," he said, favoring her with one of his most disarming smiles. "But you do, dear heart, and I had the good luck to encounter his messenger at the city gates. The man was hesitant at first to yield up his prize, but as you can see"—pulling a letter from his tunic—"I persuaded him to see reason."

Maude drew a breath sharp enough to hurt. "You took my letter? Who was it from?"

"Who was it from?" he echoed. "Now why cannot I remember the name? Was it Bertram? No . . . Barnabas? Mayhap Brien?"

"You did not have the right!"

"Of course I did, Maude. I had a husband's right. If I did not read it, how could I be sure it was not a love letter?"

"Damn you, Geoffrey!" Maude was white with fury, her hands knotted against her skirt, clenched into fists to stop herself from snatching at the letter, for she knew he'd just jerk it away, and she would not give him that much satisfaction. She'd not let him strip her of her dignity, too. For the same reason, she dared not demand the letter. He'd only refuse, and what could she do then? For God rot him, but he did have the right, and not even her brothers would deny it.

Her brothers did indeed believe that a man had the right to read his wife's mail, for she—and all she owned—was his. But that was theoretical, a belief easy to argue in the abstract. In the raw reality of Argentan's hall, Ranulf found that he could not stomach it, and he took a threatening step toward his sister's husband. "Give her the letter—now."

It was a reckless, foolhardy thing to do, and Maude loved him for it. But Geoffrey reacted as she'd known he would, smiling coldly and saying, "I think not." Rainald was on his feet now, too, for if there was going to be bloodshed, he meant to make sure it was Geoffrey's rather than Ranulf's. Robert was already in motion, though, reaching out and grasping Ranulf's arm.

"Think, lad, what you may be starting," he cautioned.

"It is easy enough to stop. He needs only to turn over her letter," Ranulf retorted, and Robert found himself staring at his youngest brother in dismay, suddenly seeing not a malleable youth but a man grown, a man who was not going to back down.

Rapidly reassessing, Robert decided to gamble upon a show of unity. "You've read the letter, Geoffrey," he pointed out, "so you have no reason to hold on to it. Why not give it to Maude?"

Geoffrey was no longer smiling. "Because," he said, "I choose not to."

Maude alone was not surprised by his refusal. Ranulf pulled free of Robert's grip, not yet sure what he was going to do, but determined to get Maude's letter, one way or another.

Amabel had jumped to her feet, hissing at Maude, "Stop this whilst you still can!" And as if coming to her senses, Maude did stretch out her arm, seeking to catch Ranulf's sleeve. But the one who stopped it was the one they'd all forgotten, Maude and Geoffrey's six-year-old son.

Henry had been playing with the puppies, oblivious at first to the angry adult voices; his was a household in which raised voices were the norm. But his mother's choked cry of "Damn you, Geoffrey!" jerked his head up, set his heart to pounding. He did not understand what was wrong, but the fury in the room was frightening. He'd often heard his parents quarrel, and hated their quarrels, sometimes even hated them, too, for the way their quarreling made him feel—as if he was lost, surrounded by strangers, with no familiar landmarks to guide him home.

This time their fighting was worse than usual, for his uncle Ranulf and his uncle Robert were caught up in it, too, all of them against his father. It was not fair, and he wanted to go to his father, to let Papa know he was not alone. But he could not, for then he'd be hurting Mama. When he could endure the conflicting urges no longer, he snatched up the fire tongs and began to jab furiously at the logs burning in the hearth. The flames shot upward, and embers and sparks were soon flying about, beginning to smolder in the floor rushes. The heat was hot on his face and his eyes were stinging, but he kept on thrusting into the fire, again and again, not even hearing his name, not at first.

"Henry! Henry, stop it!" His mother's voice sounded scared to him, muffled and scratchy. But he shook his head, continued to prod the flames, sending up another shower of cinders. His eyes were blurring and he blinked hard. When he looked up again, they were clustered around the hearth, Mama and Papa and Uncle Ranulf and Uncle Robert and Aunt Amabel, and they were all talking at once, urging him away from the fire. Instead, he moved even closer, glaring at them, biting down on his lower lip as it started to quiver. Jabbing with the fire tongs, he dislodged a burning brand, and his mother cried out as it whizzed by his cheek, thudding into the floor rushes in a sizzle of sparks.

They were demanding that he get away from the hearth, but they made no move to grab him, and he knew why. They were afraid he'd struggle and get burned. He was already closer than he wanted to be, for his skin felt scorched, and he could smell something burning . . . the floor rushes! But Aunt Amabel had seen it, too, was pouring wine into the smoking reeds. That was clever. His father was telling him to put down the fire tongs, and he wanted to, he truly did. But all he could do was shake his head again, mutely, gulping back tears. And then Uncle Ranulf was kneeling so their eyes were level, telling him about the puppies.

"Lad, you're scaring them. They fear fire. Look at them, see for yourself."

Henry glanced over at the puppies, cowering down by their mother, whimpering, and then let the fire tongs clatter to the floor. A moment later, he was caught up in his mother's arms. He wasn't sure if she was going to hit him or hug him, and she may not have been sure, either, but then she embraced him tightly, until he had to squirm to breathe. He knew he was going to be severely punished, for he'd done something dangerous and then defied them, not sins adults were likely to forgive.

But once he'd nerved himself to look up into their faces, Henry realized, with a jolt of bewildered relief, that there would be no punishment, after all. His father was mussing his hair, saying he was well roasted by now, ready for carving. He smiled at that, for Papa liked him to laugh at his jokes. But it did not seem funny to him, none of it, not even when Aunt Amabel doused the fire with wine. A silence had fallen, and he shifted uneasily, fearful that they might start fighting again. He saw, then, that they were watching his father, for he'd turned away to retrieve a letter, dropped into the floor rushes.

No one moved. All eyes followed Geoffrey on his way back to the hearth, where he held out the letter to his son. "Here, lad," he said, "give this to your mother."

THE hall was still and shadowed, like an empty stage. Henry had gotten a parental escort up to bed, for Geoffrey had surprised the men and earned himself a bit of credit with Amabel by promising his son a bedtime tale about a ravening pack of killer dyrehunds. Amabel had dismissed her wide-eyed, spellbound ladies, knowing full well they'd soon set the entire castle abuzz with embellished accounts of all they'd witnessed this night. Now she sat with Robert and his brothers around the hearth, finishing up the wine in a morose silence.

"I hope you realize that you only made a bad situation worse, Ranulf."

Robert was frowning, but it did not have the desired effect; Ranulf remained noticeably unrepentant. "I'm sorry about the part I played in scaring the little lad. But for the rest, no. Why should I be sorry for speaking up for my sister? We ought to have done it sooner, Robert, for as long as we keep silent, he'll keep on maltreating her."

"You mean well, Ranulf, but you've much still to learn. No man is going to take it well if you seek to meddle in his marriage. What do you gain by angering Geoffrey? He'll just turn that anger onto Maude, and there is little you can do about it, for you can act as her champion in the great hall, but not in the bedchamber."

Ranulf nearly spilled his wine. "If he hurts her, I swear to Christ that I—"

"What?" Robert asked impatiently. "What could you do? Kill him?"

"Not so fast," Rainald protested. "Why does Ranulf get to do it? What about me? At the very least, we ought to dice for the chance!"

"This is no joking matter, Rainald!"

Rainald gave a mock sigh. "There is nothing under God's sky that cannot be joked about, Robert. How is it that you reached such a respectable age without learning that? Look, we all agree that Geoffrey had the right to read Maude's letter. But did he also have the right to taunt her with it? I agree with the lad. She deserves better than she gets from him, and I for one am heartily sick of it."

"What would you have me say, Rainald? I do not deny that Maude is miserable in her marriage. But antagonizing Geoffrey does her no service. Bluntly put, we need him. Until we can find a safe English port, Normandy is the battlefield for our war, and we cannot hope to win it without Geoffrey's support. So the next time you two get the urge to make Maude a widow, bear in mind that your gallantry might cost her a crown."

That silenced both Ranulf and Rainald, at least for the moment, and Amabel seized the opportunity to bolster Robert's argument. "You'll not like what I have to say; I'd have you hear me out, nonetheless. I am not defending Geoffrey, but Maude is not blameless, either. She puts me in mind of a woman who salts a well and then complains when the water is not fit to drink. A few smiles and some honeyed words might work wonders in that marriage!"

Ranulf was already shaking his head in sharp disagreement. "What I most admire about Maude is her lack of pretense. Her ship never flies under false colors. She is honest even if it hurts her, and that is a rare trait, indeed."

Amabel was not won over. "A blade that cannot bend will eventually break, my lad. All I am saying is that women have no easy time of it in this world, and a woman who scorns to use the only weapons at her command makes her life more difficult than it needs be."

Now it was Robert's turn to shake his head. "I doubt that smiles or flattery could redeem Maude's marriage, Amabel. Geoffrey does not strike me as a man who could be coaxed against his will, no more than I could—"

Amabel's grin stopped him in midsentence, and he seemed so genuinely perplexed that Ranulf and Rainald could not help laughing, laughter that was cut off abruptly by Geoffrey and Maude's return to the hall.

They all tensed, but soon saw the crisis was over; Geoffrey and Maude's anger had burned itself out. They looked tired and subdued and, to Amabel's critical eye, somewhat ashamed of themselves. She'd have liked to believe that the lesson would take, but she thought it more likely that they'd just blame each other all the more; she'd never known two people so unwilling or unable to learn from their mistakes. Aloud, she asked about Henry, wanting to know if he slept.

"For now," Maude said, "but I'll look in upon him later. Robert"—avoiding Geoffrey's eye, she held out Brien Fitz Count's letter—"I'd like you to read this."

Geoffrey crossed to the table, where he poured the last of the wine into two cups, giving one to Maude. Robert passed on the letter to his brothers, and they read it together. The tension was back in the hall, feeding upon silent echoes, all that must be left unsaid.

Robert was studying his sister, troubled by her pallor. There was a brittle edge to her beauty, shadows lying like bruises under her eyes and in the corners of her mouth, and it occurred to him that shadows lay deep, too, in the corners of her life—a thought that startled him, for it seemed much too fanciful to have been his. He could not banish her shadows, but there was something he could offer, a need he could fill. He could give her hope, and he said forcefully:

"I'm much heartened by Brien's letter. It is indeed as Scriptures say, 'I was wounded in the house of my friends.' Of course the Beaumonts cannot take all the blame for Stephen's folly; he chose to heed them of his own free will. He has made more than his share of mistakes since seizing your throne, Maude, but this breach with the Church might well be the fatal one. We'll be able to sow dissension with ease, and God Willing, we'll reap enough support to harvest a crown."

That was bold talk for Robert, a man who measured his words with such scrupulous care that he could put a lawyer to shame, and Maude gave him a grateful smile; tonight of all nights, that was what she needed to hear. Ranulf and Rainald were chiming in with eager assurances of their own. But Geoffrey's voice cut through their confidence with knifelike clarity.

"Are you not putting the cart before the horse?"

Maude's fingers tightened around the stem of her wine cup. "What do you mean by that, Geoffrey?" she asked warily, and he shrugged.

"You may well be right about the seriousness of Stephen's blunder. But even if he has set chaos loose upon his land, how does it benefit you? Unless you find a way to cross the Channel, Stephen's government can be unraveling like a ball of yarn and it will avail you naught."

They were all glowering at him, but for once Geoffrey's tone was free of mockery. As hard as it was to give him the benefit of any doubt, it did seem as if he'd not meant to be malicious this time. He was right, of course, too, for nothing could be done until they broke Stephen's stranglehold upon the English ports. They could not, in fairness, fault him merely for speaking the truth, however unpalatable or ill-timed. And so they held their peace, and as always, Maude thought wearily, Geoffrey got the last word.

ON a sunlit Friday four weeks later, Ranulf led his horse from the stables. He was about to swing up into the saddle when his eye was drawn to a blaze of vivid red color. Maude might scorn embroidery and needlework, but she did enjoy gardening, and her roses were in spectacular scarlet bloom. Detouring across the bailey, Ranulf hitched his stallion and set about helping himself to some of his sister's damask roses. He picked only a few, though, before the screaming started.

Two small boys were rolling about in the dirt near the stable door. By the time Ranulf reached them, Henry looked to be the winner, straddling Geoffrey while his brother kicked and screeched. Grabbing his tunic, Ranulf yanked Henry to his feet, and then caught Geoffrey before he could flee. "Enough! What is this squabbling about?"

"He stole my sword," Henry panted, "and then broke it!"

"I did not!" Geoffrey was just as breathless and just as indignant. "It was mine!"

The disputed sword lay a few feet away, its wooden blade snapped off near the hilt. One glance was all Ranulf needed to give his verdict. "That was not your sword, Geoffrey," he said, with such conclusive certainty that his nephew stared up at him, openmouthed and wide-eyed.

"How . . . how did you know?"

Ranulf concealed a smile. "Because," he said gravely, "I made that sword myself, and gave it to your brother on his birthday last March. So you owe Henry an apology. Go on, tell him you are sorry."

Geoffrey mumbled a "Sorry" that did not sound very convincing, but it seemed to satisfy Henry, and Ranulf sent them off to play again with a promise to make wooden swords for them both. Henry came running back a moment later, though. "Uncle Ranulf . . . will you make my sword bigger?"

"Well . . ." Ranulf pretended to ponder the request, but Henry caught the glint in his eye, and they grinned at each other. The boy spun around then, to chase after Geoffrey, and Ranulf, laughing softly to himself, headed back to retrieve his horse and his roses.

He did not need to go far. Gilbert Fitz John was coming toward him, leading the stallion and carrying the flowers. "So . . . did you get the lads to make their peace?"

"At least until supper."

Gilbert laughed, playfully jerking the flowers out of Ranulf's reach. "What is your hurry? And why the roses? Ah . . . you're going courting again! The goldsmith's daughter?"

"Who else? Lora sent me word that her father left this morning to deliver a chalice to the monks at St Martin's. Since he'll not be back to Argentan till late, I thought I ought to stop by, keep her from getting lonely."

"How good-hearted of you! Will that be after you visit with the widows and orphans?"

Ranulf laughed, jabbed Gilbert in the ribs, and snatched back his flowers. But as he reached for the reins, Gilbert put a restraining hand upon his arm.

"Ranulf, wait. I've a letter that you'll want to see—from Ancel."

They'd not heard from Ancel in almost two years, not since his return to England, and as soon as Gilbert produced the letter, Ranulf grabbed for it eagerly. Gilbert was explaining that Ancel had found a man going on pilgrimage to the Spanish shrine of Santiago de Compostela, and he'd persuaded the man to stop at Argentan. "I promised him a seat at supper in the great hall and a bed for the night. But what he really wants is to talk with you, Ranulf. That was how Ancel coaxed him into taking the letter, offering him a chance to meet a king's son—even one born on the wrong side of the blanket!"

But Gilbert's banter was wasted, for Ranulf was no longer listening. After rapidly scanning the letter, and not finding what he sought, he turned aside, swearing softly.

"Ranulf?" Gilbert followed, puzzled. "What is amiss?" And then he understood. "Annora? Good God, Ranulf, is that wound still sore?"

"No," Ranulf said curtly, "it is not. But I still have a fondness for her, wish her well. Why should that surprise you? I simply wanted to know if she is content, and if Ancel ever used the brains God gave him, he'd have understood that! But no, nary a word about her—"

"What did you want him to tell you? That her husband dotes on her and she goes about her days singing? Or that she has grown thin and wan and weeps in secret?"

Ranulf whirled, eyes narrowed to glittering slits. "I said I wanted only to know if she was well!"

"If she were ailing, Ancel would have told you. But her happiness is no longer your concern. She is a married woman, and by now, it's likely she has a babe in the cradle and another on the way—"

"I know full well that Annora is another man's wife, do not need to have you throw it in my face!"

Gilbert was not perturbed by Ranulf's anger, for he knew his friend's rages were fast-burning and soon over, sooner forgotten. What troubled him was the reason for Ranulf's flare of temper. He'd truly believed that Ranulf's feelings for Annora were—like Annora herself—part of his past. "I am sorry about the sermon, Ranulf. I guess I've been spending too much time with my cousin the priest."

"Indeed you have," Ranulf agreed coolly, although the corners of his mouth were quirking. "But what I cannot understand, Gib, is why I'm still here with you when I could be in Master Jehan's house with Lora." And Gilbert grinned, stepped back, and waved him on.

Ranulf had gotten no farther than the gatehouse when he heard his name being shouted behind him. He reined in, then sent his stallion cantering back toward Gilbert. "What now?"

"Lady Maude and Lord Robert . . . they want you to come back straightaway!" Gilbert was gasping for breath; he'd sprinted all the way across the inner and outer baileys so he could catch Ranulf in time. "A courier came for her soon after that pilgrim brought Ancel's letter. I heard men say he bore a message from your father's queen. Her news . . . it must be very good or truly terrible, Ranulf, if Lady Maude is so intent upon finding you!"

Maude had never found many friends among her own sex, but the Lady Adeliza was the exception. She and Maude had taken to each other from the moment of Maude's forced return from Germany. Not so surprising, perhaps, for they shared much in common. Adeliza was German by birth, Maude by choice. They were the same age, a young queen in a land not her own, a young widow no longer at home in England, and both childless, although that would change, Maude bearing Geoffrey the sons she'd not borne for the emperor, and Adeliza—whose barren marriage had altered so many lives, especially Maude's—now in her second year with a new husband and said to be great with child. But if their circumstances had radically changed over the years, the bond between the two women had held fast, and Ranulf, ever the optimist, had no trouble convincing himself that Adeliza's news was good.

Gesturing for Gilbert to mount behind him, Ranulf headed back toward the inner bailey. Maude and Robert were too impatient to wait for him within the castle keep, and were on the outer stairs. As soon as Ranulf's horse came into view, Maude lifted her skirts and ran lightly down to him, calling out his name.

Ranulf flung himself from the saddle. "No one," he said, "is ever in such a tearing hurry to share bad news. So we must have reason for rejoicing?"

"Indeed we do! Adeliza has offered us a safe landing in the south of England."

Ranulf gasped. "At Arundel? She'd truly do that for you? Jesú, Maude, Arundel Castle is almost as formidable as Bristol!"

"Stephen thinks he has locked us out of England, but now we have the key. No more waiting, Ranulf—the time has finally come to reclaim my stolen crown!"

A sudden high-pitched yell floated across the bailey, a sound rarely heard off the hunting field. Rainald was standing in the doorway of the keep, cupping his hands to shout, "Get in here, Ranulf, so we can start to celebrate in earnest!"

Ranulf was too busy hugging his sister to pay Rainald any heed. By the time Maude broke free, laughing and breathless, Robert had reached them, with Amabel close behind. Rainald ducked back into the keep, reemerged brandishing a wine flagon. "If you're all so set upon holding the festivities out in the bailey, at least I can provide fuel for the fire!"

After that, it got very chaotic for a time. Ranulf was kissed by Maude and Amabel, shared smiles with Robert, had wine spilled on him by Rainald, and was knocked to the ground by his dyrehunds, who'd bolted from the great hall at their first opportunity. Midst much laughter, Ranulf was helped to his feet and dusted off. It occurred to him that he ought to send Lora a message, not wanting her to worry when he failed to appear, and he glanced about for Gilbert. But then Maude drove all thoughts of the goldsmith's daughter from his head, for she was saying with a fond smile:

"We have so much to do and not enough time. But this I vow to you, Ranulf—ere we sail for England, I will see to it that you are knighted."

"Maude . . . thank you," Ranulf stammered, at a rare loss for words, and they all laughed again. Maude happened then to notice Robert's squire, standing a few feet away, still holding the reins of Ranulf's horse.

"You, too, Gilbert. I'll have Geoffrey knight you both," she promised impulsively, and Gilbert's fair skin flushed as red as his hair. He was even more thrilled than Ranulf, for Ranulf had never doubted that knighthood would eventually be his. But for Gilbert, a younger son with no prospects of inheriting his family's manor, it had been far more problematic.

"How can I ever thank you?" he blurted out, and then found a way when he added, "my lady queen," for Maude would remember that she'd been recognized for the first time as England's sovereign on an August afternoon in the inner bailey of Argentan Castle.

Eventually they headed indoors, at Rainald's prodding, for he'd run out of wine. Robert and Amabel had begun to argue, low-voiced but intently, after she'd announced her intention to sail with him back to England. Ranulf and Gilbert were eager to tell their fellow squires of the honour soon to be bestowed upon them, and Maude had plans to make, letters to write, a triumph to savor. But as she turned to follow the others, she felt a sudden tug upon her skirt, and found herself looking down into the anxious face of her eldest son.

Henry had been drawn from the stables by the commotion out in the bailey. He'd kept silent, careful not to attract attention to himself, and he'd listened. But now he could wait no longer for answers, and he yanked again on his mother's skirt. "Mama? Are you going to England, to this . . . this Arundel?"

"Yes, Henry, I am," she said, and he grinned, for he loved to travel and he was especially eager to make his first sea voyage.

"When will we go, Mama? Soon?"

Maude knelt, heedless of her skirts, and put her hands on his shoulders. "I am sorry, lad, but you cannot come. It would be too dangerous. As much as I would love to have you with me, I cannot put your safety at risk."

Henry's breath stopped, disappointment warring with disbelief. His father was often gone. As much as he missed Papa, he'd learned to accept it, that Papa came and went as unpredictably as the stable cat he'd befriended when Mama had first brought him to live at Argentan. Fathers and cats were like that, not reliable like dogs. Or mothers, for Mama had always been there, and when she did go away, it was never for long. He knew better, though, than to beg. He could wheedle his way with his father most of the time, with his mother some of the time—but never when she used this tone of voice, very serious and yet patient, too, how he imagined God would talk, if ever He talked to mortal men. He bit his lip, stared down at the ground, and then raised his eyes to meet hers.

"If it is too dangerous for me," he said, "what about you, Mama? How will you be safe?"

Maude had so often prided herself on his precocity, gloried in her firstborn's quickness, his obvious intelligence. But not now; now she'd have welcomed childish incomprehension, anything but those direct grey eyes, fixed unwaveringly upon her face. "Yes . . . there will be some danger. But your uncles will be with me, and they'll keep me safe."

Henry wanted to ask why they could not keep him safe, too, but she was still using her God voice, and he didn't dare. "How long will you be gone, Mama?"

That was the question Maude had been dreading. She could not bring herself to lie to him, though, for she believed strongly that her children deserved the truth. But never had the truth been so sure to hurt. "I wish I could tell you that I'd soon be able to send for you, Henry. God knows I would have it so. But I can make you no promises, for I do not know how long it will take to win my war. I just do not know."

For Henry, it was like the time his brother Geoffrey jabbed him with a broom handle—a sharp pain in the pit of his stomach, slowly easing to a dull ache, and even after the pain went away, he still felt so hollow that it hurt.

His mother's hands had tightened on his shoulders. "Ah, Henry, do not look like that! Your father will take good care of you, and you'll have your brothers for company and your tutor and your new puppy . . ." Maude forced a smile. "And when we are together again, I'll be wearing upon my head a gilded crown, a crown that will one day be yours, lad. You must remember that whenever you feel sad, remember that shining, golden crown."

Henry said nothing. His eyes had darkened, and a few freckles stood out across the bridge of his nose. Maude got slowly to her feet, brushed dirt from her skirts. Her name was echoing again on the wind. First Rainald and then Ranulf had appeared in the doorway of the great hall, urging her not to tarry. Now it was Robert, admonishing her to make haste, reminding her of "all that must be done and done yesterday if we hope to sail ere winter weather sets in."

"We'll talk later, Henry, I promise," she said, and bent down, kissing him quickly on the cheek. She glanced back once, just before reaching the hall. Henry had not moved. Shoulders hunched forward, so pale that her lip-rouge marked his skin like a brand, he was such a forlorn little figure that Maude dared not let herself look back again.

10

SUSSEX, ENGLAND

September 1139

STEPHEN had been blessed with more than his share of good fortune; he'd been given health and high birth and a handsome face, and he'd made the most of his advantages. His life, like his marriage, had been a remarkably happy one. It baffled him, therefore, that his luck could have soured so suddenly, that his kingship should be sore beset by turmoil and treachery. He wanted only to be a good king, but his Eden was full of snakes. He could no longer trust, he who'd once trusted as easily as he breathed. The approval he craved—and had always gotten—now eluded him. He knew that he'd been judged and found wanting, and the unfairness of that judgment was a constant goad. The road to the crown had been so easy to travel; how had it ever become so mud-mired and twisting? It was almost as if the Almighty were no longer pleased with His servant Stephen.

He sensed the danger in such doubts, shared them with no others, not even his wife or his confessor. He could not let himself believe that he'd lost God's Favor. If he was being tested, he would prove himself worthy.

But why were his victories so fleeting? Waleran's scheme to cripple the Bishop of Salisbury's power had gone as planned. Yet he'd had little time to savor their success. In August, he'd been summoned to Winchester, compelled to defend himself before a Church Council convened by his vengeful brother. His advocates had been able to blunt the thrust of the bishop's charges, and no verdict had been returned, to the bishop's obvious surprise. But he had a surprise of his own for Stephen: since March, he'd been in possession of a papal bull, one naming him as England's new papal legate.

And so another triumph had turned to ashes in Stephen's mouth, for his frayed relationship with the Church would continue to unravel; Henry would see to that. But he did the best he could, sought to reassure the Church that he did, indeed, respect Church prerogatives. He even managed to cobble together a patchwork peace with his brother, at least on the surface.

Before he could catch his breath, though, the next crisis was upon him. Baldwin de Redvers had fled to Normandy after the fall of Exeter Castle. In September he came back, landed without warning at Wareham, and seized Corfe Castle. Stephen reacted with his usual verve, hastening to lay siege to Corfe. And while Baldwin de Redvers lured him west, Maude and Robert made ready to sail for the southeast coast of England.

THEY left Barfleur at dusk, for a night crossing allowed the helmsman to steer by the polestar and then to approach England's shores by daylight. This helmsman's task was a challenging one; once land was in sight, he had to hug the coast and sail into the sunrise, aiming for a stretch of beach marked only by memory. To his passengers, it seemed truly miraculous when he steered their ships into a sheltered Sussex cove, as unerringly as if he were coming home.

There were no quays for disembarking, but their ships were flat-bottomed vessels, built—like their Viking prototypes—for beaching. After waiting so long, Maude was of no mind to wait any longer, but Robert's innate caution won out over her eagerness, and he had no intention of venturing ashore until he was assured of his sister's safety. At his command, their small fleet anchored in the cove, a dinghy was lowered into the water, and its crew began to row toward the beach.

It was a harvest sky, a cloudless, crystalline blue, but the wind held a wintry tang and a thief's touch, robbing them of the warmth they had the right to expect from a September sun. It carried off Maude's veil as she leaned over the gunwale, but she did not appear to notice, her eyes never straying from the English shoreline. Ranulf was not surprised when Minna soon emerged from their canvas tent, another veil in hand. She was ashen, for she'd been seasick for much of the voyage, but she resolutely lurched toward the prow of the ship, determined to see her lady well coiffed or die in the attempt. Ranulf thought they made an odd pair, the elegant empress and the stout German widow. He could not see why Maude had chosen the stolid, taciturn Minna as a companion, and if there was a fondness between them, it was unspoken, not overt. But Minna had been there when Maude buried her first husband, when she was compelled to wed Geoffrey of Anjou, when she nearly died in childbed, and God Willing, she would be there when the Archbishop of Canterbury placed Stephen's stolen crown upon Maude's head.

Amabel's ladies had followed Minna from the tent, and much to Ranulf's amusement, began to express their dismay at the lack of quays or wharves. He laughed outright when Amabel lost patience with Agnes's whining and threatened to let her swim ashore, but when the women turned to glare at him, he prudently withdrew, joining Maude and Robert at the ship's prow. "Am I the only one," he wondered aloud, "who cannot sail from Barfleur without thinking of the White Ship?"

"I expect we all do," Maude said, and then, "What is taking so long? They ought to have been back by now!"

"Arundel is three or four miles distant from the sea," Robert pointed out calmly. "They'll be here soon."

Maude continued to fret, infecting Ranulf and Rainald with her sense of urgency. But Robert was right; it was not long before one of their scouts rode into view, well mounted upon a horse from Arundel's stables. Reining in at the water's edge, he cupped his hands, and his triumphant shout came echoing across the waves like a clarion call to battle. "All is well, my lady! Come ashore and claim your crown!"

Robert sent the women ashore in the dinghy, for they could not be expected to hike up their skirts and splash through the shallows like men. They were preparing to beach their ships so the horses could be unloaded when their escort arrived from Arundel Castle.

William d'Aubigny was in the lead, and Adeliza rode proudly at his side, mounted on a snow-white mule. The Fair Maid of Brabant was now in her late thirties, although she looked years younger, a German Lorelei, who instinctively knew what Maude had never learned—that charm could be a formidable female weapon. Her new husband shared her easygoing nature and carefree approach to life, and it was obvious, even in those first few moments, that Adeliza's second marriage was far happier than her first. William d'Aubigny shared her coloring, too; they were both flaxen-haired and blue-eyed, vibrant with health and energy. They would, Maude thought, have handsome children. And then, as Adeliza slid from the saddle, Maude stared, for her friend's mantle had fallen open, revealing a slim waist encircled by a braided belt of scarlet silk.

Adeliza saw her surprise and laughed, stretching out her hands in welcome. "Yes, I have a waistline again . . . and a robust son asleep in the solar. So you see, Maude, not only can we offer you a safe haven at Arundel, but a new subject, too!"

ARUNDEL CASTLE was situated on a high, narrow ridge overlooking the River Arun. It was strategically significant, commanding the approach between the South Downs and the sea, and a small town had grown up in its protective shadow. On the east and south it was defended by the steep angle of its slopes, on the north and west by deep ditches. Appraising its formidable defenses with a soldier's eye, Robert was comforted by what he found. Arundel would be a secure haven, just as Adeliza had promised. He could leave his sister and wife here and not fear for their safety.

They had assembled in the lower bailey to bid him Godspeed. His men were already mounted. They'd sailed with one hundred forty knights, but he was taking only twelve with him, leaving the rest to defend Arundel. Having thanked Adeliza and her husband, he kissed Maude's hand and sought to coax a smile from Ranulf, who was noticeably disgruntled at being left behind. And then Robert turned, walked toward his silent wife.

They had said their private farewells earlier that afternoon. This public leave-taking was restrained, circumspect. But he knew her too well; he could read her fear in the taut set of her shoulders, the uneasy fluttering of her lashes. "Ah, Amabel," he said softly, "you need not look so bereft. I'll get to Bristol safe and sound, will rally our men and be back ere you have time to miss me."

She managed a bright, hollow smile, for she would not send him away with recriminations echoing in his ears, would not have him regret agreeing to bring her with him. "Go with God, Robert," she said bravely.

She held on to her smile until Robert and his men rode through the gateway. Arundel did not have a tower keep; its motte was encircled by a stone wall, with lodgings built within the enclosure. It was toward that shell keep that Amabel fled, rushing breathlessly up onto the battlements, where she kept a lonely vigil, watching until her husband was out of sight.

MAUDE was usually an early riser, but during her week at Arundel, she'd been sleeping late, for she'd been staying up late with Adeliza; they had four years to catch up on. Soon after daybreak on Saturday, though, she was jolted awake by the sound of a fist thudding against her bedchamber door. As she sat up groggily, half blinded by her own hair—for she'd been too tired to bother with her customary night plait—the door was flung open. Minna started forward, indignant at this invasion of Maude's privacy; such an intrusion would have been unheard-of at the German court. But by then Ranulf was in the room, with Adeliza on his heels, an Adeliza flushed and disheveled, obviously just roused from bed. "Maude," she cried, "Maude, we are under siege!"

Maude was lodged in the gatehouse, for its upper chamber was spacious enough to satisfy even an empress's imperial tastes. She fumbled for her bed-robe as Ranulf strode to the window and jerked back the shutters. The window opened onto the west, offering a view of the village High Street, the clustered thatched houses, the steeple of the parish church, and to the south, the silvered gleam of the River Arun, swift-flowing toward the sea. But Maude saw none of those familiar sights. She saw only the battle banners catching the wind, heard only the drumming of hooves upon the sun-dried Downs above the town.

"Stephen," she breathed, staring out upon her cousin's army.

THE herald rode boldly toward the castle walls. "I have a message for the Lady Adeliza and the Lord William d'Aubigny," he called, "and my lord king says you'd best heed it well. You are sheltering the Countess of Anjou, an enemy of the Crown and a threat to the peace of the realm. The king demands that you surrender this woman forthwith, or suffer the consequences."

THE great hall was crammed with people: Arundel's harried servants and disquieted garrison, Maude's men, fearful villagers who'd fled their homes for the greater security of the castle. The latter milled about in confusion, some clutching meagre belongings, others trying to comfort wailing children and hush barking dogs, all watching their liege lady and her husband, mutely entreating Adeliza and Will to deliver them from this evil come so suddenly into their midst.

Adeliza, Will, Maude, and Ranulf had retreated from the chaos and dread in the hall, withdrawing to the privacy of their above-stairs solar. Adeliza was too distraught to sit still; she paced the chamber as if seeking escape, pausing only to rock the cradle where her infant son slept.

"How could Stephen have found out that you were here, Maude? Who betrayed us?" Adeliza kept coming back to that, as if it mattered. She seemed genuinely surprised that Stephen should have spies.

Ranulf frowned, glancing over at Adeliza's husband. Will had been conspicuously silent so far, but he was as tense as his wife, fidgeting in his chair, fingers drumming absently upon the armrest, not once meeting Maude's eyes.

It was becoming all too obvious to Ranulf that neither Adeliza nor Will had given serious thought to the consequences of their act. They'd made an impulsive offer without fully calculating the price they might have to pay, and now that Stephen was presenting the bill, they were rapidly reassessing the cost of their generosity. Ranulf had been irked by Robert's refusal to take him on that dangerous cross-country dash to Bristol, not truly believing Robert's explanation, that Maude might need him. Now her need was urgent, indeed, and Ranulf would have given anything to have Robert and Rainald back at Arundel; having sole responsibility for Maude's safety was a heavier burden than he'd been prepared to bear. But bear it he would, as long as he had breath in his body. Moving toward his sister, he took up position, as if by chance, behind her chair.

Maude gave him a quick smile; his loyalty was a luxury she was learning to rely upon. She had never doubted that Ranulf would follow her into the flames, but God help her, for Adeliza and Will were balking at the first hint of heat. She chose, as always, to face her fears head-on; if there was a betrayal coming, better to know it now. "Let Stephen do his worst," she said coolly. "He can besiege Arundel from now till Judgment Day for all it will avail him. His only hope of taking the castle would be to starve us into submission, and Robert will not give him that much time. He'll be back to break the siege ere the first frost."

She truly believed every word she said, but she'd have been more confident had she not been aware of the undercurrents in this room. And the silence that followed was a telling one. She turned in her chair, and under her level-eyed scrutiny, color crept into Adeliza's face and throat.

"I . . ." Will cleared his throat, sounding as uncomfortable as he looked. "The truth of the matter is . . . we never thought it would come to bloodshed. When Adeliza told me she wished to help you, Lady Maude, I agreed, for I knew how much it meant to her. But I did not bargain upon this, to have Stephen outside the castle walls with an army at his back. If we defy the king, we could be held guilty of treason, and all we own could be forfeit, including Arundel."

"Yes . . . your wife's dower castle," Maude said acidly, and Will suddenly found it a lot easier to contemplate turning her over to Stephen. He flushed angrily, but Adeliza forestalled his protest.

"That is not fair, Maude. Will has every right to worry about losing Arundel. We have a son to think of; Arundel is his heritage. I'll not deny that the prospect of war terrifies me . . . and not just for us. What of the villagers? If Stephen attacks Arundel, they'll lose all they have, and they have precious little to lose. They look to me for protection. If I do not keep faith with them—"

"I cannot believe what I am hearing!" Ranulf was outraged. "What of keeping faith with Maude? She trusted you! If you betray that trust, I swear that—"

"Ranulf, wait." Maude reached out, put a restraining hand on his arm. "Adeliza, I do not wish you harm. Surely you know that?" The other woman nodded unhappily, and Maude rose, closed the space between them. "I would not be the instrument of your downfall. But do not expect me to submit tamely to Stephen. Do not ask that of me. Tell Stephen that we gave you no choice, that we forced you to aid us."

"Ah, Maude . . ." Adeliza had begun to blink back tears.

Ranulf doubted that Stephen would believe it, and he could tell that Will doubted it, too. But it could be made true; their men easily outnumbered the castle garrison. He edged slowly toward the door, too desperate for qualms or second thoughts. He was reaching stealthily for the latch when Adeliza started to speak, and as he listened, he realized that he had undervalued his father's queen.

"I will not betray you to Stephen, Maude. No matter what it costs us. On that, you have my word."

"Adeliza . . ." Will had risen to his feet. "Do not be so quick to promise her salvation, for it may be a promise you cannot keep."

"Do as I suggested," Maude insisted. "If I took advantage of our friendship to seize control of Arundel, how could Stephen blame you?"

Adeliza smiled shakily. "He'd not believe it, Maude. Not even Stephen is that gullible. But there may be another way. I shall go to him, humble myself, and try to sway him with my tears. Say what you will of Stephen, he does hate to see a woman weep!"

RANULF found Maude up on the battlements of the shell keep, watching as Adeliza and a lone servant rode out under a flag of truce. A few yards beyond the castle, they were met by Stephen's escort, and headed toward the king's encampment. "She will accomplish nothing," Maude said at last. "Stephen will not heed her. Why should he?"

Ranulf agreed with her bleak assessment of Adeliza's chances, but at the moment, he had a more immediate concern. "Maude, it is not safe for you up here. You are within crossbow range; did you not realize that? What if you were recognized?"

"I do not care," she said, with sudden, defiant passion. "Let them recognize me. Let Stephen see that I am not afraid!"

ADELIZA was welcomed with courtesy, but she'd expected no less from Stephen. She'd known she'd have no chance of getting a private audience;

his barons seemed to take turns standing as sentinels between Stephen and his better instincts. She'd been resigned to the presence of the Beaumont twins, William de Ypres, Geoffrey de Mandeville, and the Earl of Northampton. But the sight of Stephen's bishop brother was an unpleasant surprise. She knew Henry invariably advised Stephen against compromise or conciliation, and when she'd learned he'd ridden into Stephen's camp just before she did, she took it as an ill omen. But she could not lose heart, not with so much at stake. Dropping gracefully to her knees before Stephen, she caught his hand in hers.

"My lord king, hear me, I beg you. My husband and I have not been disloyal to you. We did make the Lady Maude welcome at Arundel, but as my kinswoman, not as your enemy. What else could I do? She is the daughter of my late husband, may God assoil him."

Her lovely blue eyes were glistening with unshed tears; she'd always had the useful talent of crying on command. "How could I turn his child away from my door? I owed him better than that. Surely you can understand my dilemma?"

"Yes, I can," Stephen said obligingly, and she thought there was much to be said for good manners in a king. "But however well meaning you were, Lady Adeliza, that does not change the fact that you are harboring a rebel. I am not a man to hold grudges, though. If you turn her over to me with no delay, I'll forgive this lamentable lapse in judgment—provided, of course, that you never give me reason again to doubt your loyalty."

Adeliza's smile was tremulous, radiantly grateful. "We will indeed be loyal, my liege, I swear it. And I would willingly do as you bid me, if only it were in my power. But how can I betray my husband's daughter? How could I live with myself? You are known to be a man of honour, my lord king," she entreated. "Surely you understand?"

This time, though, he was not so quick to assure her that he did. "Just what would you have me do, madame?"

"Show mercy, my liege. Do not make me prove my loyalty to you by sacrificing my stepdaughter. You can afford to be magnanimous. Give her a safe conduct to Bristol, let her go in peace to join her brother. Surely that would be a gesture worthy of a king?"

Up until now, the men had been listening in attentive silence, for Adeliza's tearful appeal was undeniably entertaining. But at that, they burst into incredulous laughter, all but Stephen and his brother the bishop. Reaching down, Stephen raised Adeliza gently to her feet. "It would," he said wryly, "be a gesture worthy of a saint! I will think upon your request, Lady Adeliza. More than that, I cannot promise."

THERE was much merriment in Stephen's tent after Adeliza had been escorted back to Arundel Castle. Her proposal was so ludicrous that even the moody Earl of Northampton joined in the mockery, and Waleran, a wicked mimic, soon had them laughing until they had no breath for talking. Stephen took no part in their raillery, content to drink his wine and listen to the joking and jests, occasionally smiling at a particularly clever gibe. The bishop remained aloof, watching them with none of Stephen's indulgent good humor. When the hilarity finally showed signs of subsiding, he said, with grave deliberation:

"Actually, the woman's plea may not be as foolish as it first seems. It might indeed be to our advantage to let Maude go to Bristol Castle."

There was an astonished silence, and then an explosion of indignant sound, as they competed with one another to deride the bishop's suggestion as preposterous and absurd. But Henry was an old hand at commanding attention, and he soon drowned them out.

"Do you fools think Arundel will fall into your hands like a ripe plum? The castle could hold out for months. And what do you think the Earl of Gloucester would be doing whilst we besieged his sister? He'd be ravaging the whole West Country to lure us off; in no time at all, half of England would be in flames. Or else he'd come down on Arundel like a hawk on a pigeon, and we'd find ourselves trapped between Gloucester's army and the castle garrison."

"Ere you start giving us lessons in military tactics, my lord bishop, mayhap you'd best tell us how many battles you have won."

"I need not swing a battle-axe myself to know it can split a man's skull. I need only rely upon my common sense, which you, my lord Waleran, seem utterly to lack—else you'd see the dangers in a prolonged siege of Arundel! If we allow Maude to join Robert at Bristol, we can contain the rebellion to the west, keep London safe whilst we move against them. If Robert Fitz Roy marches to his sister's rescue, he'll be marching toward London. Or did that never occur to you?"

"A good thing it is that you sought a career in the Church, for if this is an example of your muddled military thinking, you'd not have been able to rout a flock of sheep, much less an enemy army. Once we take Maude, the rebellion ends. It is as simple as that."

"*Simple* is the word, indeed—for you, my lord! Do you truly expect Fitz Roy to bide peacefully at Bristol whilst we—"

Stephen had heard enough. Setting down his wine cup, he slipped quietly from the tent. No one noticed his departure, and the quarreling continued, unabated. He paused to admire a particularly creative burst of profanity, then moved on, trailed by a stray dog; Stephen drew children and dogs to him as if by magic. Ahead lay his mangonels, hauled into position to bombard the castle walls should it come to that. "How goes it,

Giles?" he asked, and his serjeant turned with a grin. Whatever faults others found with Stephen's kingship, he was popular with his soldiers, for he was fearless, accessible, and openhanded, and they thought those were virtues to make up for a multitude of lesser sins.

"Well enough, my liege. We've been bringing in cartloads of stones from the closest quarry. You but say the word, and it will be raining rocks all over Arundel."

"We'll see," Stephen said, raising his hand to shade his eyes against the sun's glare.

Giles saw the direction of his gaze, and volunteered cheerfully, "Oh, she is still up there, my lord, prowling those battlements bold as you please. It is almost as if she were daring us to shoot, and some of the lads would right gladly take that dare. Not," he added hastily, for he knew his king, "without such a command from you, of course."

Stephen scowled. "Make sure they understand that," he said, with unwonted brusqueness. But as he watched that distant female figure upon the castle battlements, his mouth softened into a reluctant smile. "She never did lack for courage, not Maude. I remember a day when we were hunting with her father outside Rouen. Her horse stumbled and threw her, a nasty fall, leaving her bruised and scratched. But she insisted upon getting back on her mare and continuing the hunt, damned if she did not!"

Giles joined politely in Stephen's laughter, puzzled that his lord should speak so kindly of the woman who was causing him such grief. "Look, my liege! It seems the lady has grown tired of flaunting herself and is going back inside. A pity, for we'll not find a fairer target!"

"No," Stephen agreed, "you will not. Giles . . . go fetch my herald for me. Tell him I've an answer for the Lady Adeliza."

Giles knew, of course, of Adeliza's entreaty. The whole camp did, for tents were not constructed to contain secrets. "As you will, my liege." But he did not move, halted by the odd smile hovering in the corner of Stephen's mouth. His eyes widening, he blurted out in amazement. "My lord—surely you do not mean to let her go?"

Such impertinence would have cost him dear with the old king; Stephen, it amused. Still with that enigmatic half-smile, like a man savoring a very private joke, he said, "In truth, Giles, I mean to do just that."

THE following day was unseasonably mild for October, but to the southwest, the sky was filling with fleecy cumulus clouds, which to the weatherwise, warned of a likely thunderstorm. Within Arundel Castle, the atmosphere was no less unsettled. Adeliza and her husband were still dazzled by her success. Amabel was thankful for Stephen's astonishing chivalry, but baffled by it, too, as were most of Maude's men. The villagers were just grateful for their reprieve; they'd not ventured from the castle and so had not yet discovered that Stephen's men had been indulging in that universal soldier's pastime—looting. Ranulf was confused and uneasy, for Stephen's remarkable generosity had stirred up unwelcome memories of the other Stephen, not the usurper but the cousin and friend. And Maude sheathed her emotions in ice, distancing herself from them all by the sheer intensity of her will, until there was not a soul in the castle who'd have dared to ask her what she thought of Stephen's magnanimity.

Leaving Maude to say her farewells to Adeliza, Ranulf called for his stallion and rode out alone to the king's camp. Waleran and Stephen's brother were to escort Maude to Bristol Castle, but they presented dramatically differing visages. The usually equable Waleran was smoldering, while the prickly bishop looked almost benevolent, suspiciously well pleased with himself. He certainly greeted Ranulf with uncharacteristic civility, whereas from Waleran, Ranulf got no more than a grunt. The other men were no more welcoming. William de Ypres was muttering to himself in Flemish, Robert Beaumont was glowering, and the Earl of Northampton looked truly murderous. But their baleful glares were not directed at Ranulf; they were staring at Stephen's command tent, and then at Stephen himself as he emerged into the cloud-splattered sunlight.

Ranulf stiffened. Stephen came to a halt at sight of his young cousin, and then a smile broke free, bright enough to banish the clouds. "Look at you, Ranulf! What ever happened to that gangling, raw lad I knew? By God, if you've not grown to manhood whilst my back was turned!"

"It has been nigh on four years," Ranulf said tautly. "I came to tell you that my sister will be ready to depart at noon."

Stephen nodded, and Ranulf flushed, for the older man's eyes were fixed unwaveringly upon his face, as if they could see into his very soul. The bishop had moved to join them, saying that the empress could take more time if she needed it, but Ranulf barely heard him, unable to tear his gaze away from Stephen's. He been ready for Stephen's reproaches, for his coolness, even his hostility. What he'd not expected was that Stephen should be so genuinely glad to see him.

He was so flustered that it was only when he was on his way back to the castle that the significance of the bishop's words penetrated. Stephen's allies made a point of referring to Maude by the title she herself detested: Countess of Anjou. Her own supporters accorded her the rank she much preferred, that of empress. And so, Ranulf finally realized, had the bishop.

∾

MAUDE meant to take just enough men to assure her safety; the rest would be left at Arundel to try to make their way to Bristol once Stephen's army had been withdrawn, for his safe-conduct was not all-inclusive. Maude was standing now in the lower bailey, listening as Adeliza stammered a last-minute confession. "Maude . . . I shall pray that you regain your crown; nothing would give me greater joy. But I must tell you this . . . that prayer is all we can offer from now on. My husband cannot bear arms against Stephen, for I swore to him that we'd keep faith if he let you go. I hope you can understand that?"

Adeliza held her breath then, waiting for Maude's verdict upon their future friendship, and felt a surge of gratitude when Maude nodded, for she knew only a very real affection could have wrung that concession from Maude, whose political creed came straight from Scriptures: "He that is not with me is against me." Their embrace was wordless, heartfelt. And then Maude stepped back, beckoning for Ranulf to help her mount. Her head high, her back ramrod-straight, armored in pride, she rode out to confront her enemies.

They were waiting for her, the bishop at his most courtly, Waleran making no effort whatsoever to mask his frustration or his fury. Maude was staring past them as if they were both invisible, though, staring at the man on a splendid roan stallion, tawny hair gilded by a sudden flare of sun, looking composed and confident and very much a king. Maude gave Stephen one intense, burning look, all but scorching the air between them, and then urged her mare on. But Stephen spurred his stallion forward, blocking her path. It was utterly still, all eyes locked upon them, all ears straining to hear what was said. The audience was to be disappointed, for their exchange was too brief and low-pitched to be overheard. A moment, no more than that, and then Stephen was moving aside, Maude was sweeping past him without a backward glance, and the siege of Arundel Castle was over.

As they headed west along the Chichester Road, none intruded upon Maude, for it would have taken a very brave man, or a very insensitive one, to breach her shield of silence. Ranulf, his sister's self-appointed protector, still held to his vigil, but from a discreet distance. Whistling to his dyrehunds, he slowed his stallion's pace, planning to drop back and ride with Gilbert; they'd had few chances to talk in these past turbulent days. But Amabel was beckoning to him, and he urged his mount in her direction.

"You know Stephen as well as anyone does, Ranulf. What possessed him to let Maude out of his trap? Rumor has it that the bishop is claiming credit for Maude's reprieve. Now I admit I know little of military matters; I leave that to Robert. But if the bishop's argument sounded so outlandish even to me, how did he get Stephen to swallow it?"

Ranulf laughed. "You may be sure he did not. Stephen's one failing as a battle commander is his lack of patience. He loses interest if a siege drags on too long—unless the prize is well worth the taking. And what prize could be greater than his royal rival for the throne? No, whatever stirred him to offer Maude a safe-conduct, it was not his brother the bishop."

"Well . . . what, then? A sudden fit of madness? Was there a full moon that night?"

Ranulf grinned. "I think a sudden fit of chivalry is more likely. Wait . . . hear me out. Stephen is not a man who'd willingly make war upon a woman. And at Arundel, he'd be making war upon two of them, one his own aunt and a former Queen of England in the bargain."

"Are you saying, then, that he freed Maude for Adeliza's sake? I find that rather improbable, lad."

Ranulf shrugged. "Of course it is improbable, all of it. Give Stephen credit where due; he can always surprise. He's ever been one for the grand gesture, and you must admit, Amabel, that as gestures go, this was about as grand as you get!"

Amabel caught those grudging echoes of admiration, but she did not share it. "I grant you it was gallant beyond belief. But it was also unforgivably shortsighted, Ranulf, for he had a chance to end the war ere it began, and he let that chance escape with Maude."

"Thank God he did," Ranulf retorted, so fervently that she smiled.

"Yes," she agreed, "Maude must feel truly blessed by the Almighty's Favor, for nothing less than a miracle got her safe away from Arundel. So why then is she not rejoicing in it?"

Ranulf gave her a surprised look; after all this time, how little she still understood Maude. "Because the Almighty's Favor comes disguised as Stephen's, and Maude would starve ere she'd take crumbs from Stephen's table. It is well nigh killing her to owe her deliverance to his forbearance."

Amabel marveled she hadn't seen that for herself. "I wonder," she mused, "what they said to each other . . ."

Ranulf wondered, too, and riding by Maude's side later that afternoon, he seized his first opportunity to ask her. She glanced toward him, then back to the road ahead. "Stephen said, 'Any debt I may have owed you, Cousin Maude, is now paid in full.'"

Ranulf stared at her. "So he does have an unease of conscience about you!" he exclaimed, and discovered then that he was glad it was so, glad that the Stephen who was his cousin and the Stephen who was king were not such strangers, after all.

"His conscience be damned! He owes me more than a debt. He owes me a crown," Maude said grimly, and they rode on in silence.

ON an overcast afternoon five days later, Robert rode out to meet his sister on the Bristol-Bath Road, so that her entry into Bristol could be a triumphant one. At sight of the approaching riders, Maude reined in her mare. "Well, my lords, it seems this onerous duty of yours has been discharged. You are welcome to accompany us to Bristol if you so choose. I am sure we can find a comfortable night's lodging for you within my city."

Waleran smiled sourly. "I would rather," he said, "beg my bread by the roadside."

Maude matched Waleran's smile with an acerbic one of her own. "Keep to your present course and you very well may," she said, to Waleran's fury and the bishop's amusement. He cut off Waleran's wrathful reply, saying smoothly that he would indeed accept her hospitality.

Waleran choked on an extremely virulent obscenity, and the bishop swung around to admonish the other man, only to find Waleran staring past him in dismay. Turning in the saddle, he saw why. A number of the men riding with Robert were familiar; he recognized Rainald Fitz Roy and Baldwin de Redvers and Shrewsbury's rebel baron, William Fitz Alan, and Robert's eldest son, William, who'd been holding Bristol Castle for him. But it was the identity of the two men flanking Robert that had unleashed Waleran's strangled profanity: Miles Fitz Walter and Brien Fitz Count, come to Bristol to pledge faith to their queen.

Maude saw them now, too, and laughed, suddenly, joyfully. Waleran slowly shook his head. "God forgive you, Stephen," he muttered, "for what have you loosed upon us?"

STEPHEN wasted no time in besieging Brien's castle at Wallingford. Leaving an armed force to continue the siege, he moved on to attack Trowbridge, held by Miles's son-in-law. While Stephen was occupied at Trowbridge, though, Miles outflanked the royal army, raced for Wallingford, and broke the siege. He and Robert then turned their fire upon Waleran, newly named by Stephen as Earl of Worcester.

At daybreak on November 7th, they assaulted Worcester, breaking through its defenses on the north side of the city. Fires were set, looting was widespread, and a number of the luckless citizens were taken hostage back to Bristol. Waleran arrived in his plundered town three weeks later, and in the words of the Worcester Chronicle, "When he beheld the ravages of the flames, he grieved, and felt that the blow had been struck for his own injury, and wishing to revenge himself for this, he marched with an army to Sudely," whose lord was an ally of Robert Fitz Roy. There his men pillaged and burned, and, again in the words of the Worcester Chronicle, "returned evil for evil."

And so began for the wretched people of England, a time of suffering so great that they came to fear "Christ and his saints slept."

11

BRISTOL CASTLE, ENGLAND

July 1140

FOR Stephen and Maude both, it was to be a frustrating year, one of advances and retreats, thwarted victories and inconclusive defeats, check and mate. Matilda scored a diplomatic coup in those early winter months; sailing to France, she negotiated a marriage for her eldest son, Eustace, with Constance, young sister of the French king. But that good news was soured for Stephen by a rebellion in the English Fenlands, instigated by the Bishop of Ely, who'd been nursing a grudge since the Oxford ambush. Stephen raced north, and the bishop fled south, taking refuge at Bristol.

More trouble was already flaring for Stephen. William Fitz Richard, the sheriff and greatest landholder in Cornwall, declared for Maude, and sealed his new allegiance within the sacrament of marriage, offering his daughter, Beatrice, to Maude's brother Rainald. After wedding and bedding his bride, Rainald joined his father-in-law and they set Cornwall ablaze. Stephen hastened west, and soon had them on the run. He had the greater resources, those of the Crown, and could put more men into the field than any of his enemies. But he'd begun to feel much like the "crazed firefighter" of his brother's taunt; no matter how he struggled to quench these flames, embers still smoldered, and the acrid smell of smoke hung low upon the horizon, with no end in sight.

The strife continued. Miles Fitz Walter captured Hereford and burned Winchcombe. Waleran Beaumont torched Robert Fitz Roy's favorite manor at Tewkesbury. Caught in the crossfire, the English people could only pray for deliverance. At Whitsuntide, there was a brief flicker of hope. Stephen's brother Henry decided it was up to him to act as peacemaker, and he summoned both sides to Bath. The conference was quite civil, for Maude had sent her brother Robert, and Stephen his queen. But nothing was accomplished. The war went on.

IF Stephen still held sway in much of the country, Maude's writ ran in the west, with Bristol her de facto capital. But she herself preferred to dwell in Miles Fitz Walter's riverside city of Gloucester, for there she was the mistress of her own household, whereas at Bristol, she was Amabel and Robert's guest. Since less than forty miles separated the two strongholds, Ranulf divided his days between Gloucester and Bristol. On this humid, hot Saturday in late July, he was at Bristol Castle, although not for long. After saddling his horse, he was leading it from the stables when Gilbert burst in to bar his way.

"So it is true then, what your squire said? You are going off on your own with nary a word to anyone?"

Ranulf had already had this same argument with his anxious squire, was in no mood to have it again with Gilbert. "Luke is worse than a broody hen. I am quite able to fend for myself."

"Luke has enough sense to see the danger in roaming about the countryside in the midst of a war. A pity I cannot say the same for you! What are you up to, Ranulf?"

"I have a private matter to take care of, will be back in a few days. You are making much ado about nothing, Gib."

Gilbert scowled, for he knew that stubborn set of Ranulf's jaw all too well. Following Ranulf out into the summer sun, he watched as the other man swung into the saddle, and then reached up, clamping his hand on Ranulf's boot. "At least tell me where you are going," he insisted. "If we have to search for your body, we need a place to start!"

Ranulf looked down thoughtfully at his friend. "You have a point," he said grudgingly. "If you must know, I'm bound for Shrewsbury."

"Shrewsbury? That shire is closely held by Stephen's sheriff, and he'd like nothing better than to have Maude's brother blunder into his nets! For Christ's Pity, Ranulf, why Shrewsbury? What could be worth the risk?"

Ranulf hesitated, but could not resist the temptation. "I am going to Shrewsbury's fair," he said, quite truthfully, and with the memory of Gilbert's incredulous face to enliven his journey, he spurred his stallion forward, rode laughing out of Bristol and onto the road north.

THE abbey of St Peter and St Paul was not enclosed within Shrewsbury's protective bend of the River Severn. It lay just to the east of the town, close by the red-grit sandstone span known as the English Bridge. It was not among the largest of the Benedictine monasteries, but it was a thriving one, owing a measure of its prosperity to the royal charter that permitted it to hold a fair in honour of its patron saint, Peter ad Vincula.

The fair opened each year on August 1st, lasting until sundown on the third day, and attracted merchants from Bristol and Chester and Coventry, some from as far away as London. People flocked to fairs, as much for the entertainment as for the opportunity to buy goods not available elsewhere, and Ranulf found the abbey already overflowing upon his arrival. The hospitaller squeezed him into a corner of the guest hall, though, and he spread his bedroll, made ready to pass the night.

But sleep would not come. Although he'd dismissed Gilbert's fears as if they were of no account, he knew better. His danger was real. Moreover, Maude and Robert would be furious when they found out what he'd done. Since he was unwilling to lie to them, he could only refuse to answer their irate questions, and that would fuel their fire even higher. No, he was in for a rough patch when he returned—if he returned. He had more to fear than Stephen's sheriff. The roads were full of bandits, masterless men seeking to take advantage of these troubled times, and a lone traveler was a tempting target for ambush or assault. Fortunately he'd thought to bring his dogs along, but he'd still have to keep his wits about him. Lying awake and fretful in the abbey hall, Ranulf had to admit that he was risking a great deal—and for what? Conjecture, surmise, an arrow shot in the dark.

It had taken him several months of discreet investigation, but he'd eventually found out what he wanted to know—that Gervase Fitz Clement's favorite manor was located in Shropshire, west of Shrewsbury. Once he knew "where," he set about figuring out "how," and it soon came to him: St Peter's Fair. He was gambling, though, and he knew it—gambling that the Fitz Clement household was currently in residence at the Shropshire manor, that Fitz Clement himself would have been summoned to Stephen's service, and, last, that the fair would be a powerful enough lure to draw Annora into Shrewsbury. What could happen then, he did not know. But they'd left too much unsaid between them, not even farewell. He had to see her again . . . no matter what it might cost.

The morrow promised summer at its best: sun-drenched warmth, an easterly breeze, and an iris-blue sky, feathered by wispy white clouds. Sauntering through the monastery gatehouse, Ranulf turned right along the Abbey Foregate, heading for the fairground. As early as it was, the street was crowded with his fellow fairgoers, and with others who had less innocent aims than a day of fun at the fair—pickpockets and prostitutes and tricksters mingling with the tradesmen and goodwives and eager-eyed children. Ranulf forgot his sleepless qualms, and his spirits soared. Annora would be here today; suddenly he was sure of it.

The fairground was teeming with activity. It was as if a temporary town had sprung up overnight, row upon row of wooden stalls and booths, streets of trodden grass, already thronged with the customers that were its citizens. Had Ranulf not been watching for Annora with such hungry intensity, he would have enjoyed himself enormously. There was enough variety to satisfy the most jaded appetite. There were booths offering cloth of all kinds, fresh and salted fish, wine, honey, spices, crockery, gemstones, needles, canvas, finely tanned leather, perfume, soft felt hats, mirrors of polished metal, holy relics, and hooded hunting birds, merlins and goshawks tethered to wooden perches, while off to the north, horses were being put through their paces and cattle and oxen paraded before would-be buyers. Looking upon this bustling, colorful scene, Ranulf felt much heartened, for how could Annora resist such a beguiling temptation as the St Peter's Fair?

Ranulf wandered among the booths, pausing now and then to watch the fair's numerous forms of entertainment. There were archery contests and bouts with the quarterstaff, acrobats, jugglers, and strolling musicians strumming lively tunes on lyre, lute, and gittern. There was cockfighting and a small spotted dog trained to balance upon a moving ball, and an occasional brawl, quickly broken up by the sheriff's men. The fair offered all the attractions a fairgoer could wish for—save only Annora de Bernay.

By dinnertime, the fair was at its busiest. Ranulf jostled a path toward a crowded cook-stall, bought a hot pasty stuffed with spiced pork, marrow, and cheese for himself and a plain pork pie for his dogs, washing his meal down with ale. It was getting hotter; the breeze had died down. Shortly before noon, he decided to check out the horse fair, where a race was soon to get under way. And it was then that he saw her.

He caught only a glimpse as she moved between booths, but it was enough. He heedlessly trod upon a portly merchant's heels as he sought to keep her in view, spilling the last of his ale, his breath quickening with each lengthening stride. He had her in sight again. She'd paused at a draper's stall, examining samples of samite and linen as the merchant hovered close at hand, hopeful of making a sale. She was not alone, of course, attended by a gangling groom and a young maidservant, both of whom appeared delighted by this escort duty. The girl was quite pretty, but Ranulf saw only Annora.

She was clad in a vividly red gown, with full hanging sleeves in a lighter shade of rose, a green silk cord belted at the hip, her dark hair demurely hidden away beneath a soft circular veil. She looked just as Ranulf had envisioned her in dreams and daylight yearnings these four years past, but he'd not expected her to seem so contented, so comfortable in her role as Fitz Clement's wife.

He stood, rooted, watching as she browsed from booth to booth. The merchants were very deferential, and she took it as her due, the hoyden he remembered suddenly transformed into the lady of the manor. She selected a pair of scissors and a length of green ribbon, turning her purchases over to her groom to carry. And then she stopped so abruptly that she stumbled, staring after the black-and-silver wolf-dog that streaked across her path, in pursuit of a spitting, hissing cat. Her face changed, her expression both wistful and regretful, and Ranulf knew in that moment exactly what she was thinking—of him and what they'd lost. He took a tentative step forward just as Annora turned and saw him.

Annora went white, and the combs she'd been appraising spilled into the grass at her feet. Ranulf swiftly closed the space between them, bent down and gathered up the combs; they were ivory and decorated with delicately carved flowers. "I think these are yours, my lady," he said, and Annora nodded mutely. Her eyes seemed black and bottomless, dilated in disbelief. Her groom was looking toward them, wanting to be sure his lord's wife did not need him to defend her honour. He was young enough to relish such a confrontation, and he'd soon be strutting their way, as challenging as any barnyard cock. Annora had not yet moved, and Ranulf held out the combs, saying softly, "Where can we meet?"

As Ranulf had feared, the groom was bearing down upon them. Annora snatched up the combs, so hastily that her fingers just grazed his. Thrusting the combs toward the disappointed merchant, she beckoned to her servants and moved on, toward a silversmith's booth. But Ranulf had heard her whispered words, barely more than a breath: "St Alkmund's Church."

RANULF found St Alkmund's with no difficulty; the town's weekly market was held in its churchyard. But the churchyard was deserted now, as were the streets. The fair had turned Shrewsbury into a ghost town, for its merchants were not permitted to compete with the monks, and their shops were shut down for the duration of the fair. St Alkmund's was made of stone and the interior was shadowed and cool; summer's heat seemed to stop at the church door. Ranulf walked up the nave, then continued on into the choir. Logic told him that she would not follow him right away, but he was already straining for sounds of her entry. He convinced himself so often that he heard her steps, only to find the nave empty and silent, that when she finally did arrive, she took him almost by surprise.

Ranulf had moved toward the candlelit High Altar, and when he turned back, Annora was there, framed in the arched doorway of the rood-screen. Her face was flushed; even in such dimmed lighting, he could see the color staining her cheeks and throat. He yearned to touch that hot skin, had to remind himself that he no longer had the right. Fumbling for words—any words—to break this smothering silence, he asked, "How did you get rid of your servants?"

"I did not. I told them to await me in the churchyard." Annora sounded out of breath. "When I saw that dog, I thought at once of Shadow. But I . . . I never imagined it was really him! And when I turned around and saw you . . ."

Ranulf was absurdly pleased that she'd remembered the name of his dyrehund. "I had to come, Annora," he said, and she looked at him, wide-eyed, for an unbearably long moment before saying, quite simply:

"I'm so glad."

Thinking back upon it much later, Ranulf could never be sure which of them had taken that first fateful step. But suddenly she was in his arms, and they were clinging tightly, with such urgency that further words were forgotten. They fused together, in an embrace so impassioned, so intoxicating, and so desperate that their return to reality stunned them both. It was the slamming of a door, a sound harmless in itself, but for Ranulf and Annora, fraught with the dread of discovery. There was a violence in their recoil, a tearing-away that left them momentarily bereft, unable to respond to their danger. Ranulf recovered first, flattened himself against the roodscreen and jerked his head toward the door. Annora drew a shaken breath, then stepped out to intercept the intruder.

The sight of a priest jolted Annora's conscience back to life, reminding her that sinning in a church had to be one of those wrongs God could not forgive. At the same time, she was thankful that it was not her groom or her maid, for they knew her well enough to notice her agitation. But the priest was beaming, quite oblivious of anything untoward. "Lady Fitz Clement, this is indeed a pleasure. Your man told me you were within, and I did not want you to slip away ere I paid my respects."

Annora faked a smile that would have fooled only an elderly cleric with dimming eyesight and a celibate's innocence. "Yes, I . . . I wanted to light a candle for the king's success."

The priest nodded approvingly. "I was deeply dismayed to hear of Hugh Bigod's rebellion, for he was amongst the most stalwart of the king's men. Truly, the Devil is on the loose these days, ever ready to lead the unwary astray. Your lord husband . . . he is with you?"

"No," Annora said, too abruptly, but she could not bear to talk of her husband in Ranulf's hearing. "He is still in the North with the king."

"And will return safe to you in God's good time, daughter, never fear. Now . . . may I escort you back to the fair?"

"I should be delighted for your company." Annora would have

agreed to follow the priest to Hades and back at that moment, so frantic was she to keep him from entering the choir and finding Ranulf. "Father John, could you tell my man that I'll be returning with you, and he and Joan can go ahead and meet us there, at the cook-stall? I'll be out straightaway; I left my pater noster in the choir."

She did not move until the priest started up the aisle, not returning to Ranulf until she was sure Father John was out of earshot. Even then, they waited for the sound of a closing door. Ranulf reached for her hard and pressed a kiss into her palm, silently mouthing a one-word question: *Where?*

Annora was at a loss, for privacy was as scarce as sightings of unicorns. "I do not . . . ," she began dubiously, and then brightened. "Of course, the leper hospital at St Giles!"

Ranulf's brows shot upward. "A lazar house?" he echoed in delighted disbelief, and began to laugh.

"Do hush!" Annora's fingers flew to his mouth to still his laughter, but lingered to trace the curve of his lip. "I do not mean we should meet there, for pity's sake! Just follow the Foregate until you get to St Giles. When you reach the fence, cross the road to your right and enter the woods. You'll soon come to a canal, the runoff from the abbey mill. Wait there for me."

She took his assent for granted, and hastened from the choir. But when she reached the door in the roodscreen, she paused, giving him a dazzling smile over her shoulder, so full of love that his breath stopped.

BEFORE going to St Alkmund's, Ranulf had tethered his dogs in the abbey garth, much to their indignation. He freed them upon his return, for they'd make useful sentinels for his rendezvous with Annora. Heading back to the fairground, he bought a wicker basket, a tablecloth, a wineskin, a loaf of freshly baked bread, a pot of jam, apples, and a single red rose, the same shade as Annora's gown.

With the dogs at his heels, he walked briskly along the Foregate toward St Giles. The lazar house was situated just as Annora had said, where the road forked off toward London and Wenlock. The hospital buildings and cemetery were enclosed by a wattle fence, but several of the unhappy inhabitants were squatting by the roadside, for they were not permitted to beg within the town. The sight of their ravaged flesh and hooded cloaks would have been an unwelcome reminder to the fairgoers of their own mortality, a grim spectre of stalking Death in its most grisly guise, not what the merchants had in mind for fair entertainment.

Ranulf's steps lagged as the lazar house came into view. To a man about to violate one of God's Commandments, any encounter with lepers was bound to be chilling, for many believed that leprosy was a sinner's disease. The Church sought to combat this bias by calling leprosy a "sacred malady," but Scriptures stigmatized the leper as "defiled" and "unclean," and most people were more inclined to see leprosy as divine punishment than as a manifestation of God's Grace.

Ranulf's gaze was drawn inexorably to those hunched figures, and then he strode toward them, dropped coins into their alms cups, and wished them as cordial a "Good morrow" as he could manage. Their hoarse expressions of gratitude, as much for his civility as for his charity, followed after him as he crossed into the woods, and Ranulf felt pity's taste in his mouth, as bitter as gall.

He soon reached the millrace, where he sprawled in the grass by the surging current, and tried not to think about St Giles and the poor wretches in need of its sanctuary. The sun rose higher in the sky, the dogs foraged in the underbrush for mice or moles, and eventually he heard the snapping of twigs, the muffled echoes of woodland steps.

Ranulf jumped to his feet as Annora emerged from shade into sunlight. There was a moment or two of awkwardness, but then Ranulf gave her the rose and they smiled at each other. When he asked how she'd escaped her "keepers," she looked quite pleased with herself. "I told them that I wanted to give alms at St Giles. The very thought of getting within shouting distance of a lazar house turned them greensick with fright. They started babbling that even a leper's glance was dangerous, and when I agreed to let them await me at the fair, I thought they'd both kiss the hem of my gown!"

Ranulf took her hand in his and they began to walk. They did not talk; there was no need. Without haste, they followed the millrace as it curved toward the south, leading them farther and farther from the road. The sun spangled the water, and all about them were the soothing sounds of the summer forest. They soon turned away from the millrace, moved deeper into the woods until they found a secluded, quiet clearing, shaded by trees, screened by flowering shrubs of wild holly.

Ranulf spread out the tablecloth and Annora unpacked the food, but they knew they'd not eat it. Instead, Annora removed her veil, and then slowly and deliberately began to unwind the hair neatly coiled at the nape of her neck. When she removed the last pin, she shook it loose about her shoulders, and they both understood that to be a pledge of intimacy, for only a husband or lover ever saw a woman's hair flowing free down her back. When Ranulf reached for her, she came eagerly into his arms. Her hair felt like silk; so did her skin. Her mouth was warm and sweet, her perfume scenting his every breath. It went to his head like wine. The clearing might have been crowded with their ghosts—her absent husband, all the women he'd bedded and forgotten afterward. But none of that mattered, not now. For Ranulf, there was no world beyond this cloistered glade, no woman but this one, only Annora, and when she cried out, shuddering and gasping his name, he found her climax even more satisfying than his own.

Afterward, he held her close, brushing butterfly kisses against her temples, her eyelids, the hollow of her throat, kisses so tender that tears began to seep through her lowered lashes. He tasted the salt on her skin, and was stricken by the realization that she was weeping, that he may have seduced her into a mortal sin. "Annora? Have you regrets?"

Sitting up, she flung back her hair, swiped impatiently at the tears streaking her face. "How can you even ask that? My God, if my regrets were raindrops, we'd both be in danger of drowning!"

When he reached for her this time, she pulled away. "How could we have been such fools? But no, you had to cling to Maude like a limpet, and I had to marry straightaway, so I could show you I no longer cared—Ranulf, how can you laugh?"

She glared at him, quite indignant, but Ranulf merely laughed all the more. "Because," he said, "I thought you regretted this—our love-making!"

"Oh, no," she cried, and threw herself back into his arms. "How could I ever regret this? Ranulf, this is a memory I shall have to live on for the rest of my life!"

"No," he said, "that is not so. This is not an ending, love, but a beginning, that I promise you."

She studied his face intently, and then got slowly and reluctantly to her feet. "Ranulf . . . if you are asking me to run away with you, I cannot do that." Tears were glinting again on her lashes. "I love you," she said. "I've loved you since I was old enough to know what that word meant, and I daresay I shall still love you as I draw my last breath. But I cannot be your concubine. I cannot shame my father and brothers like that. They do not deserve that, and . . . and neither does Gervase, for he is a decent man. I have the children to consider, too, and they—"

That had been Ranulf's secret dread, a festering fear that he'd dealt with by denial, an option now no longer available to him. "Have you borne this man a child, Annora?"

"No," she said, "oh, my darling, no!" She started toward him, but he was faster and caught her to him in an emotional embrace. Annora raised her face for his kiss, and then said, so softly as to be almost inaudible, "I miscarried in our second year of marriage, but I have not quickened again . . ." Although she attempted to sound dispassionate, Ranulf heard echoes of an old grief. She had mourned the child she'd lost, Fitz Clement's child, and he did not know what to say, for he could feel only thankfulness that this accursed marriage of hers was barren. He stroked her hair gently, before saying quietly:

"What children do you mean, then, love?"

"Daniel and Lucette, my stepchildren. The other lad is older, but they are just babes, and they love me well. I would not have them think of me as a . . . a wanton."

"I would not have a single soul in Christendom think you a wanton, Annora . . . and they will not. There will be no shame in our union, for it will be blessed by the Church and God, within holy wedlock."

Her eyes narrowed. "What sort of daft talk is that? Lest you forget, I have a husband already, and one is all the law and Church allow!"

"Hellcat," he said fondly. "Well, then, we'll just have to get you shed of him, will we not?"

"What do you have in mind?" she said testily. "Murder?"

"Not unless you insist." His teasing had always been able to fire her temper, and he grinned, for there was a reassuring, familiar feel to their squabbling. But he relented then, for she was getting truly angry. "I am speaking of a plight troth, Annora—yours and mine. Because we did not have the words said over us by a priest or put down in writing, your father did not bother to forswear it, I'd wager the surety of my soul on that. But the Church requires only that a man and woman pledge their vows, and we did. Which means that your marriage was not valid, for you were not free to wed anyone but me."

She was looking at him in wonderment. "Oh, Ranulf, if only that could be!" Her hope deflated almost at once, though, and she frowned again. "You know better than that. The Church will annul a marriage for princes, but rarely for the rest of us. My father and husband both stand in high favor with the king. He would never agree to annul my marriage, for what would he gain by it?"

"No, most likely Stephen would not," Ranulf agreed. "But Maude would."

Annora exhaled a ragged breath. "Be sure, Ranulf," she pleaded, "be very sure of what you say, for if it does not come to pass, my heart would surely break."

"When Maude is queen—and she will be queen, never doubt that—I shall ask her to aid us in declaring your marriage void, and then we shall be wed. This I swear to you, my love, upon the life of our firstborn son."

He was not jesting now; never had she heard him sound so serious, and she no longer doubted. "Tell me," she said, "tell me how it will be," and he laughed, drew her back into his arms, and between kisses, promised her love and lust and a lifetime in which to enjoy them. They soon sank down upon the tablecloth that served as their bed, and found in each other such passionate pleasure that it no longer mattered if it was outlawed. When they were wed, their sins would be forgiven by God; they'd already forgiven themselves.

IT was very late when Ranulf reached Gloucester. Fortunately he was known on sight by now, and was allowed to pass into the city. He was admitted into the castle with equal ease, and was relieved to learn that Maude had already gone to bed, putting off their reckoning till the morrow. He paused briefly in the great hall to exchange greetings with a few friends, deftly parried their curiosity about his absence, and then headed for his own chamber, where he was given an effusive welcome by his squire, but given, too, news not to his liking.

"Earl Robert summoned you, Sir Ranulf, just two days after you'd ridden off. He was wroth not to find you at Gloucester, for he and Lord Miles were seeking to capture Bath, and he wanted you to ride with them. Their campaign came to naught, though, for the city was well defended and they were beaten back. Lord Robert said he wants you to come to Bristol to explain yourself, and Lady Maude . . . I fear she is sorely vexed with you, too, Sir Ranulf," the boy concluded apologetically, sounding as if he and not Ranulf were the one at fault. "Ah, but I do have happier news. Sir Gilbert is here, awaiting your return."

"I'm glad you warned me, Luke. At least I'll be braced now when the storm breaks over my head! I know it is late, but I'm well-nigh starved. Think you that you could fetch me some wine from the buttery and then raid the kitchen for me?"

Luke promised to be back in a trice with food in plenitude, and Ranulf did not doubt he would, for Luke was just fifteen and overly eager to please. It still seemed odd to Ranulf, getting the sort of wholehearted devotion from Luke that he and Gilbert had given Robert. But then he would remember: he was one and twenty now, no longer a squire, Maude's mainstay. "Prop of the throne," he said aloud, liking the sound of that, and then set about unpacking his saddlebags, whistling a tune he'd picked up at St Peter's Fair, finding it as easy as that to shrug off his coming confrontation with Robert and Maude. A man caught out in a summer squall might get drenched to the skin, but the sun would soon get him dry again. Angry words seemed a small price to pay for the miracle he'd wrought in Shrewsbury.

When the door opened, he turned in surprise, not expecting Luke back so soon. But it was Gilbert. Without waiting to be asked, he strode into the chamber, sat down on a coffer, and subjected Ranulf to a scrutiny that was far from friendly. "I was going to ask if you'd seen her," he said, "but clearly you did."

"Saw whom?"

"Annora Fitz Clement. Did you truly think I'd not figure it out? Once I put my mind to it, I knew Annora had to be at the root of your folly. So I asked Miles Fitz Walter if Gervase Fitz Clement has a manor in Shropshire. It would not surprise you, I am sure, to learn that he does."

Ranulf shrugged. "What of it?"

"Do not try to lie, Ranulf; I know you too well. You went to Shrewsbury to seek Annora out, and you got what you wanted from her. Do not bother to deny it, for I can see it in your face." Gilbert's accusations had been delivered in flat, dispassionate tones, but then his outrage broke free. "Christ Jesus, Ranulf, how could you do it? How could you make a whore out of Ancel's sister?"

Ranulf had been listening in a stony silence, but at that, he took a warning step toward Gilbert, dark eyes blazing. "Watch what you say! I mean to make her my wife!"

Gilbert started to rise, then slumped down again on the coffer. This was even worse than he'd expected. "You cannot be serious," he said, but with no conviction. "Ranulf, have you lost what wits you have left? The girl has a husband!"

"Not for long," Ranulf shot back triumphantly. "Annora may have been locked into a loveless marriage, but I have the key to set her free: our prior plight troth."

Now that his first flash of anger was over, he was glad that Gilbert had guessed the truth. Having a trustworthy confidant was a luxury he'd not expected, and he gave his friend a discreetly edited account of his reunion with Annora, confided their hopes, and dwelled at length upon all the tomorrows they would share, time enough to recompense them for these lost years, a lifetime in which to wed and love and beget children and pledge fealty to his sister the queen. Gilbert listened and feared for them both. But he kept his qualms to himself, for he knew Ranulf would not have heeded them.

NIGHT had claimed Geoffrey of Anjou's capital city of Angers, and the castle was asleep. Sometime after midnight, Henry sat up suddenly in bed, jolted awake by a remembered sin. Papa's dagger! He'd been playing with it all day, but he'd not gotten his father's permission, and then he'd gone off to bed and forgotten to sneak it back where it belonged. Instead he'd left it in a window seat of the great hall, where it was sure to be found in the morning by one of the servants. And his wooden sword was down there, too, so all would know he was the culprit.

He was already in disgrace, all because of that fight he'd had with his brother Geoffrey. He still did not think it had been his fault. Geoffrey had deserved his nosebleed for the way he'd been badgering Will. Will could not help being scared of the dark; he was only four. From the superior vantage point of his seven years, that seemed very young to Henry, and he felt protective of his baby brother. When Will had begun to wake up screaming in the night, their father had given his consent for a small candle to be kept lit. That made sense to Henry, but Geoffrey could not resist teasing Will about his fears, and eventually he threatened once too often to snuff out the candle so Will could be carried off by the werewolves waiting in the dark. Henry wasn't at all sorry for hitting Geoffrey; that memory was still very satisfying. But he could not be caught in another misdeed so soon after their squabble, not after he'd promised to be good.

Well, there was no help for it, he'd have to go get the dagger. Taking care not to disturb his brothers, he edged out of bed, fumbling about in the dark until he found his tunic. It took him longer to locate his shoes, but it was October and the stone stairs were too cold for bare feet. Both of his dogs were awake by now, eager to join in the fun. He was sorry he had to shut them up in the bedchamber, but dyrehunds always seemed to bark at just the wrong time.

Henry was not afraid of the dark, not really. Anyone would be nervous creeping down a winding stairwell blacker than any cave. He kept on going, and sighed softly when he reached the great hall, for it was dark, too, but there were people here, sleeping on pallets and benches and blankets. Much to his relief, the dagger was still in the window seat, half hidden by a cushion. Now if he could just get it back to Papa's bedchamber without getting caught . . . To his surprise, he was beginning to enjoy himself, for this midnight quest was an adventure, with suspense and risk and even a worthy prize, a crusader's dagger with a ruby hilt.

Hoping that the hinges wouldn't squeak, he slowly pushed open the door of his father's bedchamber. A reassuring sound met his ears, the snoring of his father's squires. The hearth had burned low, the firelight dying down to a feeble glow. His father's favorite wolfhound, a massive beast the size of a pony, raised her head, then tipped her tail in drowsy greeting. Leaving the door ajar, Henry moved toward the coffer at the foot of the bed. He was cautiously lifting the lid when his father's voice suddenly cut through the darkness: "Just what are you looking for?"

Henry froze, shock robbing him of all speech. Before he could stammer out a response, a woman's voice came floating from the bed. "I do believe I've found it, my lord. I was but browsing. Now, though, I think I'd like to buy!"

Henry was stunned and, for a too-brief moment, joyful. Almost at once, though, he realized his mistake, one foolish enough to make him blush. How could he have thought Mama had come home? If she were back, all would know it. Crouching down behind the coffer, he tried to make sense of this. Why was a strange woman in Papa's bed? She was speaking again, an unfamiliar voice, sounding young and eager to please. Papa was laughing at what she'd said. Henry didn't like it, not at all, that Papa should be laughing in bed with this unknown woman. He wanted to go away, to forget what he'd heard. But he was trapped, unable to move until they went back to sleep. And to his horror, he now heard his father say, "Fetch me that wine cup on the table, Nan."

The bed curtains parted and a woman's tousled head poked through. She had tumbled masses of unruly flaxen curls, and Henry could not help thinking of his mother's glossy, neat braids, black as a raven's wing. Having assured herself that the squires slept, the girl swung her legs onto the floor, scampered over to the table, and snatched up a goblet. Henry had a lively curiosity about women's bodies. Not only were they formed differently than males, but people acted as if there was something sinful about female nakedness, and he still remembered a puzzling sermon he'd heard that summer, in which the priest had railed about daughters of Eve and whores of Babylon and Satan's lures. Now, though, he averted his eyes, did not look up until the woman had climbed back into bed.

"Good lass. You cannot imagine how pleasant it is to have a biddable bedmate for a change."

The girl giggled. "Your lady wife would not have fetched you wine?"

"Not unless she'd poisoned it beforehand."

Another giggle. "Surely she could not be as bad as all that? I have to admit, though, that I was right glad when she left. She could stab someone with her eyes, God's Truth! Do you think, my lord, that she will be gone long?"

"If God is merciful," Geoffrey said wryly. "No, you need not fret about my she-wolf of a wife, Nan. She's like to be bogged down in that English quagmire for years, and even if she does manage to defeat Stephen, her victory might not be worth much after she and Stephen get done with their crown-clipping."

"I . . . I do not understand."

"You do know about coin-clipping?"

"Is that not what the Jews do?"

"Not just the Jews, anyone with a sharp eye for turning a profit. They file the edges off the coin, and melt the clippings down to make a counterfeit coin. Anyone caught clipping coins in my domains does not live to regret it. But just as the clipped coins are worth less, so is a tarnished crown. For proof of that, we need look no further than the double-dealing by Hugh Bigod and Robert Fitz Hubert. Think you that either one would have dared to defy the old king like that? When pigs fly!"

The first name was vaguely familiar to Nan, the second name not at all. "This Hugh Bigod . . . was he not the king's man?"

"More than that, lass. He perjured himself to God and the Archbishop of Canterbury, claiming that Maude's father had repudiated her upon his deathbed. But he came to feel cheated, for he believed Stephen owed him more than he'd gotten, and this past June he rebelled. Stephen swooped down on him and seized one of Bigod's castles, but freed Bigod to wreak more mischief if he chose. He did, and rebelled again in August. This time Stephen decided to buy his loyalty. Can there be a better reason for rebelling?"

Raising his voice, Geoffrey launched without warning into a mimicry of a peddler's spiel. "Are you discontented with your lot in life? Has your barony begun to seem paltry and insignificant? Do you yearn for your own deer park, wine from Cyprus, oranges from Spain? Well, then, do not delay. Defy the king, gain yourself estates, castles, mayhap an earldom!"

Nan joined in his laughter, even though the humor eluded her. She laughed at all of Geoffrey's jokes, whether she understood them or not. "What of the other man, this Fitz . . . Herbert?"

"Fitz Hubert. He was one of Stephen's Flemish hirelings, mayhap the worst of a bad lot. Last October he turned on Stephen and seized Malmesbury Castle. Stephen snatched it back, but—surprise of surprises—he then agreed to let Fitz Hubert go. It seems he was a kinsman of William de Ypres, and he prevailed upon Stephen to show his cousin some undeserved mercy."

"Was that the end of it?"

"Of course not. Fitz Hubert promptly hied off to Maude at Bristol. But he soon saw he could do better on his own and by a ruse, succeeded in getting hold of Devizes Castle. When Righteous Robert—my saintly brother by marriage—sent his son to take command, Fitz Hubert drove him off. Using Devizes as a refuge, he and his brigands set about terrorizing the countryside, plundering and raping and burning as they pleased. It then occurred to him that if he'd done so well with one castle, how much better he could do with two, and he set his eyes upon Marlborough. But he overreached himself there, for Marlborough was held by a man named John Marshal, and that one could teach the Devil himself about guile."

Nan clapped her hands, like a child hearing a bedtime story. "What happened then?"

"Marshal pretended to believe Fitz Hubert's cock-and-bull tale about forging an alliance, lured our greedy Fleming to Marlborough, and cast him into the castle's dungeon. He then agreed to turn Fitz Hubert over to Brother Robert for five hundred marks. Robert dragged the Fleming back to Devizes, where he swore to hang him if he did not order the garrison to surrender. But Fitz Hubert balked and Robert, ever a man of his word, hanged him outside the castle walls. Meanwhile, the garrison had decided they did not truly need Fitz Hubert, and so they spurned all demands for surrender. Instead, they waited until Robert's forces withdrew, and then yielded the castle to Stephen, for a right goodly profit!"

Geoffrey and Nan laughed so loudly that Henry feared they'd awaken the squires. He huddled against the coffer, holding his breath, but those blanketed forms by the hearth didn't stir.

"So you see, sweet, it is every man for himself in England these days. And it'll get worse ere it gets better. Stephen and Maude have opened the floodgates, and all they can do is let the tide carry them along, whilst trying to keep their heads above water. Not that it would break my heart if the lady drowned! But whether she survives or not, she'll not be coming back to bedevil me. Now . . . enough of these English lunatics. We've more interesting matters to discuss. When are you going to make good your offer?"

"Offer?" Nan echoed coyly. "What offer was that, my lord?"

Henry did not hear his father's murmured response, only the woman's laugh. There was an intimacy to their conversation now that was different and disquieting. Making no further attempts at concealment, Henry got to his feet. He no longer cared if he was caught or not. With a deliberation that verged upon defiance, he turned away from the bed, started toward the door.

His father had once told him that ice could burn. He hadn't believed it; now he did. The coldness within him was numbing, seemed to have seeped into the very marrow of his bones. He'd never felt like this before, did not even know how to describe it. The word *desolate* was not yet in his seven-year-old's vocabulary. There was anger, too, but it was unfamiliar anger—not hot, more like the ice that burned. He had not comprehended all that he'd overheard, but he had understood what mattered. His mother was not coming back.

12

WESTMINSTER, ENGLAND

December 1140

GEOFFREY'S cynical assessment of English affairs was more accurate than he knew. Even as he predicted coming chaos, the Earl of Chester was plotting a royal murder.

Chester had not forgiven Stephen for bestowing upon Harry of Scotland the disputed Honour of Carlisle. When the Scots king's son took as his wife a half-sister of the detested Beaumonts, Chester's fury reached the flash point. He'd never been one to bother about consequences, and he had no fear whatsoever of the king's wrath—not this king—for Stephen had repeatedly shown himself to be a believer in second chances, even third, fourth, and fifth chances. Once he made up his mind to take action, Chester turned to the only man he truly trusted, his half-brother, William de Roumare.

William de Roumare was nine years older than Chester, and of a less volatile temperament. He was famed not so much for his own accomplishments as for his fortuitous dockside decision not to sail on the White Ship. Although he was ambitious, even his ambition seemed a pale echo of Chester's ravenous hunger for power and prestige. The two brothers were very close, but there was no doubt who dominated, and William de Roumare became a willing accomplice to Chester's vengeful scheme.

Their plan, as reckless as it was ruthless, was to ambush Harry of Scotland and his Beaumont bride as they made their way home from a Michaelmas visit to Stephen's court. Fortunately for the Scots prince, one of their conspirators had a weakness for wine, and did some rash bragging to a bought bedmate. The young woman was shrewd enough to realize both the value and the danger in such information, and she wasted no time confiding her perilous, prized secret to the most trustworthy of Stephen's inner circle, his queen. Matilda was appalled, but acted swiftly to frustrate Chester's murderous intent, persuading Stephen to provide

Prince Harry and Adeline de Warenne with a royal escort all the way to the Scots border.

They were then faced with a Draconian dilemma: what to do about the Earl of Chester. There was no easy answer, for this would-be assassin was also the most powerful lord of the realm. As furious as Stephen was with Chester's treachery, he and Matilda reluctantly concluded that there was no way to punish him for it. The crime had been thwarted, evidence was lacking, and who'd take the word of a drunken hireling over his high-born lord? An earl might be charged with rebellion, but a felony? No, they'd have to find another way to deal with this overmighty, unscrupulous subject, however little they liked it.

Resorting to the tactic that had become a habit by now, Stephen sought to buy Chester's loyalty. At the time of the old king's death, there had been no more than seven earls in his domains. In the five years since Stephen had claimed the crown, though, he'd bestowed no less than sixteen new earldoms. Four had gone to the Beaumonts and their kin; in the past year alone, he had created six new earls. Adding a seventh to that list, he conferred upon William de Roumare the earldom of Lincoln.

He then returned to London, confident that he'd outbid Maude and the brothers were his, but with a sour taste in his mouth, withal. He had yet to learn that for some men, "more" is never "enough." Instead of rejoicing in their new family earldom, Chester and his brother fumed, for Stephen had not included the royal castle of Lincoln in his grudging grant. And as their king rode south, they began to lay plans to remedy his omission.

CHRISTMAS EVE revelries at Westminster were lavish that year—deliberately so, as if rich fare and dramatic spectacle could somehow validate Stephen's contested kingship, as if roast goose and spiced red wine and a baker's dozen of minstrels could make people forget the burning of Worcester, the sacking of Nottingham, the newly dug graves, and the uncertain tomorrows that lay ahead. The great hall of William Rufus had been adorned with so much greenery that it resembled the forest in which Rufus had met his death, decorated with evergreen boughs and holly and beribboned sprigs of mistletoe. The meal had been so bountiful that the leftover goose and venison and bread and eel scraped from the trenchers would feed Christ's poor for days to come. The entertainment was equally extravagant: a woman rope dancer, a daredevil who juggled daggers, a Nativity play that offered not only the requisite shepherds and Magi but even a few sheep as props. Then the last of the trestle tables were cleared away and the dancing began, the irresistible, exuberant music of everyone's favorite, the carol.

Matilda danced so many carols that she began to get dizzy, and when the circle started to form for the next one, she begged off, moving to the sidelines to catch her breath. She had no need for center stage, would have been quite content to watch her husband have fun. But she was still keeping an eye upon her son and his bride; Eustace and Constance had been given permission to attend the evening revelries, although it was well past their bedtime hour. Constance had withdrawn to a cushioned window seat, Eustace had followed, and only Matilda saw what happened next, saw Eustace deliberately pour his cider down the front of Constance's gown.

Constance gave a scream, quickly choked off, and began to brush ineffectually at the spreading stain. Eustace laughed, then turned to saunter innocently away. Before he could make his escape, though, his mother was there, with a napkin for Constance and a low-voiced but stinging rebuke for him. He flushed, insisting it had been an accident, that Constance had jogged his arm. But Matilda was not mollified. Sounding like the queen and not at all like his mother, she said coldly, "Do not make your misdeed worse by lying about it, Eustace. When the carol ends, go to your lord father and ask if you may withdraw. Then go to your bedchamber straightaway, and if you wake Will, you'll have reason to rue it."

Eustace started to argue, but then thought better of it. He was not a stupid child, and he well knew which of his parents could be gotten around, which one could not. Giving Constance a baleful glance that promised future retribution, he stalked off to do as his mother bade, and Matilda turned her efforts to comforting her daughter-in-law.

Constance was the older of the two children, eleven to Eustace's ten, although none would have guessed it by appearance, for Eustace was a swaggering, handsome boy, as yellow-haired and bold as a Viking, tall for his age, and Constance's fairness was ethereal, even fey. She had the flaxen hair and blue eyes and shy nature of her elder brother the French king. Like Louis, she yearned for approval, and like Louis, she could be surprisingly stubborn. But most of the time she was quite biddable, eager to do what was expected of her, fearful of disappointing . . . fearful, too, of Eustace.

They had been betrothed that past February, wed on the last Sunday before Advent. Constance would be raised at the English court, learning the customs and ways of her new homeland, and when she and Eustace were of an age to consummate their marriage, they would share a bed. It was a common arrangement, but Matilda was already uneasy, sensing that they were poorly matched, this little French fawn and her wolf-cub son.

It was not easy to admit, for Eustace was her flesh and blood and she did love him. For some time, though, she had been troubled by what she was seeing in her son. He had known how Constance had looked forward to this evening—a chance to attend the Christmas fête, to sit at the high table and take part in the carol and wear a grown-up gown of moss-green silk. In spoiling her pleasure, Eustace had been playing no mere prank; it was a meanspirited act, the act of a bully.

Matilda had tried at first to find mitigation for her son's misbehavior, tried to convince herself that she was exaggerating the significance of his petty sins, sins common to all boys of spirit. But once her eyes were opened, she saw shadows at every turn. Her younger son had too many bruises; no child fell down that often. Four-year-old Mary had begun to shrink back whenever Eustace was nearby. Her own spaniel would not approach the boy, and Stephen's favorite greyhound was equally wary. There was an awkward incident involving a one-legged beggar who claimed Eustace had stolen his crutch, an accusation he'd hastily retracted upon learning the boy's identity. And then there was the day when Eustace was seen flinging a cat from an upper-story window. He'd been quite forthright when confronted, admitted the deed freely, explaining he wanted to see if the cat would land on its feet, as folklore held. But Matilda had been unable to repress a queasy suspicion that he'd hoped to see the cat splatter upon the hard ground below.

She did not want to bother Stephen; he had enough on his trencher as it was. After the cat episode, though, she felt she had no choice. Stephen hadn't liked what he heard, and he'd given Eustace a stern lecture about the obligations of the highborn, the need to protect those too weak to protect themselves, the duties imposed by chivalry and Christianity, duties which no king's son could shirk. Afterward, he'd assured Matilda that the lad was quite attentive and whilst denying any wrongdoing, promised to make them proud of him. Boys that age ofttimes went astray, it was to be expected, but they outgrew it, for certes he had.

Matilda very much wanted to believe him, but she could never imagine Stephen—no matter how young—tormenting small children or dumb animals. She no longer shared Stephen's implicit faith that all would always turn out for the best, and she could not help asking unsettling questions. What if Eustace did not outgrow it? What sort of king would he make? What sort of husband?

She'd engaged a new nurse for her children, one who understood that her duties included a discreet surveillance. But Constance was another matter. If her suspicions about Eustace were correct, the girl's marriage would be a wretched one. She'd become very fond of Constance, and it distressed her enormously to think of her vulnerable daughter-in-law wed to a brutal husband, and he her own son. Pray God she was wrong, that they had not done Constance a terrible injustice, for she did not believe a crown compensated for all of life's maladies. She would have to teach the lass to speak up for herself, to show more backbone. A pity the child had not come under the sway of her brother's wife, for no one would ever call Eleanor of Aquitaine docile or sweetly submissive.

Matilda had to smile at the very thought; during her stay in Paris, she'd been somewhat shocked by Eleanor's outspokenness, while envying it, too. She'd had to take a much more active part in Stephen's fight to save his crown than she'd ever envisioned, and she was proud of her accomplishments on Stephen's behalf, but it was neither easy nor natural for her to play such a role, not as it was for Eleanor.

She could not leave the hall herself, and she looked over her guests until her gaze finally settled upon Robert Beaumont's daughter Isabel, the Earl of Northampton's countess. A wife at thirteen, a mother at fifteen, she'd surely sympathize with Constance's discomfort, and when Matilda beckoned her over, she volunteered at once to assist the child in sponging off her gown, salvaging the remainder of the evening. Watching as Isabel gently steered Constance across the crowded hall, Matilda vowed to have another long, frank talk with her son, one he would not enjoy.

Matilda wanted suddenly to be with her husband. For a few hours, she was not going to fret about Eustace or Constance or Maude or that vile hellspawn Chester. For a few hours, she was going to focus upon Stephen and only Stephen, hoping that his high spirits would be contagious.

But Stephen would have to wait, for one of her guests was bearing down upon her, clearly intent upon interception. She guessed him to be about her own age, midthirties, and her initial impression was of a lord both pleasant and prosperous. While his tunic was not cut in the latest fashion, it was finely stitched and of good-quality wool, and his shoes had silver buckles. He looked like a man who smiled easily and often. He also looked familiar, but his name eluded her. He was shepherding a woman, a slim, dark creature not much taller than Matilda herself, and quite young. Had her hair been loose and her feet bare, she would have looked right at home in a gypsy encampment. She did not look at home at Westminster, and Matilda's heart warmed toward her, as it did toward all of life's misfits and orphans and lost lambs.

As they reached her, the man's name bobbed up from the depths of her memory, just in time for her to say with a smile, "Sir Gervase, it is a pleasure to see you again."

Her memory's reprieve won her a lifelong champion. He beamed, so flattered to be remembered by the queen that it was a moment before he recollected himself. "Madame, may I present my wife, Annora?"

The girl curtsied hastily, murmuring a conventional response, then raised her lashes to reveal brilliant black eyes. "The little lass . . . was that the Lady Constance?" It was soon apparent to Matilda that Constance was merely a conversational bridge, meant to get Annora Fitz Clement where she wanted to go—across the Channel to the French court, home of Constance's celebrated sister-in-law. "You met the French queen, my lady. Is she as fair as men claim? I heard that she does just as she pleases, says whatever is on her mind, and yet the French king dotes on her every whim! Can that be true?"

Matilda stifled a laugh, amused both by Annora's candor and the faintly wistful tone. She tried then to think of a diplomatic way to deflect Annora's curiosity, but Annora's husband was quicker.

"You cannot ask questions like that, lass. Queens do not gossip." His laugh was indulgent, his rebuke kindly meant, but Matilda saw it was not kindly taken; color had flared in the girl's face and the corners of her mouth drooped.

"Well . . . in truth, Sir Gervase, queens fancy gossip, too. For certes, I do," Matilda lied cheerfully. "Queen Eleanor is indeed a beauty, with green-gold cat eyes and a cat's elegant grace. She has a cat's confidence, too, and I suspect that would be true whether she wore a crown or not. She is lively and quick-witted and strong-willed and worldly, but very young, withal, only eighteen or thereabouts," Matilda concluded, satisfied that she'd given Annora an intimate glimpse of the French queen she so admired and envied, but without saying anything hurtful or too revealing.

There was still so much Annora yearned to know about the French queen, questions she could never have asked in front of her husband, for she had convinced herself that Eleanor would have been willing to brave scandal for a lover's sake. She needed to believe that not all the women in her world had their wings clipped; surely there must be a few still able to soar up into the sky, untamed and fearless and free. She smiled at Matilda, torn between gratitude and guilt. Why did Stephen's queen have to be so likable? Pray God she'd somehow survive Stephen's fall.

It was the sudden break in the music that caught their attention. The carol had not ended; it just stopped in midnote. Heads were turning toward the door, where several of Stephen's guards were scuffling with a very determined intruder. Even as they dragged him away, he was shouting that it was life or death, he must see the king.

Whether it was due to courtesy or curiosity, Stephen was almost always willing to hear a man out. "Let him approach," he commanded, and a path cleared among the dancers.

The man was exhausted, staggering with fatigue. When he sank to his knees before Stephen, it seemed more an act of physical prostration than one of protocol. "I've ridden from Lincoln, my liege, and in four days' time, too, God smite me if I lie. I come at the behest of Sir Robert de la

Haye, your castellan. I bear, too, a letter from His Grace, the Bishop of Lincoln, and a third plea from the townspeople . . ."

He faltered then, and Stephen said quickly, "Wine for this man." It was more than one hundred thirty miles to London. No man would race the Devil over winter-ravaged roads unless it truly was "life or death." Stephen waited impatiently until the man had gulped down a cupful of sweet wine, spilling as much as he swallowed. "Tell me," he demanded. "What evil has overtaken Lincoln?"

"The Earl of Chester and his brother, the new Earl of Lincoln . . . they have betrayed you, my liege. On Thursday last, they seized control of Lincoln Castle."

There were audible gasps from those listening. "That cannot be," Stephen said incredulously. "The castle could never be taken in just a day!"

"They did not assault it like honest men, my lord king. They took it by guile and perfidy. The men of Lincoln were to play camp-ball with a neighboring town, and the castellan agreed to let most of the garrison take part in the game, the honour of Lincoln being at stake. So there were only a few guards at the castle when the Countess of Chester and the Countess of Lincoln came to pay a call upon Lady Muriel, the castellan's wife. A short while thereafter, the Earl of Chester arrived to escort the ladies back to their lodging, but none suspected evildoing, for he wore no sword and had just three men with him. Once they were admitted into the castle, though, they seized weapons belonging to the garrison and attacked the sentries. One of their men then rushed to open the postern gate, letting in William de Roumare and the rest of their cohort. By the time word got out into the town, it was too late, for the deed was done."

Withdrawing several sealed parchments from the pouch at his belt, he offered them to Stephen. "These letters bear out what I say, my liege. Once they held the castle, Chester and his brother began to make harsh demands upon the townspeople. They sent out men to ransack houses and carried off food and provisions to replenish the castle larders, and if they came upon an item of value in their search for flour and salted pork, they took that, too. Several townsmen have lost horses, and rumor has it that women have been molested, although I cannot confirm that for certes; they would naturally keep silent from the shame of it."

He at last paused for breath. "My lord king, the citizens and the bishop and your castellan all implore you to deliver them from these wicked men. Highborn they may be, but they are no better than brigands, God's Own Truth. As long as they hold the castle, they are safe from retribution and well they know it. Help us, my liege. Take back your castle and return the King's Peace to your loyal subjects of Lincoln."

"You need not fear," Stephen said grimly. "This time that renegade whoreson has gone too far, and he'll soon regret it. Upon that, you have my word."

IT was late when the Earl of Chester finally mounted the stairs to his bedchamber, and his wife was already asleep. He was irked that she'd not waited up for him, but not surprised, for they'd still not made their peace after their last quarrel.

Impatiently waving aside his squire's attempts to help him undress, he stripped off his clothes, left them where they landed, and deliberately dropped his boots onto the coffer so they'd make a sleep-rousing thud—in vain, though, for his wife did not stir. Climbing into bed, he started to pull the bed-hangings, but stopped in midgesture, gazing down at the woman beside him.

It was Chester's considered opinion that his wife had inherited the worst traits of both her parents, for she had Amabel's barbed tongue and Robert's sense of moral certainty. She was also the only member of his household who was not afraid of him. She was the first woman who'd ever dared to stand up to him, and he was of two minds as to how he felt about that, or indeed, about this exasperating, prideful, vexing, exciting wife of his. All her virtues were flaws, too, in his eyes. As proud as he was of her royal blood, he was often annoyed by her stubborn loyalty to the aunt whose namesake she was. He admired her courage, admired the way she'd played her part as bait for his trap. But that same boldness of spirit kept her from being a dutiful and submissive wife. Even when she did affect that role in public, he always suspected it was done tongue in cheek.

Reaching for the bed coverlets, he pulled them back so he could look upon his wife's body, for that never disappointed him. She was a handsome young woman, bearing a striking resemblance to Maude, in both demeanor and coloring. Fortunately, though, she differed from Maude in one crucial aspect of her womanhood. The mere thought of that difference was enough to bring a smile to Chester's lips. Geoffrey of Anjou had once confided that the best place for a man to come down with frostbite was in Maude's bed. But his Maud . . . she was a lustful wench, as hot for their bedsport as he was. Sometimes it even seemed that the more quarrelsome their days, the better their nights.

Sliding over onto her side of the bed, he entangled his fingers in her lustrous, loose hair, while his other hand cupped her breast. Maud opened her eyes, looked up at her husband, and yawned. "Just once I wish you'd let me sleep through till dawn," she complained, but he could feel her nipple hardening against the palm of his hand, and when he continued to fondle and stroke her body, she soon wrapped her arms around his neck, pulling his mouth down to hers. This was the sort of sex they both liked best, sudden and hungry, with just enough hostility to give it an edge. But their lovemaking had barely begun when they were interrupted by a loud hammering on the door.

Chester raised up on an elbow, aiming a blistering stream of profanity at the door, but his squires were already sitting up sleepily, his mastiff was adding his belligerent bellowing to the din, and the pounding persisted, unabated, accompanied now by demands for admittance. Recognizing the voice as his brother's, Chester jerked the bed-hangings all the way open, and snapped, "Let him in." His body might still be quivering with thwarted need, but his brain was back in command. This was trouble.

William de Roumare looked as if he'd been roused from bed, too. He had gone gray while still in his thirties, and his tousled silver hair and ashen skin added at least a decade to his actual age. One glance and Chester felt a chill, for Will was not a man given to panic. Striding toward the bed, Roumare said hoarsely, "The king's men are in the town, and they come not as friends. Randolph, we are under attack . . . or we will be at first light."

Chester swore again, with even more heat. Maud's eyes had widened, but she said nothing, clutching the sheet to her breasts as she waited to find out their fate. Roumare envied his brother her composure; his own wife was even now having hysterics back in their bedchamber. Chester swung out of the bed, grabbing for the tunic discarded in the floor rushes. "Tell me what you know for sure," he said, pulling the tunic over his head.

"Some of our men were caught in the town. One made it back to the castle, and he says the streets are full of Stephen's soldiers. Those accursed townspeople let them in the city gates, damn their souls. Stephen is vowing to see our heads up on pikes, vowing that the siege will last till Judgment Day if need be. Randolph . . . what shall we do?"

"God rot that misbegotten, meddlesome, bungling lackwit!" Chester said savagely. "He is no more fit to rule than any beggar we'd pluck off the streets, a Beaumont puppet not worth a cupful of warm piss!" But even as he raged, his thoughts were racing ahead, clearly and coldly analyzing their danger, weighing their options.

"I will need two of our best horses saddled and ready to go," he said abruptly. "I'll take Padrig the Welshman with me, for once I reach Cheshire, I can send him on into Wales with word for Cadwaladr. He'll throw in with us if we make it worth his while, and Madog of Powys may, too. Just Padrig, though, for two men will have a better chance of getting through their lines. They must be in disarray, arriving in the middle of the night, and Stephen's captains will have no hope of imposing order till daylight. If I slip out through the postern gate, I ought to be able to get away unseen. But it has to be done now and done fast. Will, think you that you can hold out till I get back with aid?"

"God Willing," the older man said somberly. "But we are in a tight corner, indeed. Even if you succeed in getting safe away from the castle—and if I were a wagering man, I'd put my money on Stephen—what then? Mayhap we ought to give thought to surrender—"

"I'd sooner walk barefoot through Hell's hottest flames!"

"I like it not, either, but think on this, Randolph. We can always talk our way around Stephen. It means swallowing our pride. No man ever died, though, from a serving of humble pie. And what would it avail us to resist? Even if you can summon every last one of our tenants and vassals and add in Cadwaladr's Welsh hirelings for good measure, we'll still not have enough men to raise Stephen's siege."

"No, we will not," Chester admitted, "but I know where we can get them." Striding over to the bed, he caught Maud by the shoulders, claimed her mouth in a brief but passionate kiss. "For all our sakes, girl, let's hope that your kin are as fond of you as you say!"

THE feast of Epiphany was celebrated with great enthusiasm, for not only was it an important festival in its own right, it offered one last burst of brightness in the winter's dark. On this Twelfth Night, Christians bade farewell to the joy and light of Christmastide, while bracing themselves for the bleakness of the looming Lenten season of sacrifice and self-denial.

Gloucester Castle's great hall had been newly whitewashed, fresh, fragrant rushes laid down, and enough candles and torches lit to banish all but the most tenacious shadows, for Maude was determined that her Epiphany revelries be perfect in all particulars. Her cooks had prepared an elaborate feast: fresh herring, stewed capon, savory rice, a spectacular roasted peacock refitted with feathers, rissoles of beef marrow, pea soup, Lombardy custard, and nut sweetmeats, served with spiced red wine and hippocras and a sweet white malmsey. Afterward, a French minstrel from the sun-warmed South sang and strummed a gittern and recited verses from a highly popular chanson, *The Song of Roland*. But his performance was cut short by the arrival of shocking news from the North—that the Earl of Chester had seized control of Lincoln Castle.

No one had any more interest in hearing of Roland's epic deeds, and for the remainder of the evening, there was but one topic of conversation, speculation about Chester's duplicity and Stephen's likely response. Opinion was united on the former, that Chester's greed had deranged his senses, and decidedly mixed on the latter, some sure Stephen would have to retaliate, others equally certain that he would once again turn a blind eye, as he had done so often in the past. All were hopeful that this astonishing turn of events would somehow rebound to Maude's benefit.

Robert and Amabel were furious, stunned that Chester would have so risked their daughter's safety. A woman was expected to defend her husband's castle if it was besieged in his absence, but it was unheard-of to use a wife as Chester had done, as a decoy. Baldwin de Redvers was likewise outraged, for his younger sister Hawise was William de Roumare's wife. Their concern cast a pall over the festivities. Robert and Amabel soon excused themselves, intent upon dispatching a messenger to Lincoln at first light, bearing a demand that Chester get their daughter out of that castle straightaway. Miles Fitz Walter was no longer in a festive mood, either; he'd had a quarrel earlier that evening with his eldest son, and both he and Roger were still out of sorts. Once the Fitz Walters had withdrawn, too, there seemed no reason to linger. Maude dismissed the minstrels, and her guests went off to bed.

But Maude was too restless to sleep. She wandered aimlessly about her chamber, failed to find a book that could hold her interest, and finally snatched up her mantle. The great hall was already dark, beds laid out where trestle tables had stood earlier in the evening. Maude moved quietly down the center aisle, out into the inner bailey.

It was cold, but the wind had died down and the starlit sky was clear of clouds. It had snowed earlier in the week, and most of it had been trampled into a dingy grey slush. But white still glistened along the south wall, protected by Maude's garden fence. Maude liked snow, liked the way it blurred harsh edges and hid ugliness and made the world seem new and pure and pristine. Pushing open the garden gate, she sat down on a wooden bench. Her thoughts soon carried her far from Gloucester, and she started violently when a voice said, very close at hand, "Lady Maude? May I be of service?"

Maude flushed self-consciously; she hated to be caught off guard, to be watched unaware. But the interloper was a man she valued, and she bit back a dismissive retort, forcing a smile, instead. "Thank you, Brien, but nothing is amiss. I just could not sleep. What about you? Why are you not abed at such an hour?"

Brien shrugged. "I could not sleep, either," he said, and looked pleased when Maude beckoned him toward her bench. He smiled as he sat beside her, and she found herself thinking that she liked his smile, liked so much about Brien Fitz Count—his insight and his loyalty and his competence; everything he did, he did well. He did not intrude now upon her privacy, seemed content to sit in silence, until or if she chose to speak.

Maude appreciated his reticence, and soon realized that she did want to talk, after all.

"I had a letter this week from my son Henry," she said. "His own letter, the first one that was not written for him by his tutor or a scribe . . ."

Her voice trailed off, as if she'd lost interest, but Brien knew better. He studied her profile, thinking that most women benefited from the more subdued, softer lighting cast by candles or stars, but not Maude. She looked her best in the bright light of day, able to take the sun's glare full on, without flinching. "It troubled you, this letter?" he asked, and after a moment or so, she nodded.

"Henry asked me if I was ever coming back," she said, and he thought he heard her sigh. "I've not seen my sons for more than a year, Brien, nigh on sixteen months. If this war drags on long enough, I'll not even know them upon my return. They'll be strangers . . ."

He would not trivialize her pain with facile denials or comforting banalities. The truth was that she'd never get back the time she'd lost with her sons. Childhood could not be relived; children grew up, and a quest for a crown could last for years. "To be a mother and a queen, too," he said at last, "must be a burden no man could fully comprehend."

"No man needs to understand, for no man needs to bear it," she said, with more than a trace of bitterness. "What makes it so hard, Brien, is that I see no end in sight. Sometimes I find myself wondering where I will be in five years. Will I still be at Gloucester or Bristol, clinging to my shredded hopes whilst Stephen clings to his stolen crown? All I know for certes is that in five years, Henry will be almost thirteen."

"I truly believe you will one day reclaim your crown," he said softly, and she turned to look at him with a brief, bleak smile.

"I do, too," she said, "most of the time. I am not often so downhearted, for I do not let myself dwell upon my disappointments or defeats. But none of the Christmas news has been good. Lord knows, the tidings from Cornwall have been dismal. Rainald is holding on to the one Cornish castle he has left, but Stephen has the shire, and Rainald's prospects grow dimmer by the day. He has been excommunicated by the Bishop of Exeter, who blames him for the damage done to a Launceton church, and his wife . . . Rainald tries to make light of it in his letters, Brien, but others tell me the girl was so distraught and fearful at being caught up in the fighting that her wits have been affected. She weeps all the time and hears voices and cannot be left alone lest she do herself harm."

"I'd heard the lass was . . . overwrought," Brien admitted. "But just as those sick of body can heal, so, too, can the sick of mind. You must not give up hope, Lady Maude."

"I inhale hope with every breath I take," Maude said ruefully. "But lately it seems that if anything can go wrong, by God, it does. Robert is at odds with his younger son, Philip, as I expect you know; it is no secret that Robert rebuked Philip for being needlessly brutal during the assault upon Nottingham. And now he and Amabel have Maud to worry about, too. Miles is another whose temper is on the raw, and the same can be said for Baldwin de Redvers. In truth, everywhere I turn these days, I see naught but discontented, surly men and fretful wives."

"What of Ranulf?" he protested. "That lad is cheerful enough to raise all sorts of suspicions!"

"How true," she conceded. "If Ranulf were a cat, I'd be checking his whiskers for cream!"

They both laughed, and then Maude surprised herself by saying, "You've been a good friend, Brien, for longer than I can remember. You helped me get through the worst time of my life, and I never thanked you . . . not until now."

She did not need to elaborate; he understood. Their memories were suddenly functioning as one, taking them back more than thirteen years. She had been twenty-five, and no longer able to resist her father's will, agreeing at last to wed Geoffrey of Anjou. On her betrothal journey from England to Normandy, the old king had entrusted her to the custody of his eldest son, Robert, and his foster son, Brien. They had carried out the king's charge, escorted Maude to Rouen for the plight troth, and the following year she and Geoffrey had been wed at Le Mans.

"Why should you thank me? I did as the king bade, turned you over to Geoffrey of Anjou, when I ought to have hidden you away where he could never have found you."

Maude was startled. "You did what you could, Brien. You made me feel—without a word being said—that you understood, that you were on my side. That may not sound like much, but it was."

"If I had it to do over again . . ." His smile held no humor, just a disarming flash of self-mockery. "I suppose I'd do the same, however much I'd like to think I would not. But my regrets would be so much greater, knowing as I do now how miserable he'd make you. I never forgave your father for that, for forcing you to wed a man so unworthy of you—" He stopped abruptly, and a tense, strained silence followed, which neither of them seemed able to break.

Maude was staring at Brien, a man she'd known all her life, and seeing a stranger. Had she lost her wits altogether? How could she have confided in him like this? She'd long ago learned to keep her fears private, her pain secret, all others at a safe distance, yet here in a barren winter garden, she'd lowered her defenses, allowing Brien to get a glimpse into her very soul. Even worse, she'd seen into his soul, too, discovered what she ought never to have known. She felt suddenly as flustered as a raw, green girl, she who was a widow, wife, and mother, a woman just a month shy of her thirty-ninth birthday, a woman who would be queen. Getting hastily to her feet, she drew her mantle close about her throat, chilled to the bone.

"I want to go in," she said, sounding curt even to her own ears.

Brien had risen as soon as she did. "Of course," he said. An awkward moment then ensued, for he started to offer his arm as chivalry demanded, but it was no longer a simple gesture of courtesy, and they both knew it. After a discernible hesitation, Maude let her hand rest lightly on his sleeve, and they walked in silence toward the great hall.

She would later wish fervently that she'd held her tongue. But she felt compelled to prop up her diminished defenses, and so as they reached the steps, she said coolly, "You should bring your wife with you the next time you come to Gloucester. It has been too long since I've seen her."

She at once wanted to call her words back, for she saw the hurt they'd inflicted. His dark eyes searched her face, and in them she found a mute reproach. They had just shared all that they could ever have, a few brief moments of unspoken intimacy, cheapened now by her needless, heavy-handed rebuff. She understood, read his thoughts as if they were her own. But what he did not understand, and what she could never let him know, was that her pointed mention of his marriage was a reminder meant, not for him, but for herself.

"My wife will be pleased to attend you, madame," he said tonelessly.

Maude was mercifully spared the need to respond, for a commotion had erupted up on the bailey walls. Shouts were echoing on the quiet night air, a challenge offered and met. Moments later, the drawbridge was going down, a lone horseman coming through.

Sliding from the saddle, the rider tossed the reins to the nearest of the guards. "You must awaken the Earl of Gloucester and the empress, for my news cannot wait!"

He was young, weary, and disheveled, but he was exhilarated, too, by the gravity of his mission, and somewhat nervous, now that his moment was at hand. He sounded bellicose, combative, for he was anticipating a refusal. But as he braced himself for a long, heated argument, he glanced across the bailey, recognizing the woman standing upon the steps of the great hall. "Madame, thank God and His good angels!" Unable to believe his luck, he hastened forward and dropped to his knees before Maude. "I am Sir Bennet de Malpas, my lady, cousin and liegeman to my lord Earl of Chester. I bring you his urgent appeal for aid, and his pledge of fealty."

THERE was to be no more sleeping at Gloucester that night. Rumors assailed the castle, soon spilling over its bailey walls into the town. The great hall was a scene of confusion and turmoil, but all knew the solar was where the significant activity was occurring. They'd been sequestered above-stairs for hours—Maude, Robert, Miles, Brien, Ranulf, and Baldwin de Redvers—and what they decided would affect many more lives than their own.

Within the solar, there was no sympathy to spare for Chester; he had no friends in this room, and few indeed in the rest of the realm. Nor did they give credence to his sudden conversion, his belated recognition of the justice of Maude's cause. They well knew that Chester would have embraced the Devil himself in his hour of need. But all of their foregoing feelings were irrelevant to the issue at hand. They would do as Chester wanted, march to Lincoln and confront the king. They had no choice, for the chance might not come again. At Lincoln they could catch Stephen off guard, force a battle that might determine once and for all who would rule England—Maude or Stephen.

The dark had faded away, the sky lightening to a shade of misty pearl, for dawn was nigh by the time Maude returned to her chamber. Minna had turned back the bed coverlets invitingly, and put out a selection of sugared wafers and watered-down wine to break the night's fast. But Maude had no appetite. Nor could she sleep. Crossing to the window, she opened the shutters, staring down at the uproar below her.

The bailey was crowded and chaotic, at first glance resembling a fairground more than a castle ward. People were rushing about, shouting orders and yelling out questions, trying to dodge the dogs and children darting underfoot. Half the men in the castle were either in the stables or already in the saddle, for they had levies to raise, vassals to summon to arms, horses and carts and supplies to requisition, buy, or barter. Time was the enemy as much as Stephen, and speed of the essence.

Maude did not feel the cold, not on a conscious level, but then Minna draped a mantle about her shoulders and she realized she'd been shivering. The German widow was not one for fussing or coddling; Maude would never have stood for it. But Minna could not help noticing the sleepless smudges under Maude's eyes, the greyish pallor of her skin. "My lady, you look bone-weary. Can you not spare a few hours to rest?"

"I'd not be able to sleep, Minna." Maude watched as Miles Fitz Walter bade farewell to his wife, Sybil, then mounted and joined his waiting men. "Last night I told Brien Fitz Count that I saw no end in sight. Now it may well end at Lincoln, might even be over by the start of Lent."

"Does that not gladden you, madame? I ask because you do not sound glad."

"There is too much at stake for gladness, Minna." Maude swung away from the window to face the older woman. "Do you not understand? My hopes, my crown, my son's legacy—all are balanced upon the blade of a sword. My future will be decided at Lincoln, but not by me. I cannot even be there to watch whilst others decree my fate. Because the Lord God saw fit to make me a woman, I can do naught but wait."

13

NOTTINGHAMSHIRE, ENGLAND

January 1141

If winter was the enemy, January was its cruelest weapon. The weather was wet and raw, the road a quagmire of churned-up mud, the men sodden and cold and miserable. They were also uneasy, for warfare as they knew it was comprised of sieges and raids; pitched battles such as they faced at Lincoln were rare. But they kept slogging ahead, mile after plodding mile, impelled by the sheer force of Robert Fitz Roy's will. He'd already done what many would have thought impossible; in just a fortnight, he'd assembled an army formidable enough to threaten a king. When he then announced that they must be at Claybrook in Leicestershire by January 26th, his men laughed among themselves and made skeptical jokes about sprouting wings. But they reached Claybrook on that last Sunday in January, just as Robert had determined they would, and found the Earl of Chester waiting for them.

They all had the same objectives in mind—the overthrow of the king and a soldier's chance for plunder—and so there should not have been friction between the two forces. Yet there was. It was due in part to Chester himself, for he was not an easy ally, and some of the strain inevitably trickled down through the ranks. But Chester's abrasive personality was only half the problem. Riding with his Cheshire vassals and tenants was a sizable contingent of Welsh mercenaries.

Nearly seventy-five years had passed since William the Bastard had led an invading army onto English shores, but those sons and grandsons born after the Conquest did not consider themselves English. *English* was a word with negative connotations, for it referred to a people who spoke an odd tongue and clung to odd customs, a defeated people. Those of

Norman-French descent felt vastly superior to the subjugated English, and that muted their hostility. They had not been as successful, though, in subduing the Welsh. The Welsh were a vexing, unpredictable people, fiercely independent, and few of Robert's soldiers were willing to embrace them as allies—with one singular exception.

To Ranulf, Wales was a mysterious, alien land of foreboding mountains and blood feuds and Celtic craziness. Much of the time, he even forgot that he was half Welsh, for his mother had been dead for fifteen years and her gentle, elusive spirit had faded long ago into the shadows, leaving him with vague memories of a sweet smile, bedtime hugs, and a lingering fragrance of spring flowers.

All that Ranulf now knew of Wales he'd learned from Robert, whose marriage to Amabel had brought him the lordship of Glamorgan. Wales, Robert had explained, was a hodgepodge of rival realms, each ruled by its own brenin or king. The least significant of these kingdoms was in the south, where the Normans had made the greatest inroads. North Wales was known to the Welsh as Gwynedd, and ruled for the past three years by a man Robert respected, Owain Gwynedd, while the third kingdom was Powys, governed by one Madog ap Maredudd.

According to Robert, theirs was a rural, tribal society, lacking cities or castles or comforts, for the Welsh were hunters and herdsmen, not farmers. He'd found them to be a volatile people, equally passionate in their loves and their hates, uncaring of hardship, generous, vengeful, light of heart, often fickle of purpose, but always inordinately proud of their small mountainous corner of the world. Although Robert had tried to be scrupulously fair, it was clear to Ranulf that Welsh virtues were not those his brother would value, save only what Robert deemed their "marvelous, mad courage."

On those rare occasions when Wales had insinuated itself into Ranulf's awareness, he'd sometimes thought he might like to learn more about this shadowy land and its perplexing people. But he'd never truly expected to have such an opportunity. Yet suddenly here he was, riding alongside his mother's countrymen up the Fosse Way as they headed north into Nottinghamshire. The sound of Welsh, lilting in cadence and utterly incomprehensible to his ear, had begun to stir old memories, long buried, of a small boy listening sleepily as his mother talked wistfully of her homeland and family. She'd sung to him in Welsh, and he realized in surprise that he must have spoken her language, too, but all of his childhood Welsh had sunk down into the bottom depths of his brain, beyond salvaging. And he soon discovered, much to his disappointment, that Chester's Welsh hirelings spoke little or no French.

Their leaders did, of course. They were both men of importance in their own world, for Cadwaladr ap Gruffydd was the younger brother of a king, Owain Gwynedd, and Madog ap Maredudd was himself a Welsh king, Brenin of Powys. Cadwaladr attracted more attention, for he was bold by nature and not loath to speak his mind. He had a ready smile, a certain cocky charm, but Ranulf had come to mistrust charm; Stephen had taught him that. He was wary of Cadwaladr, the discontented younger brother, and Madog ap Maredudd had no interest in satisfying the curiosity of a Norman-French lordling. But on their third day after departing Claybrook, Ranulf found Gwern, who was good-natured and disarmingly forthright and spoke fluent French.

Gwern was a lean, weathered soldier of middle height like Ranulf, but swarthy as a Saracen, no longer young. He'd cheerfully admitted to "forty winters," joking that it was "pitiful, an old man like me chasing after English rebels," and when Ranulf reminded him that they were the rebels, he'd roared with laughter, obviously quite untroubled by the intricacies of English politics. From Gwern, Ranulf learned that Cadwaladr and Madog were linked by marriage and a shared jealousy of Owain Gwynedd, brother and royal rival. He learned that the Welsh scorned the chain-mail armor of the Norman knight, that their weapon of choice was the spear in the North and the bow in the South, and that Gwern hoped this war amongst the English would go on for years.

"No offense, lad, but whilst you're busy killing one another, you'll be keeping your Norman noses out of Wales!" Ranulf couldn't help laughing, and was rewarded with a miracle, for when Gwern discovered his name, he exclaimed, "The old king's son? By God, then you're Angharad's lad!"

Ranulf was dubious at first, almost afraid to believe. Gwern saw his doubt, and clouted him playfully on the shoulder. "There are no strangers in Gwynedd. Hellfire, most of us are kin of some sort. And that was quite a scandal in its day—the English king and Rhys ap Cynan's daughter. Nor was she a lass that any man would soon forget, as shy as a fawn and just as good to look upon, with hair the color of newly churned butter and a smile like a candle in the dark." He saw Ranulf's sudden grin and chuckled self-consciously. "Aye, I'll own up to it, I was mad for the girl, me and half the striplings in the Conwy Valley. Her going left quite a hole in many a Welsh lad's lustings!"

Ranulf laughed, for now he knew that Gwern was not just telling him what he wanted to hear. He had indeed known Angharad, for she'd been that rarity, a Welshwoman as fair as any Norse maid, with sun-streaked tawny hair that she'd passed on to her son. "I know nothing of her kin," he confided. "Does she still have family in . . . that valley?"

Gwern was shocked by Ranulf's self-confessed ignorance, for to the Welsh, nothing mattered more than bloodlines. "Indeed so, lad. Her father was long dead, of course, when the English king took her, and mayhap just as well. Now poor Emlyn died of a fever ten years back, and Math was slain in a border skirmish soon after. But Rhodri is hale as can be . . . your uncle, lad, and a good man he is. In fact, his firstborn was set upon coming with Cadwaladr . . . Cadell, your cousin. But Rhodri got wind of it in time. He'd buried two sons already, was not about to risk a shallow English grave for Cadell.

"I called him a good man, and God's Truth, he is, but he is an unlucky one, too. Two boys dead ere they reached manhood, a wife gone to God just two years back, a babe smothered in her cradle, another daughter who'll never find a husband . . . he's borne more than his share of sorrows. Small blame to him for wanting to keep Cadell close by the hearth!"

Ranulf was startled by the rush of sympathy he felt for this unknown uncle of his. "Rhodri," he echoed, and a forgotten memory revived. "He was younger than my mother, was he not?"

Gwern nodded vigorously. "If my memory serves, there were two years between them. He was barely thirteen at the time, and none blamed him for being unable to play a man's part, but he blamed himself, for he was right fond of Angharad. Wait till he hears I met her son!"

Ranulf was no longer smiling. "I see," he said flatly. "So her family thought she'd shamed herself by running off with the king." And although he could hardly blame Angharad's menfolk for thinking so, he resented it, nonetheless, on his mother's behalf.

Gwern's dark eyes flickered in surprise. "The shame was not hers, lad. How could she be blamed when it was not her doing? We Welsh are fairer to our women than that."

Ranulf stared at him. "Are you saying my father took her against her will?"

Gwern shrugged. "Well, he did not truss her up and throw her across his saddle. But neither did he ask for her yea or nay." He saw that Ranulf was truly shocked, and added, by way of comfort, "Kings are never ones for asking, though, are they?"

Ranulf said nothing. He'd been thinking that mayhap he might bring Annora into Wales once they were wed and Maude's England at peace again, for the idea was an appealing one, making a leisurely pilgrimage to this Conwy Valley to seek out his newfound uncle and cousins. But that would have been a fool's quest. What reason would they have to welcome him, the seed sprung from an enemy's lust? And after that, he avoided Gwern as much as possible, no longer at ease with the affable Welshman.

ON the first day of February, the citizens of Lincoln awoke to slate-colored skies and icy rain. Cursing and coughing, Stephen's soldiers grimly manned his siege machines. Slipping in the mud, they loaded heavy stones into the mangonels, sent them crashing into the castle bailey. Others labored upon the belfry, hammering out their frustrations upon the wet wood, dropping nails as they blew upon their chapped hands to ward off the cold. They had not yet begun covering the tower in the vinegar-soaked hides meant to repel fire-arrows, but unless the weather took an even nastier turn, by midweek the belfry would be ready to be wheeled up to the castle wall. Each of its four stories would shelter men, crouching within while bowmen on the top level drove the castle defenders off the wall. The belfry drawbridge would then drop down onto the battlements, they would scramble across, and the final battle for Lincoln Castle would begin.

For Stephen's soldiers, it could not come a day too soon, especially now that rumors were sweeping the city of an approaching enemy army. They wanted this accursed siege over and done with; winter warfare was, for most men, a frigid foretaste of Hell.

The rain slackened by noon, but the sky stayed dark and foreboding. Stephen did not return to his lodgings at the Bishop of Lincoln's palace until dusk. It had been an awkward arrangement at first, for Bishop Alexander's memories of the Oxford ambush were still sharp enough to rankle. He had not forgiven Stephen for his disgrace, the downfall of his uncle and cousins. But once the Earl of Chester seized Lincoln Castle, Stephen's sins began to dwindle in the bishop's eyes, and he was determined to do whatever he could to root out Chester's evil influence from his city and his see.

Supper was neither festive nor memorable, for the bishop's cooks were restricted to a Saturday fish menu. Afterward, none strayed too far from the open hearth. Stephen and the bishop began to play a game of chess; at least that spared them the need to make polite, stilted conversation. Waleran Beaumont was in a morose mood, nursing a chest cold and bored with Lincoln, Stephen, and the siege. Next time, he vowed, he'd be the one to tend to Beaumont interests in Normandy; brother Robert could have the dubious pleasure of flushing out rebels from their rat-holes. He perked up a bit, though, when William de Ypres suggested a game of hasard. Although gambling was frowned upon by the Church, the bishop's guests knew he was too worldly to take offense, and once a pair of dice was found, Waleran and the Fleming took on the Earls of York and Pembroke. Pembroke's younger brother Baldwin, the Earl of Northampton, William Peverel, and Hugh Bigod soon came over to watch, bedeviling the players and making side wagers of their own.

There was talk of the belfry, and then some speculation about the Earl of Chester's whereabouts, for rumors had begun to circulate that he was no longer holed up in the castle. By the time Gilbert de Gant joined the group, conversation had shifted to the new serving-wench at the alehouse in Danesgate Road.

Few topics were of greater interest to Gilbert than women, especially wanton ones; he was by far the youngest lord there, still in his teens. But for once he had other, more pressing matters on his mind. He wanted to discuss the rumors, for he did not understand why Stephen and his battle captains had given them so little credence. He was hesitant, though, to be the one to bring the subject up, for he was a battlefield virgin and these men were veterans. He waited until the first game ended, and while the men were summoning servants for wine and ale, he drew Baldwin de Clare aside. No matter how green or foolish his questions, Baldwin would not laugh, for his own military experience was limited to a disastrous expedition against the Welsh.

"Why is it, Baldwin, that no one believes the report of an army being sighted in Nottinghamshire? Why could it not be true?"

"I can give you one hundred and seventy or so reasons, Gilbert—the miles stretching between Lincoln and Bristol."

"Does it have to be the Earl of Gloucester? What about the Earl of Chester? Mayhap he did escape . . . ?"

"No matter, for Cheshire is nearly as far. An army on the march in the dead of winter would be lucky to cover eight miles a day. Then you have to allow for all the time it would take to raise an army. We were able to head north so fast because Stephen's Flemish hirelings were on hand; that is what he pays them for, after all. But I'd wager it would take the Earl of Gloucester a month to muster up enough men. When you then consider time for word of the siege to get out, you've now accounted for all of January and most of February. There is no way under God's sky that an enemy army could be nearing Lincoln, not unless Robert Fitz Roy taught his troops to fly!"

Gilbert was very glad he hadn't asked in front of the others; he'd have been teased about his "phantom flying army" for days to come. He looked so abashed that Baldwin took pity on him. "Come on, lad," he said, "let's go find ourselves some fun."

Gilbert grinned, ran to fetch his mantle, hoping that Baldwin's idea of fun was a bawdy-house. But before they could start their search, one of the bishop's servants was hastening into the hall. A man had just ridden in with an urgent message for the king. Should he be admitted?

Stephen welcomed the interruption; he was losing. Pushing away from the chessboard, he said, "Send him in."

As the man entered the hall, the bishop leaned toward Stephen. "I know him," he said. "That is Torger of Hunsgate, a local mercer." In answer then, to Stephen's unspoken query, he nodded. "Yes, he is reliable."

The merchant came forward, knelt before Stephen. "I bring grievous news, my liege. Those rumors of an army—Lord help us, for they were true."

The hall was immediately in turmoil, as men pushed in to hear, the dice game forgotten. Stephen silenced them, then tersely ordered Torger to continue. Drawing a steadying breath, he did.

"I was on my way to Newark, for I'd agreed to buy some woolens and silks and could not lose the deal just because the weather was foul. But I never reached Newark, my liege. I was only halfway there when I heard sounds ahead of approaching horses and men. I barely had time to get off the road and into the woods ere they came into view. They did not see me and passed on by, banners sodden in the rain, more men than I could count, mounted and on foot, heading up the Fosse Way toward Lincoln."

"You saw their banners?"

The mercer nodded. "It was the Earl of Chester. I recognized him straightaway. And the Earl of Gloucester. I saw his banner, saw his face. It was Robert Fitz Roy, my liege, I'd stake my life on it."

There was a flabbergasted silence. "How far were they from Lincoln?" Stephen asked in disbelief.

"They are less than ten miles away, my lord king," Torger said bleakly, and spoke for them all when he added, "Thank God that the rains have made the river and the fosse too dangerous to cross!"

ROBERT'S men passed a nervous, uncomfortable night camped just to the southwest of the city. The temperature plunged, and as they burrowed into their blankets in a futile search for warmth, they feared they might face snow on the morrow. But when Candlemas Sunday dawned, the sky had been swept clear of clouds by a gusting, northerly wind. Ice glazed the browned winter grass, glinted ominously midst the reeds of the soggy marshland that lay between them and Lincoln. The city was protected by the River Witham and the Fossedyke, an ancient canal of Roman origin, restored by the old king twenty years past. The river was impassable, running at flood tide. Robert hoped, though, to cross the Fossedyke at a ford known to his scouts, Lincolnshire men he'd sent out at first light. But they were soon back with disheartening news. The ford was being guarded by some of Stephen's men. The marshes along the Fossedyke were knee-deep in runoff from the storm, and the canal's water level was much higher than normal, surging with the spillover from the rain-swollen river.

Those listening were dismayed—all but Robert, who said calmly, "If we must cross this marsh, then we will," and that was enough for most of his men, who were learning to take his word as gospel. After all, they reminded one another, he'd promised the empress that he'd raise an army within a fortnight, and by Corpus, he had. He'd said that they'd meet

Chester at Claybrook on the 26th, and they had. They'd seen pig wallows less muddy than the roads of these shires, and had there been any more rain, they'd have needed an ark, and they'd gotten enough saddle sores and blisters to last a lifetime, but they'd covered more than ten miles a day, and it was the earl's doing. So if he said they'd get through this quagmire, then they would, they agreed among themselves, and they made haste to obey his order to break camp.

Their optimism lasted until they saw the fenlands for themselves, for the flooding was more extensive than any of them had expected. Robert gave them no time to reconsider and they were soon splashing through cold, murky marshwater, linking arms for leverage, coaxing recalcitrant horses, complaining that they were wetter than drowned cats, swearing when the mud threatened to suck off their boots, and shouting in triumph when they caught a dull grey gleam through the waist-high rushes ahead.

The waters of the Fossedyke ran fast and cold, surging west toward the River Trent. On the opposite bank, Stephen's sentries sat their horses in astonishment, staring across at these wet, muddied apparitions as if doubting their own senses. Robert and his battle captains drew rein at the canal's edge, trying to gauge its depth. It was, they agreed, not as shallow as it should be. But the ford must still be there, else Stephen would not have posted guards.

"Well," Robert concluded, to no one's surprise, "there is but one way to find out." But he then startled them all by saying, "It is only fair that I be the one to test it. If I seem likely to make it across, I'd welcome some help on the other side," he added dryly, and drawing his sword from its scabbard, he spurred his stallion forward into the water.

Chester was the first to react. His flaws might be beyond counting, as his enemies alleged, but none had ever accused him of timidity. "What are we waiting for?" he challenged, and charged into the Fossedyke after Robert.

Ranulf and Brien were quick to follow, but it was the Welsh prince Cadwaladr who made sure that no man would dare balk. "Come on, lads," he called out cheerfully in Welsh, "let's show these pampered English that they need not fear getting their feet wet!" And laughing as if he relished nothing more than a winter's soaking in icy waters, he plunged into the Fossedyke. The Welsh needed no further urging, scrambled down the bank and splashed into the canal.

After that, they all had to cross over, even those who most feared drowning, for they could not let themselves be shamed by these "misbegotten Welsh churls," and they waded into the Fossedyke, shivering and cursing at the first shock of frigid water on their legs. Fortunately the storm-fed current was still not too deep at the ford, and by the time they reached the opposite shore, there was no need to fumble for weapons.

Stephen's vastly outnumbered guards were already in retreat, fleeing with a frantic warning for Stephen, that the enemy would soon be at the city gates.

FEBRUARY 2ND was a holy day of special significance, the Feast of the Purification of the Blessed Virgin Mary, commonly known as Candlemas. Stephen heard Mass in the great cathedral of St Mary, and dozens of anxious citizens crowded into the church to hear the bishop celebrate the Eucharist and to study the king for clues, for some indication as to what he meant to do. They already knew he was being advised to withdraw, to leave behind enough men to hold Lincoln until he could return with a larger army. That rumor had raced through the city, faster than any fire and just as frightening, for the men and women of Lincoln would feel safe only as long as Stephen was personally taking charge of their defense.

It was not surprising, therefore, that they reacted with such alarm when Stephen's candle suddenly snapped in half as he held it out to the bishop. A simple mishap . . . or a sinister portent? Judging from the murmuring he heard sweeping the church, Stephen well knew which explanation seemed more likely to the congregation. During the remainder of the Mass, he could not keep his thoughts upon the Almighty as he ought, distracted by his anger and his disappointment. For if they were so sure that a broken candle was an ill omen, their faith in his kingship must be wavering.

Once the Mass was done, Stephen headed toward the transept door leading out into the cloister garth, waving his companions away when they started to follow. He was given only a brief respite, though, only a few moments of quiet and solitude, for Waleran soon grew impatient and barged out into the cloisters after him, with the Earls of Northampton and York close behind.

"We need to talk, my liege," Waleran insisted, "for we've settled nothing. As I told you last night, we ought not to let them force us into any rash action. We'd be foolish to take the field without enough men to make sure victory would be ours."

Stephen had heard all this before, until the early hours of the morning. "And as I told you, Waleran," he said testily, "I will not run from rebels."

"Stay here in Lincoln, then. But call up the shire levies, let us summon our own vassals—" Waleran broke off in exasperation, for Stephen was no longer listening. Turning to find out why, he saw William de Ypres striding up the walkway toward them. Ypres had scandalized the bishop by missing the Candlemas Mass, instead riding off to judge for himself the immediacy of the danger posed by Robert Fitz Roy's army. One look at his face now was enough to warn them that they'd not like what they were about to hear.

"If you're all still debating what to do," Ypres said grimly, "I can make it easy for you. We're running out of choices, for we've run out of time. That flooded quagmire everyone was so sure could not be crossed? Well, someone neglected to tell Robert Fitz Roy it was impassable."

There were exclamations at that, for by now all of Stephen's battle commanders were crowding into the cloister garth, along with the bishop and more and more of the town's apprehensive citizens. But Stephen ignored their clamoring.

"So they got across the marshes," he said, not bothering—as some of the others were—with futile denials. It mattered little if every living soul in Christendom would have sworn it could not be done; if William de Ypres said it was so, Stephen did not doubt him. "And the Fossedyke?" he asked, although he was already anticipating what the Fleming would say.

"They crossed at the ford, whilst your guards fled like women. By the time I got there, they were lighting fires to thaw themselves out. What they do next depends upon you, my liege—whether you come out to give battle or force them to besiege the city."

"Are we outnumbered?"

"As far as I could tell, but not by much. And you have the more seasoned soldiers under your command. The Welsh are worthless on the field, will break and run at their first chance. As for the Cheshiremen . . . who knows what they'll do when put to the test? If you are asking me, my liege, if we can win, I'd say you can. But I'm no soothsayer, cannot promise you victory."

"Just so," Waleran said emphatically. "Why should we risk defeat when there are other roads still open to us? I say we hold fast within the town, then send for an army that can give us certain victory. It makes no sense to take the field unless we can be sure of the outcome, and for that, we will need more than God's Favor and the good wishes of the townspeople."

The bishop was highly indignant. "My lord Earl of Worcester, you blaspheme," he said hotly, "for what power can be greater than God's Favor?"

Waleran could see the bishop was ready to launch into a lengthy lecture, and he sought to head it off with a brusque admission that he had "misspoken." But he was too late, the damage already done, for Stephen was glaring at him accusingly.

"Do you think I fear God's Judgment?" Stephen demanded. "Those men are rebels, in arms against their lawful king. How could the Almighty ever give them victory? No, I will not shrink from this battle. Better to make an end to this, here and now. We have right on our side and I am willing to prove it upon the field. I'll not cower behind these walls whilst traitors and renegades threaten the peace of my realm. We will fight and we will win."

SO sure was Robert that Stephen would come out to confront them that as soon as his men were dried off, he set about assembling them in battle array. This sparked an argument with the Earl of Chester, who insisted that he should have the honour of striking the first blow, the quarrel being his. But Robert pointed out that Maude's grievance was greater, and he prevailed.

Robert's battle tactics held no surprises, for he was a highly capable commander but not an innovative one, and he chose the traditional formation: two lines of horsemen flanking the center, which would fight on foot. The left wing, or vanguard, would lead the first assault, and for that crucial offensive, Robert shrewdly chose those men who'd had their lands confiscated by Stephen, men like Baldwin de Redvers and William Fitz Alan, men with nothing to lose. These knights, the "Disinherited," would fight under the most formidable of Robert's battle captains, Miles Fitz Walter. Chester was to have command of the center, and Robert himself took the right wing, while the Welsh were positioned out in front of his mounted knights.

Robert then made the commander's customary speech to his troops, reviling the enemy and predicting victory, for their cause was just. A prayer was said and a priest called upon the Almighty to bless their efforts with success.

By then, Stephen's army had already ridden out through the city's West Gate. Aligning his men along the slope that extended from the town wall down to the Fossedyke, Stephen thus began with a tactical advantage, for the enemy would have to charge uphill. Stephen chose to command his center, entrusting his left wing to William de Ypres and the Earl of York, who'd earned his earldom by defeating the Scots king so decisively at the battle in Yorkshire two summers ago. His right wing was, like Robert's, a division of mounted knights, leadership shared among the Earls of Worcester, Pembroke, Surrey, Northampton, and Richmond and Hugh Bigod, for none of those prideful lords were willing to defer to the others.

Because Stephen's voice was softly pitched and did not carry well, young Baldwin de Clare was chosen to speak to the troops on the king's behalf, and pleased by the honour, he began zestfully ridiculing their enemies, promising both victory and retribution. But his spirited oration was cut off in midflow by the blaring of trumpets. Not willing to wait any longer, the other army was moving to the attack.

RANULF had asked to fight under Robert's command. Never had he been so proud of his brother as in the weeks of this campaign. Robert did not have a flamboyant bone in his body; he weighed his words and pondered his actions, and in both speech and manner, showed all the élan and flair of a sedate, scholarly clerk. Even when he'd plunged into the Fossedyke, he'd made it seem perfectly natural and not particularly heroic. Ranulf loved his brother dearly, knew him to be a man of honour. But until now he'd not appreciated just what Robert could accomplish in his quiet, understated way. He yearned to tell Robert of his newfound admiration, but of course he could not, for that would have embarrassed them both. Instead, he said a special prayer for Robert's safety, and then reined in his stallion at Robert's side so they could watch together the beginning of the battle.

Ranulf had never fought in a pitched battle between equal forces, his experiences of warfare limited to Geoffrey's skirmishings in Normandy and raids upon Worcester and Nottingham with Robert and Miles. He was by turns, excited, apprehensive, fearful, and eager, and as he glanced over his shoulder, he saw those same contradictory emotions chasing across the faces of his friends. Gilbert urged his mount forward to ask, "Ranulf, think you that Ancel is with Stephen's army?"

"I hope not," Ranulf said, but he did hope Gervase Fitz Clement was fighting with Stephen, and God forgive him, but he hoped, too, that when the dead were counted at day's end, Annora's husband would be amongst them. He was too ashamed to admit it, and felt a superstitious pang of unease, for what goes around comes around and evil rebounds upon the wisher. He could not help himself, though, for the thought persisted: How much easier it would be if Annora were widowed on this Candlemas Sunday.

Miles signaled and his trumpets blasted again; the horses lengthened stride. Up on the hillside, Stephen's vanguard began a slow advance upon the enemy. The wind unfurled their banners; Waleran and Hugh Bigod were in the forefront. They had lowered their lances, preparing to joust in the French fashion, a formalized fighting that knights favored, for it looked dashing and chivalrous and rarely resulted in fatalities. But the Disinherited were not interested in tournament-style tilting. They wanted victory and vengeance and blood, and they spurred their stallions forward with wild yells, eager to sheathe their swords in enemy flesh, slamming into Stephen's knights with enough force to send horses back on their haunches.

Lances were useless in close quarters, and were hastily flung aside as men struggled to draw their swords, to defend themselves against this murderous onslaught. The Disinherited knights bore in with savage single-mindedness, not seeking to take prisoners or collect ransoms, just to slay as many of their foes as they could, and Stephen's astonished earls found themselves fighting for their lives.

It was not a fair match, men with nothing to lose against those with little to gain, and it was over with shocking abruptness. As Miles charged at a knight on a bay destrier, the horse shied away, and when it bolted, the rider let it go. And as suddenly as that, Stephen's vanguard broke and ran. The earls made no attempt to halt the flight. Instead, they joined it, and within moments, the muddy slope was emptied of all but dropped weapons and sprawling bodies. As both armies looked on in amazement, Stephen's men spurred their horses away from the field, racing toward the north with the Disinherited in triumphant pursuit.

Stephen was stunned; four of the five fugitive earls owed their earldoms to him. He could not believe they'd betray his trust like this, kept watching for them to rally their men and return to the field. But they were not coming back, Waleran and Northampton and Surrey, men of proven courage, fleeing like cravens, abandoning their king. All around him, he saw dismayed and distraught faces. Baldwin de Clare, flushed with shame on his brother Pembroke's behalf. Gilbert de Gant, wax-white and wide-eyed, looking much too young to die on this Candlemas battlefield. William Peverel, whose loyalty Stephen had once doubted, and the citizens of Lincoln, who had as much to lose as Stephen did. He read the fear in their eyes, and said reassuringly, "The battle is not over yet." Swinging about toward the distant forces of his left wing, he signaled them to the attack.

RANULF'S ears were ringing, for men were shouting and cheering as if they were spectators at a rousing game of camp-ball. He was just as jubilant, but he also felt a small, unwelcome pinch of sympathy for Stephen, deserted by the very men whom he had most reason to trust. And then the shouting changed, and he soon saw why, for Stephen's left wing was in motion, galloping straight toward them.

Ranulf unsheathed his sword, looked to Robert for guidance. But between them and William de Ypres's oncoming knights were the Welsh. They were so poorly armed that Ranulf winced as they ran to meet the attack, and felt a sudden flare of anger at Chester and Robert, for putting them in a position of such peril. He wore a chain-mail hauberk that protected him from neck to knees, and a steel helmet with nose guard. The Welsh had padded leather tunics, legs and arms bared to enemy blows, small shields, and spears to deflect sword thrusts. If he feared for them, though, they did not seem to fear for themselves, charging forward with the same beguiling, mad bravado that had sent them splashing into the icy waters of the Fossedyke.

What happened next was horrifying to Ranulf, for William de Ypres and the Earl of York and their men rode the Welsh down. It looked like a slaughter, swords flashing and bodies going under the flailing hooves, men crying out to God in three tongues: Welsh, French, and Flemish. But as the knights and Flemings raced on, many of the downed Welsh were stumbling to their feet, apparently neither mortally hurt nor much disheartened, for instead of fleeing the field like Stephen's defeated vanguard, some of them heeded Cadwaladr and Madog ap Maredudd and sprinted toward the Earl of Chester's wind-whipped banner.

It did not occur to Ranulf to wonder why he was so concerned about the safety of these alien Welsh mercenaries. He had time only for a heartfelt hope that Gwern was among those hastening to join Chester's center, not one of the bodies trampled underfoot by those battle-maddened warhorses. And then Ypres and York and their Flemings were upon them.

It was Ranulf's first encounter with hand-to-hand combat, and it changed forever his view of war as a gallant, glorious adventure. This was an ugly, desperate, deadly brawl, a drunken alehouse free-for-all, except that he faced swords, not fists, with far more to fear than bruises or a bloodied nose. He'd been trained in the use of weapons, knew how to dodge and parry blows and keep his shield close against his unprotected left side. But so did the enemy.

Almost at once, he found himself crossing swords with a yelling youth in bloodied armor. Welsh blood, Ranulf thought, and jerked back just in time, as the blade slashed past his ear. The Fleming had mottled skin, a bright-yellow beard. His mouth was contorted, his breath coming in grunts as he moved in to strike again. Their shields thudded together, and for a moment of odd intimacy, they were near enough to see into each other's eyes. His enemy's were green. Ranulf would remember those eyes and that face, for this was to be the first man he ever killed. The Fleming looked shocked as Ranulf's sword thrust through his mail, up under his ribs. Ranulf was shocked, too. He wrenched his sword free, blade dark with blood, and found that he could not swallow, had not even enough saliva to spit. He'd noticed before the battle that many soldiers carried small flasks or wineskins on their belts, had not understood the significance. He did now. Men who went too often into battle had more need of wine than any drunkard.

Some knights had gone down, for there were riderless horses milling about on the field, terrified without the familiar feel of their riders upon their backs, yet still hovering near the fighting. Like horses who'd balk at leaving their stalls even if the stable were in flames, Ranulf thought, and then decided he must be going mad, else why be thinking of stable fires in the midst of Armageddon? He had another clash with an enemy knight, inconclusive but not unsatisfactory, for they both survived it. He had just two objectives—staying alive and finding Robert—and when he did spot his brother, it was as he'd feared. Robert was being hard pressed on all sides, a tempting target for any man hoping to curry favor with Stephen.

Ranulf began to fight his way over. But he was still yards from his brother when a knight on a lathered black stallion careened into him, knocking his horse to its knees. The knight rose in his stirrups, sword poised to strike, and Ranulf swung his shield up to deflect the blow. The impact rocked him back in the saddle, and suddenly his shield was gone, the strap breaking as his stallion lurched to its feet. By then the other knight was attacking again, and this time his sword's tip caught and tore away metal rings from Ranulf's hauberk. Pain seared down Ranulf's arm. He ducked low in the saddle as the follow-through whizzed over his head. But the tide of battle shifted then, swept his foe away, and he turned again to look for Robert.

Robert's danger was even greater now. He'd been unhorsed, was struggling to protect himself from three determined opponents, one on horseback, two on foot. He'd not been forsaken by his household knights, but they were in trouble themselves, for William de Ypres knew how devastating Robert's death or capture would be, and his Flemings were jostling and cursing one another in their eagerness to get to the Earl of Gloucester.

Ranulf put his horse into a hard gallop, and the game animal plunged forward, crashing into the Flemings walling his brother in. He had no clear memory of the next moments, a blur of clashing swords and grappling bodies. His stallion, teeth bared like a huge, savage dog, raked open the neck of a screaming bay destrier, and then they were sliding in the mud, going down, and as Ranulf hit the ground, the truth hit him, too, that they were losing.

THE Earl of Chester's trumpets sounded, his banner took the wind, and his men began advancing up the muddy hillside toward the royal standard of the English king. The whole of the battlefield was open to view, for the few trees growing upon the slope had been stripped of all obscuring leaves, were now barren winter skeletons rising against the pale February sky.

They had not covered much ground before it became apparent to them all that their right wing was laboring and might not be able to hold.

Chester called for a halt. He prided himself upon making decisions that were swift and spontaneous, that "came from the gut," and he knew at once what he must do. He had the blackest eyes Brien Fitz Count had ever seen, and as his imagination caught fire, they glowed like smoldering coals.

"Stephen can wait," he said. "If we do not come to Gloucester's aid, that accursed Flemish whoreson might well prevail. But if we join the fray, we can trap his men between us, and his Flemings will scatter to the winds, intent only upon saving their own skins. Stephen does not pay them enough to die for him, now does he? Then we can turn upon Stephen at our ease, gaining so great a victory that men will be talking of nothing else for years to come!"

Brien glanced back at that seething mass of men and horses, his every instinct urging him to go to the rescue of their beleaguered right wing. How could he do nothing whilst Robert went down to defeat and mayhap death, Robert who was his friend and Maude's brother? "But what if Stephen then attacks us from behind? We could be the ones entrapped, not Ypres."

"He'll not have the chance, for even now Miles Fitz Walter must be on his way back to the field." Chester's teeth flashed white in his dark face, in a wolfish, avid smile that could already taste victory. "That Devil's whelp and I loathe each other, it's no secret. I've vowed to outlive him, if only for the pleasure of pissing on his grave. But Fitz Walter is still the man I'd want at my back, sword in hand, be it on the battlefield or in an alley of the Southwark stews," he said and gave a loud, ringing laugh. "He'll keep Stephen too busy to spare even a thought for us. On that I would wager my castle at Lincoln, my lustful little wife, and indeed, my hopes for salvation and Life Everlasting!"

"You'll be wagering your earthly life, too, and mine, and the lives of every man fighting under our banners," Brien warned, but that did not faze Chester in the least. He was already turning away, beginning to shout orders.

VICTORY was at hand. William de Ypres had fought in enough battles to read the signs. The faces of his enemies showed fatigue and fear and a despairing recognition of their own defeat. They'd not yet lost the will to fight, but slowly, inexorably, they were giving ground, being pushed back toward the cold grey waters of the Fossedyke.

The wind gave a muted warning, carrying ahead the sounds of shouting, thudding feet, echoes of a trumpet fanfare. The Flemings paid no heed, caught up in the frenzy of the battle. Ypres was one of the few who did. Cursing in Flemish, he swung his stallion about, tried frantically to alert his men to this new danger. But it was too late; Chester's soldiers were almost upon them.

The fighting was brutal, but brief. Robert's knights surged back with renewed vigor, Chester's men were eager to rout the hated Flemings so they could seek the battle's real prize—the king—and Ypres's soldiers, finding themselves outnumbered and overwhelmed, soon reached Chester's cynical conclusion: that Stephen was not paying them enough to die for him. First one and then another wheeled his horse, and then they were all in flight across the field, away from the fighting. William de Ypres and the Earl of York attempted at first to rally them, saw the futility in it, and they, too, fled.

For once the Earl of Chester got all the accolades he felt he deserved, and he found acclaim was especially sweet when it came from men who detested him. Shoving his way through to his father-in-law's side, he thrust a wineskin at Robert, waited impatiently as the older man drank in gulps.

"We're not done yet," he said, and looked about at Robert's bleeding, battered knights and his own gleeful Cheshiremen. "But bear in mind," he warned, "that the king is mine!"

AS soon as Chester's center halted its advance, Stephen guessed what the rebel earl meant to do, and he immediately gave the order to attack. His men started down the slope, swords drawn. But by then Miles Fitz Walter had halted the pursuit of Stephen's runaway earls, rounded up most of his own men, and headed back toward the battlefield. They arrived onto a scene of utter chaos. At first glance, it looked as if their center was attacking their right wing, and a few of the Disinherited briefly suspected it might indeed be so, for it was generally agreed that the Earl of Chester would double-cross the Devil on a good day. Miles needed just one look, though, to comprehend what had happened in his absence. "Seek out the king!" he commanded, and his knights charged over the crest of the hill.

Stephen's soldiers scattered as the Disinherited rode into their midst. But they did not lose heart, and quickly rallied to Stephen's side. Miles had the advantage of surprise, but they had the greater numbers, and some of the fiercest fighting of the battle now took place. Stephen more than held his own, and when he caught a glimpse of Baldwin de Redvers, he lunged forward like a man possessed, for at last his enemy had a familiar face. After months and months of combating rumors and suspicions and smoke, he now had a flesh-and-blood foe before him, a rebel baron who could answer for his treachery as Maude could not, sword in hand.

But he never reached Redvers. Gilbert de Gant was running toward him. The boy had been keeping closer than Stephen's own shadow, and he'd tried to watch over the lad when he could, knowing this was Gilbert's first battle. Now he was shouting and pointing, but the noise was too great and Stephen could barely hear him.

". . . fleeing the field!" The youngster darted forward, in his agitation forgetting to keep his sword up. A knight on a blood-streaked stallion saw and bore down on the boy. Stephen shouted a warning that Gilbert couldn't hear. But at the last moment, he sensed danger, spun around too fast, and stumbled, falling into the path of the oncoming stallion. The knight was quite willing to run him down, but the horse was not. The stallion swerved and by the time the knight circled back, Stephen was there. Facing now a far more formidable adversary than Gilbert, the man veered off in search of easier quarry.

Yanking Gilbert to his feet, Stephen brushed aside his stuttered thanks. "Christ, lad, keep your guard up if you hope to make old bones!"

Gilbert gulped and nodded and then remembered. "The Flemings . . . they are running away!"

STEPHEN had been shocked by the flight of his earls. But he took William de Ypres's defection even harder, for he'd come to trust the Fleming, convincing himself that Ypres was more than a well-paid hireling, that he truly cared who was king in a land not his own. He kept insisting that Ypres would be coming back, that he'd rally his Flemings and return to the fight. But Ypres was long gone, and Stephen found himself alone on a cold, muddy battlefield with the knights of his household and the scared citizens of Lincoln, abandoned by his own barons and his most trusted captains, surrounded by the enemy, men in rebellion against a consecrated king.

They were being assailed now on three sides, and retreated slowly up the hill. But once they reached Stephen's royal standard, he looked up at the golden lions on a field of crimson and refused to go any farther. They pleaded with him to seek safety within the city, for the battle had been fought within sight of its walls. Stephen was deaf to their urgings, and at last Baldwin de Clare cried out in anguish, "My liege, do you not understand? We are beaten!"

"I know," Stephen said. "That is why you must save yourselves now. Go and go quickly, whilst you still can."

They looked at him, and then one by one, they took up position around his standard, shoulder to shoulder as they braced themselves for the final assault. Tears stung Stephen's eyes, for they did not ask if his quarrel was good or his cause was just. He was their king and that was enough. Their steadfast loyalty made it easier to bear, the dreadful realization that he'd been abandoned, too, by Almighty God, judged as a king and found wanting, not deserving of victory.

The last moments of the Battle of Lincoln were the bloodiest. Encircled by the enemy, Stephen and his men fought off one attack after another, but his foes kept coming back, until Stephen found himself shielded by the bodies of those who'd fallen. His sword was bloody to the hilt; so was his chain mail, even his beard. When he saw William Peverel go down, he lashed out at Peverel's assailant with such force that his blade snapped against the man's shield. Almost at once one of the townsmen thrust a Danish axe into his hands, and it, too, was soon sticky with blood.

He'd taken blows, and beneath his hauberk, his body was already darkening with massive bruises and contusions, and he was soaked in sweat, as if it were a day in summer. He was so exhausted that he'd begun to feel drunk. The air itself was pressing him down, and he moved like a man walking through water. His throat had closed up, his head was throbbing, and when he brought his battle-axe down upon a man's shoulder, it seemed to descend in slow motion, to take days to slice through chain mail to the flesh and bone beneath. But through it all, he could still see his golden lions streaming above his head, gilded by the sun, the royal arms of England.

Baldwin de Clare was no longer at his side, and Gilbert de Gant was gone, too. He reeled back, panting, against the pole of his standard, intent only upon wielding his axe as long as his arms had the strength to lift it. But then he saw a familiar face, and the fatigue fogging his brain receded, enough for him to cry hoarsely, "Ranulf?" He did not trust his own senses anymore. But surely Ranulf was real? Almost close enough to touch, looking so stricken and so young, like Gilbert de Gant, who might be dead.

"Name of God, Stephen, surrender, I beg you!"

Stephen looked at his cousin, poor lad, but with no breath to speak, no time to explain why he could not do what Ranulf wanted. He shook his head and his vision blurred briefly. He nearly dropped the axe and a shadow lunged at him. When he swung the axe up again, he saw that his enemies had backed off and Ranulf was shouting like a madman at a knight sprawled at his feet, his sword leveled at the man's throat.

"My liege." This was a voice he knew, low-pitched and quiet, the way he'd heard men speak soothingly to skittish horses. A man was coming toward him across the muddy, trampled ground. There were gasps when he sheathed his sword, moved within range of that deadly Danish axe. "My liege, you've nothing left to prove," he said coaxingly. "You can surrender with honour."

"Get away, Brien," Stephen warned, and as their eyes met, the younger man reluctantly took a few backward steps. Stephen's next breath was ragged and uneven, but relieved. He'd have hated to split Brien's head open with his two-handed axe. It occurred to him that they need only wait him out, stand back and watch until he toppled over like a felled tree, too weak to keep on his feet.

And then something was happening. Voices rose, there was sudden movement, and men were scrambling to get out of the way as a horse was reined in scant yards from the royal standard. Stephen felt no surprise. He'd hunted with Chester often enough to know that the earl was always in at the kill.

Chester was in no hurry; this was a pleasure to be savored. For what seemed like forever to those watching, he regarded his foe, brought to bay under his own standard like a fox run to earth. Not so kingly now, by Christ. Swinging from the saddle, he put his hand on his sword hilt. "You can yield," he said, "or you can die. The choice is yours."

"Yield to you?" Stephen's voice cracked, for he had to force words up from a throat raw and parched. "Never," he said, and then his bruised, swollen mouth twisted into a smile, for God had not utterly forsaken him, after all.

Chester smiled, too. "So be it," he said, and then his sword was clearing its scabbard, and Ranulf flung himself forward, too late. He never even reached Chester, shoved aside by several of the earl's men. By the time Ranulf regained his feet, Chester was stalking Stephen, the steel of his blade glinting in the sun. He was grinning, looked to Ranulf as if he were truly enjoying himself. He feinted toward Stephen's left, then spun away and came in again fast, in a low, lethal lunge, and Stephen brought his battle-axe crashing down upon Chester's helmet. The blow had the last of Stephen's strength behind it, and Chester went facedown into the mud, did not move again.

The blow had broken Stephen's axe, the wooden haft splintering away from the blade. Stephen did not seem to have noticed yet, for he was still staring down at Chester's body. So were most of the men, and Ranulf was not the only one to feel disappointment when the earl moaned. And then someone—a number of men later claimed credit and Ranulf never knew which one spoke true—snatched up a large, heavy rock and hurled it at Stephen's head. It knocked his helmet askew, drove him to his knees, and a knight named William de Cahaignes, one of Robert's vassals, then threw himself upon Stephen, shouting, "I've got the king!"

Cahaignes kept yelling that, over and over: "I've got the king!" But as he wrenched off Stephen's dented helmet, Stephen somehow broke free and staggered to his feet. His head was so badly gashed that he was blinded by his own blood, and he was too dazed to draw his dagger, the only weapon he had left, yet when Cahaignes sought to grab him again, he knocked the other man's arm away.

"No," he said, "I'll not yield to you, only to Gloucester . . ."

Ranulf whirled to seek Robert, only to halt, afraid to leave Stephen alone and defenseless. But then the soldiers crowding around them began to move aside, to let a horseman pass through. Stephen was swaying, willing himself to stand erect even as the ground quaked under his feet. He watched as Maude's brother dismounted, and for a moment, they faced each other on the crest of the hill, in the shadow of Stephen's royal standard.

"Are you willing to yield?" Robert asked, and Stephen started to nod, but that slight movement caused him so much pain that he gave an audible, involuntary grunt.

"Yes," he said, but then he fumbled at his empty scabbard, with the puzzled frown of a man just awakening from an unpleasant dream. Only Ranulf understood. Pushing his way toward Stephen, he held out his sword. There were cries of protest and alarm at that, but by now, Robert, too, understood, and he raised his hand for silence. Stephen swayed again, then took several unsteady steps forward. Offering the weapon to Robert, hilt first, very deliberately, for he knew how it must be done, he surrendered to his victorious foe with his cousin's borrowed sword, and the Battle of Lincoln was over.

14

LINCOLN CASTLE, ENGLAND

February 1141

MORE than men had died at Lincoln. It seemed to Stephen that reality was a casualty, too, for nothing made sense anymore. What was he doing here in the solar of Lincoln Castle, bleeding all over the Earl of Chester's wife?

"I'm sorry," he said, but Maud was quite unfazed by the blood splattering her bodice.

"A good reason to get a new gown," she said cheerfully, continuing to daub at his gashed forehead with a wet cloth. "I think it is clean enough to bandage now. But a doctor ought to tend to it as soon as possible."

"Thank you," he said politely, although he knew his were wounds no doctor could hope to heal. He had claimed a crown, been consecrated with the sacred chrism that set him forever apart from other men, for a king was God's anointed on earth. He had believed in his right. So why, then, had he lost? Had his kingship been counterfeit from the very beginning? Had he wronged Maude and sinned against the Almighty by thwarting His Divine Will?

"All done," Maud murmured, stepping back to inspect her handiwork. Not only had her bandage stanched Stephen's bleeding, but she thought it looked rather rakish, too. Reaching for a flagon, she poured Stephen wine, relishing the incongruity of it, that she should be treating him as an esteemed guest when her husband would have cast him into the castle's darkest dungeon. But he was not here to object, and so she was taking a perverse pleasure in honouring his enemy—until it stopped being a game, until she noticed that Stephen had not touched the wine, that his blue eyes were blind and his hands clenched upon the arms of his chair as if it were all he had left to hold on to.

"I'll be back . . ." She hesitated, not knowing what to call him, for etiquette was conspicuously silent upon the subject of captive kings. She settled upon "Cousin Stephen" before giving him the only comfort she could at that moment: privacy.

Crossing the solar, she joined Stephen's gaoler in the window seat, and answered his unspoken query with a sigh. "He is in pain," she said softly, and Ranulf frowned.

"A city the size of Lincoln must have at least one damned doctor! Why is it taking so long to fetch him?"

"He'll be here soon," Maud said soothingly, and was unable to resist adding a playful "Uncle," for it amused her enormously, that she should have an uncle so close in years to her own age. "But in all honesty, I doubt that a doctor can ease what ails him, Ranulf."

"I know," he conceded quietly. "Nothing leaves so bitter an aftertaste as betrayal, not even wormwood and gall." He shook his head, still shocked by the flight of Stephen's earls, for he'd been taught that men of high birth were more courageous, more steadfast and honourable than the rest of mankind. "Ah, but you should have seen him, Maud! Men were flinging themselves at him without pause, for all the world as if he were a castle under siege, and he kept beating them back, wielding his axe like a scythe—"

Ranulf's admiring account of Stephen's defiance went no further, for he'd just remembered that Maud's husband was amongst those mowed down by that Danish axe of Stephen's. Upon their arrival at the castle, he'd informed Maud and Chester's brother of his injury, assuring them that he was not badly hurt. William de Roumare had rushed off to see for himself, leaving Maud to tend to their royal prisoner. If she was fretting about her husband's health, she hid it well, and when Ranulf now provided additional details, she listened with a faint, enigmatic smile.

"And by the time Robert bade me to get Stephen safely into the castle," he concluded, "the earl was already regaining his senses. He's like to have a god-awful headache in days to come, but he was indeed lucky, for if Stephen's axe haft had not broken, his helmet might not have saved him."

"Thank God for that hard head of his!"

Ranulf grinned, but he could not help hoping that Annora would not be so nonchalant should he ever be hit on the head with a battle-axe. He started to tease Maud about her unwifely insouciance, but she was twisting around on the seat, fumbling with the shutter. "I thought so," she cried triumphantly. "It is my father!"

ROBERT had ridden in through the postern gate in the west wall, bypassing the town just as Ranulf and Stephen had done. He was dismounting in the bailey when his daughter shot through the doorway of the keep, flew down the stairs, and into his arms. Robert hugged her tightly; of all his children, this one was his secret favorite, for Maud's cheeky, blithe spirit never failed to stir up memories of a young Amabel. "You were not harmed, lass?"

"Indeed not, Papa. In truth, I was not even scared," she confided, and it was not bravado, for she'd known Stephen would have seen to her safety had the castle fallen to him.

"I'd wager she even enjoyed herself," a new voice now chimed in, and Maud turned to grin at her elder brother Will, then stuck out her tongue as if she were still his pesky little sister and not an earl's wife.

"We will be departing on the morrow," Robert said, "and I want you to come back with us, Maud. Your mother will not believe you are truly safe and well until she sees you with her own eyes."

"Of course I'll come back with you! Do you think I'd miss being there when Aunt Maude learns that we've won?" Maud sounded so excited that Robert smiled. He knew that even among those who'd become disillusioned with Stephen's rule, the news of the Battle of Lincoln would be greeted with ambivalence, with both expectation and unease. But at least one of his sister's subjects had no doubts whatsoever. Maude's niece and namesake was utterly delighted that her aunt was—at long last—to be England's queen.

THIS was the first time that they'd been alone since the battle. Ranulf hesitated, then rose and crossed the chamber to Stephen's side. "Can I get you anything?" he asked, sounding as awkward as he felt. He'd not expected this, to be caught up in a treacherous tide of memory and regrets. He'd not expected to feel Stephen's pain as if it were his own. "Stephen? Did you hear me?"

Stephen jerked at Ranulf's touch, looked up at his cousin with clouded eyes. Making an obvious effort, he focused upon the dried blood caking the sleeve of Ranulf's hauberk. "You're hurt, lad."

Ranulf shrugged. "A scratch, although I hope it'll leave a scar I can brag about." His humor was forced, for he did not know what to say, wanting to offer Stephen comfort, realizing there was none. He opened his mouth to reassure Stephen that his life was in no danger, only to stop, defeated. What solace could Stephen derive from the promise of a lifetime's confinement? For how could they ever let him go?

Ranulf was still groping for words when the door opened and Robert entered, followed by Maud, her brother Will, and Brien Fitz Count. Stephen started to get to his feet, only to discover that his abused muscles were cramped and constricted, beginning to stiffen. Robert saw his involuntary grimace and waved him back into his chair, seating himself on the other side of the table. "I am sorry it is taking so long to find you a doctor," he began, but Stephen was indifferent to his own injuries.

"I ask nothing for myself," he said. "But I do for my wife and children. Have I your word, Robert, that they'll not suffer for any sins of mine?"

Robert's response was as prompt as it was predictable. "Of course," he said. "No harm will come to them, I promise you. Nor need you worry about your son's right to inherit the county of Boulogne, since that is Matilda's legacy."

Matilda's legacy. That was all Eustace had left now, for his paternal legacy was to have been England's crown. Nothing in Stephen's past had prepared him for this moment, for he'd been born with an infinitely deep reservoir of hope, and he'd never before experienced the sort of suffocating, dark despair that engulfed him now. It was more frightening even than the final moments of the battle, for war he knew, but desperation was an alien emotion to him. He could not give in to it, though, not here, not before these men. Grabbing for his forgotten wine cup, he drained it in several deep swallows, and then raised his head defiantly.

They were watching him intently, but he did not find in their faces what he'd dreaded—mockery or, Jesú forfend, pity. "What of Baldwin de Clare?" he asked huskily. "William Peverel and the lad, Gilbert de Gant? What befell them?"

"Baldwin de Clare suffered some grievous wounds. Peverel? That I know not, but I'll find out for you. The Gant stripling was lucky, for his injuries are trifling."

"And the townspeople?" Stephen made himself ask, although he already knew what Robert would say.

"There will be looting," Robert said matter-of-factly. "It is a soldier's right and we cannot cheat them of it. I've not been into the city yet, but I heard that many of the townsmen fled to the wharves and sought to escape on the river. They panicked and overloaded the boats, which quickly sank in those flood-tide currents. I was told that hundreds may have drowned."

"Christ pity them," Stephen said softly. He'd failed them, too, these wretched citizens of Lincoln, whose only sin was believing he could protect them. He slumped back in the seat, shading his face with his hand. How many others were going to suffer for his mistakes?

The door whipped back, banging into the wall with such force that they all jumped. The Earl of Chester's head was swathed in a wide white bandage, and his face was drawn and pinched, his skin ashen. But his dark eyes were smoldering, reflecting enough rage to prevail over any bodily infirmities, even those inflicted by a Danish axe. His gaze flicked from Stephen's face to his bandage, down to his wine cup, back to his face again. "How very civilized," he said acidly, "the victors sitting around and sharing wine with the vanquished." Striding forward into the chamber, he gave Ranulf a derisory glance in passing. "Forget whose side you were fighting on, did you, boy?"

Ranulf bristled, but Robert was close enough to put a calming hand on his arm, and he quieted. Stephen pushed away from the table, got slowly to his feet as Maud moved between them, favoring her husband with her most solicitous smile.

"You look dreadful, love, and must feel even worse, after all you've been through this day. Why not go up to our bedchamber and get yourself some well-earned rest? I'll fetch a potion for your head and—"

"I do not need to be coddled! I'm neither enfeebled nor infirm, and if I wanted a potion, woman, I'd damned well say so!"

Maud was accustomed to her husband's temper tantrums. But she did not like being reviled in front of her father and Stephen, and she snapped back, "Next time you nearly get your head split open, I will not even mention it, I promise!"

"I did not get my head split open! I took a glancing blow, and a paltry one at that!"

"Enough of this foolishness," Robert said testily, and Ranulf joined in with an unsolicited, sardonic comment about Chester's helmet, "flattened out like a Shrove Tuesday pancake." But it was Stephen who put an abrupt halt to Chester's marital quarrel.

"Do not blame your wife because you could not best me on the field. The failure was yours, not hers," he said, with such scorn that Chester's face flamed and his hand clenched on the hilt of his sword.

"You're an even bigger fool than I suspected," Chester said scathingly. "You ceased being a threat to the Lady Maude several hours ago. Now you are merely an inconvenience, and I daresay I'm not the only one thinking it a pity that you were not slain on the field. But even a minor battle wound can prove fatal afterward . . . if need be. I'd bear that in mind if I were you."

Stephen felt no fear, for at that moment, the prospect of living with defeat and disgrace was more daunting to him than death. "You'll have to rely upon your Welsh hirelings for the killing," he jeered, "since you proved that you are not man enough to do it yourself."

"You are a dead man, I swear it!"

"No, by God, he is not!" Robert's hand had dropped to his own sword hilt. Only Amabel and Maude knew him better than those in this solar, but none of them had ever seen him so outraged, or even thought him capable of such fury. "This man is my prisoner, not yours. Whatever our differences, he is still a consecrated king. And were he but a cotter's son, he'd deserve our respect for the courage he showed on the battlefield this day. Do not threaten him again."

Chester glared at Robert, but his father-in-law was one of the few men he could not intimidate and he knew it. "So be it," he said grudgingly. "But if we would hang a man for stealing a loaf of bread, why should we honour him for being ambitious enough to steal a crown? You'd do well to think on that, for I'd wager the Lady Maude sees it as I do." He did not wait for a response, shoved past his brother, who was just entering the solar, and stalked out in disgust.

His brother caught up with him at the bottom of the stairs, trailed him out into the bailey, asking questions Chester did not want to answer. He was still seething, and his head was throbbing so wildly now that he felt queasy. The bailey was fast filling with men: wounded in need of treatment, prisoners to be confined until they could ransom themselves, soldiers in search of food and ale, castle servants sent out to retrieve bodies and round up stray horses. Chester's brother had been waylaid by an irate Baldwin de Redvers, who was berating him loudly for using his sister as bait for their trap. William de Roumare was shouting back, reminding Baldwin that Hawise was his wife and he had the right to use her as he saw fit. Chester paid them no heed, and as men glanced his way, they prudently cleared a path for him.

He'd almost reached the great hall when he heard his name called out. He turned as the Welsh prince Cadwaladr reined in beside him. "Why do you look so sour? I know English customs can be right peculiar," the Welshman gibed, "but surely you do celebrate your victories? You won the day for us, so why are you not reaping your reward?"

Why not, indeed? Chester's eyes had narrowed. He looked past Cadwaladr, toward the east gate and the town. These accursed Lincoln churls had defied his authority, sent for Stephen, and joined in his siege of the castle. "You are right, Cadwaladr," he said grimly. "This town owes me a debt, and now is as good a time as any to collect it."

FROM the twelfth-century Norman chronicle of the monk Orderic Vitalis: "The Earl of Chester and his victorious comrades entered the city and pillaged every quarter of it like barbarians. As for the citizens who remained, they butchered like cattle all whom they found and could lay hands upon, putting them to death in various ways without the slightest pity."

THE wind carried into the castle hall the sound of bells, for Gloucester's churches were chiming Compline. Maude raised her head, listening until the echoes faded away. She had a book open upon her lap, but she could not focus her thoughts on its pages. This February Friday night seemed endless to her, as had each of the nights in the past month. During the daylight hours, she could keep busy enough to ignore her inner voices, but they grew louder and more insistent as soon as the sky started to darken.

Had they reached Lincoln yet? The wretched roads and winter rain were sure to have slowed them down. And once they got there, what if Stephen refused to do battle? If they had to besiege Lincoln, it could drag on for weeks, even months. How would she ever be able to endure the suspense without going as mad as Rainald's poor wife?

The hall was the heart of every great household, but at Gloucester Castle, it was beating with a sluggish, uneven rhythm these days. Maude's servants and retainers had been infected with her unease, and the other women had just as much at stake as she did, for they were wives who might become widows if fortune favored Stephen, and several—like Amabel and Sybil Fitz Walter—had sons at risk, too.

There had been a brief respite earlier in the week, when Amabel arranged a surprise celebration for Maude's birthday, but tonight the mood was somber. Maude wasn't the only one finding it difficult to concentrate upon mundane chores or idle pastimes, and when Adelise de Redvers pricked her finger and bled onto her embroidery, her outburst did not seem odd or excessive to the other women, for they understood her need to swear and fling cushions about.

Ranulf's dyrehunds had been dozing by the hearth. They jumped up suddenly and dashed for the opening door, nearly knocking down Drogo de Polwheile, Maude's chamberlain. He sidestepped just in time, and as they plunged past him, he hastened toward Maude. "My lady! Your brother has ridden in!"

"Rainald? But I thought he was still in Cornwall—"

"Not Rainald, my lady . . . Lord Ranulf!"

Maude's book tumbled down unheeded into the floor rushes. Ranulf? Jesú, what did it mean? Amabel had heard, too, and she paled visibly, stricken with the same fear, for it was too soon. What had gone wrong?

Within moments, Ranulf was coming through the doorway, with his welcoming dyrehunds at his heels and Gilbert Fitz John just a stride behind. They were both mud-splattered, and as Ranulf unfastened his wet mantle, he revealed an arm cradled in a sling. But it was his smile that Maude would long remember, the jubilant, joyful smile of a man bearing gifts of surpassing wonder, with a miracle or two stuffed into his saddlebags, mayhap even a crown.

"Robert sent us on ahead. He said I'd earned the right, that I ought to be the one to tell you—"

"We . . . we won?"

"Must you sound so surprised?" he teased, beginning to laugh. "Yes, we won! We reached Lincoln on Candlemas Eve, caught Stephen off guard, and fought the next day. We gained a great victory, Maude, by the Grace of God and the justice of our cause, with a bit of help from Stephen's craven barons."

"And Stephen?"

"He was taken prisoner, is on his way to Gloucester with Robert. Unless the weather worsens, they'll be here by Monday."

Maude had risen to meet Ranulf. Now she sat down abruptly in the nearest chair. Ranulf was assuring Amabel that Robert and her sons had come out of the battle unhurt. The other women were crowding around, excited and anxious, asking about their husbands. Ranulf was able to reassure them, too, and then Amabel wanted to know what he'd meant by "craven barons." He and Gilbert were quite happy to elaborate, taking turns lambasting the fugitive earls. But Ranulf soon realized that his sister was having very little to say. "Maude?"

She smiled up at him, then got to her feet. "It is late," she said, "and you must be bone-weary. Gilbert, too. I think we all could benefit from a good night's sleep."

Ranulf's jaw dropped. As he stared at her in astonishment, she leaned over, kissed his cheek. And then she was gone, disappearing so quickly and inconspicuously that the others in the hall did not at once notice she'd left. But Gilbert had overheard their exchange and pulled Ranulf aside. "I do not understand, Ranulf. You told her that she has won her war, that she is to be queen, and she was as calm as if she had crowns to spare. I thought we'd be celebrating till sunrise, and yet off she goes to bed, as if it were any other night!"

Ranulf was just as puzzled as Gilbert. "I expected more, too," he admitted, unable to mask his disappointment. "Mayhap it does not seem real to her yet . . ."

THE hearth fire had burned low and there was a decided chill in the air. Maude sat down on the edge of the bed, almost at once got up again. Five years and two months. Stephen had stolen more than her crown. He had taken those years, too, and she could not get them back. She had not seen her sons for more than sixteen months, and that also was Stephen's doing. She would never forgive him, never.

She moved to the hearth, for she'd begun to shiver. She'd thought of this moment so often, during all those nights when she couldn't sleep and hope dwindled down to bedrock despair, seeking to convince herself that it would truly come to pass, that she would prevail. Only now could she admit just how deep her doubts had gone, seeping into every corner of her soul.

"I won," she said aloud. "Despite Stephen and Geoffrey and even you, Papa, I did it, I won . . ." She would bring her sons to England. She need not set foot again in Anjou. And she would never again need a father's permission, a husband's consent. She was no longer just a daughter, merely a wife. She would be England's queen and Normandy's duchess—and then, the mother of a king.

The door opened quietly behind her. "Madame? You left the hall so suddenly . . . ?"

"I had to, Minna." She turned, then, for she need not hide her tears now, not from Minna. "I did not want them to see me cry."

LONDON got its first heavy snow of the season on the same evening that Ranulf reached Gloucester. The city awakened the next morning to deep snow drifts, a sky the shade of pale smoke, and random glimmerings of a pallid winter sun. Matilda's children were delighted, and dressed with record speed, spurning breakfast in their haste to plunge into the Tower's glistening, snow-shrouded bailey. Matilda followed at a more sedate pace with Beatrix, the children's nurse, was soon joined by Cecily de Lacy, her newest lady-in-waiting.

Cecily was a slender young woman in her early twenties, and still unmarried, which was highly unusual for a baron's daughter. But her father was long dead and her brother seemed unable or unwilling to provide a marriage portion of sufficient size to attract a husband, for although Cecily was appealing in a delicate, subdued sort of way, she also suffered from the "falling sickness," was subject to occasional seizures that had so far frightened off serious suitors. If she remained unwed, her brother would eventually pressure her into using her meagre marriage portion to buy her way into a nunnery, for those were a woman's choices—unless she was fortunate enough to be befriended by England's queen. Upon hearing of Cecily's plight, Matilda had taken the girl into her household, and she'd promised herself that she'd see Cecily wed to a man able to accept her affliction, for Matilda was beginning to enjoy exercising some of the prerogatives of power.

The snow was no longer pristine and unsullied, bore multiple tracks of paw prints and small feet. Eustace had coaxed or coerced his eleven-year-old wife and his six-year-old brother into helping him build a massive snow fortress; even four-year-old Mary was part of the construction crew, happily scooping out their moat. Matilda's spaniel, Stephen's greyhound, and several of the stable dogs were playing a canine version of tag. Matilda was seated on a mounting block, watching the antics of her children and dogs. She smiled at sight of Cecily, sliding over to make room on the block. "Be warned," she said, "for Eustace is likely to press us into service, too. He has his heart set upon building the biggest snow castle in all of Christendom."

"I liked playing in the snow when I was a little lass." But Cecily did not like Geoffrey de Mandeville, and it was with a distinct lack of enthusiasm that she now reported, "I glanced out the window ere I followed you downstairs, and I saw the Earl of Essex riding toward the Tower."

Matilda looked puzzled, and then smiled sheepishly. "Stephen has created so many earldoms that I've lost count of them, and I forgot for a moment that he'd bestowed one on Geoffrey de Mandeville! I do not suppose we could sneak back inside the keep ere he arrives?"

Cecily grinned, warmed by the indiscretion, proof positive of Matilda's trust. "I fear not, my lady," she said regretfully, "for the gates are already opening. But he is constable of the Tower, so mayhap he is not here to see you."

"He'll still want to pay his respects, for the man's manners are always impeccable, Cecily. He has given me no reason to be ill at ease with him, and yet I am. I wish I had not promised Stephen we'd stay at the Tower whilst he besieges Lincoln Castle. Every time I encounter my lord Geoffrey de Mandeville, Earl of Essex, I feel as if I'm the tenant and he's the landlord and I've fallen behind on the rent!"

Cecily gave a surprised giggle, for Matilda joked almost as rarely as she allowed herself to show anger. "Brace yourself then, madame," she said, "for our landlord is heading this way, and by the look of him, he has eviction in mind!"

Geoffrey de Mandeville did indeed look grim, and the good manners Matilda had admired were nowhere in evidence. "There is no way to sweeten what I have to tell you," he said abruptly, "so I'd best say it straight out. On Sunday a battle was fought at Lincoln. Your husband's barons deserted him, and the victory went to the Earls of Gloucester and Chester."

For a merciful moment, Matilda felt nothing, only a stunned sense of disbelief. "That . . . that cannot be true," she faltered. "It must be a mistake—"

"Yes, and Stephen made it! If he'd waited for reinforcements, if he'd not been set on playing the hero—"

"For God's sake, stop! Just tell me what happened to Stephen! Does . . ." Matilda swallowed hard. "Does he still live?"

"He survived the battle and was taken prisoner. But—"

"No!" Eustace had moved within earshot, unnoticed by the adults until now. "You lie!" he cried, and flung himself upon Geoffrey de Mandeville, fists flailing, kicking and yelling "Liar" over and over, as if it were the only word he knew.

The man shoved Eustace away, none too gently. The boy stumbled, regained his footing, and spat out an oath that was not at all childlike. But before he could lunge forward again, Matilda pulled him into her arms. "No, Eustace, no! He is not to blame, and hurting him will not help, will change nothing!"

Eustace twisted suddenly, breaking free. He backed up, panting, and glared at his mother as if she were now the enemy, too. "You believe him!" he accused. "But I know it is not true! Papa would not lose to those men!"

"Ah, Eustace . . ." But Matilda got no further. Her heart was beating so fast that she feared she would faint, and she could not seem to catch her breath. Cecily saw her lose color, darted forward to slip a supportive arm around her waist. By the time she'd gotten back her balance, the bailey was reverberating with shrieks and wailing, for Eustace had turned his rage upon himself. He was destroying his castle, trampling its towers and battlements, kicking snow onto his sobbing little sister and brother, screaming curses at Constance and his nurse when they tried to stop him, until at last he sank to his knees in the snow, choking on his own sobs.

Matilda had reached him by then, knelt and held him as he wept. But he soon stiffened and pulled away, angrily swiping at his tears with the back of his hand. When he scrambled to his feet, she let him go. "No, Beatrix," she said when the nurse would have followed as he bolted across the bailey toward the stables. "Let him be, at least for now."

"He survived the battle." Geoffrey de Mandeville's words were still echoing in Matilda's ears, fraught with menace. Would they dare put Stephen to death? She felt as if her head were filled with silent screaming, but she could not let herself think of Stephen's peril, not yet. Her younger children needed her. They were weeping, clutching at her skirts, terrified by her distress, their brother's frenzy. Matilda held them close, murmuring soothing sounds until they quieted, clung less frantically. Constance was hovering nearby, trembling and on the verge of tears, in need of comfort, too. And Eustace . . . she'd have to find Eustace once he calmed down.

But then what? No one would help Stephen if she did not. But how? Dear God, what was she to do?

15

GLOUCESTER, ENGLAND

February 1141

MAUDE had been waiting more than five years for this confrontation with Stephen. It had gotten her through some of her worst moments, those wakeful nights when her faith was faltering and despair hovered in the shadows. She had envisioned the scene over and over again, until it began to seem as if she were reliving a memory rather than anticipating one. She would be seated upon a dais, dressed in scarlet silk, wearing the emperor's emeralds, a gold coronet substituting for the crown that would soon be hers. The hall would be expectant, but respectful, as it had been at the German court. And then Stephen would be brought before her in chains. He would not grovel, not even in her imagination; she knew him too well to expect that. But he would be contrite, for surely she had the right to demand that much?

But when it finally came, this long-awaited reckoning, it was not at all as she had hoped it would be. It went wrong from the very beginning, for they arrived a day early, on Sunday night. Maude had already retired to her own chamber and was making ready for bed when Ranulf came racing up the stairs and pounded on her door. "Maude, dress yourself," he panted, "and make haste, for Robert has just ridden into the bailey!" He then whirled and plunged down the stairs again, leaving Minna speechless at such a blatant breach of royal etiquette.

Maude was less surprised; as much as she loved Ranulf, she'd long ago concluded that his sense of decorum was deplorable. She had no time, though, to fret about her brother's flawed manners, no time to select the jewelry and fine clothes she'd planned to wear. Instead of dressing with her usual meticulous care, she found herself hurriedly snatching up her discarded chemise and gown, then gartering her stockings while Minna attempted to rebraid her hair. Grabbing a veil, she was still adjusting it as she emerged, flushed and breathless, from the darkened stairwell into the torch-lit brightness below.

The hall was a scene of chaos. The other women had not been as punctilious about propriety as Maude, and had hastened downstairs in various stages of undress. Everywhere she looked, she saw unbound hair, bare feet, husbands and wives entwined in joyful, welcoming embraces. Her entrance went almost unnoticed in the confusion, and it was several moments before Robert disentangled himself from Amabel's arms and shoved his way through to her side. Maude reached out, taking his hand in hers. "Thank you," she said, "for winning back my throne.

"Thank you all," she added, raising her voice to be heard above the clamor filling the hall, her gaze moving from Robert to Miles and then, briefly, to Brien. They looked tired and wet and travel-stained, but triumphant, too, and one by one, they came forward to receive her praise, Miles and Brien and Baldwin de Redvers and William Fitz Alan, these men who'd wagered their futures upon her queenship, wagered and won.

It was some time before Maude was able to ask Robert the obvious question. "What of Stephen? When will he be brought in?" The answer she got was totally unexpected.

"Oh, he's already here in the hall. I could not very well leave him out in the rain, could I? Shall I find him for you?"

Maude stared at him in dismay. "Good God, Robert, you're not letting the man wander about on his own, are you? What if he escapes? What if—"

"Maude, he is being guarded," Robert said patiently. "Look . . . there he is, over by the door."

Maude spun around, saw Stephen was indeed standing by the door, flanked by his guards, like a guest politely waiting to be noticed by his hosts. "Bring him to me," Maude ordered, but she could not wait for her command to be carried out. She could not wait another moment, and she began to push through the crowd toward Stephen.

Stephen was not looking his best; his mantle was muddied, his head was bandaged, and his eyes were bloodshot, so smudged by shadows that they seemed bruised. He stiffened as Maude approached, but showed no other signs of unease. Maude halted in front of him and waited, silently daring him to defy her, for she could imagine only two possible responses: defiance or submission. But Stephen found a third way: courtesy. "Lady Maude," he said, and before she realized what he meant to do, he reached for her hand and brought it to his mouth.

Maude was outraged. It was repentance she wanted, not gallantry. Jerking her hand away, she said scathingly, "I am not the lady of the manor come to bid you welcome. I am your sovereign, and I expect you to show me the respect due your queen, I expect you to kneel!"

Stephen sought to remain impassive, but he could not keep the color from rising in his face. By now it was very quiet, all eyes upon them. "As you wish," he said, and slowly knelt before her.

She'd won, but somehow it did not feel like a victory. Maude glanced around at the encircling men. They were watching intently, too intently, and she wondered suddenly if they were remembering Stephen's magnanimous gesture at Arundel. Turning toward Robert, she demanded, "Why is this man not in irons? If the theft of a crown does not warrant it, what crime does?"

"I did not think it necessary," Robert said, rather stiffly. "He gave me his word that he would not attempt to escape, and so—"

"His word?" Maude echoed derisively. "Is that the same word that he pledged to me when he swore to accept my queenship?"

Stephen had gotten to his feet, although she had not given him permission to rise. She wanted to protest, to force him back onto his knees. She wanted to order him clapped in irons, as he so deserved. But she was stopped by what she saw in the faces of the watching men: disapproval, instinctive and involuntary, but disapproval, nonetheless. They were not comfortable when power was wielded by a woman, not at a man's expense, a man who had just acquitted himself so spectacularly at Lincoln, winning their reluctant respect in a way she knew she never could. The brotherhood of the battlefield, she thought, feeling a sharp sense of betrayal as she looked about at the silent spectators. These were her kinsmen, men who'd sacrificed and bled for her cause. If even they doubted her right to rule as a man could, how would she ever convince the others?

It was a bitter moment for her, gazing upon her defeated rival as her triumph threatened to turn to ashes before her eyes. But no, she'd not let that happen. She would prove to them that she was worthy to rule. She knew what her father would have done, and she would show them that she was her father's daughter, England's true queen—by God, she would.

"I want this man put under close guard," she said, "and I want it done now."

STEPHEN was steeling himself for confinement in one of the castle dungeons. He was relieved to find that his prison was to be a small but comfortable bedchamber in the keep, albeit with a guard posted at the door. This was the first time he'd been alone since the Battle of Lincoln, and he lay down upon the bed without shedding his clothes, grateful for the solitude.

He'd known that his encounter with Maude would be a daunting one, and so it was, for he found it very disquieting to have a woman as his enemy. He could not deflect her hostility with defiance, as he had with Chester. His dealings with Robert were free of rancor, for they both knew what was expected of them under the circumstances. Not so with Maude. None of the rules of warfare seemed to apply, for Maude neither knew nor cared what they were.

His scene with Maude had been unpleasant, but surprising, too, in a way he had not foreseen. Maude and he shared the same inability to camouflage their emotions, and the emotions he'd read on Maude's face were anger, frustration, and chagrin, not triumph. If he had not enjoyed their confrontation, neither had she. Much to his astonishment, he'd even felt a flicker of pity for her plight, for he'd suddenly seen the truth—that there would be no winners in their war. He was facing lifelong confinement at Bristol or Gloucester, and Maude was about to discover that her English subjects still did not want her as queen. She was blazing a trail on her own, and there in the great hall at Gloucester Castle, he'd realized that she did not even have a map. Whatever happened to him, he doubted that she'd reach Westminster.

Stephen folded his hands behind his head, staring up at the ceiling. But it made no sense, not that he and Maude should both lose. A ship with no helmsman would soon founder, and so would England. How could that be part of the Almighty's Plan? Was it possible that he'd been too quick to conclude that he knew the Lord's Will? What if his loss at Lincoln was not God's Judgment upon him? Mayhap the Lord God had not abandoned him, after all. The Almighty had seen fit to test Job, so why not His servant Stephen? Mayhap that was why he'd lost the Battle of Lincoln—so that he might prove his faith was strong, that he was indeed worthy to be England's king.

This was the first glimmer of light in the dark that had descended upon Stephen's world at Lincoln. The loss of hope had been a crueler loss even than his crown, for he'd never known what it was like to live without hope—not until this past week, riding as a prisoner along the muddy winter roads of his own realm. Stephen needed hope as he needed air to breathe, and he lunged toward the light. It did not take much to convince him; he was halfway down the path toward conviction by the time he heard voices at the door.

He was sitting up on the bed as the door opened. His guard stepped aside, and Stephen smiled at sight of Ranulf, beckoning him inside as if he still had that right.

Ranulf seemed ill at ease, as if he'd somehow ended up in Stephen's chamber through no doing of his own. "I . . . I just wanted to see if you need anything."

Stephen considered. "Well, how about a fast horse and a head start?" he suggested, and Ranulf grinned, pleased by this proof that Stephen's sense of humor had not been one of the casualties of Lincoln, after all.

"I've no horses to spare," he said, "but I do not come empty-handed," and with a dramatic flourish, he unhooked a wine flask from his belt, holding it aloft.

"Sir Ranulf to the rescue," Stephen joked. But when Ranulf passed him the flask, he put it down, untasted. "There is something you can do for me, lad. Persuade Maude to let me write a letter to my wife. Matilda must be half mad with worry by now."

"I'll ask Maude," Ranulf promised, wishing he could promise more. But he was remembering the obdurate look on his sister's face, and he was not at all sure that she would heed his plea, for he suspected that Stephen was the last man in Christendom likely to receive any favors from Maude.

LONDON'S justiciar and the leaders of the city's guilds came to the Tower to bid farewell to Stephen's queen, and to assure her again that Londoners were still loyal to her husband. Soon after, Geoffrey de Mandeville arrived, ostensibly to wish Matilda Godspeed on her journey to safety in the south of England. But he was not long in revealing the real purpose of his visit. As sorry as he was to see her go, he said, he understood that it was for the best. "I do think, though, that the little Lady Constance ought to stay here at the Tower."

Matilda stared at him. "I do not agree. My daughter-in-law's place is with me."

Geoffrey de Mandeville smiled and shook his head. "I can protect her, madame, make sure that no evil befalls her in these troubled times. I owe her brother that much."

Her brother. The French king. Matilda understood now. "You are indeed kind to worry about Constance," she said, as steadily as she could, "but there is no need, I assure you."

"Ah, but I insist," he said, still smiling. Matilda looked at him—so elegant, handsome, and urbane—and she had to fight the urge to cross herself, suddenly sure that she was in the presence of true evil.

MATILDA had chosen Guildford as her refuge, a fortified castle in the heart of the North Downs. It was only thirty miles from London, but they were braving February weather at its worst, and they did not reach the Wey Valley until dusk on the second day. The sky was dark and foreboding, the wind as cold and desolate as the future they faced in Maude's England. It took some time before Matilda was able to get her family settled, still longer before she could slip away to the chapel, for the younger children literally clung to her skirts these days, and although Eustace rebuffed all her attempts at comfort, he watched her constantly with bewildered, needful eyes.

The chapel was deserted, but that was what Matilda wanted most: time alone. She was so tired, in body and soul, drained by the need to be strong for her children, her household. Only at night could she give in to her fears, and even then she dared not let herself weep for Stephen, afraid that once she started, she could not stop.

Moving forward into the chancel, she sank to her knees before the candlelit altar. "Lord God Almighty, into Thy Hands and those of Thy Blessed Son I commit myself. Holy Father, hear my prayer. My husband is in great peril, forsaken by those who had most cause to be true. I would help him if only I could, but I do not know how. Show me the way. I beseech Thee, Dear Lord, to send me a sign. Reveal unto me Thy Will."

Breathing a shaken "Amen," she got slowly to her feet. But she was not yet ready to take up her burden again, and she lingered there in the quiet castle chapel, trying not to think of Constance's tear-streaked face. That hellspawn Mandeville would not harm her; Matilda knew that. But their parting had been wrenching, the child's piteous sobs echoing in her ears even after they'd escaped the Tower. For that was how Matilda saw their departure—as an escape. She did not doubt that Mandeville would have kept them all there, hostages to win Maude's favor, if not for the Londoners. But public opinion was still on Stephen's side, and even Mandeville dared not risk the Londoners' wrath by seizing Stephen's wife and children.

She'd discussed with Cecily the advisability of taking her children to Boulogne, but she was loath to leave England and she could not bear to be separated from them. If only there were someone she could turn to, someone she could trust. Stephen's brother Theobald would be sympathetic once he learned of Stephen's downfall, but what could he do at a distance? He could not rally support for Stephen, not from Blois. The bishop could, though. A prince of the Church, a papal legate, lord of some of the most formidable castles in England, he should have been her natural ally, but she'd not yet heard from him; her plea for help had so far gone unheeded. Just like Waleran Beaumont and William de Ypres and those other craven wretches who'd fled the field at Lincoln, she thought bleakly. Stephen's brother was abandoning him, too.

Had Stephen gotten her letter yet? She'd sent a courier to Gloucester, for where else would he be taken? Surely Maude would give him the letter? She could not be so cruel as to withhold it . . . could she? Matilda had begun to pace, as if trying to outrun her fears. What lay ahead for Stephen? Maude would not dare put him to death? No, God would not let that happen. Nor would Robert, surely? Stephen's life was not at risk; she must believe that. But he would be buying his life with his freedom, for they would never let him go. The old king had confined his elder brother for nigh on thirty years. His daughter was not likely to be any more merciful to Stephen.

Caught up in her own thoughts, she was slow to realize that she was no longer alone. A man was standing in the shadows, watching her. "Father Paul?" she asked uncertainly, for the silhouette did not resemble that of the portly chaplain. When he moved forward into the light, she recoiled abruptly. "You!"

William de Ypres strode toward her. "I must speak with you, my lady."

"You dare to face me after what you did! My husband trusted you and you betrayed him!"

The Fleming had not thought Stephen's queen capable of such anger. "I know."

"How could you abandon him after all he'd done for you? You owed him better than that!"

"I know," he said again, "and I am here to make amends."

"It is rather late for that," Matilda snapped. "Why are you really here? What do you want?"

"I told you—to make amends. I did your husband a grave wrong and I want to right it if I can."

Some of Matilda's rage gave way to astonishment. "You expect me to believe you? If you have a conscience, you've kept it remarkably well hidden in the years I've known you!"

"It was a surprise to me, too," he admitted, "and it is a right inconvenient discovery at this time of my life. I'd gotten along quite well without one up till now." But his humor fell flat. She continued to look at him suspiciously, and he shrugged. "If I am not sincere, why am I here? Why am I not off selling my sword—and my Flemings—to the highest bidder, to Maude?"

She opened her mouth, but she could not think of an answer to that, and for the first time, she began to take him seriously. "I do not understand what you are telling me. If you truly regret deserting Stephen, why did you do it?"

He shrugged again. "There is not much time for reflection in the midst of a battle. When my Flemings broke and ran, I tried to rally them. Obviously I did not try hard enough. But I'd not truly taken the measure of the man, not until it was too late, until I learned how he'd refused to flee, willing to fight to the death—"

"But why did he have to buy your loyalty with his blood? My husband is a good and decent man. Why could you not see that sooner?"

"Ah, but I did, Lady Matilda. Stephen has courage and a generous spirit and he is for certes one of the most likeable men I've ever met. As you say, he is a good man. But he is not a good king."

Matilda wanted to protest the unfairness of that verdict. But she did not, and after a moment, she said quietly, almost beseechingly, "Why is that? Why do men think that Stephen is not a good king? I do not understand."

"Well . . ." He frowned thoughtfully. "Suppose you had a Greenland falcon, a joy to behold, so handsome he was, whiter than a winter snowfall. A falcon that flies straighter and higher than any arrow, and twice as fast. Every falconer's dream . . . except that he falters when it is time to make the kill."

Once again, Matilda wanted to argue; once again, she did not. "Did you truly mean what you said—about helping Stephen?"

He nodded. "If not, I'd be in Gloucester by now, offering my services and men to Maude. Instead, I am here, offering them to you. I do not—" He got no further; Matilda gave a sudden gasp, clasping her hand to her mouth.

"You are my sign!" she cried. "I begged the Almighty to show me how to aid Stephen, and He did, He sent you to me!"

William de Ypres burst out laughing. "I've often been called the Devil's henchman, but this is the first time anyone ever accused me of being one of God's good angels!" He stopped laughing, though, as he realized that Matilda was utterly in earnest. "I'd not lead you astray, Lady Matilda. It may be too late. And you should know this, too—that many men may have to die to set your husband free. Will you be able to do what must be done to restore him to the throne?"

Matilda hesitated. "I cannot answer that," she said at last, "for I do not know what might be asked of me. If I could secure Stephen's freedom by sacrificing his crown, I would. But even if he agreed to abdicate—and I doubt that he would—Maude would still not let him go, for she is not a woman who knows how to trust."

"Indeed, she is not," he agreed, "and that is why we must be very cautious. Stephen survived the battle, and they must not regret it—not yet."

He was pleased to see that his bluntness had not shocked her. She was nodding somberly. "I know," she said. "That is all I can think about: Stephen's danger and Maude's controversial queenship. If I were Maude, I'd be treading with great care and speaking softly, doing whatever I could to dispel men's doubts and ease their minds."

"At least until the coronation," he said dryly. "But you do not think Maude will follow that prudent path, do you?"

"I pray to God she will not," Matilda said, "for that is the only chance Stephen has. His future, mayhap his very life, depends upon Maude's making mistakes."

IT was midmorning, but wall torches and cresset oil lamps had been burning for hours in the great hall of Geoffrey d'Anjou's castle at Angers. Although this last day of February was sunlit and clear, it was still too cold to open the shutters. A desk had been set up in a corner for study, and Henry was hunched over a primer, his face hidden by a tumbling thatch of copper-gold hair.

Geoffrey resented his brother's absorption in the book, for he felt it keenly that Henry could read and he could not. He was still learning his letters, and he was supposed to be practicing them now, copying the Christcross row their tutor had etched onto a wax tablet. But the alphabet held no charms for Geoffrey, and his parchment sheet remained blank. Instead, he'd been amusing himself by aligning and realigning his writing supplies: a pumice stone to erase mistakes, a boar's tooth to polish the parchment afterward, a small knife to trim his quill pen, a ruler to make margins, and his favorite, an inkhorn made from a real cow's horn, stuck down into a hole in the desk to minimize spills.

Geoffrey set the pumice stone on its end, was attempting to balance the ruler on top of it when he glanced up, saw their tutor heading their way. He hastily dunked the quill in the inkhorn, drew a large, crooked *A* on the parchment. Master Peter had stopped by Henry first, complimenting him for having gotten through most of the Pater Noster. Geoffrey slopped a *B* onto the page, splattering ink upon his sleeve. Fortunately Master Peter seemed in no hurry, for he was still talking to Henry, joking about his birthday next week.

Geoffrey scowled, putting down his pen. That was all anyone talked about these days, Henry's upcoming birthday. He was so jealous of the attention Henry was getting that he forgot he was likely to receive a scolding for his own lackluster efforts. But luck was with him, for Master Peter was now being called away. Instead of putting his reprieve to good use, though, Geoffrey leaned over and dribbled ink onto Henry's side of the desk. "So you are going to be eight," he said. "So what? I'll be eight in June."

Henry prudently moved his book out of ink range. "No, you will not," he said calmly. "You'll only be seven."

As much as Geoffrey yearned to refute that fact, he didn't know how. "Well . . . I'll be eight next year," he countered, and Henry grinned.

"Yes," he said, "but then I'll be nine!"

Geoffrey glowered at his brother. Somehow Henry always seemed to get the better of him. "Birthdays are stupid," he said, and pretended to stretch, taking the opportunity to prod Henry in the ribs with his elbow. Henry jabbed him back, but his retaliation was halfhearted; he was staring across the hall. Like a cat at a mousehole, Geoffrey thought, looking to see what had claimed Henry's attention. It was that lady, he decided, Papa's friend. He wished he knew why Henry disliked her so much, but Henry would not tell him, acting as if he knew a secret no one else did. Sometimes Geoffrey went out of his way to be friendly with the lady, just to vex Henry. But today it was their little brother, Will, who was doing that, holding her hand and laughing as she ruffled his hair. As soon as she moved away, Henry gave a sharp whistle and beckoned to Will, who trotted obediently across the hall in response to the summons.

"I told you to stay away from her, Will," Henry said accusingly, and Will blinked in bewilderment.

"Why? She tells me riddles, and she smells good, like flowers in the garden, like Mama. She looks like Mama, too—"

"She does not!" Henry glared at the little boy. "She is not at all like Mama!"

For once, Geoffrey and Henry were united in their indignation. "Her hair is as yellow as butter," Geoffrey pointed out scornfully, "and Mama's hair is black. You must be daft, Will, if you cannot tell the difference!"

Will's mouth trembled, and Henry was suddenly struck by an unlikely suspicion. "Will . . . do you remember what Mama looks like?"

"Of course I do! I remember better than you!" But in truth, Will did not. His mother had been gone a year and a half, and that was almost a third of Will's lifetime. It had happened so gradually that he was not aware of it, the fading of his memories. There just came a day when he could no longer call up an image of his mother's face, and now when her letters were read to him, he heard no echoes of her voice. But he could not admit that to his brothers, and he insisted, "I do remember Mama, I do!" before spinning on his heel and running from the hall.

He did not get far, colliding in the doorway with his father. Geoffrey scooped his son up into his arms, and soon had the little boy giggling. Henry and young Geoffrey watched as he strode toward them, Will gleefully riding astride his shoulders, his earlier distress quite forgotten. Setting Will back upon his feet, Geoffrey smiled down at his sons, and it was only then that they saw the letter in his hand.

"Is that from Mama?"

"Yes, Henry, it is, and a remarkable birthday gift she has for you, lad. It seems she has won her war. Your uncles fought a battle with Stephen on Candlemas, at a place called Lincoln. The victory was theirs, and Stephen was taken prisoner."

"Then Mama will be queen?" This from Henry, and "Will she come home now?" from Geoffrey.

"Yes, she will be queen, and yes, she will come back . . . in time. But England will be her home now, and Normandy, of course. Once she has been crowned, though, you'll be able to visit her. Me, too," Geoffrey said and laughed, for he'd just added a silent, "*when Hell freezes over*."

"You'll have to go away now, too, Papa," Henry said, and Geoffrey nodded, surprised and proud that Henry was so quick; he was becoming convinced that his firstborn had been endowed with an uncommonly sharp intelligence.

"Yes," he said, "I shall have to go into Normandy straightaway. Until Maude is formally recognized as England's queen and the crown is set upon her head at Westminster, the danger of rebellion remains. It will be up to me to convince the Norman barons to come to terms without delay."

Henry and Geoffrey had fallen silent, for they understood that when their father rode into Normandy, he would be riding off to war. That had escaped Will, though, for he was still focusing upon the good news, that Mama would be queen. "Will Mama let me wear our crown sometimes?"

Geoffrey hid a smile. But if Will was too young to comprehend the concept of primogeniture, his eldest son was not, as Henry now proved.

"Oh, no, Will," he said, firmly but not unkindly. "It is not your crown. It is Mama's and mine."

A MONTH to the day after the Battle of Lincoln, Maude met with Stephen's brother the Bishop of Winchester at Wherwell. It was a wet, blustery March afternoon, and they were all shrouded in wool mantles and hoods, for this kingmaking conference was being held in an open field not far from the Benedictine nunnery of the Holy Cross. The mood was almost as cheerless as the weather, for neither the empress nor the bishop truly wished to be there. Theirs was an alliance of expediency, a grudging recognition of unpalatable political realities—that Maude's claim to the throne needed the sanction of the Church, and the bishop's ambitions necessitated a cooperative relationship with England's sovereign.

At this dismal March meeting, they were to ratify already agreed-upon terms, terms Maude liked not at all, for she had reluctantly promised that "all major affairs, especially the bestowal of bishoprics and abbeys, should be subject to the papal legate's authority." In return, the bishop had vowed to recognize her as queen and pledged her his loyalty. Maude had let herself be persuaded, but she resented having to concede so much royal autonomy to gain support that should have been hers by right. She did not trust Stephen's brother the bishop, and even though she knew they needed him as an ally, she could not help despising him a little for abandoning Stephen with such alacrity. Stephen may have been luckier in wedlock, she thought, but not in brotherhood. There she'd been truly blessed, and she glanced proudly at her own brothers Robert and Ranulf and Rainald, newly come back from Cornwall.

Oddly enough, the bishop's private thoughts were not so far removed from Maude's musings. He was studying the men flanking her—Robert of Gloucester, Miles Fitz Walter, and Brien Fitz Count—and he was wondering why Maude had been able to attract men of stature and integrity whilst Stephen had relied upon self-serving knaves and malcontents, like the Beaumonts and that treacherous Fleming. If only Stephen had not been so stubborn, so shortsighted. For if Stephen had heeded his advice, he would not now be imprisoned at Bristol Castle and Maude would not be about to set his crown upon that haughty dark head of hers. He'd gotten some impressive concessions from her, more than he'd been able to coax from Stephen, but this was not how he'd wanted it to be. Yet he'd had no choice, for he had to protect the interests of Holy Church. In time, Stephen would come to understand that. Or so he hoped.

FROM the Gesta Stephani Chronicle: "So that when the bishop and the Countess of Anjou had jointly made a pact of peace and concord, the bishop came to meet her in cordial fashion and admitted her into the city of Winchester, and after handing over to her disposal the king's castle and the royal crown, which she had always most eagerly desired, and the treasure the king had left there, though it was very scanty, he bade the people, at a public meeting in the market place of the town, salute her as their lady and their queen."

16

OXFORD CASTLE, ENGLAND

April 1141

BEATRICE?" Ranulf's sister-in-law gave him a timid smile and he felt a throb of pity. At a distance, she looked like a child, a little girl borrowing her mother's gown. Up close, she looked fragile, breakable.

"I have to go, lass," Rainald said, surprising Ranulf by the gentle way he kissed his wife's cheek. "My sister has summoned me. But Ella will stay with you whilst I am gone." Beatrice smiled and nodded, but Ranulf noticed how her hands were clenching in her lap, her fingers knotting in her skirts; her nails were bitten down to the quick, several rimmed in dried blood. Ella had moved protectively to her side, and over Beatrice's bowed head, her eyes met Rainald's in a glance of grim reassurance.

Rainald was silent as they moved into the stairwell. But as they neared the bottom, he said abruptly, "She cannot bear to be alone, not even for a heartbeat."

Ranulf hesitated, not sure what he should say. Had Beatrice's troubles all begun when she was caught in that siege? Or had she always been one to shy at shadows, to see demons lurking in the dark? He knew she was a great heiress. But he knew, too, that Rainald's women had invariably been bold and lusty wenches, bawdy, cheerful bedmates, never a bird with a broken wing.

He was still pondering his response when Rainald poked him in the ribs. "So . . . what is this I hear about your turning down Maude's offer to find you an heiress of your own?"

Ranulf shrugged, for he could not tell anyone about Annora. Soon, God Willing, but not yet. "The truth? Well, my lord Earl of Cornwall," he said, playfully drawling out Rainald's new title, "I've my heart set upon a particular lady, Eleanor of Aquitaine. I hear she and the French king are mismatched, and should their marriage falter, I want to be able to put in my bid."

Once more, Rainald's elbow went into action, connecting with Ranulf's ribs. "So keep your secrets, then, lad. I'd wager you've got a light o' love hidden away somewhere," Rainald said, showing unexpected insight. "But that is no obstacle to a profitable marriage. Not that you'll need to marry for money, not once Maude— Damnation!" He broke off, giving Ranulf a rueful grin. "I let that cat out of the bag, for certes, me and my runaway mouth!"

"What?" Ranulf demanded. "What does Maude intend to do?"

"You cannot tell her I told you," Rainald warned. "She has it in mind to bestow a title upon you, too—Mortain."

"Mortain?" Ranulf echoed. "But . . . but Mortain is Stephen's."

"Not any more," Rainald said, punctuating with his elbow again.

"Christ on the Cross, will you stop prodding me? I'm not a balky horse in need of the spurs! Are you sure about this, Rainald?" When his brother nodded, he exhaled slowly. Count of Mortain. He could not deny that he wanted it. Yet he wished that his gain need not come at Stephen's expense. But Eustace still had the bulk of his inheritance intact, the county of Boulogne. When he said that aloud, though, Rainald shook his head.

"You truly think Maude will let Boulogne pass to Stephen's son? I'd say the lad has a better chance of becoming Pope than Count of Boulogne!"

Ranulf was taken aback. "That is crazed talk, Rainald! It can be argued that Stephen has forfeited Mortain, but Boulogne is Matilda's. Eustace is her lawful heir, and no court in the land would say otherwise."

"Maude's court is the only one that counts now, lad."

"No . . . Maude would not do that, Rainald. To deprive Eustace of his rightful inheritance—it would be unjust!"

"You are such an innocent, Ranulf! Do you honestly believe that Maude cares tuppence about doing Stephen justice? She hates him, lad, as I hope no woman ever hates me. You think she detests Geoffrey? Their marriage is a love feast compared to the way she loathes Cousin Stephen!"

Ranulf was not convinced, and would have argued further, but by then they'd reached the castle solar. It was already crowded with men, most of the faces familiar to Ranulf. Robert, as always, by Maude's side. Miles and Brien, also close at hand. Baldwin de Redvers, newly named by Maude as Earl of Devon. Oxford's castellan, Robert d'Oilly, and his stepson, another of the old king's illegitimate offspring.

But there were a few newcomers to their ranks, too. John Marshal, who held Marlborough Castle, although until recently, no one could be sure for whom; he'd managed an adroit balancing act for the past year, convincing both Stephen and Maude that he was on their side. William

Beauchamp, formerly one of Waleran Beaumont's most trusted captains. And Hugh Bigod, who was doing his best to pretend that no one remembered he'd perjured himself on Stephen's behalf.

Ranulf squeezed in, finding a space against the far wall. He was expecting no surprises, for he knew why Maude had summoned them—to hear the eyewitness accounts of the Church Council held last week, called by Maude's new ally the Bishop of Winchester to recognize her as England's rightful queen. She was flanked by Nigel, Bishop of Ely, and Bernard, Bishop of the Welsh see of St David's. But it was Gilbert Foliot who'd assumed the role of spokesman, and Ranulf edged over to get a closer look, for he was curious about Foliot, only thirty and already in a position of influence, abbot of the Benedictine abbey at Gloucester. Ranulf knew some begrudged Foliot his rapid rise in the Church hierarchy, attributing it to his kinship with Miles Fitz Walter; they were first cousins, once removed. But Foliot was said to have a quick wit, a nimble tongue, and a sardonic eye, all of which were in evidence now as he described for them the events of the Winchester synod.

Gilbert Foliot began with an unexpected admission, that in his youth he'd taken great pleasure in the acts of fair tumblers and ropewalkers. "But in all honesty, my fond memories of those spectacular somersaults and dazzling back flips cannot compete with the remarkable performance I just witnessed at Winchester. The bishop's mental contortions were truly breathtaking!"

He had an adroit sense of timing, waited now for the laughter to subside. "But then, he had to justify not one, but two turnabouts. He was up to the task, though. First he explained why he had been compelled to break his oath to you, my lady. As he told it, England was in chaos, and you tarried so long in Normandy that he had no choice but to accept Stephen—for England's sake. And indeed, three whole weeks did drag by between King Henry's death and Stephen's coronation."

Foliot paused again for laughter, and was not disappointed. "The suspense is becoming too much, Cousin," Miles said wryly. "How did he explain then, his abandonment of Stephen?"

"He said that whilst he loved his mortal brother, he loved far more his Immortal Father, and Stephen's defeat at Lincoln was clearly God's Judgment upon him, both as a man and a king. And so he urged his fellow clerics to follow his lead, which they did, and elected you, madame, as Lady of the English. After that, the bishop excommunicated Stephen's supporters, with special thunderbolts aimed at Stephen's steward, William Martel, who'd dared to seize the bishop's castle at Sherborne."

The word *elect* jarred with Maude; it was for the Church to consecrate a sovereign, not select one. But at least the bishop had kept faith with her, even if he did choose to pass himself off as a kingmaker. "The Archbishop of Canterbury balked at recognizing my right, claiming he could not break his oath to Stephen. He insisted upon being taken to Bristol, getting Stephen's consent ere he would agree to accept me. What of the clerics at the synod? Did any of them echo the archbishop's argument? Did any of them balk, too?"

"No, my lady," Foliot said emphatically, if not altogether truthfully. A number of the clerics had not even attended the synod, but he did not want Maude to know that, for he already had enough troubling news to tell her. "It was not the clerics who cast a shadow over the proceedings, it was the queen." Quickly amending that to "Stephen's wife," for he knew how sensitive Maude was on this particular point.

"Matilda? What could she do?"

"She sent her chaplain to the synod, a very brave priest named Christian. The bishop refused to read her letter aloud, so Christian boldly snatched it back and read it himself, much to the bishop's indignation." Memory of the bishop's discomfiture brought a brief, involuntary smile to his lips. "It was an impassioned plea for Stephen's freedom, stressing what the bishop would rather ignore, that he is his brother's keeper."

"Matilda poses no threat. But what of the Londoners? Did they obey the summons?"

"Yes, they did. But I regret to say that they were not cooperative, madame. They came to argue for Stephen's release and restoration to the throne. And the bishop had little success in winning them over. They agreed to take his message back to the city, but they warned it was likely to fall on deaf ears. London, it seems, still holds fast for Stephen."

There was silence after that, for they all knew they'd suffered a disturbing setback. Maude must be crowned at Westminster. But that could not happen until the Londoners came to their senses. Maude's disappointment was so intense that she actually felt ill, chilled to the very marrow of her bones.

"I cannot comprehend such folly. At best, they can delay my coronation, not thwart it. What do they hope to gain by antagonizing me like this? I have the blood-right to be queen, the Almighty has judged my claim at Lincoln, and Stephen is my prisoner. What else need I do to convince them? What more do they want of me?"

Maude's cry was heartfelt and found ready echoes. She heard murmurs of agreement and anger, rippling outward like waves across the crowded solar. There was one discordant note, though, a burst of laughter from the window seat occupied by John Marshal, Baldwin de Redvers, and her brother Rainald. They stopped as soon as she glanced their way, but the sound of their snickering lingered, unpleasantly so, in her memory.

Gilbert Foliot had nothing more to impart; they now knew the best and the worst of the Winchestser council. For a time, they discussed and damned the obstinacy of the Londoners, and Maude then revealed some good news from Normandy: on Easter Sunday, the Bishop of Lisieux had surrendered the city to Geoffrey. It was agreed that Miles should return to Gloucester, where he could keep watch upon the Marches, lest the Welsh seek to take advantage of English unrest. After that, the day's business was done.

Robert waited until he and Maude were alone with their brothers, Miles, and Brien. Only then did he say quietly, "I fear, Maude, that you hold Matilda too cheaply. She could be more of a threat than you think."

"Matilda? That little mouse? Surely you jest, Robert!"

"As long as she controls Kent and the coast, she is dangerous, Maude, for she could hire Flemish mercenaries, strip Boulogne bare to pay them, mayhap even blockade London—"

"She'd never have the stomach for killing, not St Matilda. She—" Maude stopped abruptly. "Rainald? You are going?"

Rainald nodded. "By your leave, Madame Queen," he said jauntily, and kissed her hand with an exaggerated courtly flourish.

"Rainald . . . ere you go, I would put a question to you. I am curious about something. What were you finding so amusing with John Marshal and Baldwin de Redvers?"

"What?" Rainald looked blank, and then shrugged, too nonchalantly. "Oh . . . that. Just a jest."

"I would like to hear it, Rainald."

The others were now watching, for Rainald's discomfort was too obvious to overlook. He scowled, ran his hand through his hair until it bristled like the quills of a ginger hedgehog. "Ah, Maude . . . it was a joke not fit for female ears. Can we not leave it at that?"

"I am not likely to swoon, Rainald."

Rainald ruffled his hair again, at a loss. If only she'd give him enough time, he might be able to come up with a less objectionable joke. But she was not about to wait, had that stubborn look he knew all too well. No, best to tell her and get it over with, but why did she have to be so damnably difficult? "Have it your way, Maude, but you'll not like it any. You asked what the Londoners wanted of you, and he . . . he said 'ballocks.'"

It was passing strange. Maude had expected such an answer, and yet she still felt as if she'd been slapped in the face. From the corner of her eye, she saw Miles and Ranulf struggling to hide grins. Were Robert and Brien laughing at her, too? "Very amusing," she said, with a smile that dripped icicles. "I want to be sure to give credit where due. Whose joke was it . . . John's or Baldwin's?"

Rainald's mouth dropped open. "I do not remember!"

"Rainald, tell me!"

"No . . . no, I will not!" he snapped, and spun on his heel, ignoring her demand that he halt, that he come back.

No one else had moved. But the slamming door broke the spell, and Ranulf leapt to his feet. "I'll go after him, Maude, talk to him once he calms down." The door banged again, and a strained silence settled over the room. Miles had risen, too. Striding forward, he kissed Maude's hand, then gave her a level look.

"You are too thin-skinned, Lady Maude. If you bleed so profusely from a mere scratch, how will you protect yourself from a much greater wound?"

"I am no fragile flower, Miles," Maude said stiffly. "You need not fear. I will meet whatever challenges lie ahead, and prevail over them."

"I do not doubt that, madame." At the door, he paused. "Even so," he said, "it was just a joke."

Robert was the next to depart. More tactful then Miles, he kept his opinion to himself, but Maude knew him well enough to read disapproval in his very reticence. She spun around, crossed to the hearth, waiting for the sound of the door's closing yet again. But it did not come, and she glanced over her shoulder, saw Brien still standing by the table.

"I suppose you think I made too much of it, too," she said, seeking to sound matter-of-fact, but sounding defensive, instead.

"Yes," he said, "but I think I understand why you did so."

Maude's smile was skeptical. "Do you, indeed?"

He nodded. "A joke about the gallows would find no favor in the house of a man who'd been hanged."

Maude took a quick step toward him. "Mayhap you do understand. Brien, this is not at all as I thought it would be. Why is it still so hard? Why are they still fighting me?"

"Nothing frightens men more than the unknown. Stephen might be discredited and defeated, but his flaws are familiar and therefore, safer."

Maude's mouth twisted. "Better a weak king than a strong queen?" she said bitterly, and Brien nodded again.

"It is so unfair, Brien! For five years, I fought to reclaim the crown that Stephen stole from me, and it cost me dear. Now that crown is within my grasp, and still there are men who would deny it to me. Miles says I am too easily wounded. Not by my enemies, by my friends, my own kinsmen. Those are the wounds that fester . . ."

"Maude." It was the first time he'd used her given name, but in the intensity of the moment, neither noticed. "You will be queen," he said, "and I will serve you faithfully until my last breath, that I swear upon the surety of my soul."

He raised her hand to his lips, and for a moment, their fingers entwined. "May I speak freely?" She nodded, but still he hesitated. "I would cut out my tongue ere I'd offend you. But there is this I must say to you, my lady. Fear cannot always be banished by force of will. Sometimes it needs to be coaxed away. Mayhap if you sought to sooth their fears with soft words . . ."

"Oh, no, Brien," Maude said earnestly, "you are wrong. I dare not, for they would take that as weakness. I must prove that I am my father's daughter, in deed and word as well as blood. It is the only way."

IF fortune had been fickle in April, it proved bountiful in May. Maude enjoyed some signal successes. Her uncle David, the Scots king, arrived. In Normandy, Robert Beaumont made a truce with Geoffrey. Geoffrey de Mandeville came to terms with her, too, and promised his aid in bringing the recalcitrant Londoners to heel. That did not prove necessary, though. A delegation of Londoners met Maude at St Albans, had a long discussion with Robert, and bowed to the inevitable. During the third week in June, Maude was given a subdued but courteous welcome into the capital, and was finally installed in the royal palace at Westminster.

ROBERT had just met with the Archbishop of Canterbury, discussing the plans for Maude's coronation. He was on his way back to the great hall when he was waylaid by his daughter. The Earl of Chester had yet to put in an appearance at Maude's court; rumor had him busy settling scores with William Peverel and the Earl of Richmond. But Maud was not about to miss her aunt's coronation, and she'd joined them at Reading. Robert was delighted to have her with them, for Amabel had been forced to remain at Bristol to watch over Stephen. He followed Maud now into the gardens, and soon unbent enough to play with her exuberant little lapdog. But this rare moment of relaxation was fleeting, for Gilbert Foliot was striding up the path toward him, with a haste that bespoke urgency.

"My lord earl, I'm indeed glad I found you. The Bishop of Winchester has arrived, and he no sooner paid his respects to the empress than they got into a right sharp argument. I thought it best to come looking for you, for they're going to be sorely in need of a peacemaker, and you're the only one they're both likely to heed."

Robert swore, profanely enough to startle his daugther. "Wherever did you learn such foul language, Papa . . . from Mama?" But her teasing was wasted, for Robert was already heading for the great hall, and she had to hurry to catch up.

"If I may be blunt," Gilbert Foliot continued, "the fault lies with the Scots king. If he were not so set upon having his chancellor named as the next Bishop of Durham—"

"Let me guess," Robert interrupted wearily. "Maude told the Bishop of Winchester that she'd approved the appointment of David's man to the Durham see, and the bishop took it amiss—badly amiss."

"You must have second sight, for that is indeed what happened. Lady Maude's temper could melt wax at twenty paces, and Bishop Henry is no meek Lamb of God. When I left, they were shouting at each other in a most undignified way, to the wonderment of a hall full of witnesses."

Robert swore again, quickening his stride, and Foliot did, too. "You know I have no great regard for Bishop Henry, my lord, but he has the right of it in this quarrel. The monks of Durham do not want the King of Scotland picking their bishop. Moreover, Lady Maude did promise the bishop that he'd have the final say in all Church appointments. As little as I like the man, I can understand his anger. It was very foolish of him, though, to scold the empress as if she were a wayward child. Any chance he may have had of prevailing ended as soon as the words 'I forbid it' passed his lips."

"He said that? Christ!"

"Papa!" Maud clutched Robert's arm, pointing. "It is too late . . . look!"

The Bishop of Winchester was stalking up the path toward them, trailed by flustered clerics. His color was so florid that he looked to be in danger of succumbing at any moment to an apoplectic seizure, and his eyes were bulging, glittering with such utter, unforgiving fury that the others stared at him in consternation; even the blasé Maud was impressed.

"Cousin? What happened?"

The bishop brushed past Robert as if he'd not spoken. But after a few steps, he stopped, turned back. "That woman," he said harshly, "has no honour."

"MAUDE, have you lost your wits?"

"I will thank you, Robert, to keep a civil tongue in your head! I owe Uncle David this. He has stood by me, never once betraying his oath. Even you swore homage to Stephen, even you. But not David!"

"David is not the problem. Did you truly say that if Henry would not invest David's man with the bishop's ring and mitre, you'd do it yourself? Tell me you did not say that, Maude!" But he saw the flush rising in her face. "Jesus God . . ."

"Robert, he gave me no choice! He forbade me, and those were his very words. 'I forbid it,' he said, whilst a hall full of witnesses looked on. What else could I do?"

"The Church does not and will not recognize lay investiture. That is a battle our father and your husband both fought with the Church—and lost!"

"You think I do not know that, Robert? But this I know, too, that he would never have dared to defy our father like that—never!"

He started to speak, stopped, and looked again at her face. His relief was enormous. Thank God she'd not meant it! The threat was foolish, but she was a novice at this, would learn. "So he goaded you into it," he said. "I can understand that, for I'll not deny that Henry can be insufferable at times. But this is a fence we must mend. He is going to expect an apology, Maude, and—"

"No!"

"Maude, you misspoke. Now you must make it right, however little you like it—"

"No," Maude said, "I will not," and he stared at her in dismay, for she sounded no less implacable than their enraged cousin the bishop.

17

WESTMINSTER, ENGLAND

June 1141

THE great hall of Westminster was said to be the largest in all of Europe, a vast timbered structure two hundred forty feet in length, more than sixty feet wide. Gervase de Cornhill had seen it before; as one of London's justiciars, he'd occasionally been summoned to attend the king. Each time he stepped across the threshold, he was awed by such earthly grandeur, marveling what mortal man had wrought. But on this humid June afternoon, his artistic appreciation was muted. He had eyes only for the woman seated upon the dais. She did look verily like a queen, he conceded, and a right handsome one at that. Pray God that she'd prove reasonable as well as comely. He glanced at his comrades, saw the same unease upon their faces. It was a sad day indeed for London when a good man like Stephen could be supplanted by a woman.

Once they'd been summoned, they knelt before Maude. They'd agreed that Gervase should speak for them, but when he started to introduce himself, a familiar male voice cut him off, saying, "Ah, but we know you well, Master de Cornhill." The Londoners stiffened, watching apprehensively as Geoffrey de Mandeville sauntered up onto the dais to stand at Maude's side.

His presence there was not a total surprise, for rumors had been circulating for a fortnight that Maude had made it well worth his while to switch sides. They'd been hoping it was not so, for he was no friend to London or its citizens. He'd been hostile to their commune from the first, had often used his power as the Constable of the Tower to intimidate and coerce, and his animosity now had a personal edge, for his father-in-law had been killed last month when a demonstration for Stephen had turned violent. But once Maude gave him leave to rise, Gervase strode forward purposefully, and launched into his prepared plea, that she should restore to them the laws of good King Edward, the sainted Confessor, whose reign had become enshrined in legend as a Golden Age in the brutal aftermath of the Conquest.

"My lord father ruled London for thirty-five years. His reign was peaceful and prosperous, and when he died, men called him the Lion of Justice in tribute to his enlightened and righteous kingship. Are you saying now that his laws were so onerous, so oppressive that you need relief from them?"

"No, madame, indeed not," Gervase said hastily, and launched into a well-rehearsed explanation that stressed the Londoners' reverence for the old ways, the old customs, while insisting that they were not disparaging the laws or courts of good King Henry, may God assoil him. When he was done, Maude said that she would take their request under consideration, a response that could promise all or nothing. But Gervase was already sure what her eventual answer would be, for as he studied her face, he'd come to a troubling conclusion. This new queen of theirs had no liking for the capital of her realm.

He had to persevere, though. "Madame, we have another petition to put before you. We beseech you to ease the burden our city is laboring under. We have been told that a new royal tallage is to be imposed upon us. But we are not able to meet this demand, for the city coffers are well nigh empty—"

"And why is that, Master de Cornhill?"

Gervase blinked. "Madame?"

"I asked why the city coffers are so bare. No, you need not fumble for an answer. I already know. For the past five years, your money has been propping up Stephen's monarchy. Dare you deny it?"

Gervase shifted from foot to foot, hoping she was posing a rhetorical question. When he saw that she was not, he said haltingly, "Madame, he . . . was the king. What choice did we have?"

"Oh, indeed you had a choice. When he sought to usurp my crown, you could have barred the city gates to him!"

"Madame, that was not for us to do. We are not kingmakers."

"Since when?" Geoffrey de Mandeville queried, and Gervase tensed, for he knew from personal experience that the earl's smile was never so disarming as when he was about to draw blood. "Your sudden modesty is commendable, Master de Cornhill. But if my memory serves, that is exactly what you and your cohorts claimed, that it was the Londoners who'd brought Stephen's kingship into being. And you in particular have been remarkably loyal to the man. Not only have you been urging your fellow citizens to keep faith with him, you've been doing some interesting almsgiving: to the Lady Matilda down in Kent."

Gervase wasn't the only one taken by surprise; so was Maude. "What?" she exclaimed, turning to stare at her new ally. "Are you sure of this, my lord of Essex?"

"Quite sure, madame. Master de Cornhill has been generously aiding Stephen's wife in her efforts to engage Flemish hirelings . . . for what purpose we can only speculate about. Unless he'd care to tell us?"

"Madame, that is not so! It was not at all as the earl makes it sound. I agreed to lend the queen a sum of money, and she pledged one of her Cambridgeshire manors as collateral. It was purely a business transaction."

"How very reassuring. Knowing that your treason was done for profit and not principle certainly sets my mind at ease!"

"Treason? Madame, I did not—"

"Yes, Master de Cornhill, you did. You are accomplices in Stephen's usurpation, all of you Londoners who aided and abetted him in his treacherous quest for my crown. If not for your disloyalty, he'd never have become king. You rejoiced in his theft, and supported his outlaw kingship without conscience qualms. Even after God's Judgment had been passed upon him at Lincoln, you still balked at recognizing me as England's true sovereign. I ought to have been crowned months ago, but you made that quite impossible. And now you dare to ask me to remit your taxes? Better you should seek out Stephen in his Bristol prison, for you'll get no such reprieve from me!"

"Madame, I entreat you to be fair, to—"

"I've heard you out. That is fairer than you deserve. Go home, Master de Cornhill, and tell your friends that a bill has come due, five years late, payable upon demand."

THEY'D gathered to hear Ranulf's report of his reconnaissance mission into London. He was relishing the attention, and spun out for them a vivid account of his reconnoitering. "I think I might have a promising career as a spy," he boasted, "for I was able to mingle freely without arousing any suspicion. But it is just as you feared, Robert. I wandered about the marketplace; I tarried in alehouses and taverns and the cookshop down by the river. I even paid a visit to the Friday horse fair at Smithfield. No matter where I went, the talk was of Maude and it was blistering hot. They are angry and fearful and some of them are defiant, too. They accuse Maude of being overweening and unwomanly, of seeking to bleed them white and destroy their commune. They are even quoting from Scriptures, that 'The Lord will be a swift witness against those that oppress' and 'All wickedness is but little to the wickedness of a woman.' I've never seen London in such a furor. Maude has stirred up a hornet's nest for true this time."

"I know," Robert conceded. "This is why I've asked you all here. We have a problem for certes. Maude seems set upon doing herself grievous harm, and we must find a way to limit the damage. We have to act, for she is losing the Church, the Londoners—"

"Her mind," Rainald said acerbically, and Robert glared at his brother.

"This is no time for joking, Rainald."

"Who is joking? I think she has gone stark, raving mad! How else explain it? It cannot always be her time of the month, can it? But what do you propose, Robert? I see no means of silencing her, shy of stuffing a gag in her mouth, and she pays you no more heed these days than—"

"This serves for naught," the Scots king interrupted impatiently, and Rainald yielded, grudgingly deferring to the other man's greater age and rank. "I am not here to mock my niece, but to determine why she has gone astray and figure out how to correct her course."

"I was thinking," Ranulf said pensively, "that it might be that her first taste of power has gone to her head. She has never had any, after all, not until now. Wine always hits a man harder if he is not one for drinking. Mayhap it is like that for Maude . . ." He trailed off, a little shy before the Scots king, and was pleased when Brien concurred.

"I know I am not her kinsman, as the rest of you are, but I think Ranulf might well be right. Lady Maude has always been compelled to obey, as a daughter and a wife, even as a widow. If you cage an animal up from birth, it takes time to adjust once it is finally set free."

"What are you both blathering about?" Rainald was scowling. "We all have to obey our betters. You think I have always done just as I please? My father kept me on a tight lead, I assure you! But I did not go helling about like a lunatic after he died, did I?"

"No," Brien said coolly, "but then no one ever told you that one of your 'betters' was to be a lad of fourteen."

Rainald showed signs of pursuing the argument, but David headed him off. "I think the true problem is that Maude was not schooled in kingship. She seems to believe that royal power is absolute, and her father ought to have taught her better than that. It was not enough merely to name her as his heir. She needed guidance as much as she did a husband, and she did not get it. In a sense, we are paying now for Henry's shortsightedness."

There was a moment of circumspect silence, none of them wanting to say what they were all thinking—that David's heavy-handed clash with the monks of Durham had not helped any, either. "We seem to be in agreement," Robert said, "that something must be done. But what? It occurred to me that we ought to summon Miles back from the Marches. Maude respects his opinion."

"She respects you, too, Robert," Ranulf insisted, and Robert shrugged.

"Mayhap so, but she is not listening to me much these days."

Rainald reached across the table for the wine flagon. "Well, I think Brien ought to be the one to talk to Maude. Come now, Brien, you need not look so surprised. It makes sense, after all. Anyone with eyes to see knows you fancy her, so Maude must know it, too. If you—"

He stopped abruptly, for Brien had just jerked the wine flagon out of his reach. "Let it be," he said, in a voice low-pitched and dangerous, "or you'll have reason to regret it."

It was suddenly very tense. Ranulf was fascinated, for although it was almost universally agreed that Brien was a man of uncommon honour, he'd heard others say, too, that he made a bad enemy. But he'd not seen that side of Brien. Not until now.

"Rainald, not another word! Do you ever think ere you talk? At times I'd swear your tongue and brain cannot possibly be connected!"

"The man just threatened me, Robert! I'm supposed to ignore that?"

Robert leaned over and grasped the younger man's wrist. "You heed me and heed me well. Nothing is easier to start and harder to stop than rumors of scandal. I do not ever want to hear you slander our sister's good name again. Is that understood?"

Rainald was accustomed to giving his temper free rein. But the hostility was repressive, walling him in on all sides. "I can see I am not wanted here," he said, and shoved his chair back. No one tried to stop him as he stalked toward the door and pulled it open. Almost at once, he recoiled. "Maude!"

"However did you know I was outside, Rainald? I'd not even knocked yet . . ." But Maude's smile wavered as she stepped into the room. For the men, it was like watching a shield crack after taking an unexpected blow, for in the instant that her defenses were down, they saw with unsparing clarity her surprise, her suspicion, and her hurt.

"You are getting forgetful, Robert. You neglected to let me know we'd convened a council for this afternoon. Is it not lucky," she said tonelessly, "that I happened by?"

Robert got slowly to his feet. "I asked them here, Maude. I am troubled by your recent actions and I thought it best to tell them of my qualms ere I sought you out."

"That is true," David agreed, "as far as it goes. But I cannot let him take all the responsibility upon himself. I share his qualms, too, lass. I suspect we all do."

"I see. So . . . now that you've had a chance to tally up my shortcomings, have you reached any conclusions? Is there any hope for me at all, or should I just abdicate at the first available opportunity?"

"You cannot abdicate until after your coronation," Rainald muttered, "and if you stay true to form, you're likely to offend the Archbishop of Canterbury so mortally that you'll end up having to crown yourself!"

"I am sorry that you find my behavior so shameful, Rainald. But you've not always been so critical, have you? As I recall, you said nary a word of protest when I bestowed the earldom of Cornwall upon you!"

Rainald flushed, but before he could retaliate, Robert said swiftly, "Maude, we need to talk about this. I've tried to tell you of my concern, but you seem to have defective hearing these days. I labored long and hard to win the Londoners over, and in one angry audience, you undid all my efforts. They are now convinced that having you as queen will be putting a cat amongst the pigeons, and it need not have come to that. You are making enemies faster than I can count them, and I do not understand why!"

"No, you do not understand . . . none of you do!"

But when she would have turned away, Ranulf stopped her. "Tell us, then," he entreated. "Make us understand. Maude, we are not the enemy. Surely you know that?"

She looked at him, and then nodded. "Yes," she admitted, "I know . . ." The anger had drained out of her voice, but so had the animation. As they watched, she walked to the window, stood staring out at the regal silhouette of Westminster Abbey. "If Stephen had taken me prisoner at Arundel, all resistance would have ended within hours of the word's getting out.

You'd have been loath to do it, but you'd have made your peace with him. What else could reasonable men do?"

She swung back to face them, and was reassured by what she saw, for they were listening intently. "But what happened after Lincoln? Stephen and I had submitted our claims to trial by combat, and I prevailed. That should have been enough . . . but it was not. Still men balked, still they refused to recognize my right. How many of Stephen's barons have come to my court? Where are these craven souls who abandoned Stephen at Lincoln? Robert Beaumont hastened to make a truce in Normandy—with Geoffrey. But neither he nor Waleran has made any peace overtures to me. Neither have the Earls of Northampton or Surrey or Pembroke. Even Chester's brother has kept his distance, and that after you saved his skin at Lincoln!"

"Maude, I know they have been slow to submit to you, but they will in time. You must have patience—"

"Robert, I have been patient for more than five years. And where has it gotten me? When my Norman barons learned of Stephen's defeat at Lincoln, did they rush to acclaim my victory? You know better—they offered my crown to Stephen's brother Theobald! And what did he do? He tried to strike a deal with Geoffrey. If Geoffrey'd accept Theobald's claim to Tours and agree to set Stephen free, Theobald would then recognize him as Duke of Normandy and King of England—Geoffrey, not me!"

"But Maude, Geoffrey did turn Theobald down!"

"For the love of God, Rainald! Are you so blind that you cannot see? How do you think that makes me feel? How many times do they get to spit in my face? Stephen was crowned within three weeks of my father's death. More than four months have passed since our victory at Lincoln, and I am still waiting for my coronation. That is four more months away from my sons . . . or did you never think of that? Henry is old enough to make the journey, even if the younger lads are not. I wanted him to be here for my coronation, to watch the archbishop set upon my head the crown that will one day be his. But the Londoners have denied me that. And yet you wonder, Robert, why I love them not? Just put that question to my eight-year-old son if you truly need an answer!"

"Maude, I do understand," Robert said. "I do not begrudge you a moment of your anger. I am simply saying that you cannot always act upon that anger. You've proven that you have the courage and perseverance and will to rule England. Now you must show the English that you have the discipline, too."

Maude said nothing, but her silence was a concession of sorts, and they took heart from it. She'd made mistakes—too many, in truth—but she'd learn from them. Encouraged, Robert crossed the chamber and kissed his sister's hand with deliberate formality, subject to sovereign.

Ranulf came over, too, only his was a brotherly kiss upon her cheek. "You'll see," he said. "It will get easier once you are crowned."

Maude gave him a weary smile. "I hope so, Ranulf," she said, "for there has been precious little joy in this queenship so far."

EMERGING from his tent, the Earl of Northampton stood motionless for a few moments, gazing upon Matilda's encampment. Newly hired mercenaries mingled with Matilda's vassals, William de Ypres's Flemings, and the earl's own men. Not quite a month had passed since he'd offered his services to Stephen's queen. He'd have come much sooner had he not dreaded facing her. Cynics might assume that he was motivated by the arrival at Maude's court of his stepfather and hated rival, the Scots king. But it was more complex than that, for he'd been deeply shamed by his flight at Lincoln. He was a proud man, one who'd been held up to public ridicule, and his disgrace was a gnawing cancer in his vitals. He owed Stephen a debt of honour, and he was here in the lush Kent countryside in an attempt—however ill advised—to repay it.

Matilda had made it easy for him; her need was too great to indulge in the luxury of reproaches or recriminations. But if his welcome was warmer than he deserved, the position he was expecting to fill—Matilda's mainstay—was already occupied.

The earl found it baffling that William de Ypres had not offered his sword to the highest bidder. He was equally astonished to see how high the Fleming had risen in Matilda's estimation. They made the oddest pair imaginable. There was no question, though, of her trust, and he had to admit that Ypres seemed to accord Matilda what he'd rarely shown other women—respect. But if Matilda had faith in the Fleming, Northampton did not, and he was determined to watch over Stephen's queen, whether she wanted such protection or not.

Stopping a soldier, he asked about Matilda's whereabouts, and it was no surprise to be told that "She is conferring with the Fleming, my lord."

Matilda and Ypres were walking together not far from her tent, heads down, so intent upon their discussion that they did not at once notice the earl's approach. When they did, Matilda greeted him gravely, looking so pale and tired that he felt a prickle of unease. "Have you heard anything, madame? No word about the king?" For that was his secret fear; he marveled sometimes that there had been no regretful announcement from Bristol Castle, breaking the sorrowful news that Stephen had been stricken by a mysterious mortal ailment.

"No . . . no word. I've had just the one letter from Stephen, nothing since then." Matilda looked toward the Fleming, back to Northampton. "Willem thinks the time has come."

The intimacy of the Flemish "Willem" vexed him, but the earl did not hesitate. "I think that he is right, my lady. You've sought to reason with the woman. You promised her that Stephen would abdicate, and pledged castles and hostages as surety. What more could you offer?"

"She did not believe me," Matilda said sadly. "And mayhap she was right, for I could not be sure Stephen would have agreed."

"Nonetheless, you did try to avoid bloodshed, my lady. Not only did she spurn your plea, she would deny your son his just inheritance. Ypres is right, and surely you know that. So why do you hesitate?"

Soldiers had begun to move closer, straining to hear. Some of them glanced away shyly as their eyes met Matilda's; others grinned and doffed their hats. Neither Ypres nor Northampton would understand her reluctance. Even if she'd tried to tell them, they'd not comprehend, for they knew war and accepted its consequences and its casualties. It was not that easy for her. It was a sobering realization, that men would die because of her decision, and her husband might well be one of them. She fumbled at her throat for the reassuring feel of her crucifix. Thy Will be done. But how did she know if it was God's Will . . . or her own?

"So be it," she said. "I agree, Willem. Tomorrow . . . at first light."

GERVASE DE CORNHILL was one of London's wealthiest merchants, as his Bishopsgate Street house unblushingly proclaimed. It was newly built and of stone, which made it a rarity in a city of wood and timber, constructed after the fashion of a lord's manor, with a spacious great hall, a private solar, even a privy chamber instead of the usual outdoor latrine. When the men began to arrive, they were welcomed by a young maidservant and offered not ale but wine, the beverage of the gentry. If some of them thought that Gervase was getting above himself, others were impressed by his affluence, and all hoped that good might come out of this urgent evening conclave.

Rohese was not supposed to be in the hall, but she was too curious to keep above-stairs. She was afraid that she might be sent home if London's troubles were as bad as her cousin Gervase feared, and she did not want to go; life was infinitely more interesting since she'd been chosen to attend Gervase's wife, Agnes. She'd not been sure at first just what "attending" meant, but it turned out to be easy enough: assisting with Agnes's grooming, taking care of her clothes, accompanying her in public, and keeping her company in private, just as young women of good birth did for the queen and ladies of rank. No, Rohese definitely did not want to lose so agreeable a sinecure, and so she lingered in the shadows, intent upon eavesdropping, for her future and London's had become one and the same.

"If Gervase sees you, he'll send you above-stairs straightaway," Agnes warned, but she was an indulgent mistress, and instead of banishing Rohese to the bedchamber, she soon found herself answering the girl's eager queries about their influential guests. It was indeed a gathering of distinction, she said proudly. There were several former sheriffs, some past and present aldermen, a magistrate, John Fitz Ranulf, and three members of the powerful Buccuinte family.

"Oh!" Rohese was staring at two newcomers to the hall. "By the saints," she hissed, "who is he?"

"That is Osborn Huitdeniers, no friend to Gervase, but too important not to include. He is a justiciar like Gervase and—"

"No, not the balding, stout one! The other, the young one!"

Agnes laughed. "Oh, you mean Thomas! He is a kinsman of Osborn's, and his new clerk. He was studying in Paris, but came home last year when his mother died, and his father then got him this position with Osborn. That is his father over there, Gilbert Becket, one of the former sheriffs I mentioned. He was quite prosperous once, but lost most of his property in the great fire a few years back and never recovered . . ."

But Rohese was no longer listening, for she had no interest whatsoever in the sire, only in the son. Snatching a platter from the maidservant, she swayed gracefuly across the hall. Up close, she found Thomas Becket even more attractive, tall and elegant, with fair skin and gleaming dark hair. Favoring him with her most seductive smile, she offered him wine, but to her disappointment, he politely declined. She was not so easily discouraged, though, was mustering her forces for a counterattack when Gervase happened to glance her way, and that was that for her flirtation with Master Thomas Becket.

"I thank you all for coming," Gervase said, striding to the center of the hall, "and I'll waste no time getting to the heart of the matter. I fear for our city under that spiteful woman's reign. London will be no more than a royal milch cow, milked dry for the Queen's Exchequer, and that will be the least of our troubles. Geoffrey de Mandeville is looking for any excuse to avenge the slaying of his wife's father, and when we complain to our new queen, I can assure you that it will be Mandeville she heeds, not us. Let me speak bluntly. London will suffer untold hardships if the *empress* ever sits upon Stephen's throne, for she—"

"Have you God's Ear, Gervase? You know something the rest of us do not? Why do you use words like *if* and *ever* when you speak of her queenship? I'd say that is no longer in doubt. The Bishop of Winchester has already proclaimed her as 'Lady of the English.' Her coronation is but a formality, and an inevitable one at that."

"Inevitable? I think not, Osborn. That is why I have summoned you here tonight, to remind you that she has not been crowned yet. It is not too late to save our city . . . if we have the courage to act and act now."

There were murmurings at that, and Osborn Huitdeniers said forcefully, "I did not come to hear talk of treason!"

"How can it be treason to support our lawful king? Stephen is God's anointed, not Maude. I say we keep it that way. She cannot be crowned if the city rises up against her. So there is still time—"

"You think we want that alien woman as our queen? I do not, for certes. But still less do I want to see bloodshed."

"Sometimes, John, there is no other choice. Maude reminded me that her father was called the Lion of Justice. Well, let me tell you about the justice he meted out to Luke de Barré. Most of you may not know of this, for it happened in Normandy. Some of the old king's barons had rebelled against him, and it took months ere he was able to put the rising down. Waleran Beaumont was amongst the rebel prisoners. He was young, though, not yet twenty, and the king was persuaded to take pity upon him; he was eventually set free and even restored to favor. But Luke de Barré was not so lucky, for the king commanded that his eyes be put out with red-hot awls. Men thought this was unjust, as Luke de Barré was not one of the king's vassals and thus was not forsworn, not guilty of treason. But he was a poet, and he had offended Henry by his mocking, scornful verses. Even the Count of Flanders pleaded on his behalf, to no avail. The king would not yield; Barré had made men laugh at him, he said, and there could be no forgiveness for that. As it happened, the sentence was never carried out . . . because the poor wretch preferred death to blindness and beat his head against the wall of his dungeon until he died. But the king did not relent. And this I can tell you for true, that Maude is his daughter. We'll get no more mercy from her than Luke de Barré did from Henry."

His story seemed to have the desired effect. Men shifted uneasily in their seats; a few blessed themselves as inconspicuously as possible. Osborn felt a chill; the sheep, did they not see that Gervase was leading them right to the cliff's edge?

"What does the fate of a Norman lord have to do with us?" he demanded. "I do not deny that the empress is a vexing and overweening woman. But she is not going to destroy our city. That is for us to do—if we heed reckless men like Gervase de Cornhill! What will happen to us if we do rise up, as he urges? She will retreat, only to come back with an army and lay siege to London. How long could we hold out? Who is going to come to our aid? I do not suppose that Stephen commands too many men from his prison chamber at Bristol!"

"I admit there is a risk, but if we take a stand, others will join us. No one wants that woman as queen, and men would be heartened by our defiance. They would rise up, too, would—"

"And if they did not? What would befall us then? If the empress is even half as vengeful as Gervase claims, she would exact a dreadful price for our rebellion. Let Gervase talk about long-dead Norman poets. I say we talk about history closer to home—Lincoln! Is there a man here who does not know what that city suffered after it was taken by the empress's army? Do you truly want to see London reduced to the same pitiful straits?"

The spectre of the ravaged ruins of Lincoln was a powerful deterrent. Although Gervase continued to argue, he soon saw that he was swimming against the tide. He'd wager that most of the men agreed with him, but they needed more than hope ere they'd commit to such a perilous course. He subsided, slumping down in his chair as the discussion ebbed and flowed around him. If the fools would not listen, what more could he do?

Thomas Becket had taken no part in the debate, listening intently but voicing no opinion of his own. When it was clear that Osborn's arguments were going to carry the day, he asked his clerk to fetch him more wine. Thomas rose obligingly, and it was then that he saw the monk being ushered across the hall toward Gervase. He paused to watch, sensing something out of the ordinary was occurring.

"Silence!" Gervase shouted suddenly. "I've just gotten an urgent message from Bermondsey Priory, and it changes everything. It seems there is a new player in this game. Brother Anselm here has come at the behest of Prior Clarembald to bear witness. He says that Queen Matilda and William de Ypres have led an army out of Kent, and they are ravaging and burning south of the river!"

That announcement unleashed brief pandemonium. "Quiet!" Gervase cried, over and over until he got his way. "Let Brother Anselm tell us what he knows."

"It is true," the monk said calmly; he alone seemed untouched by the chaos permeating the hall. "They spared our priory, but others were not so fortunate. If it were not full dark, you could see the smoke along the horizon. And by the morrow, they'll be in Southwark."

"As I said," Gervase repeated triumphantly, "this changes everything. The queen is sending us an unmistakable message—that we have as much to fear from her wrath as we do from Maude's."

"It is so unfair! How can people hope to survive, trapped between two armies! What can we do?"

"Is it not obvious? We ally ourselves with the queen, we keep faith with Stephen, and we show Maude the mettle of true Londoners!"

This stirring declaration set off a burst of cheering. Osborn shuddered, seeing his rental houses and his luxurious Thames Street home going up in flames, a lifetime's work lost, and for what? "Let's not be hasty! We must think this through, must—"

"What was it you'd asked, Osborn—who would come to our aid? Well, now we know—Queen Matilda! I say we send word to her straightaway!" And this time Gervase prevailed. Agreement was swift and almost unanimous. On this Midsummer's Eve, London cast its fate with Stephen's queen.

JUNE 24TH, the Nativity of John the Baptist, was also known as Midsummer's Day. It was a popular festival, celebrated with bonfires and flowering garlands and torch-lit processions. Westminster's great hall was hung with St John's wort, rue, roses, and vervain. The palace cooks had been laboring all morning to produce a truly spectacular meal, a trial run for Maude's coronation banquet, and the air was redolent with the aromas of simmering venison stew and roast swan and freshly baked bread. As noon approached, the guests were escorted into the hall, then to their designated seats at the linen-draped trestle tables, while youths hurried to offer lavers of scented washing water and hand towels.

It was not until the first course was served—a savory rabbit soup—that Maude had the opportunity to question Robert about the Bishop of Winchester's conspicuous absence. "When you saw him this morn, Robert, did he tell you he'd not be attending? What excuse did he offer?"

"I did not see him, Maude. He has left Westminster."

"Without a word to me? Where did he go?"

"I do not know. I have to admit, Maude, that I'm troubled in this disappearance of his. I know you do not like hearing it, but we have to make our peace with the man . . . and it will not be easy if we cannot even find him."

Maude set her spoon down. "Most likely he's gone off to one of his manors to brood, waiting to be coaxed back. I understand that was his usual routine whenever he did not get his own way with Stephen. I never expected to be in sympathy with Stephen, but I can well imagine what he must have gone through after denying Henry that archbishop's mitre he so craved. It amazes me that he had the backbone to hold fast . . ."

She waited until a server had removed her soup bowl before turning back toward her brother. "Now . . . what of the rumors about Ypres? Is it true that he plundered and burned manors and villages south of the river? Have you been able to verify that yet?"

"My scouts have not returned, but Geoffrey de Mandeville says it is true enough, and he ought to know." Robert lowered his voice, for the Earl of Essex had been given a seat of honor at the high table. "I've heard it claimed that half the whores in Southwark spy for him, and I'd not be surprised, for little gets past him."

Maude found it difficult to admit she'd so misjudged Stephen's queen. She was baffled, too, for she would never have expected Matilda to put Stephen's life at risk. But this was neither the time nor the place to discuss Matilda's astonishing metamorphosis, and she contented herself with saying only, "I thought Matilda had more common sense."

The conversation at their table was now focusing upon the continuing saga of the Earl of Chester's lordly banditry. He'd claimed proprietary rights over most of the prisoners captured at Lincoln, and those unlucky souls had been bled for exorbitant ransoms, not always in money. Young Gilbert de Gant had been compelled to wed Chester's niece as the price of his freedom, and William Peverel had been forced to yield Nottingham Castle. But if the table talk was true, it seemed that Chester had pulled off an even more outrageous coup. He'd lured his old enemy the Earl of Richmond into an ambush, cast the man into one of his dungeons, and neglected to feed him until he'd agreed to turn over Galclint Castle.

As usual, Chester's utter indifference to public opinion stirred amazement, amusement, disapproval, and possibly even envy. Maude's feelings were not so ambivalent, though; her response was anger, pure and simple. Once her coronation was over and she could concentrate upon matters of state, she meant to teach the outlaw earl a sharp lesson in the powers of the Crown. He seemed to think he was above the laws of the land, and for that, she blamed Stephen. Her father would never have tolerated such arrant breaches of the King's Peace, and neither would she.

She glanced down the table now toward her niece. Maud was giggling at something Ranulf had just said. If she was distressed on her husband's behalf, she was concealing it remarkably well. Maude still thought it prudent to divert the conversation away from Chester's manifold misdeeds, and she signaled for silence.

"I have good news to share. I received a letter this morn from my husband. He writes that the city of Caen has yielded to him, as have Verneuil and Nonancourt, and he predicts that by summer's end, he will control all of Normandy west of the River Seine."

Audible ripples of approval and relief eddied about the hall. All were war-weary and impatient for the succession dispute to be settled. Maude was not the only one who resented Stephen's barons for their stubborn reluctance to come to terms with political realities.

The venison stew was being ladled onto trenchers when a flustered youth was admitted to the hall, insisting that he had an urgent message for the Earl of Essex. Geoffrey de Mandeville rose at once, and Maude watched with interest as they conferred. So did Robert, for it had occurred to them both that Mandeville's spy system might have unearthed information about Matilda's whereabouts or intentions. When the earl turned around, they knew at once that whatever he'd just learned was calamitous, for the color had faded from his face, and he was not a man to be easily shaken.

Striding swiftly back to the high table, he said, "The Londoners are rising up against you, madame. They are massing in the streets, making ready to march on Westminster."

"No . . . they would not dare!"

"Yes," he said flatly, "they would. You can believe it or not as you choose, but I do. This lad's master is a local merchant, a man who's given me reliable information in the past, and he is not likely to make a mistake of this magnitude."

Osborn Huitdeniers's servant had trailed the earl to the dais, and he nodded vigorously. "It is true, my lady, I swear it," he assured Maude solemnly. "By the time I reached Ludgate, the church bells had begun to peal throughout the city, calling men to arms. Listen . . . can you not hear?"

Maude and Robert tilted their heads, and indeed, they could hear the distant, muted chiming of church bells. As stunned as Maude was, she rallied fast and got hastily to her feet, still clutching her napkin. "Thank God for the warning! But we'll have to act at once if we hope to repel them. Robert, the command is yours—"

"What command?" Geoffrey de Mandeville snapped. "We're facing a mob, not an army. That is not a fight we can win. But we ought to be able to get away ere they—"

"Run?" Maude was flabbergasted. "Never!"

Robert was on his feet, too. "Maude, he is right. Not only are we outnumbered, but our wives and daughters are with us. If we'd been able to reach the Tower . . . but we could never hope to keep them out of Westminster and Christ pity us if we try!"

By now those at the high table knew of their peril. Men were pushing their chairs back. Ranulf had already reached Maude's side, with Brien just a stride slower. Maude's niece was leaning over Rainald's wife, coaxing her to rise, but Beatrice seemed incapable of moving; she'd begun to make soft whimpering noises, sounding eerily like a mewing kitten. Maude saw the truth of Robert's words in their stricken faces, but her every instinct fought against flight. "Is there not some way that we can resist?"

Robert shook his head. "Even if we could hold them off for a time, there is another army on the loose, just across the river. How long do you think it would take the Londoners to open their gates to Matilda and Ypres? No, Maude, if we stay, we doom ourselves." He glanced around at the hall, now in a state of spreading confusion. Fear stood poised to strike, and nothing was more contagious, as he well knew. If they hoped to head off utter panic, they'd have to act swiftly. "I will tell them," he offered, "if you wish."

"No," Maude said, "it is for me to do." Wondering how she would ever find the words, she moved toward the edge of the dais. "Be silent so you may hear me," she urged, "for there is something I must say."

THE retreat from Westminster was done "without tumult and with military order" according to a chronicle favorable to Maude's cause. One much more sympathetic to Stephen described a "panic" and a "disorderly flight." The truth lay somewhere in between.

Maude and her coterie got away safely to Oxford, but some of her adherents veered off on their own. The Londoners surged into a ghost palace: food still heaped on trenchers in the deserted great hall, chairs overturned, doors oddly ajar, open coffers, burning candles and silence. A few of the angry citizens were disappointed to have won by default; most were relieved. They celebrated by ransacking the palace, carrying off clothes and bedding and belongings left behind, and some sat down to enjoy Maude's interrupted meal. As word spread into the city, people flocked into the streets again, to cheer and hug and marvel at the ease of their triumph, while church bells were rung with joyful exuberance, until all of London reverberated with the clamorous, silver-toned sounds of victory.

THEY had gathered at Eastcheap to wait. At this time of day, the marketplace ought to have been thronged with people looking for bargains, moving from stall to stall, examining the fresh fish, choosing the plumpest hens, buying candles and pepper and needles. The stalls were open, but the fishmongers and cordwainers and butchers were doing no business, despite the growing crowd. The sun was hot, flies were thick, and the odors pungent; no one complained, though. They talked and gossiped among themselves, strangers soon becoming friends, for the normally fractious and outspoken Londoners had forgotten their differences, at least for a day, united in a common purpose and determined to revel in their triumph, for they were pragmatic enough to understand this might be their only one. Now they joked and swapped rumors and waited with uncommon patience, and at last they heard a cry, swiftly picked up and echoed across the marketplace: "She is coming!"

People had been clustered at the bridge, lining both sides of the narrow street. But Matilda had not expected a crowd of this size. Nor did she expect the sudden cheer that went up as she came into view. Her mare shied and the Earl of Northampton kicked his stallion forward, ready to grab her reins if need be. William de Ypres was content merely to watch; he'd learned by now that Matilda was better able to take care of herself than most men realized. Matilda soon got her mare under control, and reined in as the spectators pressed forward. She found herself looking out upon a sea of friendly faces, and she smiled at them, wishing she could thank each and every one, these Londoners who'd fought for Stephen as his own barons would not.

"We have made a beginning this day," she said. "With your help, good people, we shall set my husband free and restore him to England's throne."

18

GUILDFORD, ENGLAND

July 1141

WILLIAM DE YPRES was taken at once to the queen's presence, despite the lateness of the hour. Not for the first time, Matilda found herself marveling at the Fleming's stamina. He was past fifty, his hair thinning into a silver fringe, his skin as rough-hewn as bark from constant exposure to sun, wind, and winter gales. He was fighting age, though, as fiercely as he'd fought all his foes, continuing to expend his energy with the reckless abandon of a twenty-year-old. Matilda knew he must be greatly fatigued, for he'd been in the saddle since dawn. But she knew, too, that he'd never admit to it. Ignoring his protests, she insisted upon ordering him a meal from the kitchen and then stood over him while he ate it. It still surprised her, that she could have become fond of a man so likely to burn in Hell's hottest flames.

Casting aside a drumstick, Ypres reached for a napkin. "Can we forget about chicken now and talk instead of crowns? I have news, my lady, about your enemy the empress. My scouts were right; she did indeed head for Oxford. But she did not tarry there for long, and she and Brother Robert were soon riding west in all haste."

Matilda stiffened. "Bristol?"

"No . . . Gloucester, most likely to confer urgently with Miles." Ypres caught the echoes of alarm in her voice and gave her a level, faintly admonitory look. "That is not a fear you ought to dwell upon, madame. It serves for naught."

"I know," Matilda admitted. "I have no reason to think Maude capable of outright murder. And . . . even if desperation did drive her to it, I cannot believe that Robert would ever agree. But such comforting certitude comes more easily to me during the daylight hours. Alone at night, I begin to hear whispers in the dark . . ."

"I cannot swear to you, madame, that you have no cause for fear. Nor will I deny that you have put your husband in greater peril. But had you done nothing, he'd have no chance whatsoever of regaining his throne or his freedom. Remember what he was facing: a lifetime's confinement with no hope of reprieve. With the stakes that high, I'd willingly gamble my life on the outcome, and from what I know of your husband, I suspect he would, too."

Matilda smiled wanly. "You do find your own way, Willem. Anyone else would have reassured me that Stephen's life is not truly at risk. You assure me, instead, that he'll go to his grave bearing me no grudge."

Ypres grinned; he was always encouraged whenever Matilda essayed a jest, however tentative or forced, for he'd initially feared that she lacked any humor whatsoever. She'd moved to the solar window, gazing out at the summer darkness. After a few moments of silence, she said, "I have news of my own. I had a clandestine visit from Stephen's brother whilst you were gone."

Ypres showed no surprise. But then, he was the most cynical soul she'd ever met, always expecting the worst of men and rarely disappointed. "The bishop is seeking to mend fences, is he? Let me see . . . he did not want to forsake Stephen, but he had no choice, for he had to put the good of Holy Church above all else, however deeply it pained him."

"If I did not know better, I'd swear you were there, Willem, for that is exactly what he said. By the time he was done, he'd even managed to make his betrayal seem almost heroic."

He'd rarely heard her sound so bitter. "It was easy enough to guess what he would say. But what of you, madame? What did you tell him?"

"I wanted to spurn his hypocrisy," Matilda confessed, "to curse his treachery and revile him as Cain. Instead, I made myself smile. I let him clasp my hand and I lied, I said I understood. And then I told him the truth, that we need his help."

"We do," he said succinctly.

"I know. And to save Stephen, I'd have made a deal with the Devil himself." Matilda paused. "In truth, I think I did."

WORD soon spread of Maude's return to Oxford. She wasted no time, conferring with her uncle David, the Scots king, and then summoning the others to the castle solar. They were heartened to find Miles at her side, for he had the gift of the best battle commanders, that ability to banish doubts and exorcise the spectre of defeat by the sheer contagious force of his own self-assurance. His presence seemed to have bolstered Maude's spirits, too; she looked tired and thin, but resolute. "We have made mistakes, most of them mine," she said, surprising them by her candor. "Fortunately, mistakes can be made right, and that is why I have called you here."

That had not been an easy admission for Maude to make, but she could not deny, even to herself, that she bore much of the blame for this sudden downturn in her fortunes. She still believed that her grievances were justified. She'd not been able to argue, though, with Miles's blunt assessment of her plight: had she paid more heed to Robert's cautious counsel, she'd have been spared the humiliation of being chased out of her own capital by those misbegotten, knavish Londoners. They, at least, would pay for their treachery. Geoffrey de Mandeville would see to that. And she told them then of her proposed pact with the Earl of Essex, one which would grant him the sheriffdoms and justiciarships of London, Middlesex, and Hertfordshire, would promise him the Bishop of London's castle at Stortford, and agree to make no peace with the Londoners, his "mortal enemies," without his consent.

That was not well received. There were murmurings, disapproving frowns, and Brien said skeptically, "Is it wise to give Mandeville so much power? When I think of men worthy of trust, he is not the first one to come to mind."

"We do not trust him, either," Maude conceded, and Miles stirred laughter by saying brusquely:

"I'd wager that even the man's own mother did not trust him! But we do need him. We cannot allow the Londoners' rebellion to go unpunished. The sooner we regain control of the city, the sooner we can get our lady crowned. Stephen's kingship has been a stinking corpse for nigh on six months now. I say we bury it once and for all."

That was the sort of tough, confident talk they needed to hear. But they needed answers, too, and John Marshal was not shy about seeking them. "That sounds well and good. But ere we go looking for shovels, what about the chief mourner at this funeral? What about the Bishop of

Winchester? Geoffrey de Mandeville told me that one of his spies trailed the bishop to the queen's castle at Guildford."

Until now, Robert had taken no part in the discussion. There was a deliberation in his movements that bespoke exhaustion, and he was carrying all of his fifty-one years heavily these days. "We heard the same rumor," he said. "We have decided, therefore, that I should seek out the bishop in Winchester, do what I can to soothe his wounded pride and assuage his anger. We can only hope it is not too late. But if he does mean to ally himself with Stephen's queen, better we find out now. We need to know our enemies."

"Speaking of enemies," Miles prompted, glancing toward Maude and Robert, "ought we not to tell them about Stephen?"

Robert took up the challenge with obvious reluctance. "When we reached Gloucester, I sent to Bristol for my wife. She brought troubling news. On two different occasions, Stephen was found out in the bailey, each time after dark. Clearly we erred in taking him at his word. He cannot be trusted."

Maude had been arguing that all along, and it was hard to resist a tart "I told you so." Even a fortnight ago, she wouldn't have. But how could she decry their poor judgment now . . . after the London calamity?

Stephen had none to defend him. The men still admired his battlefield bravery, but much of their sympathy had been left in the dust on the London-Oxford Road. Even Ranulf acknowledged the danger. Shifting uneasily in his seat, he asked, "What will you do?"

"We shall see to it," Maude said coolly, "that he does not get a third chance to escape."

STEPHEN jerked upright on the bed. The dream's terrors were already fading; he no longer remembered what had set his heart to racing, caused the sweat to break out on his skin like this. So much, he thought, for sleeping during the day. But what else was there to do? Who would have guessed that a prisoner's greatest foe would be sheer boredom?

Getting to his feet, he wandered restlessly about the chamber. Because he'd been lucky enough to have been born male and a king's grandson, he'd passed his adult years doing as he pleased. He'd been spared Maude's painful lessons in obedience—until now. The room was stifling. On a hot July day like this, he would have been out hunting. How many more months would he be caged here, tethered like one of his own falcons?

Finding himself at the table, Stephen picked up a book, soon set it down again. He knew there were those who read for fun, but that was a pleasure which still eluded him. The window was unshuttered; he could see men-at-arms crossing the bailey, a groom unsaddling a lathered gelding, several black-clad Benedictine monks. These months of enforced celibacy had given him a new respect for those men who willingly chose to deny the hungers of the flesh. Not even for the love of God could he have forsaken the love of women.

He sat down in a chair by the window and tilted it back at a precarious angle. Thoughts of Matilda were invariably bittersweet. This past week had been particularly difficult, for their sixteenth wedding anniversary was approaching. He refused to let himself believe, though, that he might never again make love to his wife. Without hope, he could not endure, nor keep faith with God.

If this ordeal was indeed a test, if he must prove himself to the Almighty as a true Christian and a worthy king, he could not let himself despair. He could not doubt that he would eventually prevail.

Church bells were pealing in the distance. What was Matilda doing at this hour? Was she still in England or had she taken their children back to Boulogne? He knew she'd be loyal to her last breath. Nor did he doubt her courage or resourcefulness. He'd never believed that women were weak; his mother had effectively dispelled that male myth early in his childhood. But Matilda could not be his salvation, for she labored under the same burden as Maude. A woman could not act alone. She could not lead men into battle. Maude's claim to the crown depended upon support from men. She'd never have been able to mount a serious challenge to his kingship if she'd not had Robert to fight her battles in England and Geoffrey to fight them in Normandy.

But Matilda had no Robert of Gloucester or Geoffrey of Anjou. The men she ought to have been able to turn to—his brothers—were unable or unwilling to come to her aid. Theobald was too far away to be of assistance, and Henry too treacherous. Nor could he expect men like the Beaumonts and the Fleming Ypres to rally to Matilda, men who'd so shamelessly abandoned him on the battlefield. No, he did not see how he could win—barring a miracle—and it seemed very presumptuous to expect the Almighty to intervene actively on his behalf. If the opportunity arose again, he'd risk an escape. But his best hope was that Maude would lose, that she'd blunder badly enough to confirm all those queasy suspicions about her queenship. Maude or a miracle—his was, Stephen acknowledged wryly, a most unlikely battle plan.

A shout floated up through the open window, and he tipped his chair back still farther, craning his neck to see. A rider was coming through the gatehouse—a courier from Maude? Of all the crosses he had to bear, his sense of isolation was surely the most onerous.

It was all the more frustrating for being a new burden. Up until a month ago, his guards had kept him apprised of the happenings beyond

Bristol's walls. Even his enemies had never denied his charm, and it had been easy enough for him to disarm his young gaolers with his affability and his humor. Only one guard had been immune to his friendly overtures, a burly freckled youth from Shropshire whose cousin had been one of the Shrewsbury garrison hanged at Stephen's command. The hostile Godwin had still been a source of news, though. He'd been the first to tell Stephen that his brother the bishop had betrayed him, and when the Londoners capitulated, he'd come at once to gloat.

But without warning, it all changed; the well went dry. Now Stephen's questions went unanswered, deflected with shrugs and silence. He was baffled by their sudden reticence. If Maude had been crowned—as surely she must by now—why were they so loath to tell him so?

Confinement had sharpened his senses, and he heard the muffled footsteps on the stairs long before a key turned in the lock. He was puzzled, for supper was still hours away, but pleased. To a man as gregarious as Stephen, solitude was a punishment in and of itself.

The first man into the chamber was a disappointment, though—Godwin, the embittered Shropshireman. The second guard was a stranger to Stephen, but he smiled at sight of the third, for he'd become fond of Edgar, a painfully shy youth whose stoop-shouldered height and harelip had earned him a cruel nickname from his fellow guards: "Scarecrow."

Edgar did not return Stephen's smile. He looked so ill at ease that Stephen glanced instinctively toward Godwin. When he did, he set his chair down with a thud, staring in disbelief at the dangling chains.

Godwin smiled grimly. "I'd begun to despair of this day ever coming, but it was worth the wait, by Corpus, it was. I daresay you think a king deserves shackles of silver. But you'll just have to make do with the sort used on common folk like my poor cousin."

Stephen shoved his chair back with enough force to overturn it. Although he'd not yet spoken, it was impossible to misread the defiance in his stance, and Edgar said hastily, "Please, my lord, do not resist. They'll just summon more men to hold you down . . ."

Stephen had taken a backward step, his eyes flicking from the chains to the closest weapon at hand, a pewter candlestick. But Edgar had spoken the simple truth; this was not a confrontation he could hope to win. He slowly unclenched his fists, then stepped forward and held out his wrists for the manacles.

STEPHEN'S rage had sustained him until the guards withdrew. But as soon as he was alone, his shoulders slumped and he sank down in the window seat. The shackles were surprisingly heavy and had already begun to chafe his skin. He jerked the chain suddenly and futilely, wincing as the iron bit into his wrist. Like a hobbled horse. Better to have died on the field in Lincoln than this.

Edgar came back at dusk, alone and apologetic, carrying Stephen's supper tray. Stephen was still sitting in the window seat. He ignored the food, seemed equally indifferent to Edgar, and the youth became flustered under his aloof, uninterested gaze. Even if Stephen's friendliness was false, as Godwin claimed, it mattered to Edgar that this man, a crowned king, remembered his name, looked upon his harelip without flinching, and when caught out in the bailey, concocted a story to deflect suspicion from Edgar, who'd forgotten to lock his chamber.

"Look, my lord, I've brought you these," he said nervously. "With your permission, I can wrap these rags around the irons. That will keep them from rubbing your wrists raw."

Stephen met Edgar's imploring eyes, and nodded curtly. Edgar knelt, began to fumble with the rags. "I am so sorry, my lord. It does not seem right to me, shackling you like this. I do not blame you for trying to escape, for any man would. But it gave them an excuse, you see. Mayhap once the empress is able to be crowned, she will relent—"

"What are you saying, Edgar? Maude has not been crowned yet? Why not?"

Edgar hesitated. "If I tell you, my lord, please do not let anyone know you heard it from me. The empress cannot be crowned, for the Londoners rebelled and chased her out of the city."

"Christ Jesus! Have they forgotten what befell Lincoln?"

"They are safe enough from the empress's wrath, at least for now. They have your lady wife to protect them, need not fear as long as she holds London."

"Matilda holds London?" Stephen leaned forward, grasped Edgar's arm. "Who is helping her? The Beaumonts? My brother? Name of God, lad, tell me!"

"It is the Fleming, my lord. No one knows how your lady won him over, but she—"

"Ypres? You are telling me the truth, Edgar? You swear it is so?"

Edgar nodded solemnly, and Stephen pulled away, leaning back in the window seat. Edgar waited a moment or so, before asking tentatively, "Do you not want me to fix your manacles, my lord?" Stephen merely shrugged, as if the chains no longer mattered, and then startled Edgar by laughing.

Edgar's eyes were wide, for he could find no humor whatsoever in Stephen's plight: a consecrated king shackled like a felon. "My lord?"

"For the past six months, Edgar, I've been telling myself that as much as I needed a miracle, it was foolish to expect one. But I'd forgotten," Stephen said, beginning to laugh again, "that I had my own miracle all along. I married her!"

BRIEN FITZ COUNT was standing upon the battlements of Oxford Castle, watching as the day died away. The sun was haloed in brightness, deepening from molten gold to a fiery copper-red, and seemed to have set the river on fire. Gazing down at that shimmering, sunset-tinted current, Brien found himself thinking of past battles, remembering rivers that had run red with the blood of the wounded and the slain.

He was so caught up in his own thoughts that he did not at once hear his name being called. By the time he did, Maude was coming up the battlement wall-walk toward him. "I've been searching all over for you," she said. "I'm glad I finally thought to look up!"

He made room for her at the embrasure and together they watched as the sun disappeared beyond the distant hills. "Did you arrange matters with Geoffrey de Mandeville's vassal?" he asked, and Maude nodded.

"Yes, a man named Hugh d'Ing. Mandeville is sending him to Normandy to obtain Geoffrey's approval of our pact, and then on into Anjou to get my son's consent. Henry will enjoy that," Maude said with a smile, "for this will be his first official act as heir to the throne."

By now the vivid sky was past its peak, the colors beginning to fade. Brien turned away from the embrasure, focusing all of his attention upon Maude. "Did you say you were looking for me, my lady?"

"Yes . . . I wanted to talk to you about an earldom."

Brien smiled. "In all the years I've known Miles, I've never seen him so joyful. Is all ready for the ceremony?"

"Yes . . . on the morrow I will confer upon Miles the earldom of Hereford. It is no more than he deserves, for he has been amongst my most stalwart supporters. But so have you, Brien. It would give me great pleasure to grant you an earldom, too. Will you not reconsider?"

When he shook his head, still smiling, Maude moved closer, looking up intently into his face. "But why, Brien? You have been steadfast, a loyal ally and as dear a friend as I could hope to have. Why will you not let me reward you as I've done the others?"

Brien was no longer smiling. "I want no reward for serving you. If I can offer you nothing else, I can give you this—the certainty that I seek only to help you claim the crown that is your birthright."

As their eyes met, Maude found she could not look away. "Ah, Brien," she said, almost inaudibly, "I begin to think you could be more dangerous to me than Stephen." Her words seemed to surprise her as much as they did Brien, for color suddenly burned its way up into her face and throat. He drew a sharp breath and then reached for her hand, bringing it up to his mouth. To anyone watching, it was a perfectly proper gesture of respect, but Maude knew better, and she freed her hand from his clasp. She did not draw away, though, not until a sudden shout echoed from the West Gate: "Riders coming in!"

Maude and Brien moved back to the battlements, peering down through the gathering dusk at the approaching horsemen. They were still some distance away, just crossing the bridge, but Maude recognized the rangy grey stallion in the lead, for it was her brother's favorite mount.

"It is Robert!" she exclaimed. "I do not like this, Brien. Such a rapid return from Winchester does not bode well for us."

ROBERT soon confirmed the worst of Maude's forebodings. In a solar poorly lit by smoldering cresset lamps, he told them that his mission had failed. The Bishop of Winchester was, he reported, as slippery as any eel, impossible to pin down without a forked stick. The bishop had refused to return with him to Oxford, but he'd denied conniving with Matilda to restore Stephen to the throne. He'd insisted that his only concern was the welfare of Holy Mother Church, disclaimed any ambitions of his own, contended that he bore Maude no grudge for her intemperate behavior, provided that she kept faith in the future, and, Robert concluded bleakly, "I believed none of it."

"I daresay the bishop knows far more of Scriptures than I do," Maude said, "and I am not sure if this comes from the Book of Matthew or Luke, but the message itself is beyond dispute: 'He that is not with me is against me.'"

She paused, her gaze sweeping the solar, moving from face to face. She found what she sought: a unity of purpose and a grim resolve to do what must be done. What had been lost in London would be recouped at Winchester.

"Stephen's kingship died at Lincoln," she said. "I agree with Miles, that burial is long overdue. Well, God Willing, we shall hold the funeral in Winchester."

19

WINCHESTER, ENGLAND

July 1141

WILLIAM DE CHESNEY finally located his brother Roger in a shabby alehouse on Gold Street, in unseemly proximity to the Church of All Saints. "What sort of peculiar folk do you have in this town? I stopped a monk on the street, asked him the whereabouts of the bishop's palace at Wolvesey, and damn me if else, but he spat into the dirt at my feet!"

Roger laughed. "There is a sea of bad blood between the bishop and the brothers of Hyde Abbey. For more than six years, he has been blocking their election of a new abbot. Why, you ask? Very simple, lad. As long as they lack an abbot, Bishop Henry gets to control their revenues."

Will shook his head ruefully. "If men only knew how easy it was to commit legal larceny, banditry would be cut in half overnight. That fits, though, with what I've heard about Bishop Henry, that he loves money overly well. I came to Winchester seeking a position in his household as you suggested. But first I ought to ask you this: Is he miserly with those in his service? If so, I'd rather look elsewhere."

"You need not fret about that. He is tightfisted for certes, but he is also shrewd enough to understand that a man gets only what he pays for in this life. Serve him well and he will reward you as you deserve. Let him down and you get no second chance. So . . . what say you?"

Will shrugged. "If I'm going to sell my sword, it might as well be to the Church. Mayhap the bishop will put in a good word for me come Judgment Day!"

His brother laughed again, scattered a few coins onto the table, and they sauntered out into the sunlight. This was Will's first visit to Winchester, and Roger insisted upon acting as his guide, keeping up a running commentary as they ambled along High Street, also known as Cheap or Cheapside. The castle was situated in the southwest corner of the city, and had supplanted the old palace as a royal residence. Bishop Henry had sweet-talked Stephen into turning the palace over to him—"back in the days when they were still talking," Roger said with a grin. He also held the bishop's palace at Wolvesey, off to the southeast, and had embarked upon an ambitious building project to make Wolvesey the wonder of Winchester.

Will liked what he saw: a city prosperous and thriving. While Roger didn't know the exact population, he estimated it to be between six and eight thousand, which made it one of England's larger cities. It had its own fair, its own saint, and a proud history, for it was once a Roman settlement, later the capital of the Saxon kingdom of Wessex, and several English kings had tombs within the great cathedral. So many bells were chiming that it sounded as if there were a House of God on every corner, and indeed there were too many parish churches to count, Roger reported, as well as the priory of St Swithun, the nunnery of St Mary, and just beyond the walls, Hyde Abbey. "But," he added, "there are alehouses and bawdy-houses, too, lad, and I might be coaxed into taking you on a sinner's search after dark!"

They bought apples from a peddler, fended off a tenacious street beggar, then stopped to watch as several small boys threw mud upon a man in the pillory. He raged and cursed, but could not defend himself from the onslaught, for once a man's hands and head were locked into the wooden frame, he was effectively immobilized. The Chesney brothers saw no reason to spoil the boys' fun, but when a drunkard was attracted by the commotion and started scrabbling around for good-sized rocks, they sent him reeling on his way. Shaming a prisoner was permitted, even encouraged, but stoning was not, for the pillory was a punishment for petty crime; serious offenders could expect the gallows out on Andover Road. The entertainment over, Roger and Will continued east along High Street, past the royal palace that was now the bishop's stronghold, where they lingered to flirt with a pretty girl strolling by. It was midday, therefore, by the time they reached the Water Gate that gave entry into the precincts of Wolvesey Palace.

Their leisurely afternoon ended abruptly, though, upon their arrival at Wolvesey. The atmosphere was charged with tension, and Roger de Chesney was ushered at once into the bishop's private quarters in the West Hall. No one challenged his brother, and so he followed, too. Will was expecting luxury—the bishop's lavish lifestyle had long provided fuel for gossip—and the chamber furnishings did not disappoint. The walls were hung with rich embroiderings; the bed was vast in size, piled with feather-filled pillows and silk coverlets; a polished oaken table held gleaming silver candlesticks, an ivory chess set, and several leather-bound books. What startled Will was not the elegant surroundings, but the man standing in the midst of them: a thin, nondescript figure clad in the anonymous black habit and cowl of a Benedictine monk.

"My lord?" Roger seemed baffled by the monk's presence, too; he sounded very dubious.

"Of course it is me," the bishop said impatiently, jerking back the hood of his cowl. "Why did you take so long to answer my summons?" He gave Roger no chance to respond. "Never mind, for we've no time to waste. That accursed woman is approaching Winchester with an army."

Roger drew a quick, comprehending breath. "You'll not be waiting around to welcome the empress into the city, then?"

The bishop frowned; he could never understand why so many men insisted upon joking about matters of life-or-death urgency. "Why else would I be wearing this monk's cowl? It will enable me to slip out of the city undetected, and by the time Maude reaches the East Gate, I ought to be well on the way to my castle at Waltham. I will then seek aid from my own vassals, from my sister-in-law and the Fleming. But it will be up to you, Roger, to hold Wolvesey and the palace until we can break their siege. Can I rely upon you?"

Roger nodded. "I will do my best, my lord bishop."

"Good man." Turning aside, the bishop unlocked a small casket and tossed a pouch toward Roger. He caught it deftly; it had a reassuring heft and clinked loudly as he tucked it away.

"My lord . . . this is my brother William. He wishes to serve you, too." The bishop glanced over at Will, nodded briefly. But before he could dismiss them, Roger said hastily, "Your Grace . . . wait. I must be clear about what you expect of me. You once told me that if we found ourselves under siege, I was to take whatever measures I must to hold out. Is that still your wish?"

The bishop gave him a level look. "'Silent leges inter arma.' That was said by a great man, Roger, a Roman statesman named Cicero. 'In time of war, the laws are silent.'"

UPON her arrival in Winchester, Maude took up residence in the castle. She then summoned the bishop to her presence. The bishop's men stalled for time, sending forth the bishop's response, that he "would prepare himself." Once they were certain that his delay was in fact defiance, Robert dispatched one of his men with a formal challenge. He sent a spear thudding into the gate of Wolvesey Palace, and the siege of Winchester began.

ON Saturday noon, the second day of August in the Year of Christ 1141, Waleran Beaumont, Count of Meulan and Earl of Worcester, arrived in

Winchester to make his peace with the Empress Maude. Waiting with two of his household knights to be admitted into the castle's great hall, he sought to sound jaunty and nonchalant. "Well, here I go . . . into the she-wolf's den. Say a prayer for my pride, which is about to be shredded into salad and served up to Maude for dinner." There was too much truth in the joke for humor, though; this was an ordeal he was dreading.

To his surprise and relief, he discovered that his anticipated submission had been more painful than the actual event proved to be. It was not an experience he'd want to repeat. He felt that Maude kept him too long on his knees, and she made no effort to conceal her satisfaction. But he'd expected to be bleeding profusely by now, knowing what a lethal weapon her tongue could be. He remembered—in disheartening detail—telling Maude that he'd beg his bread by the roadside ere he'd acknowledge her as queen, and he well knew that Maude also remembered. So as grateful as he was for her unlikely restraint, he marveled at it, too.

Mayhap those Londoners had done the country a good turn, scared some sense into her. But no . . . it would not last. If ever there was a woman unable to learn from her mistakes, it was this one for certes. No more than Stephen could. If the Lord God plucked him out of his Bristol prison on the morrow and restored him to power at Westminster, nothing would change. He'd still go on forgiving men he ought to hang, promising more than he could deliver, failing to keep the King's Peace. Maude and Stephen, a match made in Hell. What was it Geoffrey de Mandeville had once said—a lifetime ago? Ah, yes, that Maude would listen to no one and Stephen to anyone. Had there ever, he wondered, been a war like this? Was there a single soul—not related to them by blood or marriage—who truly wanted to see either one of them on England's throne?

Maude interrupted his morose musing with a pointed query. "Are you here, my lord earl, to assist in the siege of the bishop's strongholds?"

"No, madame, I am not," Waleran admitted. "I shall be returning to Normandy straightaway." Forcing himself to add a politic "With your permission, of course. I promised your lord husband that I would aid in his campaign."

Geoffrey or Maude—that was verily like choosing Sodom over Gomorrah. How much the old king had to answer for! If only he'd named Robert of Gloucester as his heir, how much grief and misery they all could have been spared. Being born out of wedlock seemed a minor matter indeed when compared with Maude's unwomanly ways, Geoffrey's perverse humors, and Stephen's well-meaning weakness. No, by the Rood, he'd had enough. He'd do what he must to safeguard his holdings in France, but if he never saw these English shores again, so much the better.

He knew Maude would make him pay for his past allegiance to Stephen, and so he was not surprised when she demanded that he turn over to her the Worcestershire abbey of Bordesley, for it had been founded on royal desmesne lands given to Waleran by Stephen, and Maude refused to recognize Stephen's right to make such grants. Waleran yielded with what grace he could muster, which wasn't much.

"As you will, madame," he said grudgingly. "I shall inform the abbot that—" He got no further, for Maude was staring past him, half rising from her seat on the dais. Turning, he saw her brother striding up the aisle toward them.

"Maude . . ." Ranulf was laboring for breath; he'd come on the run. "The window," he panted, "look!"

Maude darted down the dais steps, with her uncle David and Waleran close behind. The shutters were open wide. Maude leaned out and then gasped, for the blue summer sky was sullied by an ominous cloud of billowing black smoke.

HIGH STREET was thronged with agitated people, some running toward the fire, others fleeing it. Ranulf and Gilbert realized almost at once that they should not have taken their horses. They had to keep reining in to avoid trampling the men and women surging into their path, and as the scent of smoke reached the animals, they began to balk. After his mount shied and Gilbert banged his head against an overhanging alehouse pole, Ranulf signaled for a halt.

"We'll make better time on foot," he said, swinging from the saddle. He was handing the reins to his squire when he heard the screaming. The crowd was scattering, people ducking into doorways of the shops lining both sides of the street. Ranulf followed their example, but then he saw her: a young girl sprinting toward them, her hair streaming out behind her, her skirts smoldering.

Several people were shouting, telling her to roll on the ground, but she was too terrified to heed them; Ranulf doubted that she even heard. A woman tried to catch her arm as she ran by, her fingers just falling short. Ranulf had better luck. Flinging himself forward, he sent the girl sprawling, then scooped her up and dropped her into the closest horse trough. She thrashed about wildly, drenching Ranulf, too, and when he lifted her out, sputtering and choking, she clung to his neck and sobbed. She was even younger then he had first thought, only ten or so, her entire body shuddering with every breath she took. Her wet hair was in his face, had an unpleasant burnt smell, but he couldn't tell if she was trembling from fear or pain or both.

By now several would-be samaritans had gathered around, and when he asked, a gangling youth in a bloodied butcher's smock identified her as "Aldith, the wainwright's lass." His squire was standing a few feet away, having somehow managed to keep their frightened horses from bolting, and Ranulf entrusted the weeping child into his care. "Take her back to the castle, Luke. This lad here will help you and then find her family . . . right?" The butcher's apprentice nodded shyly, and the crowd parted to let them through.

The royal palace was just a few streets ahead. Already, Ranulf could feel the heat, could see the flames shooting skyward along the north side of High Street. Several shops and houses were ablaze, and the fire was moving with deadly speed. Even as he watched, flames leapt across the narrow width of the closest side street and ignited a thatched roof. When he reached the siege site, he stopped in shock, unable to credit what he was seeing. Firebrands were being shot from the palace walls, launched from mangonels in a sizzle of sparks and cinders, raining death down indiscriminately upon citizens and soldiers alike.

The scene meeting his eyes was chaotic. Men were shoving and cursing, coughing whenever smoke blew their way, loading mangonels with heavy stones as archers sought to drive the enemy off the battlements. In the midst of so much urgent activity, it took him some time to find Robert. His brother's face was streaked with soot and sweat, his eyes red-rimmed, his voice hoarse from shouting orders. At sight of Ranulf, he said wearily, "Can you believe it? Those whoresons set fire to their own city."

"I saw this done once before, in Normandy. The Breton commander put Lisieux to the torch rather than have it fall to Geoffrey. But he was a mercenary, whilst Bishop Henry . . . Jesú, Robert, he is a man of God!"

"Tell that to those people out on High Street, watching their homes and livelihoods go up in smoke." Others were clamoring now for Robert's attention: his own captains, a man who claimed to be the city's royal reeve, some of the imperiled merchants . . . and a tearful nun. "Sister? You ought not to be here—"

"My lord earl, you must help us! Our nunnery is afire!"

Robert swore softly. "I'll do what I can," he said, seizing her elbow and steering her toward the greater safety of the barricades.

Ranulf's first impulse was to follow, but he'd promised Maude that he'd report back to her straightaway. He hesitated, and then John Marshal solved his dilemma for him. "I've just heard that the fire is spreading to the west, and I own two houses on Scowrtene Street. I could use some help if it turns out to be true."

Ranulf didn't care for Marshal's peremptory tone, but he didn't take it personally, for those who knew him joked that Marshal would be barking orders to St Peter himself if ever he made it to Heaven's Gate. Moreover, Scowrtene Street was on the way back to the castle, and so he and Gilbert trailed after John Marshal as he hastened along High Street, using his elbows and shoulders to clear his path.

By now the turmoil was spreading as fast as the fire. Most of the shops had family dwellings above-stairs, and frantic men and women were trying to save all they could, staggering out of their threatened houses with whatever belongings they could carry away. Others were desperately seeking to contain the fires: dousing nearby homes and shops with water, forming bucket brigades. Brooks ran down the center of several streets, but they were shallow, meandering streams, meant to sweep away garbage dumped into the streets, never to quench a conflagration such as this.

Ranulf marveled at the courage of the people. They kept plunging into smoke-filled buildings to retrieve what they could, and when they heard that St Martin's Church in Fleshmonger Street was ablaze, they rallied to the rescue—the elderly and the young as well as the able-bodied—all responding to the priest's frenzied plea for help.

John Marshal had quickened his pace, beginning to curse, for smoke was spiralling up ahead. By the time they reached the corner, Marshal's worst fears were confirmed: one of his houses was already in flames and the other seemed likely to be consumed, too. The neighborhood residents were trying to save the rest of the street by soaking down the roofs. Some were demanding more drastic measures, insisting that they must pull down those houses already doomed in the hopes of creating a fire break. John Marshal at once allied himself with the men arguing against it, for his second house was among those to be sacrificed. Under normal circumstances, he would easily have prevailed, for he was a baron, a man with a notoriously quick temper and a sword at his hip. But the circumstances were anything but normal, and these men were in danger of losing all they had.

The argument raged on, and might well have come to blows if not for the screaming. It was high and shrill and filled with too much terror to ignore. They turned toward the sound as a woman lurched into their midst, falling to her knees. "You are lords," she sobbed, "you can save him . . ."

John Marshal pulled away when she plucked at his arm; his sense of chivalry was stunted in the best of times. Ranulf was more obliging, but she was almost incoherent and he did not know what she wanted of them. It was not until she gasped out the word *pillory* that one of the men understood. "Oh, Christ! There was a man locked in the pillory—"

The woman sobbed again. "I could not get him free . . ." She choked, clutching now at Ranulf. "Hurry," she pleaded, "please hurry!"

Ranulf was already in motion, running back toward High Street, the others at his heels. Turning the corner, he came to a horrified halt. The closest house was ablaze, and collapsing rafters had fallen upon the pillory, setting it afire. The man was engulfed in flames; even his hair was on fire, and there was a sickening stench of burning flesh. But he was still alive, his mouth contorted in a silent scream. Ranulf lunged forward, but the heat drove him back. When he tried again, Gilbert grabbed him by both arms.

"It is too late, Ranulf!"

"We cannot let him burn to death!" Ranulf wrestled free, but by then John Marshal was there, shoving him aside as he drew his sword.

Ranulf shouted, but the sword was already thrusting downward. It was a clean, powerful stroke, decapitated the man with one blow. Splattered with blood, Ranulf stumbled backward, fighting queasiness. The other men looked sick, too; one had doubled over and was vomiting into the dirt. Several were trying to keep the woman from seeing, to no avail. She screamed just once, then crumpled to the ground, almost at John Marshal's feet. Sheathing his sword, he said matter-of-factly, "I'd hope that someone would do as much for me." They watched him in silence, stunned not so much by his act as by the realization that he was utterly unaffected by it.

WITH the coming of night, the city took on an eerie, awful beauty. Flames lit up the darkness for miles, smoke shrouded the town in a garish orange haze, and each time the wind shifted, embers drifted down like fiery snowflakes. It was past midnight, but no bells were chiming the hour; too many churches lay in ruins. A few fires still burned, but the worst seemed over. Ranulf fervently hoped so. Never had he been so exhausted. Finding an overturned horse trough, he sank down upon it, not looking up until he heard footsteps crunching through the ashes and debris.

Brien did not have to proclaim his fatigue; his slow, uneven step did it for him. Upon recognizing Ranulf, he limped over, and Ranulf made room for him on the trough. "Did you hurt yourself?"

"I fell off a ladder." Brien did not elaborate, and Ranulf did not probe. They'd all seen sights this night that they'd want only to forget. They sat in silence for a time, absorbed in thoughts neither wanted to share. But then Brien's head came up. "Horses," he said, and they watched as riders emerged from the shadows. A moment later both men were on their feet, Maude's name an unspoken echo between them.

They reached her even before she reined in, insisting that she should not be there, that it was too dangerous, that she must return to the castle where she'd be safe. Maude heard them out with unusual patience, and then said simply, "I could not wait any longer, had to see for myself. Do you know where Robert is? And is it true that St Mary's nunnery could not be saved?"

"No, it all burned." Brien moved closer to Maude's restive mare, fighting the urge to reach for her reins. "I do not mean to belabor the point, but some of the bishop's men might still be loose in the city, and if you were recognized—"

"Brien, enough!" Maude frowned, but as she gazed down into his face, her mood changed abruptly, and she surprised them by yielding. "If it will ease your mind, I'll return to the castle. But I want you both to come back with me. You look as if either one of you could be toppled over by a feather, and little wonder, after such a night as this . . ."

Maude's guards could not hide their relief, and hovered protectively around her when she insisted upon a pace slow enough to accommodate Brien and Ranulf. As they walked along High Street's smoldering trail of misery, Ranulf found himself wondering what would become of these people, burned out of their homes and their shops. Winchester was in for a wretched winter, he concluded bleakly, just as a shower of sparks blew across their path, spooking the horses. Maude was a good rider and soon quieted her mare. But then she looked up uneasily at the sky. "Tell me I am wrong," she said, "tell me the wind is not rising."

They could not, for they felt it, too. The wind was indeed picking up. Flames that had almost died down were surging back to life, embers kindling anew, flames burning higher and hotter, putting the city again in peril.

THE fire raged through the night and into the following day. Driven by gusting winds, the flames razed much of Winchester north of High Street. By midmorning, airborne embers and cinders had soared over the city wall onto the shingled roofs of Hyde Abbey. The monks managed to save most of their livestock. But their church, chapter house, infirmary, kitchen, and stables were burned to the ground.

THE sky was an overcast, ashen shade, the air humid and still, as if the night's firestorm had never been. Daylight revealed a scene of widespread desolation: ashes and rubble and charred fragments of shattered lives. Maude was shocked and shaken by what she saw. Had she been asked about a king's responsibilities, she would have said that he must safeguard the subjects of his realm, for Scriptures spoke of saving the poor from the sword and feeding the hungry. But faced with the reality of it—a city in ruins, people homeless and in despair—she was suddenly at a loss. What could she possibly do to ease suffering on a scale like this?

She was accompanied by William Pont de l'Arche, sheriff of Hampshire and castellan of Winchester's royal castle, by her brothers and Miles and Brien, all of whom had argued in vain against this expedition, and by the newly arrived Archbishop of Canterbury, who seemed stunned by what he was finding.

Maude and the archbishop had wanted to visit the burned-out nuns of St Mary's, but Robert balked at that, for the nunnery was perilously close to both siege sites. He was so adamant that they had to content themselves with an offer of shelter until the nunnery could be restored. But who would rebuild the shops and homes of the townspeople? It was a question that shadowed Maude as they inspected the scorched wreckage of High Street, a troubling one, for she had no answer.

William Pont de l'Arche proved to be too knowledgeable a guide, for he had fought the fires all night long, and there seemed to be no tragedy that he'd not heard about, no sorrow that had escaped him. He pointed out a blackened shell where a child had died. He reeled off the casualty list of the city's churches—at least twenty, he said, mayhap more. He showed them the spot where the pillory prisoner had met his gruesome death, and he told them what had occurred at St Mary's Church over in Tanner Street. The priest had rushed back inside to retrieve the holy relics—St Swithun's tooth and straw from the Christ Child's manger—and had been overcome by smoke. When three parishioners attempted to rescue him, the roof collapsed, trapping them all inside. "Our city will never be the same," he said mournfully, and there were none to refute him.

People were wandering about like sleepwalkers, as if the full magnitude of their loss had not yet sunk in. Many clutched bundled-up clothes, candlesticks, blankets, whatever they'd been able to snatch from the flames. Some merely stared blankly at Maude as she passed by. Others sought to get close to her, and when her guards kept them away, their voices echoed after her, crying out their fear and their grief and their pleas for help. She ordered her chaplain to distribute alms, but it seemed a futile gesture, offering good wishes to one bleeding to death, and Maude felt a rush of relief as they neared the castle, for there was naught she could do. But then she drew rein abruptly, common sense forgotten.

The woman might have been Maude's own age, but childbearing and hard work had aged her beyond her years. She had three boys clinging to her skirts, a baby in her arms, and she was weeping silently, rocking back and forth as if oblivious to the devastation around her. It was the children who'd drawn Maude's eye, for they all had curly reddish-copper hair—the same shade as Maude's sons'. The smallest had looked to be about three, and in him, Maude saw her own youngest son, for Will had been just three when she left to claim her crown, when she saw him last . . . nigh on two years ago.

The woman's husband had been searching through the charred timbers for anything worth salvaging. He straightened up slowly, belatedly becoming aware of the royal cavalcade. "This was my apothecary shop," he said. "Over there I kept my mortar and pestle, and in the back, my brazier. Some of my customers came all the way from Southampton, for no one had a better selection of herbs and spices and soothing potions. Ginger and clover and antimony and wormwood and henna and camphor and calamine and hemlock . . ." Squatting down, he sifted ashes through his fingers, looking up at Maude with a lopsided smile. "Not much for a lifetime's toil, is it? Our house is gone, too, for we lived above-stairs. Not that we lost everything: Alice found a ladle and our fire tongs did not burn. Fire tongs," he repeated, and began to laugh hoarsely, a painful, rasping sound that caused those listening to glance away.

A small crowd had gathered, and Robert nudged his mount forward, offering them the only comfort he could, a grim promise that the men responsible for burning Winchester would pay a terrible price for it. Maude's guards urged her on toward the castle, but she kept looking back over her shoulder, and at last reined in her mare. She was fumbling with a ring as Miles rode up beside her. As their eyes met, he shook his head. "Why not?" she demanded. "You saw them, Miles. They lost everything!"

"I know," he said. "But do you have rings for them all?" sweeping his arm to encompass the rest of the ravaged city.

Maude looked away. "You know I do not . . ." she conceded, and they rode on in silence. They'd almost reached the castle before she spoke again. Although he caught her words, he did not understand them, and gave her a quizzical, questioning look. "I was just remembering an old German proverb," she said in a low voice. "'In time of war, the Devil makes more room in Hell.'"

WINCHESTER'S great fair was held annually on August 31st, the Eve of St Giles, on the hill of the same name just east of the city. Gunter had not missed a St Giles Fair for the past ten years; it was one of his most profitable markets. He'd expected this trip to be particularly rewarding, for his cart was loaded with goods sure to appeal to discriminating fairgoers: staples such as razors, scissors, and spindles, supplemented by luxuries like incense, perfume, parchment, and quicksilver.

His sojourn in Winchester was to be special for another reason: his daughter was accompanying him. He'd been reluctant to expose Monday to the perils of the road, but it seemed riskier to leave her home alone, for she was twelve now, balancing precariously on the border between childhood and womanhood, not yet ready to cross over, but close enough to see the other side. Gunter's doubts had been swept away by her excitement;

to Monday, this trip to Winchester was as great a gift as she'd ever been given.

Gunter's disappointment was acute, therefore, when he learned that Winchester would be holding no fair this year, for his loss was twofold, as both merchant and father. Monday was inconsolable, all the more so because she'd come so close; they'd been within ten miles of Winchester when they encountered people fleeing the city.

She was no longer weeping, but her eyes were still swollen and her voice held a betraying tremor. "I do not understand, Papa. Even if the fair was called off this year, why could we not go on into the city? At least I'd get to see it!"

"It would be too dangerous, girl. You heard what we were told, that half the town is in ruins and a siege is still under way. Think you that I'd have brought you to Winchester had I known that the town would be full of soldiers?"

Monday sniffed into her sleeve, obviously not convinced. Gunter glanced at her occasionally from the corner of his eye, but she'd averted her face, and all he could see was a curve of flaxen hair. She was getting too old to wear her hair loose like that. More and more, he regretted not having remarried after Isolda died; it was no easy task, raising a lass alone. "Here, girl, you take the reins for a while," he said. She was always pestering him to let her do that, but now he got only a shrug, and she slid over on the seat as if she were doing him a great favor.

"Pull up, lass," Gunter said suddenly, and beckoned to the couple trudging along the side of the road. "I can see your woman is with child. She can ride in the cart with us." His offer was gratefully accepted, and the woman was soon seated next to Monday, her husband walking briskly beside Gunter. He was young and brawny, looked as if he could hold his own in a brawl, an important consideration in these lawless times. Now that they had three males in their party—Gunter, his hired lad, and the stranger—Gunter felt somewhat safer, for bandits and masterless men were less likely to prey upon travelers able to defend themselves.

Gunter's generous gesture was indeed bread cast upon the waters, for his new companion had more to offer than youth and muscle and a stout oaken staff, thick enough to crack a man's head wide open. Oliver was a Winchester man, born and bred, able to provide Gunter with a vivid eyewitness account of his city's troubles. He and his wife were luckier than most, though, for they had kin willing to take them in until the siege ended and life got back to normal.

"We're going to Alton," Oliver confided. "Clemence will stay with her brother until I can fetch her home."

"And you? You're not staying with her?"

Oliver shook his head, casting a regretful glance toward the cart. "The babe is not due for another three months, not till after Martinmas. Pray God that the fighting will be long over by then. In truth, I am loath to leave her, but I must go back. I will lose my job if I do not."

"I'd not think there'd be much work, not if the fire was as bad as I'd heard . . .?"

"It was," Oliver said somberly. "I just hope I live long enough to see the bishop stripped of his finery and turned out of the city. If it were up to me, I'd send him on pilgrimage to Jerusalem, with bare feet and hairshirt and no bread but what he could beg. But there is not much chance of that. The great never seem to pay for their sins, at least not in this lifetime."

"Then you want to see the empress win?"

Oliver smiled mirthlessly. "What I want is to repair my house, bring my wife home in time for her to give birth there to our child—a son, God Willing. I want to see the bishop punished, but I doubt he will be, for the Church tends to its own. And I want this accursed war to end. Let Maude rule or Stephen—you think I care? Am I ever likely to see Westminster? Hellfire, I've never even seen Southampton, and that's but twelve miles away."

"I'll own up that I'm not losing any sleep over the outcome, either. I thought it was for the best when Stephen claimed the crown. But if a king cannot keep the peace, what good does he do us? The roads were never so dangerous whilst the old king was alive—"

"Gunter? Is something amiss?"

"It may be," Gunter said, and there was suddenly so much tension in his voice that Oliver felt an instant unease. The older man was staring off into the distance, his eyes narrowed against the sun, riveted upon the horizon. "Do you see it? It would take a lot of men and horses to churn up that much dust." Making up his mind, he swung around toward the cart, yelling for his hired man, asleep in the back. "Wat, bestir yourself! I want to get the cart off the road, into that grove of trees, and fast!"

Oliver helped him lead the horses across the field, while Clemence and Monday clung to the cart as it swayed and bumped over the rough ground. "Is this truly necessary, Gunter? Even if it is an army, most likely it is Geoffrey de Mandeville, since they're coming along the London Road. It was known in the city that the empress has summoned him to aid in the siege."

Gunter gave the young townsman the pitying gaze of a seasoned traveler for a rank novice. "The Pope himself could be leading that army and I'd still burrow down till they'd passed by. It matters little if they be friend or foe. Would you trust your wife with a tamed wolf?"

Once they'd hidden the cart amid the sheltering trees, Gunter and Oliver crept forward to watch the road, hunkering down in the under-brush. After a while, the high grass began to ripple, and Gunter swore as his daughter crawled up beside them. "Get back to the cart," he ordered, but then he grabbed her arm, pulling her down again, for it was too late. "Stay still," he warned, and as they watched from their hiding place, the army's scouts and advance guard rode by, sun glinting on the chain links of their armor, lean and fit and sun-browned and fascinating—at least to Monday, who'd never before seen men who looked like the heroes in her favorite minstrel songs, the ones about gallant knights errant who had amazing adventures and never failed to rescue highborn ladies in peril.

After the advance guard passed, the army followed, men-at-arms and mounted knights. Monday was so enthralled that it almost made up for missing Winchester. She wished she could squirm closer to the road, but her father held her in an iron grip. "Oh, look, Papa!" she whispered. "A lady rides with them!"

"Nonsense," he said curtly, but when he raised up on his elbow, he saw that she was right. "Jesus wept," he murmured, "it is the queen!"

Oliver gaped at him. "How can you be sure?"

"I've seen her before, once at the St Ives Fair and twice in London. It is Stephen's queen and no mistake."

Oliver had gone very pale. He stared after Matilda, and when Monday glanced his way again, she was startled to see tears in his eyes.

"Papa?" she whispered. "Why is he so distraught? Why does he weep?"

"For Winchester, lass," he said softly. "He weeps for Winchester."

20

WINCHESTER, ENGLAND

August 1141

THE citizens of Winchester were still sifting through the ashes and charred debris of their homes and shops when the queen's army descended upon them. Her forces augmented by more than a thousand Londoners, men from her lands in Boulogne and Kent, and the bishop's vassals and tenants, Matilda posed a formidable threat, and

Maude and Robert at once dispatched urgent messages to Geoffrey de Mandeville, the Earl of Chester, to all their allies not already in Winchester. Matilda was accompanied by several earls, but she entrusted the command of her army to William de Ypres, and he at once cast a net around the city, blockading all of the major roads leading into Winchester. With luck and knowledge of local terrain, a lone rider could still get through the lines. But cumbersome supply convoys were snared like flies in cobweb, and hunger soon stalked the streets of the beleaguered town. The besiegers had become the besieged, and the trapped citizens of Winchester could only pray for divine deliverance, entreating the Almighty to spare their city the fate that had befallen Lincoln.

WILLIAM DE YPRES was returning from a foray into Winchester. That was not as reckless as it sounded, for their arrival had forced Maude's men to withdraw into the city, thus raising the siege of Wolvesey. He had been admitted into the palace by a postern gate in the outer wall, and as he'd gazed down from the battlements at the deserted city streets, he'd marveled that the smell of smoke was still so acrid, three weeks after the fire. Looking out over the ruins of Cheapside, he'd laughed exultantly, for the scent of victory was in the air, too.

Riding back to Matilda's encampment south of the city walls, Ypres encountered William de Warenne, Earl of Surrey, who reported gleefully that yet another of Maude's supply convoys had been captured. They'd soon be scouring the city streets for stray cats and dogs, he predicted, and as the siege dragged on, they'd be eating mouse soup and rat stew and thanking God for it.

"As much as I'd love to see Maude gnawing on a mouse leg," Ypres grinned, "it is not likely. In a siege, the townspeople starve first, for what food there is goes to the army. Ere the castle larders get bone-bare, they'll try to break out of the trap. I'd say in a fortnight or so . . . assuming, of course that they do not get help from some of Maude's missing barons. Any chance of a few of your kinsmen showing up on the wrong side, my lord?"

There was no real malice in Ypres's gibe; it was merely force of habit. It did no damage, though, for Warenne was not thin-skinned about the propensity of his kindred for fence-straddling. Waleran and Robert Beaumont were his half-brothers, the Earl of Warwick was his first cousin, and his sister was the wife of the Scots king's son and heir, so their family history did indeed present a complex mosaic of contrary and uncertain loyalties. Warenne's own allegiance to Stephen was shadowed by past conflicts and an outright betrayal: he was one of the earls who'd fled the battlefield at Lincoln. Like Ypres and Northampton, he was seeking now to make amends for that abandonment, and for that very reason, Ypres trusted him. Shame was a powerful inducement, even more of a goad than self-interest.

They were passing Holy Cross, the hospital founded by the Bishop of Winchester to aid men indigent and infirm. The hospital had been far luckier than Hyde Abbey and the nunnery and much of Winchester, for the fires set by the bishop's men had never spread south of the city; protected now by Matilda's army, Holy Cross seemed likely to be one of the few buildings to survive the siege intact.

Warenne glanced back at the hospital precincts, floating above the fray like an island haven in a storming sea. "I do not understand," he said, "why the queen refused to stay at Waltham. She'd be safer for certes at the bishop's castle, and more comfortable, too. Why did the bishop not insist upon it?"

"The queen has a mind of her own, or so rumor says," Ypres said blandly, but his mouth was twitching in an involuntary smile, for he was hearing again Matilda's private comment, that she'd sooner seek shelter in a lazar house than under her brother-in-law's roof. "She says she can do more good in our camp, and I'd be the last one to dispute that. She comforts the wounded, prays for the dying, never misses an opportunity to remind them—ever so gently—that they are fighting for their lawful king . . . and if she asked them to sprout wings and fly into Winchester, at least half would start flapping their arms for take-off!"

Warenne laughed. "She does inspire devotion in the unlikeliest of men! Let's hope that is a trick Maude never learns, for if—" Breaking off in surprise. "What is going on?"

By now they'd reached the camp, and both drew rein, for men were bustling about, horses being unsaddled, additional tents being set up. "It looks," Ypres said, "as if we have gained some new allies. Your brother Leicester?"

Warenne shrugged; he knew Robert Beaumont wanted to see Stephen restored to the throne, but he also wanted to protect what was his. Dismissing their escorts, they dismounted before Matilda's tent, entered, and halted abruptly at the sight that met their eyes: Matilda sharing a wine flagon with the Earl of Northampton and Geoffrey de Mandeville, Earl of Essex. Matilda greeted them with a tight smile, saying, "The Earl of Essex has come to pledge anew his allegiance to my lord husband."

"In truth," Geoffrey de Mandeville said placidly, "my allegiance to the king never wavered. But when the Bishop of Winchester ordered all Christians to accept the Countess of Anjou as queen, I felt compelled to obey, as a good son of the Church, however little I liked it. You can well imagine my relief when the bishop recanted, for I was then free to follow my own conscience, to do whatever I could to gain the king his freedom."

Warenne looked dumbfounded by the sheer effrontery of it, but Ypres was delighted; his only regret was that the bishop was not present to hear himself blamed for Geoffrey de Mandeville's defection. As for the unrepentant defector, he seemed equally indifferent to Warenne's amazement and Ypres's amusement. He was already on his feet, kissing Matilda's hand with ostentatious gallantry. "By your leave, my lady, I ought to get my men settled in."

Northampton had risen, too. "I will keep a close eye upon him, madame," he promised as soon as the Earl of Essex had departed, and ducked under the tent flap. Warenne followed, leaving Ypres alone with Matilda and her lady-in-waiting, for Cecily had stubbornly insisted upon providing Matilda with female companionship, mindful of the proprieties even in the midst of war.

Matilda was staring down at her hand with an expression of distaste, as if she could still see the imprint upon her skin of Geoffrey de Mandeville's mouth. Ypres helped himself to some of the wine, then refilled the women's cups. "I suggest a scrubbing with lye soap for your hand, a few flagons of hippocras for the foul taste in your mouth. You ought to be very proud of yourself, my lady. I am, for certes. The temptation to spit in his face must have been well nigh irresistible—"

"No, Willem, you are wrong," Matilda said earnestly. "It never even occurred to me. I dared not offend him or let my true feelings show, not as long as he holds . . ."

The rest of her sentence was lost in the depths of her wine cup. Ypres was about to finish her sentence for her with the obvious answer—the Tower of London—when Matilda said, "Constance." He looked away quickly, lest she read his surprise in his face, for he did not want her to know he'd almost forgotten that Mandeville had abducted her son's child-wife. Matilda set the wine cup down, snatching up a parchment. "He even brought me a letter from Constance! The gall of the man!" She sputtered indignantly, muttering something under her breath that he'd have taken for an obscenity—had it been anyone but Matilda. "He is still posing as Constance's protector," she said, shaking her head in disbelief, "promising to return her to me as soon as her safety can be assured."

"And what promises did he demand from you? What price does he put on his resurrected loyalty to the Crown?"

"He wanted me to match all that Maude had given him at Oxford. Which I did, of course. It is passing strange, Willem. The more I lie, the easier it gets."

"Did I forget to warn you that sinning can be habit-forming?" But Matilda found no humor in his joke. She looked down at Constance's letter again, and he said, quite seriously this time, "You are doing what you must, my lady."

"I know," she said. "But what if it is not enough, Willem? What if it is not enough?"

AS Ranulf crossed the castle's inner bailey in response to his sister's summons, he slowed to watch the crowd lined up outside the kitchen's door. When they'd begun giving out bread, most of the supplicants had been women and children, for the townsmen had been shamed at having to rely upon charity and had sent their wives to collect their share. But that was no longer so. On this overcast afternoon in early September, most of the people in line were males, for no man wanted his woman or child out on the streets, not anymore. The danger was too great. Matilda's blockade had brought more than hunger to the citizens of Winchester. Once she'd lifted the siege of Wolvesey, their town had become a battlefield. The bishop's men prowled the battlements of both his strongholds, shooting at anything that moved, even venturing out occasionally to clash with the enemy, and they included the townspeople in that hostile category, for Winchester had backed Maude, not their bishop, and he was not likely to forgive or forget. The city was now split into two broken halves, divided by the blackened boundary of Cheapside; the bishop's men held the south side, and Maude's forces the castle and the damaged neighborhoods north of High Street. There were daily skirmishings, daily deaths, and many feared that the worst still lay ahead of them.

Miles and Robert were standing on the steps leading up into the great hall. The tension between them was unmistakable, and not a surprise to Ranulf, for their rivalry was no secret, exacerbated by the very real differences in their natures and their approach to war; both men were capable battle commanders, but Robert was inherently more cautious than Miles, and that made conflict all but inevitable.

Ranulf was near enough now to catch the gist of their argument, low-voiced but intense, nonetheless. He'd heard it all before, for Miles had been very vocal about his desire to fight fire with fire, insisting that they take advantage of the castle's high ground to hurl firebrands down upon their enemies. He'd not been convinced by Robert's counterargument, that if the winds shifted, the rest of the city could burn, and he'd not taken defeat with any measure of grace, continuing to complain long after the issue had been rendered moot by Matilda's arrival upon the scene.

They turned as Ranulf approached. He opened his mouth to remind them that Maude was waiting, instead heard himself say belligerently, "Robert was not the only one loath to put the city's survival in peril. So was Maude."

Miles was caught off balance; he'd long ago tagged Rainald as the family hothead, not Ranulf. He recovered quickly, though, and said caustically, "I daresay Stephen would have balked, too, and where did his misguided mercy get him?"

"We are wasting time," Robert said impatiently, and turned on his heel. Miles and Ranulf followed in a strained silence. The others were already in the solar: Maude, her uncle the Scots king, Rainald, Brien, Baldwin de Redvers, William Pont de l'Arche, and John Marshal.

"We've been waiting for you," the usually urbane David snapped; the siege was rubbing raw the nerves of even the most phlegmatic among them.

Miles was irked, but not enough to contradict a king. Straddling a seat, he said, "We need to talk about that mob down in the bailey. I know charity is a virtue, but we can no longer afford to be quite so virtuous."

Maude frowned. "It is not a womanly weakness to feed hungry children, Miles!"

"I did not say it was, madame. But it is an indulgence. We've already cut our daily portions in half, and even that may not be enough. You've not been in a prolonged siege, and I hope to God you never are, for it is an ordeal no woman ought to endure."

"He is right, my lady," Baldwin de Redvers said emphatically. "I am indeed grateful that you were not at Exeter during Stephen's three-month siege. My men ended up eating their horses, and when the well went dry, they had to put out fires with wine, until that ran out, too. Had they not surrendered when they did, they'd have been drinking their own piss."

Maude was not impressed; she hated it when men treated war as their own private province, acting as if suffering were a uniquely male experience that no woman could hope to comprehend. She was particularly vexed by Baldwin's contribution, for he'd escaped at the start of the siege, leaving his wife behind in the castle. She yearned to point that out, but she resisted the temptation, contenting herself with a cool reminder that "Our well has not gone dry. Moreover, we are expecting aid any day now."

They had reason for optimism, for they'd sent out writs to Geoffrey de Mandeville, the Earl of Chester, his brother the Earl of Lincoln, the Earl of Warwick, the Earl of Oxford, and Hugh Bigod, among others. Robert created a stir, therefore, by saying suddenly, "What if aid does not come? Mayhap we ought to consider a withdrawal."

"No!" Maude's indignant cry was echoed at once by other voices, all expressing the same urgent argument—that Maude could not afford two successive defeats. After the disastrous setback she'd suffered in London, she must prevail here in Winchester. She dared not lose again.

Robert did not dispute them, merely waited them out. "I am not saying that we should retreat. I am saying, though, that we need a plan should it become necessary."

"Why would it?" Rainald demanded. "Even if a few of these lords do not keep faith, they could not all fail us! Once we have more men, we can force a battle, put an end to this damnable war once and for all."

"We have to settle this, Robert," Maude agreed. "If I were to withdraw, people would see it as running away. And what of the townspeople? What would happen to Winchester once we'd abandoned it to Ypres's Flemings?"

"In war, madame," Miles said calmly, "soldiers expect to be rewarded for the risks they take. When a city falls, it is plundered by the victors. So it was at Lincoln, so it would be at Winchester."

Maude started to protest, stopped herself just in time. What could she say, after all? She had indeed accepted the suffering of the citizens of Lincoln as a necessary evil, war's ugly aftermath. So why could she not do the same for Winchester? Was the suffering real only if she could see it for herself? But she had never seen suffering like this before—hungry babies and homeless women and a city in ruins. She could not admit that, though. They would neither understand nor approve. Compassion was a woman's frailty, one she dared not show, for it would but confirm their qualms about her fitness to rule.

John Marshal was lounging against the wall, arms folded across his chest, seemingly oblivious to the tensions and undercurrents swirling about the solar. When he spoke up now, heads turned in his direction. "As I understand it, the good news is that reinforcements are on the way, whilst the bad news is that we may run out of food ere they get here. So we ought to be thinking how to feed ourselves in the meantime . . . unless we really do want to empty out the stables."

Baldwin de Redvers took that as a jab at his siege story. "I suppose you have a way to do that?" he scoffed, and was startled when Marshal nodded.

"I may," he said, "I just may." He glanced around to make sure they were all listening, and only then did he tell them what he had in mind.

It was very quiet after he was done speaking. Maude was regarding him thoughtfully. "You'd be taking a great risk, Sir John."

He responded with a shrug, a laconic "If I were not willing, my lady, I'd not have offered."

Maude admired his audacity, but she was not about to second-guess Robert or Miles on a matter of military judgment. She was turning to find out what they thought of John Marshal's scheme when the door burst open and Gilbert Fitz John plunged into the room.

"Forgive my bad manners, my lady," he said, "but this news could not wait. Geoffrey de Mandeville has betrayed us. That whoreson Judas has gone over to Stephen's queen!"

"FOOD is getting scarcer by the day in Winchester," William de Warenne reported. "They cannot hold out much longer, not unless they get help and soon. And in truth, I doubt that aid will be coming. Those who can stomach Maude's queenship are already with her. The others are reluctant bridegrooms at best, being dragged to the altar against their will. If they think there is a chance that the wedding might be called off, they'll go to ground faster than any fox you've ever seen! Men like my cousin Warwick and Hugh Bigod are not about to spill their blood on Maude's behalf. They're not likely to get within a hundred miles of Winchester, not as long as the outcome is in doubt."

The other men agreed with his optimistic assessment. Matilda alone kept silent, listening uneasily as they shared stories of the siege: rumors of sickness in the city and dissention in the castle, accounts of livestock being butchered for food, a word-of-mouth tale about a pack of starving stray dogs chasing down a drunkard—or was it a child?

That was too much for Matilda. She understood the strategy—to force Maude's army into a fight it could not win, with hunger the weapon of choice. An effective weapon, for certes, but an indiscriminate one. Was she the only one troubled by that?

"I have a question," she said, so abruptly that they all turned to stare at her. "Those who are suffering the most during the siege are the citizens of Winchester. Women and children, priests, pilgrims—they are supposed to be spared. Those are the rules of war, are they not? But these rules do not stop the shedding of innocent blood. So how do you keep from thinking of them—the innocents? Please . . . I truly need to know."

There was an awkward silence. She looked from one to the other—from the Fleming Ypres to her brother-in-law the bishop, to the Earls of Northampton, Surrey, and Essex, to William Martel, her husband's steward—and saw the same sentiment on the faces of these very unlike men: discomfort that she should ask such a foolish question and reluctance to offend her by saying so.

The bishop took it upon himself to allay her qualms. "It is always distressing to see Christians sorely afflicted, Matilda, my dear. But it is not given to mortal men to understand the workings of the Almighty. It is as Scriptures say, that 'Now we see through a glass, darkly, but then, face to face.' All will be revealed to us in God's good time."

This was not the answer Matilda had been looking for. The men realized that, but only William de Warenne ventured to improve upon the bishop's effort. After a brief hesitation, the young earl decided he could best serve his queen by candor. "I am not qualified to argue theology, madame. But I can speak as a soldier. In war, men do what they must to stay alive . . . and sometimes they do what they later regret. Am I sorry for the suffering of those you call the innocents? I am. Do I think much about their suffering? No, in all honesty, I do not. What good would it do? The people in Winchester will be no less hungry because I pity their plight."

She should have known better. What had she expected to hear? Matilda nodded politely, and saw their relief. After a few moments, the conversation resumed. They were still certain that they need not fear reinforcements from Scotland and Normandy. Maude and Robert would have been leery of bringing a Scots army across the border. Nor would Maude have entreated Geoffrey to come to her rescue. The men laughed at the very thought, agreeing that Maude would starve first. Matilda said nothing. She seemed composed, but she'd begun to fidget with her wedding band, as she invariably did whenever she was under stress. That was how well Ypres had come to know her during this unlikely alliance of theirs; even her nervous habits were familiar to him. He watched her twisting and tugging at her ring, and he would have comforted her if he could, but he'd rather she grieve for the townspeople of Winchester than mourn for Stephen.

The bishop was proposing a plan to divert a stream that flowed past the castle when there was a sudden commotion outside. Warenne was the closest and the most curious, and ducked under the tent flap to investigate. He was back almost at once, wide-eyed and incredulous. "This," he exclaimed, "you all have to see for yourselves!"

The camp was in turmoil, and in the very midst of it—seated astride a sleek white stallion, surrounded by an armed escort, and reveling in the uproar—was none other than Randolph de Germons, Earl of Chester. They were all taken aback, none more so than Matilda. She stared at Chester in disbelief, not finding her voice until he started to swing from the saddle. "No!" she cried. "Do not dismount, for you'll not be staying. You are not wanted here."

Chester looked truly surprised, and she hated him all the more for that, for the arrogance that allowed him to imagine his betrayals would be overlooked, his treachery forgotten. "That is a strange jest, madame," he said coldly, "one likely to offend rather than amuse."

"I assure you I find no humor in your presence here, my lord earl. I want you gone from my sight. How much more plainly need I speak than that?"

Chester was enraged. Angry color scorched his face, and he communicated so much tension to his stallion that the animal kicked out suddenly, causing the closest spectators to scatter. The earl yanked savagely on the reins, glaring at Matilda. "You are distraught, madame, do not know what you are saying. But I cannot indulge your whims, not with so much at stake. The king's need is too great. I think it best that I speak with you, my lord bishop."

Matilda spun around, but the bishop was as deliberate as Stephen was impulsive, and his face was impassive, his thoughts his own. She was never to know what his response would have been, for William de Ypres had sauntered forward, brandishing a drawn sword and a smile so full of mockery that it was in itself a lethal weapon, conveying mortal insult without need of any words whatsoever.

Words he had, though, each one aimed unerringly at Chester's greatest vulnerability—his pride. "I can speak for the bishop," he said, "for every man jack here. We heed but one voice in this camp—that of the queen. Now that flag of truce means no more to me than it would to you, but our lady is a woman of honour. So thank God for her forbearance and ride out, my lord earl, whilst you still can."

Chester showed no fear, only fury. "You fools," he snarled, "you shortsighted, pompous fools! Mark this day well, remember that you had a chance to save your king. Instead, you heeded a woman and a foreign cutthroat, and sealed his doom. He'll stay chained up at Bristol till he rots, and glad I'll be of it!"

Chester spurred his stallion without warning, and men dived out of his way as the horse plunged forward into the crowd. His men hastily followed, retreating in a hail of hostile catcalls and curses.

Matilda had moved away, jamming small fists into the folds of her skirts as she sought to regain her composure. When she turned back to face the men, she was braced for disapproval. "If you say I ought to have accepted his offer, I cannot dispute you. But I could not help myself. I could not pretend that I believed his lies, that I did not despise him. I can only pray that I have not harmed my husband . . ."

"You did not," Ypres said, with an assurance that she envied.

"You think not, Willem . . . truly?"

"I think spurning Chester was for the best. I'll not deny that I enjoyed it immensely. But it was still a wise move, for the man would have been a constant source of trouble. Not even a saint could fully trust him, and our men are far from saintly. We'd have had an army of hungry cats, so intent upon watching the rat in our midst that Maude would be forgotten!"

The bishop smiled at that, then nodded. "It is rare indeed when the two of us are in agreement about anything under God's sky," he said wryly, "but we do agree about the Earl of Chester. He would have been a dangerous distraction, more of a hindrance than a help. The man has proven himself to be thoroughly untrustworthy, an unscrupulous self-seeker who serves only himself."

Matilda stared at her brother-in-law in amazement, for he seemed to have spoken utterly without irony. She'd been incensed not just by Geoffrey de Mandeville's treachery, but also by his cynicism. In offering his aid, he'd made no attempt to convince her of his good faith, sardonically sure that her need would outweigh her anger. He was not blind to ethical boundaries—as was Chester—merely indifferent to them. But as she looked now at Stephen's brother, she realized that he was quite unlike those two renegade earls. It would never occur to him that others might consider him an "unscrupulous self-seeker," too. He truly believed himself to be on the side of the angels, a pious man of God, defender of Holy Church, burdened with a feckless, ungrateful brother, a foolhardy king. And Matilda found his sincerity even scarier than Mandeville's mockery or Chester's amorality.

Chester was being damned now from all sides, with great zest and considerable venom. Soldiers were not accustomed to censoring themselves. But few of them were comfortable cursing so freely in front of their queen. Matilda's presence was inhibiting, therefore, and she knew it. Turning aside, she started back toward her tent, smiling at Warenne's colorful way with words; he'd just described Chester as "able to slither under a snake's belly with space to spare." That got a laugh from Geoffrey de Mandeville. "To give the Devil his due, though, he roots out secrets like a pig going after acorns. How many men know about the king yet? Bristol must be swarming with Chester's spies! He—madame?"

Matilda had darted forward, grabbing Mandeville's arm. "Know what? Has something happened to Stephen?"

"My lady, we did not mean for you to hear . . ." William de Warenne stammered. "I am truly sorry!"

"For what?" Mandeville demanded. "Unless . . . you mean she does not know?"

Warenne shook his head, looking more miserable by the moment.

"Know what?" Matilda repeated. "What are you keeping from me?" She had her answer not from either man, but from Chester himself, for his parting taunt came back to her then. "Chains," she echoed, "oh, Sweet Jesus, no!" Whirling around, she sought the one man she trusted not to lie to her. "Have they put my husband in irons? Willem . . . answer me!"

Ypres was already beside her. "Yes," he said, "it is so. He has been shackled since mid-July or thereabouts."

"Why did you not tell me?"

That was a difficult question for him to answer; he'd had so few protective urges in his life that he did not know how to justify such an alien emotion. "I did not see what good it would do for you to know," he said gruffly.

"You had no right to keep this from me—no right!" Tears had begun to sting her eyes, but she made no attempt to hide them, to wipe them away. What man among them would not have wanted a wife who'd weep for his pain? "Whatever happens to Stephen," she said tautly, "I must be told. You are fighting to free your king. But I am fighting to free my husband. Do not ever forget that."

RANULF FITZ ROY and John Marshal led a force of three hundred knights, crossbowmen, and men-at-arms out of Winchester's North Gate and onto the old Ickniell Way, toward Andover. It was still dark, dawn more than an hour away. The men were silent, tense. They had less than ten miles to go, but every one of those miles would be fraught with peril.

John Marshal's plan was not only dangerous, but controversial, too. He'd proposed setting up an outpost at Wherwell, where the River Test could be forded. Once they had control of the Andover Road, they would be able to escort supply convoys safely into Winchester. They would have to fortify the crossing, but that could be done with surprising speed; when a castle was under siege, timber countercastles were often put up by the attacking army. This would be far riskier, and to protect their men while they were building a temporary stronghold, John Marshal meant to take over the nearby nunnery of the Holy Cross. The nuns would be sent to safety in Andover until the nunnery could be returned to them, and would be compensated for their dispossession. But Maude and her allies would be bringing the wrath of the Church down upon them for this intrusion into a House of God, and the Archbishop of Canterbury, already irate at being trapped in the siege, would not be easy to placate. It was a measure of their desperation that they'd approved John Marshal's daring stratagem.

Maude had not been so willing, though, for Ranulf to lead this high-risk mission, and had quarreled hotly with her brother over it. But Ranulf had insisted and he'd prevailed. The argument he'd made was a valid one, that John Marshal was a good man to have on their side in battle, but not the ideal candidate to negotiate with a convent of nuns. But there was more to his motivation than concern for Holy Cross and its Brides of Christ. Ranulf was in need of diversion—however dangerous—for his nerves were fraying under the strain. He was still an optimist, still believed that Maude would win her war. But they'd come so close! Just three months ago, he'd been lodged at Westminster Palace, anticipating his sister's coronation, and Annora was within his reach, if not yet his grasp. Now she seemed to slip further away with each passing day of this accursed siege. Maude had lost ground that it would take them months to regain. He was trying not to blame Maude for this, but those were months he could never get back, months in which Annora would be sharing Gervase Fitz Clement's life and bed, instead of being where she belonged—at his side and in his bed.

Easing his stallion, Ranulf now slowed its pace until Gilbert caught up. "I still say you ought to have stayed back in Winchester," he grumbled. "You act at times as if I cannot be trusted out of your sight!"

"Well . . . the last time you ventured into a nunnery, you got yourself arrested!" Gilbert glanced up at the greying sky, for they'd outrun the night, would be racing the sun to Wherwell. "What are the chances, you think, of Ancel's being in the queen's encampment?"

"More than likely," Ranulf conceded. "We know Northampton is there. So why would Ancel not be with his liege lord?"

"It could be that he has seen the error of his ways, is now ready to acknowledge Lady Maude as his rightful queen."

"As if you believe that!"

Gilbert shrugged. "I will if you will," he offered, and got from Ranulf a reluctant grin. They rode on, bantering, into a waiting ambush.

They had no warning, for the terrain was ideally suited for concealment, the road narrowing and curving as it wound its way up into the hills, bordered by deep woods, tangled oak and beech and yew providing perfect camouflage for the soldiers who now rushed out to the attack.

There was instant chaos, horses rearing up, men swearing, hastily drawing swords, reeling back under the onslaught. What followed was not so much a battle as a wild mêlée, confusing and random and deadly.

There was no organized retreat, no orders given. It was each man for himself, doing his best to stay alive. Assailed from both sides of the woods, Ranulf's companions bunched together for protection, spurring their horses mercilessly, for those who halted were quickly struck down, dragged bleeding from their mounts, trampled and left for dead as the running battle surged up the road, until it reached the moss-covered walls of the Wherwell nunnery.

Warned by the sounds of conflict, two nuns and the porter were struggling to close the doors of the gatehouse. They jumped aside just in time as the first horsemen swept by them into the convent grounds. As the nuns and porter watched helplessly, their nunnery was invaded by armed men, all striving urgently to kill one another.

Ranulf's stallion swerved suddenly, almost unseating him. Steering with his knees until he was able to snatch up the reins, he glanced back and gasped, for had his horse not veered off so sharply, he'd have ridden down a small child. It was quite common for nunneries to take in children as boarders or pupils, and several youngsters had been drawn outside by the commotion. This particular child was in the greatest peril, for she'd toddled directly into the path of the riders galloping through the gateway.

Fighting to swing his stallion about, Ranulf yelled, "Run, lass!" But she was frozen with fear. Crouching down in the dirt, she disappeared into the dust clouds being swirled up by the flying hooves. When Ranulf got a glimpse of her again, her little body was being cradled by one of the nuns, and he was never to know if the nun had gotten to her in time.

Nuns had come running out of their dorter, from the bakehouse and the buttery. Not all the women wore the black habit of the Benedictine Order, for widows often lodged in nunneries, renting themselves a safe haven away from worldly temptations and turmoil. But the real world had intruded upon them with a vengeance on this second Tuesday in September. Some of them screamed, fled back into the nearest buildings. Others stood rooted as the battle raged around them.

John Marshal slashed and cut his way toward the church. "Take shelter inside!" he shouted, shoving aside the priest who tried to block the doorway. Flinging themselves from their horses, his men sprinted after him into the church. Ranulf had just traded blows with a young Fleming, their swords coming together with numbing force, clashing in a shiver of sparks. When the Fleming's horse stumbled, Ranulf spurred his mount toward the church, too.

He never made it. A dog lunged toward them, barking ferociously. The stallion reared, lost its footing, and went down. When Ranulf tried to throw himself clear, his spur caught in the stirrup. He hit the ground hard enough to drive all the air out of his lungs, yanked desperately to free his spur, and rolled away from the horse's flailing hooves. Before he could regain his feet, a soldier was standing over him, wielding a bloodied mace. His helmet took the brunt of the blow, undoubtedly saved his life. But the impact was still strong enough to stun. His vision blurred, and he saw the mace start to descend again through a wavering red haze, powerless to deflect it. The blow never landed. Someone grabbed his assailant's arm, spoiling his aim. "Do not kill this one, you fool! Look at his horse! He'll be able to pay a goodly ransom!"

RANULF'S arms were pinned behind his back, bound with leather thongs. He and the other prisoners, those judged worthy of ransoming, had been dragged over to the almonry, shoved against the wall, and held under guard. Ranulf's head was throbbing so wildly that his slightest move set the world to whirling around him. He closed his eyes tightly until the dizziness subsided. When he opened them again, he could think only of those ancient Roman circuses, for the comic and the tragic had merged into a scene as bizarre and compelling as any he'd ever witnessed.

Bodies lay sprawled at odd angles. Horses milled about in panic. Convent dogs barked hysterically. Plundering had already begun. Soldiers had broken into the abbess's dwelling and the guesthouse in search of valuables. Others were ransacking the buttery for wine. Not far from Ranulf, two youths were squabbling good-naturedly over a lute, while a third staggered under the weight of a massive coffer. When he broke the lock, revealing neatly folded veils, wimples, and habits, his friends roared with laughter at his chagrin. There was an almost festive air about the looting, but sporadic fighting still continued. John Marshal and the men with him had managed to barricade the church, and some of the Flemings were attempting to force their way inside. And through it all, there echoed the screams of the nuns and children.

Ranulf tugged at his bonds, to no avail. He'd have to concoct a false identity, for if they learned he was Maude's brother, he'd not have a prayer in Hell of being ransomed. Mayhap he could claim to be a knight of her household; that would explain why she'd be willing to buy his freedom. It was hard to think clearly, though, when his head was pounding like a drum. As he tried to contrive an alias, one that would alert Maude as to his true identity, more riders rode through the gateway. As they passed Ranulf and the other prisoners, his heart skipped a beat, for he recognized William de Ypres, and he did not doubt that the Fleming could also recognize him.

Ypres beckoned to several of his captains. After conferring briefly with them, he started toward the church. He'd not ridden far before a nun ran out to intercept him. She was an elderly woman, barely five feet tall, plump and pink-cheeked, as unlikely a foe as he could imagine. But she displayed no fear whatsoever, boldly blocking his horse's path, and when Ypres reigned in, she cried fiercely, "God will curse you forever if you do not stop this from occurring!"

Ypres assumed that she was blaming him for shedding blood in God's Acre. But when she warned that "There is no greater sin than to defile one of His daughters!" he understood. "Where?" he said, and she pointed toward the stables.

The horses had already been led from the barn, for they were among the most prized of all plunder. It was not empty, though. In a shadowy back stall, two men crouched over a struggling, thrashing figure. One was kneeling on the girl's outstretched arms, a hand clamped over her mouth to stifle her screams, while his partner was tearing away her habit. They were so intent upon their prey that they did not at once realize they had an audience. Their recoil was almost comical, therefore, when Ypres queried, "I trust I am not interrupting anything of importance?"

They whirled, groping for their weapons, weapons that went untouched as soon as they recognized the identity of this intruder. They knew Ypres on sight—and by reputation—every man in his army did. The young nun gasped for breath, then pleaded with Ypres to help her, but he kept his eyes upon the men.

Ypres seemed in no hurry, gazing down at them impassively. "She is a pretty bit, what I can see of her. So . . . if she's what you want, go to it. In all fairness, though, you ought to know this. The last time one of my men raped a nun, I cut off his cock and fed it to him."

The nun understood none of this, for Ypres spoke in Flemish. "Please," she sobbed, but without hope, for this cold-eyed man on a grey stallion did not have the look of a saviour. It seemed miraculous to her, therefore, when her assailants suddenly let her go, scrambled to their feet, and fled the stables. Her relief gave way almost at once to a new jolt of fear; what if this foreign knight meant to finish what his men had begun? She clutched at her ripped garments, and when she dared to look up again, she started to weep in earnest, no longer doubting her deliverance, for Ypres was gone.

As he rode out of the stables, Ypres was met by one of his captains and the elderly nun, now gripping a pitchfork, much to his amusement. "Your lamb is within, Sister," he said, "scared but unsullied." She gave him a hard, hostile look, then brushed past him into the stables. Ypres laughed. "That old lady," he said, "loves us not."

His captain grinned. "I truly thought she was going to run those fools through!"

"No loss if she had. When you can buy a woman for a fistful of coins, why do these dolts have to muck about with nuns? Now . . . what is happening in the church?"

"Some of them have holed up inside, refusing to surrender. Marshal is amongst them, and that one will hold out till we're all too old and feeble to fight."

"Patience," Ypres said, "is a nun's virtue, not mine. Let's make it easy on us all, Martin. Find some kindling."

Ranulf had tensed as Ypres emerged from the stables, fearing that at any moment, the Fleming would glance his way. He was not close enough to hear the orders being given, but he soon saw what they meant to do, and began to struggle frantically against his bonds, until one of his guards came over and threatened to slice off an ear if he did not keep still. Ranulf slumped back, for by now it was too late. Ypres's soldiers had flung blazing torches onto the porch, were shooting fire arrows into the shutters, up onto the roof shingles. Ranulf watched in horror as the church began to burn, for he was sure that Gilbert was one of the men trapped inside.

WHEN he'd raced into the church, Gilbert had thought Ranulf was right behind him. By the time he discovered his mistake, the other men were hastily barring the doors and latching the shutters, dragging altars over to blockade the entrances. With daylight cast out so suddenly, the church was plunged into darkness. It was hot and uncomfortable inside, crowded with anxious men and two terrified nuns, who'd had the bad luck to be in the chancel when John Marshal seized control. The atmosphere was grim, for they knew they could not hold out for long. Their only hope was to offer so much resistance that their attackers would decide it was not worth the effort to overcome them. Under John Marshal's command, they managed to beat back two assaults. But one of the doors was beginning to split under repeated blows, and when they opened a shutter for their crossbowmen to fire out, a torch was tossed through into the nave. They were able to quench it, but they could still smell smoke, and they soon discovered why—the church was afire.

WHEN John Marshal ripped up an altar cloth and soaked it in the holy water font as protection against the smoke, Gilbert did the same. And when the smoke and flames became too intense, he followed Marshal's lead again, and they retreated up the stairs to the dubious shelter of the bell tower. He was not long in regretting it, not long in realizing he'd made the greatest mistake of his life. The heat was getting unbearable. Smoke was seeping up into their sanctuary, and they could hear the crackle of the flames below; it sounded to Gilbert as if half the church were ablaze. "My lord," he said, "if we stay up here, we'll die for certes. We'd best surrender whilst we still can."

John Marshal blotted sweat from his forehead with a corner of the altar cloth. Raising his head, he stared at Gilbert. "You take a step toward that door, and I'll kill you myself. We are not going to surrender."

Gilbert's mouth dropped open. Was the man serious? Marshal was regarding him with unblinking, inscrutable eyes. "What are you saying, that it is better to be roasted alive than surrender?"

"I have no intention of being roasted," Marshal said calmly. "That door ought to keep out the worst of the smoke for now. This church is stone, will take a while to burn. We can wait them out—as long as we do not panic. I cannot speak for you, Fitz John, but I'm not one for panicking."

Gilbert had never doubted his own courage, but he was not willing to dice with Death, not like this. He'd watched from one of the tower windows as men reeled out of the flames, coughing and choking. Some were spared, some were not. But a quick sword thrust was not the worst of ways to die. Being trapped in a burning building with a lunatic suddenly seemed a far worse fate. "We'll be doomed if we stay up here!"

"No," Marshal said, "we will not," and to Gilbert's dismay, he sounded faintly amused. "God favors risk-takers. He'll not let us burn."

Gilbert was speechless. He watched warily as Marshal moved toward a window, having made up his mind to bolt for the door at the first opportunity. But then Marshal gave a triumphant cry. "What did I tell you? They are riding off!"

"Truly? God be praised!" Gilbert darted over, joining Marshal at the window. The older man was leaning out recklessly, laughing. But then he screamed and stumbled backward. Gilbert was stunned, not sure what had happened. Had he been hit by an arrow? There was a sudden stench; although he'd encountered it only once, the night the man in the pillory had died, he'd never forget it—the smell of burning flesh. Marshal had dropped to his knees, making no sound now, rocking back and forth in agony. When Gilbert bent over him, he got his first look at Marshal's face, and his stomach heaved. "Christ," he choked. "Your eye . . . it is gone!"

NUNS had rushed from hiding in a futile attempt to save their church. Ypres's soldiers held them back, and they watched in despair as flames swept through the nave. When the roof collapsed, they wept and then prayed. But their prayers went unheeded, for the wind was swirling fiery embers up into the sky. A shower of cinders drifted down into the cloister garth, and some of them landed upon the dorter roof, setting the shingles afire.

By then the enemy was gone. William de Ypres saw no reason to tarry any longer in the ravaged abbey. He was disappointed that John Marshal was not among the men who'd fled the flames, but the whoreson was probably halfway to Hell by now, he said, for no one was getting out of that inferno alive. Halting the looting, he dispatched some of his men back to camp with their wounded and dead, their prisoners, their captured horses and booty. The others he took with him, for the town of Andover lay just a few miles up the road, too tempting a target to resist. They'd reached the river ford when they heard the bells pealing in the distance. His men were puzzled as to the source of the sound, but Ypres merely laughed. "Do you not know what that is?" he said. "Those are funeral bells, tolling for Winchester!"

RANULF'S balance was still unsteady and he stumbled frequently. But his emotional equilibrium was even more precarious. He no longer cared about his own peril. He realized that Winchester was now doomed, but it did not seem to matter anymore. There was but one image filling his brain: a burning church. He'd watched Gilbert die, as hideous a death as he could imagine, and a needless one. If he'd not been so stubbornly set upon taking part in this lunacy, Gilbert would still be alive.

Surrounded by other prisoners and guards, Ranulf was alone with his grief and his remorse. He trudged along in a daze, not noticing when he was prodded to keep pace. When a knight reined in beside him, he paid the man no heed. Not even the sound of his own name could cut through his fog.

"Ranulf! Christ Jesus, have you gone deaf? Ranulf!"

Ranulf stopped, but the sun was in his eyes. The man's face was dark and sharply sculptured and familiar. "Ancel?"

Ancel slid hastily from the saddle. "I want a word with this man," he said curtly, waving away the closest of the guards. "I could not trust my eyes at first," he confessed, pitching his voice now for Ranulf's ears alone. "Why would you risk your neck like this? Did you truly expect to take us by surprise? A starving city is a natural breeding ground for spies! You ought to—Ranulf? What ails you? Do you even hear me?"

"I hear you."

Ancel's narrow black eyes probed Ranulf's face, then roamed over his hauberk in search of blood, finally finding it encrusted along Ranulf's temple, half hidden by the tousled blond hair. "More fool I," he said. "How badly are you hurt?"

"I am not the one . . ." Ranulf swallowed with difficulty. "Gilbert is dead. He was in the church."

Ancel paled, then spun around to stare at the distant smoke billowing up behind them. When he turned back, his eyes glistened with unshed tears and his hands had balled into hard fists. "God rot them all!" he spat. "Stephen and Ypres and yes, that precious sister of yours!"

Ranulf blinked. "Annora?"

"Not my sister," Ancel hissed, "Yours! Just how clouded are your wits? Can you fend for yourself?"

Ranulf started to nod and winced. "I think so . . . why?"

Instead of answering, Ancel turned his attention to his horse. He seemed to be adjusting the girth strap, but Ranulf soon saw what he was really about: he'd moved so that his stallion now blocked the closest guard's view. "Hold still," he said, and Ranulf felt his bonds giving way. Ancel swiftly stooped, slid his dagger into the top of Ranulf's boot. He gave Ranulf no chance to respond, swung up into the saddle, and urged his stallion on, not looking back.

Ranulf lagged farther and farther behind, biding his time. His chance came as the road dipped, for the ground fell away to the right, and he crouched, then slid down into the hollow. Some of the other prisoners saw him go. He did not think, though, that they'd give him away. Had any of the guards noticed? But his fear of capture was soon forgotten, for his head was spinning again. Long after his enemies had moved on, he lay there in the hollow, his cheek pressed into the grass, his fingers digging into the dirt as he prayed for the pain to pass.

IT was almost dark by the time Ranulf was within sight of the walls of Winchester. Maude's men still controlled the fields within arrow-shot of the city, and he approached the North Gate without fear. He was admitted at once, and it was like plunging down into a well, for the citizens had heard of their calamitous defeat at Wherwell, and they were understandably terrified. They trailed Ranulf to the castle, but when they sought his promise that his sister would not abandon them, he had no assurances for them, only a heart-wrenching and exhausted surge of pity.

Maude came running down the steps of the great hall, flung her arms around Ranulf. Even through his numbed fatigue, he was surprised, for he'd never known her to be so unrestrained in public. "Thank God," she cried, "oh, thank God . . ." Stepping back, she sought to compose herself, gave up the struggle, and embraced him again. "We were so afraid you were dead!"

By then, Robert had reached them. "I do not know," he said, "when I have ever been so glad to see anyone as I am to see you, lad." Turning, he called to a man just coming through the doorway of the hall, "Fetch Lord Rainald! Tell him his brother is alive!" After a second, closer look at Ranulf, he added, "And find the doctor!"

"I have no need of a doctor," Ranulf insisted, even as he wondered where he'd find the strength to climb those few steps into the hall. "You know, then, what happened?"

"We know," Maude said, and while her words might have referred only to the ambush, Ranulf could see in her eyes what they truly encompassed—her anguished acknowledgment that Wherwell was a devastating setback for her queenship claims and for Winchester, possibly a death blow.

"A few men were able to get back to Winchester," Robert said, "like you. But there are not many survivors. Most are either prisoners or slain. What of John Marshal, Ranulf? Do you know what befell him?"

"He is dead." Ranulf's voice thickened. "So is Gilbert," he said, "and it should have been me."

THE dream was fragmented, foreboding, and filled with dark undercurrents more frightening than overt menace. Ranulf awoke with relief, which lasted only until memory came flooding back. Waking or sleeping—he was no longer sure where lurked the worst nightmares. The room was shadowed; it seemed to be night, and for a troubling moment, he could not remember which night it was. Wednesday . . . it had to be Wednesday, for Tuesday night he did remember. The doctor had given him a potion to ease his pain, but he'd drunk little of it and tossed and turned restively till dawn. Maude had sat up with him; that he remembered, too. Stretching out, he tried to will sleep to return, and when it did not, he sought to coax it along with a flagon of wine. Eventually he did sleep again, a shallow, uneasy doze instead of the dreamless stupor he craved. And then it was morning, and his guilt-ridden grieving began anew.

He'd gotten up and dressed, but although his earlier bouts of nausea had abated, he still had no appetite, and when his squire brought him bread and cheese for breakfast, he left it untouched. Luke hovered nearby, eager to serve, but Ranulf wanted no comfort, no solace, wanted only to be alone.

When the door opened suddenly, he did not even glance up. It was Maude. "I am glad you are awake," she said, "for you have a visitor."

"I do not need the doctor again. I still have some of that concoction he brewed up for me, betony and feverfew and God knows what else. Anyway, my head feels better, probably because I did not drink it all down."

"Your head may be better, but your good humor is breathing its last."

Ranulf turned to stare at her, unable to believe she could be joking. She was smiling, the sort of smile he'd not seen on her face since the siege began. "We may have been defeated at Wherwell," she said, "but we did not lose as much as you think. See for yourself." Opening the door wider, she stepped aside and Gilbert walked into the room.

He looked dreadful. An ugly welt seared across his forehead, blistered and raw, as red as his hair. His eyes were swollen and puffy, his lashes and one eyebrow had been singed off, and when Ranulf flung himself off the bed, he recoiled, hastily holding up his hand to stave off the embrace. "Easy," he cautioned. "I'm not up to one of your bear hugs yet. I've peeled off more skin from this arm than an onion."

"You're a ghost," Ranulf said, "by God, you are! Not even the Devil himself could have come through that fire unscathed!"

Gilbert grimaced. "Scathed I am," he said. "Broiled might be a better way to put it."

He was trying hard for levity, too hard. His smile contorted, and when Ranulf grasped his good arm and steered him toward the bed, he sank down upon it gratefully. Luke poured wine and then disappeared; they didn't even notice that Maude had also discreetly vanished. "Between us, we used up the luck of a lifetime at Wherwell," Gilbert said hoarsely. "For all I knew, you were dead, too. When Lady Maude told me you were safe, I could scarce believe her."

"I had a guardian angel, one you happen to know: Ancel. I can see, though, that Maude already told you about my adventures—except for the part about me retching in a ditch, since I did not share that golden moment with her. But do not keep me in suspense, Gib. How did you escape from that inferno?"

"John Marshal and I took refuge in the bell tower. When it began to look as if we'd end up as smoked hams, I suggested we yield. He responded as any reasonable man would, that he'd kill me if I tried."

Ranulf choked on his wine. "You are joking!"

"No, and neither was Marshal."

"Name of God, Gib, are you going to leave me twisting on the hook? What happened?"

Gilbert gazed down into his wine cup, frowning. "Something horrible happened," he said quietly. "The fire had not yet reached the upper story of the tower, but it had spread to the roof. It was only afterward that I figured it out. I think the heat was so intense that the lead on the roof started to melt. When Marshal leaned out of the window, some of the molten lead splashed him in the face." He shuddered at the memory, gulping down the rest of the drink. "I've never seen anything like that, Ranulf, hope to Christ I never do again. His skin just . . . just melted like candle wax. But the worst was his eye. It was burned away, as if scooped out with a spoon, leaving nothing but an empty socket . . ."

Ranulf's mouth was suddenly dry, and he reached quickly for his own wine. "No wonder you looked so greensick! That poor soul. So that was when you escaped? But how? What did you do?"

"What I did was nearly get us both killed. I tried to go down the stairs. You've never lacked for imagination, Ranulf. Envision what it would be like to be stuffed into an oven, for that was the tower stairwell." He gestured self-consciously at his burns. "You can see for yourself. I slammed the door shut just in time. Next, I tried shouting for help, but no one heard. So I did the only thing I could think of: I rang the bells."

Ranulf was riveted. "I heard it," he said, "I did!"

"Fortunately, so did the nuns. They are remarkable women, Ranulf. I'd not have blamed them for turning a deaf ear to my pleas. Jesú, look what we brought down upon them! But as soon as they saw me at the tower window, they did all they could to save us, dragging bales of hay from the stables. I anchored the bell rope, knotted it around Marshal's waist, and lowered him down. When he got to the end of the rope, he cut himself loose and fell onto the hay. I said the most fervent if brief prayer of my life and followed."

"You mean Marshal was still in his right senses? An injury like that would have driven most men mad!"

"Oh, he is mad," Gilbert said, very seriously. "Only a madman could lack all fear as he does. I swear to you that he was not afraid up in that tower. I saw it in his face, and that scared me for certes! But crazed or not, he is as remarkable in his own way as those nuns. I cannot even imagine the sort of pain he must have been in. He was soon burning up with fever, too, and sick as a dog. I had to keep reining in the horse so he could puke. And by the time we got there, he—"

"Got where, Gib? Back up to those bales of hay and start over."

"The nuns did what they could, smeared our burns with fennel and goose grease. We dared not stay there, though, for Ypres would be coming back. The nuns said he'd ridden off to raid Andover, and—as we discovered—he burned it to the ground. I could not take Marshal back with me to Winchester, and he insisted upon going to his castle at Ludgershall. That made some sense to me; his wife could tend to him there. As we were starting out, we got lucky and stumbled onto a loose horse from the battle. I do not know how far Ludgershall is from Wherwell—about ten miles, mayhap more. But it was without doubt the longest journey of my life. We got there, though, Marshal suffering in silence all the way. As I said, an amazing man. I admire him mightily, but I much prefer that it be at a distance from now on!"

Ranulf was quiet, marveling. Leaning over, he emptied the last of the wine into their cups. "I'll grant you that Marshal must have been suffering the torments of the damned. But what of your own pain? Have you even seen the doctor yet?"

"I think the nuns and Marshal's lady did right by me, as much as any doctor could do. I will let him tend to me, though, if you insist. But later. Now . . . now I just want to sit here and get drunker than I've ever been before. I know we're fast running out of food, but how is the wine holding up?"

"I'll tell Luke to bring up enough wine to fill a bathtub. That way you can drink it or bathe in it or both." Ranulf smiled crookedly. "My God, Gib, why did you come back? Why did you not stay at Ludgershall?"

"Earl Robert is my liege lord," Gilbert said, as if that explained all, and for him, it did. "And I'd rather take my chances with you and Lady Maude than our friend Marshal. For all the trouble you've gotten me into, not once did you ever trap me in a burning tower . . ." Gilbert had lain back on the bed; his voice was blurring, his odd, lashless eyelids drooping. Just when he seemed to be asleep, he murmured, "I feel like I escaped from Hell . . ."

Ranulf reached out, taking the tilting wine cup from Gilbert's lax fingers. "That you did, Gib," he said softly. "From Hell back to Purgatory."

21

WINCHESTER, ENGLAND

September 1141

"MY lady?" Minna's self-control was impressive; she'd had a lifetime's practice in curbing unruly emotions. But even her vaunted composure had been affected by the strain of the siege, and she could not completely conceal her anxiety. "Has a decision been reached?"

Maude closed the bedchamber door. "Yes," she said. "We are withdrawing from the city on the morrow. We have no other choice, Minna. It has become painfully clear that we can expect no aid. Of all the lords we summoned, we've heard from none but Chester. And whilst he claims he is making ready to march on Winchester, none of us are willing to wager our lives upon his good faith. If he truly meant to help, he'd have been here by now."

"Could King David not send to Scotland for more men? Or Lord Geoffrey . . . ?"

"By the time they could get here, we'd all have starved. We've talked it over and agree that we must try to break free. Matilda's men have blocked the roads to the south and east, and now that Ypres has taken over the Wherwell nunnery, he holds the Andover Road, too, in the palm of his hand. But we think the road west—the Salisbury Road—remains open. We've decided that I should go out first, ahead of the army, and ride hard and fast for John Marshal's castle at Ludgershall. Robert believes that would be the safest way."

Although Minna said nothing, Maude quickly added, as convincingly as she could, "You need not fear for me, Minna. I will be with Brien and Rainald, and they'll not let me come to harm."

Minna did not doubt that Brien and Rainald would do all they could to protect Maude, but would it be enough? What if the road was not still passable, as they hoped? Or if they could not outrun pursuit? It would serve for naught, though, to give voice to her fears; her lady well knew the dangers. Forcing a smile, she sought to sound rueful as she said, "I ought to have heeded you, my lady, and stayed at Oxford Castle with Lady Beatrice and Lord Ranulf's wolf-dogs. It is good of you to resist reminding me of my folly, but I do not want you to fret on my behalf. I'll be quite safe here at the castle."

"That might have been true if Stephen were commanding this siege, but I would never entrust your safety to a man like Ypres. No, Minna, I'll not leave you behind."

"My lady, you must listen to your head, not your heart. I am an old woman, past fifty. Once you go out that West Gate, you must ride for your life. I could never keep up with you, would be an anchor dragging you down."

"That is why I have arranged for you to ride with the Archbishop of Canterbury and his retinue. They will have a flag of truce, and the greater protection of God's Cross. You'll be safe with them, Minna. You at least will be safe."

Minna was at a loss. What Maude needed to hear—that the men who mattered most to her would not be in peril—she could not say, for it would have been a lie. "What will happen come morning, my lady?"

"Once the archbishop departs, the army will ride forth, led by Miles and my uncle David. Robert will then bring up the rearward. I tried to talk him out of it, Minna, I tried so hard . . . but he would not listen. He insists upon commanding the rear guard."

"I know naught of military matters, my lady. Is that so dangerous?"

"He means to delay pursuit as long as possible, Minna, so that I might have time to get away. He would not admit it, but I know that is what he intends to do. Robert always lays claim to the heaviest burden, the greatest risk, and if any evil befalls him because of me, I do not think I could live with it . . ."

"I will pray for him, madame," Minna said earnestly. "I will pray for us all."

"Pray for the poor people of Winchester, too, Minna. May Almighty God protect them," Maude said softly, "for I cannot."

IT was no longer night, not yet day. Dawn was still hovering beyond the horizon, although faint glimmerings of light had begun to infiltrate the eastern sky. Torches were flaring in the castle bailey, giving Maude one last glimpse of the taut, shadowed faces of her kinsmen and liegemen. Farewells had already been said, muted and measured and private, and once she'd mounted her mare, Robert confined himself to a grave "Godspeed."

Meant as a benediction, it sounded more like an epitaph. Ranulf salvaged the moment, though, by drawling, "The first one to reach Ludgershall gets to go to church with John Marshal." Since Gilbert's account of his bell-tower interlude had not only circulated throughout Winchester, but was fast passing into legend, that got an edgy laugh. Maude looked at her brothers, her throat constricting, and then urged her mare forward, toward the opening gate.

Once they passed through the city's West Gate, they turned onto the Salisbury Road. Maude did not look back at Winchester; she did not dare. Never had she felt so powerless, and she envied the men their weapons, their male right to self-defense. She'd thought she knew all of the burdens imposed upon her because she'd been unfortunate enough to have been born female, but they'd not gone a mile before she discovered yet another of Eve's afflictions: that her very skirts were hampering her escape. She was riding sidesaddle, for women of rank rode astride only on the hunting field, and although she was an accomplished rider, sidesaddles were not meant for a flat-out gallop at full speed. As she could not match the men's pace, they had to slow their mounts to accommodate her mare, and Maude's fears for Brien and Rainald soon rivaled her dread for those she'd left in Winchester. If they were pursued, they'd never be able to outrun the enemy. But she knew they'd not abandon her, no matter how badly her mare lagged behind. Had she doomed them, too?

The road was an ancient one, of Roman origin, the major route to Sailsbury and the West. They would follow it until they reached Le Strete, a raised causeway also dating from Roman times. There they would cross the River Test, and then turn off onto a narrow trackway that would take them safely past Andover, on to Ludgershall Castle. Maude tried to focus her thoughts upon the hard, perilous ride ahead of them, but her brain would not cooperate; it kept conjuring up bloody images of dead and dying men. Would Robert and the others be able to fight their way free? How much time had passed? Daylight was nigh, the sky a soft, milky shade of grey. What would this day bring for Winchester, for them all?

The countryside was hilly and the road was rising. When they reached the crest, they drew rein abruptly, for the road below was blocked by a large log. There weren't that many soldiers in the camp, just enough to keep watch or halt a supply convoy. They were not as alert as William de Ypres would have wished, for they did not appear to have posted a guard, and they were rolling sleepily out of their blankets, cursing to find their fire had gone out during the night, yawning and stretching and then gaping up at the riders above them.

For seconds that seemed endless, both sides stared at one another. And then Brien grasped Maude's arm. "Do not stop," he said, "no matter what!" As soon as he saw she understood, he spurred his stallion forward, led his men down the slope into the enemy encampment.

Lacking spurs, women riders carried small leather whips. Maude rarely used hers, and when she brought it down now upon her mare's withers, the horse shot forward as if launched from a crossbow. Gathering momentum as they swept down the hill, the mare did not falter as they approached the barricade, soared up and over. Maude thought one man had grabbed for her reins as she galloped past, but she could not be sure, for it all happened in a blur. She heard shouts and swearing, another sound she'd never heard before but would never forget—the metallic, lethal jangle of clashing swords. She did as Brien had bade, urged her mare on until the noise had begun to fade behind her and the road ahead was clear. Only then did she ease her mount and look back at the enemy camp.

The battle was already over. But it had been as bloody as it was brief. Outnumbered, on foot, and just roused from sleep, these careless young sentinels had been no match for Brien's armed knights, handpicked for their killing capabilities. Bodies lay crumpled in the road, half hidden by the tall grass, slumped across the log barricade. There were no survivors, for there could be no witnesses. They'd suffered but one casualty of their own, and they left him where he'd fallen, amidst his enemies, for on this Sunday September morn, debts owed to the dead had to be deferred.

They paused only long enough to set free the tethered horses. Rainald was cursing his own clumsiness. He seemed more aggrieved by the damage done to his hauberk than to his arm, and submitted, grumbling, as Maude hastily bandaged his wound with her silk veil. She was about to mount her mare again when Brien rode up.

"You are not hurt?" Much to her relief, he shook his head. He slid his sword back into its leather scabbard, but not before she saw the blood smeared upon the blade.

"Can you ride astride like a man?" he asked. "I urge you to attempt it, for speed may well be our salvation."

Although she'd only ridden astride during an occasional hunt, Maude did not hesitate. "I will," she said, and when they brought forward the slain knight's stallion, she let Brien assist her up into the saddle. As they turned the mare loose, Maude felt a pang, for the graceful grey palfrey was her favorite mount.

"I am sorry," Brien said, "but we cannot spare the time to switch saddles."

Maude was surprised and touched that in the midst of all this carnage and chaos, he'd remembered her fondness for the filly. "I pray," she said, "that by day's end, the greatest of my regrets will be for a lost mare."

DESPITE the early hour, the citizens of Winchester turned out to watch as Miles led his army out of their city. Logic had told them this day was coming, but they seemed stunned, nonetheless, now that it was finally here, for they'd had to believe all the more fervently in God's Mercy, knowing they could expect none from William de Ypres and his Flemings. But neither the Almighty nor the empress was answering prayers on the second Sunday in September. On one of the sacred days of the Church calendar, the Exaltation of the Holy Cross, the Apocalypse was at hand.

As Robert approached his stallion, the man holding his reins spoke up. "I am Ellis, my lord, groom here these ten years past. I fear for my family now that you are going. What shall I do? How can I keep them safe?"

"There will be looting," Robert said, "afterward. Stay off the streets if you can. Bar your doors and shutter your windows. Do nothing to call attention to yourself. I can tell you no more than that."

Ellis still clutched at Robert's reins. "My lord," he said, "I have daughters."

Robert felt anger flare, anger at a world in which so many men saw war as sport. He'd fought when it was necessary, killed when he must, but never had he taken any pleasure in it. "Hide them away," he said, knowing how inadequate an answer that was, yet having no other advice to offer. He could do nothing for Ellis, nothing for Winchester.

His men were mounted and waiting. They looked tired and tense and of a sudden, younger than their years. Never did men seem so vulnerable to him as when they were about to go into battle under his command. He glanced again at their faces, then drew a sharp breath. "Ranulf!" He beckoned and his brother nudged his stallion forward. "What are you doing here? You agreed to ride out with Miles!"

Ranulf shrugged. "I overslept."

Robert's reaction was hopelessly conflicted—enormous pride in Ranulf warring with an urge to grab hold of the younger man and shake some sense into him. "I should think that one fool in the family would be enough. You just be sure to get through this unharmed, or Maude will never forgive me."

"Come on," Ranulf said. "I'll race you to Ludgershall."

THEY'D come more than eight miles and were almost upon Le Strete; it was on the other side of the hill. Rainald signaled for a brief halt to ease their horses, and unwittingly earned Maude's undying gratitude. She shifted gingerly in the saddle, seeking inconspicuously to tuck her skirts in under her legs. When Brien glanced her way, she mustered up a smile, for she was determined to keep her discomfort hidden as long as possible. Hopefully, it would not occur to them that skirts were not meant for riding astride. Nor were they likely to realize that her stockings were gartered at the knee, that with nothing between her inner thighs and the saddle leather, the constant jouncing had soon rubbed her skin raw. She was already chafed and blistered, and they had hours of hard riding ahead of them—if they could get safely across the River Test.

That was still in doubt, for they'd run into two of Ypres's scouts a few miles back. Brien's crossbowmen had brought one of them down, but the other had been luckier and had vanished into the woods. Their greatest danger lay just ahead at Le Strete, for there the Salisbury Road was joined by the one from Wherwell. If the scout had succeeded in giving the alarm, Ypres's men could be waiting for them at the river crossing.

Maude was not the only one thinking of that. Brien moved his horse close so they could talk. "The man on the roan is a local lad, who'll guide us across the downs to Ludgershall. He says there is a ford at Leckford, but it is too close to Wherwell for us to risk it. There is a royal manor at Le Strete, a handful of houses, and a bridge. If we can get across it without being seen by Ypres's men, they'll not know which path we took. Are you ready to ride as if the Devil were on our tails?"

She nodded. "If I had to choose between Ypres and the Devil, I'm not sure which one I'd pick. Let's outrun them both."

FOR Ranulf and Gilbert, the Battle of Winchester was chillingly familiar. It was as if they were reliving that frantic skirmish on the Wherwell Road, for once again they were being assailed from all sides, caught up in a surging, frenzied tide of thrashing bodies, panicked horses, and bloodied weapons. Only this time there was no abbey to take shelter in, just the road ahead and the enemy behind.

Robert was urging them to stay close together and to keep going, and they did their best to heed him, for his was the one voice of reason in a world gone mad, a world filled only with their enemies now that their retreat from Winchester had turned into this wild rout.

Miles had known they'd be pursued; what suspense there was lay in the timing of the attack. But he'd not expected his men to crack under the assault. It happened, though, and with shocking suddenness. His army had disintegrated as more and more men lost heart in this unequal struggle, sought salvation in flight, and Robert's rear guard found itself on its own, fighting a desperate and valiant delaying action in a war already lost.

The battle raged along the Salisbury Road. The fugitives from Miles's broken command were being chased down, bodies were being looted, and riderless horses seemed to be everywhere, circling about in confusion. Ranulf's own mount was tiring; it had begun to shorten stride. He had to strain now to find Robert midst the crush of men and horses. They would have to make a stand soon; if not, they'd be cut to pieces. But where? The road was sloping up again. He glanced over his shoulder, seeking Gilbert, and was jolted to discover he'd lost his squire.

He twisted around in the saddle. Some yards back, a chestnut stallion was flailing about on the ground, unable to rise. It had a white blaze and foreleg, and so did Luke's palfrey. As little as that was to go upon, it was enough for Ranulf, and he swung his horse about.

He soon spotted Luke. The youth was on his feet, although he seemed dazed by his fall, and did not respond to Ranulf's shout. But he'd drawn the attention of these men searching a nearby body for valuables. Recognizing him as easy prey, the men moved in confidently.

Their cockiness almost cost them dearly. They scattered just in time as Ranulf's destrier plunged into their midst. But they did not go far. Instead, they spread out and began to circle warily, swords and pike at the ready. Ranulf aimed his stallion at the closest of his assailants. Blood spurted, the man's sword thudded to the ground, and he recoiled hastily. Ranulf turned to confront the others, only to find them in retreat, too, for he was no longer alone; Gilbert was coming toward them at a gallop.

"You came back for me!" Luke lurched forward, tripped, and nearly fell under the hooves of Ranulf's stallion. Ranulf saw no blood, but the boy's face was the shade of curdled milk. "I hurt my arm," he said, sounding apologetic, as if his injury was somehow his fault. "I fear it is broken."

Ranulf and Gilbert exchanged troubled looks. They could not leave the lad here, injured and on his own. But never could they have ridden away, abandoned Robert to his fate. They wasted no time in discussion, caught a loose horse for Luke, put his foundering chestnut out of its suffering, and hastened after their beleaguered comrades.

The battle had swept past them, over the crest of Winchester Hill. They spurred their horses up the road, glancing back to make sure Luke was following, and came upon the last bitter moments of the ill-fated seven-week siege of Winchester. It ended there at Le Strete, when Robert's struggling rear guard collided with a contingent of Flemings coming down the Wherwell Road, ended in one final flurry of doomed resistance, dying, and defeat.

THE longest and most desperate day of Maude's life was at last drawing to a close in the inner bailey of Ludgershall Castle. She was trembling, so great was her fatigue, and when she was helped from the saddle, she feared that her legs would not support her. Brien came to her rescue, offering his arm for support. She thought he looked exhausted, too. They all did, men and horses alike, drenched in sweat and choked with the reddish dust of the dry September roads. She allowed herself a moment's indulgence, borrowed Brien's strength. Then she squared her shoulders, and moved to meet the man just emerging from the tower keep.

She was not surprised that John Marshal was up and about, rather than languishing upon a sickbed. She knew the man well enough to have been sure that if he was not dead of his wounds, he'd be on his feet. She thought she was prepared for the extent of his injuries, but she was not. Her breath stopped as she saw his face. She forced herself not to avert her eyes, feeling that she owed it to him to look without flinching upon the wounds he'd gotten in her service. His eye socket was covered by a pus-stained bandage, and from hairline to beard, his skin was raw and red and encrusted with scabs, slathered with goose grease. But she knew he'd have scorned her sympathy; in that, they were alike. So she said only, "Do you think you can find room for some unexpected guests?"

His mouth twitched. "I've never yet turned an empress away from my door." A woman had come from the keep behind him, and he said, "Madame, may I present my wife, the Lady Adelina?"

Adelina made a graceful curtsy. Maude took one look and liked her not, for she was small-boned and fair-haired and flower-fragile—like Matilda. But when Marshal's men began to crowd around, assailing them with questions, it was Adelina who saw Maude's utter exhaustion. "I'll not have it said that the mistress of Ludgershall does not know how to welcome a highborn guest," she chided. "Explanations can wait. If you'll be good enough to follow me, my lady . . . ?"

Maude did, gratefully, and by the time she was seated upon the bed in John and Adelina's private chamber, she'd completely revised her unfavorable impression of Marshal's wife. Adelina brought her a laver of scented washing water, a soothing salve for her sunburned face, a flagon of spiced and sweetened wine, all the while carrying on an easy conversation that was oddly comforting in and of itself, for she asked no awkward questions and gave Maude no time to dwell upon Winchester's fall and the men who might be dying even now on her behalf. When she urged Maude to stretch out on the bed, Maude did not demur, although she insisted that she'd never be able to sleep.

"Just rest then," Adelina said. "Supper can wait." She'd already helped Maude to strip off her gown, lamenting its bedraggled condition and the fact that Maude was too tall to wear one of her own gowns. "Never you mind, though. We'll clean and mend this one for you. I'll look in on you later, my lady. Now I must tend to John. The doctor said I should soak his bandage in vinegar and change it often."

"It is a wonder," Maude murmured, "that the pain did not drive him mad . . ."

"Most likely because we kept him drunk for days . . ."

Adelina's voice was lulling. Maude closed her eyes. When Adelina leaned over the bed and touched her shoulder, she thought at first that she'd just fallen asleep. But as she sat up groggily, she saw the night sky framed in the bedchamber's open window.

"Madame, I am indeed sorry to awaken you, but I was given no choice. Your brother and Lord Brien insist upon leaving at once for your castle at Devizes. I urged them to let you sleep the night through, but they say the danger is too great for you here."

Maude asked no questions, but she could not suppress a gasp when she swung her legs over the bed, for even that slight movement was painful. Her hair was trailing down her back, the true measure of her fatigue, for Adelina must have unbraided it while she slept on, unaware. As Maude tried again to get to her feet, Adelina gave a soft cry. "There is blood on your chemise! Did your flux come upon you of a sudden?"

"No, I had to ride astride like a man, but I lacked the undergarments that men wear, and my thighs blistered badly."

"How can you ride on to Devizes, then? That is nigh on twenty miles!"

"I can and I will. I must. And you cannot tell the men, Adelina. I do not want them to know."

The other woman nodded reluctantly. "Then you must let me do what I can to ease your discomfort," she said, and turned aside to ransack a coffer by the foot of the bed. With gentle, deft strokes, she rubbed an herbal ointment into Maude's blistered, abraded skin, then fashioned bandages from a pillowcase, and she understood when Maude's "thank you" seemed grudgingly given, saying, "Those are words that catch in my John's throat, too. He finds it hard to admit a need."

Maude did not know what to say to that, for it seemed to require a confidence in return. But Adelina did not wait for a response, instead crossed the chamber to retrieve Maude's gown. She was helping to lace it up when Brien and Rainald sought admittance.

Maude looked from one to the other. "Why must we leave Ludgershall in such haste? What is it that you're so loath for me to know?"

Rainald cleared his throat. "Marshal sent a few of his men toward Winchester to find out what happened. Only one of them has gotten back so far, but after hearing what he learned, we knew we dare not stay here, for this will be the first place they think to look once they start searching for you in earnest. We've got to get you as far away as we can, as fast as we can. It will not be easy for you, but—"

"You think I care about my comfort? Just tell me, was there a battle?"

Brien nodded. "Ypres and the queen's earls fell upon our army soon after they rode out along the Salisbury Road. Marshal's scout says they scattered to the winds, every man for himself. He says not even the archbishop was spared, that the clerics were roughly handled, their horses stolen."

"Oh, dear God," Maude whispered. Minna. And what of Ranulf? Miles and David and all the others. "Tell me the rest," she said, "the worst. Tell me about Robert."

"We do not know for certes," Rainald said, but he no longer met her eyes, and it was Brien who told her the truth.

"Marshal's scout says that Robert's men did not bolt like the others. They fought a running battle as far as Le Strete, where they were surrounded and overwhelmed by Warenne and Ypres and his Flemings." Brien saw her shudder and started to reach toward her, then let his arm fall to his side. "They would have wanted to take Robert alive," he said. "I swear to you that is true."

Maude swallowed with a visible effort. "You are saying, then, that either Robert was captured or he was slain."

Neither man spoke, but she had her answer in their silence, and she shut her eyes, squeezing back her tears. She would be able to weep soon, hidden by the darkness, riding through the night toward Devizes, but not now, not yet. She would leave Ludgershall dry-eyed and unbowed. She would not shame Robert with her tears.

CECILY watched anxiously as Matilda moved again to the tent entrance, but she no longer urged her mistress to attempt to get some sleep; she knew that Matilda would be up until dawn if need be, until she got the word about Maude. Rising, she poured a cup of wine and carried it across the tent. The other woman accepted it absently, continuing to gaze up at the star-dusted dark sky. "There is a fire in Winchester," she said. "See . . . over to the east."

"Come back inside, my lady," Cecily pleaded, "ere you catch a chill. Try to put the town's troubles from your mind. It does no good to dwell upon what cannot be helped."

Matilda let the tent flap drop. "Stephen kept his army from pillaging and raping in Shrewsbury," she said. "There must have been something I could have done . . ."

"And why did the king's soldiers heed him at Shrewsbury? Because he'd just hanged ninety-four men from the castle battlements and they feared not to! My lady, this is the way of the war. We need not like it, but accept it we must. What other choice have we?"

"What you say makes sense, Cecily. But I doubt that I will ever understand. The Londoners were so fearful for their city, so afraid that Maude would wreak havoc upon their homes and families. How, then, could they have been amongst the first to despoil Winchester?"

"My lady, I cannot answer that. But this I do know, that you have nothing to reproach yourself for. You seek only to free your lord husband from unjust confinement, and against all the odds, you have prevailed. This day he has won his liberty and it was your doing!"

Matilda felt a prickle of superstitious dread. "We do not know that, not yet. If Maude escapes, all this suffering and dying will have been for naught. The war will go on, and . . . and Stephen's life might well be forfeit, because of me."

"That will not happen. She has been taken prisoner, I know she has!"

"I would to God I could share your certainty," Matilda said wearily. "But she seemed sure to be taken at Arundel, too, and then again at Westminster, did she not?"

"The king's gallantry spared her at Arundel and blind luck at London, luck that is fast running out."

Matilda sat down at the table, pushed the candle aside, and leaned forward, resting her head upon her arms. But almost at once she straightened up. "Did you hear that? More men coming in . . ."

Her senses had been betraying her all night, hearing sounds that echoed only in her head. But this time she was right, and she was on her feet, waiting, by the time William de Warenne and William de Ypres pushed their way into the tent.

Warenne looked dirty and tired and jubilant. "God has shown us such favor, madame, for what a victory we had!"

"I know that," Matilda interrupted. "But what of Maude? Is she captive?"

Ypres shook his head. "I regret not. That woman has the most unholy luck. She ought never to have been able to slip through our net, yet she somehow did. You need not fear, though, for we'll soon track her down. We have men on her trail even now—"

But Matilda was no longer listening. "Then we lost," she cried. "Can you not see that? Without Maude, we gained nothing!"

Neither man seemed fazed by her despair. They looked at each other and grinned. "Ah, but we did," Ypres said. "Maude may have flown the nest, but we plucked her tail feathers for certes!" And turning, he lifted the tent flap. "Bring him in."

The man escorted into the tent was a stranger to Cecily. He was no longer young, for his brown hair was well salted with gray, and save for an ugly bruise under his left eye, he seemed unhurt. What struck her most forcefully was his composure; if not for his bound wrists, she'd never have known he was a prisoner. "Lady Matilda," he said calmly. "It is always a pleasure to see you, although I would rather it be under different circumstances."

Matilda was staring at him in shock. "Robert," she breathed, so softly that only Cecily heard, and her eyes widened.

"My lady, is this man the Earl of Gloucester?"

"This man," Matilda said unsteadily, "is Stephen's salvation." Her voice was muffled, midway between laughter and tears. Reaching for the Fleming's hand, she held fast. "How good God is, blessed be His Name. And bless you, too, Willem, for you've given me back my husband!"

22

NEAR DEVIZES CASTLE, WILTSHIRE, ENGLAND

September 1141

WHEN Maude's lashes flickered, a voice said, "She is coming around." She wondered hazily what Brien was doing in her bedchamber. The light seemed glaringly bright, and it actually hurt to look up at the sky. Sky? Her eyes opened wide, and she discovered that she was lying on the ground, a mantle wadded up under her head. "Brien . . . ?" How far away her voice sounded, how weak. "Brien, what happened?"

"You fell from your horse. You do not remember?"

"No." She bit her lip. "No . . ."

His fingers brushed her cheek, her forehead. "You're feverish, and little wonder, after all you've been through these three days past—"

"Why did you not tell us you were ailing, Maude?"

Maude blinked and Rainald's face came into focus over Brien's shoulder. "You said it was too dangerous to stay any longer at Devizes—"

"Yes, but I had it in mind to get you to Gloucester alive!" Rainald patted her shoulder, awkwardly tender. "No matter, though, for we've gone only a few miles. I'll send back to Devizes for a horse litter."

A horse litter was used only by the aged and the infirm, the helpless.

Maude's flush deepened. "You risked your lives for me," she said huskily, "and I've let you down . . ."

"Maude, that is not so!"

"I agree with Brien, Sister. You've done right well for a woman. And that," Rainald added hastily, "is but a joke!"

"Rainald . . . thank you for seeing to my safety."

He shrugged, then smiled. "I reckoned it was time I started earning my earldom. Brien, make sure she stays put whilst I see about the horse litter."

Maude did lie still as he moved away, although her compliance was due to exhaustion. "Brien," she said, so softly that he had to lean closer to hear, "I thank you, too. I owe you more than I could ever repay, mayhap even my life. You've been so loyal, and I . . . I did not even give you an earldom like Rainald!"

Her smile was hesitant, her jest no less tentative. But Brien knew what she was really asking—why he'd been so loyal. He even knew what she would never let herself ask—why he cared. Reaching out, he entwined the tip of her long black braid around his fingers, remembering the way her hair had looked in John Marshal's bedchamber, tumbling loose and lush and free about her shoulders. "I admire courage above all else," he said, "and you are as brave as you are beautiful, as brave as any man and braver by far than most. Loyalty is the least that you deserve."

To Maude's horror, tears filled her eyes. "What will I do, Brien, if Robert is dead?"

"You will grieve for him, and then you'll go on."

That was a lie, for Robert was their linchpin; without him to hold it together, her cause would falter, fall apart like her army at Winchester. But she was grateful to Brien for believing that she was strong enough to survive without Robert. "He is alive," she insisted. "Robert and Ranulf and Miles . . . they are all alive. I am sure of that, Brien." And if that was a lie, too, it was one they both needed to believe.

SLEEP had always come easily to Stephen. He could catnap at a moment's notice and it was a rare night when the day's troubles invaded the safe shadow-realm of his dreams; even in sleep, he was not one for violating sanctuary. But that had changed abruptly in mid-July. The irons clamped upon his wrists had done more than chafe his skin and shrink his space; they also clanked loudest at night. Dragged down by their weight, he snatched what sleep he could, never more than skimming the surface. And so it took only the slightest sound—a stealthy footfall muffled in the floor rushes—to bring him upright in the bed, wide awake and wary. Before he could speak, though, a shadow flitted forward. "Make no noise, my lord, for I cannot be caught here. It is me—Edgar."

Stephen's eyes were adjusting rapidly to the dark. "For you to come calling in the middle of the night, Edgar, you must have news that is very good or very bad. Which is it, lad?"

Edgar hesitated. "In truth, my lord, it could be either." Squatting in the floor rushes by the bed, he said, "You must know what I overheard in the hall. Lady Amabel got word tonight from the empress."

"From Winchester?"

Edgar shook his head. "Winchester has fallen to your queen. The empress fled the city on Sunday morn, and escaped by the Grace of God and a fast horse. She reached Gloucester last night, weary unto death but luckier than many, for her army's retreat turned into a wild rout. Men lost their weapons and shed their armor and hid themselves howsoever they could. Lord Miles and the Scots king and the Earl of Devon and Lord Ranulf—they are all unaccounted for, their whereabouts unknown."

Stephen was quiet, taking it all in. "You omitted one name from that list of missing men. What of Robert Fitz Roy?"

Edgar's voice hoarsened. "No one knows . . . not yet. He did not run like the others, fought off the Flemings until they trapped him at the River Test. But in giving the empress time to escape, he may well have doomed himself, and she fears the worst. So does his wife. Poor lady, I heard her in the chapel, weeping as if her heart would break—"

"Are you sure it was Amabel? I'd have thought she had more sense than that. Tears are a woman's weapons and she ought not to squander them needlessly."

Edgar was shocked by the levity, enough to venture a timid reproach. "A widow's grief ought not to be mocked, my lord. God would not approve."

"Amabel is no widow, lad. Robert is not dead. They'd have been loath to see him even bruised, much less mortally hurt. They took him alive, you may be sure of that, for Robert is my ransom . . . a king's ransom," Stephen said and laughed suddenly, jubilantly.

"I hope so, my lord. Indeed, I do hope so," Edgar said, sounding so dubious that Stephen gave him a quizzical look.

"I'd not blame you if you did not, lad. I understand that you are loyal to Robert—"

"Oh, no, my lord, it is not that! I wish the earl well, admire him mightily. But . . . but if I had money enough, it would be your freedom I'd buy, not his."

Hearing what he'd just blurted out, Edgar blushed, shamed by his disloyalty to Robert. He owed his lord better than that. And Stephen was the enemy, the possessor of a stolen crown. Yet none of that mattered, not anymore. "Earl Robert is my lord," he said softly, "but you are my king."

Stephen smiled. "Should you not be glad, then, for me? You do understand what this means? To gain Robert's freedom, Maude will have to give me mine. She'll like it not, but she'll do it, for she'll have no choice."

Edgar nodded solemnly. "I know that, my lord. But . . . but what if the earl was not taken alive? What if he was struck down in the battle?"

"Then Maude's queenship hopes were struck down, too. She cannot win without him."

Edgar squirmed uneasily. "But . . . well, people without hope . . . they might . . ."

"What are you so shy of saying, lad . . . that I might soon follow Robert to the grave? I have more faith in Maude than that. If she were capable of outright murder, I'd have been dead months ago."

Edgar was not reassured. He knew Stephen was more worldly than he, but he suspected that he'd had far more experience with desperation than ever Stephen had. "What if the empress was not consulted beforehand? What if some of her men took it upon themselves to rid her of her only real rival? If you were dead, my lord, I daresay most men would accept her as queen."

Now that he'd finally confessed his fears, Edgar looked up quickly to catch Stephen's reaction. To his amazement, Stephen seemed quite unperturbed, almost amused. "It does not pay to borrow trouble, lad. If you do, you're sure to end up with more than your share. I am not going to be smothered in my sleep or poisoned or take a convenient tumble down the stairs."

"How can you be so sure?"

"Because I believe in happy endings! If the Almighty had meant for me to die, I'd have died at Lincoln. What would be the purpose of my confinement if I were slain now, with vindication just within my reach? No, lad, the Almighty would never be so cruel."

Edgar didn't argue, although Stephen's benevolent Deity did not sound at all like the one he'd been taught to revere and fear, Jehovah, God of Wrath. He had a multitude of reasons for envying Stephen—his health and high birth and handsome face and devoted wife—but he found himself envying above all else Stephen's utter certitude, his sunlit faith in what he'd just jokingly called a "happy ending." Edgar could not imagine what it would be like to dwell in a world so free of shadows. But then his own world was one in which he was known—to all but Stephen—as Scarecrow.

"I'd best go," he said, "ere I am missed. I'll not see you on the morrow, my lord, for it is not my turn to guard you. But if I hear anything more about Earl Robert or the battle, I'll find a way to get word to you."

Stephen shoved his pillow behind his shoulders, knowing he'd never be able to get back to sleep. He had long, wakeful hours ahead, but they would be a gift, a private time alone in which to rejoice, to thank the Almighty, and to anticipate a reunion with his wife. "Edgar . . . think you that you might like to see London one day? If so, you need only seek out my steward, William Martel, and identify yourself. You'll have a place in my household waiting for you as long as I am king. You have but to come and claim it."

Edgar was mute, awed by the offer and all it encompassed. Reaching the door, he opened it cautiously, glanced back over his shoulder, grinned, and then was gone. The memory of that rapt, shining smile lingered, though, for it was the first time that Stephen had seen Edgar smile without bringing up his hand to shield his cleft lip.

FROM the castle solar, Matilda could catch a glimpse of Winchester's streets. People were out and about, the city slowly getting back to normal. But the damage done by the siege was even more extensive than she had first feared. On this sun-warmed September morning, she found herself dreading the coming of winter, knowing what suffering it would bring to Winchester.

Turning from the window, she studied the men seated at the solar's table. They were tense, expectant—except for Robert. He seemed quite calm; she suspected that he'd gotten a better night's sleep than she had, and her anger flared without warning. If not for Robert, Maude's claim would have flickered out by now, a candle quenched and cast aside. But anger was a luxury she could not afford, not yet. Instead she smiled; she was learning to use smiles as shields.

"I trust you've thought about our last conversation?" she queried, pointedly but still polite. Robert smiled, too, a noncommittal smile that was as meaningless as her own, saying nothing, and her brother-in-law stirred impatiently.

"What is there to think about? We've made you a remarkable offer, Robert. You need only renew your allegiance to Stephen and take your rightful place in the government—as his second-in-command. How could you even contemplate turning down an opportunity like that?"

Robert glanced from the bishop to Matilda, then over at Ypres. They'd promised to give him a vast amount of power. He wondered impersonally if they meant it, if it was bribe or hoax. "As you say, Cousin Henry, a 'remarkable offer.' But it is not one I can fairly judge under the present circumstances. Set me free and I shall give it the consideration it deserves."

He saw their faces change as they absorbed his answer, saw their disappointment and anger and—from Ypres—a grim glimmer of amusement. "I will not betray my sister," he said quietly. "You ought to have known that."

Matilda's eyes narrowed. "I will not apologize for trying to halt this needless, bloody war. I am sorry, Robert, that you cannot see the harm you are doing, sorrier than I can say. But so be it."

"I think you made a fool's choice," the bishop said brusquely, "but you are the one who'll have to live with it. So . . . let's talk of a trade: your freedom for Stephen's. That should be simple enough to arrange. There is a pen and inkwell on the table, and plenty of parchment. The sooner you write to your sister, the sooner you—"

"I cannot do that."

They stared at him. "Why not?"

"I cannot agree to a trade on those terms. I am but an earl, whilst Stephen is a consecrated king. I would have an inflated sense of my own worth, indeed, were I to believe I was a king's equal. If Stephen is to be freed, it is only fair that the men taken prisoner with me at Le Strete should be freed, too."

There was an astonished silence, broken by Ypres. "Set them free, without ransoms? Never whilst I draw breath!"

He sounded so indignant that Robert knew at once he must have captured one or more highborn prisoners himself. "Those are the only terms that I can accept."

"I hardly think you are in a position to dictate terms!" the bishop snapped. "I think it is time for some plain talking. You've been very well treated so far, Cousin, but that can change. We know that Maude clapped Stephen in irons. I daresay we can find some for you, too, if it comes to that."

Robert remained impassive. "We all do what we must."

Ypres leaned across the table. "You'd do well to remember that I am no friend to you, Fitz Roy. Moreover, I've always looked upon mercy as a character flaw."

"Willem!" Matilda confined herself to that involuntary objection, not willing to reprimand Ypres in Robert's presence. The bishop had no such scruples, and aimed a withering look in the Fleming's direction.

"You are but wasting your breath and our time, Ypres. He knows full well that we'll not be torturing him to break his will. Matilda would never abide it, nor would I. Let's talk, instead, of confinement. Not the kind you'd enjoy, Cousin. And not in England, either, where you might find friends foolhardy enough to attempt a rescue. No . . . if you force us to it, we'll send you to Matilda's lands in Boulogne. I'd advise you to think on that prospect long and hard: a lifetime alone in the dark, with no hope of escape."

Robert was not intimidated. But neither was he defiant. Sounding eminently reasonable, as if he were merely pointing out a hitherto overlooked fact, he said, "And whilst I was rotting away in a Boulognese dungeon, what do you think would be happening to Stephen?"

AMABEL picked up a pen without enthusiasm. She'd been taught to read and write in her youth; lacking a son, her father had lavished unusual care upon the education of his daughters. Writing was a clerk's task, though, and she'd had little practice at it. But this was not a letter she dared dictate to a scribe; she no longer trusted her own discretion.

To my daughter Maud, Countess of Chester, greetings:

I would that I had word for you of your father's fate, but it has been three days now since I joined Maude at Gloucester, and we've heard nothing. I fear I shall go stark mad if we do not soon

Reconsidering, she scratched out that last sentence. Gripping the pen again, she wrote:

Miles Fitz Walter reached us yesterday, in a sorry state indeed—bruised and bleeding and hungry and dispirited, having made his way alone to Gloucester after his command shattered. And last night a message arrived from Gilbert Foliot, the abbot of the Benedictine monastery here. He was one of the churchmen with the Archbishop of Canterbury, and reports they were ill used, their horses stolen, their belongings rifled; those impious knaves even robbed the archbishop of a silver cross. But they were not harmed, and Abbot Gilbert vows to bring Minna back with him as soon as he can provide a safe escort—you remember Minna, that dour German woman of Maude's? We still do not know, though, what befell Ranulf or the Scots king; pray God they were able to escape as Miles did.

Her pen hovered above the parchment as her attention wandered, and ink dripped down onto the letter. She could not seem to control her thoughts anymore; every road led her back to Robert and that wretched river crossing at Le Strete.

Your brothers Will and Philip are back at Bristol, keeping a close watch upon Stephen, but I brought Roger with me. He is so sure that Robert is alive and unhurt, but a priest would not be likely to lack faith, would he?

She got no further. Her head came up, the pen slipping from her fingers. Her maid had heard it, too. Casting aside her sewing, she said, "Something is amiss below-stairs." But by then Amabel was already halfway to the door.

The great hall was lit by smoking torches and an open hearth fire. Coming from the dark of the stairwell, Amabel squinted at the sudden brightness. Maude and Rainald and Brien and Miles were clustered in a circle, utterly intent upon a new arrival. She could tell only that he was of middle height, for her view was blocked by those crowding around him, but her heart leapt in a sudden, desperate surge, a hope that plummeted as Rainald moved aside, revealing the man in their midst. She thought Ranulf looked ghastly, his face bloodless and haggard, dark eyes glazed and unfocused—until he glanced her way.

"You are a welcome sight—" she began as he strode toward her, but Ranulf cut her off, as if his safety were of no matter.

"Robert was taken prisoner at Le Strete," he said. "But he was not harmed, Amabel, I swear he was not."

"Be sure what you say, Ranulf. For God's Pity, be very sure!"

"I am sure," he insisted. "I was there. I saw him surrender."

"You were there?" she echoed blankly. "And you left him? You just rode off and left him? Jesus wept, how could you?"

His face twitched, as if he'd taken a blow. "It . . . it was too late," he stammered, "was all over by the time I got there . . ."

He sounded as wretched as he looked, and somewhere in the back of her brain, she perceived his pain, acknowledged her own unfairness. But she did not want to be fair, not anymore. Robert had toiled his entire life striving to be fair, and where had it gotten him? "He would never have abandoned you," she cried, "never! You know he—"

"How dare you!" Maude's voice was choked, so great was her fury. "Ranulf would have given his life for Robert! If you must blame someone, blame me, then. But not Ranulf, damn you, not Ranulf!"

"You are right—for once. The blame does belong to you, Maude, and I'll not cheat you of any of it!"

Maude stepped closer, grasped Amabel's arm. "I care not if you make a fool of yourself. But Robert would. You owe him better than this."

The realization that Robert would indeed have disapproved of her behavior only stoked Amabel's rage all the higher. "You are right again," she said, with a tight, brittle smile. "Twice in a row—a record for certes." She pulled free of Maude's hold then, so violently that she stumbled backward, and when she felt a steadying hand upon her arm, she started to lash out at this new enemy. It was only when she heard his indrawn protest of "Mama" that she glanced up at his face, recognized her youngest son.

"Let's go to the chapel, Mama," he urged, "and pray for Papa's safe deliverance."

Roger was still new to his calling, painfully earnest in his priestly dignity. To the rest of the world, he may have seemed like one of God's Chosen, but to Amabel, he was a lost lamb, and she did not object when he tugged her toward the door. "But if prayer does not gain Robert's release . . ."

It was an unspoken threat, and a needless one. Maude would do whatever she must to pay Robert's ransom. Those in the hall knew that. But they knew, too, what his freedom would cost—for Maude, for them all, and for England.

THE bishop had settled in at Wolvesey, for it had not been badly damaged by the siege, unlike the royal palace, which was in ruins. Declining his hospitality, Matilda chose to stay at the castle, and people were soon lining up outside the kitchen, for the threat of starvation no longer hung over the city, but hunger was still Winchester's unwelcome guest. Robert was gone, though; William de Ypres had escorted him to the greater security of Rochester Castle in Kent, deep in the heartland of Matilda's English domains. It was mid-October before Ypres reported back to Matilda, and the news he brought was not good: Robert was still refusing to end his own captivity by setting Stephen free, not without additional concessions they were unwilling to make.

They were seated close by the hearth in the great hall, for there was a chill of early winter in the air. Stretching his legs, cramped from long hours in the saddle, Ypres complained, half humorously, "It is extremely irksome, having to respect someone I dislike so heartily. But I cannot deny the man's courage. If he was cut, he'd likely bleed ice!"

Matilda did not find Robert's fortitude quite so admirable; she didn't share Ypres's conviction that courage was the defining measure of a man. "If we agreed to free the other prisoners—"

"You cannot do that! When a man takes a highborn prisoner, he expects to profit from it. That is the way it's always been. You cannot change the rules with no warning, not without risking rebellion. My lady . . . Gloucester is engaging you in a clash of wills; do not let him win. He thinks he can outwait you, that you're so eager to get Stephen back that nothing else matters. Prove him wrong."

"How?"

"Simple. Make him want his freedom just as much as you want Stephen."

Matilda shook her head. "I do not like the sound of that, Willem."

"I am not suggesting we hang the man up by his heels, although the idea does have some merit. But we need not make his confinement quite so comfortable, either. He is being treated more like an honoured guest than a prisoner of war, allowed to have visitors, to write letters, to go into the town if he chooses; last week he even bought some blooded horses! I know what you are about to say, that he gave his sworn word he'd not attempt to escape. And I'll concede that he's probably the one man in Christendom whom I'd trust to keep such a preposterous oath, for he has always been insufferably prideful whenever honour is involved. But your generosity is leading you astray. He can afford to balk, to reject your terms, for what is it costing him? I say we change that, impose a price he'll not be willing to meet."

Matilda frowned. "I will think upon what you've said, Willem. I know my brother-in-law agrees with you. I will admit that my patience is fast shredding thin. If Robert does not see reason soon . . ."

A servant was hovering close by, ready to refill their wine cups. Once the man withdrew, Matilda shook off her disappointment and sought to sound more cheerful as she said, "We did have an unexpected stroke of luck last week. We intercepted a courier from the Scots king on his way to Gloucester with a message for Maude."

"So David finally surfaced for air, did he? Well, we knew he'd not been taken prisoner, and I found it unlikely that a king would be lying dead in a ditch and no one know of it. Where is he now . . . and more to the point, does he intend to rejoin Maude?"

"By now he ought to be back in Scotland. His letter was dated on the 22nd of September, and by then he'd gotten as far north as Durham. To hear him tell it, he had as many narrow escapes as Maude—it must run in the family. Twice he was cornered and bribed his way free. His letter was sparing of details, so I assume he still had enough men to defend himself, and his would-be captors must have decided it was easier to take what was offered. The third time that he ran into trouble, he was recognized. But the knight in charge turned a blind eye, let him go by, for he just happened to be David's godson! I have to confess that I am glad he got away; he is my uncle, too, after all. What gladdens me even more is that he will be staying up in Scotland where he belongs. He said as much to Maude, tactfully, of course. Still, the meaning seemed clear enough, that from now on, Maude is on her own."

That was what Ypres was hoping to hear. Pulling his seat closer to the fire, he listened with amusement as Matilda related the bishop's latest undertaking. He'd sent his men to scour through the ruins of Hyde Abbey, sifting the ashes until they'd recovered those abbey treasures that had survived the flames. He'd gotten back enough melted gold and silver to pay for the soldiers he'd hired, Matilda reported, much to the outrage of the monks.

Ypres was still laughing when the message arrived. Matilda gazed down at the seal of the Countess of Gloucester and all else was forgotten. Ypres had tensed, too, and watched intently as she read Amabel's letter. He could not read her face as easily as he once had, for she was belatedly learning a queen's skill at camouflage. But it seemed to him that she'd gotten paler, and when she glanced up, her eyes gave away her unease.

"Amabel has heard rumors that we've threatened to drag Robert off to Boulogne. She reminds me that Stephen is being held at her castle, in her custody, and she vows that if any harm whatsoever comes to Robert, she will send Stephen where even God could not find him—to Ireland."

As threats went, that was a daunting one. "You know the woman," he said, "as I do not. Is this a bluff? Or is she capable of carrying out her threat?"

"Amabel? Oh, yes," Matilda said, without hesitation, and Ypres slouched back in his chair, reconsidering their options. They'd have to tread with care, for if Gloucester's wife knew her Scriptures—an eye for an eye, a wound for a wound—Matilda was not likely to follow his advice and strip Gloucester's confinement down to the bare bone. Jesú, would she be desperate enough to give in, to let Gloucester win?

Matilda was studying Amabel's letter, but her initial disquiet seemed to have ebbed away. She looked pensive now, not dismayed, and as he watched, he saw a smile flicker about the corners of her mouth.

"What is it?" he said sharply. "What do you have in mind?"

"I am thinking," she said, "that we've been going about this the wrong way. We have been negotiating with the wrong people, Willem. We've been seeking to come to terms with Robert and Maude, when the one we ought to have been bargaining with is the woman who holds Stephen—the woman who wants her husband back just as much as I want mine."

23

BRISTOL, ENGLAND

November 1141

THE first of November was not a comfortable day for travel. Rain had been falling intermittently since dawn and the wind had been constant, blustery and biting. Eustace did not care about the cold; he was so tense he barely felt it. He looked occasionally at his mother, but more often at William de Ypres, for he was very much in awe of the redoubtable Fleming. When Ypres happened to glance in his direction, Eustace stiffened his spine and raised his head, hoping that Ypres would notice how well he rode. He wished he had a stallion as spirited as Ypres's chestnut, but his horse was a docile gelding. Wolf-bait, he thought scornfully, longing for spurs like Ypres and the other men wore. Despite his disappointment with his placid mount, it was still easy to pretend that he was the one leading an army to Bristol, not Ypres and his mother. If only theirs were a real rescue mission. He was sure they could catch the enemy by surprise, assault the castle and set Papa free. A pity Mama was so timid, so loath to see bloodshed.

Feeling her son's gaze upon her, Matilda gave him a quick smile. Eustace knew it was meant to reassure, but he resented it for that very reason. "I do not need to be coddled, Mama," he said indignantly. "I am not a bairn like Will and Mary, and I am not scared to be a hostage, not at all."

"I know that, Eustace." Matilda found herself yearning for bygone days, when the distance between them was never so great that it could not be spanned by a hug. After some moments, she said, choosing her words with care: "It will all be over in a matter of days. Upon our arrival at Bristol, your father will be set free. He and Willem and Robert's eldest son will then ride straightaway for Winchester. Once they get there, Robert will be released. Leaving his son as his pledge, he will hasten to Bristol. You and I will then be escorted safely back to Winchester, and Robert's son will be freed. So you see, Eustace, we'll scarcely have time to unpack, will be reunited with your father at Winchester by week's end."

"It sounds as if none of you trust each other very much," he said, with a cynicism that seemed too adult and knowing for his eleven years. Matilda was troubled by it, but she could not contradict him.

"One another," she corrected automatically, "not 'each other.' And you are right, lad. Trust never entered into it."

He slanted a sidelong glance her way. "Will she be at Bristol, too . . . the Angevin slut?"

Matilda was no novice at motherhood, knew full well that she was being tested. "I like it not when you use such unseemly language, Eustace. Moreover, you are mistaken as well as rude. Maude's husband is the Angevin. She is of Norman and Scots stock. Nor is she a slut."

Eustace's lower lip jutted out. "Then why do men call her that? I've heard them," he insisted.

"I do not doubt it. But that does not make it true. When people want to insult a man, they cast slurs upon his courage. But the worst they can say about a woman is to impugn her chastity. It is unfair, though, for no scandal has ever sullied Maude's good name. Whatever her other failings—and I find them plentiful—she is not a wanton."

Eustace was not convinced, but he prudently refrained from saying so. He didn't really want to quarrel with his mother, not today. "Will she be there or not, Mama?"

"No, she will not. She has withdrawn to Oxford Castle, will be awaiting Robert there upon his release. I suspect she could not bear to see your father ride forth as a free man."

Eustace felt a momentary disappointment, for he'd envisioned himself confronting her, this troublesome, wicked woman who'd dared to make war upon his father. "Mama . . . after Papa is free, what happens then? Will Maude give up, go back to her husband, and leave us in peace?"

Matilda kept her eyes on the road ahead. "I doubt it," she said bleakly. "I very much doubt it."

MATILDA had never been to Bristol, and she was both impressed and chilled by the fortified defenses of town and castle, protected by two rivers and a deep man-made ditch. They would never have been able to free Stephen by force. Thank God and His Holy Son that it had not come to that. Now they passed unchallenged into Robert Fitz Roy's great citadel, and when they dismounted in the inner bailey of the castle, the Countess of Gloucester was awaiting them. Following Amabel inside, Matilda found a hall crowded with curious, wary, and hostile onlookers. But one glance was all she needed to see that the only man who mattered was not in their midst.

Whirling upon Amabel, she demanded, "Where is my husband? Why is he not here?"

Her suspicions were insulting, but Amabel was willing to overlook the affront, for she could identify with Matilda's fear. "Stephen is waiting for you in the solar. He wanted your first meeting to be private." And ushering Matilda and Eustace across the hall, she herself led them up into the stairwell.

Matilda soon moved ahead, lifting her skirts and taking the stairs two at a time. When Eustace would have followed, Amabel blocked his way. "Give them a few moments alone, lad, ere you enter." Eustace stared at her in astonishment, for this woman was the enemy. Did she truly think he'd do as she bade him? But to his fury, she refused to move aside when he sought to push past her, effectively trapping him in the narrow stairwell.

Matilda was not aware that her son had been waylaid. By the time she'd reached the door, she was breathless and flushed. Nine months he'd been a prisoner, to the very day. How would he look? Could a man like Stephen survive confinement with no scars on his soul? Her heart was pounding. Reaching for the door latch, she shoved inward.

Stephen was standing by the window. It had occurred to her that he might have gained weight, an active man suddenly forced into idleness. Instead he seemed to have lost weight. His face was thinner, his cheekbones noticeably hollowed, and he had more grey in his hair than she remembered. But his eyes were crinkling at the corners, alight with such a blazing blue joy that her throat tightened and she found herself thinking that no crown was worth more than Stephen's smile. He moved so fast that before the door could close behind her, he had her in his arms, holding her so hard it hurt a little. She clung tightly, raising her face so he could claim her mouth, not even realizing she was crying until he'd begun to kiss away her tears.

"I was so afraid," she confessed, "that this day would never come."

"I never doubted," he assured her, encircling her waist and pulling her even closer, "never."

She'd worried as much over his mental state as she had over his physical danger. "Truly, Stephen?"

"Truly," he said and grinned. "With you and God both on my side, Tilda, how could I lose?" He kissed her again, hungrily. "But I'd pawn my crown right now for a bed."

"Yes," she agreed, "oh, indeed, yes . . ." Giving him so ardent a look that his joke lost all humor. But at that moment, there was a loud banging on the door, followed by their son's angry entrance.

"That meddlesome woman would not let me in!" Eustace's outrage flamed out quickly, though, at sight of his father. He was suddenly uncertain, oddly ill at ease.

Stephen felt no such shyness. "Look at you, lad," he marveled. "You are taller than your mother!"

Eustace nodded, very pleased that his father had seen it at once, just how much he'd grown. "I am glad you are free, Papa," he said, sounding rather formal even to his own ears, but surely he was too old now for open displays of affection? Stephen thought otherwise, and once Eustace found himself caught up in his father's embrace, he forgot his qualms and clung no less urgently than his mother had done.

Amabel gave them as much time as she could, but she could not wait long, not with so much at stake. "I am sorry to intrude," she said, "but the sooner you are on the way to Winchester, Stephen, the sooner I'll have my husband back. Now there is someone else waiting to see you." And she stepped aside so William de Ypres could enter the room.

The Fleming paused, almost imperceptibly, before crossing the threshold. In his entire adult life, he could not remember ever offering an apology for any act of his, and he was not sure how to go about it. But if they were to put the ghost of his Lincoln betrayal to rest, he'd have to say a few words at graveside. "I owed you better than you got," he began awkwardly, "and for what it is worth, I did regret it. But by then, it was too late."

"Regrets always are," Stephen said. He felt Matilda's hand tighten on his arm, and he covered it with his own before turning his gaze back to Ypres. "It is passing strange," he said, "how confinement has affected my memory. For the life of me, I cannot seem to remember anything at all about your conduct at Lincoln. Yet I have a very clear and vivid recollection of the great service you did me at Winchester . . . and I was not even there!"

Amabel, watching from the doorway, said nothing. She was still furious with her sister-in-law. But somewhat to her surprise, she experienced a sudden, sharp pang of pity for Maude, who had right on her side, but little of Stephen's generosity and none of his charm.

MATILDA'S dream was at first fanciful and then increasingly erotic. Stirring drowsily, she opened her eyes and discovered this dream was—at long last—real. "Are you getting hungry again, my love?" she murmured, and Stephen laughed into her hair.

"I did not mean to wake you. I was just taking inventory of treasures I've been too long without. I ought to warn you, Tilda, that we are likely to create something of a scandal, for I may not let you leave this bed for days."

"Promise?" she said and he laughed again, drawing her in against him until they lay entwined, two halves made whole. "I was so proud," she said, "of the way you accepted them back into the fold, all the sheep who had strayed . . . Willem and Northampton and Warenne and the others."

"'Willem'?" he echoed, as if affronted by the intimacy. But she caught the playful tone, and bit him gently when he traced her mouth with his fingers.

"It was easy enough," he said lightly, "for I believe in redemption. I would that I could say I also believe I am my brother's keeper, but that saintly I am not, sweetheart."

She saw through the flippancy, for she knew that of all the betrayals he'd suffered, none wounded so deeply as his brother's defection. Shifting so she could cradle her head in the crook of his shoulder, she said, "I think Henry will be loyal from now on . . . in his own, odd way. At least you need not fear any more dalliances with Maude. He's burned that bridge for certes."

"Along with most of Winchester," he said, "and I wonder if he spares any regrets for the city when he mourns all his losses."

"Speaking of loss," she said softly, "I came too close to the abyss, Stephen. You must promise me that you'll never put yourself so at risk again. You have nothing to prove, for not even your most bitter enemies have ever questioned your courage. No more Lincolns, my love . . . promise me."

"Such a promise would be hollow, Matilda, unless it came from the Almighty. I cannot promise you that I'll never come to harm. I can pledge to you that I will not be so careless of my own safety in the future. Lincoln was . . . my Antioch, but that is not a mistake a man makes twice."

Lincoln and Antioch. The similarities between the two sieges had occurred to Matilda almost at once, so striking were they. The crusaders capturing Antioch, Stephen besieging Lincoln Castle. Both armies then caught by surprise, confronted by a large enemy force. Stephen's father had abandoned the siege, rode away from Antioch and—fairly or not—into infamy, disgrace that not even his subsequent martyr's death had fully expiated. Stephen had chosen to stay and fight. It was Matilda's belief that he'd been paying off his father's debt, but she had not expected him to see that for himself, as he was the least introspective of men.

He sensed her surprise and said wryly, "Solitary confinement gives a man plenty of time to think. What else was there to do?" Reaching for her hand, he kissed her fingers, one by one. "I do not have too many memories of my father, Tilda, for I was only five when he took the cross again, at my mother's insistence. But I do have one very strong memory of a church, probably the cathedral at Chartres. He was telling me about Antioch, and what I remember was the sadness in his face . . ."

Raising up on her elbow, Matilda brushed her lips against his cheek. What a heartless wife Adela had been, that she could have valued her husband's honour above his life. She was no longer threatened, though, by her indomitable mother-in-law, for Adela's shadow had receded in the three years since her death in the cloistered quiet of a Marcigny nunnery. Matilda supposed most people would say her life had been a great success. Daughter, wife, widow, mother, and nun—she'd never failed to play the part expected of her, and lived long enough to see one son as a prince of the Church, a second as Count of Blois and Champagne, and a third as England's king. But when Adela died, few had grieved for her.

Stephen had been stroking her hair, sliding his hand down her back, along the curve of her hip. Before his caresses could become more intimate, she laced her fingers through his, holding his hand still against her thigh. "Stephen . . . we need to talk about betrayals, those beyond forgiving."

"Geoffrey de Mandeville?"

"Yes. I realize that you can take no action against him now, not yet. But he must be punished for what he did. I entreat you to see that he is, to hold him accountable for his treachery."

"Of course I will. Jesú, the man abducted Constance! Moreover, he abandoned you when your need was greatest. Do you truly think I could ever forgive him, Tilda?"

"Forgiveness comes easily to you, my love, sometimes too easily." Her smile was tender enough to take any sting from her words. "You are not a man to nurture grudges, and I admire you greatly for that. But Mandeville owes us a debt that cannot be remitted. Promise me, Stephen, that you will harden your heart against him. He is not deserving of clemency, yours or the Almighty's."

She kissed him then, a kiss so soft and seeking and full of promise that he began to laugh. "What is hardening at the moment," he said, "is not my heart!"

She laughed, too, and gave herself up gladly to the joys of the marriage bed, those pleasures of the flesh that were so sweet and mayhap sinful, for the Church said passion was suspect, even if sanctified by wedlock. But it seemed a strange sin, indeed, that of loving her husband overly well, and she could not believe it was one to imperil her soul. "I've been so wretched without you," she confided, and those were the last words she got to say for some time thereafter.

Later—much later—as they lay at ease in each other's arms, he could not resist teasing her about her "sudden thirst for blood." Dropping a quick kiss on the tip of her nose, he said, "Can this truly be my Matilda? My gentle little wife who would not even frown at a mangy dog or a surly beggar? Can this be the same woman who now plies her seductive wiles with a skill that Salome might envy?"

Matilda was unperturbed. "If I remember my Scriptures," she said placidly, "Salome did her dance of the veils for the head of John the Baptist. But I do not want you to kill Geoffrey de Mandeville, Stephen." She turned her head on the pillow and smiled at her husband. "Just ruin him."

UPON Robert's arrival at Oxford, Maude celebrated his freedom with a lavish supper of roast swan, stewed venison, baked lamprey, and a sugared subtlety sculptured to resemble a unicorn. Wines were poured freely, her minstrel entertained them between courses, and all did their best to act as if they truly had cause for rejoicing.

Afterward, they retired to the solar, ostensibly for privacy, but also because they could keep up the pretense no longer. The castellan, Robert d'Oilly, and his stepson, yet another of the old king's by-blows, had excused themselves as soon as they could, leaving behind a fractured family circle.

Rainald thought those remaining were as glum a bunch as he'd ever had the bad luck to encounter. Robert was so quiet one would have thought he'd taken a holy vow of silence whilst he was captive. Amabel and Maude were being polite to each other, but it was the kind of courtesy to set a man's teeth on edge. And Ranulf was brooding again. He was usually good company, cheerful and obliging. But something was sitting heavy on his shoulders these days, over and above his natural chagrin at Maude's rout from Winchester. Whatever it was, though, he was keeping it to himself. Rainald had made one attempt to find out what was festering, only to have the lad snap at him like one of those blasted dyrehunds.

Ranulf was staring intently into the fire, and did not even notice when Rainald leaned over and helped himself to his brother's drink. It would be a shame to waste good wine, he reasoned. His gaze roamed the chamber, flitting over his wife, sitting meek and mute in the window seat, before coming to rest on Maude. She and Robert were hunched over a chessboard, but neither of them seemed to have much interest in the game. Rainald felt pity stir and looked away hastily, lest she read it in his face, for he knew she'd forgive him almost anything but pity. He did feel sorry for her, though, damned if he did not. He did not even blame her anymore for botching things so badly. Mayhap it was just not meant to be. At least he'd done better than most, for he'd gotten an earldom out of it all. If he could hold on to it. Getting to his feet, he reminded them that he was leaving for Cornwall on the morrow and bade them goodnight, remembering just in time to take Beatrice with him.

Amabel soon went off to bed, too; she was finding the atmosphere in the solar just as oppressive as Rainald had. Ranulf was the next to make his escape, claiming he had to let his dogs out, and Robert and Maude were left alone with a flagging chess game and a silence heavy with all that lay unspoken between them.

Maude pushed her chair back. "I cannot concentrate upon this game. I am truly glad to have you safe, Robert. But tonight I feel as if . . . as if we'd struggled and panted and clawed our way up a mountain, only to stumble just as we neared the summit and fall all the way down, landing in a bloodied, bruised heap at the bottom. What in God's Name do we do now?"

"I suppose," he said, "we start climbing again."

"How many of our men will have the heart for it?" Rising, she began to pace. "To come so close and then to have it all snatched away like this . . . it is so unfair, Robert, so damnably unfair!"

"Life is unfair," he said, sounding so stoical, so rational, and so dispassionate that she was suddenly angry, a scalding, seething, impotent rage that spared no one—not herself, not Robert, not God.

"You think I do not know that? When has life ever been fair to women? Just think upon how easy it was for Stephen to steal my crown, and how bitter and bloody has been my struggle to win it back. Even after we'd caged Stephen at Bristol Castle, he was still a rival, still a threat . . . and why? Because he was so much braver or more clever or capable than me? No . . . because I was a woman, for it always came back to that. I'll not deny that I made mistakes, but you do not know what it is like, Robert, to be judged so unfairly, to be rejected not for what you've done but for what you are. It is a poison that seeps into the soul, that makes you half crazed with the need to prove yourself . . ."

She stopped to catch her breath, and only then did she see the look on Robert's face, one of disbelief and then utter and overwhelming fury, burning as hot as her own anger, hotter even, for being so long suppressed.

"I do not know what it is like?" he said incredulously. "I was our father's firstborn son, but was I his heir? No, I was just his bastard. He trusted me and relied upon me and needed me. But none of that mattered, not even after the White Ship sank and he lost his only lawfully begotten son. He was so desperate to have an heir of his body that he dragged you back—unwilling—from Germany, forced you into a marriage that he knew was doomed, and then risked rebellion by ramming you down the throats of his barons. And all the while, he had a son capable of ruling after him—he had me! But I was the son born of his sin, so I was not worthy to be king. As if I could have blundered any worse than you or Stephen!"

Maude was stunned. She stared at him, too stricken for words, not knowing what to say even if she'd been capable of speech. Robert seemed equally shattered by his outburst: his face was suddenly ashen. He started to speak, then turned abruptly and walked out.

THE night was bitter-cold and starless, the sky choked with clouds. Maude leaned into the embrasure, gazing down into the darkness of the bailey. She knew her presence on the battlements was making the guards uneasy. They kept their distance, but she could feel their eyes following her, curious, probing, wondering what she was doing up here, alone, at such an hour. She wondered, too.

It may have been memory that had drawn her up to the battlements. Shivering each time the wind caught her mantle, she remembered watching a summer sunset from this very spot, Brien at her side. Not so long ago, just a lifetime. Brien was back at Wallingford Castle now, not far away, twelve miles or so. As if distance mattered, as if what kept them apart could be measured in miles. She did not often let herself think of Brien, of what might have been and what could never be. But she did now, deliberately and unsparingly. She wiped away tears, and thought of them all. Robert, who'd turned into a stranger before her eyes. Robert, whom she'd trusted and taken for granted and never really known. Ranulf, who'd lost the earldom she'd promised and mayhap much more. Rainald, who'd profited, too, from her quest—a mad wife and a precarious hold upon a corner of Cornwall. Geoffrey, whom she'd loathed from the very day of her wedding, because it was easier to hate him than to hate her father. And her sons, growing up without her. Her sons, whom she'd not even seen in more than two years.

She lost all sense of time, and when the sky began to pale, it was with shock that she realized she'd passed the entire night out on the battlements, standing guard over the wreckage of her ravaged kingdom. The cold seemed to have penetrated into her very bones, yet for hours she'd not even been aware of it. She watched as the shadows receded and daylight slowly gained the ascendancy. Only then did she turn away from the battlements, go to find her brother.

As early as it was, Robert was already up and dressed, attended by a sleepy squire. The bed curtains were closed; Amabel still slept. But after one glimpse of Robert's face, Maude was sure his night had been as wakeful as her own. The squire soon remembered an urgent need to be elsewhere, and muttering about bringing his lord cider and bread to break his fast, he made a swift, discreet exit.

Maude was still trembling with the cold, and she knotted her hands together to still their tremors. When Robert gestured toward the bed, she nodded and kept her voice low, no more wanting to awaken Amabel than he did.

"I am sorry, Robert. I do not say that as often as I ought, but never have I meant it more. You have been my rod and my staff, more loyal than I deserved. You would have made a very good king."

His shoulders twitched, in a half-shrug. "Well, better than Stephen, for certes," he said, with the faintest glimmer of a smile.

"Our father was a fool," she said, and he did not dispute her.

"Robert." Her mouth was suddenly dry. "I am never going to be queen, am I?"

"No," he said quietly, "you are not."

She'd known what he would say. But his uncompromising, honest answer robbed her of any last shreds of hope. She averted her face, briefly, and he, too, looked away, not willing to watch the death of a dream.

"I'd best go now, ere Amabel starts to stir." She gave him a smile so pained that he winced.

"Maude." She turned back to face him, slowly, and he said, "You are not giving up?"

"You know better than that, Robert. I may have lost, but I'll not let Henry lose, too. I shall fight for my son as long as I have breath in my body. He must not be cheated of the crown that is his birthright."

She saw sympathy in his eyes, and what mattered more, respect. "I will do whatever I can," he vowed. "to make sure that does not happen." And in that moment, she realized the truth—that he'd been fighting for Henry all along.

24

DEVIZES, ENGLAND

March 1142

THE Countess of Chester arrived the day after her aunt and father held an urgent council at Devizes Castle. Maud needed to take but one meal in their company to conclude that something was amiss, for her senses were finely attuned to emotional undercurrents. As soon as she could, she lured her mother away, and after some bantering about the tedium of the Lenten menu, she demanded to know why "Aunt Maude and Papa and the others look like mourners at a particularly dreary wake."

Amabel settled herself in the window seat. "They have cause, child, for they have had to swallow their pride, and that goes down much harder than salted fish. They have decided to send envoys to Maude's husband, asking Geoffrey to aid them in overthrowing Stephen."

Maud's eyes widened. "Were they sober at the time? I cannot believe they'd turn to Geoffrey!"

"Well, they did. Which proves, I suppose, just how desperate they are."

Maud was still incredulous. "I would have sworn upon my very soul that Aunt Maude would never have agreed, no matter how great her need!"

"For herself, I daresay she would not. But there is very little she would not do for her son."

Maud sat down abruptly, suddenly realizing the full magnitude of what her aunt had lost at Winchester. "It is not fair, Mama. She ought to have been queen!"

"Most people thought otherwise."

Amabel's tone had an edge sharp enough to slice bread, or so Maud thought. She was sorry that her mother and her aunt were so often at odds, for they were the two women who mattered most to her, but she was insightful enough to understand why it was so, and pragmatic enough to accept it. Diplomatically steering the conversation away from hidden family reefs, she said, "I understand now why Uncle Ranulf was in such a black mood. He trusts Geoffrey even less than he likes him, and he once told me that if he was given a choice between befriending Geoffrey and trying to tame a polecat, he'd take the polecat every time!"

"Do you remember that Bristol goldsmith's son, Maud . . . the wretch who was caught setting all those fires? When he was asked why, he said he just liked to watch things burn. Well, Geoffrey likes to set tempers afire, and he does it right well. But Ranulf's 'black mood' cannot be blamed on Geoffrey's coming, for he has been troubled for some weeks now. Even Robert commented upon it, and men are usually blind to any wound that does not bleed."

Maud's curiosity was piqued. She was quite fond of Ranulf, no less fond of intrigue, and later that afternoon she set herself a dual task—to ferret out Ranulf's secret and to console him if she could.

She was halfway up the stairs to Ranulf's chamber when she bumped—quite literally—into her uncle's young squire. Luke recoiled, stammering incoherent apologies, for his natural shyness became almost paralyzing in the presence of self-assured, flirtatious young women like Maud. Eventually, though, he managed to suggest that this would not be a good time to seek out Lord Ranulf.

"Has he a woman with him?" she asked, and when he blushed at her bluntness but shook his head, she gave him a bewitching smile and continued on up the stairs. In his haste to escape, Luke had left the door ajar. She was about to knock when she heard the voices, as angry as they were audible.

"I swear by the Rood, Ranulf, that you've gone utterly daft! Let's suppose you are able to evade bandits and the king's men and get safely to Shrewsbury. What then? How are you going to contact Annora? Hope she comes into town ere the year is out? Or do you just intend to ride out to her husband's manor and ask him if you can borrow his wife for a bit?"

"Damn you, Gilbert, this is none of your concern!"

"Someone has to keep you from dying so young and so needlessly!"

"I've had enough of your meddling!" Ranulf jerked the door open, only to find himself nose to nose with his niece. "Maud! What are you doing out there?"

"I should think it would be obvious. I was eavesdropping, of course." She stepped forward into the room and winked at Gilbert. "My turn to talk some sense into him."

"Good luck," he muttered, giving the door a satisfying slam on his way out.

"I want no lecture, Maud," Ranulf warned, but his rudeness fazed her not at all. Perching on the edge of the bed, she arranged her skirts decorously and then smiled sweetly.

"Sermons are for church. I'd much rather talk about your tryst with . . . Annora, was it? The girl to whom you were once plight trothed? Such fidelity is rare indeed in our world and must be rewarded. First of all, I need to know what she is like. My husband—and most men, if truth be told—seem far more interested in what is between a woman's legs than between her ears, but—"

"Maud!"

"Since when are you offended by plain speaking? Just tell me if this lass of yours has a brain in her head. Does she have the wits to read between the lines of my letter?"

"What letter?"

"The one I plan to write to her husband, telling him how much I miss my dear friend Annora and how I yearn to have her visit me. Is she clever enough to need no further prompting?"

"Yes," Ranulf said slowly, "she is. But what of your husband, Maud?"

"Ah . . . so Annora's husband supports Stephen, then? That should pose no problem, though, for Randolph is taking no part in the war these days. His creed at the moment seems to be, 'May the pox take Stephen and the plague take Maude.' He may be no friend to Stephen, but he is still the most powerful lord in the realm. Annora's husband will be greatly flattered that the Countess of Chester is so fond of his wife, and when I suggest that I send an armed escort to bring Annora safe to Chester Castle for a visit, he'll snap at the offer like a starving trout! Nothing is so alluring," she added playfully, "as a crown of some sort."

"You make a most convincing argument," Ranulf conceded, "but when I asked about your husband, I was not thinking of his political affinities. I was wondering how he'd react upon learning that yours was the guiding hand behind our . . . tryst, did you call it?"

She waved away his objection with a graceful, airy gesture of dismissal. "What makes you think he'd even be there? As soon as he heard that Stephen had gone north to forbid a tournament at York, he became more nervous than a treed cat, fearing that Stephen might try to reclaim Lincoln Castle whilst he was in the neighborhood. He and his brother have been holed up at Lincoln since the beginning of Lent, making sure the castle could withstand an assault. But even if he were at Chester, he'd be no hindrance to us. Randolph brings great passion to what interests him, utter indifference to what does not. He'd never even notice your dalliance—not unless you were indiscreet enough to make love in the great hall!"

Ranulf sat down beside her on the bed. "It means more than I can say, that you do not pass judgment upon us, that you have offered to help. But if I let you do it, we'd be ensnaring you in our sin."

Maud laughed. "I assure you that I'll have so many sins of my own to answer for come Judgment Day that any secondary sins will count for very little!"

He shook his head, laughing, too, in spite of himself, and said again that he could not accept her help. Maud merely smiled, knowing that he would.

ANNORA supposed she should have been nervous as the distant walls of Chester came into view. She was, after all, answering a mysterious summons from an utter stranger, and intending to commit adultery if she was right about the real reason for the Countess of Chester's sudden avowal of friendship. But she was not nervous at all, so sure was she that she would find Ranulf waiting for her in Chester.

People stopped to watch as she rode through the hamlet of Handbridge, recognizing the Earl of Chester's badge upon the sleeves of her escort, impressed and curious. Annora liked the attention, and she smiled graciously when they stared and pointed, playing the great lady with zest—Eleanor, Queen of France and Duchess of Aquitaine, on her way to a rendezvous with a royal lover.

Crossing the wooden bridge that spanned the River Dee, Annora entered the city through Bridge Gate, and rode into the castle bailey. The Countess of Chester was awaiting her on the steps of the great hall, coming forward to greet her as Annora was assisted from her mare. Annora recognized Maud at once, so strongly did she resemble her aunt, the empress. She hastily dropped a respectful curtsy, and was then enveloped in an affectionate, perfumed embrace.

"Dearest Annora, how good of you to come!" Maud was enjoying herself enormously. Linking her arm in Annora's, she led the other young woman across the bailey, giving such a flawless performance that none would ever have doubted she'd just been reunited with a cherished childhood friend. "I see you brought no maid," she observed, adding a soft, approving "clever lass" before assuring Annora that her own maid would be pleased to be of service.

"I may have forgotten to mention in my last letter that a dear kinsman of mine might be visiting. I am sure you will remember him," she said blandly, but Annora was no longer listening. At that moment, there was no one in her field of vision—or her world—but Ranulf, just emerging from the great hall out into the daylight, blond hair gleaming in the sun, dark eyes shining with excitement, triumph, and such tenderness that Annora's own eyes misted and she moved to meet him with a light step and a secret smile.

MAKING sure they were unobserved, Ranulf and Annora ducked into the stairwell. They had discovered, by trial and error, that the one place where they could be ensured privacy during the daylight hours was in Maud's bedchamber. As soon as they were inside, Ranulf slid the door's bolt into place, an act that never failed to give him pleasure, for it was—however briefly—a means of shutting out the world.

Annora wrapped her arms around his neck, tilting her face up until her mouth was temptingly close to his own. It was not an invitation he could resist. Between kisses, they backed toward the bed, where Ranulf pulled her onto his lap. Turning her head so he could kiss her throat, she sighed. "How could a week go by so quickly, Ranulf? I said I'd be away just a fortnight, so our time together is already half over . . ."

"This time," he corrected. "There will be other visits, sweetheart. And we can write to each other, for Maud has offered to pass on your letters. That well nigh drove me mad, not being able to contact you. But with Maud on our side, it will be much easier for us from now on."

"But how long must we wait, Ranulf? I know you say we'll be together eventually. And I know, too, that you'd not lie to me. Yet I cannot help wondering if you're not lying to yourself. Maude had her chance and botched it. In this life, how many people get a second chance?"

"We already have," he reminded her, "when we found each other again at Shrewsbury's fair. And Maude will have another chance, too. I told you that Geoffrey will be crossing the Channel, bringing us enough men to keep Stephen on the defensive until he can be defeated. Once that happens, you and I can share our lives, as it was meant to be. You must believe that, Annora; you must not lose hope."

"You have enough hope for both of us," Annora gibed, but she was smiling. "Whatever do I see in you? No one else can make me as angry as you do. You are impulsive and impractical and so stubborn that—"

Ranulf stopped her words, effectively and pleasurably. When Annora got her breath back, she gave a low, shaken laugh. "You ought not to have interrupted me, for I was going to admit that I am utterly besotted with you, for better or worse."

"Are you? Prove it," Ranulf challenged, and she set about convincing him, with such success that he was soon unfastening the lacings of her gown. She was reaching up to unbraid her hair, knowing how he loved it loose and free-flowing, when they were jarred by a sudden, sharp knocking on the door. Sitting up, they hastily adjusted their clothing, waiting to see if the knocking would stop.

It did not. "Ranulf, it is me—Maud. Let me in."

As soon as Ranulf unbarred the door, Maud swept into the chamber. She never just entered a room; she made an entrance. This one was more dramatic than usual, for her face was flushed and her dark eyes were flashing. "Men," she exclaimed, "are the most vexing creatures in Christendom—never around when you want them, always underfoot when you do not. My husband, who is supposed to be at Lincoln, has ridden into the bailey."

Ranulf and Annora's instinctive alarm passed as soon as they saw that Maud was irritated, not fearful. They hurriedly smoothed the rumpled bedcovers, were making a final check for incriminating evidence when they heard Chester's voice blaring in the stairwell, loud enough to rival any hunting horn. "Maud? Where the Devil are you?"

Like his wife, Chester never simply entered a room, instead hurling himself across the threshold as if he were about to launch an assault. But he was not in a rage; quite the contrary. Taking hold of Maud's hands, he grinned down at her cheerfully. "Glad to have me home, girl?" Not waiting for her response, he kissed her exuberantly, bending her backward in a passionate embrace, one that seemed likely to lead straight to their bed—had he not caught movement from the corner of his eye and realized they were not alone.

"Who are you?" he asked, staring at Annora in surprise; he'd yet to notice Ranulf.

"This is Annora Fitz Clement, Randolph, one of my oldest friends. I am sure you must remember how often I've talked about her in the past."

"Of course I remember," Chester insisted, his eyes flickering over Annora, without any real interest. "I trust you are enjoying your visit with Maud," he added politely, if unenthusiastically, and then swung around as Ranulf stepped forward.

They knew no reason why Chester should look so startled at sight of Ranulf, for he was Maud's favorite uncle. But it was quite clear to them all that Chester did not expect to find Ranulf here. "Why are you not with Maude, now of all times?" he demanded. "It is an incredible stroke of luck, for certes, but she must act swiftly if she is to take full advantage of—Why are you looking at me so oddly? Unless . . . you do not know, do you? You've not yet heard about Stephen!"

"I heard he went north," Ranulf said warily. "What else should I know?"

Chester shook his head impatiently. "Stephen left York after Easter. He'd gotten as far as Northampton when he was stricken with a fever, the kind that burns hotter than any fire, that consumes a man like kindling." Chester saw Ranulf's shock and he smiled, grimly, wtih infinite satisfaction. "He is said to be dying."

STEPHEN had never been trapped in a nightmare like this one, for it would not end. Somehow he knew it was a dream, and he kept trying to wake up.

But it was as if he were caught in a riptide, being dragged farther and farther from shore and safety. He would not give up, though, and struggled on toward the light.

When he finally broke free, he found himself in a stranger's bed in an unfamiliar bedchamber. Even his body seemed to belong to someone else, for the coverlets were weighing him down like lead and his lungs wheezed and heaved as if he were starved for air. He wanted to say that he was thirsty; the words stuck in his throat. When he tried again, they emerged as the thinnest and weakest of whispers.

"Stephen? Thank God All-merciful! Henry . . . Henry, come quickly!" This voice was a woman's. The face bending over him was pale and tear-marked. "My love, do you know me?" Matilda pleaded, and when he mouthed her name, she fumbled in the blankets for his hand. "You've been so ill," she said, almost inaudibly. "The doctors despaired. Do you . . . remember?"

"I think so . . ." His lips were chapped and raw, blistered by fever. "You kept calling to me," he said hazily. "I followed the sound . . ."

And then his brother was there, shouldering Matilda aside in his urgency. "Stephen, listen to me. You've not been shriven, for you've been out of your senses with the fever. You must make your confession to me now, so you can go to God cleansed of your sins."

"Am I dying?"

Matilda made an involuntary movement, quickly checked. But the bishop did not flinch. "I hope not," he said, "I truly hope not. But we cannot put your immortal soul at risk, for we are all in God's Hands, and I would not be so presumptuous as to promise you what only He can decree."

"I agree." Stephen's voice was slurred and scratchy, and when Matilda put a cup to his lips, he drank gratefully, greedily. "I want to be shriven. But not by you, Henry." He looked up at his brother, the corner of his mouth curving as he added, "You already know . . . too many of my guilty secrets . . ."

The bishop was not amused. "Very well," he said stiffly, "if that is your wish. I shall fetch your confessor straightaway."

Matilda saw that half-smile of Stephen's through a blur of tears, for she was suddenly hearing her own words, so often directed at her light-hearted husband in gentle, bemused reproach, that he'd be jesting verily upon his deathbed.

"Tilda." Stephen cut his eyes toward the cup she still held, and she helped him to drink again. "Thank you," he said, and then, softly, "Do not be afraid. I am not going to die."

She swallowed. "You promise?"

"Yes," he said, and squeezed her hand before giving her another ghostly shadow of a smile. "It would give you too much pain and my enemies too much pleasure."

MAUDE'S shrinking circle of partisans had been summoned back to Devizes Castle on a wet, warm day in mid-June. As they gathered in the great hall, waiting for the council to begin, there were gaps in their ranks, missing faces. The Scots king had elected to remain on his own side of the border. Rainald was still in Cornwall, trying to save his imperiled earldom. More dubious allies like Hugh Bigod and Geoffrey de Mandeville's brother-in-law the Earl of Oxford were keeping their distance. But Miles Fitz Walter was there. So were Baldwin de Redvers and the exiled lord of Shrewsbury, William Fitz Alan. From Wallingford had come Brien Fitz Count, and from Marlborough, John Marshal, the worst of his wounds hidden behind a rakish eye patch.

As they waited for Maude and Robert to join them, they swapped stories about the dangers of the road these days. Roving bands of outlaws were springing up like dragon's teeth, for there was no more fertile soil for banditry than a realm in the throes of civil war and anarchy. They then shared the latest rumors about Stephen's health. By now they knew the worst—that those early reports of his death had been regrettably premature. While he'd been laid up at Northampton for the entire month of May, word filtering south was that he was expected to recover. They indulged in some grim, gallows humor at Stephen's expense, but their jests were labored, for Stephen's death would have won them a kingdom. Few in this war-battered and bleeding land would have had the stomach to continue the struggle on behalf of Stephen's young son Eustace.

And so they cursed Stephen's luck and sheer stamina, and cursed, too, the doctors who'd tended to him and the priests who'd prayed for him. But by common consent, they did not discuss the reason for their presence at Devizes on this Trinity Sunday—to hear Geoffrey's answer. It had taken three months for Maude's envoys to bring back her husband's response, and they did not think that boded well for their cause.

When Robert and Maude entered, with Ranulf following a step behind, their faces were somber enough to confirm the worst. Miles was the one to put it into words, saying with a soldier's bluntness, "Geoffrey balked at coming, did he not?"

To their surprise, Maude shook her head. "No, he did not refuse," she said, but then added reluctantly, ". . . outright. He says he is loath to break off his campaign in Normandy, for he has met with considerable success. He is willing, though, to consider it, if we can convince him that his presence in England could truly mark a turning point in our war to overthrow Stephen. But he says the only opinion he can trust is Robert's, and so he insists that Robert come back to Normandy to discuss it in person."

"A long and dangerous trip," Robert said morosely, "and most likely a futile one. Geoffrey does not want my counsel, he wants my help in his war. Too many Normans view Angevins as spawns of the Devil. With me riding at his side, some of them might be more willing to accept his lordship. I do not doubt that he'll be lavish with his promises, but I do doubt that we'll ever see him set foot on English soil."

It was unlike Robert to be so imprudent; speaking out so harshly in public about a man they needed to win over was impolitic at best. There could be no more convincing proof of Robert's discontent than this uncharacteristic outburst, and the men exchanged disappointed glances, seeing yet another opportunity slipping away from them.

Once again it was Miles who gave voice to their misgivings. "I daresay you are right, Robert, to suspect the man's good faith. But a reed-thin chance is still better than none, and if you do not even try to persuade him, we'll never know if you might have prevailed or not. I urge you to think again ere you refuse."

"There is no need for that," Maude said, sounding very tired. "Robert has agreed to go."

"Yes," Robert said tersely, making no effort to hide his frustration. "Geoffrey has left me no choice. So . . . I will sail for Normandy and I will do my utmost to gain his support. But I expect—nay, demand—something from all of you in return. Whilst I am gone, I want your sworn oaths that you will see to the safety of my sister, let her come to no harm."

They responded without hesitation, promising to protect Maude in Robert's absence. Maude said nothing, but hot blood scalded her face and throat. Ranulf noticed, understood, and sympathized, for he knew how she hated any reminder of her special vulnerability as a woman. He was impressed now by her restraint, for it was not so long ago that she would have rebuked Robert sharply for shaming her by his unwanted solicitude, however well meant. But she was not the same woman who'd blundered so badly that she'd gotten herself chased out of her own capital city. She had learned from her mistakes. It seemed bitterly unfair to Ranulf that she had learned too late. They could not give up, though. It might be too late for Maude, but not for her young son. They must do whatever it would take to claim the English crown for Henry—even if that meant doing the bidding of Maude's hated Angevin husband.

MATILDA was very glad to be back in London; more and more, it seemed a haven from the troubles besetting the rest of her husband's realm. On this morning in early July, she was performing one of her more pleasurable duties as queen: bestowing largesse upon the neediest of her subjects. Her servants loaded a cart with jars of honey, sacks of flour, baskets of eggs, loaves of bread, woolen blankets, even a few toys—whipping tops and balls. Matilda then mounted her favorite white mule, and she and Cecily and her escort set out to deliver her bounty to London's two hospitals.

St Giles in the Fields was a leper hospital just outside the city walls, founded by a queen, Maude's mother. Matilda felt great pity for those poor souls afflicted with such a fearful malady, although she found it exceedingly difficult to look upon their dreadful deformities. But she forced herself to smile and show none of her revulsion when they came forward to thank her, and afterward she confided to Cecily her awed admiration for Maude's mother, who had kissed lepers and washed their ulcerated sores with her own hands to demonstrate they were still beloved by God.

Cecily agreed that such a woman well deserved to be known as Good Queen Maude, although she could not help adding mischievously that it explained much about the Empress Maude, child of such a disparate mating—a notorious lecher and an earthly saint. Matilda laughed, commenting that Stephen's parents were surely an oddly matched pair, too, but then her smile faded, for she found herself thinking of yet another incompatible couple—her brash young son Eustace and Constance, his timid French bride.

From St Giles, Matilda continued on to the hospital of St Bartholomew, situated next to the Augustinian priory of the same name in West Smithfield. St Bartholomew took in the needy and orphans as well as the sick, and it was for the orphans that Matilda had brought tops and balls. Her own children had puppets and wooden swords and dolls and whistles. But toys were a luxury, and she knew the skinny, solemn youngsters at St Bart's were unlikely to have had any but makeshift playthings—scraps of rope and stones and hollow reeds. She was warmly welcomed by the hospital's master and nuns, but the memory she took away with her was of the shrieks and laughter of boys playing with their first real ball, a pig's bladder filled with dried beans.

They reentered the city through Cripplegate, headed back toward the Tower. Matilda's progress was a slow one, for people flocked to her as she passed by, seeking to find out if the king was fully recovered from his near-fatal fever. If the questions directed at her were occasionally intrusive or overly familiar, Matilda did not object; had the Londoners not been so forthright and cocky, they never would have dared to defy Maude. And so she waved and smiled and assured them that the king was on the mend, of good cheer, and eager to take up the reins of kingship again.

Just how eager Stephen was, she was soon to discover. Upon her arrival at the Tower, she hastened up to the royal apartments on the top floor of the soaring, whitewashed keep. There she found her husband sitting around a table with his brother and William de Ypres and William Martel, his steward. They had a large map spread out before them, but that was not what caught Matilda's attention; it was the charged atmosphere, one of barely suppressed excitement. "You look," she said, "like foxes who've just found a way into the hen roost. What has happened that I do not yet know about?"

There was a time when she would never have spoken up so boldly, but now she did not even hesitate, taking it for granted that she had earned the right to share in their decision making. And of the men, only the bishop thought her candid curiosity was unseemly, but even he held his tongue, tacitly acknowledging that Matilda would not be retreating back into the shadows. For better or worse, he conceded, hers had become a voice to be heeded.

"We have gotten some very interesting news, Tilda." Stephen leaned back in his chair, smiling at her. "Maude's brother has gone to Normandy to meet with Geoffrey. Robert sailed for Barfleur a week ago."

"Leaving the hen roost unguarded," William de Ypres said happily. "I never thought I'd owe Geoffrey of Anjou such a debt of gratitude!"

Matilda's first reaction was unease. Stephen might be ready for the rigors and risks of an active campaign, but she was not; her memories of his Northampton illness were still too raw. But she did not confess her qualms, for fear was a wife's burden, to be borne alone. "What are you planning?" she asked, and Stephen beckoned her toward the map.

"Robert sailed from there—from Wareham—putting his firstborn in command. But the son is not the man his father is, and he promptly went back to the greater comforts of Bristol, leaving the castle poorly garrisoned. If we capture it, we can deny Robert a safe port for his return."

"Where is Maude now . . . still at Devizes?"

"No, she is back at Oxford Castle, with Miles Fitz Walter, Baldwin de Redvers, and Ranulf, amongst others, keeping a close watch upon her. Robert seems to have been so worried about her safety that I'd almost think he had second sight!"

Matilda did not share Stephen's smile. "That does not sound like an unguarded hen roost to me."

"No . . . not yet. Maude is well served at the moment. That is why I do not plan to besiege Oxford after we capture Wareham. No, there is our next target," he said, "Cirencester. For however devoted Maude's men are to her, they're not likely to stay cooped up at Oxford if their own lands in the west are threatened. My raid on Cirencester will draw them away from Oxford, and then," Stephen said, with a grim resolve he'd not often shown, "we take Maude captive and end this accursed war once and for all."

25

OXFORD, ENGLAND

September 1142

OXFORD, like Winchester, had two royal residences, the eleventh-century castle by the river and the "king's house" just north of the city walls. The latter was the more comfortable of the two, but Maude always chose to stay at the castle, for its castellan, Robert d'Oilly, was a loyal supporter and kin by marriage, his stepson being one of Maude's numerous half-brothers.

Even by English standards, it had been an unusually wet summer and autumn. But this 26th day of September dawned dry and clear and mild. Ranulf was standing on the steps of the great hall, savoring the sun as men passed in and out of the bailey. More riders were coming in, a dozen or more—not an uncommon sight these days, for only foolhardy or desperate travelers braved the roads alone. As they dismounted, Ranulf started forward, catching a glimpse of a familiar figure.

At sound of his name, Bennet de Malpas turned around, his dark face lighting up with a grin of ready recognition. Ranulf was not surprised that Bennet should be so well mounted and armed, for he was one of the Earl of Chester's household knights, the man entrusted by Chester with that urgent appeal for Maude's help. He and Ranulf had struck up a casual friendship on their wretched winter march to Lincoln, and renewed acquaintance this past April at Chester Castle. He seemed genuinely pleased to see Ranulf now, although he was deliberately vague about his current task, saying only that he'd been to Coventry at the earl's behest.

Ranulf would have loved to learn more about Bennet's mysterious mission for the earl, for he was morbidly curious about Chester's doings; he'd never been able to resist turning over rocks, even if he knew he'd not like what lurked beneath them. But Bennet would not be revealing any of the earl's secrets. Although Chester might not practice what he preached, he demanded complete discretion and utter loyalty from those who served him. Ranulf could only hope that Chester was not casting his nets wide enough to entangle Maude, and he said cautiously, "What brings you to Oxford, Bennet?"

"I am performing a double duty, first off to Coventry for the earl and then on to Oxford for his countess. Lady Maud entrusted me with a letter for the empress. I also have one for you," he said, turning aside to root in his saddle bag.

Ranulf took his letter with a nonchalance he was far from feeling, for he was sure Maud had included a letter from Annora along with her own. After an unobtrusive check to assure himself that Maud's wax seal had not been tampered with, he tucked the letter inside his tunic, and summoned up a distracted smile. "I missed that. You were saying . . . what?"

"Is it true that the Earls of Hereford and Devon are no longer with the empress?"

Ranulf's mouth tightened. Chester must have more spies than a dog had fleas. The mere mention of the earls' defection was enough to stir up his anger again, for Miles and Baldwin had promised Robert that they would put Maude's safety before all other considerations. But he was not about to unburden himself to a man who'd carry his complaints straight back to the Earl of Chester. "They were naturally disquieted when word reached us of Stephen's raid upon Cirencester," he said, striving to sound offhand, untroubled. "But they will be returning to Oxford once they are sure that their own lands are not in peril."

"I am glad to hear that, and so will my lady. She was concerned lest her aunt be put at risk by their departure. Now . . . I'd best seek out the castellan. As I mean to ask his hospitality for my men and myself, I ought not to be tardy in paying my respects."

"I am afraid you are too late, Bennet. Sir Robert was taken ill last month, and he was not as lucky as Stephen. He died a fortnight ago."

Bennet had watched too many men die for death to take him by surprise. Nor did he see any point in mourning a man he'd never met. "I am sorry," he murmured, with perfunctory politeness. "Mayhap I ought to look for lodgings in the town, then . . . ?"

"Indeed not. There is more than enough room. Come on, I'll take you to my brother." The word *brother* never failed to echo oddly in Ranulf's ears whenever he applied it to Rob d'Oilly, for it seemed such an intimate way to refer to a stranger. They were not actual strangers, of course, more like acquaintances who happened to share the same blood. Ranulf sometimes wondered how many other half-brothers of his might be scattered throughout England and Normandy, sons not even his father had known he'd sired. Any man who could claim more than twenty bastards was bound to have missed a few.

Leading Bennet into the hall, Ranulf watched the other man from the corner of his eye, anticipating Bennet's surprise when he first saw Rob d'Oilly. In truth, Rob's appearance could still unsettle him, too, so uncanny was his resemblance to their father: the same stocky build, the same ink-black hair and deep-set eyes. Rob did not have the old king's commanding presence, though. He was—Ranulf had discovered—just what he seemed to be, an affable, well-meaning man of wealth and privilege and modest ambitions, of whom the worst that could be said was that he was obstinate at times and too impulsive; his vices, like his virtues, were inhibited by his lack of imagination.

Bennet did a comical double-take upon being introduced to Rob, for no one who'd ever met the old king would have forgotten him. Recovering his aplomb, he was expressing his condolences for the loss of Rob's stepfather when he was interrupted by a sudden shout, loud enough and urgent enough to turn all heads toward the sound. When it came again, Ranulf and Rob both moved swiftly across the hall, with a curious Bennet on their heels.

A rider had just reined in his mount in the crowded bailey. As the man flung himself from the saddle and ran toward them, Ranulf watched with foreboding, for Hugh de Plucknet was well known to him, a quick-tempered but intensely loyal Breton, one of Maude's most trusted household knights. Hugh had departed at first light for Wallingford Castle, bearing Maude's letter to Brien Fitz Count. So why was he back so soon? What had caused him to abandon his mission for Maude and return to Oxford in such haste? Ranulf was already sure he was not going to like Hugh's answer.

"The king is leading an army up the Abingdon Road, heading straight for Oxford!"

Rob gasped, then began to assail Hugh with questions. Was he sure it was Stephen? Where had he seen them? Could he have been mistaken? How many were there?

Ranulf paid no heed, for he knew the interrogation was a waste of time; Hugh was not a man to conjure up phantom foes. But what now? Would Maude be better off slipping out of the city whilst there was still time? But where could she go? Wallingford lay to the south. If she tried to reach Brien's castle, she'd be riding right into Stephen's army. No, she'd be safer staying in Oxford. The town was well protected by two rivers, the Cherwell on the east, and on the south and west, the great river known as Isis in Oxford, as the Thames elsewhere. The city's walls were of stone, its defenses augmented by a deep outer ditch. And the castle itself presented a formidable challenge. He'd almost convinced himself that they could easily withstand a siege when Bennet pulled him aside, thrust the Countess of Chester's letter into his hand, and asked him to see that the empress got it.

Ranulf stared at him in amazement, unwilling to believe that Bennet truly intended to ride off, indifferent to Maude's danger. But Bennet was beckoning to his waiting men, telling them to mount up. "What are you doing? Jesú, Bennet, we will need every man we can get to stave off Stephen's attack!"

Bennet shrugged. "I wish the empress well. But I am not about to risk my life for her. Ranulf, this is not my fight."

And with that, he signaled again to his men, put spurs to his stallion, and cantered across the bailey toward the drawbridge, leaving Ranulf with an unenviable task—telling Maude that Stephen would soon be at the city gates.

MAUDE was keeping vigil upon the roofed ramparts of the castle keep. South of the city, where the River Cherwell flowed into the Thames, the late Robert d'Oilly's uncle had built a raised clay causeway, known to locals as Grandpont. Ranulf and Rob had aligned their men to block this causeway, for the rivers themselves were impassable. Swollen with the run-off from the heavy rains, they'd spilled over their banks, flooding the adjacent meadows. The September sunlight was dazzling, but still not able to lighten the swirling depths of the water, a dark grey-green like the moss on cemetery tombstones.

There were sporadic flashes of brightness as the sun reflected off the swords and chain-link hauberks of the soldiers. Arrows were being intermittently launched across the river, to the accompaniment of taunts and jeers. Some of the citizens had come out to join in this dangerous sport, daring the enemy to attack. Their more prudent brethren were patrolling the city walls, making ready to repel the invaders should they somehow manage to surmount the fast-flowing barrier of the Thames. There were some who'd escaped, like Bennet de Malpas and his men, out of the city's North Gate. But most were not willing to abandon their homes, to abandon hope. Facing down a king's wrath and a large hostile army, Oxford remained defiant.

Maude was attended by several of her household knights, by Adam of Ely, her clerk, and William Marshal, a blunt-spoken priest who shared some of the steely qualities of his better-known brother, John. Maude had been impressed enough with Will's abilities to have named him as her chancellor, but at this particularly precarious moment, he was the wrong brother. It was John Marshal whom she needed, arrogant and pitiless and scarred and miles away, like all the others who had taken Stephen's bait.

Just before noon, Ranulf returned to the castle. While the kitchen cooks hastily prepared a meal that he could eat quickly, he joined Maude up on the keep battlements. Rob was sure, he reported, that Stephen's men would not be able to cross the Grandpont. Their bowmen were likely to prove almost as formidable as the river. The city gates were under guard and the townspeople seemed determined to resist, not cowed or disheartened.

"You sound confident," Maude said when he was done speaking, "but your words are at variance with what I see in your face. Do not keep your qualms from me, Ranulf. We owe each other better than that."

He gave her a quick, tense smile, one that acknowledged the validity of her complaint. And then he told her the truth, why he'd really come back to the castle—not for roast chicken and ale, but for the superior view from the keep roof.

"I do not understand. What are you looking to find?"

"A missing king. Stephen has been able to bring together a redoubtable force. Most of his barons and vassals seem to have answered his summons. I saw William de Warenne and Geoffrey de Mandeville and the Earls of Northampton and Pembroke, amongst others. Even his brother the bishop is across the river, doing God's Work with a mace these days. But I looked in vain for Stephen, and that troubles me more than I can say. Just where is he, Maude?"

DOWNRIVER from the Grandpont, Stephen stared across at the surging, wind-churned current. After several moments, he stooped and pitched a stone out into the water, watching as it splashed and sank. "This is the secret ford?" he asked skeptically. "It looks to me like a crossing fit only for fish."

The man at his side nodded vigorously, stubbornly. "The river can be forded here, my liege," he insisted. "I swear it upon the tears of the Blessed Mother Mary. It is just deeper than usual because of the rains."

Stephen looked at the man's earnest face, then back at the river. "This is probably not one of my more rational decisions," he said at last, "but I say we risk it."

William de Ypres shrugged. "Why not? It is as good a day to drown as any, I suppose."

"If Robert Fitz Roy could cross the Fossedyke at flood tide in the dead of winter, then we ought to be able to survive a September dunking in the Thames. Besides," Stephen smiled suddenly, "if the Almighty meant for me to drown, he'd have let me sail on the White Ship."

"Even God can change His Mind," Ypres pointed out, but he was already gesturing to one of their scouts. "Tell my lord Earl of Northampton and the others that we are going to cross at the ford. Have them stand ready to move onto the Grandpont."

Mounting his stallion, Stephen glanced at his waiting men, handpicked by Ypres and eager to reap the bounty that victory would bring. "Now," he said, and plunged into the river. Their guide had not lied. There was indeed a ford there, but it was not for the faint of heart; the current was strong and the water level dangerously deep for such a crossing. Splashing toward the shore, swimming at times, Stephen's stallion scrambled up onto the bank, and the others soon followed. Only one man had been swept from his saddle, and he'd managed to grasp his horse's tail, holding fast until he could regain his footing in the shallows. Stephen looked them over, his eyes moving from face to face, shadowed by their conical helmets. Satisfied by what he found, he unsheathed his sword. "A gold ring," he promised, "to the first man into the city!"

They were soon spotted by sentries up on the city walls, who hurried to sound the alarm. But by then it was too late. Rob d'Oilly's men were not expecting a flank attack on their own side of the river. They recoiled in confusion, and as Rob and his captains frantically tried to regroup, the main body of Stephen's army came charging across the causeway and into the fray. Assailed from two sides, the defenders broke rank and sought to retreat back into the town. But when the guards up on the walls opened the South Gate to admit them, Stephen's soldiers surged in, too, and the battle for Oxford was suddenly being fought in the streets of the city.

FROM the keep battlements, Ranulf and Hugh de Plucknet and the others had watched helplessly as Stephen and Ypres bore down upon Oxford's defenders. Racing to aid their beleaguered comrades, they were halfway down Pennyfarthing Street when the first fugitives from the battle fled into the town. Warned by the noise ahead, Ranulf slowed his stallion. The men with him reined in their mounts, too, just as the wind brought to them one of the most dreaded of all cries: "Fire!" As soon as they saw the smoke swirling up from the direction of Southgate Street, Ranulf and Hugh looked at each other in appalled understanding. "Christ, they are in the city!"

Swinging their mounts about, they galloped back to the castle. There was no need for words; they all knew what must be done if they hoped to survive Stephen's assault. Fortunately, Maude had anticipated disaster, and servants were already heating water in huge cauldrons. Once it reached the boiling point, they carried it up onto the wall-walk on either side of the gatehouse, knowing they'd have no margin for error and but one chance.

Oxford was in chaos. The citizens had no training in the skills of war, and many of them panicked now, fleeing from Stephen's pursuing soldiers instead of defending themselves. Stephen's men were throwing torches into shops and onto roofs, and people were soon stumbling out of their barred and shuttered houses, coughing and choking. Some tried to take refuge in St Frideswide's Priory, clambering over the monastery walls when the monks refused to open their gate. Knights on war-horses rampaged through the streets, and a few unlucky souls were trampled when they fell under the plunging hooves.

There was some resistance offered, and the fighting was bloodiest in Great Bailey Street, where Rob d'Oilly and his knights were attempting an ordered retreat back to the castle. Once they were within sight of its walls, the drawbridge was lowered and they sprinted desperately for safety. When the enemy followed, seeking to rush the castle gates as they had the town's gate, the men up on the walls poured scalding water down into their midst. There were terrible screams, most scattered, and several rolled on the ground in agony. Before the attackers could try again, the castle defenders raised the drawbridge.

Rarely had a city been captured with such ease. Stephen could afford to be magnanimous, and sent some of his men to help put out the fires they had set, thus sparing Oxford the massive fiery destruction that had devastated Winchester. But when a town was taken by storm, it was turned over to the victorious army for their sport. Knowing what to expect, some of Oxford's women had fled, hiding themselves in the woods or seeking refuge in the nearby nunnery at Godstow and the priory at Osney. Oxford's shops were located mainly in Northgate Street and High Street, and these neighborhoods were pillaged first. Private homes could be plundered, too, and often were, for crimes were not crimes if committed in war. The townsmen concealed their valuables as best they could, feared for their wives and daughters, and prayed for Oxford.

Not all the citizens were so distraught, of course. Some were relieved, for the suffering of those trapped in a besieged city could be terrible. Now at least they need not fear starvation. And the alehouses and brothels in Gropecunt Lane would thrive under the occupation.

They were in the minority, though, and most of Oxford passed a nervous, wakeful night, the quiet broken by the brawling of celebrating soldiers, by laughter and cheerful cursing and, occasionally, a woman's screams. In the morning, the city reeve, the prior of St Frideswide's, and several members of the merchant's guild made their way to the king's encampment and pleaded for an audience with Stephen. When they finally returned, they brought comforting news for their anxiously waiting colleagues. The king had assured them that he held no ill will for the citizens of Oxford, and as long as they cooperated fully with his army, they'd not be harmed. All he wanted was the castle and the woman trapped within.

MAUDE stood at the open window in the upper chamber of the castle keep, looking out at her cousin's army. It was three years, almost to the day, since she'd gazed out upon a similar scene at Arundel Castle. But there were deadly differences between that siege and this one. Robert would have been able, then, to come to her rescue. Now he was in Normandy and unaware of her peril. Nor was Stephen going to set her free, send her safely on her way in another act of mad gallantry. Oxford was not Arundel. This time there would be no reprieve.

26

CÉRENCES, NORMANDY

November 1142

WINTER came early that year to Normandy. Upon his arrival at Cérences, the latest Norman stronghold to yield to his father, Henry was delighted to find a dusting of snow upon the ground. He'd spent several hours collecting enough to build a snow fort and two days later, it remained intact out in the bailey, not yet melted. Although a blazing fire burned in the open hearth, the great hall still held a chill. Henry had a wax tablet propped up on his knees, and a bone stylus clutched in his fingers. He was supposed to be practicing his declensions of Latin nouns and adjectives, for he'd promised that his brief visits to his father's sieges would not disrupt his studies, but he'd gotten no further than amicus magnus and amici magni.

He knew what came next—amico magno—but instead he scratched Bastebourg into the wax, followed by Trevieres, Villiers-Bocage, Briquessard, Aunay-sur-Odon, Plessis-Grimoult, Vire, Tinchebray, Teilleul, St Hilaire, Mortain, and Pontorson. He had just space enough to add Cérences. He'd not made a conscious effort to memorize his father's conquests, but he'd followed the campaign so closely that he now knew the names of the captured castles as well as he did the names of the servants who tended to him back in Angers.

They were getting easier, these victories. Cérences had surrendered at once. Glancing across the hall, Henry studied his father and uncle as he should have been studying his Latin. He knew about their quarreling; all of Normandy knew. One more castle. It was always one more castle. They would triumph and then they would argue and his father would make Robert more promises, promises few thought he had any intention of keeping. Henry did not understand the rules about lying. His tutor said that lying was a grievous sin. But his father often joked that life without sinning was like food without salt, pure but tasteless. As far as Henry could figure, some lies were harmless, some were necessary, and some were unforgivable. But what if people could not agree which was which?

Men kept coming into the hall, seeking shelter from the frigid November wind. Some of them Henry knew from past visits to siege sites. Fulk and Hugh de Cleers were rarely far from his father's side. But his uncle Hélie was usually as far away from Geoffrey as he could get; men jested grimly that they could teach Cain and Abel about brotherly rivalry.

Tonight Hélie was dicing with Henry's cousin Philip. Philip's family ties were tattered, too, these days; Henry hoped his father would never look at him the way he'd caught Robert looking at Philip, with disappointment too deep for words. Henry did not like Philip; he was moody and sarcastic and insisted upon calling Henry "Nine and Eight" after hearing Henry explain that he was nine years and eight months old. Henry didn't mind being teased—his father teased him all the time—but he did mind being mocked; to his thinking, those eight months mattered.

He did like the man watching the dice game, one of his uncle's knights. He'd been put off at first by Gilbert Fitz John's odd appearance, for he had but one eyebrow and no eyelashes. But Gilbert never failed to smile at sight of Henry, he'd patiently answered Henry's questions about the fire at Wherwell nunnery, and Henry no longer even noticed his scars.

Geoffrey was usually the focal point of all eyes; that was a role he relished. Tonight he was sharing center stage with a new arrival, a man unfamiliar to Henry, a tall, fair-haired lord with a loud laugh and a tendency to run roughshod over any conversation but his own. Men seemed willing to listen to Waleran Beaumont, though, for he'd just come from Paris and was well informed about the great scandal sweeping the French court.

Henry already knew about the scandal, for they'd been gossiping about little else back in Anjou. The Queen of France's younger sister, Petronilla, had fallen in love with the Count of Vermandois. Count Raoul de Péronne was the French king's cousin and his seneschal. He was fifty to her nineteen, an age that seemed vast indeed to Henry, but it was not the age difference that troubled people; it was not so uncommon for men to take much younger wives. The problem was that Raoul already had a wife. Petronilla would have him, though, wife or no, and she'd gotten her sister the queen on her side. Eleanor in turn had won over her husband,

and to please her, King Louis set about finding a way to get rid of Raoul's unwanted wife. The Bishop of Noyon, who happened to be Raoul's brother, declared himself willing to dissolve the marriage on the grounds of consanguinity, and Louis found two other compliant bishops to go along with him. The marriage was invalidated, the countess and her children packed off to her uncle, and Petronilla and Raoul married before the ink was dry upon his annulment decree.

Unfortunately for the newly wedded pair, Raoul's repudiated wife was not without allies of her own. Her uncle was none other than Count Theobald of Blois and Champagne, Stephen's brother and long a thorn in the French king's side. Theobald had promptly appealed to the Pope, and the verdict was now in. According to Waleran Beaumont, the papal legate had reaffirmed the validity of Raoul's marriage, excommunicated the guilty lovers until Raoul agreed to take back his lawful wife, and suspended the three bishops who'd been so overly eager to please their king.

The news created a sensation, for it was sure to have dramatic repercussions. Yet none doubted the accuracy of Waleran's account, for he was kin to the love-stricken count; Raoul de Péronne was his uncle. And when he added that the French king was so enraged by Theobald's meddling that he was swearing upon Christ's Cross to take a bloody vengeance upon the count's lands in Champagne and Blois, none doubted that, either, for it would not be the first time Louis had gone to war on his wife's behalf. Just a year ago, Louis had led an assault upon Toulouse, which Eleanor claimed through her grandmother. The claim was questionable, and the campaign so ill planned and poorly executed that it soon resulted in Louis's ignominious retreat back to Paris, nursing a nasty wound to his pride.

It was clear to Henry that these men held the French king in no high esteem, and he tucked his newfound fact away for future reference: that a man ought not to love his wife overly well, for if he did, other men would laugh at him. The rules about men and women were just as confusing as the code about lying. Wives were supposed to obey their husbands, but not all of them did. Not his mother, for certes! But the French queen not only did as she pleased, she got her husband to do what she wanted, too. That was a trick his mother had never learned; Papa begrudged her so much as a smile. Henry wondered why the French king was so eager to do his wife's bidding, and he found himself suddenly curious about Eleanor, this woman who seemed to play by her own rules and get away with it. Once he was old enough, that was what he meant to do, too.

The men were still joking about the scandal, but the festive mood ended abruptly when Waleran asked Geoffrey which castle would be assailed next. "Avranches," Geoffrey said promptly. He did not look at Robert as he spoke, though, and Henry tensed, for he was learning to read storm signals in faces as well as cloud formations. Papa and Uncle Robert were on another one of their collision courses. He kept hoping that eventually Uncle Robert would wear Papa's resistance down; either that or they'd run out of castles to besiege. But each time they clashed, he feared that their quarreling would flame out of control, end with his uncle's giving up in disgust. And that must not happen. Papa had to agree. For Mama to ask for his help, her need must be dire.

He was watching them uneasily for signs that trouble was brewing when servants ushered a stranger into the hall. Henry had never seen anyone look so bedraggled; his face was reddened and chapped by the cold, his clothing torn and filthy. But he was no beggar, for as his mantle parted, Henry glimpsed a sword riding low on his hip. He sat up hastily, understanding the significance of what he'd just seen. This pitiful wretch was a courier, one bearing a message worth risking his life, health, and horse for.

Geoffrey had already pushed his chair back, getting to his feet. But the man never even glanced his way. Stumbling forward, he sank to his knees before Maude's brother. Robert's first, fervent hope was that this messenger was from Maude, for he was becoming more and more worried by the silence echoing across the Channel. The seal on the letter, though, was not hers.

"You come from Brien Fitz Count?" he said, and the man nodded numbly.

"I swore to him that I'd get to you as quick as I could, but my ship was caught in a gale and blown off course. We finally came ashore in Flanders. And then I did not know where you were campaigning—" He stopped, realizing he was rambling, putting off the moment of revelation. "The empress is in grave peril, my lord. Three days before Michaelmas, Stephen swooped down on Oxford, forced his way into the city, and lay siege to the castle."

Robert stared at him, appalled, then tore the letter open and read rapidly. When he looked up, his face was flushed with outrage. "They left her? Miles and Baldwin de Redvers and the others . . . those fools just rode off and left her to fend for herself?"

The messenger nodded again, bleakly. "Stephen lured them off by raiding Cirencester, all but Ranulf Fitz Roy and my lord Brien at Wallingford. But he lacks the men to break the siege."

Robert already knew that; Brien's letter had been brutally honest about the gravity of the danger Maude was facing. "Michaelmas," he said, and then, "Jesus God!" for that meant Maude had been under siege for six weeks. The castle could fall to Stephen any day now—if it had not already fallen. Swinging around, he pointed an accusing finger at Maude's husband. "This is your fault, too! If not for your damnable delays and excuses, I'd have been back in England in time to keep this from happening!"

"And just what do you think we've been doing here—playing chess with real castles? We have been waging a campaign to conquer Normandy for my son, and I'd say that matters as much as your endless and futile skirmishings in England!"

Robert made an enormous effort to master himself, clenching his teeth until his jaw muscles ached. "How much time will you need to make ready?"

"More time than you can afford to spare. I am not about to break off this campaign and go chasing off to England on a misguided mercy mission. There are too many malcontents eager to take advantage of my absence," Geoffrey said with a pointed glance in his brother Hélie's direction. "You'd best sail on your own, Robert, and I'll join you when and if I am able."

"If you are able?" Robert echoed scathingly, no longer bothering to mask his contempt. "Your wife is facing a lifetime's confinement and you cannot even bestir yourself to ride a mile on her behalf? Just out of curiosity, is there anyone in Christendom whom you'd risk your selfish skin for—anyone at all?"

"Not for that bitch at Oxford," Geoffrey snapped. "And spare me your self-righteous wrath. The last I heard, men pray to God for expiation of their sins, not to the Earl of Gloucester. If I must choose between Maude and my son, that is as easy a choice as any man ever made. Normandy is Henry's legacy, and I am going to see that he gets it, which is more than I can say for Maude and her pitiful efforts to claim the English throne. You dropped the crown at her feet after Lincoln, and she had only to pick it up. But she threw it away, and I might forgive her for that—if it were not Henry's crown, too. So whatever trouble she is in, she brought it upon herself, and not even you can deny it, not if you're half as honest as you claim to be."

"I'll not deny that Maude made some serious mistakes. But she shows more honour and courage in a single day than you can hope to find in a lifetime!"

"You've overstayed your welcome, Brother-in-law," Geoffrey said, and there was a quiet menace in his voice that was more daunting than threats or bluster. Robert did not look in the least daunted, though, and the men began to crowd in closer, some to intervene if need be, others to get a better view. But they soon moved aside, for Henry had shoved his way into their midst, using his elbows like weapons, kicking his uncle in the shins when Hélie did not let him through. Hélie let out a startled oath and grabbed for the boy, but Henry ducked under his outstretched arm and flung himself forward. Fists clenched at his sides, chin up, and head high, he stepped between his father and uncle, his defiant stance all the more poignant for the glimmer of blinked-back tears.

"You need not go, Papa," he said tautly. "Let Uncle Robert take me."

There were murmurings at that, pity and surprise and a few suppressed smiles. Hélie, his ankle still smarting from Henry's blow, laughed outright. "I can just see you, sprout," he gibed, "toting a sword taller than you are!" and Geoffrey turned upon him in a fury.

"You are the last one in Christendom qualified to give my son lessons in manhood!" he snarled, and Hélie gave an indignant gasp. But before he could retaliate, Henry urged again:

"Let me go, Papa." It was not a demand, but neither was it an entreaty, and Geoffrey reached out, putting his arm around the boy's rigid shoulders.

"Come over here, lad, where we can talk. The rest of you men find some other way to entertain yourselves," he said sharply. Steering a resistant Henry toward the comparative privacy of a window seat, Geoffrey was uncertain what to say next; it wasn't often he found himself so thoroughly discomfited. "You were not meant to hear what you did. We did not realize you were in the hall. I know you are confused, lad, but you're too young to understand what can go wrong between a man and his wife—"

Henry pulled away, so abruptly that he stumbled. He wanted to run, but he stood his ground, for there was no escaping what he'd overheard. His mother was in danger and his father did not care.

Father and son were so intent upon each other that they'd not even realized Robert had joined them, not until he said quietly, "This is not about your wife, Geoffrey. It is about his mother."

Geoffrey started to speak, stopped himself, and Henry seized his chance. "When you told me what happened at Winchester, Papa, you said Mama had lost her chance to be queen. You said that from now on, she was fighting for me. I ought to be there, then. I ought to be in England so men can see me. With Mama trapped, they need a reason to keep fighting. I can help Uncle Robert rescue her, I know I can."

Geoffrey was silent for several moments, regarding the boy in thoughtful reappraisal. "I am not saying you are wrong, Henry. But I am saying it would be too dangerous."

"Do you think Stephen would hurt me?" Henry challenged, and Geoffrey cursed himself for all the times he'd mocked Stephen's soft heart in his son's hearing.

"There are other dangers, Henry," Robert pointed out. "Just getting to England would be hazardous, for November is a bad month to cross the Channel."

Henry looked from his father to his uncle, back at his father again. "Yesterday I heard some of the castle servants talking about a funeral for one of the stable lads. He went skating last week on the pond in the village, but the ice was not thick enough and he drowned. I like to skate on the ice, too, Papa, have my own pair of bone skates. I could drown crossing the Channel as Uncle Robert fears . . . or I could drown back in Angers, if I was unlucky like that stable lad."

Geoffrey's mouth twitched. "God help me," he said, "I've sired a lawyer! Henry . . . you go back to the hearth and get warm whilst your uncle and I talk about this."

Seeing that further argument was futile, Henry reluctantly retreated, casting them several anxious looks over his shoulder. The two men watched him go, enemies suddenly allied in their concern for one small, stubborn boy. "If you'd not been so quick to start your sermon," Geoffrey said, "I'd have told you that I'm willing to spare some men for Maude's rescue. I can probably part with two hundred or so, more if you can wait."

"I cannot," Robert said tersely. "Every day brings Maude closer to capture. But what of the lad? You are going to let him go with me?"

"Am I that obvious? Yes . . . I am."

"Are you sure?"

"Of course not," Geoffrey said, an edge creeping back into his voice. "Maude and I may not have agreed on much, but we do on this—that we cannot coddle the lad. So . . . I am trusting my son to you, Robert, and to Stephen." Another smile tugged at the corner of his mouth. "God pity him if Henry did fall into his hands, for that lad of mine would talk him into abdicating by sundown!"

"I'll keep him safe," Robert said. "I can promise you that."

"No," Geoffrey said, "you can only promise that you will try. Look at him over there, watching us like a hungry hawk, whilst pretending to play with those dogs of his. He is still so young . . . Come on, let's tell him ere I change my mind."

Henry had knelt to pet his dyrehunds. But he straightened up abruptly as they started toward him. "Well," Geoffrey said, "I'd not advise a man to buy a horse sight unseen, so I suppose the same holds true for kingdoms. You'd best check out the wretched English weather for yourself, lad, make sure it is a realm you want to rule."

Henry swallowed, his pulse quickening with an emotion that was not excitement and not fear, yet oddly akin to both. "I can go? Truly?" And when his father nodded, he swallowed again before saying, "Uncle Robert . . . we will be in time?"

"I do not know, lad," Robert admitted. "I hope so."

That was not the answer Henry had been expecting. He'd wanted reassurance, had gotten, instead, an uncompromising adult reply, honest and unnerving. He could not have articulated the awareness that came upon him now, but he sensed, however instinctively, that when he sailed for England, he'd be leaving the greater part of his childhood behind.

"I hope so, too," he said, striving to match his uncle's matter-of-fact tones. A moment later, though, he blurted out, "I want to take my dogs with me," no longer sounding like a young king in the making, just a nine-year-old boy afraid for his mother.

THE wind was banging against the barricaded windows of the keep, the wooden shutters creaking and groaning under the onslaught. It sounded to Henry as if the storm were besieging Corfe, and having better luck than Uncle Robert was at Wareham. The chamber was dimly lit and cold; on awakening that morning, he'd found his washing laver iced over. In the three weeks that he'd been at Corfe, he'd come to hate it, trapped inside much of the time by the wretched weather. People were convinced this was going to be the worst winter in years, for there had already been three heavy snowfalls and it was only the second week in December. Not that Corfe had gotten much of the snow; it was too close to the sea. A few miles inland, the roads were drifted over, but at Corfe and Wareham, they'd been buffeted by wind-lashed sleet and freezing rain.

"Wolf! Lass!" That was all the encouragement his dogs needed. Piling onto the bed, they crowded Henry toward the edge, but he didn't mind. The last time he'd opened the shutter, he'd looked out upon a sky clogged with leaden clouds, dusk at midday. His uncle was at Wareham, just four miles to the north, as he'd been most days since they'd forced a landing there. They'd taken the town, but the castle still held out, and that was why Henry was stranded at Corfe, waiting for Wareham to surrender.

He'd tried a few times to write to his father, but he'd not gotten very far, a smudged page or two blotched with ink smears and crossed-out words. It was not that he lacked for material to write about. The Channel crossing had been a rough one, and he was proud of the fact that he hadn't gotten seasick like many of the men. Their original plan had been to land at Southampton, but some of the sailors balked, for that was their home port. So their fleet had come ashore at Wareham, and Henry had watched from a ship in the river harbor as the town was captured. In the weeks that followed, his uncle let him visit the siege whenever the weather permitted, as long as he kept well out of arrow range. No, he could have filled a dozen letters with what he'd seen and heard in the past month. But he was too troubled to write.

His uncle had explained to him that the besieged garrison had appealed to Stephen for aid, agreeing to surrender if he did not come to their rescue. The rules of war gave them that right. Henry understood that, or tried to. He understood, too, his uncle's strategy: he was using the castle at Wareham as bait, hoping to draw Stephen away from Oxford. Such tactics had always worked in the past, for Stephen had rarely found the patience for a long siege; that was not his nature. So far, though, he had not taken the lure, and with each passing day, it seemed more and more likely that he was willing to sacrifice Wareham if it meant he gained a far greater prize—Maude.

When Henry had confronted his uncle with these fears, Robert had acknowledged their validity. But he'd explained, then, the grim truth—that the three hundred men with him were not enough to raise the siege at Oxford. He'd need a far greater force to expel Stephen's army, sheltered behind the city's walls and newly dug earthworks. Unless they could provoke Stephen into coming out to meet them, as he had at Lincoln, Oxford Castle seemed doomed, for certes.

After that stark revelation, Henry's fears took a far darker turn. He'd spent a lot of his time at Corfe thinking of his mother, holding on to memories as elusive as the fireflies he chased every summer. It had been more than three years since he'd seen his mother. What if he did not recognize her? Even more unsettling was the thought that she might not recognize him; he'd been only six then and he was nigh on ten now. He fretted, too, about what she was enduring at Oxford. People were always interrupting conversations as he came by, but he already knew what they did not want him to hear—that her food supplies must be running very low by now, for the siege was into its third month.

But after his uncle admitted that they could not just ride to the rescue the way he'd expected them to do, he could not bring himself to write to his father, who'd shrugged off his mother's peril with the scornful words, "Whatever trouble she is in, she brought upon herself." And each day when he awoke, his first conscious thought was always the same. Would it be today that the castle fell? Today that his mother was taken prisoner? His worry about recognition seemed a small care, indeed, when measured against the dread that he'd never see his mother again.

His dogs were rooting in the coverlets, for he'd eaten bread and jam in bed for breakfast and spilled enough crumbs to warrant their attention. Wolf gulped down the last morsel, then began to bark. The female dyrehund joined in, and a moment later Robert entered the chamber.

"Wareham Castle surrendered to me this morning," he said, not sounding at all like a man who'd just gained a significant victory.

Henry scrambled down from the bed. "What will you do now?"

"What I'd hoped to avoid—lay siege to Oxford. We've got to muster as many men as we can, so I've summoned all our allies to meet me at Cirencester."

"Will you take me with you to Cirencester?" Henry asked, and was very relieved when his uncle nodded. "Uncle Robert . . . you do not think we'll be able to rescue Mama, do you?"

Robert debated the merits of a kind lie versus a cruel truth, but he waited too long to make up his mind, and his hesitation confirmed the worst of Henry's fears. He turned away, knelt by the closest of his dogs, and buried his face in the dyrehund's thick, silvery ruff. "If Stephen captures the castle, will he hurt my mother?"

"No," Robert said swiftly, "he would not harm her. Not Stephen."

Henry glanced up, eyes wide and very dark in the candle-lit shadows. "But he would not let her go," he said, and Robert slowly shook his head.

"No, lad," he admitted. "He would not let her go."

27

OXFORD CASTLE, ENGLAND

December 1142

It was snowing again. From his vantage point up on the castle battlements, Ranulf gazed out upon a frigid, frozen landscape of barren, foreboding beauty. Stephen had set up his quarters at the king's house north of the city walls. Much of his army was billeted within the town, but he'd established an outer defensive perimeter, and at night it looked as if the city were ringed with flames. Now it was midday and the blowing snow hid the smoldering campfires. So much snow had fallen in December that it even covered up the uglier scars of the siege: the newly dug graves in the outer bailey, the churned-up, pitted earth where mangonel missiles had landed, the ruins of the stables, which had been ignited by a flaming arrow more than a month ago. The snow muffled sound, blurred vision, and transformed the familiar and known into another world altogether, one pristine and alien and eerily, deceptively tranquil.

Ranulf did not remain up on the battlements for long; the wind soon drove him to seek shelter inside. Not that it was so much warmer indoors. As their food supplies had dwindled, so, too, had their fuel. Their firewood had been consumed weeks ago. These days they kept fires burning only in the great hall and the kitchen, but even so, they'd slowly stripped the castle of most of its furniture. Stamping snow from his boots, Ranulf hastened toward the open hearth. Other men were taking their turns there, too, thawing out. Only the ailing had the privilege of staying put, and there were always a few blanket-clad figures crouching close to the flames, for their increasingly Spartan diet and the constant cold were taking an inevitable toll.

The faces around him were grim and pale and gaunt, for hunger had become the enemy lurking within, Stephen's remorseless accomplice. They had not been as careful with food as they ought in the beginning, confident that aid would be forthcoming. By Martinmas, though, they were on strict rationing, and Maude had contributed greatly to the men's morale by insisting that portions be shared equally; the highborn usually claimed more than their just due.

As the provisions in their larder were depleted, they'd killed the castle livestock, one by one, and then their horses. Ranulf had hated that. But they had no more grain to feed the animals, and less and less to feed themselves, so it mattered little whether he liked it or not. If the siege dragged on for another month, he might have to make a wrenching decision about his dyrehunds. So far he'd been sharing his own meagre allotment with them, and even if men thought it was foolishly sentimental of him, they kept their opinions to themselves, for he was a king's son and the empress's brother. But that could all change if the spectre of starvation became a real danger.

Moving reluctantly away from the hearth, Ranulf began to look for Hugh de Plucknet. It took a while, for it was hard to distinguish one bundled form from another. Eventually he found Hugh slouching morosely in a corner, playing a game of merels with Alexander de Bohun, the Angevin captain of Maude's household knights. Alexander aligned his pieces in a row just as Ranulf joined them, and both he and Ranulf braced themselves for Hugh's complaints; the hotheaded Breton was a notoriously poor loser. Now, though, he did not react at all, demonstrating anew how the siege was sapping their spirits.

They made room for Ranulf in the window seat, but no one bothered to talk; it expended too much energy and what was there to say? Beyond the castle walls, the world went on as usual, but they no longer seemed to have a part in it. Ranulf in particular found the isolation hard to endure; it was, he thought, like a foretaste of death, the smothering silence of the grave.

They'd had but one outside contact since the siege began. A daring archer had gotten himself admitted into the city, waited till dark, and then shot an arrow over the castle wall, with a letter from Brien Fitz Count wrapped around the shaft. Brien assured them that he'd sent for Robert. He'd had no luck luring Stephen out to do battle, but he'd been doing all he could to harass and harry Stephen's occupying army, engaging in hit-

and-run raids, disrupting Stephen's supply barges as they paddled upriver past Wallingford. But Stephen ignored the challenges, and rerouted his supply trains overland.

And since then, nothing. October had yielded to November and then December. The snows came and the noose tightened. What, indeed, was there to talk about?

Alexander was too restless to sit for long and soon wandered off. Ranulf and Hugh were trying to muster up enough enthusiasm for another game of merels when Rob d'Oilly headed their way. Never the most articulate of men, he seemed even more tongue-tied then usual. "Did Maude tell you about our talk?" When Ranulf shook his head, Rob frowned and worried his thumbnail between his teeth. "I spoke to her last night. I told her that . . . that we ought to consider surrendering."

Ranulf's "No!" merged and echoed with Hugh's equally impassioned protest, and Rob flushed. "I do not want it that way," he insisted, "God knows I do not. But there comes a time when resistance for its own sake makes no sense. We're past the point of hope, and are merely prolonging our own suffering. I understand if you do not want to hear that, but it must be said. And Maude knew that, too, for she did not argue."

"She agreed with you? I do not believe that!"

"Well, she did not say it in so many words, Ranulf, but she listened to what I had to say and made no protest. If you want my opinion, I think she is losing heart for this struggle. Women are not meant for hardships and privation, after all. They despair more easily than men—"

"You're raving! Maude is braver than any man I know!" Ranulf snapped, and Hugh chimed in, no less indignantly, arguing that Maude would starve ere she'd surrender.

"Then why is she acting so oddly? Why did she say nothing when I talked of surrender? And . . . and there is more, Ranulf. When I came to her chamber this morn, she was behaving in a most peculiar manner. She and Minna . . . they were sewing!"

Ranulf and Hugh exchanged astonished glances, and then both burst out laughing. "Good God—sewing? That is indeed proof of madness!"

Rob bridled, his face getting even hotter. "Do not mock me till you've heard it all. The room was in utter disarray, the coverlets thrown on the floor, the bed stripped, coffers open as if they'd been searching for something. And there they were, sewing away in the midst of all this chaos, so intently you'd think they were getting paid by the stitch. And mind you, they were not mending old clothes, or even making new ones. They were cutting up and hemming bed sheets!"

"Sheets?" Ranulf said blankly. "Are you sure, Rob? What could they possibly make out of bed sheets?"

"That is what I've been trying to tell you." Rob frowned again, lowered his voice, and said uneasily, "I've thought upon it and I can come up with only one answer—a burial shroud."

RANULF did not share Rob's anxiety about Maude's emotional state; he knew their sister better than Rob. He was curious, though, about those mysterious bed sheets. But when he sought Maude out, she shrugged off his curiosity with a cryptic smile, saying she'd explain that evening, after Vespers.

The twilight service was held in the chapel adjoining St George's Tower. It was well attended; most men found that their piety increased in direct proportion to the urgency of their need. Once it was over, Ranulf accompanied Maude and Minna across the snow-drifted bailey, back to Maude's chamber in the upper story of the keep. There they found Alexander de Bohun, Hugh de Plucknet, William Marshal, and Adam of Ely, Maude's clerk, awaiting her return. They were soon joined by William Defuble, another of Maude's knights.

Ranulf could not help smiling, thinking they made an odd sight, indeed: muffled in mantles up to their ears, their breath frosting the air as they searched for seats; the castle's chairs, benches, and stools had long ago gone up in smoke. Rob d'Oilly was the last one to arrive. As a rule, Maude did not like to be kept waiting. Tonight, though, she seemed quite tolerant of Rob's tardiness, which confirmed Ranulf's suspicions—his sister had something in mind, and he'd wager the surety of his soul that it was not surrender.

"I have been giving thought to what you said, Rob, and I have decided that you are right. Our men have put up a gallant defense, but they have endured enough. The time has come to put an end to this. If you offer to surrender the castle, you ought to be able to get generous terms from Stephen, a promise that the garrison goes free."

Rob looked relieved, the other men stunned. "Maude, no!" Ranulf exclaimed. "It may seem hopeless, I'll not deny that. But you cannot give up. If you surrender, you'll be shut away from the world for the rest of your life. Stephen will never let you go!"

"I am not giving up, Ranulf. And I have no intention of surrendering to Stephen. But it is obvious by now that we have no reasonable hopes of being rescued. Robert would never abandon me. If he has not come to my aid, it is because he cannot. So it is up to me to save myself—if I can—by escaping from the castle."

"My lady, I doubt neither your resolve nor your enterprise, and for certes, not your courage. But this time I fear you are well and truly trapped. You cannot very well fly over the castle walls, and every gate is watched night and day by Stephen's sentries, even the little postern in the west wall."

"No, Hugh, I cannot fly over the wall," Maude agreed, with just the hint of a smile. "But I could be lowered down from St George's Tower onto the iced-over moat. The marshes must be frozen solid by now, and the river, too. If I am right, I ought to be able to cross in safety. If I am wrong . . ." A slight shrug. "As I see it, I do not have much to lose."

She did, of course. She was putting up the highest of all stakes—her life. But Ranulf would have made the same wager, had he been the one facing a lifetime's imprisonment. "You are proposing, then, to walk right through Stephen's lines? That is without doubt the maddest idea I've ever heard. When do we try it?"

Maude looked at him and laughed. "Tonight . . . after it is full dark."

"Would it not be safer to wait until the snow stopped? To be out and afoot on such a night . . . you'd have as much to fear from the weather, Maude, as from Stephen's men."

Marveling at his slowness, Maude said patiently, "What better cover could I have, Rob, than a snowstorm? Stephen's guards will not be able to see beyond the noses on their own faces, and they'll be too cold and wretched to be showing much zeal for sentry duty. With but a bit of luck, we ought to be well-nigh invisible. Show them, Minna."

Even as Minna reached into the closest coffer, Ranulf had a sudden epiphany. "The sheets!" he cried, bursting into enlightened laughter. Hugh began to laugh, too. The others remained perplexed—until Minna straightened, holding up her handiwork for them to see: a hooded mantle as white as milk . . . or newly fallen snow.

By now they were all laughing. Maude passed the white cloaks around for their admiring inspection. "I count four of these remarkable garments," Hugh said, "and since two are already spoken for, I hereby lay claim to the third. Who gets the last one?"

Alexander de Bohun looked irked that it should even be open to question. But before he could speak, Maude headed him off. "I would like you to remain at the castle, Alex, so you might assist Rob in striking a deal with Stephen." The words themselves were bland; the real message was relayed as their eyes met. They'd been together long enough to read each other without difficulty, and Alexander understood at once what Maude was telling him—that she wanted him to keep Rob from making any costly errors in the negotiations with Stephen. He did not like it any, but he did not argue; he shared her doubts about Rob's judgment.

"The fourth man has to be a local lad," Ranulf pointed out, "someone who knows every lane and deer track in the shire. Stephen's sentries are not going to be the only snow-blind ones out there. Without a truly trustworthy guide, we're likely to wander around out in the woods till we freeze to death."

Their eyes all turned toward Rob, who was quiet for a few moments, his brow furrowed in thought. And then he smiled. "I know just the man you need. He was born and bred in Berkshire, could probably find his way to Wallingford in his sleep. And he is cocky enough to jump at the chance to show off his tracking skills. Moreover, he has a brother or a cousin—I'm not sure which—who took vows at St Mary's Abbey. You will be heading for Abingdon first?"

Maude nodded, moved to the coffer chest, and drew out a small leather-bound book. "Rob, I want you to keep this safe. There are two letters hidden in the binding, one to Robert, telling him that this was my doing and my choice, and one to my sons . . . just in case."

They looked at one another, the edgy laughter stilled, acknowledging in their sudden silence the magnitude of the risk and the slim likelihood of success.

THEY gathered in an upper chamber of St George's Tower shortly before midnight. The only light was a flickering oil lamp, and when they were ready to unlatch the shutters, Minna prudently blew upon the sputtering wick, for darkness was their only defense, the continuing snowfall their only hope.

Their preparations had been made. Hugh had a small sack filled with dried meat, Ranulf carried flint and tinder, Maude a pouch in which coins had been wrapped in cloth to keep them from clinking, and the men had wineskins hooked to their belts. The farewells had already been said, and Maude had coached Rob in how to deal with Stephen's demands. "Tell him," she instructed, "that you ask nothing on my behalf, that your concern is for the safety of the garrison. That way he cannot accuse you of lying later, once he learns I am gone."

Their guide was a skinny, undersized youth, barely twenty, with an unkempt shock of fair hair, so blond it looked white, and as incongruous a name as they could imagine: Sampson. At first glance, he seemed an unlikely candidate for such a dangerous mission. But his slender build was deceptive; he was as lean and lithe as a greyhound and as eager to hunt. "Are we ready?" he queried jauntily, sounding for all the world as if they were embarking upon a grand adventure instead of attempting to cross through enemy lines in the midst of a snowstorm. "I'll go first," he offered, swinging his legs over the window ledge. A moment later, he was gone, climbing down the rope so rapidly that he made it look easy.

Ranulf was the next to go. "If any of you whoresons eat my dogs once I'm gone, I'll come back from the grave if need be to make you pay," he warned, and launched himself out into space to the accompaniment of joking threats about dyrehund stew. His trip was a lot rougher than Sampson's had been; buffeted by the wind, he was bumped bruisingly against the tower, and slid the last few feet, leaving rope burns on his palms.

Hugh was already shinnying down the swaying rope. Alexander and Rob were to lower Maude slowly once the men had climbed down, and Ranulf and the others watched nervously now as she started the perilous descent. The wind tugged at her cloak, blew back her hood, and at one point, the rope jerked, plummeting her briefly toward the ground before the men above were able to brace themselves again. By then she was close enough for Ranulf and Hugh to catch. She leaned against Ranulf, struggling to regain her breath as Hugh cut away her rope harness. No one spoke—they dared not risk it—but the same thought was in all their minds. It was not a comfortable feeling, being on the wrong side of the castle walls.

Their first test of faith was the castle moat. With Sampson in the lead, they stepped out gingerly onto the ice, and when it held, they shared tense smiles. It was bitterly cold, but the wind was not constant. A sudden gust would send snow swirling across their path, stinging their eyes and skin, but then it would subside. If not for the castle wall rising up at their backs, Ranulf would have been utterly disoriented, for all recognizable landmarks were camouflaged or buried. But Sampson showed no hesitation, striking out boldly as if following the King's Highway. Peering into the impenetrable blackness ahead, he whispered, "We're coming up on the millstream." Ranulf and the others could not see a foot in front of their faces, so dark was it. They could only put their trust in Sampson, and they trailed after him out onto the ice again, for the millstream was just where he'd said it would be.

Off to the east and west, they could now see smoke rising, and Sampson plotted a course that would take them between these enemy campfires. They had agreed that Stephen's sentries would not likely be patrolling on a night like this; for certes, any man with sense would be keeping as close to the fire as he could get. They felt sure they had logic on their side. But they knew, too, that gambles are won by luck as much as logic.

The drifts were deep, and it was more tiring than any of them had anticipated, their pace a slow and laborious one. The marshes were hidden under a blanket of soft snow, but the ground was frozen so hard that it was difficult to remember these same meadows had been under water when the siege began.

They crossed a second stream with encouraging ease. Ranulf guessed they had come no more than half a mile, but already the castle had disappeared into the darkness. Visibility was so poor that Hugh walked straight into a tree, a mishap that might have been comic if not for the fact that he gashed his cheek on a splintered branch, just missing his eye, more proof—as if they needed it—of how vulnerable they were out here, for any mistake was likely to be lethal.

Sampson was in the lead, with Ranulf and Hugh close behind, breaking a trail for Maude, who was hampered by her skirts. When Sampson stopped abruptly, flinging up his hand in warning, they froze as a rider materialized out of the night. His stallion's hoofbeats made no sound upon the snow; moving with a ghostly grace, it seemed more like a phantom spirit than a flesh-and-blood animal, an illusion enhanced by its odd color, the shade of pale smoke. The rider was enveloped in a dark mantle, his face shadowed by a peaked hood, and he seemed no more real than his mount. There was a fey, dreamlike quality to the encounter—until he turned his head and looked in their direction.

No one moved. No one even blinked. For seconds that lasted longer than years, he seemed to be staring right at them. And then he shook his head, like a man trying to clear cobwebs from his brain, made a sketchy sign of the cross, and rode on. No one spoke for another eternity. Had he decided he could not possibly have seen what he'd first thought? Had he concluded that these spectral white shapes were but a figment of his imagination? Or had he only sensed a presence, instinct overruled, then, by reason? They would never know.

As soon as they dared, they pushed on, blessing Maude's foresight, her camouflaging white cloaks. They'd not gone far when they saw a gleam through the trees up ahead. Quickening their steps, resisting the urge to keep looking over their shoulders, they halted on the riverbank, staring in silence at the icy grey surface of the Thames.

The moat and millstream had been obstacles to be overcome, but the Thames would be their grave if Maude's gamble failed, if the ice was not solid. Trying not to think of the depth and power of that frigid current, trying not to remember how unusual it was for the Thames to freeze over, they clasped hands and slowly ventured out onto the ice. As they moved farther from shore, they could hear snapping sounds as the ice settled, and first one and then another would pause, eyes straining for cracks. Each footstep was an act of hope, an expenditure of courage. They had almost reached the far bank when Ranulf's boot skidded. In the fragmented instant before his body hit the ice, they all saw it break under his weight, pitching them into the ink-black water. There was a thud that could surely have been heard back in Oxford, and then . . . nothing. The ice held firm, and a few moments later, they had achieved a rare distinction: they would be able to say in all honesty that they had crossed the River Thames without even getting their feet wet.

"That was fun," Maude said faintly, and caught the flicker of shaken grins. By common consent, they sought the shelter of a massive oak. Hugh pulled out his wineskin and passed it around. Maude drank so deeply that she choked; the wine was heavily spiced, burned its way down her throat, but she welcomed the heat, for never in her life had she been so cold. She'd not expected to be so tired so soon. She estimated they'd come about a mile or more. Which meant they had at least another five miles ere they reached Abingdon. "I am rested," she lied. "Let's go on."

The ground was sloping upward, and the snow was knee-deep in spots. It was like trying to run through water. The wind had shifted, was coming now from the south, and seemed intent upon blowing them back to Oxford. They stumbled repeatedly, clutching at one another to keep from falling. The trees were glazed in ice; branches broken off by the weight of the snow crunched underfoot and occasionally sent one of them sprawling. Hugh's hands were growing numb; he tucked them into his armpits in an attempt to warm them, deciding that gloves might not be such an effete fashion, after all, even if they were worn only by women and princes of the Church. Panting and shivering, they struggled on, until at last they reached the crest of the hill.

"Look," Maude said softly, pointing back down the hill. The blowing snow was already drifting across their trail; soon all signs of their tracks would be gone, blotted out as if they'd never passed this way.

"By God," Hugh murmured, sounding awed, "we just might make it!"

"You did not think we would?" Maude asked, and he shook his head with a grin.

"Not a chance in Hell," he admitted cheerfully, and Maude turned away hastily, moved almost to tears by their fealty and their reckless, rash gallantry. And there in the December darkness on this snow-clouded, silent hill, she beheld a glimmer of illuminating light, the realization that such loyalty could only be earned, not commanded, no matter who claimed England's crown.

It took them another six hours to reach Abingdon, and by the time they were within sight of the abbey walls of St Mary's, they were in danger of losing the night. Leaving Ranulf and Maude to hide in the woods, Sampson and Hugh trudged out to seek admittance from the porter at the gate. Maude and Ranulf were both acquainted with Abbot Ingulph, had dined with him at Oxford Castle that summer, and Maude did not want to implicate him in her escape; while Stephen was not usually given to searching for scapegoats, it was difficult to predict what a man might do when reeling from the blow Stephen was about to take.

So they had concocted a cover story for Sampson and Hugh, which explained their urgent need for horses without stirring up suspicions. Sampson was going to claim that he'd left Rob d'Oilly's employ before the siege began, and now served Hugh, who'd taken on Bennet de Malpas's name for the occasion, Ranulf's sardonic contribution to the fable. Sampson's cousin, Brother Joseph, would know better, of course, but Sampson swore he'd not say so, and they were fast learning to accept whatever the slight young soldier said as gospel, for he'd gotten them this far, had he not?

The snow had stopped several hours ago, but began again as soon as Hugh and Sampson were out of sight, and this time the flakes were not soft and lazy, floating wisps of white lace. This dawn snowfall was wet and icy, pelted against their skin like sleet. Hugh and Sampson had shed the white cloaks that had so effectively disguised their mantles, and Maude and Ranulf made a little tent of them, huddling together in a futile search for warmth. They took turns talking, keeping each other awake, for exhaustion was on their trail, even if Stephen was not. And they could not be sure of that, either. Discovery and capture were still very real threats. That sentry might have reevaluated what he'd seen and decided to give the alarm. Or they could have the bad luck to run into one of Stephen's patrols, now that daylight was nigh. Or Hugh and Sampson might fail, be unable to buy or borrow horses. There were any number of ways disaster could descend upon them, and between them, Maude and Ranulf thought of them all, seeking to scare away sleep.

The last night-shadows were in retreat and the wind was picking up as they heard approaching horses. Ranulf unsheathed his sword, drawing Maude in behind him. Moments later Sampson and Hugh rode into the clearing, mounted upon matching bay geldings, grinning from ear to ear. They'd agreed that it would be too suspicious to seek four horses, and now Sampson swung nimbly from the saddle, tossing Ranulf the reins. As soon as he'd assisted Maude up behind her brother, he vaulted onto Hugh's mount, and confidently pointed out the direction they were to take. Putting spurs to their horses, they set off at as fast a pace as the weather and their double burdens would allow, leaving in the snow for the villagers to find and puzzle over, four hooded white cloaks.

Wallingford Castle was nine miles away, so close and yet so far. Sampson was taking no chances, though, and steered clear of the Abingdon-Wallingford Road in favor of a safer cross-country route that he followed as unerringly as a bloodhound on the scent of prey. So it was almost noon before the castle at last came into view.

Wallingford was one of the best-defended strongholds in England, and they were challenged as soon as they came within bow range of its massive walls. "Open up," Ranulf shouted, "for the empress!" a claim so unexpected and so startling that the guard forgot all about caution and popped up to peer over the wall embrasure.

"The empress is trapped at Oxford," he shouted back. "What sort of lunatic trick is this?"

Maude's teeth were chattering too much for speech. Reaching up impatiently, she pulled back the hood of her mantle so the skeptical guard could see her face. There was a strangled sound up on the battlements, which might have amused her had she not been so very, very cold. She would later realize that Brien's men had acted with impressive dispatch, but now it seemed to take an extraordinarily long time before the drawbridge began to lower and the gate swung open to admit her.

Crossing into the bailey, they rode into utter pandemonium. Men were coming on the run from all corners of the castle, and they were mobbed as soon as they reined in. A dozen eager hands reached up to help Maude dismount, but her muscles were so numbed and cramped that she stumbled and had to grab at the nearest arm to keep from falling. When she faltered again, Brien was there to catch her. As soon as he felt her trembling, he jerked off his own mantle and wrapped her in it before escorting her into the great hall, leaving Ranulf, Hugh, and Sampson to fend for themselves.

Maude was dazed by the furor. She had often been the center of attention, but never before the object of such intense and unbridled enthusiasm. Every man in the hall was beaming at her, admiring, marveling, approving. She was being assailed from all sides with shouted questions and lavish praise; it was unseemly behavior and she reveled in it.

Ranulf and Hugh and Sampson were fighting their way toward her, overwhelmed by so much goodwill; men were slapping them on the back, spilling wine on them with overeager generosity, inadvertently keeping them from what they most wanted: to thaw themselves out by that blazing hearth. Maude was so close to the flames that she was in danger of being singed. She was thirsty and hungry and half frozen and so fatigued she felt lightheaded. But none of that mattered. She was quite content to stay right where she was, in Brien's arms, surrounded by laughing, exultant men, men who were calling her Queen Maude as if they truly meant it, rejoicing in her triumph and making it their own.

Brien was holding her as if he had no intention of letting her go, dark eyes never leaving her face. "You are the most amazing woman," he said, and laughed, too happy to hide it, to keep up the pretense between them any longer. Maude smiled at him as her own defenses dropped, realizing what was happening and not caring, not now, not anymore.

"My only regret," she said, "is that I'll not be there to see Stephen's face when he finds out I've bested him!" That set them all to laughing, and this time she knew the jokes were at Stephen's expense, not hers.

"If I do not sit down soon, I'm likely to fall down," she confided to

Brien, for she could admit to physical frailties now; she'd earned that right. His arm tightened around her shoulder, and when he called out for a chair, so many men volunteered that Maude began to laugh. Never had she felt like this, so in harmony with her world, so at ease with herself. It was a wonderful feeling, had been a long time coming.

She smiled again at Brien. But he was no longer gazing down into her face with such flattering and heartfelt joy. He was looking over her shoulder, and although he showed no overt signs of tension, Maude saw enough subtle indications—a tightening around his mouth, a flickering of his eyelids—for her to turn around, seeking the source of his stress.

A woman was coming toward them. She was about Maude's age, although without Maude's statuesque carriage or her elegant, high-cheeked handsomeness. Maude's features were boldly stated, her coloring as dramatic as her demeanor. This woman's appeal was as delicate as it was conventional, delineated in gentle, muted shades, hair a pale ash-brown, golden lashes, eyes a soft, misty blue, eyes that were as clear as spring water and as transparent, giving Maude an unwanted glimpse into the very depths of her woman's soul. There was pain in the look she now gave Maude, pain and fear and a quiver of hopeless hatred.

"Welcome to Wallingford, madame," she said tonelessly. "Welcome to my husband's home."

STEPHEN felt more than triumph as he watched the castle drawbridge being lowered; he felt a quiet but intense sense of vindication. Judging from the comments he overheard as they rode into the bailey, he knew his men were experiencing emotions no less jubilant and a good deal more vengeful. As much as he'd wanted to take Maude prisoner, he had no desire to see her humiliated, and in that, he was clearly in the minority. His brother in particular was anticipating Maude's surrender with more pleasure than seemed becoming for a man of God. Stephen hoped Henry would not gloat too openly, but he could not very well say anything. Not only would that infuriate his brother for days and even weeks to come, but it would reinforce the lingering suspicions of his other allies, that he lacked the old king's implacable will and unforgiving royal memory. It would be a great relief once he no longer had to compete with a ghost; in ending the threat Maude posed, he hoped, too, to put her father to his long-overdue rest.

Rob d'Oilly was awaiting them upon the steps of the great hall, standing with a tall, burly man whom Stephen recognized as the captain of Maude's household knights. But there was no sign of Maude, and Stephen's smile faded. "That is odd," he said, "I would have wagered any sum that Maude would be the first one we'd see."

"It is not so surprising," the bishop countered. "She is facing utter ruin, confinement for the rest of her days. Little wonder she might want to put off the moment of surrender as long as possible."

"After all this time, Henry, do you know Maude as little as that? The greater her defeat, the more determined she'd be to meet it head-on. I do not like this, not at all. Mayhap she is ailing? That might explain her sudden capitulation. In truth, I'd expected her to hold out until the last morsel of bread had been swallowed."

Rob d'Oilly drew a visibly bracing breath. He was obviously not looking forward to this coming confrontation, and that was the true measure of the difference between them, Alexander de Bohun thought, with just a trace of disdain, for he was relishing what lay ahead. His eyes flicked past Stephen to the familiar faces behind him: the cutthroat Fleming, the swaggering Warenne whelp, that sour pickle Northampton, whose smiles always looked borrowed, and Winchester's ungodly bishop, as smug as a cat with a mouse between its paws. No, he was glad now that his lady had asked him to keep her brother from blundering. He'd not have missed this for all the whores in Babylon.

Rob d'Oilly's sin was not in being nervous; it was in letting it be seen. He was determined, though, to follow the proper code of conduct for such occasions, and as Stephen dismounted, he stepped forward stiffly, knelt and formally offered his sword. "Oxford Castle is yours, my liege."

Stephen accepted the sword with appropriate gravity and did not keep Rob on his knees any longer than need be. Say what you will about the man, Rob thought, he knew how to play his part. But he did not yet know that Maude had rewritten the ending. And when he did?

"Where is the Countess of Anjou?" the Bishop of Winchester demanded, and Rob found himself—oddly enough—taking umbrage on Stephen's behalf, that his partisans should feel so free to usurp his role. He hesitated and was not sure whether to be relieved or resentful when Alexander de Bohun spared him the dangerous duty of revelation.

"You were expecting to find the empress here?" Alexander queried blandly. "You are in for a disappointment, then."

There was a brief moment of stunned silence, and then, uproar. Stephen had to shout to make himself heard above the din. "How witless do you think we are? She must be here—unless she has learned to fly! Now where is she? I'll have the truth from you," he warned, adding ominously, "one way or another!"

Rob gulped, saying nothing, but thinking all the while of the garrison hanged at Shrewsbury Castle. Alexander was not as easily intimidated; he even smiled. "I do not expect you to take my word for it. See for yourselves."

Several of the men seemed ready to fling themselves at Alexander de

Bohun and Rob, threatening to beat the truth out of them if need be, and Rob took an involuntary backward step. But Stephen stopped them with a peremptory gesture, "Search the castle," he commanded. "Take it apart stone by stone if you must, but find her!"

They took Stephen at his word, all but tore the castle apart. Rob and Alexander de Bohun and the rest of Maude's men were herded into the great hall under guard. Those who showed too much pleasure in the frantic search were soon nursing bruises and split lips, and Rob warned them hoarsely that prudence was the order of the day. Sidling up to Alexander, he asked softly if they ought not to remind Stephen of his promise to free the garrison. But Alexander shook his head. "No, just stay quiet till their fury burns out. Only once has Stephen sent men to their deaths in a rage, and it is said he later regretted it. I do not doubt Ypres or the bishop would hang the lot of us before breakfast without blinking an eye, but Stephen will not let them take out their anger on us—if we are half as lucky as the empress!" It was sound advice and Rob took it. For the remainder of the search, he and his men kept as low a profile as they could.

"The bitch is gone," the Earl of Northampton reported, sounding as if he could not believe his own words. "We've looked in every corner and cranny of this accursed place. If she is still here, she is in one of those fresh graves out in the bailey, for we've not missed so much as a mousehole."

Stephen turned away without answering. His brother was beside him now, ranting in his ear again. Listening to Henry was like pouring salt into an open wound. Swinging about, he headed for the stairwell, taking the stairs two at a time up to the chamber he'd been told was Maude's. His spurs struck sparks against the stone steps, and his heart thudded in rhythm to the dirge echoing in his brain. *Gone. She is gone. But how? Christ on the Cross, how?*

Maude's chamber had been demolished, bedding slashed, coffers spilled open, her clothes strewn about, ripped into rags. William de Ypres had backed a heavyset woman against the wall, pinning her by her wrists. Her hair had been shaken loose, falling over her face in salt-and-pepper dishevelment, and there was blood welling in the corner of her mouth. But she showed no fear, and that seemed to goad the Fleming all the more.

"Where is she, old woman? You'd best tell me now, whilst you still have a tongue to talk!"

"I do not know! And if I did, I'd never tell you!" she spat, before calling Ypres a name that sounded German to Stephen, and clearly no compliment.

"Let her go, William," he said angrily, and Ypres spun around to protest, but saw something in Stephen's face that silenced him. Moving to an overturned coffer, he picked up a woman's chemise, tore it in half, and flung the pieces contemptuously at Minna's feet.

Minna expelled an audible breath as Ypres stalked out, watching Stephen warily as he moved about the chamber. "I know who you are," he said. "You have been with Maude for a long time. It surprises me that she could leave you behind like this. Had she no fear for your safety?"

"She knew you'd not harm a woman," Minna said calmly, retrieving the torn chemise and using it to daub at her bleeding mouth.

"Did she, indeed? I find it passing strange," Stephen said, with sudden bitterness, "that my enemies value my virtues more than my friends do."

Minna continued to watch him closely, rubbing her chafed wrists now that Ypres was not there to see. "I was not lying," she insisted. "I do not know where my lady is."

"I do," Stephen said, "Wallingford. Where else could she go? But I need to know how she did it. You owe me that much."

He did not truly expect her to answer him, but she did, saying readily, "She had us lower her from St George's Tower, down onto the ice outside the walls."

"And then what? She just walked past my army?" Stephen asked incredulously, and she nodded proudly. "I see . . . so you are telling me she escaped from a besieged castle in the midst of a snowstorm. I suppose I should say that if she could endure such an ordeal, take such a mad risk, then she deserved to get away. But I will not. I cannot," he said, his voice cracking with rage, and another emotion, one more raw and revealing than anger.

Minna was folding the bloodied and shredded chemise neatly, as if it were still a whole garment and not a fragment beyond salvaging. "Even if you had captured my lady," she said, "you would not have won your war."

He turned to look at her, and she continued quietly. "You'd only have gained yourself some time. The empress is fighting for her son, and even if you were to confine her in the Tower until she died, men would still see young Henry as the rightful heir."

"That may well be," he said at last. "But Maude had best understand this, that I am fighting for my son, too."

AT Wallingford, Maude was still enjoying her newfound celebrity status. The garrison could not do enough for her, and on the few occasions when she'd ventured beyond the castle walls, the townspeople flocked around her, the way Londoners had once trailed after her mother, "Good Queen Maude," on her visits to the city's lepers and Christ's poor. Maude was no saint, nor did she want to be one. But she'd been popular with her German subjects, and it had stung her pride when the English acknowledged her so grudgingly, with suspicion and scorn instead of approval. So there was a healing balm in this belated acceptance, even though she knew that nothing had truly changed. Men might praise her courage, admire her intrepid escape, but they were still not willing to obey her.

The sun was blinding on the snow, so bright that it hurt Maude's eyes. Some of the younger men were having an exuberant snowball fight, but they waved and held their fire until she'd safely passed by. As soon as she entered the hall, a young page offered to fetch her an almond milk custard from the kitchen, and when she declined, he confided that the cooks were planning a special Christmas Eve subtlety in her honour: they were baking a cake shaped like Oxford Castle, surrounded by sugared snow. Up in her bedchamber, Maude found she'd been given extra pillows, and yet another gown was spread out on the bed, a soft wool in a flattering shade of green. As Maude was too tall to borrow any clothes from Brien's wife, he had engaged some of the townswomen on her behalf, and to judge by the way her wardrobe was expanding, they must be sewing day and night. Maude had never been treated so well as she had during her stay at Wallingford, and she wanted nothing so much as to get as far away as she could.

Ranulf was in the solar, decorating it with mistletoe and evergreen boughs. Smiling at sight of his sister, he said "Catch!" and tossed Maude a wafer. It was hot from the oven and filled with honey, the aptly named angel's bread. "If Robert does not get here soon," Ranulf confessed, "I'll not find a horse big enough to bear my weight. I've not been able to stop eating, spend more time in the kitchen than the cooks!" He was pleased when she laughed, for he knew she was not as cheerful as she would have others believe. He suspected that her victory had left a sour aftertaste in her mouth, and he thought he knew why. But Maude would never admit it, mayhap not even to herself.

"I saw Sampson in the stables this morning, Maude. Flying higher than any hawk, is that lad. He says he's coming with us back to Devizes, sounding like a man offered a post guarding Heaven's Gate!"

"Actually, he approached me first, said he had a yearning to see more of the world than Wallingford. I was going to take him with us, anyway, though, for I do not care to think what might have befallen us without him."

Sitting down, she helped herself to another wafer. "Ranulf, I've been thinking about the ransoms. We might as well send word to Stephen now, find out what we must pay to free Rob and Alexander and Minna and the others. I know Brien wants to wait till Robert arrives, but surely Stephen knows by now where I am."

Ranulf sat down across from her; so simple an act as sitting in a chair was a pleasure after all those weeks of feeding their furniture into the fire.

"You are not worried about your safety here, Maude? There is no need, you know. Robert was already gathering an army to march to your rescue when he got Brien's message about your escape, and so he should reach us any day now. And you may be sure that Stephen knows he is on his way. But even if Stephen were foolish enough—or furious enough—to assault Wallingford this very morn, he'd have no chance of taking it ere Robert arrives. If the worst happened and he somehow captured the town as he did Oxford, he'd never be able to take the castle. And Brien has his larders well stocked. I'd wager we could hold out at Wallingford till spring and beyond if need be!"

He'd meant to reassure her, but the look on her face was one of dismay. It was painfully obvious that she found the prospects of a Wallingford siege even more daunting than the dangers she'd braved in escaping from Oxford. She would, he suspected, flee barefoot out into the snow rather than be trapped here with Brien and his wife, and he understood why; thinking of Annora, he understood all too well.

The door burst open and Hugh reeled into the room. "Riders approach," he panted, "under a flag of truce!"

Maude and Ranulf both flew to the window, fumbling with the shutters. For all his bold talk, Ranulf felt a chill that was not caused by the sudden infusion of cold air. Was Stephen making a demand that Brien give Maude up? He leaned out the window, so recklessly that Maude and Hugh grabbed for his belt to anchor him. "I can see them now," he reported. "They are Stephen's men, for certes. Either a messenger or an escort—Holy Mother!"

He was blocking Maude and Hugh's view, and they could only wait impatiently until he withdrew safely back into the solar. As soon as he turned, they knew his news was good. "It is Minna! Stephen has sent her back to you, Maude!" His grin widened. "And damn me if else, but he threw in my dyrehunds, too!"

MAUDE was sitting beside the hearth in her bedchamber while Minna brushed out her long, dark hair. It had been quiet for a while, a comfortable quiet; they were finally talked out. Moving to the table, Minna poured wine for them both, then went back to brushing Maude's hair.

Maude sipped the wine without enthusiasm; it was a malmsey, too sweet for her taste. "Did you ask for Ranulf's dogs?"

Minna shook her head regretfully. "In truth, I never thought of them," she admitted. "No, that was Stephen's doing."

Maude set her wine cup down, turning so she could look into Minna's face. "Did he take it hard . . . my escape?"

"Yes," Minna said, and Maude smiled.

Another silence settled over the chamber. Minna had begun to hum under her breath, a German song from her youth, and it was like a cat's purring, proof of Minna's contentment. "What a Christmas this will be, madame. It would be well-nigh perfect if only Lord Robert were here. Do you know what sort of festivities are planned? I asked that woman, but she was not very forthcoming."

Minna's loyalty was a fierce and elemental force; it took no prisoners. She managed to make the innocuous phrase "that woman" sound as damning as anything Maude had ever heard. She hid a smile in her wine cup, for there was a primitive, sweet pleasure in it, but it was a forbidden pleasure, nonetheless, one she dared not indulge. "You might as well call her what she is, Minna—Brien's wife."

"I know," Minna said, but she could not resist adding a muttered comment under her breath, which seemed to fault Brien's wife for an odd sin, indeed, that she shared Maude's name. Maude said nothing, but she could feel heat rising in her face.

It had happened on her third night at Wallingford. She'd gone into the solar to retrieve a book, and she was already in the room before she realized she was not alone. They were standing in the shadows, beyond the reach of the cresset lamp. Brien had his hands on his wife's shoulders; his back was to Maude, and he was speaking too softly for her to hear, but his tone was soothing. His wife's face was turned up toward his, and it was wet with tears. Maude froze, not wanting to be there, to witness this intimate moment. She'd taken a stealthy backward step when the other Maude's voice rose, just enough for her words to carry clearly across the solar. "How lucky for you, Brien, that I was christened Maude, for you need never fear crying out the wrong name in bed." Maude never knew how Brien responded, for she heard nothing after that but the blood pounding in her ears as she slowly retreated toward the door. She could not have borne it had they turned and seen her, but she was spared that, at least. Yet the memory lingered, one she would never share with another soul, not even Minna.

"I've never been able to abide women like that, Minna. The ones who flutter their lashes and coo like doves whenever a man walks by, just the sort of woman Geoffrey would fancy."

"Just remember, my lady, what God has given you and denied her. Her marriage is barren, whilst you have three healthy sons."

That gave Maude pause. "Sons I never get to see," she said, and at once regretted it, for even to her ears, that sounded suspiciously self-pitying. "I am so thankful, Minna, to have you back with me. We've traveled a bumpy road together, too many miles for us ever to go our separate ways."

Minna smiled, began to hum again. Within moments dogs were barking out in the bailey. "That sounds like Ranulf's wolf pack," Maude said. The barking did not subside; the other castle dogs were joining in. "Minna . . . do you think it could be Robert?" Maude was on her feet, re-tying the lacings of her gown, and Minna was brushing her hair back, preparing to pin it at the nape of her neck, when they heard the footsteps on the stairs.

It was Ranulf and Brien, and Maude knew at once that her hunch had been right. "Robert?" she asked eagerly, and they nodded in unison. Ranulf's emotions always ran close to the surface; Brien's did not. Now, though, the same expression was mirrored on both their faces, a look of jubilation and joy that was somehow expectant, too, the sort of inner excitement that hinted at secrets and surprises. But Maude had no time for curiosity, for Robert was coming in behind them, and then she was in his arms, being held in a wordless embrace, one that said what they could not.

"These narrow escapes of yours," Robert said, "are becoming the stuff of legend."

Maude laughed. "Ah, Robert, I cannot begin to tell you how the sight of you gladdens me!"

"I have to admit," he said, "that you truly surprised me with that miraculous midnight escape of yours. But I have a surprise of my own." He looked back toward Brien then, and nodded.

Maude watched, puzzled, as Brien pulled the door all the way open. And then she gasped, "Dear God!" for her son was standing in the doorway.

Henry's qualms about not being recognized now seemed very foolish to him, for he was suddenly sure that his mother would have known him anywhere, on any street in Christendom. He liked the way her hair fell loose about her shoulders, black and shiny like the polished jet in the hilt of his uncle's dagger, and he liked it, too, that she did not pounce on him, swooping him up in one of those tearful, perfumed embraces that squeezed the air out of him. He did not want her to act like the mothers of his friends. She said his name, making it sound like the "Amen" that ended prayers, and he was drawn forward into the room, straight as an arrow toward its target.

"We were coming to rescue you," he explained, with just a trace of reproach, "and we would have, too. But you were too quick, Mama. You rescued yourself." Had she known he was on the way, she said, she'd have waited, and she laughed. He laughed, too, and then she was hugging him, and instead of being embarrassed, he found himself hugging her back.

Henry was not shy, and he was soon settled cross-legged across from his mother in the window seat, talking a blue streak: asking about her trek through the snow, interrupting to brag a bit about his own adventures, then wanting to know if she'd been scared, if she'd gotten lost, if she'd mind that he went to bed later tonight, since he was not tired at all, and there was so much still to share.

Minna and the men watched and listened and then, one by one, discreetly slipped away. Brien was the last to go. He'd seen Maude look more beautiful than she did at this moment. Ironically enough, he'd always thought she had never looked fairer than on the day of her wedding to Geoffrey. But never had he seen her look happier. "Merry Christmas, Maude," he said softly, and closed the door, leaving her alone with her son.

28

DEVIZES CASTLE, ENGLAND

June 1143

JUNE was a good month for Maude; her son was back at Devizes Castle. His visits were never long enough, left her yearning for more. But boys of Henry's age did not belong with their mothers. Only a man could teach them the navigational skills they would need to reach the distant shores of manhood. Or so Society and the Church dictated. Maude had reluctantly acquiesced, entrusting Henry into her brother's keeping, for motherhood could not compete with kingship. No matter what she must do or endure or sacrifice, it would be worth it—on the day her stolen crown was placed upon Henry's head. That, she did not dare to doubt.

On this sultry June Saturday, Ranulf and Hugh de Plucknet had taken Henry on a hunt in the royal forest of Melksham, and they did not return till dusk, grimy and sweat-soaked and tired and triumphant. This was Henry's first hunt, and his enthusiasm was so intense that his audience knew it was witnessing the birth of a lifelong passion. One of his arrows had helped to bring down a hart, and with each telling, the tines on the stag's antlers grew more numerous and awesome. Maude listened patiently as he relived the hunt for her, praising the lymer hounds and recounting the chase and describing in detail the moment when their quarry turned at bay. But when he started to explain how a skilled tracker could determine a stag's size by the shape of its droppings, Maude called a halt.

"Deer droppings? That explains why you smell so ripe," she teased, and Henry grinned, for being dirty and bedraggled was part of the fun. "Go bathe and then you can come back and teach me all about the mysteries of deer dung," she promised, and he began grumbling good-naturedly about taking a bath, bargaining for a lesser washup, not conceding defeat until Ranulf weighed in on Maude's side.

"You need not bathe, Harry, not as long as you stay downwind at supper," he suggested, and Henry grinned again, for he was old enough now to laugh at himself. But Maude turned to look at her brother in surprise.

"'Harry'?" she echoed. "Where did that come from?"

"You did not tell your mother yet, lad? He wants to be called 'Harry' from now on."

Just as Henry had feared, his mother's brows slanted downward in a disapproving frown, and he said hastily, "Why not, Mama? I've always hated Henry; it sounds like the name of a priest or . . . or some peddler's nag. It is just not a heroic name, Mama. I like 'Harry' much better, and that is the way the English say Henry, and since I'm to be king of the English, I ought to have an English name, and—" At that point, he broke off, not having run out of arguments, just out of breath. But before he could rally, Maude shook her head.

"Henry is what you were christened, and Henry you will remain. Nicknames are undignified."

Ranulf started to speak, stopped himself. Henry was not as prudent. His disappointment was too sharp to swallow; instead, he let it out in anger, saying accusingly, "That is not fair! It is my name, not yours!"

"That is so," Maude conceded coolly, "but it is also so that you are ten years old. Once you are grown, you may call yourself whatever you choose. Until then, you must make do with Henry."

The obdurate look on her son's face was one she was becoming all too familiar with. "It is not fair," he said again, but this time as defiance, not complaint, and when Maude showed no signs of relenting, he turned away abruptly, deliberately knocking over a chair on his way to the door. But he did not get far. His mother's voice froze him in his tracks.

"Henry, I will not abide such churlish behavior, and you well know it. Go and take your bath—now!"

Ranulf had watched in astonishment, and as soon as Henry had gone, he admitted, "That is the first time I've seen the lad flare up like that. Has he done this before?"

"Yes, I am sorry to say. Once when he did not get his way, he broke a pitcher."

"So . . . he inherited his share of the infamous Angevin temper, after all."

"Tempers can be controlled. Geoffrey controls his. No, Ranulf, these fits of temper are not a tainted legacy of the blood. Henry was not given to tantrums, not whilst he was in my care. These sprang up in my absence like weeds, and took root once he saw how well they worked. I suppose it was only to be expected, for Geoffrey was always overly indulgent with our sons, and whilst he was off waging war in Normandy, there were few to say no to Henry or his brothers. That is another reason why I agreed to put Henry into Robert's keeping, for I knew Robert would never brook disobedience or deliberate mischief."

"Indeed not," Ranulf agreed ruefully, remembering his own apprenticeship under Robert's tutelage; his brother was even more of a disciplinarian than Maude, with no tolerance for tomfoolery. "Robert will set the lad straight if anyone can. But if you do not mind my meddling, I think you were too hard on him about the name. What harm in letting him call himself Harry? Did you never want to change your name? I did, for certes!"

"Truly?" Maude sounded so puzzled that it was obvious this particular childhood craving had eluded her altogether. "What did you want to be called?" she asked curiously, and Ranulf hesitated.

"I'll tell you only if you promise not to laugh. I was so bedazzled by the hero's exploits in *The Song of Roland* that—Maude, you are laughing!"

"No, I am not," she insisted, untruthfully and unconvincingly. "Roland Fitz Roy . . . I cannot believe our father countenanced that!"

"You do not think I ever asked Papa? No, that was whilst I was still a page in Stephen's household, and if memory serves, he called me Roland for nigh on a fortnight—and with a straight face, too—till the whim passed."

"He would," Maude said tartly, but she fell silent after that, and Ranulf hoped she was pondering what he'd said; if Geoffrey had to learn how to rein Henry in, she needed to learn how to slacken those reins. Changing the subject, he asked her about Geoffrey's last letter, and she told him of her husband's victorious siege of Cherbourg. All of Normandy south and west of the River Seine was now his, she reported, but with a discernible lack of enthusiasm. He understood why; as much as she wanted to see the duchy conquered for Henry, it had to rankle—that Geoffrey was succeeding spectacularly in Normandy, whilst her English campaign was mired down in controversy, buffeted by setbacks and shadowed by defeat.

From Normandy, their conversation shifted to the latest news from the French court. Urged on by Eleanor, the French king had invaded Champagne to punish Count Theobald for championing Raoul de Péronne's repudiated wife, and the resulting carnage had been shocking even to an age inured to bloodshed and civilian casualties. When the French army had swept into the town of Vitry-sur-Marne and laid siege to one of Theobald's castles, the frightened townspeople had taken refuge in their church. But when the town was fired, the wind shifted and the flames spread to the church. Within moments, it became an inferno, and few escaped; more than thirteen hundred bodies were later found in the smoldering ruins. The young French king was a horrified eyewitness, and his sleep was said to be haunted by those dying screams even now, six months after Vitry's fiery death throes. But the king's anguished conscience had not bidden him to withdraw his troops from Champagne, and the campaign continued.

It was, Ranulf and Maude agreed, incredible folly—fighting a war to vindicate an illicit love affair. When her own peace was troubled by memories of the terrible suffering in Winchester, Maude confided, at least she knew her cause was just; her son's kingship was worth fighting for, even dying for.

Henry chose that moment to reenter the chamber. His mother and uncle scowled at sight of him, and his disgrace stung anew, for their good opinion mattered greatly to him. "You could not possibly have taken a bath already," Maude said suspiciously, and he readily admitted that he had not.

"The servants are fetching the bathwater. But I did wash my face and hands and even my neck . . . see?" he said, tugging aside his tunic to show a patch of newly scrubbed skin. "I came back, Mama, to say that I was sorry for being rude."

Maude's mouth softened. "You deserve to be forgiven, then. But do you know what I would value as much as an apology? Your promise that it will not happen again."

Henry hesitated. "I'd rather not, Mama," he said at last. "I cannot be sure I could keep that promise. And if I could not, then my sin would be twofold—rudeness and bad faith, too."

"Very scrupulous of you, Henry," Maude said dryly. "But I would suggest that you try to mend your manners in the future, that you try very hard."

"I will, Mama. I will not throw any more chairs about. And I'll make no more mention of names, will not ask you again to call me Harry," he said solemnly, and then heaved a wistful sigh. "Papa will agree, and I'll just have to settle for that."

Ranulf coughed to camouflage a laugh, while Maude wavered between exasperation and amusement. "I may not know as much about military tactics as your uncles, but that is one I do recognize—divide and conquer, no?" Henry grinned at being caught out, and she beckoned him forward. "Fortunately for you, your uncle Ranulf has been pleading your case, and he would have made a worthy lawyer, for he convinced me that Harry is a fitting name for an English king."

"Thank you, Mama! And you, too, Uncle Ranulf!" Henry beamed at them both. "But you'd best write and tell Uncle Robert that you agree. I asked him last week, and he looked at me like I'd lost my wits!"

Henry had no time to savor his triumph, for a sudden commotion had erupted out in the bailey, demanding investigation. Darting across the chamber, he knelt on the window seat and leaned recklessly out the window. "Armed riders," he reported breathlessly, "lots of them! And one of them is your friend, Uncle Ranulf—Gilbert Fitz John!"

GILBERT bore an urgent summons for Ranulf and Maude's household knights. "You know, my lady, how Stephen tried to recapture Wareham Castle, but backed off once he saw how well defended it was. He has since moved into Wiltshire, and he is now at Wilton."

Ranulf and Maude exchanged glances, for Wilton was only twenty-one miles from Devizes. "What does Robert think he has in mind? An attack on us?"

"Possibly. Earl Robert's spies have warned him that Stephen has sent out writs, summoning his lords and vassals to Wilton. In the meantime, he has taken over the nunnery, is using it as an outpost whilst he builds a castle. He could then isolate Salisbury, since the river crossing is at Wilton, and threaten all our holdings in the west. But he has made a grievous mistake, madame, for Wilton cannot withstand a siege, not yet."

"Robert means to take him by surprise?"

Gilbert nodded. "He sent me to fetch you, Ranulf, and as many men as Lady Maude can spare. He wants us to ride on to Marlborough and alert John Marshal. He and Lord Miles will join us there, and then swoop down upon Wilton without warning." Gilbert smiled grimly. "God Willing," he said, "it will be another Lincoln."

WILTON was situated at the conflux of the Rivers Nadder and Wylye. It had a prestigious past, for it had once been a royal borough of the Saxon princes. It was still an important town, with a thriving market, the wealthy and renowned abbey of St Mary, which regularly drew pilgrims to its shrine of St Edith, and the hospital of St Giles, founded by a queen, the old king's Adeliza.

But Stephen's arrival had shattered the security and threatened the prosperity of its citizens. The market had attracted customers from all the neighboring villages, but no more, for few were willing to visit a town occupied by soldiers. The local tradesmen suffered, too, and their shops remained shuttered. The town's Jews had been the first to flee, for they knew from bitter experience that they were the most vulnerable in times of upheaval. Some of the citizens—those with daughters or young wives—had sent their families to the greater safety of Salisbury. The dispossessed nuns had found shelter at the nearby nunnery in Amesbury. Most of the townspeople, though, had nowhere to go.

And so they kept indoors as much as possible, watched the slow progress of Stephen's castle, and prayed that once it was done, he and his men would ride off and leave them in peace. But as soured as their luck seemed to them that June, it was about to get far worse.

The first day of July got off to a bumpy start for Stephen; he had an uncomfortable audience with the abbess of St Mary's Abbey, and his charm and promises had not placated her in the least. Then one of their scouts reported that armed riders had been spotted to the north. Since the three closest castles in that direction—Ludgershall, Marlborough, and Devizes—were all hostile, Stephen dispatched the Earl of Northampton and a contingent of Ypres's Flemings to investigate and engage the enemy if need be. He was just sitting down to dinner with his brother the bishop in the abbey's great hall when a bleeding youth burst in, breathlessly gasping out his bad news as he stumbled toward them. The Earl of Northampton had run into trouble, for the force was larger than they'd expected. They'd skirmished with the enemy and were attempting to retreat back toward the town, but they needed help, and fast. By then chairs were being shoved back, trenchers pushed aside. Within moments, the hall had been emptied of all save the bishop, his clerics, and servants. The other men were already out the door, shouting for their horses.

Galloping out of the abbey precincts, Stephen led his men up East Street and onto the road north. It was a hot day, the sun at its zenith, for it was almost noon, and their horses kicked up clouds of dry, choking dust. Stephen could feel sweat trickling down his ribs, and even before the town receded into the distance, his head had begun to throb under the weight of his helmet. Fighting in the heat of high summer was almost as debilitating as a winter campaign. But he was usually impervious to the discomforts of weather, and he wondered if he was beginning to feel the aches and woes of age; after all, he was forty-seven now, and his youth was long gone.

"I'm getting too old for all this excitement," he said wryly to William de Ypres. But the Fleming, who seemed as ageless to Stephen as Wiltshire's eternal oaks, merely glanced over at him with a bemused frown, his every thought already focused upon the coming conflict. And then they heard it, the clamor of fighting up ahead. Spurring their horses, they charged forward.

They came upon a scene of chaos and impending catastrophe. Northampton and his men were in retreat, with their foes in close pursuit. "Holy Christ," Stephen breathed, for he knew at once what he was seeing. This was no foray into hostile territory, no scouting expedition to test Wilton's defenses. He was facing an enemy army, and even before he saw it, he knew whose banner they were flying. Only one man could have assembled a large fighting force with such deadly speed and accuracy—just as he'd done at Lincoln.

Ypres had come to the same appalled conclusion. "God smite him," he swore, "it is that misbegotten hellspawn, Gloucester!"

Stephen hastily unsheathed his sword. By now Northampton's men were almost upon them. Within moments, they'd been sucked into the battle. There was so much confusion that men struck down their own comrades by mistake, for it was no easy task, identifying the enemy in the midst of a maelstrom. Dust clogged their throats, stung their eyes, and the glare of the sun on the metal of chain mail and swords was blinding. Horses reared up, savaged one another as they collided, and when they fell, dragged their riders down with them. Stephen was soon splattered with blood. So far none of it was his . . . yet. But they were outnumbered, off balance, and if defeat was still inconceivable, it was also inevitable.

"My liege, you've got to get away whilst you still can!" William Martel had fought his way to Stephen's side. "You cannot let them take you—not again!"

"He is right!" Although Ypres was close enough to grab Stephen's arm, he had to shout to make himself heard. Knowing Stephen's stubborn streak was apt to surface at the most inconvenient times, he was already anticipating opposition, and rapidly assessing the arguments most likely to convince. Scorning appeals to common sense or safety, he chose to remind Stephen, instead, that "You promised your queen! You vowed no more Lincolns!"

Stephen realized the truth in their entreaties, but flight was an alien instinct, for his code of chivalry had always been long on gallantry, short on realism. His hesitation was almost fatal; a shout went up, one of recognition. "Jesú, the king! There, on the roan stallion!" Ypres seemed almost ready to snatch at his reins, and the other man's urgency prevailed over Stephen's own doubts. Swinging his destrier about, he gave the command to retreat.

As Stephen raced his qualms and his enemies back toward Wilton, his steward flung himself into the breach, fighting a desperate rearguard action to save his king from capture, just as Robert had done for Maude at the Le Strete crossing. Because of William Martel's courageous, doomed stand, Stephen and Ypres and the others were able to reach Wilton. By the time Robert had fought his way into the town, it was too late. Wilton was afire and Stephen was gone.

Robert refused to believe it. At his urging, his men fanned out through Wilton's narrow streets and lanes, forcing their way into homes, shops, and churches. They concentrated their search upon the commandeered nunnery, and soon flushed out fugitives from the battle. They dragged out sanctuary seekers from the town's eight churches, infuriating the parish priests. And they discovered coffers and chests for the plundering at the abbey, belongings left behind by Stephen and his men. But they could only confirm the worst of Robert's fears, that Stephen had indeed escaped.

At the guildhall, Robert was timidly accosted by Wilton's leading merchants, seeking to deter him from taking out his anger upon their town, in case he was so inclined. They were much relieved to find that he was not, although the damage done—deliberate or not—was already considerable; a number of the houses were in flames and his soldiers had engaged in some selective looting even as they pursued the hunt for Stephen.

The merchants, eager to curry favor with their new conqueror, were able to provide eyewitness accounts of Stephen's flight. He had ridden into the town at a flat-out gallop, they reported, pausing only to warn the bishop of his peril. He and the Fleming and the Earl of Northampton had then raced off down the road to the south, with the bishop and his retainers not far behind. They were not sparing their horses, could not long maintain such a killing pace, they predicted, but Robert spurned their crumbs of comfort, for he knew Stephen's brother had a castle less than ten miles away at Downton, where they could obtain fresh mounts.

He went through the motions, sending John Marshall off in pursuit. But it was an empty gesture and he knew it. Stephen had only to avoid the main roads, then circle back and head for safety at Winchester. He'd had his chance and it had come to nothing. In time, he'd accept the loss with grudging grace—but not now, not yet.

Miles was herding prisoners into the marketplace, arguing all the while with several indignant priests. At sight of Robert, the bolder of the two strode over to lodge a complaint against this breach of sanctuary. Robert responded for once not as a diplomat, but as a hunter robbed of his prey, and he rebuffed the priest with a brusque reminder that not all churches could claim the right of sanctuary. The priest retreated, but his banner was snatched up then by a new adversary, no less determined.

"My lord earl, a word with you!" The voice was educated, peremptory, female, and furious. Bearing down upon him was a tall, stately nun, garbed in the stark black of the Benedictine order, coming at such a brisk pace that her flowing garments and wimple caught the wind, giving him the incongruous image of a ship under full sail. He knew without being told that this was the abbess, a woman with a legitimate grievance. But he was in no mood to hear her out, and he started to turn away, leaving Ranulf to mollify her if he could.

He'd taken but a few steps, though, before he heard his name echoing across the square, and this was a voice so familiar that he spun around in astonishment. He'd not noticed the second nun. As Ranulf deftly intercepted the abbess, her companion cried out again, "Robert, wait!"

He did, for she was family, Hawise Fitz Hamon, his wife's younger sister. "What are you doing here?" he demanded. "We heard all the nuns had been moved to the convent at Amesbury."

"I came back with the abbess, hoping to shame the king into returning our abbey to us. What we got for our pains, though, were smiles and fair words. And now . . . with your men swarming over the nunnery like bees at a hive, I shudder to think what we will find. We need to fight the fires you started if the town and abbey are not to burn to the ground."

"It is being done," he said, and she turned, saw that Ranulf was indeed responding to the abbess's demand. But she did not seem satisfied, continuing to glare at her brother-in-law, arms akimbo, chin jutting out, looking eerily like Amabel, camouflaged for some unlikely reason as a nun.

"It will take our nunnery years to recover from this outrage," she said angrily, and he reminded her, no less sharply, that the abbey's adversity was Stephen's doing, for he was the one who'd seized it for his own purposes.

"Of course Stephen is at fault," she snapped. "But what does that matter now, with our town in flames and the abbey plundered? Look around you, Robert, at what you and Stephen have brought to Wilton. What did we do to deserve this misery? You think that burned-out wainright cares whether the crown goes to Stephen or Maude? I assure you his only worry is how he is going to feed his family now that his shop has been gutted. Ask the draper in Frog Lane, his shelves plucked bare and every scrap of cloth stolen. Ask my sisters in Christ, forced to take refuge in Amesbury whilst God's Acre is turned into a killing ground!"

"Hawise, enough! Innocents suffer in war. You think I do not know that? I sympathize, but—"

"Sympathy makes a poor gruel, Robert, fills no empty stomachs. Just tell me this, in all honesty. How much longer is this accursed war to continue?"

"I thought," he said bitterly, "to end it here and now—at Wilton. Suppose you answer a question for me, Sister Hawise. Tell me why the Almighty chose to let Stephen escape, to let the war go on."

She looked at him in silence, having no answer for him. But he'd not expected one.

AS hot and dry as July was, August was even more parched and scorching. A people usually starved for sun now had too much of it, and the crops began to wither in the fields. To a troubled, lawless land came new woes in this eighth year of Stephen's reign—a fear of famine.

MATILDA was walking across the garth toward Westminster's abbey church, accompanied by Cecily, and her confessor, Christian. The subject was one dear to her heart, the distribution of alms to Christ's poor, but she found herself increasingly distracted, for Eustace and Constance were quarreling again.

They had the sense to keep their voices low, but Matilda could still hear more than she wanted to. Constance's usual weapon was silence, a tactical retreat into an inner fortress where Eustace could not follow. But this afternoon, she was speaking up, insisting stubbornly, "I did not!" "Yes, you did!" Eustace countered, with the certainty he brought to all issues, and Matilda shot them a warning glance over her shoulder.

She did not seek, though, to learn the nature of their quarrel, for she well knew they disagreed over trifles. Their arguments were superficial, their differences so deep they burned to the bone. Eustace was thirteen now, Constance a year older, and they were getting dangerously close to the day she dreaded, the day when they were old enough to share a bed as man and wife. She already knew the marriage was a mistake; consummation would be throwing clods of dirt upon the coffin.

"Eustace!" There was so much alarm in Constance's cry that Matilda spun around, half fearful of what she would see. But for once Eustace was not the cause of his young wife's dismay; she was staring across the garth at the men just emerging into the sunlight, her blonde fairness fading into an ashen, greyish pallor. Eustace pulled her in behind him, at once protective and defiant, for in this alone were they utterly united: in their shared loathing for Geoffrey de Mandeville.

Mandeville never even noticed them. He was carrying on an intense, angry conversation with William de Warenne, but he broke off at sight of Matilda and strode toward her. "I am glad you are here, madame. Mayhap you can talk some sense into the king."

Matilda's reply was icy enough to defy the oppressive August heat. "It is not my place to question the judgment of the King's Grace, my lord earl."

Mandeville did not have the sort of incendiary temper that started so many fires for the Earl of Chester. But it burned deep if not hot, and Matilda suspected that he stored away grievances for kindling. His dark eyes narrowing, he said with lethal courtesy, "Correct me if my theology is flawed, madame, but I was taught that infallibility is an attribute of the Pope, not the King of England."

The temptation to lash back was a strong one, but Matilda had never lacked for control; she could wait. Her pressing need now was to learn the cause of his anger. Fortunately a more reliable source was approaching, and she hastened to intercept William de Ypres so they could speak together in private, with the candor queens were rarely allowed.

Ypres was no less provoked than Geoffrey de Mandeville, and he did not keep Matilda in suspense. "We finally heard from Robert of Gloucester, damn his soul. He has offered to ransom William Martel—for Sherborne Castle."

"Oh, no . . ."

He nodded bleakly. "Without Sherborne, we cannot hope to challenge Gloucester's hold upon the western shires. It is too great a price to pay for any one man, but your husband, God save him, means to pay it, and I doubt that even you, madame, can talk him out of it."

"I am not sure," Matilda confessed, "that I would want to try. We owe William Martel so much, Willem! If not for him, Stephen would have been captured for certes. How can we turn our backs on him now?"

"A king owes other debts, too, madame—to his supporters, to the men who've fought and bled for him, and to the subjects he rules. I'll not pretend that I care tuppence for the English people, but I know that you and the king do, and yielding Sherborne Castle will prolong the war. Even Stephen admits as much."

"What would you have him do, Willem? Abandon the man who sacrificed himself so he could escape? You know Stephen could never do that."

"Yes, I do know . . . and so does Gloucester. But why does the cup always have to be brimming over or empty? Why will half measures never suffice? Offer a lesser ransom for Martel, one we can afford to lose, and in time, Gloucester will let him go. A year or two in confinement against the loss of Sherborne—I'd say that was a fair bargain."

"But you'd not have to pay it, Willem. If you were the one being held in a Bristol dungeon, can you honestly say you'd not want Stephen to offer the sun and moon for your release?"

"Of course I would," he said impatiently. "But I am not the King of England . . . am I? It seems to me, madame, that we had this same conversation once before, in a Guildford chapel more than two years ago. Not much has changed since then, has it? That hawk still will not hunt."

MATILDA found Stephen in the church, standing before the tomb of the sainted Confessor, the last but one of the Saxon kings. He'd just lit a candle, but at sound of her familiar footsteps, he turned so abruptly that the flame guttered out. When she was almost close enough to touch, he said softly, "I have to do this, Tilda. I cannot let Will barter his freedom for mine."

"I know."

"Do you think I am wrong?"

She was silent for some moments, considering. "As your wife, I would gladly give a dozen Sherbornes to gain Will's release. As your queen, I have doubts. It is a difficult decision, Stephen, and I am glad it is not mine to make."

Stephen reached out to her then, entwined her fingers in his. "It was not difficult for me. You must understand that. For me, it was an easy choice, for it was the only choice."

"I know," she said again, and coming into his arms, she clung tightly, resting her cheek against his chest as she sought to comprehend the ultimate irony, she who had no irony at all in her soul, that the qualities she most loved in Stephen were the very ones that were crippling his kingship.

29

TOWER OF LONDON

October 1143

GEOFFREY de Mandeville had lost track of time, could not be sure how long he'd been held as a prisoner in the stronghold that had so recently been his. On those rare occasions when his rage receded enough for calculation, he thought it must be nigh on a fortnight, for it had been Michaelmas week when he'd arrived at St Albans for the king's council, unsuspecting that he was riding into an ambush.

He still felt a sense of disbelief, remembering that moment when the king had turned upon him without warning, ordering his arrest. He'd not even been able to resist, for Stephen had managed to separate him from his men before springing the trap. Of course Stephen was now in trouble with the Church, for the arrest had taken place within the abbey grounds, and the outraged abbot had viewed this as sacrilege. But he could take little consolation from that, for he'd been dragged off to London in chains, forced to order his garrison at the Tower to submit, and then thrown into one of his own dungeons. And now he waited, alone in the darkness, for the king to decree his fate, his world in ruins, and nothing to sustain him but his hatred.

WHEN he was brought before them, dirty and unkempt, blinking like a barn owl in the sudden surge of sunlight, Matilda was taken aback; could this pitiful wretch of a prisoner and the elegant, prideful Earl of Essex be one and the same? What shocked her even more than how far he'd fallen was the joy she took in it. Moving to her husband's side, she stared coldly at Geoffrey de Mandeville as he was shoved to his knees before them.

Stephen was experiencing the same unfamiliar emotion: satisfaction in an enemy's suffering. "You do not look as if you've enjoyed your stay here at the Tower, my lord earl. But then I doubt that my daughter-in-law enjoyed her stay, either."

Mandeville's eyes were gradually adjusting to the light, and when he blinked now, it was in surprise. "Is that what all this is about—the little French lass? No harm came to her, I saw to that. So I imposed my hospitality upon her for a while . . . what of it? That seems a minor sin, indeed, when compared to some of the other betrayals you've forgiven, including those of your own brother. You'd need a tally stick to keep count of all the times he has switched sides!"

Stephen scowled, and so did Matilda and William Martel. But the gibe did find an appreciative audience of one: a laugh floated from the window seat, where William de Ypres was comfortably sprawled, whittling upon a stick of white beech. His amusement seemed genuine, but his blade flashed all the while, paring the wood down to splinters.

"Had you betrayed only me," Stephen said, "I might have forgiven you. But you wronged my wife and Constance, and there can be no forgiveness for that."

Geoffrey de Mandeville said nothing, merely glanced toward Matilda and then away. But that look, brief as it was, was chilling in its intensity, its malevolence, for until that moment, Matilda had not known what it was like to be an object of hatred.

"If I pleased myself, I'd keep you caged here at the Tower till you rotted. But you are luckier than you deserve," Stephen said coolly, "for a number of your fellow barons have argued for clemency. And so I have decided to offer you a choice. If you cooperate, I will set you free."

Mandeville shifted awkwardly, for Stephen had not given him permission to rise and his calf muscles were cramping. "And what will this . . . cooperation of mine cost?"

"You've already yielded the Tower. Surrender as well your castles at Pleshy and Saffron Walden and I'll give you your freedom."

Mandeville took time to think it over, as if seeking to convince someone—if only himself—that there was an actual decision to be made. When he nodded, Stephen gestured and the guards jerked him to his feet. "I've a word of warning for you," he said, "and you'd best take it to heart. You'll be getting no second chances."

Mandeville paused at the door, balking when the guards would have pushed him through. "You may be sure," he said to Stephen, "that I will remember."

Once Mandeville was gone, Stephen took Matilda's hand and steered her toward the settle. "A pity Henry was not here to see that," he said, surprising them all, for he did not often express a yearning for his brother's company.

But the bishop had made possible Geoffrey de Mandeville's downfall, and Stephen was grateful. In a maneuver as guileful as it was adroit, Henry had contrived to have the hostile Bishop of Ely charged with Church irregularities, thus compelling him to journey to Rome to defend himself. With the Bishop of Ely absent from England, Stephen no longer needed Mandeville to keep peace in Bishop Nigel's Fenlands, and he'd at last been able to punish the earl as he deserved.

The reckoning had been no less gratifying for being so belated, and Stephen knew his brother would have enjoyed it immensely. But Henry, too, was now on the way to Rome, seeking to persuade the new Pope to reappoint him as a papal legate.

An even more unlikely source now echoed Stephen's regrets. "I wish the bishop were here, too," William de Ypres said, "for I'd wager that he'd have agreed with me—that Geoffrey de Mandeville ought not to have seen the light of day again in this lifetime."

"Are you still fretting about that, Will?"

"I am, my liege. I know you think you've pulled his fangs by taking the Tower and his strongholds away from him. But a defanged snake is still a snake, and my experience says you kill it when you can; you do not let it slither away just because all the other snakes are pleading for mercy."

Stephen slanted an amused glance in the Fleming's direction. "I do not think my barons would like your calling them snakes, Will—scales and forked tongues notwithstanding!"

"I am not jesting, my lord king. Why do you think Hugh Bigod and the others were so keen to speak up for Mandeville? You think any of that lot would truly care if you hanged him higher than Haman? They do not want you to punish Mandeville too harshly because they fear that the next time, it might be one of them whose double-dealing comes to light."

"Your view of mankind is bleak enough to disturb even the Devil," Stephen joked. "I am not denying that there is some truth in what you say; even Mandeville's Vere and Clare kindred do not seem overly fond of him. And I'll not deny, either, that they get downright disquieted at the prospect of one of their own being treated like any other felon or brigand. But no man ever died from the bite of a toothless snake, Will. What trouble could he stir up now? He cannot go crawling off to Maude, not after his betrayal at Winchester. That lady is far less forgiving than I am, and all of Christendom well knows it!"

"I cannot argue with anything you've said," Ypres admitted. "I can only tell you that when I first learned to hunt, I was taught that if you go after dangerous prey—like wild boar—you never strike unless you are sure your blow can kill."

"Sometimes it is enough," Matilda interjected, "for a blow to maim, Willem," and the Fleming did not demur. But neither was he convinced, and because they knew that, the disgraced earl's presence seemed to linger on in their midst, long after he'd been returned to his prison cell.

NATURE that year was unrelenting. An arid, sweltering summer had brought a poor harvest to a land already ravaged by four years of war, and to add to the miseries of the English people, winter came early. Even for November, the weather was unusually wretched: day after day of icy downpours, gusting winds, and sleet. By early December, the first snow of the season had blanketed half the country, and Annora was thankful when the walls of Lincoln at last came into view, for there a hot meal, a soft bed, and a lover's embrace awaited her.

RANULF had been awake since dawn, cocooned in coverlets, blissfully content to lie abed on this frigid December morn, watching the young woman asleep in his arms. It was easy to pretend they were snowbound, that the world beyond the boundaries of his chamber did not exist, easy to convince himself that their love affair was a secret from even the castle servants, for Annora's bed was in Maud's chamber and who but Maud would know where she really slept? It was always easy to hold on to his hopes while holding on to Annora, too. It was even possible to forget the living, breathing impediment to their union, Annora's husband—almost.

Annora stirred eventually, giving him a sleepy smile. "I love waking up with you," she murmured, leaning over to claim a kiss. "But I almost did not get to come, for Gervase was uneasy about my being out on the roads, even with Maud's escort."

Ranulf frowned; any mention of her husband, however fleeting or casual, was sure to sour his mood. "Because of Geoffrey de Mandeville's arrest?" he asked, and when she nodded, he drew her in against him, propping pillows behind their heads.

"It is passing strange, Annora. Stephen reached manhood at my father's court, had ample opportunities to learn the lessons of kingship from a master. Whatever his other failings, Papa understood the uses and perceptions of power, and his mistakes were few, indeed. He knew how to handle men, whereas Stephen . . . with the best will in the world, he just lurches from one blunder to another."

"Because he arrested Mandeville at his court, the way he did with the Bishops of Ely, Salisbury, and Lincoln? I grant you that does make him a dubious host," Annora teased, "but why is that so damaging to his kingship?"

"Because it makes men think he cannot be trusted, because it makes him look weak—"

"Be fair, Ranulf! No one—not even your sister—could fault Stephen's courage."

"Nor do I. I said men think him a weak king, not a cowardly one. I am not saying that Mandeville did not deserve to be arrested, but there was something sly about the way it was done. That might not matter if men respected Stephen as they did my father. But they do not, Annora, for they do not fear him . . . and fear and respect are horns on the same goat."

Annora was rapidly regretting ever having brought the topic up, for she had no interest in hearing Ranulf hold forth upon the flaws in Stephen's kingship; she got enough of that from her husband, who was increasingly disillusioned with his king's failure to end the war. "Can we not talk of something besides politics? I would much rather hear about the doings in Winchester, for," she added hopefully, "was there not some sort of scandal involved?"

The recent calamity in Winchester was a sore subject with all of Maude's partisans. But Ranulf knew how much Annora loved gossip, and so he overcame his reluctance, told her the rather sad and sordid story of William Pont de l'Arche, his young, fickle wife, and the Flemish mercenary, Robert Fitz Hildebrand. The former castellan of Winchester's royal castle had taken advantage of the Wilton debacle to regain control of the stronghold, and then appealed to Maude and Robert for aid. They'd dispatched Hildebrand—to their eternal regret—for welcomed as an ally by William Pont de l'Arche, he'd promptly set about seducing the latter's wife, and with her connivance, his men overpowered the castle garrison, cast the cuckolded husband into his own dungeon, and then struck a deal with the bishop and Stephen. All in all, it was a sorry tale, a deplorable commentary upon the way this war was unraveling the country's moral fabric, and Annora found it highly entertaining.

"How do you know this Robert Fitz Hildebrand seduced the castellan's wife? Mayhap she was the one seduced him," she suggested impishly, and then demonstrated that she was not lacking in seduction skills herself. They kissed and rolled, laughing, to the very edge of the bed, where they kissed again. But then Annora bolted upright and let out a piercing scream. "A rat! Ranulf, a rat bit my hair!"

As he started to look, she grabbed his arm. "Wait—get your sword first!" she insisted, and then, indignantly, "Ranulf! Why are you laughing?"

"Because," he said, "you're about to meet a rare Norse rat," and she peered cautiously over the edge of the bed, frowning at sight of the dog looking gravely back at her.

"I knew no rat would dare venture into the chamber with Loth here. He's the best hunter of Shadow's sons. I once saw him take down a deer all by himself," Ranulf bragged, reaching out to ruffle the dyrehund's thick fur. "When your hair swung down, he probably thought you were playing with him."

"Tell him, please, that I was playing with you, and three are not wanted in this game." Annora frowned again; she liked dogs, but there was something unnerving about this one's unblinking stare. "What did you call him—Loth? Wherever did you get an outlandish name like that?"

She was at once sorry she'd asked, for she'd unwittingly given Ranulf an opportunity to expound upon one of his more peculiar passions—his love of reading. It was called *The History of the Kings of Britain*, he informed her, written by an Augustinian canon named Geoffrey of Monmouth, and dedicated to Robert. The book was the most remarkable one he'd ever read, tracing English history back through the ages. He'd especially fancied the story of Arthur, King of the Britons, the people known today as the Welsh. He'd gotten Loth's name from the book, he explained; Loth was Arthur's brother-in-law, and with Arthur's help, he'd become King of Norway. So what better name for a Norwegian dyrehund?

Annora agreed politely that Loth was indeed an inspired choice, only half listening, for she neither shared nor understood Ranulf's enthusiasm for books. Her brothers had been taught to read and write—against their will—for her father had an almost monkish respect for education. When she'd wanted to learn, too, jealously intent upon following in her brothers' footsteps, he'd indulged her, as always, even though their priest had insisted that women had no need for worldly knowledge. She'd soon lost interest, would not have persevered had Ranulf not come into her life when he did, Ranulf who truly took pride in being able to wield a pen like a common clerk. Now, of course, Annora was thankful for her education, scanty as it was, for her rudimentary skills enabled her to write to Ranulf and to read his letters. But as he continued to extol the virtues of this Geoffrey of Monmouth's book with its oddly named heroes—Brutus, Arthur, Merlin, Loth—her eyes glazed over and her jaw began to ache from the yawns she was suppressing.

Not wanting Ranulf to know he was boring her, she took diversionary measures, with such success that they soon attracted Loth's attention. Puzzled and protective, the big dog rose to his feet, head cocked to the side as he tried to make sense of the strange noises coming from the bed, not moving away until he had satisfied himself that all this sudden thrashing about did not put his master in peril.

RANULF and Annora's idyllic stay at Lincoln Castle came to an abrupt end the next day with the unexpected arrival of Maud's husband. Their unease was soon dissipated, though, for it was apparent that Chester had no recollection of ever having met Annora before. Ranulf, of course, he did remember, greeting the younger man with a caustic "You here again? It is well that you are Maud's uncle or else I might start wondering why you seem to be underfoot all the time." But the insult was offhand; he had weightier matters on his mind than baiting Ranulf. "Set the servants to packing what you need," he instructed his wife, "for I am taking you back to Cheshire, and I want to depart on the morrow."

Ranulf and Annora were dismayed, Maud irked. "Why?" she demanded, and Chester scowled.

"It ought to be enough for you that I say so." His complaint was perfunctory, though, for he was in suspiciously high spirits. Maud regarded him warily, knowing from past experience that he was never so cheerful as when contemplating the troubles of others. And indeed, his black eyes were agleam with the perverse pleasure that people so often take in being the bearer of bad news. "Like ancient Egypt, we have a plague loosed upon us," he declared dramatically. "Geoffrey de Mandeville has rebelled."

His revelation was fully as explosive as he'd hoped, and he found himself fending off questions faster than arrows. "If you'll all stop talking at once," he protested, "I'll tell you what I know. Mandeville took advantage of Bishop Nigel's absence to seize the Isle of Ely and capture Aldreth Castle. He then advanced upon Ramsey, drove the monks out, and took over their abbey."

"Do you truly think he'd dare to lay siege to Lincoln Castle, Randolph?" Maud asked skeptically and he shook his head.

"Not likely. But until Stephen tracks the whoreson down, there'll be a lot of bodies found floating in the Fens. It is an outlaw's Eden, a murky, deadly maze of salt marshes and quagmires and bogs. If Stephen goes in after Mandeville, he'll never come out," Chester predicted and smiled at the thought.

"Well, I am flattered," Maud murmured, half mockingly, half flirtatiously, "that you were so concerned about my safety."

"No one takes what is mine," he said, "be it a lamb, a wife, a sack of flour from my mill, a felled tree from my woods. Let Mandeville steal and plunder all he pleases on his way to Hell, but if he makes me his enemy, he is an even greater fool than Stephen. No, lass, better you should keep to Cheshire and away from the Fens. Until Mandeville's body is rotting on a gallows for all to see what befalls rebels, there will be no peace in these parts, nothing but blood and tears and the wailing of widows."

It was a phrase that seemed to echo out of Scriptures, trailing a whiff of fire and brimstone. But what startled Ranulf was not that Chester was prophesying ruin and perdition, it was that he appeared to relish the prospect. Ranulf felt repelled when he realized why: that the Earl of Chester saw Geoffrey de Mandeville's mad, doomed rebellion as an opportunity in bloody guise, a chance to set his own snares and pursue his own prey while Stephen hunted in the Fens.

THE next day, Chester and the women departed at first light with a formidable armed escort. But Ranulf was not among them, for a messenger had arrived soon after Chester did, bearing urgent word for Annora. Her husband had heard, too, of Mandeville's rebellion, and Lincoln was too close to the Fenlands for his peace of mind. If the Countess of Chester would be good enough to provide Annora with an escort again, Gervase would meet her along the route. Maud dispatched a courier to let Gervase Fitz Clement know that she and Annora would be heading west in the earl's company, suggesting that they rendezvous at Coventry. Gervase's letter vexed Ranulf even more than his disappointment at having their tryst cut so short. It was as if the man had reached across the miles to claim Annora as his own, and he had to stand aside and let it happen.

Nor could he accompany them on their westward journey, for he dared not risk Gervase's learning that he'd been in Annora's company. Even the most complacent, trusting husband would not accept "happenchance" as the explanation upon finding his wife with the man she'd been pledged to wed.

Annora and Maud were both uneasy about his striking out on his own, but Ranulf had a more potent armor than his chain-mail hauberk—the invincibility of youth—and he'd assured them that he'd keep to the main roads, take no needless risks, and send word straightaway upon his safe arrival at Devizes. He set out the day after their departure, taking the Fosse Way toward Newark. There he would follow the road south to Grantham, where he would swing off onto the cross-country road that would take him through Leicester, Coventry, and on to Gloucester.

The roads were even worse than he'd expected, for temperatures had plunged and treacherous ice patches were not always noticeable until it was too late. It had taken Ranulf a full day to travel the fourteen miles to Newark, and as he left the town behind the following morning, the sky was overcast, as leaden and bleak as his mood. More snow seemed in the offing, but he hoped he'd be able to reach Grantham before the weather turned truly foul.

Even in winter, there should have been travelers on the road, but it was virtually deserted; he covered more than five miles without seeing another soul. Loth had ranged off into the bushes, having caught an enticing scent, and Ranulf halted his palfrey, giving it a rest until the dog returned. Gazing at the empty stretch of road, he found himself worrying just how serious this rebellion of Geoffrey de Mandeville's was. Fear was clearly on the prowl.

He was not sure at first what he'd heard, and he tilted his head, listening intently. It came again and this time he had no doubts—it was a scream. Turning his stallion about, he followed the sound into a copse of trees off to the side of the road.

He came out onto a frozen meadow, where a hunt was on. The quarry, though, was not deer or rabbit. Two men were trying to run down a young girl. There was a second child, too, but the men had no interest in him, and when he slipped on the ice and fell, they veered around him, continuing their pursuit of the girl. She'd been attempting to reach the woods, but the snow was hampering her flight, and they were gaining on her with every stride. When she risked a glance over her shoulder, she dodged suddenly, making a desperate detour out onto the ice of a small pond. The men halted at the edge, cursing, for the ice would never support their weight; as light as the girl was, the surface was creaking ominously under her feet. The men swore again, for by the time they circled the pond, she would have gotten into the woods, where it would not be so easy to find her.

At first glimpse, one of the men bore a superficial resemblance to Gilbert, for he was a redhead, too, and tall enough to look down upon most men. His partner in crime was lean and spare and dark, lacking either the redhead's brawn or his conspicuous coloring. But he was the dominant of the two. As the redhead continued to stand at the pond's edge, thwarted and fuming, he swung back toward the boy.

The child was just getting to his feet. Pouncing upon him before he could scramble out of reach, the man stopped his struggles with a blow across the face and then crooked his arm around the boy's throat, shouting, "You'd best come back, girl, or I'll snap the whelp's neck in two, by God, I will!"

The girl looked back and froze on the ice, steps away from safety. The boy squirmed, bit the hand clamped over his mouth, and cried, "Run, Jennet!" He paid a price in pain for that, kicked futilely as he was snatched off his feet, and then gagged as the pressure on his windpipe increased. The girl's face was contorted in horror; she seemed unable to move, and the man grinned, sensing victory.

"If you care about the cub," he warned, "you get over here now!" Jerking his head toward his partner, he said, "Go around the pond so you can head her off if she runs for the woods."

The redhead was accustomed to taking orders and was starting to obey when he caught movement from the corner of his eye. He turned and his jaw dropped open. He wasted several precious seconds, staring, eyes wide and mouth ajar, as Ranulf's stallion raced toward them, before blurting out, "Holy Jesus! Ned, behind you!"

The man called Ned was of a different mettle than the befuddled redhead. The shock of seeing an armed knight bearing down upon him must have been considerable. But his reaction was instantaneous. Without hesitation, he threw the child into the path of the oncoming stallion.

Ranulf yanked on the reins and the palfrey swerved, with not a foot to spare. But the horse's sudden plunge carried it onto a glaze of iced-over snow. It skidded, started to slide sideways, and went down.

Ranulf flung himself from the saddle, and was fortunate enough to land in a snowdrift. For a heart-stopping moment, he could not see where his sword had fallen, then spotted it ensnared in a hawthorn hedge. The prickly spines inflicted deep scratches upon his wrist and hand as he snatched it out, but that was the least of his problems, for the men were almost upon him.

He was surprised at their boldness, for he'd had a few encounters with brigands of their ilk, and they invariably backed off from any confrontation with a knight, preferring easier prey. They may have been enraged over the loss of the girl, for both children had seized their chance to flee. Or they may have been hungry enough for Ranulf's horse and trappings to forget caution. Whatever their motivation, they were closing in fast, and he got a second, nasty surprise, for they were better-armed than he'd expected. The big redhead had a rough-hewn wooden club studded with nails, and Ned had a sword, an unusual weapon for one of these outcast, masterless men.

It was a basic tenet of faith with men of Ranulf's class that a knight, trained in the ways of war since boyhood, could easily vanquish lesser foes, as much a belief in the superiority of blood and breeding as in the benefits of battle lore and killing competence. Ranulf had accepted this comforting conviction, too, but no one seemed to have told his assailants that they were inferior adversaries.

The thrust he aimed at Ned should have been lethal. It never connected, though, for Ned parried the blow with startling skill; whatever he was now, he'd once been a soldier, for no man handled a sword like that by chance. Moreover, they understood the concept of teamwork, and only Ranulf's quick reflexes saved him when they bore in again. Fending off Ned, he whirled just as the redhead swung his club. Unlike them, he had the protection of chain mail, but had that blow landed, it would have broken bones. Instead, he was the one to draw blood. Not a mortal wound, but the redhead yelped and sprang backward so hastily that he nearly fell. Ranulf could not take advantage of it, though, for the other man was circling, ready to strike.

They'd taken his measure, too, were more wary now. The redhead, in particular, seemed leery of getting within range of Ranulf's blade. They backed off a bit, talking strategy, not realizing that Ranulf understood them, for unlike many of Norman-French descent, he spoke English—not well, but enough to get by. While they were planning their next move, he retreated slowly toward the closest tree. He was ready for them when they attacked again, and they were forced to pull back, cursing and bleeding. But he was bleeding, too, and his fall had done more damage than he'd first thought, for his knee was stiffening up, slowing him down. Panting, his sword poised for their next assault, he realized that he was in the fight of his life and the odds were not in his favor.

The children were nowhere to be seen, probably long gone—if they were wise. His horse was not in view, either, and the distant road was still deserted—not that any passersby were likely to have intervened. But he saw then that there was one about to join the fray, for Loth had backtracked to find him, and was coming now at a run, a dark streak against the snow, silent and swift, hackles up, as fearful and blessed a sight as ever filled Ranulf's eyes.

The dog made no sound, but alerted by instinct, perhaps, the redhead started to turn just as Loth launched his attack. The man yelled, but had no time to react, for the dyrehund was already upon him. As the animal leapt at him, he recoiled, slipped on the ice, and went over backward. His next scream was one of pain, for Loth had clamped his powerful jaws upon the redhead's thigh, shaking the man's body to and fro as if he were prey, as Ranulf had seen him attack deer.

When the redhead shrieked, Ned whirled in his direction. It was a natural reaction, but one that doomed him, for in the brief moment that he was distracted by the dog, Ranulf lunged, burying his blade in the other man's back. Ned's knees buckled. Ranulf's second thrust all but decapitated him, and blood spurted out like a crimson fountain, splattering Ranulf with gore.

Swinging his sword up, Ranulf turned then to aid Loth, but the dog had no need of assistance. The redhead's screams were mingling now with the dyrehund's fierce, guttural growling. He'd dropped his club when he'd fallen, and had tried then to kick the dog away. Loth released his hold upon the man's mangled thigh and, seizing an ankle, began a promising effort to cripple his quarry. Unable to break free of those ravening jaws and razor teeth, the man was writhing in pain as he desperately tried to reach his club, which lay tantalizingly close, but just beyond his groping fingers.

Ranulf kicked the club into the bushes, then reached down and dragged Loth off. It took the man a moment to realize he was no longer under attack, and he continued to claw the snow for his club, kicking feebly at a dog who was no longer there. Ranulf was having trouble restraining Loth; even when he pulled the dyrehund up onto his hind legs, the dog did not desist his struggles, choking and snarling as he fought to get back to his kill. The redhead had now scrabbled to his hands and knees, his breath coming in wheezing, gasping sobs. Somehow he lurched to his feet, screaming anew as pain jolted through his crushed ankle. Hobbling, stumbling, weaving like a drunkard, he fled in terror, leaving a blotched and bloody trail across the snow. He'd not get far; Ranulf had seen the terrible gaping wound, the shredded flesh of the man's thigh.

Reaction now set in and Ranulf started to shake. Still clutching Loth's collar, he sank to his knees. Blood was everywhere, splashed across the front of his hauberk, caking his boots. The churned-up snow was bright red, and Loth's silver muzzle seemed to have been dipped in scarlet; so had his chest. The dyrehund was trembling, too; he whimpered and nuzzled Ranulf, smearing blood across Ranulf's cheek and into his beard. Ranulf pulled the dog closer, wrapped his arms around Loth's heaving sides, and held tight.

When Loth growled, Ranulf raised his head, automatically reaching again for his sword hilt. The boy was standing ten feet away, poised to take flight. Ranulf guessed he was about nine or so, but small for his age, reed-thin and meagre. He seemed all eyes; they dominated the pinched little face, a striking shade of blue-green, glassy with shock. He looked at the body, swallowed, and asked, "Is he dead?"

"Yes."

"And the other . . . the one the dog bit?"

"Most likely he'll bleed to death," Ranulf said honestly.

The boy was quiet for a moment, staring at Loth. "Good," he said, and then recoiled when Ranulf seemed about to rise. He did not go far, though, backing off a few more prudent feet. "Are you bad hurt?"

"No, not bad," Ranuld said and waited, feeling as if he were trying to tame some wild, woodland creature, ready to bolt at any moment.

"Why?" the child asked suddenly. "Why did you help us?"

Ranulf considered several different answers, and then twitched a shoulder in a half-shrug. "I had nothing better to do."

The boy's eyes widened even further. But he seemed to take reassurance from the joke, for he slowly edged closer. "I am Simon," he said solemnly, and after Ranulf introduced himself and Loth with equal gravity, Simon held out a small fist for the dyrehund to sniff. In view of what the child had watched the dog do, Ranulf thought that was a commendable act of courage. Simon peered intently into Ranulf's face, then glanced back at Loth. "We know where your horse is," he said unexpectedly. "It ran into the woods and its reins snagged on a bush. My sister found it."

Ranulf wondered why they hadn't tried to catch the stallion for themselves, and then realized that to these children, a horse would be as exotic an animal as an elephant. He still did not know why they were out here alone, but did not doubt that he was looking at the sort of poverty he'd rarely encountered; Simon's clothes were so ragged they showed glimpses of skin and his worn leather shoes were held together with cord. Getting stiffly to his feet, Ranulf said, "Can you take me to the horse?"

The child nodded, but hesitated. No longer meeting Ranulf's gaze, he asked, "Do you have any food?" Adding quickly, "Not for me, for Jennet."

"Yes, I do," Ranulf said, as matter-of-factly as he could manage, and with the child hovering just out of reach, he limped across the meadow toward the woods. Even if he'd had a shovel, the ground was too hard to dig a grave, so he left the body of the outlaw where it had fallen. Simon seemed to share his view that the man did not deserve a Christian burial, for the boy did not glance back, either.

Simon's sister looked so like him that they might have been twins if not for the age difference; she had the same vivid blue-green eyes, the same light hair of an indeterminate shade that was either a pale ash-brown or a dirt-darkened blonde, and like him, she bore the signs of malnourishment. Ranulf imagined she was about thirteen, yet she was smaller than his nephew Henry, so frail and wan that he ached for her. More than the boy, she comprehended the full horror of what they'd been spared, and he was impressed by the bravery she'd shown in staying to watch the outcome of the battle.

He had bread and cheese in his saddlebag, and they fell upon it ravenously, with a hunger he'd never known. He waited until they'd devoured every crumb before asking what they were doing by themselves on the Newark-Grantham Road, and got an answer that dismayed him. They were on their way, Simon confided, to their uncle Jonas in Cantebrigge.

"God Almighty, you cannot be serious! Not only is Cantebrigge at least eighty miles from here, but it is less than twenty miles from Ramsey Abbey, which has been seized by rebels. You cannot go to Cantebrigge!"

Anxiety had given his voice an angry edge, and the children reacted with immediate fear, backing away. "We are going to Cantebrigge," Jennet cried, "we must! And we will, we will go!"

Ranulf hastily changed his tack. "I did not mean to shout," he said soothingly, while rapidly reviewing his options. There was another ten miles or more to Grantham; Newark was less than five. "Speaking for myself, I've never felt so battered or bone-weary. Luckily, I know an inn in Newark where we can get a decent meal and mayhap even a bone for Loth."

They conferred together, speaking too swiftly for him to catch their words; his grasp of English did not allow for nuances or even slurred speech. When they turned back, Simon came forward until he was close enough to be grabbed; it was, Ranulf recognized, a declaration of trust. "We've nothing better to do," he said, with what was almost a smile.

RANULF had already attracted attention at the inn the preceding night: a lone knight and a dog the likes of which none had seen before. When he and the wolf-dog returned, drenched in gore and with two beggar children in tow, he created a sensation. But their curiosity was to remain unsatisfied, for he offered no explanations and all that blood somehow discouraged prying.

The innkeeper was as amazed by Ranulf's request for two rooms as he was by his alarming appearance. A private room was an almost unheard-of luxury, except for the highborn; it was usual for strangers to share not only a chamber but a bed, and it seemed utterly bizarre to him that Ranulf should want to squander a room upon bedraggled urchins who ought to be bedding down out in the stables with the lord's fine palfrey. He confined himself, though, to a timid protest, which Ranulf ignored, for he thought Jennet would be fearful sharing a room with anyone but her brother, so soon after the thwarted rape.

As much as he needed a bath, Ranulf knew better than to ask for one, not in a small, shabby inn in the midst of winter. The innkeeper was able to scrounge up some soft soap of mutton fat and wood ash, and he washed himself as best he could with cold water and a burlap towel. When the children crept downstairs to join him in front of the fire, they were still filthy, but so unself-conscious that he realized bathing was for them done only in summer, if at all. They'd shared their lives with him by now, offered up in hesitant bits and pieces as they'd made the slow trek back to Newark, and the more they'd told him, the less he'd wanted to know.

Simon and Jennet were children of the Fens, having lived all of their brief years in the bleak isolation of the Lincolnshire salt marshes, more cloistered than in any convent. Their mother was long dead and Jennet had insisted so vehemently that their father was a "free man" that Ranulf knew he must have been a runaway villein, a serf bound to the land. Their world had been a wattle-and-daub hut out in the Fens; all they could say was that it had been north of Sleaford. There they'd dwelled, just this side of starvation, their father fishing for eels and sometimes taking water reeds into Sleaford to sell for roof thatching. But he'd not taken them; until Ranulf had shepherded them through Newark's streets, they'd never seen a town. As far as he could tell, the only people they ever saw were other fishermen and their families, mayhap an occasional peddler—until the day the outlaws came.

They took turns relating the horrors of that day, with the detached composure of emotional exhaustion. How their father had sensed danger and sent them off into the marsh to hide. How they'd waited out in the wind-ripped bogs for their father to fetch them, huddling together for warmth as gulls shrieked overhead and night came on. How they'd seen the smoke, and when they dared to venture back, they found their home in flames and their father's body sprawled by the hen roost. The hens were gone, of course, as was the pig that was their prized possession, and every scrap of food that Jennet had salted away and stored for winter. And whatever the brigands hadn't carried off had been burned in the fire.

They did not seem to know how long they'd lingered in the ruins, and Ranulf did not press them; better such memories were mercifully blurred. They'd buried their father and eventually hunger had driven them to undertake this lunatic quest of theirs—to seek out their only kinsman, their father's younger brother Jonas, plying his trade as a tanner in the distant town of Cantebrigge.

Stretching his legs toward the fire, Ranulf massaged his aching knee and watched the children as they ate their fill, probably for the first time in their lives. It was a Wednesday fast day, but he'd made a conscious decision to violate the prohibition against eating flesh; he could always do penance once he got back to his own world. Now it seemed more important to feed Simon and Jennet the best meal he could, and the innkeeper had served up heaping portions of salted pork, a thick pottage of peas and beans, and hot, flat cakes of newly baked bread, marked with Christ's Cross. To Ranulf, it was poor fare, and he ended up sharing most of it with Loth. But Simon and Jennet savored every mouthful, scorning spoons and scooping the food up with their fingers, as if expecting to have their trenchers snatched away at any moment. And Ranulf learned more that night about hunger and need than in all of his twenty-five years.

What would become of them? How could they hope to reach Cantebrigge? And if by God's Grace, they somehow did, what if this uncle of theirs was not there? They'd never seen the man, knew only what their father had told them, that soon after Simon's birth, a peddler had brought them a message from Jonas, saying he'd settled in Cantebrigge.

That confirmed Ranulf's suspicions: two brothers fleeing serfdom, one hiding out in the Fens, the other taking the bolder way, for an escaped villein could claim his freedom if he lived in a chartered borough for a year and a day. It was a pitiful family history, an unwanted glimpse into a world almost as alien to Ranulf as Cathay. But like it or not, he was caught up now in this hopeless odyssey of Abel the eelman's children. In an unusually morose and pessimistic mood, he wondered how many Simons and Jennets would be lost to the furies unleashed by Geoffrey de Mandeville's rebellion.

That was mere speculation, though. These ragged, half-starved orphans were all too real, flesh-and-blood burdens, weighing ever more heavily upon his peace of mind. All through supper, he'd been silently debating his conscience, seeking to convince himself that he'd done what he could, that he was not responsible for them. But when the meal was done, he heard himself saying reluctantly, "If you are truly set upon going to Cantebrigge, I'll take you."

RANULF had been surprised and vexed that the children had not shown more enthusiasm for his offer. It was no small sacrifice he was making, after all, for he had more to fear than Mandeville's brigands; Cantebrigge was the king's borough, and so were most of the towns they'd be passing through on their way south. But the children's acceptance had been subdued, even wary, and he'd gone off to bed in a thoroughly bad humor. In the morning, though, he'd awakened to find Simon and Jennet asleep on the floor by his bed.

This journey was likely to be as expensive as it was dangerous; it was already draining his purse. He might have to stop at Wallingford on his way west and borrow money from Brien, for he'd had to buy a mule for the children, and mantles, too, for their cloaks might better serve as kitchen rags. He'd already decided that if—God Willing—he ever got home again, this Cantebrigge detour was a secret he'd share only with Loth, for he well knew that his misguided chivalry would make him a laughingstock. Who would ever understand why he'd gone to so much trouble for the children of a runaway serf?

Their pilgrimage was an excruciatingly slow one. The children were fearful at first of riding the mule, and even though they were traveling along the Great North Road, it was rough going, pitted and rutted by the winter weather. Moreover, daylight hours were dwindling away, dusk infiltrating now by late afternoon. and in every town or village, they ran into rumors of Mandeville's depredations. Raiding throughout Cambridgeshire, up into Lincolnshire, he was spreading terror and laying waste to shires already suffering from famine. He'd gathered together a motley army: his own vassals and tenants, unemployed men-at-arms, bandits lured to his banner by his promises of money and livestock and women, all for the taking. Ranulf heard stories of pilgrims ambushed, merchants robbed, villages plundered and burned. How much of it was true and how much was hearsay, he had no way of knowing.

At Grantham, they were forced to stay over an extra day, waiting out a freezing rainstorm. When they finally reached Stanford, they were delayed again, this time to find a barber for Simon. The boy's jaw had begun to swell, for he had a rotted tooth which should have been pulled months ago. He bore the pain in good spirits, though, and carefully tucked away his yanked tooth as a keepsake. In truth, both children were starting to enjoy their first foray into the world beyond the Fens. They did not realize their danger, so utterly had they come to trust in Ranulf's protection, and they were fascinated by the castle at Stanford, the timbered town houses of two stories, their first market. Every day brought new and strange sights, and each night an inn awaited them, where there'd be a warm fire and all the food they could eat and then a safe night's sleep on pallets in Ranulf's chamber. Ranulf marveled at first that it took so little to content them, until he realized that those who'd had nothing expected nothing, and he began to worry that he was unwittingly teaching them an unfair lesson—to hunger for more than they could ever hope to get.

By their second week on the road, they were in Cambridgeshire, and much too close to Ramsey's captured abbey for Ranulf's comfort. But at Huntingdon, they had a stroke of luck, for they were able to join a caravan of merchants bound for London to sell their wares, men who'd banded together for protection against Mandeville's cutthroats and their own fears. They were more than happy to have Ranulf ride with them; the sword at his hip guaranteed his welcome.

They parted company at Caxton, the merchants continuing south, Ranulf and the children turning off onto the Cantebrigge Road. There were fewer than ten miles to go now, and his relief was considerable, for he'd heard a very disturbing tale from some of the London-bound merchants—that Mandeville had raided the town of St Ives. Ranulf found that hard to believe, for St Ives was a prosperous borough, site of a famed fair. Surely Mandeville did not have enough men or enough nerve to attack a town? Rumor or not, though, it was unsettling, and he was grateful that he'd soon be able to turn his young charges over to their proper guardian. What he would do if the uncle could not be found, he did not know, for that was a dilemma he'd resolutely refused to address, preferring to fall back upon his innate optimism.

But as those last few miles began to ebb away, so did Ranulf's confidence, and he found himself struggling with a sudden sense of foreboding, wondering what they would find in Cantebrigge. Yet he never expected what awaited them around a bend in the road: a sky full of smoke.

Ordering the children to hide themselves until he returned, he began a cautious investigation. It was almost dusk, but to the east, the sky glowed, and within a mile, he knew why—the city of Cantebrigge was afire. The first structure to come into sight were the stone walls of the castle, and then the rippling grey surface of the River Granta. The town lay just beyond, wreathed in smoke. Ranulf had been in Cantebrigge before, during his father's reign, and as he looked now upon the charred and blackened shell off to his right, he knew it had once been a church, even remembered the name: All Saints by the Castle. Reining in his stallion, he stared at the ruins in shocked silence. All Saints was well away from the town; flames could not have spread that far. To have burned, the church must have been deliberately torched.

He was close enough now to see people wandering about, and it was like being back in the smoldering streets of Winchester, watching as dazed survivors stumbled about aimlessly in the wreckage of their lives. Loth growled softly, looking up at Ranulf with anxious eyes, for the scent of death was in the air. But it was then that Ranulf noticed the castle portcullis was up and the gates ajar. So it was over. The dying was done; the grieving only just begun.

Ranulf did not want to go any farther, to see any more. There would be bodies in the rubble of those smoking houses and looted shops. There would be bloodstains in the streets, but no screaming or wailing, not yet. When grief came so suddenly, the bereft were silent, too stunned for tears. He'd been at Lincoln, at Winchester, at Oxford. He knew what he'd find.

A slight, stooped figure was trudging up the street toward the castle, his priest's cassock befouled with blood. He seemed unaware of his surroundings, but as he passed Ranulf, his step slowed and his aged eyes focused upon the younger man's face. Recognition was mutual, and as dangerous as it might be, Ranulf did not deny it. Instead, he swung from the saddle to stand in the street beside the old man, chaplain for more years than he could remember at his father's royal castle of Cantebrigge. "Father Osmond," he said, "are you injured?"

"The blood is not mine." If the priest was surprised to encounter the old king's son in a town under Stephen's dominion, he gave no sign of it. "I never thought," he said, "to see such suffering, to see the innocents struck down in God's Sight. There was killing even in the churches, where people had fled for refuge."

He was far more feeble than Ranulf remembered, and he reached out, put a steadying hand on the priest's elbow. "When did this happen?"

"Last night. They came in the night like thieves, but they came to kill. Some of the people were able to get into the castle, but the others . . . the ones caught in their houses, their beds . . ." His mouth trembled; he had a priest's familiarity with death, but not like this.

"I looked upon evil, Lord Ranulf. We saw the Devil's work. They showed no mercy, forced householders to divulge where their valuables were hidden, then cut their throats. They plundered St Radegund's nunnery and raped honest women in front of their husbands. They deliberately burned churches and stole from God. They spared neither the young nor the old nor the weak, and their killing was wanton, done for the sport of it. And when they rode off, they took all our livestock and they loaded carts with their plunder and they carried off women, even some of the nuns. I know war and this was not war. Not even the infidel Saracens could be so cruel, so deserving of damnation . . ."

Ranulf, too, had thought he knew war. But never had he seen the sort of savagery the priest had just described. An outlaw army, composed of brigands and felons, the very dregs of the gutter, led by one who feared neither man nor God. And if he'd taken a different road, he and Jennet and Simon might have run right into them. "Who was it?" he said, already knowing what the priest would say.

"The Devil's spawn. That son of perdition, Geoffrey de Mandeville."

30

DEVIZES CASTLE, ENGLAND

January 1144

THE drawbridge was lowered at once for Ranulf, and by the time he'd dismounted, his squire was racing across the inner bailey. "Where have you been, my lord? We'd given up all hope of ever seeing you again!"

"I had my own doubts, too, Luke. But how did you know I was in trouble? I did not tell my sister when I'd be returning."

"The empress had a letter from the Countess of Chester. Lady Maud was uneasy, not having heard from you as promised. And when you missed Christmas, we knew something was wrong. The empress wanted to send men out to search for you, but we did not know where to begin. My lord . . . may I speak freely? I do not know why you go off on these mysterious journeys of yours, and it is obvious that you do not want me—or anyone else—to know. But I would take your secret to the grave, that I pledge upon my honour and hopes of salvation. In Stephen's England, life has become too cheap for a man to venture out alone."

Ranulf was touched and gave the younger man a quick smile, although he avoided making Luke any promises. "If you'll take our mounts into the stable," he said, "I'll get the children inside where they can thaw out." At that, Luke abandoned his polite pretense of ignoring his lord's unlikely traveling companions, but Ranulf deflected his curiosity with a murmured, "I'll tell you about it once I've seen my sister."

He led them toward the great hall, Simon and Jennet keeping so close to Ranulf that they were in danger of treading upon his heels. They'd almost reached the door when his nephew came bursting through it. "I knew you'd come back safe! But Mama has been fretting night and day over you, Uncle Ranulf, and she'll likely scorch your ears for scaring us so. Of course if it was me, I'd have gotten my rump blistered, so you'll be getting off easy!"

Ranulf laughed and ushered all three children into the hall. "Over to the hearth," he directed, before adding, "Harry, I want you to look after Simon and Jennet whilst I seek out your mother."

He'd become oddly protective of these orphans of the Fens, but he had no qualms now about entrusting them to Henry. His nephew had his share of swagger and was not one for backing down when challenged; in Bristol, he and Miles's youngest son, Mahel, had gone from being rivals to outright enemies after a rough-and-tumble game of hot cockles. But as much as Henry liked his own way, he did not take unfair advantage of his privileged position. As young as he was, he seemed to understand that it was no more sporting to bully a servant than it would be to shoot a nesting bird, and Ranulf had concluded that a child was indeed more than the sum of his parents, for he did not associate a sense of fair play with Geoffrey, nor with his sister, either, for all that he loved her.

"You be on your best behavior with them, Harry, for they've never been in a castle before. Nor do they speak any French."

"It is lucky then, that I've learned a little bit of English."

Ranulf was not deceived by the boy's offhand manner—he could recognize bragging in reverse when he saw it—and he made sure that his nephew got the praise he was craving. Turning then, to Simon and Jennet, he switched over to stilted English. "This is my nephew, the Lord Harry. He'll stay with you till I get back." They could not hide their dismay at being separated from him, even briefly, but he knew they'd do as he bade them; they were as trusting as Loth and far more obedient.

There was no need, though, to hunt for Maude. She was already rushing into the hall, a mantle hastily flung over her shoulders. "Ranulf, thank God! I thought you were dead, too!" A quick, convulsive hug; he could feel her trembling, her tension. She looked exhausted, her skin stretched as taut as her nerves, so pallid she might have just risen from a sickbed. Stepping back, she still held on to his arm, her fingers gripping hard enough to hurt. "Why were you visiting Maud in secret? And why in God's Name did you go off on your own like that? Where have you been?"

"Cantebrigge," he said simply, and she went even paler. Before she could speak, he drew her toward the hearth, appropriating a couple of chairs. "I know we've much to say to each other, and I am indeed sorry for worrying you. But first there is a story I must tell you, one I'd hoped to keep to myself. I brought back company—those two scared fledglings Harry has taken under his wing."

As concisely as possible, he related then his adventures since encountering Simon and Jennet on the Newark-Grantham Road. "We finally reached Cantebrigge," he concluded, "on the day after Mandeville's raid. The town was still smoldering; it was Winchester all over again. And I could find no one who'd even heard of Jonas the tanner. If he'd ever been there, he was long gone."

He grimaced in remembered frustration. "So . . . I took them back with me. What else could I do, Maude? They could never fend for themselves, would soon starve—if worse did not befall them. And the people of Cantebrigge had nothing to spare; the last thing the town needed was more orphans."

He was talking faster than usual, partly from embarrassment and partly to keep Maude from interrupting until he was done. So far she'd listened in silence, although she'd occasionally shaken her head at the risks he'd taken. "I thought," he said, "that we could ask the priests in Devizes and Bristol for help. They might know of a family willing to take Simon and Jennet in, mayhap one who'd lost a son—"

He stopped in surprise as Maude jumped to her feet. "I cannot talk about this," she said sharply, "not now!" And before Ranulf could react, she spun away from him, exiting the hall so rapidly that it was almost as if she were fleeing. Ranulf was nonplussed. He'd been braced for gibes and raillery, knowing full well that few would understand his compassion for a runaway serf's children. But he'd counted upon Maude to be more indulgent, if only because women were taught to be tolerant of male folly. The rebuff stung all the more, then, for being unexpected.

Staring after Maude, Ranulf started at the sound of "Uncle Ranulf," for he'd not noticed as Henry edged unobtrusively within eavesdropping range. The boy looked unhappy, much too mature for his years. "Mama is not angry with you," he said. "She has been grieving ever since we heard, and—"

"Jesú," Ranulf breathed, for his sister's words had suddenly come back to him, taking on a new and sinister significance. "I thought," she'd cried, "you were dead, too!" Ranulf started to speak, had to swallow first. "Who?" he asked hoarsely. "Who died, lad?"

"The Earl of Hereford."

"Miles?" Ranulf sank back in the chair he'd just vacated. "How? I did not know he was ailing."

"He was not. He was slain on Christmas Eve . . . by mischance. He'd gone hunting in Dean Forest, and one of his companions misfired an arrow. It hit him in the chest and he died there in the woods."

"What a meaningless way to die . . ." It occurred to Ranulf, then, that most deaths seemed meaningless these days; for what greater good had the citizens of Cantebrigge died? "May God forgive his earthly sins," Ranulf said softly. He'd never shared Maude's fondness for Miles. But the political ramifications of his death were far-reaching and dangerous. He'd been one of Maude's most powerful and steadfast supporters, one she could not afford to lose.

"Uncle Ranulf, there is more. Mama got a letter yesterday from my father. He wants me to come back home."

Ranulf sat upright. "And she agreed?" he asked, too surprised for discretion.

"Not at first. Not until I . . . I told her that I wanted to go." Henry's lashes swept down like shields, but not in time, and Ranulf felt a wrenching pang of pity for the boy. He wanted to assure Henry that missing his father was no cause for guilt, but he knew it was futile; in this war of tangled and torn loyalties, Henry's conflicted battlefield was his heart.

Simon and Jennet had trailed timidly after Henry, and Ranulf summoned them over. "You will be staying here for now," he said, and they nodded solemnly, for they never asked questions, their faith even stronger than their fear. No one had ever shown such utter confidence in him; it was both a great compliment and a great burden.

Leaving them with Henry, he started to go after Maude. He stopped, though, before he reached the door. He knew now what had sent her fleeing from the hall—his careless talk of "losing a son." She'd not thank him for following her. She was as shy of showing her pain in public as her ten-year-old son. But Harry would outgrow his emotional skittishness. For his sister, it was too late.

STEPHEN hastily gathered an army to put down Geoffrey de Mandeville's rebellion. But Mandeville refused to do battle and retreated deeper into the Fens. Stephen set about erecting castles in an attempt to contain the bloodshed. He then marched north in the hopes of catching the Earl of Chester's garrison off guard at Lincoln Castle.

For most of England, it was neither a happy nor a peaceful spring. Maude's partisans were still mourning Miles. Stephen's supporters were troubled by his failure to bring Geoffrey de Mandeville to swift, summary justice. In Yorkshire, the Earl of Chester was pillaging the lands of the rival Earl of York. And in the Fens, the killing continued.

BY May, the royal gardens at Westminster Palace were in bloom, and Constance was able to pick an armful of primroses and daisies and violets, intending to surprise her mother-in-law with the first bouquet of the season. But she was the one who got the surprise, for she found Matilda in tears. Constance froze, jolted by fear. Eustace had gone north with Stephen to Lincoln Castle, having persuaded his father that he was old enough, at fourteen, to witness his first siege. But it never even occurred to Constance that he might be in peril. Dropping the flowers, she ran toward the bed. "Maman, what is wrong? Nothing has happened to Papa Stephen?"

Matilda sat up, wiping away tears. "No, child, no. The last I heard from Stephen, he and Eustace were quite well, although sorely vexed because the siege was going so poorly."

Constance sighed with relief. She might loathe her husband, but she adored her in-laws, felt far closer to them than to her own parents. She'd been just eight when her father died; she remembered only a gross mountain of flesh, a man grown so corpulent that he could no longer ride a horse or fit onto a throne, known to the more irreverent of his subjects as Louis le Gros. Her mother had been a remote, detached figure, seldom seen and soon gone; after quarreling with her lively and willful young daughter-in-law, the dowager queen had conceded the field to Eleanor, withdrawing to her own dower estates and wedding again in unseemly haste. While Constance was fond of her brother, the French king, and dazzled by the siren he'd married, she'd been on the periphery of their hectic, whirlwind lives. She'd not learned what it was like to belong until she'd come as a child bride to this alien land of England.

Perching on the foot of the bed, she asked shyly, "Why then, are you so sad?"

"I had bad news this morn. The castle at Rouen surrendered to Geoffrey of Anjou on the 23rd of April."

Constance did not know what to say, for surely Matilda must have expected this; the city itself had yielded back in January, and all knew the castle would eventually fall, too. "I suppose," she ventured, "this means Lord Geoffrey will claim the duchy for himself?"

"He has already done so, Constance . . . and with the blessing and full consent of the French Crown."

"My brother has agreed to recognize him as duke? But . . . but why?"

"Because Geoffrey agreed in his turn to cede Gizors and the Vexin to Louis," Matilda said, truthfully but tactlessly. She at once regretted her candor, for Constance blushed deeply, as if she were the one shamed by her brother's diplomatic double-dealing.

"I . . . I am so sorry, Maman," she stammered, and Matilda hastily reached for her hand, giving it a reassuring pat.

"You have nothing to be sorry for, child. I am the one being foolish, for I knew this day was coming. I ought not to have let it disquiet me so. But this bodes ill for England, for any faltering hopes of peace. Even if Stephen were able to drive Maude and all her kith and kin into the sea, that would not end the war . . . not now. Too many of Stephen's barons have holdings in Normandy."

She did not elaborate, nor did she need to. Constance understood. With England and Normandy now severed, the English barons were confronted with a hard choice. If they recognized Geoffrey as their liege lord in Normandy, they risked having their English estates confiscated by

Stephen. But if they balked at acknowledging Geoffrey, that would place their Normandy lands in jeopardy. Loyalty to Stephen kept Matilda from admitting it, but Constance knew what she feared—that men would conclude it was more dangerous to antagonize Geoffrey than Stephen.

"Do not fret, Maman. Papa Stephen will win his war, for surely the Almighty must favor him over that shrewish woman and her accursed Angevin husband. Back in Paris, all knew the Angevin counts sprang from the Devil's loins. Papa Stephen will prevail, you'll see. He'll have a long and peaceful reign and . . . and by the time Eustace follows him to the throne, no one will even remember Maude's name."

She'd meant to offer comfort, but Matilda frowned and looked away, and Constance caught her breath, stunned by what she'd seen for an unguarded moment in her mother-in-law's eyes. She detested Eustace, and Matilda loved him, but they shared the same secret unease, the same unspoken doubts about what kind of king Eustace would be.

MAUDE had seen little of Robert and Ranulf that summer; they'd spent most of it in the saddle, chasing after Stephen. After some skirmishing around Malmesbury, Stephen had moved on to lay siege to the nearby castle at Tetbury. Robert and Miles's eldest son, Roger, had then swooped down upon Tetbury. But Stephen's outnumbered barons had refused to fight, and he'd broken off the siege, once again thwarting Robert's hopes of forcing a resolution upon the field of battle.

After the disappointment at Tetbury, they returned to Gloucester and Maude joined them there during the last week in September. As glad as she was to be reunited with her brothers, she found it strange to be at Gloucester Castle without Miles.

This was her first visit since Roger had inherited his father's earldom of Hereford, and he entertained Maude far more lavishly than Miles had ever done, which only underscored the differences between the brusque, frugal, pragmatic father and his extravagant, impulsive, fun-loving son. Roger was as quick-tempered as Miles, and like his father, he was fearless on the battlefield. He had inherited the same russet coloring, too, although he was handsomer than the rough-hewn, freckled Miles. But he lacked his father's mettle, the flinty force of character that had made Miles such a formidable ally, a man to be reckoned with. The better Maude got to know Roger, the more she liked him—and the more she missed Miles.

She also missed Rainald and Brien, for she'd seen neither one for months. Rainald was still in Cornwall, fighting a dogged, lonely battle to defend his imperiled earldom. And Brien was equally hard pressed, for since the fall of Oxford, Wallingford had become a beleaguered island in a hostile sea, a target for frequent attacks and sporadic sieges by the king's men. So far Brien was grimly holding on, but his tenants could no longer till their fields or harvest their crops, and he staved off utter ruin only by seizing the provisions he needed to keep Wallingford going. His loyalty was costing him dearly, and Maude wanted to help him so badly that it was like a hollow, empty ache, but there was little she could do.

After supper, the conversation focused upon the continuing depredations by Geoffrey de Mandeville and his lawless band. The men had news that Maude had not yet learned: Mandeville had been wounded in late August while besieging Burwell, one of the castles Stephen had thrown up to keep him in the Fens. It was a hot day and when he rashly removed his helmet, he'd been struck by an arrow. But once again he'd had Lucifer's own luck, Robert reported, for they'd heard the wound was not serious. Mandeville would soon be on the prowl again, unless Stephen took more aggressive action to bring him to bay.

They were in agreement, though, that Stephen would not do so. Maude put it most trenchantly: "Stephen ought never to have let Mandeville elude him in the Fens. Blockading the marshes with castles was the easy way—ever Stephen's way. But my father would have followed Mandeville into the very bowels of Hell if need be." She paused, then, her eyes coming to rest upon her brother. "So would you, Robert," she said, and he smiled in surprise.

"You are right about our father," he agreed. "He'd never have allowed a rebel to escape his wrath, no matter how long it took to track him down. But Stephen has the attention span of a summer dragonfly. He alights, begins a siege, loses interest, and flits away in search of a new target. Only twice has he mustered up enough patience to flush out his prey—when he lay siege to Baldwin de Redvers's castle at Exeter and then at Oxford, when he thought he had you trapped, Maude. I suppose we ought to be thankful, though, that he is so easily distracted, else Wallingford—and mayhap even my castle at Bristol—might have fallen to him by now."

In the past, Ranulf would have defended Stephen. Even if he'd not spoken up, he'd have wanted to. But that was before he'd ridden into the smoking ruins of Cantebrigge. Rising abruptly, he glanced about for Loth, found the dog scratching in the floor rushes under the table, hoping to unearth a dropped morsel or discarded bone. Whistling for the dyrehund, Ranulf let him out into the castle bailey.

When he returned to the hall, the gathering had broken up into smaller groups. Amabel was conversing with Roger's young wife, Cecily, and Sybil, Miles's widow. Robert and Maude were talking with Gilbert Foliot, the abbot of Gloucester's great monastery of St Peter's. Across the hall, Roger was sharing a joke with Hugh de Plucknet, or so Ranulf assumed, for they were laughing. Closer at hand, Gilbert Fitz John had begun a game of tables with Alexander de Bohun, and Ranulf wandered over to watch his friend play. It was not long, though, before Hugh was beckoning to him.

"How would you fancy a foray into the town?" Hugh asked as soon as he and Ranulf were alone in the window seat. "Earl Roger says there is a new bawdy-house on Here Lane, just beyond the North Gate. You want to come with us after the women and Abbot Gilbert go up to bed?"

Ranulf raised an eyebrow, for he believed a husband owed his wife discretion, if not fidelity, and chasing after whores within shouting distance of Roger's own castle seemed a foolproof way to set the entire town gossiping, gossip sure to find its way back to Cecily's ears. He could not help glancing across the hall at Cecily, a plump, pretty girl with a throaty giggle, not yet twenty and already six years a wife. Although Ranulf would never shame Annora like this once they were finally able to wed, he decided that Roger was old enough—at twenty-one—to master his own conscience.

"Why not?" he said, and when he next caught Roger's eye, he nodded to convey his interest in taking a tour of Gloucester's best whorehouse. Roger grinned and began to drop such heavy-handed hints about the lateness of the hour that Ranulf and Hugh dared not look at each other, lest they burst out laughing.

Fortunately, indications were pointing to an early evening. Robert had begun to yawn and once Amabel noticed, she'd shepherd her sleepy husband up to bed. Cecily was still much too bright-eyed and chipper, but Maude was more promising, for a messenger had just arrived from Devizes, bearing a letter. She seemed so pleased that Ranulf knew the letter must be from her son or Brien, and as she excused herself to read it, he signaled to Roger and Hugh that they'd soon be on their way.

And indeed, Sybil was already bidding her family and guests goodnight. Robert and Amabel were starting to follow when Maude cried out, turning all heads in her direction. "Do not go, Robert, not yet. I've news you must hear." Maude glanced again at the letter in her hand. "Geoffrey de Mandeville is dead."

As they all crowded in close to hear, she told them what Brien had written. "Brien says that either Mandeville's wound was more serious then he claimed or it festered. Whichever, that was an arrow directed by God, for he died a fortnight ago."

There was a somber silence after that, for damnation was much more fearful than death, even when the man deserved it as much as Geoffrey de Mandeville did. He'd died excommunicate, and even a deathbed repentance was denied him, for the Bishop of Winchester had decreed in his waning days as a papal legate that only the Pope could absolve a man guilty of crimes against the Church.

They all knew, of course, that an excommunicate could sometimes escape his dreadful fate, for Miles had. He, too, had died accursed by the Church, cast out after a bitter clash with the Bishop of Hereford. But he'd had a powerful advocate in his cousin Gilbert Foliot, and after he was struck down on that ill-fated Christmas Eve hunt, the monks of Gloucester had quarreled with the canons of Llanthony Priory over which House would have the honour of burying him.

But they all knew, too, that there would be no such reprieve for Geoffrey de Mandeville. No priest would speak up for him. None would offer prayers for his salvation. His body would lie unclaimed, unable to be buried in consecrated ground. His title and lands would be forfeit, his family shamed. His name would be anathema, a curse to frighten children. And his soul would be forever lost to God, damned to the hottest flames of perdition.

No one spoke for a time. It was left to Ranulf to pronounce Geoffrey de Mandeville's epitaph. None of them had ever heard him sound as he did now, implacable and unforgiving. "Even if Mandeville burns in Hell for all eternity," he said, "that would not be long enough to atone for his sins."

31

CHESTER, ENGLAND

June 1145

THE Benedictine abbey of St Werbergh held a three-day fair every year upon the Nativity of St John the Baptist. It was not a gainful time for the merchants of Chester; they were not allowed to sell their wares for the duration of the fair. But the monks profited handsomely from the rental of the booths and stalls set up in front of the abbey's Great Gate, and people flocked to the fair from all over Cheshire.

The Earl of Chester was not present to open the fair, but his countess acted in his stead, and was warmly welcomed by the monks, for the earl was a generous benefactor to the religious houses in his domains. His enemies jeered that Chester knew his only hope of ever getting to Heaven was to buy his way in, but whatever his motives, the monks were appreciative of his bounty and lavished enough courtesy upon Maud to satisfy a queen.

Maud reveled in the attention, chatting with the merchants, making an occasional purchase as she wandered among the booths, scattering alms to the beggars and children following in her wake, and appearing not to notice as Ranulf and Annora lagged farther and farther behind.

They were attracting stares, too, for Ranulf was trailed by his canine bodyguard, and Annora was proudly showing off her new pet. Pausing to allow two small boys to admire the silvery-grey puppy, she gave Loth a bite of her meat pie; she'd become the dyrehund's biggest fan since learning how he'd come to Ranulf's rescue on the Newark-Grantham Road. After explaining to the curious children that the pup was Loth's son, she picked the little dog up, laughing as he licked her cheek. "I've thought of a name for him," she announced. "Since you gave him to me on the Feast of St John the Baptist, I shall call him John."

Ranulf made a face. "That is no fitting name for a dog!"

"This from the man who burdened one of God's beasts with a name like Loth?" Annora gave the dyrehund the rest of her pie and slipped her arm through Ranulf's. "Where did your squire go?"

"He's over there, watching that bout with the quarter-staff." Although she'd voiced no objections to Luke's presence, Ranulf felt compelled to add, "I finally had to promise Maude that I'd not go off on my own again. She knows about us, Annora, or at least suspects. You might say we've entered into an unspoken pact. She does not ask what she'd rather not know for certes, and I agree to take Luke with me." He shrugged apologetically, but Annora surprised him.

"You think I mind? I only wish you had a dozen Lukes to keep you out of trouble. Or better yet, a dozen Loths! If not for him, I shudder to think what might have befallen you and those poor waifs. Were you ever able to find a home for them?"

"I thought I had. A Southampton merchant heard about them whilst in Bristol to buy wine and offered to take them in. He seemed worthy and had a heartrending story about a stillborn baby and a grieving wife. But it was all lies. He was no vintner, Annora. He ran a bawdy-house on the Southampton docks, and he meant to sell Jennet's maidenhead to the highest bidder, then force her to whore for him whilst he put Simon out on the street to beg. He'd probably have crippled the lad first, since a lame beggar makes more—"

"Jesú, Ranulf, they did not—"

"No, praise God, but only because the man was careless. Thinking the children were asleep in the back of his cart, he talked freely to his servant about what awaited them in Southampton. Jennet heard and she and Simon fled at their first chance. Fortunately they'd not gone far, and they were able to get safely back to Devizes, scared out of their wits, and who can blame them?"

He shook his head grimly. "After that, I was wary of trusting to the kind hearts of strangers. But Robert's chaplain eventually found a brewer and his wife who had no children, and since he spoke well of them, I agreed."

"But you do not sound like a man relating good news," Annora said, and he shook his head again.

"I was in Bristol a few weeks later, and I stopped by to see how they were getting along. They were toiling away in the brewery like galley slaves, free labor for the good brewer. He could not understand why I was so wroth. Surely I had not expected him to treat a villein's children like his own blood?"

"So you took them back to Devizes." Annora was frowning in thought. "Surely there must be something we can do. What if you offered a corrody for the lass?" Almost at once, though, she saw the flaw in that. "But then, no nunnery would accept a villein's daughter, would it?"

"No, not likely. Besides, they ought not to be separated. All they have is each other."

"And you," Annora pointed out. "How long ere they start calling you Papa?"

Ranulf called her a brat, but he did not mind her teasing, for it was just that—teasing. Annora was one of the few people who not only understood but approved of his efforts on the orphans' behalf. To others, the fact of the children's low birth was all that counted. But to Annora, what mattered was their youth and their need. Ranulf had never known anyone so protective of children as she. She was not indiscriminate; she had met children she'd not liked. But she'd never met a child she would not help. "I wish I could take them," she said, and sighed regretfully. "I know I could find a place for them on our Shropshire manor. But we cannot risk it. All we'd need would be for my husband to hear them chattering about the heroic Lord Ranulf, who catches arrows in his teeth and walks on water!"

The joke went awry, though, the word *husband* dragging it down like an anchor. Ranulf said nothing, but his silence spoke volumes. Annora at once realized her mistake and set about remedying it. Once she'd coaxed him into a better humor, he told her the rest. Back at Devizes, the children were safe and earning their keep, Jennet in the laundry and Simon in the stables. He had hopes, though, that better lay ahead. One of the grooms seemed smitten with Jennet, and since she was nigh on fifteen now . . .

Annora smiled, seeing where he was heading. He would provide a marriage portion for Jennet, she'd wed the stable groom, Simon would go to live with them, and all would be well. It was just like Ranulf, she thought; with him, a happy ending was always a foregone conclusion. But such was the power of his faith that when she was with him, she found herself believing in happy endings, too.

At her urging, Ranulf bought them both cups of apple cider, and they wandered over to watch a man entertaining the fairgoers with a trained monkey. Annora was more interested in Ranulf's gossip, though, than the monkey's antics. "Of course I remember John Marshal," she said, "that madman who trapped poor Gilbert in the burning church belfry. Why? What has he been up to now?"

"For the past year he has been feuding with a neighbor, Patrick Fitz Walter, the sheriff of Wiltshire. It was a mismatch, for Patrick was much more powerful, especially after gaining the earldom of Salisbury. So John decided it would be prudent to make peace, and to prove his good faith, he offered to wed Patrick's sister."

"I thought Marshal had a wife?"

"Not for long. He is getting his marriage annulled, having discovered that he and his wife are related within the prohibited degree and have thus been living in sin for the past fifteen years."

"You mean he is casting his wife aside like a worn-out pair of boots?" Annora exclaimed, and was indignant when Ranulf laughed.

"I was laughing," he defended himself, "because those were Maude's very words. She'd taken a liking to John's wife and—Annora? Did you hear someone call out my name?"

Even as she shook her head, the cry came again, urgently. "Lord Ranulf!" One of Maud's ladies-in-waiting was gesturing frantically. "The countess has been taken ill!"

Shouldering his way roughly through the crowd, Ranulf found his niece clinging for support to a draper's booth, surrounded by alarmed attendants, flustered monks, and curious onlookers. Her face was wax-white, her skin damp with sweat, and her eyes glazed with fear. "Take me home," she gasped, and when he lifted her up in his arms, he saw the blood staining her skirt.

RANULF knew as soon as Annora came slowly down the stairs from Maud's bedchamber. "She lost the baby," he said, and she nodded, reaching out to him for comfort. He held her close for a time, until her trembling stopped. "I did not even know," he confessed, "that Maud was with child."

"I do not think even her husband knew yet. She'd missed only two of her fluxes."

"Can I see her?"

"The midwife is still up there." When Annora raised her face to his, it was wet with tears. He was touched that she should be grieving so for Maud's loss, but then she said, almost inaudibly, "You cannot imagine what it is like, Ranulf, no man can. Her baby was dying inside her womb, where he should have been safe. She could feel him slipping away, and she knew when it happened, for she suddenly felt so empty. And afterward . . . afterward she will blame herself. No matter how hard she tried to hold on to him, she ought to have tried harder . . ."

Ranulf was too shaken for speech. This was no past pain she was describing; it was so recent that it was still raw. "Annora . . . did you miscarry again?"

"Yes," she whispered. "A fortnight before Christmas."

"Jesus God . . . and you never told me?"

"What good would it have done, Ranulf? Could you have come to comfort me? Could we have mourned together?" She met his eyes levelly, almost accusingly. "As for the question you cannot bring yourself to ask, I do not know if it was yours. And do not look at me like that! I did not betray you by sleeping with my husband. You may lay claim to my dreams, but I live in the real world—with him."

She'd often had cause to regret her intemperate tongue, but never more so than now. She could not deny what she'd said, though, for she'd spoken nothing less than the truth. "I ought to go back up to Maud," she mumbled remorsefully, and was turning toward the stairs when he caught her arm.

"Annora, wait. You do not believe we'll ever be able to wed . . . do you?"

He sounded angry, but she did not need to see blood to know she'd inflicted a heart wound. Tears filled her eyes. "Sometimes," she said softly. "Sometimes I do . . ."

THE summer was hot and dry and discouraging for those who believed in Maude's cause. Geoffrey was faced with a rebellion in Anjou, led by his own brother. In England, Robert suffered a political defeat and a personal calamity when Faringdon Castle fell to Stephen. Robert had built Faringdon, strategically situated on the London-Bristol Road, at the behest of his son Philip, who hoped to cut communications between Stephen's garrisons at Malmesbury and Oxford. But that July Stephen laid bloody siege to Faringdon, and when Robert was unable to come to the beleaguered stronghold's aid, Philip was so enraged that he defected to Stephen.

DESPITE such setbacks—or perhaps because of them—Maude kept a particularly lavish Christmas court that year. The great hall of Devizes Castle was ablaze with candlelight and swirling color, for another carol was beginning. Standing on the steps of the dais, Ranulf watched the dancers whirl by. Familiar faces, the stars in Maude's firmament.

Rainald and Beatrice had come from Cornwall, and were harvesting a crop of congratulations, for Beatrice had given birth that summer to their first child. Rainald had confided to Ranulf his disappointment that it was a lass and not a son, but he'd wasted no time suggesting to Baldwin de Redvers that his infant daughter would make an ideal bride for Baldwin's young heir. Rainald was now dancing with such exuberant verve that Ranulf assumed Baldwin had been amenable to the proposal. Beatrice was not in the carol circle, but Ranulf had seen her earlier that evening, drifting about in the shadows. Motherhood had not anchored her to reality any more than marriage, he thought sadly, for she seemed as unsubstantial to him as a puff of smoke.

Robert and Amabel were not dancing; they were sitting together in a window seat, more like spectators than participants in the Christmas revelries. Although all were taking great care to make no mention of Philip, he was the uninvited guest at dinner, the unwelcome intruder in their midst, his betrayal the unspoken topic of conversation. None might ask Robert outright, but people still wondered and speculated. Even those like Ranulf, who knew of Philip's troubled relationship with his father, did not understand what had driven him to an act so desperate and so despicable. Ranulf doubted that Robert understood, either.

When the carol ended, the dancers continued to mill about, awaiting the next one. Patrick Fitz Walter and John Marshal were nearby, exchanging mordant banter; marriage may have made them allies, but not friends. John Marshal's new wife stood beside them, smiling placidly at their verbal sparring. She was not as handsome as Marshal's discarded wife, but she was undoubtedly fertile; Marshal had been bragging to one and all that his bride was already pregnant. Ranulf wondered if the Lady Sybil's complacency was due to that early pregnancy; if so, she must be conveniently forgetting that the cast-off Adelina had borne Marshal two sons. But then, Sybil was an earl's sister, and just as that fact explained her marriage, it also guaranteed its survival.

While Marshal's new marriage had made him an object of curiosity, Brien Fitz Count was the one attracting the most attention, the heartiest congratulations, and the most lavish—if puzzled—praise. Brien had just proved that he could wield a pen as well as a sword on Maude's behalf; he had written a political treatise in support of her quest for the crown, marshaling arguments like armies as he sought to discredit Stephen's kingship. He was, of course, preaching to the converted, but his efforts had been well received even by men of scholarly bent, such as Gilbert Foliot, the erudite abbot of Gloucester's great abbey. The others were impressed, but bemused, too, by Brien's foray into such alien territory; with the exception of Robert and himself, Ranulf doubted if there was a man in the hall who'd even read a book in its entirety, certainly not for pleasure. Tonight, though, they were all claiming to have read Brien's, counting upon his good manners to keep him from putting them to the test.

Watching as Brien shrugged off compliments with self-deprecating humor, Ranulf felt sympathy stirring, for he knew only one opinion mattered to Brien; his book may have been offered to the world, but it was meant for Maude. She had already thanked him, circumspectly, for his wife had accompanied him to Devizes and never strayed far from his side. It occurred to Ranulf that Brien's renowned courtesy was camouflage for a profoundly unhappy man. There had always been a streak of melancholy in his nature, even in the best of times. How must it be for him now—a man of honour forced outside the law to feed his people, an idealist with no faith in his fellow men, ruining himself for a woman he could never have and a cause that, however worthy, was soaking England in blood.

Ranulf drew in his breath sharply; looking into the depths of Brien's soul, he'd looked, too, into his own. He at once repudiated the vision. It was true that smoldering images of Cantebrigge had not faded from his memory. But as much as he lamented the suffering of the English people, he still believed Maude's cause was just, her war could be won. And he and Annora would not be like Brien and Maude, lovers left with nothing but regrets for what might have been. No, by God, that would not be their fate, too. He would not let himself lose hope, not like Annora.

Ranulf could not deny, though, that his mood was far from festive. Sometimes he could feel his faith slipping away from him, and he feared the day when he could not hold on. It was no coincidence that he framed his thoughts in Annora's words; six months afterward, he was still haunted by her confession, her miscarriage, and the realization that she had wanted the child—even if it were not his. Looking around for a wine bearer, he took refuge, instead, in the happiness of a friend, hastening over to join Gilbert Fitz John and his wife.

Even a stranger could have guessed that Gilbert and Ella were newly wedded, for the glow had yet to fade. Often a landless knight was never able to wed, unable to provide for a family. But Gilbert's marriage had been made possible by Ranulf's persuasive tongue and Maude's generosity. Unable to bestow an earldom upon her youngest brother, she had compensated as best she could by giving him lands under her control in Wiltshire. When he'd asked for a manor on Gilbert's behalf, she had agreed, and Gilbert and Ella were wed in November, just before Advent. Gilbert's bride was so like him that they could have been siblings. Ella was as good-natured and practical and easily satisfied as her new husband, and they were mirror images—male and female—of each other, both of them fair-skinned, freckled redheads, tall and sturdy and perfectly matched.

"Why so downhearted?" Gilbert asked before Ranulf even opened his mouth; he'd always been able to read Ranulf with ease. "The news from Anjou is not bad?"

"Not at all. Geoffrey swiftly put down the rebellion and he's now giving his rebel barons reasons aplenty to rue their folly. Apparently Hélie thought he'd be able to talk his way out of trouble, but Geoffrey has never been one for forgiveness. He cast Hélie into a dungeon at Tours, and is likely to keep him there until Hélie goes grey . . .

He seemed to lose track of his thoughts, and his sentence trailed off. Following his gaze, Gilbert saw that he was staring at a newcomer to the hall. "You know that man, Ranulf?"

"Yes, I do. He is in my niece's service."

Gilbert was astute about shaded meanings. "You are saying he is loyal to her, not Chester?"

Ranulf nodded. "Maud has her own attendants, most of whom came with her from Robert's household at the time of her marriage. They are utterly devoted to her, none more so than Nicholas. I'm surprised that she'd give him so simple a task as delivering a letter to her parents. He always seemed the sort," Ranulf joked, "to be skulking around at midnight on life-or-death missions."

As they watched, Nicholas was ushered toward Robert and Amabel. Within moments, it was obvious that something was wrong. When Robert started toward Maude, Ranulf hastened to intercept him. But before Ranulf could speak, Robert said in an urgent undertone, "Not now, lad. Meet me in my chamber after the guests have gone to bed. And till then, say nothing."

That was hardly reassuring. Ranulf watched uneasily as Robert drew Maude aside for a brief colloquy, one that left her looking tense and preoccupied. When he sought her out he got only a whispered, "Not here, Ranulf . . . later." After that, Ranulf could only wait and worry.

RANULF was puzzled by the composition of the after-hours council: Robert and Amabel, Maude, Rainald, and Brien. If Robert's news was a family matter, why include Brien? And if it was political, why were Baldwin de Redvers and John Marshal and Roger Fitz Miles excluded?

Robert was leaning back against a trestle table, Amabel at his side. "I know my behavior must have seemed odd tonight, but what I have to tell you cannot leave this chamber. Until it is common knowledge, we can say nothing, lest my daughter be put at risk. She has sent us a secret warning. After the Christmas revelries, the Earl of Chester and his brother are journeying to the town of Stanford, there to make their peace with Stephen."

Rainald swore explosively. Brien was close enough for Ranulf to hear him suck in his breath, but he said nothing, keeping his eyes upon Robert and Maude. Ranulf was astounded, for he knew, if any man did, how much Chester scorned Stephen. "Why? Why now?"

"Maud says that after Faringdon Castle fell, Chester concluded that Stephen cannot be overthrown. He decided to make the best deal he could, whilst Stephen still needed him as an ally." Robert's shoulders had slumped; his face looked pinched and grey in the subdued light. "My son Philip acted as the go-between," he said heavily, and no one spoke after that, not knowing what to say.

The silence was full of foreboding; they all knew what this unholy alliance could mean. Chester's holdings rivaled the Crown's; nigh on a third of England lay within his domains. Ranulf rose and began to prowl the chamber. His sister was standing utterly still in the shadows, so none could see her inner turmoil. Ranulf glanced toward her, and then away. With Chester as an active ally, Stephen seemed likely to prevail. Henry would not be left with nothing, for even if Maude did fail, Geoffrey had not. The duchy of Normandy would one day be Henry's. But Ranulf knew that would not be enough for Maude, not ever enough. Her own dreams were dead. Ranulf did not think she could bear to see Henry's dream die, too.

32

CHESTER CASTLE, ENGLAND

June 1146

AFTER opening St Werbergh's Fair on her husband's behalf, Maud and her guests returned to the castle for dinner. When coaxed by the women, Ranulf agreed to escort them back to the fair once the meal was done. But it was hard to muster up much enthusiasm for fairgoing, not when he kept remembering that a year had passed since the last fair, another year lost. How could he blame Annora if her faith sometimes faltered?

Servants were ladling venison stew onto their trenchers. Breaking off a chunk of bread, Ranulf glanced over at his niece. "So . . . how is the grand alliance going?" While that still sounded faintly sarcastic, it was considerably more tactful than his usual description of Chester and Stephen's peace—as a Devil's deal.

Maud smiled into her napkin before saying demurely, as befitting a dutiful wife, "My poor Randolph . . . he has exerted himself tirelessly to prove his good faith—first taking Bedford Castle for Stephen and then assisting Stephen and Ypres to build a stockade at Crowmarsh so they could cut off supplies to Wallingford. But even after all he's done, he says that Stephen's barons are still wary and suspicious."

"I wonder why," Ranulf said dryly. But his humor was hollow; he did not find anything amusing in Chester and Stephen's accord. It was far too dangerous to be laughed away, as Brien could testify, after a harrowing spring under siege. "Have you heard about Philip's latest outrage?"

Maud's lip curled contemptuously. "Philip who?" she said coolly.

"Your black-sheep brother seems bound and determined to dishonour himself beyond redemption. I'm sure you know that Maude and Robert offered to negotiate with Stephen? We hoped we might be able to take some of the pressure off Brien . . . to no avail. Stephen granted Rainald a safe-conduct to come to his court; that was the only concession he was willing to make, though. But Philip saw a chance to wreak more havoc and ambushed Rainald on his way to Bristol, took him prisoner, and brought him back to Stephen's court in chains."

"How treacherous," Annora interrupted, "and how shameful!"

"Stephen agreed with you. He was infuriated that Philip should have dared to defy his safe-conduct and he released Rainald at once. Rainald returned home in high dudgeon, vowing vengeance upon Philip if it takes a lifetime, and Philip . . . I suppose he went off to sulk."

Maud shook her head scornfully. "My brother Will always claimed Philip was a changeling, and more and more, I do believe him. This I can tell you for certes, Ranulf—that God might one day forgive Philip for the pain he has inflicted upon our family, but I never shall."

Ranulf and Maud lapsed into a morose silence after that, and Annora hastily cast about for a new topic, one distracting enough to keep them from dwelling upon Philip's betrayal. "Is it true that the Church is preaching a new crusade?"

Ranulf's attention was immediately caught and he nodded vigorously. "On Easter Sunday at Vézeley, in Burgundy, the Abbot of Clairvaux read a papal bull urging all Christians to rescue the Holy Land from the infidel. Thousands thronged to hear him speak, and the French king was amongst the first to take the cross."

"A pity Stephen was not stricken, too, with crusading fever," Maud said wryly. "In truth, I can think of any number of lords whose souls would benefit from a sojourn in the Holy Land. I am surprised, though, that Louis is so keen to go. The last time Randolph's brother was in Paris, he said Louis could not bear to have Eleanor out of his sight. How will he cope once a thousand miles stretch between them?"

"Fortunately for Louis," Ranulf said with a grin, "his beautiful queen has taken the cross, too."

Maud was startled, but not astounded, for women had participated in the First Crusade. Some had been loyal wives, others less reputable, for even God's army had attracted its share of camp followers. As a girl, Maud had loved to hear tales of these female pilgrims, women braving hardships and danger for the same mixed motives that drew men to the Holy Land—the curious and the devout, the daring and the pious, the wanton and the faithful, seeking God's Grace or gold, salvation or adventure. Maud could not say which of these categories Eleanor of Aquitaine fit into. She knew only that she felt a sharp surge of envy, a hunger to leave the familiar behind, to strike out boldly toward the unknown as the young French queen meant to do.

Annora's reaction was far different: disbelief and then painful disappointment. She'd long idealized Eleanor, the only woman who seemed able to hold her own in a man's world. They were almost of an age—Eleanor just two years younger—and she'd reveled in Eleanor's triumphs, admired her independent spirit, and when faced with difficult decisions, she'd silently ask herself what Eleanor would have done. This was the first time that her idol had let her down, and she frowned at her cooling stew, her appetite gone. "But Queen Eleanor just had a baby last year," she pointed out plaintively, half hoping the reminder would prod Ranulf into admitting this was another of his dubious jests.

Her lover gave her a questioning smile, and she saw her point had eluded him. "Her baby," she repeated, more forcefully. "Eleanor has an infant daughter now. I would not think she'd want to leave her babe so soon, not after so many years of a barren marriage . . ."

This elicited only a shrug, more male incomprehension. Nor did Maud seem to understand, either, for she laughed when Ranulf quipped that he doubted Eleanor could find the nursery without a map. Annora knew, of course, that queens were not expected to be doting mothers; circumstance and protocol and practicality all conspired to distance a royal mother from her child. The babe would be suckled by a wet nurse, swaddled and comforted and cuddled by servants, a royal pawn to play in the marriage game, for daughters were often betrothed before they could walk, bred to be brides for foreign princes. Annora supposed it was possible that a queen might prefer not to get too attached to a child she was soon to lose. But she'd still expected more from Eleanor, the same devotion she would have given to a babe of her own.

Neither Ranulf nor Maud noticed her preoccupation, and were soon talking about the Bishop of Winchester's latest feud, this one with no less a personage than the Archbishop of Canterbury; Bishop Henry blamed the latter for the Pope's refusal to reappoint him as a papal legate. Annora spooned her stew listlessly, paying the conversation no mind until she heard her own name.

A servant was nearing their table, announcing that a man had just ridden in, asking to see Lady Fitz Clement. As her eyes met Maud's, Annora nodded, but she felt a sudden unease, for only her husband knew she was at Chester, and she'd been gone less than a week, not long enough for him to be writing to her—not unless something was wrong. Borrowing some of Ranulf's optimism, she sought to convince herself that all was well with her father, brothers, stepchildren, husband, and dog in the endless interval before the servant ushered the new arrival into the hall.

Maud was signaling for the final course of fruit-filled tarts as she caught her first glimpse of Annora's visitor. One glimpse was all she needed, so strong was the family resemblance. Even before she heard Annora's strangled cry of "Ancel!" she'd realized that this enraged, swarthy stranger was Annora's brother, and she hastily sought Nicholas's eye, sending him a surreptitious message to be on the alert for trouble.

Ranulf and Annora sat, frozen in their seats, as Ancel strode toward the high table. After one burning glance at Ranulf, Ancel aimed his accusing gaze at his sister. Ignoring Maud and the others in the hall, he said abruptly:

"I had business in Shrewsbury for my lord earl and thought to surprise you. I was the one who got the surprise, though, for your husband informed me that you were off visiting your 'dear girlhood friend,' the Countess of Chester. I found that puzzling, for as far as I knew, you'd never even laid eyes upon the woman. But as I was sitting there, listening to that poor fool Gervase boast that you and the countess were closer than sisters, one of your stepsons came running into the hall, chased by a Norwegian dyrehund."

Ancel's eyes flicked then, to Ranulf. "Did you think I'd forgotten about those accursed dyrehunds of yours? Outside of Norway, that is a beast as rare as the unicorn. But I still fought against facing the truth. All the way to Chester, I kept trying to convince myself that I was wrong, that my suspicions were unjustified. In my heart, I knew I was befooling myself, but I . . ." His mouth twisted, he took a great gulp of air, and then lashed out, "I did not want to believe that my little sister was a whore!"

"Ancel, enough!" Ranulf pushed his chair back, coming swiftly around the table toward the other man. "We need to talk," he said, "but not here. Let's find some privacy—"

He got no further; it was then that Ancel lunged at him. Caught off balance, Ranulf reeled backward, crashing into the table. He would later figure out that he hit his head upon one of the trestle legs. Now, dazed and bleeding, he knew only that he was thrashing about in the floor rushes, trying to keep Ancel from throttling him.

The table had gone over, spilling food into the laps of the startled diners, setting off so much screaming and swearing that the entire hall reverberated with angry clamor. Loth had been scavenging under the table for scraps. With a muffled roar, he fought his way clear of the tablecloth's smothering folds. Fortunately for Ancel, though, Maud had enough presence of mind to grab the dog's collar as he erupted from the wreckage. Annora had been splashed with hot gravy, but she did not yet realize she'd been burned, so intent was she upon reaching Ranulf and Ancel.

By the time she did, it was over. Nicholas and several of Maud's household knights had pounced upon Ancel, pried his fingers from Ranulf's throat, and dragged him away. Annora gasped at her first sight of Ranulf, for he was bleeding profusely. Snatching up a napkin, she pressed it to his gashed forehead. By now Luke was there, too, and between the two of them, they helped Ranulf to his feet.

"Are you bad hurt?" Maud paused only long enough to assure herself that Ranulf's cut was superficial before launching her assault upon Ancel. "How dare you force your way into my home and attack my kinsman? Just who do you think you are—an avenging angel from Hell? This is none of your concern—"

"My sister is shaming our family! But what would you know of dishonour? No decent woman would make herself an accomplice to adultery. Only another slut would—"

Ancel never saw the blow coming. Nicholas moved in, quick as any cat, burying his fist in Ancel's midsection. As Ancel groaned and doubled over, Nicholas brought his knee up, with lethal aim. It was as brief and efficient and brutal a beating as Ranulf had ever seen, over before he could react, before many in the hall even knew what was happening. It confirmed all of Ranulf's suspicions about Nicholas, made him wonder what such a man was doing in his niece's service.

But as Ranulf turned toward Maud, he found her quite unmoved by the violence. She was watching with grim satisfaction as Ancel sank to his knees, choking for breath, and Ranulf saw her for the first time as

Chester's wife, not Robert's daughter. "You may be thankful that I am forgiving of the half-witted," she said scathingly, "else your folly would have cost you your tongue."

Ancel's beating had unbalanced Annora's loyalties, and she flew to his defense now, glaring at Maud and Nicholas as she warned, "Do not threaten him!" When she tried to help him up, though, he shoved her away.

Ignoring Ancel's cursing, Ranulf reached down and jerked him to his feet. "You are such a fool, Ancel. You know I love your sister. If you'd given me a chance, I'd have told you that I mean to make her my wife."

Ancel spat out a mouthful of blood, then called Ranulf a misbegotten bastard, a foul Judas, a false friend. But what chilled Ranulf was seeing in Ancel's eyes such utter, implacable hatred.

Ancel swung away, starting unsteadily for the door. When Annora's protest went unheeded, she hurried after him. As Ranulf started to follow, Maud caught his arm. "He is in no mood to listen to you," she said. He knew she was right. But as soon as she was done daubing away his blood, he hastened from the hall.

He found Annora standing alone out in the bailey, watching as her brother rode away without looking back. When Ranulf reached her, she turned with a sob, buried her face in his shoulder, and wept. He comforted her as best he could, reassuring her that he loved her—which was true—and that Ancel would calm down and see reason, which was not.

"He'll never forgive me," she wept, "never. He said so, said my disgrace would break our father's heart . . . and he is right, Ranulf, it would!" She sobbed again, then shuddered. "What if he tells my husband? What if he tells Gervase?"

Ranulf did not know what to say. He'd just lost a lifelong friend, had seen a twenty-year friendship die in the span of seconds. But he feared now that he was losing far more.

33

NORTHAMPTON, ENGLAND

August 1146

WHAT sort of knavery is Chester up to now?"

Stephen had just come from a lengthy private audience with the earl, but he had to admit, "I do not know, Henry . . . not yet. I can tell you what he has asked of me—that I accompany him on an expedition against the Welsh—but I am not sure if he has something more nefarious in mind."

If Stephen had doubts about Chester's intentions, the others had none at all. "You cannot go into Wales with that evil man," Matilda cried, at the same time the bishop protested, "Utter madness!" and William de Ypres blistered the air with Flemish obscenities.

"Should I interpret that as two 'nays' and one 'undecided'?" Stephen asked, smiling faintly, but he was the only one who found the joke funny. "I did not agree," he said defensively. "I said that I'd have to think about it." And before they could object again, he told them of Chester's proposal. The earl's lands had been coming under attack by the Welsh, and he wanted Stephen's aid in restoring peace to the Marches. If Stephen would agree, he'd provide the men and supplies, insisting that the king's presence would be enough to intimidate the Welsh.

Ypres snorted. "From what I've heard, the only king likely to overawe those Welsh lunatics would be the King of Heaven—not England."

For once, Stephen's brother was in full accord with the Fleming. "If Chester is having Welsh troubles, let him sort them out with his new kinsman," Henry said skeptically. "He's just betrothed his niece to that renegade Welsh prince who marched with him against Lincoln, so let him turn to Cadwaladr for help, assuming he really needs it—which I doubt."

"You are not seriously considering it, Stephen?" Matilda moved to her husband's side, gazing up anxiously into his face. "Relying upon Chester's honour would be like taking the Devil on faith. You cannot do that Stephen, you dare not!"

"Sweetheart, do not distress yourself so. Whilst I do not think I ought to dismiss his request out of hand, I have no intention of riding into an ambush with nothing to protect me but Chester's goodwill."

"It gladdens my heart to hear you say that," Matilda confided. "I know we must do what we can to keep Chester content, but not at the risk of your safety. If he wants your help in Wales, he must be willing to do his part. Let him agree to provide hostages—men whose lives matter to him—and mayhap then I'll believe this Welsh campaign of his is an honest endeavor, not some sort of treacherous snare."

The bishop nodded approvingly; although he still felt Matilda exercised undue influence over his easygoing brother, he was willing to admit that she was more sensible than most of her sex. "Let him yield Lincoln Castle, too," he said, "as he ought to have done months ago."

As Stephen glanced toward William de Ypres, the mercenary shrugged. "I doubt that I'd trust Chester even if the Archangel Gabriel himself vouched for the man. But it cannot hurt to put him to the test. I agree with Madame Queen and the bishop. Let Chester offer up proof of his good faith, and then we'll see."

Stephen nodded, heartened by such unanimous agreement. "It is settled, then," he said. "We'll tell Chester our terms on the morrow. After that, it is up to him."

AS the Earl of Chester strode into the castle hall the following morning, Bennet de Malpas and several members of his entourage hastened to intercept him. He was walking into a lion's den, they warned. Northampton was aswarm with his enemies, and they were stirring up the hive by ranting about the dangers of his Welsh expedition, for word had gotten out that he wanted the king to go into Wales.

As he listened to Bennet and Ivo, the castellan of his castle at Coventry, Chester was surveying the hall. They had not exaggerated; it was thronged with men who'd thank God fasting for a chance to do him harm. The Earl of York, whose lands he'd repeatedly ravaged. Gilbert de Gant, who'd been forced to wed his niece after being captured at Lincoln. William Peverel, Lord of Nottingham and cousin to Stephen, a man with a temper to rival that of his fiery royal grandsire, William the Bastard. That poisonous Fleming Ypres. Friends of the absent Earl of Richmond, who'd starved in one of Chester's dungeons until he agreed to yield Galclint Castle. The Earl of Northampton, dragging his disapproval around like an anchor. Even Robert Beaumont, who'd been rarely at Stephen's court since his twin came to terms with Maude and Geoffrey.

Die-hard foes, the lot of them. Only one of the barons was likely to offer any support: the Earl of Hertford, his sister's son. Most men would have been daunted by such odds. Not Chester, though; he relished turmoil, thrived on controversy, and he was looking forward to imposing his will upon these men who hated him so.

"It is getting on toward noon. Why are we delaying dinner? And where is the meddlesome little bitch?" He had no need to be more specific. They knew he meant Matilda, for every man in his service was aware of the grudge he bore Stephen's queen; he was not one to forgive a public humiliation, especially at the hands of a woman. They explained now that Matilda had been called away when one of her ladies was taken ill. The pale, shy lass, Bennet disclosed, the one who had fits, but Chester was no longer listening; his interest in the Cecilys of this world was nonexistent. Beckoning them to follow, he headed for the dais, where he offered Stephen a perfunctory obeisance.

"I understand we are holding dinner for the queen. We have time, then, to discuss our Welsh expedition. How soon can Your Grace be ready to go? The sooner the better, for Wales turns into a quagmire once the autumn rains begin."

Stephen frowned. He could hear troubled murmurings from those within earshot, and he wanted to assure them that it was not so; it nettled his pride that anyone should think—even briefly—that he might be Chester's dupe. But they'd all agreed that the confrontation should be private, for Chester was too volatile to be trusted in a public setting. His brother was already nudging him, silently mouthing the warning words "Not now." Annoyed by the reminder, Stephen said brusquely:

"We have much to talk about, but I prefer to wait until a time of my choosing."

"Why wait? We can settle it right quickly," Chester insisted. "Just tell me when and I'll take care of the rest. As I told you, I'll provide the men."

The mutterings were louder now, and distinctly alarmed. Men were pressing in around them, Chester's enemies in the forefront. "The king would not accompany you across the hall, much less let you lure him into Wales so you could ambush him!" Few would have dared to accuse Chester so openly, but William Peverel had never lacked for nerve. Seeing that some thought he'd overstepped himself, he said angrily, "Why not say it? It is what we are all thinking!"

"Why should I care what you think?" Chester sneered. "Your opinion is not important enough to matter to anyone, least of all to me. And as usual, you're wrong, for the king *is* coming into Wales. Tell them, Your Grace," he demanded, swinging around on Stephen. "Let them hear it from you if they doubt me!"

"What would you have me say? I did not agree to go, merely to talk further—"

"You did agree! By God, you did!"

"Indeed I did not!"

Both men sounded equally indignant, equally sincere. Most simply assumed that Chester was a convincing liar, but the bishop suspected it was more complicated than that, for he knew how hard it was for Stephen to turn people down. Even with one he disliked as heartily as he did Chester, he'd still temporize, hear the applicant out with the affable courtesy he denied to no man, be he baron or blacksmith. He'd left the door ajar, whether he meant to or not; the bishop would wager any amount on it. And for a man like Chester, who tended to hear only what he wanted to, that cracked door would beckon wider than Heaven's Gate. "We'd best discuss this in private," Henry said hastily, but it was already too late. Fueled by grievances and fanned by suspicions, Stephen and Chester's accord was going up in flames.

This was exactly what Stephen had hoped to avoid, and he was furious with himself for letting Chester force the issue—which made him even more furious with Chester. "I told you that I would think about your request, no more than that. After due consideration, I have decided that I am willing to join you in Wales—provided that certain conditions are met."

Chester was silent for a moment, cursing himself for not putting an end to Stephen's kingship when he'd had the chance at Lincoln. If only his aim had been truer! "What conditions?"

"Bluntly put, your history does not inspire trust. I do not think it unreasonable to expect a show of good faith on your part. I want Lincoln Castle back. And hostages—of our choosing. I think that is a fair—"

"Fair? It is outrageous! I come seeking your aid—the aid you owe me as your liegeman—and what happens? You lie to me and then spit in my face!"

"I did not lie to you! Nor do I see why you object to these conditions. If you have been honest with me, why not provide hostages? What risk to them—as long as you are true to your word?"

"It is insulting, an affront to my honour!"

To Chester's fury, that evoked a burst of derisive laughter from most of the men. Stephen smiled scornfully and Chester tensed, ready to lunge for his throat. But others were now joining in the fray. Bennet de Malpas put a restraining hand on Chester's arm, for they were hopelessly outnumbered. William de Ypres had shouldered his way to Stephen's side. "I never knew you had such a droll wit, my lord earl," he gibed. "Surely that was a jest—your complaint about affronted honour?"

That prompted more laughter, which stilled, though, when William Peverel at last made himself heard above the uproar. "Treason!" he shouted. "He meant to betray the king!" And that stark cry of "Treason" was quickly taken up by others, until the entire hall seemed to echo with this deadly denunciation, the one accusation no king could ever ignore.

"You fools!" Chester raged. "I did nothing wrong!"

"Prove it, then," Stephen challenged. "Accept my terms."

"Rot in Hell!"

Faced with such defiance, Stephen had no choice. "Arrest him," he ordered. Resistance would have been futile and possibly fatal, but no one had expected Chester to realize that, too. He surprised them all and disappointed more than a few by an unwonted display of common sense—he let himself be taken.

Afterward, there was jubilation among Chester's enemies. But others were more ambivalent, asking themselves if suspicions alone were enough to justify a charge of treason. Even some who rejoiced in Chester's downfall were still troubled by the way he'd fallen. If so great and powerful a lord as Chester could be arrested without proof of wrongdoing, who amongst them was safe?

MAUDE and Ranulf arrived at Bristol Castle in midafternoon. The summer sky was just starting to darken when Nicholas rode in. His unexpected appearance jarred Ranulf; barely two months had passed since his confrontation with Ancel and the memory was still raw. For a moment, he let himself hope that Nicholas might be bringing a letter from Annora, routed through Maud. But he knew better, knew that Nicholas was here on a far more urgent mission than the delivery of a clandestine love letter, and his suspicions were soon confirmed. Summoned hastily to the privacy of the castle solar, he and Maude and Rainald and Amabel listened in astonishment as Robert read aloud his daughter's letter, a laconic account of her husband's arrest at Northampton.

There was an amazed silence once he was done. "Has the man gone daft?" Rainald said at last. "How could even Stephen blunder this badly?"

"Just be thankful, Rainald, that he has," Robert said earnestly. "We need not fear any more sheep straying from our fold now, not after the way Chester was sheared."

"There will be no more defections, for certes," Maude agreed. "I do not understand why Stephen keeps making the same mistakes. Does he not realize how weak and sly it makes him appear—breaching the King's Peace to arrest men at his own court?"

"First the bishops, then Mandeville, now Chester. If he keeps on like this, he'll have to send out his sheriffs to fetch his dinner guests. 'Come and dine with the king, get to see the royal dungeons, too!'" Rainald was always one to laugh at his own jokes; the others were too preoccupied for levity.

"I wonder," Maude said thoughtfully, "if Chester was guilty."

They all did. It was easy enough to agree upon the obvious—that Chester's refusal meant nothing, for even if he'd been as innocent as one of God's own angels, he'd have balked at a public submission. But beyond that, they could only speculate. None disputed Ranulf, though, when he observed wryly that a man could rarely go wrong suspecting the worst of Chester.

"I find it difficult to give him the benefit of any doubt, too," Robert admitted. "My daughter seems to think he was not plotting evil—for once. Of course he'd not be likely to confide in her if he was setting a snare. But he is having trouble with the Welsh; that was no lie."

"I suppose he could be innocent," Ranulf conceded grudgingly. "And if so, it would be the ultimate irony—that he'd be punished for the one sin he did not commit!"

There was laughter and then Maude surprised them with a comment that showed just how far she'd traveled down the road toward self-awareness. "No, Ranulf," she said, "the ultimate irony is this—that for all the harm Stephen and I have tried to do each other, our worst wounds always seem to be self-inflicted."

AN autumn rain was making life miserable for any Londoners who had to be out in it. Within the palace at Westminster, it was drier, but the mood was as dreary as the weather. Stephen had been closeted all morning with his wife, his brother, and William de Ypres, gloomily assessing their options. They agreed that they had but two choices, neither of them palatable.

If they kept Chester in confinement, they risked a rebellion by his vassals and tenants, who'd reacted with outrage to their liege lord's arrest. Moreover, Chester was garnering support from unexpected quarters. The Cheshire Church was speaking out strongly on behalf of so generous a patron. Naturally his brother was among the most vocal of his defenders, as was his nephew, the Earl of Hertford. But others were arguing for his release, too, respected lords like the Earls of Derby and Pembroke. It had not helped, either, when the Welsh took advantage of Chester's disgrace to raid into Cheshire. As unlikely as it seemed, Chester was becoming a figure of sympathy.

The longer Chester was imprisoned, the more problems he posed. But if he was set free, they well knew what to expect. He'd never forgive Stephen for this, never. Even if he was as guilty as Cain, he'd still see himself as the one wronged. When Ypres pointed this out, no one disputed him, and he took the opportunity to argue further against Chester's release. "If you snared a wolf, would you let it go just because the rest of the pack was on the prowl?"

"Spare me your hunting homilies," the bishop said brusquely. "They do not address the issue at hand. I like the thought of freeing Chester no more than you do, but I see no other way. How do you expect the controversy to abate as long as we keep him in the Tower?"

"Nor can we bring him to trial," Matilda said, "for we have no proof to offer of his treachery. So in all fairness, Willem, how can we continue to hold him?"

"Kill him, then. Let him have a convenient mishap, fall down a flight of stairs or catch a fatal fever."

Matilda wanted to believe this was one of Ypres's unseemly jests, but as she met his eyes, she was chilled to see that he was in deadly earnest. She'd always known that he was lawless at heart, a man who'd passed most of his adult life perilously close to the dark side of damnation. She'd convinced herself that he'd pulled back from the brink, that salvation might still be within his grasp. But in recent months, he'd begun showing flashes of an erratic temper, his humor had soured, and he was either drinking more or not holding it as well. She did not know what was troubling him, was not even sure she wanted to know, for she suspected that she was not equipped to deal with his demons. But she was worried, nonetheless.

Stephen and the bishop had been offended by Ypres's cynical suggestion, and they were taking turns berating him for his murderous advice. He listened in silence, not looking in the least contrite. As soon as she could interrupt the castigating flow, Matilda urged them to "Let it be. Willem erred, you were understandably affronted, and told him so. Now can we get back to the problem at hand? I agree with Henry. I think we must set Chester free."

There was an unusual asperity to her tone and all three men looked at her in surprise. Stephen felt remorse stirring anew; she may have been far more tactful than his acid-tongued brother, but he knew how dismayed she'd been by Chester's arrest. He'd repeatedly tried to explain that it was not his fault, and she'd professed to believe him, but he still fretted that she blamed him for the debacle.

Sometimes so did he, usually late at night as he sought to convince himself that Chester was the one at fault; it was then that he heard the insidious inner voices, insisting that his uncle the old king would never have gotten himself into such a bind. These voices sounded depressingly like his brother's, for Henry was still reproaching him for not taking command of the situation before it got out of control. He never tired of pointing out that a private confrontation would have posed few risks; if Chester had balked at proving his good faith, Stephen need only have refused to go into Wales, and that would have been the end of it.

Now there seemed no end in sight. But how could he admit that he'd blundered when he did not know what he could have done differently? Even if he were given a chance to relive that scene in Northampton's great hall, the outcome would likely be the same, and that realization was the most troubling of all.

"I botched it," he said abruptly. "I know that. Chester will bear me a lifelong grudge. I know that, too. But I cannot change what is already done. I can put a high price on Chester's freedom, though, high enough to make him think twice about incurring the wrath of the Crown again."

He sounded as if he truly believed what he said, that it was possible to intimidate Chester into submission. For his sake, Matilda tried to believe it, too. Even the bishop held his peace. Ypres reached for his wine cup and drained it, in an unspoken sardonic salute to the phantom presence in their midst, the man they were at such pains not to mention, the late, unlamented lord and rebel, Geoffrey de Mandeville.

BY the time the negotiations for Chester's release were completed, winter was upon them. It had not yet snowed, but the fields were bleak and the ground frozen as Chester and his brother rode west. William de Roumare had brought Chester's favorite white palfrey and an impressive armed escort so that he could return to Cheshire in the style befitting an earl. But he knew it would take more than resplendent trappings to blot out the memories of the past few months.

Roumare kept glancing uneasily at his brother's profile, as hard and unyielding as the barren countryside around them. Chester had been publicly shamed, clapped in irons, treated like a common felon. To gain his freedom, he'd been forced to swear a holy oath that he'd not bear arms against the king. He'd had to offer up a number of highborn hostages as pledges for his future loyalty, among them his nephew Gilbert de Clare, Earl of Hertford. And most galling of all, he'd had to surrender his castles at Lincoln and Coventry.

Roumare had expected Chester to be wild, afire with homicidal intent. The brother he knew ought to have been raging and raving and cursing, making threats and vowing vengeance with every breath he drew. That sort of frenzied fury would not have disturbed him unduly; it was just Chester's way, and he was prepared for it.

Instead, he'd encountered a stony silence, so unlike Chester that he was becoming genuinely alarmed. Like William de Ypres, he, too, was haunted by memories of Geoffrey de Mandeville, the rebel earl who'd died an outlaw, accursed by all. Looking again at Chester, Roumare shifted in the saddle. He was not a fanciful man, but he seemed to feel the rage radiating from his brother, hot enough to scorch. Hot enough, too, to consume all common sense? Was Randolph so hate-maddened that he'd follow Mandeville's bloody road to his doom?

"Randolph . . ." He cleared his throat, nudged his stallion closer to his brother's mount. "You must tell me," he urged, "what you mean to do."

Chester's eyes flicked toward him, opaque and unblinking and blacker than pitch. "I mean to do all in my power," he said, "to gain the throne for Maude's son."

STEPHEN celebrated Christmas that year in his newly recovered castle at Lincoln. The citizens, freed from six years under Chester's yoke, welcomed Stephen joyfully, as their liberator, and he rewarded them with lavish pageantries, festivities that heralded his victory over Chester as much as they did the Nativity of the Christ Child. The people were so bedazzled by the royal revelries that they accepted with aplomb Stephen's decision to defy local superstition and wear his crown within the city, even though that was traditionally held to be bad luck.

The high point of the Christmas court was the elaborate ceremony in which Stephen knighted his eldest son and invested him as Count of Boulogne. Eustace would be seventeen in the spring, and he made a favorable impression upon Lincoln, for he was as tall and tawny-haired as Stephen, and looked like a fine young king in the making—from a distance. That heretical thought was Matilda's. It had come unbidden, casting a shadow over the pleasure she'd been taking in the evening. It was an unbearably lonely feeling, for she could not confide her qualms to another living soul. How could she ever admit that she harbored such doubts about her own son?

THE Christmas fête had been over for hours, but Matilda was still clad in her elegant court gown with its long, hanging sleeves and decorative silk belt that reached below her knees. A fur-trimmed mantle trailed from her shoulders, shielding her from the cold as she made her way to the small chapel in the east tower of the keep. She'd promised Stephen that she'd not be long, but she needed time alone with the Almighty, needed the peace of mind that could come only from entrusting her troubles to a Higher Power.

The chapel was in the upper story of the tower. Wall sconces still burned, and the scent of incense lingered on the air. She was not expecting to find anyone there, for the priest had retired for the night. But a man was standing before the altar. He spun around at sound of her footsteps, almost as if he were fearing an ambush, and she saw that it was William de Ypres.

"Willem!"

"I suppose I am the last man you thought to find here."

"Well . . ." She did not know how to answer, for he was right, but to admit that seemed insulting.

"You never speak ill of people if you can help it, do you? We both know that if I turned up missing, you'd mount a search in the town's alehouses, taverns, and whorehouses. You'd expect," he said, "to find me in the gutter, not in church."

His words were slurred, his eyes swollen, and she shivered, realizing that he was drunk. But he was also in pain. "Your need brought you to church tonight," she said softly. "He is there for all of us, Willem. He loves the sinner as much as He hates the sin."

To her consternation, he laughed, a harsh, grating sound that caused her to shiver again. "If that is a suggestion that I mend my ways," he said, "I have already started down that road. I got as far as Boxley, too, for all the good it did me . . ."

Matilda was not comfortable being alone with him in this dimly lit chapel, for she was timid around drunkards; they tended to be loud and often quarrelsome and alarmingly unpredictable. His last words were so garbled that she was not sure she'd heard him correctly. "Boxley?" she echoed uncertainly. Forcing a smile when he did not respond, she repeated, "Boxley? Where is that, Willem?"

"In Kent." He moved toward her, steady on his feet but with a telltale stiffness in his carriage, the rigid posture of a man concentrating carefully upon the commands his brain was sending his body. "I just founded a Cistercian abbey there," he said, and laughed again, mirthlessly, at her dumbfounded expression.

Matilda's initial amazement gave way almost at once to delight. She and Stephen had rewarded Ypres lavishly for his loyalty; he had been given such vast holdings in Kent that his enemies complained he was its earl in all but name. Even so, founding an abbey was an incredibly generous gesture, one which went well beyond the usual largesse bestowed upon the Church by its more pious or repentant sons.

"Willem, how wonderful! You seem so . . . so worldly sometimes that I feared you'd not given sufficient thought to your immortal soul. This is a worthy thing you've done, and I admire you for—"

"Do not!" At her startled recoil, he said again, more calmly this time, "Do not, my lady. There is nothing admirable about a bribe, especially one that failed."

Matilda blinked. "I do not understand."

"It is simple enough. I sought to make a deal with God. I'd give Him a House for His monks if He would give me back—" He bit off the rest of his words, would have turned away had she not caught his arm.

"Give you back what? Willem, tell me! Give you back what?"

He looked at her for a moment that seemed endless before saying hoarsely, "My sight. I am going blind."

"Sweet Jesus," Matilda breathed. "I did not know . . ."

"I did not want you to know." His voice was flat, almost hostile. "I did not want your pity."

"It is not pity! Willem . . . Willem, listen to me. I know it seems like meagre comfort, but the Almighty does not give us burdens too heavy to bear. Let Him help you carry it. And let us. Stephen and I will do all we can—"

"Will you?" His mouth contorted, in a bitter parody of a smile. "Even after I'm of no more use to you?"

Matilda understood, then, the true source of his fear; it was rooted in his turbulent and bloody past. His father had been the Count of Ypres, his grandsire Count of Flanders, but he was tainted by the Bar Sinister, not his father's heir, just his bastard. He'd been unwilling to accept so limited a destiny, though, had fought for Flanders, lost, and been forced into English exile. At fifty-six years old, all that he had, he'd won by the sword, by his ruthless will and superior skills as a battle commander. No wonder he was so afraid now, she thought. It was not Death he dreaded, not even the loss of light; it was being helpless, unable to defend himself in a world that had never been anything but hostile.

"You are a wealthy man, Willem. Surely you did not fear that your estates would be forfeit if you were no longer able to fight for Stephen?" she said, although she well knew that was precisely what he'd feared. "You've earned whatever we've given you. Speaking for myself, I could lavish royal favors upon you from now till Judgment Day and I would still be in your debt. You gave me back my husband!"

As she spoke, he'd retreated into the shadows. No longer able to see his face, she reached out, took his hand between her own, and held tight.

But later that night, she lay awake and fretful in Stephen's bed. Her husband slept peacefully beside her, snoring slightly, for he'd turned onto his back. She'd told him nothing of her conversation with Ypres; the Fleming was not yet ready to reveal his secret, even to one as sure to be sympathetic as Stephen. Matilda tucked the covers more securely about Stephen's chest, then gently smoothed his hair; it was well streaked with silver. Her own hair was beginning to go grey, too, for she was forty-one now. Tonight, though, she felt as if she were much older, burdened with more troubles than she could even count.

Lying next to Stephen, she closed her eyes tightly, but the images would not go away. Ypres in the chapel. Eustace as he knelt to receive knighthood, his face upturned and eager. And Chester, a dark presence in the shadows, malevolent and unforgiving. Surely Chester could not be indifferent to the fate of his hostages, one of them his own kinsman? Would he truly risk his nephew's life by rebelling? Stephen insisted that not even Chester could be so reckless, so ruthless. But what if he was?

AS soon as Stephen withdrew, the Earl of Chester launched a fierce attack upon the city of Lincoln. But Stephen had left a strong garrison behind, and with the help of the citizens, they were able to beat back the earl's assault.

Thwarted at Lincoln, Chester then attempted to recapture Coventry. Stephen hastened to break the siege, was wounded in the fighting that followed, and had to withdraw. But he soon returned and put Chester to flight, the earl narrowly escaping with his life. Although hard pressed by Stephen, Chester continued his rebellion, and was accused by the chronicle Gesta Stephani of exercising "the tyranny of a Herod and the savagery of a Nero."

34

DEVIZES, ENGLAND

May 1147

STEPHEN gave Chester's chief hostage a choice: gain his freedom by surrendering his castles. The Earl of Hertford reluctantly yielded the strongholds and once free, joined his uncle's rebellion. Chester was the young man's maternal uncle; his paternal uncle, the Earl of Pembroke, argued that his nephew's forfeit castles should have gone to him. When his claim was denied, he withdrew from court and made plans to seize the disputed castles. Stephen struck faster than the disaffected earl, captured his castles at Leeds and Tonbridge, then laid siege to the earl himself in his seacoast fortress at Pevensey. Once again Stephen had demonstrated his abilities as a soldier, but his political skills were less impressive: by alienating the influential Clare family, he threw more logs onto the fires set by Chester.

Chester's rebellion was to have far-reaching consequences for a number of people, Ranulf and Annora among them. Now that Chester was an outright enemy of the king, Annora's husband refused to allow her to continue her visits to the Countess Maud. Ranulf and Annora were still able to use Maud as a conduit for their letters, but there were no more trysts; that well had dried up. They would need to find another reliable go-between. So far, though, Ranulf's ruminations had yielded no candidates. When Rainald asked for his help in Cornwall, he was quite willing to join his brother's Cornish campaign, if only to take his mind off his trouble with Annora. He was gone more than two months, would have remained longer, but a messenger caught up with him after Easter, bearing an urgent summons from his sister. Maude needed him back at Devizes as soon as possible—if not sooner.

AS Ranulf dismounted in the inner bailey of Devizes Castle, Hugh de Plucknet hurried out to greet him. "Thank God you've come! The empress has been as fretful as a wet cat, awaiting your return. In all the years I've known her, never have I seen her so disquieted, not even when we were trapped at Oxford."

"What has Stephen done?"

"Not Stephen—Lady Maude's son."

"MAUDE? Hugh had some cock-and-bull story about Harry coming over here to fight Stephen! Surely that cannot be true?"

"I would to God it were not!" Maude said fervently. "But alas, it is. Henry got it into his head that it was time for him to play a more active part in our efforts to overthrow Stephen. So he found a few young Norman and Angevin lords eager for adventure, hired some Breton mercenaries, and set sail for England—"

"Geoffrey let him do this?" Ranulf interrupted incredulously, and Maude shook her head.

"Geoffrey knew nothing of it, no more than Robert or I did. No, this mad escapade was Henry's doing and his alone. He landed at Wareham, sent a messenger to Devizes with his greetings, and then began his war."

"Good God Almighty," Ranulf murmured. His nephew was all of fourteen.

"They attacked Cricklade first, were easily driven off. They then tried to lay siege to a castle at Purton, again failed. It was only to be expected: a raw lad, not enough men, no siege weapons. But it quickly got worse, for he'd paid his soldiers with promises, and they were growing impatient. What money he had was soon spent, and he had no choice but to appeal to Robert and me for aid. It was then that I fear I made a greivous mistake, Ranulf."

"Why? What did you do?"

"We ordered Henry to cease this foolishness and return to Normandy. That affronted his newfound manhood and he balked like a mule, flatly refusing to go home. Robert was furious and persuaded me that we dared not indulge him, that he must be brought to heel straightaway. We would not give him so much as a farthing, but instead of bringing him to his senses, we only goaded him into further defiance. Off he went in a prideful rage, and there was nothing I could do to stop him. I could not very well hold him prisoner here. He'd never have forgiven me."

"No, probably not," Ranulf agreed. "What happened then?"

"That is just it, Ranulf—I do not know what is happening! We heard that Henry's men had begun to abandon him, that his mercenaries were clamoring for payment. What if they all forsake him? Or even worse, if he is betrayed and turned over to Stephen? What if—"

"Maude, stop scaring yourself. This serves for naught. You and Robert did only what you thought was best for the lad, what would get him safely back to Normandy. And with most fourteen-year-olds, it would have worked." Honesty compelling him to add, "Of course most fourteen-year-olds would not be out hiring mercenaries or assaulting castles. I assume you want me to go after him?"

She swallowed, nodded, then swallowed again. He found it astonishing that a woman so indifferent to her own safety, whose bravery had so often bordered upon recklessness, was coming undone now at the mere thought of danger to her son. "Do you know where he is?"

"He went back to Wareham. He has always been fond of you, Ranulf. I think he'll listen to you—he must! Tell him that I will get the money he needs to pay off his men, but he must sail for Normandy straightaway."

"I'll leave at first light," he promised. "Now you must stop blaming yourself, Maude. You were just trying to teach the lad a lesson, one he badly needed to learn."

"I know," she said softly. "But what if the lesson proves fatal?"

TRUE to his word, Ranulf departed at dawn the next morning, with an armed escort large enough for safety, not large enough to slow him down. It was close to fifty miles to Wareham and the roads were muddy, for it had been a rainy spring. They still made good time, not stopping for the night until they'd reached Gilbert Fitz John's manor on the Dorsetshire border. When they left on the morrow, Gilbert rode with them.

Sunset-tinted clouds were trailing the sun as it started its slow descent toward the western horizon. They were almost upon Wareham; the wind was sharper and damper now as they neared the sea. Riding at Ranulf's side, Gilbert glanced curiously at his friend's profile. "What sort of response," he asked, "do you expect to get from Henry?"

"I'm not sure," Ranulf admitted. "Most likely he'll be defensive, even defiant. Nothing is more tender than youthful male pride."

"Remember us at fourteen? You, me, and Ancel—the Unholy Trinity, Annora liked to call us. Not that our tomfoolery could hold a candle to young Henry's undertaking. Not once did we ever think of invading England!"

Although it sounded as if Gilbert were just rambling on, Ranulf knew he had deliberately forced Ancel's name into the conversation. He kept his eyes on the road, saying nothing, but Gilbert was not discouraged by his silence. "Surely you'll be able to patch things up with Ancel," he insisted. "The fact that he has not revealed what he knows—do you not think that is a hopeful sign, Ranulf?"

"He'll not forgive me, Gib. Nor will he be forgiving Annora, and of all her brothers, he was her favorite . . ."

Ranulf said no more, and this time Gilbert took the hint, let the matter drop—for now. He was not about to give up, though, meant to make peace between his friends, no matter how long it took. "Have you figured out another way to meet with Annora? A pity Chester had such a wretched sense of timing. If not for his falling out with Stephen, his wife's pregnancy would have been a perfect excuse for Annora to stay with her awhile."

"Pregnancy?" Ranulf swung around in the saddle. "Maud is with child again?"

"You did not hear? Ah, but you've been off in Cornwall; I forgot. Lady Maud wrote to Earl Robert and Lady Amabel last month. The babe is due in September, I believe." He grinned suddenly. "So we know how Chester celebrated his release!"

Under his breath, Ranulf called Chester a foul name; it might not be logical, but he found himself bearing a very personal grudge against the earl whose rebellion had played such havoc with his love affair. "May the Almighty bless Maud with an easy birth and a healthy child," he said, and then raised his hand to halt his men, for Wareham lay just ahead.

"May the Almighty favor me, too, Gib, in my coming talk with my nephew. God Willing, I'll be able to coax him into sailing with the tide for Normandy."

RANULF was pleased, but surprised, too, by the warmth of Henry's welcome. He'd been expecting to find a youngster despondent and possibly defiant, in need of some face-saving comfort. But as improbable as it seemed, his nephew appeared to be in high spirits, genuinely glad to see him, and apparently unperturbed to be stranded in enemy territory. He insisted upon personally ushering Ranulf and Gilbert and their men into the hall, very much the young lord of the manor as he directed the castle cooks to prepare a meal for these new arrivals.

Servants were stoking the fire, for Wareham was near the sea and the spring evenings were still chilly. Settling Ranulf and himself before the hearth with wine and wafers, Henry regarded his uncle over the rim of his wine cup. "So," he said, "Mama sent you?"

Ranulf nodded. "Your mother is the most courageous woman I know, Harry. But you've managed to accomplish what Stephen and all the might of the English Crown could never do—you've scared her half to death."

"That was not my intent," Henry protested, although without heat. He seemed older to Ranulf than fourteen; for better or worse, he was growing up fast—and in a hurry to hasten the process along. Ranulf's own world had not changed dramatically or drastically in the three years since he'd last seen his nephew; he was still living on hope. But those three years had wrought significant changes in Henry. It was too early to tell if he was going to inherit Geoffrey's height, but he was already sprouting up, almost as tall as Ranulf and obviously proud of his new stature. He was still in that awkward stage, the perilous no-man's-land of adolescence; the curve of his cheek was smooth and beardless, but his voice had steadied, and he seemed to have outgrown the coltish clumsiness so common to boys his age. How, Ranulf wondered, was he to deal with this stubborn man-child, too clever for his own good, too young to let loose, too old to rein in.

Henry took the initiative. "I suppose," he said, "that you think I've gone stark mad?"

"No . . . it is understandable and commendable that you'd want to do your own fighting. But Scriptures say that for everything there is a season, a time for every purpose under Heaven—and it was not yet your time, lad."

"I know," Henry conceded, with disarming, cheerful candor. "I botched it badly."

"And . . . and you are not troubled by that?"

Henry shrugged. "Next time," he said, "I'll do better."

Ranulf was very relieved that the boy was being so reasonable, and yet something was not quite right about this. Harry was being too reasonable, too complacent in defeat. There was a piece missing from this puzzle, but how to find it? "Your mother is now willing to give you the money you owe your men—provided that you agree to end this campaign and return to Normandy."

"That is kind of Mama, but I no longer need her help. I've already paid my men."

Ranulf stiffened. "Where did you get the money? Harry . . . you did not turn outlaw?"

"Of course not, Uncle Ranulf! How could I hope to win the hearts of my English subjects by stealing their purses?"

"Then I repeat—where did you get the money, lad?"

Henry's amusement was unmistakable now; silvery glints of laughter swam in the depths of sea-grey eyes. "You need not fret," he said, "for I kept it a family matter. After Mama and Uncle Robert refused to help me, I turned to my other kinsman. I got the money from Stephen."

Ranulf inhaled his wine, choked, and began to cough. Struggling for breath, he managed to croak out, "Not . . . joking?"

Henry grinned. "I am quite serious. I sent a messenger to Cousin Stephen, explaining that I was out of funds and asking for a loan to get back to Normandy. My man said that he read my letter, laughed until he was blinking back tears, and then agreed to give me the money, provided that I not overstay my welcome!"

Henry laughed soundlessly, eyes alight with both triumph and mischief. But then he took another look at his uncle and became solicitous. "You're still red as a beet and you've spilled all your wine. You sit and catch your breath, Uncle Ranulf, whilst I fetch some more."

As soon as Henry went off in search of a servant, Gilbert hastened over. "Ranulf, what is going on? You look poleaxed; what did he tell you?"

Ranulf was still coughing. "You'll never believe who is financing this expedition of Harry's—none other than the man he was attempting to overthrow."

Gilbert's jaw dropped. "Stephen?"

Ranulf nodded and coughed again. "I've always thought of Harry as Maude's son. But for a moment there, it was as if I'd been given a glimpse of Geoffrey at fourteen. For certes, the lad did not get his sense of humor from my sister! She'll be appalled when she hears about this, for it is not in her nature to understand it. Nor will Robert. But I daresay Geoffrey will find it hilarious." He shook his head, but the corners of his mouth were already twitching, and he was soon laughing himself.

Gilbert could not help laughing, too. "Remember that old joke . . . the one about the lad who killed his parents and then asked the king's court to show him mercy because he was an orphan? But whatever possessed Stephen to agree? Other men suffer from recurring ailments like the ague fever or toothache or boils. With Stephen, it is always these fits of misguided chivalry!"

Ranulf grinned. "I'll admit that Stephen would be beguiled by the sheer audacity of the lad's request. But I suspect that he sees his generosity as common sense, not chivalry. So far Harry has been more of a nuisance than a real threat, and Stephen may have considered the money well spent just to get rid of him. He's not a man to take a fourteen-year-old foe very seriously, or to wish the boy harm . . . not until he grows up some. So he probably—"

Alerted by Gilbert's expression, Ranulf broke off, but not in time. Henry had heard. "Sorry, Harry. No offense meant."

"None taken," Henry said equably. "I know Stephen gave me the money to get rid of me. I was relying upon that."

"And you are going home?"

Henry nodded. "It would not be fair to take the man's money and then renege upon our bargain. I am returning to Normandy as soon as I've bade my mother farewell." His pause was deliberate, for as young as he was, he was already developing a sense of timing. "But," he said, "I will be back."

35

DEVIZES, ENGLAND

July 1147

THE foal was the color of cider, wispy mane and tail as fair as flax. It tottered about the stall like a landlubber just getting its sea legs, and the men laughed at its endearing clumsiness, while marveling, too, for they knew that in a few fleeting hours, this hobbled little colt would be able to gallop after its mother as if it had been born with wings. The foal had finally found what it had been instinctively seeking. Nosing its mother's udder, it began to suckle.

Reaching over, Ranulf clapped one of the grooms on the shoulder. "Good work, Godric. The empress will be very pleased with you, for she sets quite a store by this mare of hers."

Godric smiled bashfully, and mumbled something they couldn't catch. His shyness always came as a surprise, for people assumed that anyone so big would be aggressive, too. But his rawboned, hefty appearance was deceptive, burly camouflage for a gentle soul. He never shrank from the dirty jobs, was generous in offering his help to those who needed it, whistled softly to himself as he worked about the stables, and Ranulf had concluded he was that rarity, a man utterly content with his lot in life.

The most persuasive testimony to Godric's genial nature was the reaction of the other grooms. They might well have been jealous to see him thrust into royal favor. Instead, they were lavish now with their praise, telling Ranulf and Hugh enthusiastically how the foal had been stillborn, "limp as an empty sack," until Godric had somehow brought it back to life, "kneading the little fellow like he was a lump of bread dough and then blowing air into his nostrils till he began to breathe on his own." It was, they all agreed, a sight to behold.

Ranulf and Hugh thought so, too, and heaped more plaudits upon Godric, until he was squirming with pleased embarrassment. He continued to insist that he'd done nothing out of the ordinary, but he became even more flustered when Ranulf seemed about to go.

"My lord . . . wait! I . . . I need to talk to you," he stammered. "You know that my wife is with child?"

Ranulf nodded encouragingly, then waited patiently for Godric to find his tongue. "My lord . . . it is like this. Jennet and me, we talked it over and . . . and if the babe be a son, we want to name him after you. But . . . but if you think we'd be getting above ourselves, you just say so . . ."

Hugh was snickering. Ignoring him, Ranulf smiled at the groom. "If you and Jennet are sure," he said, "I would be pleased to share my name with your son."

Godric beamed, and Ranulf warned Hugh off with a sideways shake of his head. Hugh shrugged and followed him from the stables. Both men flinched as they stepped out into the sun-scorched bailey. It was only midmorning, but the temperature was already soaring. The air was as heavy as it was hot, and breathing it was like inhaling steam. "Jesú," Hugh gasped, "we might as well climb into the kitchen's oven and get it over with! A man could drown out here in his own sweat. So . . . will you be offering yourself up as godfather to the groom's whelp?"

He'd meant it as a joke, and was taken aback when Ranulf snarled, "Just let it lie!" Ranulf was not usually so thin-skinned. It was this accursed heat, Hugh decided and magnanimously forbore to take offense.

Ranulf's continuing involvement in the lives of these lowborn Saxons was a puzzle for certes, but one he was not likely to solve.

One puzzle led to another, putting him in mind of an odd rumor circulating that summer. "You were recently at Bristol, Ranulf. Is all the talk true about Earl Robert's double-dealing son? Has he taken the cross to atone for his sins?"

Ranulf nodded. "Philip was stricken with a mysterious malady at Easter and nearly died. He vowed to make a pilgrimage if God would spare him, and sailed for Normandy as soon as he got his strength back. The French king's army started for the Holy Land after Whitsuntide, and I suppose Philip hopes to catch up with them. It is well and good to honor the Almighty, but I think it a pity he did not see fit to make peace with his father ere he left."

"I daresay Philip was too shamed to face the earl, and if he was not, by God, he ought to be! So . . . the French king is on his way to Jerusalem? And he truly did take his queen with him? Talk about inviting the snake into Eden! I suppose, though, that if she were mine, I'd not want to leave her behind, either. You think she's why so many men are clamoring to take the cross? The last I heard, Waleran Beaumont, William de Warenne, and William Peverel, amongst others, had all vowed to join the Crusade. What about you, Ranulf? Are you not tempted to go soldiering for Christ, too?"

The temptation was greater than Ranulf was willing to admit—to leave England and this bloody, unending civil war and his own troubles behind in the dust and join a bright, shining quest for God, offering adventure and salvation and a chance to see the holy city of Jerusalem. He was spared the need to answer by a sudden shout up on the battlements. Riders were being admitted.

Hugh's curiosity had shriveled in the heat, and he continued on toward the hall, only to stop once he realized Ranulf wasn't following. "Ranulf? You know these men?"

"One of them," Ranulf said warily. Why would Ancel be seeking him out? By now, Ancel had seen him, too. Halting his men, he dismounted swiftly. Ranulf started toward him, and they met in the middle of the bailey. "Ancel? Why are you here? Annora is not ailing, is she?"

"No. She is quite well."

Ranulf could think of only one other reason for Ancel to be at Devizes: to make peace between them. There was nothing conciliatory about his demeanor, but apologies had always gone down hard with Ancel. Ranulf was willing, though, to take that first significant step. "I am glad you've come, Ancel. Let's get out of the sun and find a quiet place to talk."

"I am not staying, Ranulf. I came only to give you this." Holding out a sealed parchment. "It is a farewell letter from Annora."

Ranulf made no move to take the letter. "I do not believe you."

"As I recall, you did not want to believe me, either, when I told you she'd wed Fitz Clement. But you need not take my word. Read it for yourself."

This time, when he thrust the letter forward, Ranulf reached for it. The seal was Annora's and unbroken. "What did you do, Ancel? Did you threaten to go to her husband?"

"It is not my doing. I would that it were. But she turned a deaf ear to me, did not come to her senses until she got with child."

Ranulf was stunned. "Annora is pregnant?"

"Yes, and she has promised God that she'll sin no more. She may have been willing to risk her immortal soul for you, but not this babe." Ancel paused, glanced at Ranulf's stricken face, and then away. When he spoke again, his voice no longer held such a hard, hostile edge. "Annora insisted that she was as much to blame as you, and I daresay it is true. Fools, the both of you, but I'd not see her hurt. Or you, either," he added grudgingly. "Fortunately, Annora's husband and our family know nothing of her infidelity, and God Willing, they never will. Be thankful for that much, that this dangerous passion of yours wrecked no lives."

Ranulf said nothing. The bailey was shimmering in heat, the sky a bleached bone-white, the color of his face. Ancel started to turn away, then stopped. "If you love her, Ranulf," he warned, "you let her be."

ANNORA'S letter was not as brutally blunt as Ancel had been, but the gist of her message was the same. She told Ranulf that she was with child, the babe due in November, at Martinmas, reminding him—needlessly—that they'd not lain together since Ancel caught them last summer at Chester. She'd not let herself hope at first, she wrote, so afraid she'd miscarry again. But she was into her fifth month now, she could feel the baby moving within her womb, and she did not think God would take this child, too, not if she repented. She'd promised the Almighty and Ancel that she'd not see him again, and she meant to keep that vow. She wanted Ranulf to know that she'd truly loved him, but it was not meant to be. She'd long known that, suspected that he had, too. He must try to understand. She wished him well, and asked him to burn this letter once he'd read it.

Ranulf did not burn her letter, not at first. Instead, he tormented himself by reading it over and over, until her words were embedded so deeply into his memory that he'd never be able to get them out. How could Annora give up like this? If she loved him, how could she just walk away? What of the baby, though? How could he expect her to abandon her child? And if she could somehow keep the babe, would he be willing to accept

Gervase Fitz Clement's child as his own? But what if she miscarried again? An ugly thought, one that shamed him when it kept coming back.

He remembered a conversation he'd once had with a soldier wounded at the Battle of Lincoln. The man's arm had been so badly mangled that the doctors had been forced to amputate it, and he'd told Ranulf that his arm had continued to ache even after it was gone. And after another sleepless night of phantom pain, Ranulf knew what he must do. He had to see Annora. They had to talk. What that would accomplish, he could not say, even to himself. He knew only that it could not end like this.

IT was very early, a few stars still glimmering in the dawn sky. Ranulf had saddled his horse himself, for the grooms were not yet up and about. The bailey was deserted, save for the guards up on the battlements. He had hoped to be long gone by the time the castle was stirring for the day. But as he swung up into the saddle, he heard his name being called.

Luke was running across the bailey. "My lord, wait!" Coming to a halt in front of Ranulf's stallion, blocking the way. "You cannot go off on your own like this," he insisted. "I know what you mean to do. You are seeking out your lady. I saw him the other day—her brother. I was in the town when he rode by, after leaving the castle. And since then, you've been like a man with a wound that'll not stop bleeding. I am not prying, in truth I am not. It is your safety I care about. You know you can trust me. Take me with you. I'll need but a few moments to saddle up—"

"No," Ranulf said. "This I must do alone."

"My lord, forgive me for saying so, but that is madness! The risk is too great. Let me come—"

Ranulf turned his horse, circled around Luke, then spurred it forward. Luke could only watch, defeated, as the stallion cantered across the bailey. "At least take Loth with you!" he shouted, but he could not be sure if Ranulf even heard him, for he did not look back.

LUKE'S fears proved unfounded, for Ranulf reached Shrewsbury without incident. The town was crowded with fairgoers, but he was able to persuade the hospitaller at St Peter's to find him a place in the abbey guest hall, just as he'd done during his last visit to Shrewsbury Fair, seven years ago.

The next morning, he rose early and headed for the fairground. The August sun was hot upon his face, the Abbey Foregate thronged with cheerful, laughing people eager for the pleasures of the fair. Ranulf soon inhaled the aromas of hot meat pies and freshly baked bread; he could not even remember the last time he'd eaten. All sorts of activity swirled around him. A knot of children were shrieking at the antics of a trained monkey; the sheriff's men were dragging off a pickpocket caught in the act; merchants were calling out their wares. But for Ranulf, it was a scene haunted by memories, blighted hopes, and regrets.

As he moved between the booths, he kept catching glimpses of Annora, not the woman he hoped to find today, but a carefree, reckless girl clad in scarlet, a ghost from a bygone fair, living on in memories he'd take to his grave. As soon as he'd remembered that St Peter's Fair was imminent, he'd had to come, knowing he'd have no better chance to encounter Annora. It had worked once; why not again? But he'd not anticipated how painful it would be—revisiting his past.

He saw the dog first. Annora's pup had grown into a handsome, grey-black animal, not as large as Loth, who was uncommonly big for a dyrehund, but very like his sire in all other particulars, the reason why Ranulf had dared not bring Loth with him. A dog that looked so much like the Fitz Clement dyrehund would have been dangerously conspicuous.

Annora was accompanied by a giggling young girl, about thirteen or so. When Annora called her "Lucette," Ranulf realized this was her stepdaughter. Seeing her with Annora gave Ranulf a jolt; for the first time, she was real to him. His eyes were drawn irresistibly now to Annora's skirts. She was already starting to show, and basking in the benevolent, approving smiles people reserved for expectant mothers. She was wearing an apple-green gown, a shade he'd never seen on her before. It suited her, for she looked at ease, quite content—until she glanced over, saw Ranulf standing by the silversmith's booth.

Ten feet or so separated them, but Ranulf could still see how fast the blood drained from Annora's face. Lucette also noticed, and plucked at Annora's sleeve. "Mama?" That, too, came as a shock to Ranulf. But then he realized that Annora—nigh on eleven years wed—was probably the only mother Lucette remembered. "Mama, are you ailing? You're so pale! Papa! Mama is sick!"

A man at one of the nearby stalls turned, made haste to rejoin them. Ranulf had never seen Annora's husband before. He was not at all the horned demon of Ranulf's jealous imaginings, just a compact, ruddy-faced man in his forties, with enough laugh lines to attest to an agreeable nature, hair shorter than was fashionable, a neatly trimmed beard showing signs of grey. "Nan? You do look ill of a sudden. Is it the babe?"

Annora swallowed. "I . . . I am well. Truly, Gervase, I am. It is just so hot . . ." She managed a feeble smile, all the while keeping her gaze riveted upon Ranulf. Gervase and Lucette were fussing over her, insisting she move into the shade, signaling for a vendor to bring her a cider drink. As Ranulf watched her, it seemed to him as if the distance were widening between them, although neither one had moved. Color was slowly coming back into Annora's face; she no longer looked so terrified, but her eyes were wide and dark, filled with mute entreaty. Ranulf took a backward step, then turned and walked away.

RANULF left Shrewsbury that same day. He had no set destination in mind, wanting only to put as many miles as he could between himself and Gervase's "Nan," Lucette's "Mama." He was not ready to go home, though, and rode in the opposite direction, taking the road that led north.

It had not been a conscious choice, and he was halfway to Chester before he realized where he was heading. He was to be disappointed, for Maud was not at Chester Castle. She and her lord husband were awaiting the birth of her child upon one of his Welsh manors, the earl's servants reported, and only then did Ranulf remember that his niece was less than a month away from her lying-in.

He could have continued on into Wales. But he was done with acting upon impulse, without thinking first, for where had it ever gotten him? He was not going to burden Maud with his troubles at a time when she ought to be thinking only of her baby. He lingered a few more days at Chester, and then slowly, reluctantly, started back toward Devizes.

The borderlands were lawless in even the best of times. But once again, Ranulf rode unscathed over some of the most perilous roads in Stephen's realm. It may have been that indifference was the most formidable armor of all, that bandits somehow sensed the danger in attacking a man who felt he had nothing left to lose. It may have been no more than happenchance, sheer good fortune. Whatever the explanation, Ranulf reached Devizes safely in early September, bone-tired and disheveled and heartsick.

NIGHT had long since fallen by the time Ranulf dismounted in the bailey of Devizes Castle. He was handing the reins to a stable groom when Hugh de Plucknet came hastening out of the hall, a swaying lantern held aloft. "Is that you, Ranulf? Good God, man, where have you been? We'd begun to despair of ever seeing you alive again. Do you . . . do you know?"

"Know what?" Ranulf asked, but without interest. "Whatever your news, Hugh, hold it till the morrow. Tonight I want only to get myself up to bed." It was not to be that easy, however, for a woman's figure was framed in the open doorway of the hall, familiar even in shadow. Ranulf heaved a weary sigh, cursed his wretched sense of timing, and moved to meet his sister.

"Maude, I know you are furious with me for going off as I did," he said abruptly, hoping to delay her lecture. "I promise I'll hear you out, offer you all the apologies you want, but not now, not tonight."

Maude looked as exhausted as Ranulf felt, her dark eyes ringed with sleepless shadows, but he could find no traces of anger in their depths. "I am not going to reproach you," she said. "But I must talk to you, Ranulf, and it cannot wait."

Whatever she had to tell him, he did not want to hear, not more bad news, not tonight. But Maude would not be denied. Once they were alone in her dimly lit solar, she seemed in no hurry to unburden herself, instead fretting about the flickering candles, insisting upon pouring wine for them both, until he lost all patience and demanded to know what could not wait till the morrow.

Maude turned slowly to face him. "I have grievous news for you," she said haltingly. "The day after you rode away on your own, your friend Gilbert Fitz John arrived, stopping over on his way to Bristol. When he learned that you'd gone off alone, he was so dismayed that he insisted upon going after you. He sent a message to Robert that he would be delayed, and then he and Luke and their escort set out after you."

"I do not understand," Ranulf said uneasily, "why they did not overtake me, then, for I tarried along the way. But I did not see them at Shrewsbury, nor on the road."

"They never got there, Ranulf. They'd ridden less than ten miles when a fox chased a rabbit out onto the road, spooking their horses. The others were able to get their mounts back under control, but Gilbert was not so lucky and he . . . he was thrown."

Ranulf's mouth was suddenly dry. "Was he bad hurt?"

"I am so sorry," she whispered, "so very sorry. He broke his neck in the fall. Ranulf, he is dead."

36

DEVIZES, ENGLAND

October 1147

"Ranulf . . ." Maude hesitated, unsure how to proceed. Her every instinct urged against trespassing across emotional boundaries, for she respected the privacy of pain as few others did. But she'd begun to feel as if she were witnessing a drowning, and her greatest fear now was that her lifeline would fall short.

"Ranulf . . . you know that a wound can fester if it is not tended, spreading its poison throughout the entire body. Grief can fester like that, too. My chaplain says that you refused to talk to him again."

"I had nothing to say to him."

"You have nothing to say to anyone these days. That is what worries me." She waited, soon saw he was not going to respond. He'd picked up the fire tongs and was prodding the hearth back to life, his face hidden; all she could see was a thatch of fair hair, gilded by firelight. Maude watched him in silence for several moments, and then said purposefully, "Luke thinks that you blame him for Gilbert's death."

As she'd hoped, that got his attention. "That is not so," he said hotly. "I do not blame Luke!"

"I know," she said. "You blame yourself." She closed the space between them, reaching for his arm. "Ranulf, listen to me. It was not your fault. How could you know that Gilbert would follow you to Shrewsbury? What befell him was tragic, but it was an accident. It could as easily have happened on the Bristol Road—"

"But it did not." The words were wrenched from Ranulf, against his will. He at once repudiated them, saying huskily, "Maude, just let it be."

She studied his face, and then reluctantly loosed her hold upon his arm. "I want you to go to Bristol," she said. "I want you to find out how Robert's plans are progressing for our new offensive against Stephen."

He frowned. "Why me? Why not send Hugh or Alexander?"

"Because," she insisted, "I want to send you." At the door, she paused, glancing back over her shoulder. "If you cannot talk to me," she said, "mayhap you can talk to Robert."

MAUDE was wrong. Robert was the last one Ranulf could have confided in. What could he say, that because of his adulterous affair with another man's wife, his best friend was dead? Even if he no longer deserved it, he could not lose Robert's respect. He despised himself, though, for his moral cowardice. He'd not been able to bring himself to face Gilbert's widow, Ella, and now he could not bear for Robert to know the truth about him. What was that if not the worst sort of cowardice?

But Ranulf's shattered spirits flickered and the ache in his chest eased somewhat as the walls of Bristol came into view. Even if he could not unburden himself to his brother, just being with Robert would be a comfort. He could cling to Robert's abiding calm like a shipwrecked sailor, like so many others in need. Robert was always there for them all, a refuge for the lost and the disheartened and the damned. Mayhap Maude had known what she was about, after all, in sending him to Bristol.

The east gate of the castle swung open as soon as Ranulf identified himself. He and his men dismounted in the bailey, and he handed the reins of his stallion to Luke. "If you'll unsaddle him for me, lad, I'll seek out my brother and see about getting us all fed."

That sounded good to his tired and hungry men, and they headed for the stables, eager to get this final task over with. Luke nodded and followed, cheered by Ranulf's smile; he'd not seen it for weeks. The bailey was oddly empty, no servants in sight. But Ranulf knew the layout of Bristol Castle well enough to find his way blindfolded; for the past eight years, it had been his second home. The stone tower of the keep rose up against the western sky, crested by sunset clouds, the most likely place to find his brother. He was halfway there when a familiar figure appeared in the doorway, cried out his name, and then started toward him at a run.

Puzzled, Ranulf quickened his pace. "Will?"

By the time Robert's firstborn reached him, he was flushed and panting, badly winded by even so short a sprint, for he was as indulgent in his habits as his father was sparing, and he'd begun to develop a paunch while still in his twenties. He was in his thirties now, several years Ranulf's senior, cheerful and gregarious but not redoubtable, a sapling stunted by his sire's formidable shadow. Ranulf had rarely seen him so flustered, for he'd inherited Robert's equable temperament, if not his capacity for command. "How did you get here so fast?" he demanded. "We just sent a man out this morn. Where is Aunt Maude? She did come with you? Christ Jesus, surely she understood—"

"Understood what? Will, you're raving. Start over—at the beginning."

Will gulped in a great lungful of air. There was an autumn chill in the bailey, but beads of sweat had broken out upon his forehead. "You got no message, then? No, of course you did not. What was I thinking of? No man could get to Devizes and back in but a day—"

"Will! Name of God, man, what is wrong?"

"It is my father. It came upon him without warning, a sudden fever . . ." Will's mouth trembled and he struggled to blink back tears. "Christ pity us all, Ranulf, for the fool doctors . . . they say Papa is dying!"

RANULF was slumped in a window seat of his brother's bedchamber, his muscles cramped and stiff from so many hours of immobility. He'd lost track of the days, could not have said how long he'd been at Bristol. He measured time differently now; nothing mattered but the dwindling number of Robert's labored breaths. Night had fallen again, but the chamber was still crowded; men who'd come to bid their dying lord farewell lingered as long as possible, loath to let go.

Baldwin de Redvers stumbled away from the bed, blowing his nose in a napkin. William Fitz Alan was the next to go, head down, face wet. Each day brought more of them, Robert's friends and vassals. Robert had insisted that longtime servants be admitted, too, and men-at-arms who'd bled for him and would have died for him now if given the chance.

The men usually withdrew at sunset; that was the family's time. Ranulf knew the priests would not go far, though—just in case. Few kings had so many clerics at their deathbeds, but Robert had been one of the Church's most generous benefactors. He'd founded a Benedictine priory in Bristol, established a Cistercian abbey at Margam in South Wales, and he'd shown particular favor to the abbeys of Tewkesbury and Gloucester and Neath. Gilbert Foliot and Abbot Roger of Tewkesbury were in daily attendance, praying first for Robert's recovery and then, when the doctors could not bring down his fever, for his immortal soul.

Ranulf had seen fever scramble a man's wits, but so far, Robert remained conscious and coherent. After he'd been shriven of his earthly sins, he'd made his will, provided for alms to the poor, asked to be buried at his Bristol priory, and sought promises from his liegemen that they'd be as loyal to his son as they'd been to him. He was dying, Ranulf thought, as he'd lived, competently and quietly and with dignity, and Holy God Above, what would they do without him?

Amabel was sitting on the bed beside her husband, his hand clasped in hers. When she was not bending over to whisper private endearments or encouragements, she was watching his heaving chest, almost as if she were willing his every breath. She was younger than Robert, who'd celebrated his fifty-seventh birthday that summer, but she seemed to have aged years in a matter of days. Ranulf could not look long upon her face, so naked was her grief.

Maude was standing by the bed. Silent tears were spilling over again; she made no attempt to wipe them away, did not even seem to notice. Robert's children were clustered at the foot of the bed, as if afraid to stray too far. Roger's pallor was accentuated by his dark priestly garb, but it was the son, not the priest, who occasionally choked back a sob. Hamon's eyes were red-rimmed, his shoulders hunched and fists knotted in a futile defiance of Death. And Will sat, frozen, upon a coffer he'd dragged near the bed. He was about to come into his own, into great wealth and power. But he looked dazed, like a man soon to be cast adrift with no land in sight.

There were missing faces in the circle, loved ones whose absence grew more ominous as Robert's strength waned. Brien was under siege again at Wallingford. Robert's second son, Richard, was in Normandy, Rainald in Cornwall. Maud was on her way from Wales. And they all took great care not to mention Philip.

The room was shuttered against the cooling evening air, but Ranulf could still hear a muffled pealing in the distance. The churches of Bristol were tolling passing bells for their stricken lord on this All Hallows' Eve. Getting wearily to his feet, he approached the bed. Robert had been sleeping for much of the day. Ranulf knew he should be glad, for Robert's sake, that they were so close to the end, but he also knew he'd have done whatever he could to gain Robert more time, even if it prolonged his suffering. His brother's face was gaunt, burning with false, feverish color, his hair soaked in sweat. A thin white scar angled up into his hairline. Passing strange, but Ranulf could not remember ever noticing it before. How could he have missed it? Now he'd never know how Robert had gotten it. Why that should matter so much, he could not explain, but suddenly it did—enormously.

Reaching over, he gently touched Amabel's shoulder. As their eyes met, she drew a shuddering breath and covered his hand with her own; her skin was hot and her fingers had a perceptible tremor. When they looked back toward the bed, Robert's eyes were open.

"Are you thirsty, love?" It was not so much a question as entreaty, so great was Amabel's need to do something for him. When he nodded, Maude turned swiftly toward the table, poured hastily, and thrust a dripping cup into Amabel's hand. Ranulf watched as Amabel helped Robert to drink, tears filling his eyes. Robert saw and when his whisper drew Ranulf closer, he said, faintly but distinctly:

"Not . . . not just my little brother . . ."

The others may not have understood, but Ranulf did and his throat closed up. Robert was saying what they'd both always known, that the bond between them was more than brotherly. He could have been one of Robert's own sons, and he would mourn Robert all his days, as he'd never mourned his father.

Swallowing tears, he sought in vain to steady his voice enough to respond. Robert's eyelids were drooping again and when Maude whispered wretchedly, "Ranulf, we're losing him," he could only nod wordlessly. It was then that the door burst open.

A mantled, hooded figure flew toward the bed. "Papa? Papa, it's me!" Jerking back her hood, Maud turned a white, anguished face toward her mother. "For the love of God, Mama, tell me I'm not too late!"

She sank to her knees by the bed as Robert's lashes flickered, searching for his hand midst the coverlets. He no longer had the strength to talk, but his eyes sent her the only message that mattered—one of recognition. Maud sobbed in relief, then cried out sharply, "Randolph, hurry!"

That turned all heads toward the door. So intent were they upon the bedside drama, they'd not noticed that the Earl of Chester had followed his wife into the chamber. Dressed in somber colors, his demeanor no less decorous, he greeted Amabel gravely, then stepped forward to pay his respects to his dying father-in-law.

His courtesy was flawless and so rarely seen that his audience could not help marveling at it, for he was not a man to care about propriety. Ranulf and Maude exchanged speculative glances, never doubting that his wife's grief was not enough motivation to get him to join in Robert's deathbed vigil. There had to be more to it. And when he turned then, toward Maude, kissing her hand with ostentatious deference, they knew what it was. This was Chester's dramatic declaration of good faith, public proof that he was now dedicated to the Angevin cause, an ally to be trusted in the war against Stephen.

Maud tore herself away from the bed to embrace her mother. "Randolph," she repeated urgently, "where is she?" Still playing the role of the attentive husband, he jerked the door open and a moment later ushered a young woman from the stairwell. Maud reached out and when the wet nurse placed a small, swaddled bundle into her arms, she swung back toward the bed. "Look, Papa," she pleaded, "look at your first grandson!"

Robert did, and even as she saw the light dimming in his eyes, Maud was sure that he'd understood and died trying to smile at her son.

NOVEMBER swept October away in a deluge of early-winter rain, which did not slacken as the week wore on. London began to resemble a city under siege by nature; its citizens ventured out-of-doors only when they had no choice, the streets soon looked like deserted swamps, and the rain-swollen Thames became the enemy in their midst, threatening to flood with each high tide.

A fire roared in the hearth of the king's chamber in the uppermost story of the Tower keep, but it could not banish the damp, only held it briefly at bay. Although it was midafternoon, the sky was smothered in so many rainclouds that the day's dull light was already ebbing away, and Stephen, his wife, and William de Ypres had pulled their chairs close to the fire.

"I took care to mention no names, Will, but I've been consulting physicians about your . . ." Stephen paused tactfully. ". . . your problem."

"No need for such delicacy, my liege. Say it straight out, that I'm fast going blind." Ypres smiled as he spoke, but it was a smile to make both Stephen and Matilda wince.

"But that is just it, Will," Stephen said earnestly. "There might be hope for you. According to the doctors, there is a means of treating your sort of eye ailment. You're losing your sight because a film is forming over your eyes, like a cloud passing across the sun. By taking a needle—preferably a gold one—and sticking it into the white part of the eyeball, on the edge of what they call the . . . the cornea, it is possible to pierce the film. And once the pupil becomes black again, you'll regain your sight."

Stephen had carefully memorized what the doctors had told him, so that he might properly explain it to Ypres. But he saw now that his efforts had been wasted. Matilda could not repress a squeamish shudder, and Ypres was shaking his head with another of those ghastly, grimacing smiles.

"I've heard about that procedure," he said. "It is usually performed by traveling doctors, who go from town to town offering their services to those in need of miracles. Sometimes it even seems to work and the patient can see again—at least long enough for the doctor to collect his fee and move on. No, my liege, it was good of you to bother on my behalf, but I'd have to be crazed as well as blind ere I'd let any man plunge a needle into my eye."

"I'll admit it sounds stomach-churning, Will, but I wish you'd at least talk to the doctors. We could send to Arundel for Adeliza's physician, a man named Serlo, said to be as good a healer as you'll find in all of England. Or there is Robert Beaumont's physician, known as Peter the Clerk—"

"No."

Even then, Stephen would have persevered had he not caught Matilda's eye. "As you wish," he said reluctantly. "There is just one more thing I want to say, and then we'll speak no more on it. I value your counsel, Will, no less than your sword-arm. There is probably not a man alive who knows more than you do about battle lore and siege warfare. When you first revealed your ailment, you said you might go back to Flanders. I would hope that you'll stay here, where you are so needed."

It was one of the few times they'd seen the Fleming with his defenses down, reacting without the jaded cynicism that served so well as his shield. He cleared his throat, faked a cough, and muttered gruffly that he'd stay, then. Matilda rose, let her hand rest lightly on his shoulder for a moment, smiling over his head at her husband.

The door banged open without warning, so loudly that they all jumped. "I've been looking all over the Tower for you, Papa!"

"Eustace! We thought you were staying in Winchester for another week, lad."

"I was, but—"

"Eustace, you're soaked clean through! Come over to the fire and dry off."

Eustace frowned impatiently but allowed his mother to steer him toward the hearth. When she insisted then that he remove his wet mantle, Stephen intervened with a grin. "I think the lad has something to tell us, Tilda, for he looks about to burst. Go on, Eustace, give us your news."

"Did you hear about Robert Fitz Roy?"

"That he is ailing?" Stephen nodded. "Yes, we heard, but—"

"He is dead," Eustace interrupted, unable to wait any longer. "Papa, he is dead!"

They did not react as he'd hoped. Instead of being jubilant, they seemed dubious. "Are you sure, lad?" Stephen asked slowly. "When I was stricken with that fever at Northampton, rumor had me dead and buried about twice a day till I recovered, and—"

"This is no rumor. Uncle Henry sent a spy to Bristol to find out if his malady was life-threatening, and he well-nigh rode his horse to death getting back with his news. Robert died on Friday last, the 31st of October, soon after Compline. The entire town is in mourning, people weeping in the streets and grieving as if they'd lost their Holy Saviour—the fools!"

"I'll be damned," Ypres murmured; he and Robert were of an age, and the sudden death of his old adversary was an unwelcome reminder of his own mortality. Shaking it off, he forced a laugh. "And it was not even my birthday!"

Eustace laughed, too. "I'll get us wine," he offered, "so we can celebrate in proper fashion." On balance, he was disappointed by their tepid response to such momentous news. His mother was making the sign of the cross, and his father had yet to say a word. Eustace glanced gratefully at Ypres; at least he understood. Raising his cup, he said, "Let's drink to Robert Fitz Roy . . . and his speedy descent into the hottest depths of Hell!"

"Robert is not likely to go to Hell, lad," Stephen said. "For all our differences, he was a man of honour."

"Honour?" Eustace echoed indignantly. "What honour is there in trying to steal our throne? Jesú, Papa, do you never speak ill of anyone? I suppose you'd even find some good to say of the Devil!"

Stephen lowered his wine cup to stare at his son. "I'd hardly equate Robert Fitz Roy with the Devil," he objected, sounding more hurt than angry. "A man can be our enemy, Eustace, and still be a decent sort."

Eustace's lip twitched. He seemed about to retort when Ypres said coolly, "Fitz Roy was a worthy foe. We can be glad that he is dead without making a monster of him." Eustace flushed and gulped the rest of his drink. Matilda could not help noticing that he was stung by Ypres's rebuke, not Stephen's, and she sighed softly.

"That poor woman," she said, and her son looked at her in disgusted disbelief.

"Not you, too, Mama! Jesus God, how can you muster up even a shred of pity for Maude after all she—"

"Watch your tone when you speak to your mother!"

Matilda reached over, putting her hand on her husband's arm. "I do not think Eustace realized how rude he sounded . . . did you, Eustace?" she said evenly, waiting until he gave a shamefaced shake of his head. "As it happens, I was not speaking of Maude. I was thinking of Robert's widow. After forty years as the man's wife, she must be utterly bereft."

A strained silence filled the room. Stephen glanced from one to the other, not liking what he found. His wife looked very pensive, a sure sign she was troubled; Ypres was deliberately noncommittal, and Eustace was sullen. Stephen's eyes lingered on his son. Without meaning to, they'd let the lad down. He'd come hell-for-leather from Winchester with his news, thinking he was bringing them a wonderful gift, only to have them not even bother to unwrap it.

"This is a day we'll always remember," he said, as heartily as he could. "Your news changes everything, lad. Chester's defection no longer matters now, for Maude is burying the one man she could not afford to lose. Her claim to the English crown breathed its last when Robert did. It is over. At long last, it is over."

37

DEVIZES, ENGLAND

January 1148

So it is over . . . just like that? No regrets, no looking back, sail off into the sunset—what a simple way to end a war! A pity we did not think of this ere so many men died for you, but better late than—"

"Ranulf, enough!" Maude was livid. "I did not say it was over. It will never be over, not as long as I draw breath, and you, of all men, ought to know that. But we can no longer remain in England, and you ought to know that, too. Dear God, Ranulf, do you think I want to go? Back to Normandy, back to Geoffrey? What more proof can you have of my resolve than this—that I am forcing myself to do something so repugnant? This is a strategic retreat, not an abdication."

"You can talk all you want about continuing the fight from Normandy, but that is what it is—just talk. If we flee England, we are conceding defeat, conceding the crown to Stephen!"

"That is not so! I would never abandon my son, never!"

"Harry has Geoffrey to fight for him in Normandy. He needs you to fight for him in England! But you've grown weary of war, tired of the struggle."

"No!"

"Then why are you using Robert's death as an excuse to give up, to run away? If you do that, then what has it been for—the sacrifices and the battles and the dying—all for what?"

Maude was stunned by the attack. She'd never seen him like this, all nerve ends and raw rage. "You are not being fair, Ranulf! Whether you want to admit it or not, Robert's death changed everything!"

"Mayhap for you, but not for me." When she would have argued further, he flung up his hand. "There is nothing more to be said. If you are set upon deserting those who fought and bled for you, I cannot stop you. But do not expect me to follow you, and do not expect me to forgive you."

She stared after him in shock, too angry and hurt to call him back.

RAINALD was still groggy, for he'd not slept well the night before. "Maude, you're not making sense. You say he is gone? Gone where?"

"If I knew that," she said impatiently, "I'd not need your help. After you went up to bed last night, Ranulf and I had a terrible argument. I told him that I dared not remain in England now that Robert was dead. The dangers are so obvious; it never occurred to me that he might not understand. But he flared up in a wild rage, accused me of betrayal and cowardice and God knows what else, and then slammed out of the room as if it were on fire."

Rainald blinked sleepily. "You're still not making sense. Ranulf has always had a good head on his shoulders. Surely he sees how precarious your position has become. I like Will well enough, but he could no more fill Robert's shoes than he could get himself elected Pope. Brien has a plateful of his own troubles, and that whelp of Miles's is too green to be much help in fending off Stephen. Ranulf knows all that, not being a fool. So why is he balking?"

"Ranulf . . . is in a lot of pain," Maude said reluctantly; she did not feel she had the right to give away Ranulf's secrets.

Rainald nodded knowingly. "He always did think Robert could walk with the angels. But why are you so distraught about all this? So you quarreled and he went off in a sulk. He'll be back once his temper cools and then—"

"No," Maude interrupted, "I do not think he is coming back. He said nary a word to me. He just rode away at first light, was long gone by the time I sought him out to make our peace."

"What makes you think he is not coming back?"

"He gave his dogs away."

Rainald sat up abruptly. "Are you sure about that, Maude?"

"He gave his breeding pair to Hugh de Plucknet and his young bitch to Luke. He took only Loth, and rode away without a backward glance. Now you tell me, Rainald. Does that sound like a man who's just gone off to sulk?"

"No," he admitted, "no, it does not. Well . . . what we must do is figure out where he is likely to have gone. You gave him several manors here in Wiltshire, so we ought to send a man there first. What about that friend of his, Gilbert Fitz . . . whatever? Ah, no, he was killed; I forgot. Wait—I have it! I'll wager that we'll find him at Chester with Maud."

"And if he is? What then?"

"I go and bring him back, of course." After a moment to reflect, though, Rainald realized how impractical that would be. "I guess I cannot drag him back by the scruff of the neck," he conceded. "So . . . what do you want to do?"

"There is not much I can do, Rainald. If we can find him, I can write and entreat him to return. Otherwise, I can only hope he'll come back of his own accord."

"You dare not wait too long, Maude."

"I know," she said, "I know . . ."

MAUDE stood on the battlements of Arundel Castle, watching as Rainald rode away. A grey February fog had rolled in from the sea, and he and his men were soon swallowed up in it. Maude did not move, though, until Adeliza tugged at her arm, urging her back inside.

MAUDE had chosen to sail from Arundel so she might bid Adeliza farewell. It was also a closing of the circle, a means of punishing herself for her failure, ending up where she had begun.

Adeliza was embroidering as they talked, her needle flashing in the firelight. Maude had offered to help, but now her own sewing lay forgotten in her lap. The more she studied Adeliza, the less she liked what she saw. The other woman was pale, even for February, and alarmingly thin; always inclining toward the voluptuous, she seemed almost gaunt now. Maude's first reaction was to ascribe these troubling changes to the travails of the birthing chamber. In the eleven years since she'd wed William d'Aubigny, she'd been almost constantly pregnant, giving birth to seven surviving children and two stillborn.

"You are not with child again, are you?" Maude asked uneasily, for at Adeliza's age—her own forty-six—childbed was all too often a woman's deathbed, too. Adeliza cast her an oddly secretive, sideways look, then shook her head. "But you are ailing," Maude persisted, and this time she got no denial. Adeliza sewed in silence for several moments while Maude waited to see if more information would be forthcoming. When it was not, she reached over and touched the other woman's wrist. "I'll not pry," she promised, "but whatever you choose to tell me will never leave this chamber."

Adeliza continued to stitch, but color had risen in her cheeks. They were speaking German, the language of their youth, and the words themselves called up memories of an old intimacy. "Did I ever tell you, Maude, about the Flemish monastery founded by my lord father? It is at Affligham, near Alost, has a house for monks and one for nuns. My brother has written to me that he is thinking of taking holy vows there. It is my heartfelt wish to do the same."

Maude was speechless, so great was her surprise. It was not at all uncommon for widows to retire to a convent to end their days. But Adeliza was a wife and a happily wedded one, or so Maude had thought. And if she renounced the world, she'd be renouncing her children, too, the youngest still a babe in her cradle, the oldest not yet nine. Maude could easily understand a woman's urge to abandon the marital bed. So, too, could she comprehend the appeal of the cloister, so orderly and serene and reassuring in its very simplicity. But she could never have turned her back upon her children—not even for God.

Floundering for words, she said hesitantly, "What does Will think of this, Adeliza? You would have to get his permission ere the Church could accept you, would you not?"

"Yes." Adeliza kept her eyes upon her work, a cushion adorned with delicately drawn roses. "He thinks it is a foolish female whim, one that will pass. But it will not."

"Are you truly sure this is what you want, Adeliza? You seemed so contented with Will." Maude paused, but Adeliza ignored the hint. Maude watched her in bafflement, then tried again. "And what of your children? They are so young, little more than babies . . ."

"I am a queen, not a cotter's wife. There are more than enough hands to tend to their needs, to see that they want for nothing. Do not make it sound as if I am forsaking my family, Maude. I have been as good a wife and mother as I know how. I did no less for your father, as his consort and his queen. And I was a dutiful daughter, marrying as my father bade me. I have always done what was expected of me. Now—in the time remaining to me—I would follow my own heart."

"I was right, then. You are ill."

"Yes," Adeliza said calmly. "But you must not grieve for me, Maude. Death is just the door to Life Everlasting."

Maude frowned, struggling with her pain and her rebellious instincts; she knew nothing of surrender. "You are very dear to me," she said at last, "and you must let me help you." Her mind was racing, although not fast enough to outrun her grief. A doctor—she would find Adeliza the best doctor in all of Christendom. But almost at once she remembered Master Serlo, Adeliza's personal physician; if he could not help her, no mortal healer could. "Do you want me to talk with Will? Mayhap I could persuade him to let you take the veil . . ."

Adeliza concealed a smile, for Maude had hardly endeared herself to Will, would probably be the last one he'd be likely to heed. "It helps," she said, "to know that you understand," and then raised her head inquiringly, for a servant was hovering in the doorway.

"There is a visitor," he said deferentially, "for the empress," and Maude's lacerated heart took a sudden, joyful jump. Ranulf! But the man eventually ushered into the chamber was Brien Fitz Count.

IT was the first time that they'd been alone in a long while. Maude wished that she'd had some warning, wished that she'd had time to prepare herself, wished that she were not wearing this drab dark gown. "You got my letter, then?" she asked, and at once felt foolish, for why else would he have come to Arundel?

"Yes, I did," he said, just as needlessly. "Did Ranulf come back?"

"No, and we had no luck in finding him. Rainald and Maud have promised to let me know if they hear from him. I'd be grateful if you would, too."

"Of course I will." He looked tired and sounded dispirited. "I do not understand about this falling-out with Ranulf. It does not seem like him at all."

"Ranulf gave up a great deal to support my claims to the English crown. And now . . . now he fears it was all for nothing."

"No," he said, "it was not for nothing." Removing his mantle, he moved toward her. "You saw Maud," he said, "and Rainald, and you've come to Arundel to bid Adeliza farewell. But you were going to leave without seeing me."

Maude swallowed. She could feel her face getting hot, but she owed him the truth—this once. "I could not, Brien. It would have been too painful."

"Are you sorry, then, that I came?"

"No," she said softly, "no . . ."

"I have something for you." Reaching into his tunic, he drew out a soft pouch. It was finely stitched in her favorite shade of green, with silken drawstrings. Nestled within was a small coin, threaded upon a delicate gold chain. Maude's eyes misted as she gazed down at the keepsake, a silver penny minted at Bristol in her image, with her name and title engraved in Latin around the rim. Lady of the English, the queen who might have been.

"Thank you," she whispered. "Thank you, Brien."

He hesitated and then gave her one last gift—his jealousy. "Are you going back to Geoffrey?"

She did not pretend to misunderstand. "Not if I can help it." Her fingers clenched around the silver coin. "I have no choice, Brien, but to go. When Robert died, it all started to crumble. It was only a matter of time until I'd have fallen into Stephen's hands, and what good could I do Henry from an English prison? I was even in danger of losing Devizes.

We'd seized it from Stephen, but he'd taken it from the Bishop of Salisbury, and the new bishop is now demanding its return to the Church. Ranulf accused me of losing heart, but I did not, I swear I did not. I am not giving up."

"I know that. So does Ranulf. You are doing what you must—for your son's sake. There is nothing you'd not sacrifice for Henry." The corner of his mouth curved in a melancholy smile. "Who would understand that better than me?"

Maude shook her head. "Do not make me sound heroic, Brien. There is nothing heroic in defeat, nothing admirable in failure."

"You did not fail, Maude."

"No? Then why am I fleeing this accursed country like a thief in the night? More than eight years and God alone knows how many deaths, and what have I to show for it all?"

"Normandy," he said succinctly. "And do not tell me that was Geoffrey's doing, for you made it possible. You kept Stephen so busy defending himself that you gave Geoffrey the time he needed to win Normandy. That was as much your triumph as it was Geoffrey's. Do not let him tell you otherwise."

She summoned up an unconvincing smile. "I was never one for listening to Geoffrey," she said. "Thank you . . . for your abiding friendship and your faith in me, your faith in Henry. He is not old enough, not yet. But he will come back. He'll lay claim to our crown. And he will prevail."

"I never doubted that," he said, "for what son of yours could ever lack courage or fortitude? He'll be back for certes. But you will not . . . will you?"

"No," she admitted, "I will not. England may not have broken my spirit, Brien, but it did break my heart." It was a feeble attempt at a joke, holding too much truth for humor, and to her dismay, she found she could no longer blink back her tears. When he reached for her, she did not pull away, and they stood for a long time in a wordless embrace, while the fire burned down and the shadows advanced, for night was coming on.

SLEET was pelting the beach, and the ship rocked from side to side as Adeliza's men pushed it out of the shallows, then splashed hastily back to shore. Maude clung to the gunwale, with a white-faced Minna standing resolutely at her side. Alexander de Bohun, William Marshal, and the others were already heading for the canvas tent, and Maude now insisted that Minna seek shelter, too. "Go on," she urged. "It looks like a rough crossing."

Waves were starting to break over the bow. Back on the beach, the wind was blowing sand about and buffeting the onlookers, most of them servants from the castle and curious villagers. They soon were in retreat, until only three hardy souls remained: Brien and Adeliza and Hugh de Plucknet, who'd wed an English heiress but insisted upon seeing Maude safely to Arundel. She would miss Hugh. So many she would miss. So many she mourned.

The sky was as grey as the sea, splattered with clouds. The sleet stung her face and her eyes blurred as the shore started to recede. Adeliza and Hugh were trudging toward their horses, but Brien still stood at the water's edge, staring after the ship. Maude was trembling with the cold, but she stayed there on the pitching deck until the blue of Brien's mantle was no longer visible and England began to fade into the distance.

38

CANTERBURY, ENGLAND

March 1148

MATILDA knelt before the High Altar in the cathedral church of the Holy Trinity and prayed for peace. The choir was chilled and damp, but she stayed on her knees until her back began to ache. She should have been happy, for fortune seemed to be favoring Stephen at last. There were rumors, as yet unconfirmed, that Maude was preparing to leave England. Matilda herself was fulfilling a long-cherished desire; she'd acquired thirteen acres of land from the canons of Holy Trinity, Aldgate, so that she could establish a hospital to treat London's poor and pray for the souls of her dead children. And she and Stephen had finally been able to go ahead with their plans to found a Cluniac abbey at Faversham. But her satisfaction was shadowed by Stephen's continuing quarrel with the Archbishop of Canterbury, a clash of will made all the more ominous by the new Pope's obvious sympathy for the Angevin cause.

Archbishop Theobald's intransigence was all the more infuriating to

Stephen because he saw it as rank ingratitude; he and Matilda had done their utmost to secure the See of Canterbury for him, at Stephen's brother Henry's expense. Stephen had long insisted that Theobald was much too quick to acknowledge Maude after the Battle of Lincoln, and he'd soon convinced himself that Theobald was a secret Angevin partisan. Theobald was, after all, once the Abbot of Bec, the monastery that Maude favored above all others, and when Theobald had hastened over to Paris last May to meet with the Pope, Geoffrey of Anjou had just happened to be there, too. Coincidence or conspiracy? Stephen was sure he knew the answer.

Matilda had been less suspicious, loath to think ill of so pious and godly a churchman. But she was no longer so willing to give the archbishop the benefit of every doubt, not since the furor over the York See. The Pope had deposed the current Archbishop of York, Stephen's nephew, and then chose his own candidate, who thus became the first English archbishop ever to be consecrated without the consent of the king. To Stephen, it was a slap in the face—and Theobald had delivered it, for he'd supported the Pope wholeheartedly, exercising his considerable influence on behalf of the Pope's man.

Stephen had been provoked into taking drastic action of his own, urged on by his brother, who blamed Theobald for thwarting his reappointment as papal legate. When the Pope summoned England's bishops and abbots to a Church Council at Rheims in March, Stephen forbade the clerics to attend. Warned that Theobald meant to defy the ban, Stephen had then taken his court to Canterbury and put his ports under guard. But Theobald managed to slip through the royal net. Accompanied only by one of his young clerks, Thomas Becket, he'd arranged to board a small fishing boat in a secluded cove, and survived a perilous Channel crossing to be accorded a hero's welcome by the Pope and his fellow clerics.

Matilda sympathized with Stephen's indignation, but she was troubled by this widening breach with the Church; no good could come of it. Making the sign of the cross, she rose wearily to her feet; she tired more easily these days than she was willing to admit, even to Cecily, who awaited her now in the nave.

She should have said a prayer for Cecily, too, for all her attempts to find the other woman a worthy husband had come to naught. Most men were leery of Cecily's falling sickness; her fits scared them more than her marriage portion tempted them. The only ones who seemed willing to take advantage of Matilda's generosity were not the sort of men likely to make Cecily content. And Matilda's disappointment was tainted by guilt, for in a small, selfish corner of her soul, she was glad that Cecily remained unwed, so deeply had she come to rely upon the younger woman's loyalty and devotion.

As they left the church, it began to rain, and they quickened their steps. A sheltered passage led from the cloisters to the Archbishop of Canterbury's great hall, sparing them the worst of the weather. Shaking moisture from their mantles, they hastened into the hall, and then stopped in surprise, for a raucous celebration seemed to be in progress.

Trailed by a puzzled Cecily, Matilda made her way toward the dais. Just hours earlier, the atmosphere in the hall had been as cheerless as the rain, for they'd learned only that morning of the archbishop's daring escape. What, Matilda wondered, could have happened to dispel all the gloom?

As she tried to catch Stephen's eye, she was grabbed from behind, and found herself enveloped in a breath-stealing bear hug. Her son was grinning down at her; at eighteen, he was already as tall as his father and towered over the diminutive Matilda. "She is gone, Mama," he laughed. "The bitch is gone!"

"Are you sure, Eustace?"

He nodded and steered her protectively toward the dais. "She sailed for Normandy a fortnight ago. We ought to have heard ere this; too often, Papa is poorly served. But all that matters now is that Maude is no longer a threat. My only regret is that she never had to answer for her sins."

"I doubt that she came away unscathed from this war, Eustace. No one did," Matilda said, and held out her hand to her husband. Reaching down, he swung her up onto the dais, as jubilant as their son, for the passing years had tempered neither his capacity for exuberant rejoicing nor his faith in happy endings.

"It took us more than eight years, Tilda, to drive Maude from our shores, but she has finally gone back where she belongs—to Geoffrey—and I am not sure which of them I pity the more!"

"I am so glad," she avowed, "so very glad that it is finally over." But honesty compelled her to add a realistic qualifier: ". . . at least until Maude's son is old enough to renew the war."

Her men regarded her indulgently. She would always remain earthbound as they soared up toward the heavens, and whilst they pitied her lack of wings, they could not teach her to fly. "I may have to borrow money occasionally," Stephen joked, "but I flat-out refuse to borrow trouble. Maude's son is but a raw lad, not worth losing sleep over."

"You worry too much, Mama. How much danger can Maude's meagre whelp be?" Eustace scoffed. "With men as with horses, breeding always tells."

"Indeed it does," Stephen agreed, smiling fondly at his prideful heir. He'd long wanted to follow the Continental practice, have Eustace crowned in his lifetime. What better way to please his son and secure the succession? And what better time than now, with Maude in exile and her supporters in disarray?

Matilda smiled at them both. "It would be so wonderful," she said wistfully, "to have peace at last . . ."

HENRY I's royal manor at Quevilly, a suburb of Rouen, was adjacent to Notre-Dame-du-Pré, a priory of the great Benedictine abbey of Bec. Upon her arrival in Normandy, Maude chose to lodge in guest quarters at the priory rather than at her father's palace or in Rouen's formidable castle. And it was here that she was reunited with her husband, after a separation of more then eight years.

They were alone. Minna had reluctantly withdrawn, giving Geoffrey a baleful glance that catapulted him back in time, a time he did not want to remember, much less relive. Reaching for a wine flagon, he offered Maude wine and a sardonic smile. "I see the English climate has not mellowed your Minna any."

Maude accepted the wine, ignored the sarcasm. Outwardly composed, inwardly she felt hollow, so tense it actually hurt to breathe. Much of it was nervous anticipation at seeing her sons again. But it was Geoffrey, too. Just the sight of him brought back too many ugly memories, churned up old emotions that had been stagnant, becalmed during her years in England. Why could this man disquiet her so? Why did she let him?

There was no longer a need for pretense, for the polite conversation they'd exchanged in front of the prior and Minna: queries about health, condolences over Robert's death, those little courtesies that society expected of a man and woman nigh on twenty years wed. Geoffrey sat down in a high-backed chair, stretching long legs toward the hearth. It surprised her that he still looked so young. But why not? He was only thirty-four. She felt so much older, decades older.

Geoffrey was regarding her over the rim of his wine cup, an old trick of his, one that invariably made her shift self-consciously. "Since you chose to stay with the monks at the priory rather than with me at the castle," he said dryly, "I suppose that is your subtle way of hinting that you are not overeager to sleep in our marriage bed."

Maude sipped her wine. "I can assure you, Geoffrey, that I want to be in your bed just as much as you want to have me there."

An eyebrow shot up, another familiar mannerism. "A jest . . . from you? You have changed, dear heart!"

"Jesú, I hope so!" she said, with such intensity that he stopped in the act of pouring more wine and stared at her. "I do not want to go back to the battlefield that was our marriage, and I cannot believe that you do, either, Geoffrey. I do not want to be held hostage to memories anymore, or to keep paying for past mistakes. I want . . ." She faltered then, for what did she want of this man? Her husband, her intimate enemy, poisoner of her peace. But how long ago it all seemed. What had happened to that wronged young wife, so choked with helpless hatred? England had happened.

"Can it be," he said, "that you are offering to make peace, Maude?"

She swallowed a sharp retort. "And if I am?"

"You ask too much." But he was smiling faintly. "Suppose we start with a truce . . . see how many days that lasts."

His humor still held its buried barbs; they did not sting as much, though, as she remembered. "I'll try if you will, Geoffrey." Setting her wine cup down, she leaned forward. "Tell me of our sons."

"They are good lads, for the most part. Geoff has a temper and Will is somewhat lazy, has to be prodded. As for Harry's flaws . . . well, I need only remind you of last year, when he decided that invading England would be a marvelous way to get through the boredom of Lent. But why not judge for yourself?"

Maude stiffened. "They are here? You brought them?"

"The younger lads. Harry had gone off into town, but I left him word that you'd arrived."

Rising, he looked down at her, and she realized that some things would never change; she still had no idea what he was thinking. But when he smiled, it caught unexpectedly at her heart, for it was so like Henry's smile. What of her younger sons? Would their smiles be familiar, too? Would they know her? For so long, she'd yearned for this reunion, so why did she feel so nervous? He was holding out his hand. "I am ready," she lied, and let him help her to her feet.

WHAT shocked Maude the most was that she would not have recognized her own son. When she'd last seen Will, he was a chubby-cheeked child of three, and that was the image she'd kept in her mind for the past eight and a half years. But that little boy was forever lost to her, replaced by a russet-haired stripling in his twelfth year, as skittish as a young colt.

Geoffrey—or Geoff, as he'd brusquely corrected her—was no less unfamiliar, for great was the gap, too, between a five-year-old and one not far off from fourteen. Geoff had the same fair coloring as his brothers: bright, curly hair, a sprinkling of freckles, and wide-set grey eyes; no matter how troubled her marriage had been, not even Maude's most virulent enemies could ever have challenged Geoffrey's paternity. Geoff had some of his father's swagger, too. He was leaning against the wall, arms folded, eyes guarded, for Maude had yet to recover from her initial misstep, when she'd remarked, before she could think better of it, that he bore a strong resemblance to Henry.

Geoffrey was also leaning against the wall, their poses too similar for coincidence; it was obvious to Maude that her sons sought to emulate him in all particulars, and that was not a comforting thought. This was not going well, not at all. The boys were wary, not readily tamed, and conversation was painfully stilted. They were just shy, Maude told herself, and that would pass. "I almost forgot," she said, with forced cheer. "I brought you back presents from England."

Putting Henry's gift aside, an ivory and ebony chess set, she gave Will his gift first, a rare lodestone that acted as a magnet. Will seemed pleased, but her present for Geoff was not as successful. It was a book handsomely bound in red leather, *The Song of Roland*; she'd remembered Ranulf's saying how much he'd enjoyed Roland's adventures as a boy. Geoff thanked her politely enough, but then added snidely, "Harry is the only one who likes to read."

"And the only one with manners, too," Geoffrey observed. Although he'd spoken with a smile, it was clearly meant as a reprimand, and Geoff mumbled an apology. But it was Geoffrey he wanted to placate, not her. They were strangers, these sons of hers. Beloved strangers. Blessed Lady Mary, was it not enough that she'd lost her crown? Was she to lose her children, too?

Geoffrey was not surprised by the awkwardness of this meeting, nor that Will seemed so diffident, Geoff so sullen. He'd expected as much, for Will had no surviving memories of his mother, and Geoff resented what he saw as favoritism to his elder brother. But what Geoffrey had not expected was that he should actually feel a prickling of pity for Maude, laboring to bridge an eight-and-a-half-year gap in the space of a single afternoon.

They were all relieved by a sudden commotion in the outer chamber, welcoming the distraction. A moment later the door flew open and Maude's firstborn burst in upon them. "Mama!" It had been almost a year since she'd seen Henry last, and he'd taken several consequential steps toward manhood in those intervening months. Had he not been her own, she'd have guessed him to be older than fifteen, for his shoulders were beginning to broaden, his voice had deepened, and he had none of the uncertainty, the gangling awkwardness of a boy growing into a man's body; he seemed to have bypassed that stage altogether. But he still looked blessedly familiar and blessedly at ease with her, as he demonstrated now by striding forward eagerly and giving her a hearty, welcoming hug.

With Henry there, conversation no longer flickered like a spent candle; it flared brightly, feeding upon his enthusiasm, his obvious pleasure in having his mother home. During the next hour, the talk ranged far afield, touching upon a variety of topics. Maude's voyage from Arundel. Memories of Robert. Archbishop Theobald's dramatic arrival at Rheims. Henry's new stallion. The latest news from the Holy Land, a bloody massacre of German crusaders by the infidel Turks. The Pope's proposed elevation of their ally, Abbot Gilbert Foliot, to the bishopric of Hereford, an action sure to outrage Stephen. For it always came back to that, to Stephen and a stolen crown.

"I'd hoped to hold out for a few more years, until you were old enough to confront Stephen yourself," Maude told her son, and Geoffrey could only marvel, for implicit in her apology was an admission of failure. He almost made a gibe about her newfound humility, remembered their tenuous truce just in time. Henry had turned aside to let Will show him how the magnet worked. But at his mother's regretful words, he glanced up with a quick smile.

"You've nothing to reproach yourself for, Mama. Without Uncle Robert, how could you have continued the war? But what you began, I will finish."

Maude had assumed that years must pass before Henry could mount a serious challenge to Stephen's sovereignty. Looking now at her son, though, she realized that she'd not long keep him in Normandy. He was already racing headlong toward manhood and his destiny, to be decided upon an English battlefield. It seemed such a cruel irony that she'd finally gotten him back, only to have to let him go, much too soon.

Picking up Geoff's discarded book, Henry began to leaf through it, and the book immediately became a gift of great value to his brother. He tried to snatch it back, and a brief scuffle ensued, which revealed to Maude that Henry liked to tease, and that Geoff's jealousy was a banked fire, ready to flare up at the least provocation. Theirs was a bond much in need of mending, if it was not already too late. Geoffrey ought to have taught them better. But then, what did he and Hélie know of brotherly love? It saddened her that her sons should be rivals, not the steadfast allies her own brothers had been.

Almost as if he'd read her thoughts, Henry said suddenly, "Where is Uncle Ranulf? I assumed Uncle Rainald would stay behind in Cornwall, but surely Uncle Ranulf came back with you?"

"No . . . he did not."

Henry's disappointment was keen, for Ranulf was his favorite uncle. "Why not? I do not understand, Mama. Where is he, then?"

"I do not know, lad," Maude admitted unhappily. "I do not know."

39

CHESHIRE, ENGLAND

March 1148

RANULF was not sure where he was—somewhere along the Cheshire-Shropshire border—but it did not really matter, since he did not care where he ended up. Like a ship that had snapped its moorings, he just went wherever the wind blew him.

When he'd ridden away from Devizes Castle in such a rage, he'd wanted only to put as many miles between himself and his past as possible. But he could outrun neither his grief nor his guilt, and after a fortnight of aimless wandering, he'd realized what he needed to do if he was ever to have any peace of mind again. It was what he ought to have done as soon as he learned of Gilbert's death. He had to face Gilbert's widow and ask her forgiveness.

It had taken him a week to gird himself for it, and then another week to find her, for she'd returned to her father's manor near Hereford. But if he'd hoped for absolution, he'd come to the wrong woman. Ella's widowhood was too new to allow for perspective, too wretched to allow for mercy. Anger was easier than acceptance, and she blamed Ranulf. Gilbert had confided in her about Ranulf's clandestine affair with Annora Fitz Clement, and she reasoned that if not for his ill-fated passion for another man's wife, her husband would not have died. And Ranulf could not argue with her, for he believed that, too.

Afterward, he truly was a lost soul. He'd slowly drifted toward the north, indifferent to direction or destination, rousing himself only enough to make a wide detour as he neared Shrewsbury. Eventually he would run out of money. Although Robert had bequeathed him a generous legacy and he still held the Wiltshire manors Maude had given him, he would have to return to claim them, and that he was not yet able to do. And so he continued his erratic odyssey through a countryside blighted by war, no longer even sure what he was fleeing, sure only that he could not go back.

On this blustery March Monday in Lent, he'd covered less than ten miles, for the night before he had drunk too much, picked up a prostitute, and tried to blot out his pain with cheap red wine and bought caresses. All it gained him was a miserable morning-after, the worst headache of his life, and an ugly scene with the girl, who'd sought to steal his purse while he slept. Hours later, he still felt queasy and shaken. His head was throbbing, he'd not been able to tolerate the weight of his hauberk, and for most of the day, the mere thought of food was repellant.

By midafternoon, he'd begun looking for lodgings. But the few villages he passed through were no more than hamlets and Chester was at least fifteen miles away, if not more. He was beginning to think he'd have to bed down out in the open when he encountered an elderly shepherd tending a handful of scrawny sheep. The man was fearful at first, for strangers were suspect in these parts; the border shires had never known much peace. But the fact that Ranulf spoke English reassured the shepherd somewhat, and after he'd stopped Loth from chasing off the man's mangy dog, he got the directions he needed. Ahead lay the hamlet of Broxton, where a narrow lane forked off from the Chester Road, toward the west. If he followed it for a few miles, he'd reach the village of Farndon, and the priest there would put him up for the night.

It was a relief to know there would be a bed at the end of his journey, for the wind was rising and dusk settling in. Ranulf kept a wary eye on the sky as he rode; getting rained upon would be the final indignity of this utterly dismal day. Off to the side of the road, he caught sight of a grove of alder trees and he guided his stallion toward them, for alder trees were usually found near water. After dismounting, he led his horse forward, waiting while it drank its fill. Loth had ranged on, but Ranulf didn't worry, knowing the dyrehund would not go far. Kneeling by the pond, he splashed water onto his face, and then cupped his hands so he could drink, too.

A watering hole just off a main road was a bandit's dream come true, an ideal place to ambush thirsty travelers . . . and Ranulf should have known that. He did know that, but his hangover had dulled his caution as well as his senses. Oblivious of his surroundings, he did not notice as the men emerged stealthily from hiding. Only when his stallion snorted in alarm did he look up, and by then, it was too late. They were almost upon him, and before he could get to his feet, one of them lunged forward, an upraised cudgel poised to strike.

Ranulf flung himself sideways, and the cudgel missed by inches, so close that he felt a rush of air on his face as it plunged downward. Kicking out, he was lucky enough to rip the other man's leg with his spur, and the man jumped backward with a startled oath. That gave Ranulf enough time to regain his feet, but not to draw his sword. It was only halfway out of the scabbard when the second bandit struck. The blow was hard enough to stagger him, but he felt no pain, and did not realize at first that he'd been stabbed, not until he saw the bloodied blade of the outlaw's dagger.

There were three of them, and they knew what they were about. One grabbed for the reins of Ranulf's horse; the other two closed in on Ranulf. He yelled for Loth, then grappled with the man brandishing the cudgel. A deadly sort of dance ensued, in which he struggled with one assailant while trying at the same time to keep the man's body between him and the knife-wielder.

For a few frenzied moments, he actually managed it, immobilizing the one man in a bear hug, fending off the other's thrusting dagger. The third man was still trying to stop the frightened stallion from bolting, but he'd soon join the fray, too. Desperation had lent Ranulf strength, but there was blood on both men, his blood, and he was being forced away from the pond, exposing his back to the knife. The second bandit saw his chance and moved in for the kill.

The light was fading and Ranulf did not see what happened next. The man seemed to trip, for suddenly he was not there anymore. Ranulf heard a scream, snarling, and then the sounds of a wild struggle, as the outlaw and Loth thrashed about in the shadows. But Ranulf's reprieve was brief. He was weakening fast, and when his boot slipped in the mud, he went over backward into the pond.

His assailant landed on top of him. He'd lost his cudgel in the fall, but wasted no time groping for it in the shallows. Instead, he grabbed Ranulf's hair and shoved his head under the water. Ranulf fought frantically to get free, but each time he gulped a lungful of air, he was pushed under again. The water was rapidly turning red, and then black, and he was spiraling down into that darkness, unable to break his fall.

He was almost unconscious when the killer's grip slackened, but his body fought to survive even as his brain clouded, and he battled his way back to the surface, back to life. Gasping for breath, he had no strength to resist when he was seized again. As easy to drown as a newborn kitten, he choked and sputtered and sucked in as much air as he could in the moments he had left. But he was not being pushed down into the pond's depths. Another bandit had waded into the water, was dragging him toward the shore. It made no sense to him. In his mind's eye, he saw himself rolling clear, scrambling to his feet, getting away. Instead, he vomited weakly into the wet grass, bracing for the bite of steel as the outlaw's blade found his throat.

"Easy, man, easy." The voice was friendly, the words French. He'd heard his attackers as they sought to subdue him, their speech guttural and oath-laden and unmistakably English. Making an enormous effort, Ranulf turned over onto his back.

The bandits were gone. In the deepening dusk, he could make out the blurred outlines of a peddler's cart, blocking the road. A muscular youth stood several feet away, a hefty club in one hand, a chain in the other; at the end of the chain was one of the most fearsome dogs Ranulf had ever seen, as broad-chested as a mastiff, as black as the darkening sky. A second stranger was kneeling by Ranulf's side. As their eyes met, he repeated:

"Easy now. You've swallowed half the pond and you're bleeding badly. But the danger is past. Those craven knaves took off like rabbits. I'd like to think the mere sight of my brother and me was enough to strike fear into their evil souls, but I suspect it was Cain there who put them to flight!" He chuckled and then gave an exclamation of dismay. "What are you doing? Just lie still, get your breath back."

Ranulf ignored him. "My dog . . . where is my dog?"

The youth in the shadows moved forward as Ranulf struggled to sit up. "Over there," he said, pointing off toward his right. "There is naught you can do for him, though. He's dead."

"No," Ranulf exclaimed, "no!" Unable to rise, he crawled over to his dog. Loth lay on his side, tongue protruding, the fur on his chest matted and dark with blood. Ranulf's rescuers had followed, were urging him away from the body. Ranulf never heard them. Cradling Loth's head in his lap, he buried his face in the dog's ruffled fur and wept.

RANULF awoke to pain and a wrenching sense of loss. He remembered at once: the ambush by the pond, his panic as his lungs filled with water, bursting for air. Loth's death. But that was his last memory, holding the dyrehund's limp, lifeless body in his arms. After that, nothing.

Opening his eyes, he squinted up into midday sunlight. He was outdoors, wrapped in blankets before a smoking fire, wrapped, too, in makeshift bandages. The pain had begun to recede, but never had he felt so weak. He willed himself to move again, propping up on his elbow so he could look around. His movement attracted immediate attention: a low growl, disturbingly close at hand, a quick "Down, Cain!" and then, "Josce, he's awake!"

Last night's Good Samaritan was bending over him. He looked to be about Ranulf's own age, in his late twenties, with a pleasant, bluff face, thick sand-colored hair, and uncommonly green eyes. "Well, you're back with us at last. How are you feeling? Never mind, foolish question. You look puzzled. Do you not remember what happened?"

"Only some of it. Did I . . . pass out?"

His benefactor nodded. "You were set upon burying your dog, even if you bled to death doing it. We tried to talk some sense into you, for you were hardly in any condition to be digging graves and there was always the chance those swine might come back. But I'll say this for you; once you get an idea into your head, you plough that furrow, no matter what. Fortunately you then swooned dead away—bad choice of words—ere we had to bury you with the poor beast. So we bundled you into the cart, stopped your bleeding as best we could, and set up camp once we'd gone far enough to feel safe from pursuit."

Raising his voice, he beckoned to his brother. "Josce, fetch the man some of our dinner. You need to eat, even if you have to force it down. Ah, I almost forgot—we found your horse. And . . . and I did bury the dog for you. You set such store by him . . ." He paused, sounding the way men often did when caught out in a kindness—somewhat embarrassed. "I thought you might want this," he said, holding up Loth's leather collar.

Ranulf took it, squeezing back tears. When he looked up again, the youth called Josce was offering a wineskin. Ranulf swallowed and discovered it held a pungent, tart cider. Josce watched him drink, then said, "From what we saw, your dog chewed up that wretch something fierce ere he got stabbed. That one'll be limping off to Hell, and feeling those teeth ripping into him every time he hears a dog howl."

"Loth saved my life," Ranulf said, "and so did you. I'd have drowned for certes if you had not come to my aid. I thank Almighty God for you both. May He bless you with His Bounty for the rest of your days."

Josce smiled oddly, as if at a private joke Ranulf could not be expected to understand. He was the younger of the two brothers, no more than twenty, and none would have taken them for kin. He was taller, leaner, far more intense, as taut as a notched bow and as ready to fire. "I wonder," he said, "if the memory of your blessing will soon catch in your throat like a fish bone, gagging you whenever you remember making it."

Ranulf frowned. "Why should it? I owe you both my life. How could I not be grateful?"

Josce shrugged. "You'd best give credit where due, to my softhearted brother. If it had been up to me, I might well have ridden by, keeping my eyes on the road."

"No, you would not," his brother contradicted. "Never in this lifetime."

Josce shrugged again. "Mayhap not," he conceded. "Kill a weasel and every man's chickens sleep safer at night. I might even have fished you out of that pond. But after that, I'd have left you to fend for yourself. It was my brother's foolhardy notion to load you into our cart, to tend your wounds as if you were our own kin. So if thanks are owed, you pay them to him, not me."

"I see," Ranulf said, although he did not. Josce seemed to be going out of his way to be belligerent. Why?

Josce's brother was no longer smiling. "Josce feared that if you died of your wound and were found in our cart, men would blame us for your death," he explained somberly, but Ranulf still did not understand.

"Why would you be blamed? Because you are . . . peddlers?"

Josce smiled, without humor. "No . . . because we are Jews," he said, and laughed bitterly then, at Ranulf's involuntary recoil. "From your look of horror, I assume you've never been in the company of . . . what do you Gentiles like to call us? The Devil's minions? Servants of Satan?"

He was not far wrong, for Ranulf had never had any dealings with Jews. He knew of them, of course. They'd come over to England from Normandy after the Conquest. Most were moneylenders, for they were not permitted to join the craft guilds. They were often accused of usury, of coin-clipping, and sometimes suspected of profaning the Eucharist, stabbing the Host till it bled. Four years ago in Norwich, an even more unspeakable accusation had been made, that they had crucified a Christian child in an unholy mockery of the Passion of Christ. The Norwich sheriff had not believed the charge, taking the town's Jews into the castle to shelter them from a mob's fury. But his skepticism had not stopped people from flocking to the church where the boy was buried, or from proclaiming him a sainted innocent, a martyr to the True Faith.

Ranulf had not believed the Norwich accusation, either. He'd never shared the view so many did, that the Jews were Christ's enemies in their midst, doing the Devil's bidding to corrupt unwary Christians. For if they were truly so evil, he reasoned, his father would not have protected them. And the old king had, granting them a charter which gave them the right to live freely in England, to hold land, to have recourse to royal justice. If his father, a man so quick to suspect the worst, had not feared the Jews, why should he?

And yet . . . and yet, they were still aliens and infidels. They might look like their Christian neighbors, speak French as well as any Norman baron, but the fact remained that they were dangerously different. They rejected the concept of Original Sin. They did not believe in the Holy Trinity. They denied the divinity of Our Lord Christ. They faced the horror of Eternal Damnation without flinching, without fear for their immortal souls.

For an unnerving moment, Ranulf felt an instinctive unease; he was, after all, utterly at their mercy. But then common sense reasserted itself. These men had saved his life. They had chased after his horse, bandaged his wound, even buried his dog. What more proof did he demand of their goodwill?

"I have my vices," he said, "but ingratitude is not amongst them. I admit I was taken aback, merely because I've never known any Jews. But if it did not matter last night, it ought not to matter today." He smiled wryly. "I do not remember your asking if I was a Jew ere you came to my aid. I am deeply grateful to you both, owe you a debt I can never repay."

The elder of the brothers smiled, too. "I'll settle for a name. I am Aaron of Bristol. Josce, as you know, is my brother. What do men call you?"

"Ranulf . . . Ranulf Fitz Henry." Ranulf's new identity was not assumed for their benefit. He'd stopped calling himself the king's son the day he rode away from Devizes.

AARON and his brother were indeed peddlers, as Ranulf had guessed. Filling their cart with woolens imported from France, with needles and thread and metal mirrors, they routinely made the perilous journey from Bristol up to Chester. They were on their way back to Bristol when they'd stumbled onto the ambush, and Aaron insisted that Ranulf ride with them till he recovered his strength. They'd cleansed his wound with honey, applied a plantain poultice to stop his bleeding; they were, of necessity, knowledgeable in the healing arts and well supplied with life-saving medicinal herbs. But he still needed a doctor's care, Aaron stressed, for the danger of infection was always hovering close at hand. Fortunately, the knife blade seemed to have missed any vital organs. Ranulf had been amazingly lucky, Aaron concluded, and Ranulf heartily concurred.

Ranulf slept through most of the day and the night that followed. The next morning they made him as comfortable in their cart as they could, and headed for home. They were both Bristol-born and -raised, and very thankful that Bristol had so far been spared the suffering of Winchester and Oxford and Lincoln and the other English cities caught up in this accursed civil war. Aaron had a wife and young son awaiting him at home, and he cheerfully passed the time extolling the virtues of his Belaset and their two-year-old Samuel. Josce walked alongside the wagon, brusquely declining Ranulf's offer to ride his stallion, leaving it to his brother to carry the conversational burden.

Aaron was happy to oblige, and Ranulf found himself being given a rare glimpse into a hitherto hidden world; what surprised him the most was that it was, in so many ways, a familiar world, too. Aaron's concerns were those of any Bristol citizen: pride in his son, worry over the war, anxiety lest the new Earl of Gloucester not prove himself to be the man his father was, for Bristol's continuing safety depended upon his strength.

Slowly, though, distinctly Jewish details began to emerge. Ranulf learned that Jews did not eat pork, which was considered unclean. The Jewish Sabbath was not Sunday as in the Christian faith, but sundown to sundown, Friday to Saturday. And dogs were not often found in Jewish households; their formidable Cain was an object of curiosity back in the Bristol Jewry. Although Aaron didn't say so, Ranulf was sure that the dog's name had come from Josce, a sardonic swipe at those who claimed all Jews bore the Mark of Cain.

Ranulf had never ridden in a cart before. It was an experience he could have done without, so jolting and rough a ride that he soon scrambled out to walk beside Josce, fearing that the constant jouncing might break his wound open. After that, Aaron insisted upon pausing frequently, ostensibly to rest their horse, and Ranulf gained new appreciation for his tact.

As they grew more comfortable with Ranulf, the brothers began to talk more frankly of politics. Aaron praised the old king for keeping the peace and putting his Jewish brethren under the protection of the Crown. Josce pointed out, though, that the king profited handsomely from the presence of the Jews in his realm. "Think of us," he said sarcastically, "as a herd of milch cows, which the king alone has the right to milk."

Aaron's opinion of Stephen was one Ranulf had often heard voiced in the Christian community, too, that he was "good-hearted, but as easily swayed as a weather vane." On the whole, he said, Stephen was favorably disposed toward the Jews, but he could be most unfair when his pride was pricked by the Lady Empress, his foe. And he told Ranulf of the experience of the Oxford Jews. When the empress held the city, she'd imposed a levy upon the Jews there, and when Stephen recaptured Oxford, he demanded that they pay three and a half times the amount of her levy, as punishment for obeying her unlawful command. Ranulf remembered when Maude had decided to impose that levy; it had seemed a good way to raise much-needed money. He'd never given a moment's thought to Oxford's hard-pressed Jews. Listening now to Aaron, he wished that he had.

They did not debate theology; that was too inflammatory a subject. Aaron said only that Jews and Christians shared a belief in the same God, the God of Israel, and by unspoken consent, they ventured no further. But as Josce slowly thawed toward Ranulf, he could not resist regaling him with facts sure to startle.

It was eye-opening to Ranulf to learn that Jews were by their own laws forbidden to break bread or drink wine with Gentiles. Obviously this was not strictly enforced, for the brothers had been sharing their meals with him for two days now. But it was disconcerting, nonetheless. He was surprised, too, by Josce's revelation that English Jews, no matter where they lived, could be buried only in the Jewish cemetery in London; he had to admit that seemed like an undue burden to impose upon people already mourning a loved one.

What Ranulf found most astonishing, though, was Josce's mischievous description of the Rite of Abraham, which involved snipping away the foreskin from the most vulnerable part of the male anatomy. By now he'd discovered that Josce's humor was as perverse and unpredictable as Geoffrey of Anjou's, and he half suspected that he was being teased, until Aaron confirmed that they did indeed circumcise their young sons. It was, Ranulf decided, one more reason to be thankful he'd been born into the True Faith, but he did not let himself pursue that line of thought. He did not want to think of Aaron and Josce as Jews, for he did not want to think of them as doomed, forever lost to God's Grace.

It was a strange interlude for Ranulf, the first time in two months that he'd formed any bond with another human being, other than an occasional tumble in a harlot's bed. It did not seem real somehow, that so much could have happened—have changed—in such a brief time: that he'd come so close to death, that he'd lost Loth, that a good Christian could look upon Jews with respect, even friendship. The respite ended that night, though, as they made ready to bed down by the fire. It was then that Aaron mumbled sleepily that with luck, they might be able to reach Shrewsbury on the morrow.

Ranulf jerked upright, brought back to reality with a jolt. "I cannot go to Shrewsbury!"

They sat up, too, regarding him curiously in the flickering firelight. "Ranulf, I've told you from the first that you need to have that wound tended by a doctor. There is one in Shrewsbury, also a monk at their abbey said to be skilled in the use of healing herbs. But we'll not find another one till we reach Hereford or Gloucester, and it would not be wise to wait that long."

"I cannot go to Shrewsbury, Aaron. Wise or not, I cannot."

"Why not?"

Ranulf hesitated. He could not tell them about Annora, the unforgivable botch he'd made of his life. But he owed them more than evasion or rebuff. "I was not completely truthful with you ere this."

"What a surprise," Josce murmured dryly, and his brother scowled in his direction.

"Not now, Josce. What did you lie about, Ranulf?"

"It was not a lie, more like a . . . a sin of omission." Did Jews know about such things? Now was not the time, however, to elaborate upon the finer points of Christian doctrine. "When I called myself Ranulf Fitz Henry, that was indeed my father's given name. What I omitted was his title—Fitz Roy."

There was a brief silence as they absorbed this. Josce whistled softly, and Aaron said carefully, "You are saying, then, that you are one of the old king's . . . natural sons?"

"One of his bastards," Ranulf said bluntly. "No need for delicacy, Aaron. But you see now why I cannot go into Shrewsbury. The town and castle are held by Stephen, and I've been fighting for my sister. I cannot risk being recognized." That had never kept him away from Shrewsbury in the past, an inner voice jeered, but Aaron and Josce could not hear it, and they took his excuse at face value.

"No, I suppose you cannot," Aaron agreed, sounding worried. "The problem is that we have business dealings in Shrewsbury. Mayhap if we let you off ere we reached the town and then came back for you afterward . . . ?"

"That is a right generous offer, but I'd not impose further upon your goodwill. You've a wife eager to welcome you home, Aaron. It would be ill done on my part if I repaid your kindness by making her fret over your safe return."

Aaron could not deny that he was impatient to get back to Bristol and Belaset. "I will not feel easy in my mind, watching you go off by yourself. There is a doctor in Chester, but that is too long and dangerous a ride on your own. Have you no friends or kindred closer at hand?"

Ranulf shook his head, but he knew Aaron was right. It would indeed be foolhardy to ride all the way to Chester, as weak as he was, and without Loth to watch over him. Pain rippled toward the surface; he resolutely pushed it back into the depths. In any event, he had no intention of going to Chester; he was not yet ready to deal with Maud's curiosity or—worse—her pity. After some reflection, he had the answer.

"William Fitz Alan," he said triumphantly. "He used to be castellan of Shrewsbury Castle, until Stephen chased him out. But he still holds a castle at Blancminster, on the Welsh border. I'd be sure of a welcome there, and if he does not have a doctor in his household, he'll send for one." Best of all, there'd be no awkward questions, no prying, no pity, for Fitz Alan was an ally, not a friend.

"As you will," Aaron agreed dubiously. A wounded man going off into the Marches alone . . . not a reassuring prospect. But it was not his choice. It was Ranulf's. Rolling over into his blankets, he comforted himself with the thought that come morning, Ranulf might change his mind.

Ranulf did not, though. He arose determined to seek out Fitz Alan at Blancminster, and after a hurried breakfast, he stood beside them in the road, not sure how to say farewell. How could he just ride off? But he knew they'd have been insulted had he offered them money. There must be something he could do for them . . . and then he smiled, for he knew what it was.

"Thanking you seems a meagre response, indeed, for giving me back my life. I will remember you, Aaron and Josce of Bristol, and wish you well all your days. And if—God forbid—you ever find yourself in trouble on one of your trips to Chester, get word to the Countess of Chester and she will come to your aid, for I will let her know what you did for me. She makes a good ally, does my niece," he said, and his smile twisted awry. Too good an ally. How selfish he'd been to entangle her in his adultery. But surely God would forgive her, when his sin was so much greater?

"That is most generous," Aaron said, and Josce made a jest about friends in high places, but he looked pleased, too. It was no small boon Ranulf was offering; to be a Jew was to ride always along the cliff's edge, and in Chester, where no Jews dwelled, there would have been none to speak up for them. Aaron came forward, Josce following, and they helped Ranulf up into the saddle. He smiled again, wished them Godspeed back to Bristol, and then turned his stallion toward the west, toward Wales.

The brothers stood in the road, watching him ride away. He looked back once, waved, and Aaron waved, too. Somewhat to his surprise, so did Josce.

"I ought to have wished him good luck," Aaron said suddenly. "I wish I'd remembered."

Josce nodded. "He'll need it."

40

THE WELSH MARCHES

March 1148

RANULF had been to Blancminster once before, with Robert, and he remembered that it was sixteen miles northwest of Shrewsbury. That would make it, by his reckoning, fourteen or fifteen miles due west. Even if he kept his mount to a slow canter and stopped often, he should still be able to reach Fitz Alan's stronghold before dark.

He soon realized, though, that this would be the longest fifteen-mile ride of his life. He had to halt and rest frequently, and each time it became more difficult to get back into the saddle. By noon, he was already wondering why he'd been such a fool, and if he'd had it to do over again, he'd have elected to ride into Shrewsbury with Aaron and Josce, and let Annora and his overblown pride and Stephen's sheriff be damned. But that was a regret four hours and five miles too late. All he could do now was to make the best of a bad bargain.

With that in mind, he resolved to seek the first shelter he could find, no matter how shabby or meagre. But the narrow road was deserted, the land uninhabited. He passed no hamlets, not even an occasional secluded cottage. Villages did not thrive in the shadow of the border, for this was bloody, disputed ground, English today, Welsh yesterday, who knows on the morrow. Ranulf felt as if he were riding through a ghost country, watched by unseen eyes, and his unease increased apace with his exhaustion. He plodded on, telling himself that he must be almost there, that the castle was likely to come into view at any time, just around the next bend in the road. But what he encountered was a river, swollen with the spring thaw.

He drew rein, staring in dismay at the expanse of muddy brown water. The River Dee snaked its way south from Chester, twisting and doubling back on itself like a fugitive seeking to throw off pursuit. Could this be the Dee? If so, he was miles to the north of where he'd hoped to be. How could he have gone so far astray?

Oddly enough, his very fatigue enabled him to slough off his despair; he was just too tired to be truly alarmed. He would, he decided, camp there by the river for the night. Come morning, he could decide whether to retrace his path back to the Chester Road or follow the river south toward Blancminster.

He'd been accustomed from boyhood to caring for horses, but never had such simple tasks exacted such a toll. By the time he'd unsaddled and watered his stallion and tethered it to graze, the sun was retreating west into Wales. Making a fire was an even more laborious effort, for first he had to gather and shred birch bark and dry moss to use as tinder, and then find a hard stone to strike sparks against his dagger. Once he finally got a fire going, he forced himself to eat some of the bread and salted fish he'd gotten from Aaron. It troubled him that he had so little appetite; he knew that was not a good sign.

It was not yet dark, but he laid out his blankets by the fire, wincing as he pulled his hauberk over his head. The interlocking metal links weighed more than twenty pounds and seemed to have gotten heavier as the day dragged on, but if he'd been wearing it on the Chester Road, it might have deflected that outlaw's dagger. Rolling up his tunic, he slowly unwound the bandage Aaron had fashioned from a shirt, fearing what he would find. Red streaks radiated outward from the wound, like spokes on a wagon wheel, pus oozed around the edges of the plantain poultice, and the lightest touch of his fingers caused pain. Aaron had prophesied true when he'd argued the need for a doctor's care. Well, God Willing, he'd find one on the morrow.

Ranulf awoke with a start. The sky was still dark, speckled with stars above his head. The air held a damp chill, but he'd flung the blankets off in his sleep, and when he touched his face now, his skin felt as if it were afire. Trying not to panic, he lay back upon the blanket. A fever was not always fatal. He was ill, there was no denying that. But he might be better by morning. If not, then he'd spend another day here, recovering his strength. There was no need to fear, not yet. He kept telling himself that until he finally fell asleep again.

He slept fitfully for the next few hours, but as the fire burned down, his temperature soared. Sweating and shivering by turns, he drifted in and out of a feverish sleep. His dreams were suffused with heat and hectic color, full of confusion and vague, unspecified menace. And when he was prodded awake in midmorning, he still seemed to be in that world of shadows and sinister foreboding, for two men were standing over him and one of them had a lance leveled at his throat.

Bandits! That was his first guess, followed almost immediately by—No, Welsh—for their faces were clean-shaven, mustached. There was no comfort in that realization, though, for the Welsh were just as likely to slay him—a Norman-French knight—as outlaws would. He swallowed dryly, taking care not to move, not flinching even as the spear dipped lower, hovering scant inches now from his chest. They were regarding him impassively. Did they understand French? And even if they did, what could he say to keep that spear from continuing its downward thrust?

"I am a king's son," he said hoarsely, "and worth more alive than dead." Not even a flicker crossed those inscrutable faces. He repeated himself, in English this time. Again, no response, and that spear never wavered. Powys lay across the river, but the name of its ruler eluded him. The man had fought with them at the Battle of Lincoln; why could he not remember? Seizing upon the one name he did recall, Cadwaladr's brother, the King of Gwynedd, he said hastily, "Owain Gwynedd!" At last he got a reaction; at least Owain's name meant something. "I was seeking Lord Owain out," he improvised, "with a message from the English king. Lord Owain will want to hear it."

Did they understand? Impossible to tell. He lay very still, watching the spear as they conversed briefly in Welsh. He could taste sweat on his upper lip, hoped they knew it was from fever, not fear. Why it should matter what they thought of him, he could not have explained, but it did, if only because these enigmatic Welshmen might well be the last men he'd ever see.

They seemed to have reached a decision. The spear was shifting, being withdrawn. Ranulf's sword had already been claimed while he slept. Reaching down, one of the men drew Ranulf's dagger from its sheath, then produced a thin leather thong, which he used to lash Ranulf's wrists together. And Ranulf expelled a shaken breath, knowing now that he had gained himself some time. How much time was still very much in doubt.

THEY followed the river upstream to a ford, splashed across into Wales, and then headed north. The road narrowed until it became little more than a deer track. They were in hill country now. The woods had not yet begun to show spring buds, and wherever Ranulf looked, he saw bare, wintry branches rising up, stabbing at the sky. Each time he swayed in the saddle, he grabbed the pommel, somehow managed to hold on. He was soon drenched in sweat, though. His ears were echoing with the labored, rasping sound of his own breathing. And by afternoon, a dark stain was spreading across his tunic.

When one of the Welshmen noticed the bleeding, he gestured toward the road ahead and then held up five fingers. Ranulf interpreted that to mean they had only five more miles to go. He clung to that hope as tightly as the saddle pommel. Five miles was not so very far. He could endure another five miles. In the past few months, life had lost its sweetness and he'd lost his way. But no longer. Death was once again the enemy, his indifference and apathy drowned in a Cheshire pond. And as his captors led him deeper into Wales, he clutched at that—his will to live—as his armor, his shield against whatever awaited him in this alien land.

The sun vanished with surprising swiftness, and the sky was soon the color of smoke. A hill loomed out of the twilight dusk, encircled by a timber palisade. As they rode toward it, it slowly took on a familiar shape, materializing into an English-style castle. But it was garrisoned by Welsh; mustached faces were peering over the palisade as the gate swung open to admit them.

Ranulf suddenly knew where he was—at Mold, the Welsh stronghold of Robert de Montalt, steward to the Earl of Chester. He remembered hearing of its fall, captured by Owain Gwynedd after a fierce three-month siege. Castles were not native to Wales, unknown until Marcher lords such as Montalt began to encroach across its borders, buttressing their claims with fortresses of timber and stone. So this must be Mold, Ranulf reasoned, Owain Gwynedd's conquered castle. But as they rode across the deep ditch that separated the inner and outer baileys, Ranulf had another flash of memory. Mold had more than one name. According to William Fitz Alan, the Welsh called it Yr Wyddgrug—"the burial mound."

Ranulf had to be assisted from the saddle. Once he was on his feet, his bonds were cut. Leaning heavily upon his guard's arm, he was taken into the great hall. A number of men were standing by a huge open hearth, and he knew at once which one was Owain Gwynedd. He needed neither throne nor crown to proclaim his rank; the man himself was impressive enough to require no external trappings of authority. It helped that he was tall and tawny-haired, for his were a people more commonly dark and slightly built. But Ranulf knew his impact could not be explained away as easily as that. God had granted Stephen a handsome face and athletic body, too, but not a king's "presence." Whereas his own father—stout and bowlegged and balding—had been able to dominate any gathering, to awe and intimidate by the sheer force of his royal will.

When Ranulf was brought forward and forced to kneel before Owain Gwynedd, the Welshman regarded him thoughtfully. "There was no message from the English king, was there?" he said, in accented but understandable French. When Ranulf shook his head, he smiled slightly. "And are you truly a king's son?"

"So they did understand me . . ."

"Enough to get you here. What happens next remains to be seen." Owain had dark-grey eyes, a direct, incisive gaze. "Who are you? And more to the point, who'd want to ransom you?"

"I can afford to ransom myself." Did his voice sound as odd to Owain as it did to him? Slurred and strangely muffled, as if coming from a great distance. "I am what I claimed to be—the son of an English king and a free woman of Wales."

Owain smiled again, this time with ironic amusement. "Welsh blood? How convenient."

"But true. My mother was Angharad ferch Rhys. She lived in your domains . . . the Conwy Valley . . . and my uncle dwells there still, Rhodri ap Rhys . . ."

Ranulf had just expended the last of his family lore, but what little he knew was apparently enough, for the Welsh king no longer looked so skeptical. "Rhodri ap Rhys is your uncle? A good man, I know him well." He gestured then, giving Ranulf permission to rise. Ranulf made a game try, lurching to his feet, but then the ground seemed to fall away and the room began to tilt alarmingly. The next that he knew, he was on a bench, choking on a mouthful of mead. He sputtered, waved away the wineskin, and Owain leaned over him, holding up his hand, the palm smeared with red. "How were you hurt . . . and when?"

"Cheshire bandits, four days ago . . . I think." Surely it was longer than that? He was being urged backward now, onto the bench, and he was quite willing to obey. Mayhap if he closed his eyes, the hall would stop spinning.

Owain stepped aside, beckoning to one of his men. "Fetch a doctor straightaway." Glancing back at Ranulf's chalky pallor, he added prudently, "And a priest."

RANULF knew he was very ill, but he was too weak to worry about it. He wanted only to sleep, yet people would not leave him alone. When they were not changing his bandage, they insisted upon piling wet compresses onto his forehead and chest, or spooning hot liquids into his mouth. He'd protest peevishly, yet they paid him no heed. They were patient and persistent and engulfed him in a sea of Welsh, not a word of which he understood. Sooner or later, though, they would go away, allowing him to slide gratefully back into oblivion.

Ranulf had lost all sense of time. He could not have said whether it was hours or days later when he opened his eyes, saw Owain Gwynedd standing by the bed. "I . . . I am not doing so well, am I?" he whispered, and the Welshman shook his head.

"The doctor says your wound has festered."

"Am I going to die?"

"You are in God's Hands, lad, as are we all."

Ranulf pondered that evasive answer. "I think," he said, "that I'd best see a priest . . ."

Owain nodded. "I've sent to Basingwerk Abbey for one who speaks French." Ranulf seemed to be trying to speak again and he leaned closer so he could hear.

"If . . . if I die, will you let the Countess of Chester know?"

Owain nodded again. "I've sent word to your uncle Rhodri, too," he said, and Ranulf lay back, too weak to talk further, but oddly comforted by Owain's assurance that if he did die, his kin would be told.

RANULF'S dreams trapped him in a fever-induced world of darkness and loss. Sometimes he was in familiar surroundings, back at Devizes or Bristol. More often he was under siege again at Oxford, watching Winchester go up in flames, thrashing about in a murky Cheshire pond. And always . . . there was trouble. Maude was in danger and he could not protect her.

Annora was lost and he could not find her. He kept hearing her cry his name, but she was always out of sight, out of reach. Gilbert was trapped in that burning church, and he could do nothing. Again and again those he loved needed his help. Again and again he failed them.

His father was there, too, a remote figure never quite in focus. Robert, keeping his distance, looking sad and disappointed. And a gentle ghost, more than twenty years dead: Angharad, his mother. He'd not dreamed of her for years, and her face was indistinct, shadowy, but he knew it was she. He recognized the bright hair, the low-pitched voice, the soothing sounds of her Welsh. Unlike the other apparitions in these terrible dreams, she did not disappear when he reached out to her. Instead, she took his hand and held tight. He held tight, too, and she stayed with him. Through the worst of the delirium and fever and pain, he could sense her presence, a beacon in the dark, guiding him home.

THE room was shuttered, but even the dim rushlight hurt Ranulf's eyes. He was wondering where he was and why he felt so weak when a woman bent over the bed. She held a basin of water, dipped a cloth into it, and laid it upon his forehead. Her touch was sure, her fingers cool against his skin. He studied her through his lashes; she seemed somehow familiar and yet he could not remember seeing her before. "Who . . . are you?" The sound of his own voice startled him, for his words emerged as a croak. She was even more startled. She gasped and her hand jerked, spilling water onto the bed coverlets. When she spoke, her voice sounded strangely familiar, too, but he did not understand what she was trying to tell him. "I am sorry," he mumbled. "I speak no Welsh . . ."

More Welsh rang out, but this voice was male. Joining the woman at Ranulf's bedside, a greying, burly stranger beamed down at him. "We'd about given up on you, lad!" This Ranulf understood, and it puzzled him for a moment, before he realized that the man was now speaking French. Turning away, the man switched briefly back to Welsh, and another figure emerged from the shadows, this one a young girl, no more than fourteen or fifteen. "Ranulf . . . men do call you Ranulf? No, do not try to talk. For more days than I can count, we were sure each breath you drew was like to be your last! You do not know me?" The query followed by a hearty, booming laugh. "How could you? I am Rhodri ap Rhys, your uncle. And these are your cousins, Rhiannon and Eleri."

"Your . . . your daughters?"

"My lord king's message said that you were in a bad way. I thought it best to bring my lasses along, so that at least they'd have a chance to bid you farewell. And glad I am that I did. I'm not sure you'd have made it if not for Rhiannon here."

Rhiannon murmured in Welsh, and her father patted her on the arm before turning back to Ranulf. "She speaks no French, but she still suspects that I'm bragging on her. I'm just speaking God's Truth, though. Even after the doctor gave up, my girl did not. She never left your bedside if she could help it. She prayed for you and talked to you and held your hand, so you'd know, she said, that you were not alone."

"Tell her," Ranulf whispered, "that I did know . . ."

His young cousin had squeezed between Rhodri and Rhiannon so that she could get a better look at Ranulf. "Papa, his eyes are closed! He . . . he is not dead, is he?"

"No, child. He is sleeping again, that is all."

Rhiannon leaned over, brushing her fingers lightly against Ranulf's cheek. "He feels cooler," she said. "Papa, do you truly think he will recover?"

"Yes, lass, I do. But I did not," he admitted, "until now."

RANULF would have few memories of the days that followed. Mostly he slept. Owain Gwynedd was gone, back to his royal manor at Abergwyngregyn. The monk-priest had returned to his brethren at Basingwerk. Declaring that Ranulf no longer needed his care, the doctor, too, departed. But each time Ranulf awoke, his uncle and cousins were there.

He came to rely upon it, that they'd be close at hand whenever he needed them. Rhodri straddled a chair by the bed, translating French into Welsh and back again, demanding that Ranulf eat all the food he brought over from the castle kitchen, putting Ranulf in mind of a shepherd hovering over a lamb long given up for lost. When the boredom of the sickroom became too much for Eleri, she slipped out to explore the castle grounds and flirt with the garrison. But she volunteered to wash Ranulf's hair, tried to talk him into letting her shave off his beard so he would look "properly Welsh," and borrowed a lute to play for him at night before he fell asleep. And he was convinced that in all of Christendom, he could not have found a more devoted nurse than Rhiannon.

Unlike Eleri, Rhiannon never seemed to tire of her vigil. During the day, she was always within the sound of Ranulf's voice, and after dark, she slept on a pallet by his bed so that she could hear him if he needed her in the night. It did not matter that he could not understand what she said; he lay still, listening to the ebb and flow of her soft-spoken Welsh, as lulling as the familiar patter of rain upon a roof, and he knew that he would not die in this alien place called Yr Wyddgrug, the "burial mound." His cousin Rhiannon would not allow it.

WHEN Rhodri opened the shutters, spring sunlight flooded the chamber. After a fortnight in the semi-gloom of a sickroom, Ranulf was dazzled by this sudden blaze of brightness. "Another week in here," he told Rhodri, "and I'd have been blinder than any bat."

Rhodri swung around to glare at him. "Do not joke about that—not ever!"

Ranulf blinked. "What did I say amiss?"

His bewilderment was not feigned, too sincere to doubt. "You truly do not know, Ranulf?"

"Know what?"

"That Rhiannon is blind."

"No . . . that cannot be! She has been taking care of me, bringing me food, even pouring me wine . . . I saw her do it!"

"You sound just like all the others," Rhodri said impatiently, "those who believe that to be blind is to be utterly helpless. Do not deny it, Ranulf. When you think of a blind man or woman, you think of a beggar, seeking alms by the roadside."

"It is not that," Ranulf insisted, not altogether truthfully. "You just took me by surprise. It never occurred to me that . . . that she could not see. She did not stumble or bump into things or— And I am proving your point," he said, and Rhodri nodded.

"You'll learn, lad," he said tolerantly. "But do not start treating her any differently now that you know. My girl cannot abide pity." Moving toward the bed, he looked down pensively at Ranulf. "I've a question to put to you. You're on the mend for certes. But do you think you're strong enough yet to travel? I think you'd do well enough in a horse litter, but if you'd rather wait a few more days, we can. It is up to you."

"Where would we be going?"

"Why, home, lad. Back to the Conwy Valley, to Trefriw. You'll stay with us whilst you regain your strength. You've grown up in your father's world. Now it is time you got to know your mother's world, too."

"I do not understand," Ranulf confessed. "I am a stranger to you, the son of your enemy. Why have you opened your hearts to me like this?"

Rhodri was puzzled, for the answer was so obvious. "Because," he said, "you are my sister's son."

41

GWYNEDD, WALES

May 1148

FOR Ranulf, Wales was one surprise after another. He'd known it was very unlike England, a land of deep, trackless forests, jagged mountain peaks, sky-high icy lakes, barren moorlands, and no towns or cities. He had not known, though, that it was so beautiful, a country of untamed grandeur and lofty, soaring vistas, and for the first time, he understood why his mother had never stopped looking back.

He was surprised by how well his Welsh kin lived. Wales was a much poorer country than England, but even by English standards, Rhodri ap Rhys had a comfortable home in the hills overlooking the Conwy Valley, where his cattle grazed—for the Welsh were hunters and herdsmen, not farmers. As in England, the great hall was the heart of the manor. The kitchen and private quarters were set apart, but otherwise, the layout of a Welsh manor house was not drastically different from its English counterpart. Reassured by the familiarity of his new surroundings, Ranulf hoped to make a quick recovery, and learn a little Welsh in the process.

His convalescence was to last far longer than he'd anticipated. He'd assumed—unrealistically—that he'd be up and about in a matter of days, but he soon realized that it was going to take weeks to regain his strength, a frustrating outlook for a man who'd never been gravely ill before.

He had better luck with Welsh, picking it up with what appeared to be impressive ease and remarkable speed. He let himself bask in the admiration of his newfound kin for a while, and then confessed that his mastery of Welsh was not as amazing as it seemed, for he'd spoken the language in childhood. He'd thought it had disappeared into the darkest depths of his memory after his mother died, he admitted. But all he'd needed was to fall into a Welsh well. His own forgotten Welsh had to bob up to the surface if he had any hope of keeping afloat, he laughed, and when his cousins and uncle laughed, too, he felt inordinately pleased, and not just because he'd made his first successful joke in Welsh. Their approval was already beginning to matter to him.

That was the greatest surprise of all—how fast he'd become so fond of this hitherto unknown family of his. It went well beyond the natural gratitude he might have expected to feel. Memories of his mother had come flooding back along with his bygone Welsh, and that was part of it, but not all. He liked them enormously, as simple as that.

He remembered that his uncle was two years younger than Angharad, which put Rhodri in his midforties. His hair was short and already so grey that it was impossible to tell if he'd once been flaxen-haired like Angharad. He was not tall, but he had a powerful wrestler's build, and it was no surprise when he boasted that in his youth he'd excelled in the sport, equally popular on both sides of the border. He was one of the most affable men Ranulf had ever met, cheerful and expansive, with a serene good humor that Ranulf found truly remarkable once he learned about his uncle's past. Other men, if they were lucky, had merely a passing acquaintance with tragedy. But Rhodri had a long and intimate relationship.

He was the sole survivor of four siblings, having lost his sister to the English king, his two elder brothers to untimely deaths. He and his wife, Nesta, had been blessed with six children, but three had died in childhood, and his last son, Cadell, had died in a fall from his horse two days before his twentieth birthday. Cadell had outlived his mother, though; by then Nesta was already six years dead and Rhodri wed again to a neighbor's widow. Enid was a classic Welsh beauty, dark and sultry, and it was obvious that Rhodri adored this voluptuous young wife of his, too much ever to put her aside—even though she had been unable to give him a son. A man who'd buried so many loved ones, a man with a barren wife, no male heir, and a blind daughter—such a man might well have despaired of his lot. But Rhodri bore his losses with the patience of Job, and Ranulf could only marvel at his uncle's faith and fortitude and life-affirming optimism.

A bed had been set up for Ranulf in the great hall, screened in at night so he could sleep. He liked this arrangement, for it enabled him to observe comings and goings in the hall, practice his Welsh on all who came within range of his bed, and get to know the three very disparate women of his uncle's household.

Enid was a pleasure to watch, gliding gracefully about like a sleek, dark swan, indolent, incurious, accommodating as long as it did not inconvenience her too much, as placid and lovely to look upon as a Welsh mountain lake. She was the mistress of the manor, but she seemed quite content to delegate her responsibilities to her stepdaughters. She was not the wife Ranulf would have wanted for himself, but he did envy Rhodri the way her eyes sparkled as soon as her husband walked through the doorway, and he could not help wondering if Annora smiled so sweetly for Gervase Fitz Clement.

Fourteen-year-old Eleri won Ranulf over at once, for she seemed like a younger, Welsh version of his favorite niece. Like Maud, Eleri was lively and playful, with a penchant for practical jokes and a taste for mischief. She was a pretty girl, with dimples, dark eyes, and a heart-shaped face framed by pale ash-brown hair that looked shot through with silver in bright sunlight. She was her father's pet, and was not above taking advantage of that when it suited her purposes. She treated Enid with an amused indulgence that few fourteen-year-olds could have carried off, doted upon her father, signified her approval of her new kinsman, Ranulf, by teasing him unmercifully, and was utterly and fiercely devoted to her elder sister.

Rhiannon did not resemble Eleri in either appearance or temperament, but she returned the younger girl's devotion in full measure. Ranulf guessed her to be in her midtwenties. She was taller than Eleri, slim and straight-backed. Her hair was her most striking feature, a rich russet shade of chestnut, and like Eleri, she'd gotten their mother's brown eyes. If Enid was a swan and Eleri a frisky kitten, Rhiannon put Ranulf in mind of a young doe, wary and elegant and as careful as her younger sister was carefree. She was deliberate in all that she did, but whether that had always been her nature or was the result of her affliction, Ranulf couldn't tell. He prided himself upon being a good judge of character, but Rhiannon eluded him at every turn, for he kept colliding with his own presumptions about the blind.

Ranulf had been told about his cousin's accident. She'd been struck in the eye by an ice-encrusted snowball, and within a year, the sight in her other eye had begun to fail, too. That was often true, the doctors had explained to Rhodri, but they could not explain why it was so. All he knew was that at the age of eight, his daughter had gone blind.

Ranulf could imagine few crosses heavier to bear than that of blindness, and it followed, then, that those so stricken would be lost souls, drowning in darkness, tragic and pathetic and helpless. He still thought Rhiannon's plight was tragic. But she was certainly not pathetic, nor was she helpless.

She startled him with occasional flashes of wry humor, for humor and blindness seemed utterly incompatible to him. She puzzled him by her stubborn insistence upon doing things for herself when it would have been so much easier to let others help. She made him feel self-conscious, for he had to keep censoring himself, lest he inadvertently say something she might find hurtful or offensive. And again and again she amazed him by her eerie ability to act as if she were sighted.

Blindness was not an uncommon affliction in their world, but Ranulf had no firsthand experience of the malady; those fortunate enough to have families to care for them rarely ventured out on their own. The only blind people he'd ever seen were beggars, for that was the brutal choice they faced: begging or starving. Who, after all, would hire a blind man? What could he do? Nothing, of course.

Ranulf would once have answered that question in the negative, too. But no longer, not after watching his cousin at Trefriw. Rhiannon assisted her sister and servants in running Rhodri's household. She crossed the hall with sure steps, detouring around the center hearth without hesitation. She invariably recognized her father even before he called out to her, and when neighbors began to drop by, eager to get a glimpse of Rhodri's long-lost English nephew, she greeted them by name. She mended clothes, and while she needed to have her needle threaded for her, she then reached into her sewing basket and selected the proper spool of thread. She changed Ranulf's bandage without fumbling, poured him wine without spilling it, and whenever he spoke to her, she turned and looked toward him so attentively that he found it hard to believe those wide-set dark eyes could be sightless.

And so he studied Rhiannon in mystified fascination, awed by what he could not understand, but his bafflement was a barrier between them—until the evening when she checked upon him before retiring, crossed to the table by his bed, and exclaimed, "Your candle has gone out!" And as he watched in amazement, she carried the candle over to the hearth, returning a moment later with her hand cupped protectively around the flickering flame.

This was too much for Ranulf. "How in hellfire did you do that?" he blurted out. "How could you know the candle was no longer lit?"

"Have you never heard of second sight?" she murmured, so earnestly that it was a moment before he realized he was being teased. When he laughed, she did, too, and then she explained that the quenched candle gave off no heat. At the time, he was amused by her wordplay, relieved that he'd not affronted her, and intrigued by the simple logic of her answer. Later, though, he would look back upon this incident as a turning point for them both.

Having discovered that Rhiannon was so matter-of-fact about her blindness, Ranulf felt free to satisfy his curiosity, sure now that it would not be at her expense. She readily revealed her secrets. Trefriw was the only home she'd ever known; was it so surprising that she should know it so well? As long as the household members took care not to shift furniture around, she could move about with confidence. Nor was there anything magical about her ability to recognize others; she knew the sound of their footsteps, as she knew the sound of their voices. She did not overfill a wine cup because she crooked her finger over the rim and poured until she felt the liquid at her fingertip. Her sewing spools were notched so that she could tell if the thread was white or black. She sewed tags into her clothes so that she would not make the mistake of wearing a garment inside out. She knew that venison was being served for dinner by the smell of roasted meat. She needed her fingers and ears to play her harp, not her eyes. There was no sleight-of-hand, she insisted, none of the "tricks of the trade" practiced by traveling jongleurs. It was just a matter of learning to heed her other senses, to rely upon memory, and to be patient.

She'd made it seem so easy, and yet Ranulf knew it was not. He no longer saw her achievements as uncanny, even miraculous. But once he understood just how hard-won her victories were, he felt such admiration for her courage and perseverence that pity was crowded out. He thought of her now as "Cousin Rhiannon who is blind," not as "blind Rhiannon," and so began what was to be one of the most rewarding and significant friendships of his life.

IT took Ranulf a month to recover, and another month until he began to feel like his old self again. Each time that he broached the subject of his return to England, his uncle and cousins raised such strenuous objections that he let the matter drop. It was easy enough to do, for he did not know where he wanted to go once he left Trefriw. He was content to let the days slide by, and before he knew it, the summer was slipping by, too.

THERE was much about Welsh law that caused Ranulf to marvel, for this small, mountainous land was a crucible of political heresy. Of all the states in Christendom, in Wales alone did secular law take precedence over canon law, and the Welsh diverged from their Church's teachings on a number of controversial issues. The Welsh took the provocative view that a failed marriage was a mistake to be remedied, and offered generous grounds for dissolution. Even more remarkably, women were given the same right as men to walk away from an unhappy marriage. Maude would have loved Wales, Ranulf thought, for Welsh women could not be forced into marriage against their will, nor did the husband invariably get custody of the children when a marriage did end, as was always the case elsewhere.

Of particular interest to Ranulf were the laws regarding illegitimacy. Here, too, the Welsh were breaking new ground. In Wales, unlike the rest of Christendom, if a bastard-born child was acknowledged by the father, that child then enjoyed equal status with those children born within wedlock. This staggered Ranulf. Robert could have claimed the crown if England had such an enlightened law, and how much suffering they all could have been spared if only that had been so! But he was thankful that another Welsh law was not in force across the border, for in Wales, a youth reached his legal majority at age fourteen. Lord help them all if his nephew Harry could have claimed to be lawfully on his own at fourteen!

It was this latter law which explained the presence in Rhodri's household of several boisterous teenage boys. A Welsh youngster might legally reach manhood at fourteen, but he still had a lot to learn, and so it was the Welsh practice to place him in a local lord's service to receive his training in arms, similar to the English squire's apprenticeship. Sixteen-year-old Padarn had been with Rhodri only a fortnight, and was still settling in. Ranulf could not help noticing how uncomfortable the youth was in Rhiannon's presence, and when his cousins wanted to show him their favorite spot for an outdoor meal, he picked Padarn to accompany them, hoping that time spent with Rhiannon would allay the boy's qualms.

Padarn and Eleri had raced their horses ahead, leaving Ranulf and Rhiannon to follow at a more sedate pace. Rhiannon was riding pillion behind Ranulf, and she soon announced that they were nearing the waterfall. The sound of rushing water came clearly to Ranulf's ears, too, but he could not resist teasing her about her "second sight," for that had become a running joke between them. Rhiannon agreed that second sight was indeed a useful skill, especially for those who lacked "first sight," and he reined in his stallion to look upon this waterfall his cousins so loved.

Rhaeadr Ewynnol it was called, "the Foaming Fall," and well worthy of the name on this mid-August Friday, for the river was running high after a fortnight of steady rain. The dropoff was not steep, but spectacular in the sunlight, as churning white water spilled over mossy green rocks, down into a dark emerald pool below. Ranulf thought it a sight to behold, and felt a pang of regret that Rhiannon could see it only in memory. Helping her to dismount, he tethered his mount to an overhanging branch, and then cried out in alarm, "Rhiannon, stop!"

To his surprise, both his cousins laughed. "What did you fear," Rhiannon asked, "that I would walk right over the cliff? I can tell as I approach the edge by the movement of the air."

She'd long since established her credibility with Ranulf, but Padarn looked skeptical, and Eleri saw that. "Go on, Rhiannon," she urged. "Show them how you can sense things they can only see."

As Ranulf and Padarn looked on in puzzlement, Eleri led her sister away from the bluff, and then gently spun her around. They watched as she started to cross the clearing, but when she headed toward a large oak tree, only Eleri's vehement gesture kept Ranulf from calling out a warning. It was not needed, for Rhiannon stopped just in time.

"There is something ahead of me," she said, and after reaching out and encountering the scratchy feel of bark, she grinned suddenly, triumphantly. But she could not explain to them how she'd known of the tree's presence, able to say only that she'd sensed an obstacle looming before her. She called it her "inner vision," and whilst it was not always reliable, she admitted, especially with objects close to the ground, it had spared her many a bruising fall, for certes.

Padarn was so captivated by this mysterious skill of Rhiannon's that he had to try to master it, too, and keeping his eyes tightly shut, he lurched around the clearing, crashing into trees and stumbling into thickets like a stag in rut. He was, of course, showing off for Eleri, but he got more than he bargained for when he tumbled headfirst into a blackthorn bush. Once she stopped laughing, though, Eleri was so solicitous that Ranulf suspected the boy counted his scratches well earned.

Spreading their blanket under Rhiannon's oak, they unpacked their basket. Eleri had wheedled their cook into yielding up roast chicken, thick chunks of goat cheese, ripe plums, and cider; there was even a round loaf of newly baked bread, primarily for Ranulf's sake, for the Welsh did not eat nearly as much bread as their English neighbors. Borrowing Ranulf's dagger to dig a thorn out of Padarn's thumb, Eleri began teasing him about his "lamentable lack of inner vision."

Padarn bridled, pointing out that "inner vision was a poor trade, indeed, for the loss of sight," and then flushed deeply, glancing toward Rhiannon and then away.

When he began to stammer apologies, Rhiannon insisted it was not necessary. "You did but speak the truth, lad, for none would choose darkness over light. The choice is to live in that darkness with some measure of grace and contentment . . . or not. I am more fortunate than many, for I can take comfort in the love of my family, in my faith in God's Mercy, and in the knowledge that at least my blindness has spared me the need to learn embroidery."

Padarn sputtered, choking on his cider. Eleri poured him another cup, adding that Rhiannon never had to weed their garden, either, and Ranulf chimed in with a reminder of all the money Rhiannon saved her father on candles. When Padarn joined, somewhat sheepishly, in their laughter, Ranulf knew he'd been right about the boy; he was worth the extra effort.

Padarn was studying Rhiannon intently, as if seeing her truly for the first time. "May I ask you a question . . . a serious one? What is the worst of being blind?"

Ranulf had wondered that himself. He expected Rhiannon to need time to think it over, but she answered immediately. "Other people. It would be much easier to accept my blindness if only they could accept it, too. But they shy away as if it were contagious. Or else they assume that since I cannot see, I cannot hear, either, and they shout as if I were quite deaf."

"Or they do not speak to her at all," Eleri said indignantly. "Rhiannon will be standing right at my side, but I'll be the one they ask, 'Has she always been blind?' God Above, but the world is full of fools!" And in the clearing by Rhaeadr Ewynnol, there was none to dispute her.

Later, after the food had been eaten, Eleri and Padarn set off to hunt for wild blackberries. Ranulf found a hedgerow of blooming honeysuckle and collected a handful of the fragrant blossoms for Rhiannon. "What else?" he asked quietly, and she understood at once.

"Waking up and not knowing if it is day or night. Even now I find that disquieting. I miss seeing smiles, for they are conversational clues, are they not? I also miss seeing things which cannot be touched, like butterflies or a night sky. But I think the dreams were the most troubling, Ranulf, the ones in which I was able to see again. They'd seem so real, so very real, full of color and light. But then I'd awaken and I was still blind."

"I had dreams like that after my mother died," Ranulf said. "Waking up was like losing her all over again."

"Mourning dreams," Rhiannon said pensively. "I'd never thought of it that way, but you are right. I was mourning my lost sight as you mourned your mother."

It occurred to Ranulf that they'd been about the same age, too. "You mentioned color in those early dreams, Rhiannon. Can you remember it, then?"

"I think so," she said, but she amended that, then, to, "Well, I remember red. But the other colors have faded. Papa tries to prod my memory, but he cannot seem to describe color in terms that are not . . . colorful." She smiled, so swiftly that Ranulf almost missed it. "He talks about bright and dark and pale, which is not very helpful."

Ranulf watched her breathe in the scent of honeysuckle. How to explain color? "Give me your hand," he said. Once they were on their feet, he led her away from the tree, out into a patch of summer sunlight. "Tilt your face up," he said, "and tell me what you feel."

"The sun," she said promptly. "I feel its warmth."

"What you are feeling," he said, "is yellow. Green is the sound the wind makes, rustling through the trees. If we walked down to the riverbank and you put your hand in the water, you'd feel the cool color blue. To remember red, you need only stand in front of the hearth. And a winter snowfall, silent and cold and pure . . . that is white."

Rhiannon was delighted. "Do not stop now," she entreated. "What of purple? Silver?"

"Next you'll be asking after plaid," Ranulf joked, but once they were settled back on the blanket, he did his best to oblige her. "Do you know what a sable pelt feels like . . . soft and lush? Well, that is purple. Silver is . . . silk. Brown is a steady, dependable color . . . like dogs."

Rhiannon laughed and clapped her hands. "Let me," she cried. "If dogs are brown, then cats are . . . green!" Ranulf laughed, too, and they expanded the game, deciding that harp music was green, too, that anger was red and pride blue. Ranulf did not know whether he'd actually helped Rhiannon to form a mental image of these colors, but he was sure he'd given her something she'd had too little of—fun.

Sharing the last of the cider with him, she shared, too, memories of her childhood. Her mother would have fetched for her, protected her, coddled her, but Rhodri would not allow it. He had encouraged her to defy the dark, to get up when she fell, to find out for herself what was possible and what was not. He'd taught her to ride, to play the harp, to turn her head in the direction of voices when she was spoken to, as a sighted child would have done. He'd taught her that she could be blind and self-reliant and proud. The great pity, Ranulf thought, was that he could not teach the rest of the world that, too.

Over these past few months, he'd told her of his own childhood, of Stephen and Maude and Robert and the war. But he'd told her nothing of his grieving or his guilt, and so he was taken utterly aback when she asked suddenly, "Ranulf, who is Annora?"

The silence lasted so long that she grew uneasy. "I did not mean to pry," she apologized, and he reached across the blanket, patted her hand.

"You just took me by surprise, lass. How do you know about Annora?"

"I know only that you cried out her name when your fever burned so high. Even if I'd spoken French, I could not have made sense of your mumblings. But the name I did hear—often enough to remember. I can tell, though, that some wounds heal more slowly than others. We need not speak of her."

"No," he said, "I will tell you, Cousin Rhiannon. After all that you and your family have done for me, you have the right to know."

And as if that secluded riverside clearing were a confessional, he told her about Annora, sparing himself nothing. She listened in silence, her thoughts hidden from him, for he'd kept his eyes upon the surging power of Rhaeadr Ewynnol until he was done. He waited, then, for her response, as an accused man might await a jury's verdict, steeling himself for her disappointment, her condemnation, even revulsion. When he looked into her face, though, he saw only sadness.

"I am sorry," she said at last, "for your friend's death. I am sorry, too, that you blame yourself for it."

"I was such a fool, Rhiannon. I truly believed that Annora would be able to divorce her husband and marry me, that wanting was enough to make it so. I never considered the consequences, not until it was too late."

"I do not pretend to know much of such matters," she said slowly.

"But I would guess that most men—and women—share that same failing." She hesitated. "Annora . . . do you still love her?"

He nodded, remembered such a gesture meant nothing to her, and said, with some reluctance, "Yes . . . I do."

Rhiannon was quiet for a time. "And if you had it to do all over again, would you?"

This time his answer was immediate—and explosive. "Good God, no!"

"Well, then," Rhiannon said, "there is hope for you yet!"

Ranulf stared at her, and then gave a startled and rueful laugh. "Who would have guessed," he said, "that a butterfly could bite?"

"This one can," she said tartly. "What would you have me say, that I'd want you to go on lusting after a married woman? The Lord God will forgive any sin if it is truly repented, but people who keep repeating the same sins must try His Patience for certes!"

Ranulf forgot and nodded again. "I do repent my sins, Rhiannon. And I mean to learn from my mistakes. I owe that to Gilbert."

"I think learning from past mistakes would be a fine thing," she said softly, and then she tilted her head, listening. "Eleri and Padarn . . . they are coming back."

Ranulf heard the voices now, too, the playful bickering that passed for flirtation among the very young. "You have just enough time," he said, "to bless me and tell me to go forth and sin no more."

She turned her face toward him, with a smile that offered its own sort of absolution, and he reached for her hand. "Come on, Cousin," he said. "Let's go home."

42

CHESTER CASTLE, ENGLAND

September 1148

MAUD?" The Earl of Chester plunged through the doorway of his bedchamber. "Where are you, girl?" Striding over to the bed, he jerked the hangings back, then glanced about in puzzlement.

"Maud?" A moment later, his wife emerged from the corner privy chamber. She was fully dressed, her hair neatly braided, but she looked so pale and drawn that even her unobservant husband noticed. "Queasy again, eh?" he said, and she regarded him balefully.

"No, I spend so much time crouching over the privy hole because I like the view!"

Chester scowled, but held his peace, reminding himself that a woman had to be humored whilst she was breeding. "Well, I've news sure to cheer you. You've a visitor."

"I'm not up to seeing anyone," Maud said, settling herself gingerly upon the bed. "Unless it is my mother or His Holiness the Pope, tell them to come back later."

"This is one visitor you'll want to see," Chester insisted, and before Maud could stop him, he opened the door, shouting into the stairwell. "Come on up!"

"Randolph!" Maud was furious, but it was too late. Already she could hear footsteps on the stairs. Reluctantly swinging her legs over the side of the bed, she pushed her husband's arm aside when he offered his help. "You never listen," she scolded softly, "never—Jesú!" Her morning sickness forgotten, she shot off the bed. "Ranulf!"

Chester watched with a smile as his wife and her uncle embraced. "I told you," he said smugly, "that you'd want to see him!"

AN autumn rainstorm was drenching the Conwy Valley. Each time the door to the great hall was opened, damp drafts blew in, guttering the candles. But flickering candles were no inconvenience to Rhiannon, and she continued to sew. Eleri had pinned a strip of flat wood to the material to guide her stitches, but even so, it was slow, laborious going. "How does it look?" she asked as Eleri's steps drew near. "Do I have to rip out this row, too? Tell me the truth."

"It does not have to be perfect," Eleri chided, moving closer to see.

"Yes," Rhiannon said, "it does." Once her sister assured her that the stitches were even, she bent over her handiwork again, concentrating so diligently that she did not at first notice her stepmother's approach.

"What are you making, Rhiannon?"

"A belt for Ranulf. He told Papa that his birthday is in November."

"Why not let me make it for you? I could do it much faster."

"I am sure you could, Enid," Rhiannon said evenly. "But I want to do it myself."

"Are you so sure he is coming back?"

"Of course he is. He promised he would."

"It might be better if he does not."

Rhiannon stopped sewing. "I thought you liked Ranulf," she said in surprise.

"I do like him. We all do . . . too much, I fear."

"I do not understand."

"We welcomed him into our home, our hearts. It was easy enough to do, for he is very likable. He filled an empty place at our table . . . Cadell's place. But he is not Cadell and this is not his world. Sooner or later, he will choose to return to the world he knows."

"That need not be so," Rhiannon protested. "He seems happy here. He could decide to stay."

"Ah, lambkin . . . you are fooling yourself."

That was Rhodri's pet name for Rhiannon. She never liked her stepmother to use it, especially in such solicitous, sympathetic tones. Theirs was an awkward relationship, not friends, no longer enemies . . . although that had not been true in the beginning. Rhiannon had, by her own admission, reacted badly to her father's decision to remarry. Her mother was just dead a year and Rhiannon was not ready to accept another woman in Nesta's place. Nor had Enid known how to deal with a blind stepdaughter. Her kindnesses seemed condescending, her good intentions invariably went astray, and her patience hovered on the border between sainthood and martyrdom; only her bafflement rang true.

Looking back upon those first troubled months, Rhiannon could admit now that Enid was unfairly cast as the wicked stepmother, guilty of missteps and gaffes, not mortal sins. But she was—quite unknowingly—serving as a scapegoat, for that was the year that Rhiannon collided with reality, the brutal reality that men feared blindness only a little less than they feared leprosy. She was old enough by then for marriage and motherhood. Her father could find no suitable husband for her, though. A blind wife was a contradiction in terms, a bizarre joke, a curse besotted men might fling at one another in an alehouse brawl. At eighteen, Rhiannon had finally understood just how barren her future was to be, and she'd taken out much of her heartbroken rage and frustration upon her beautiful, well-meaning, obtuse stepmother.

Seven years had passed since then, and they'd long ago made their peace, for whatever their differences, they both loved Rhodri. But Rhiannon would never have chosen Enid for her confidante, and she resented Enid now for voicing her own secret fear. She knew that Enid was right, that Ranulf was unlikely to stay in Wales. Saying it aloud, though, gave her a superstitious shiver. Hoping that her silence would communicate her unwillingness to discuss it further, she bent over her sewing again.

But Enid was never one for taking hints. "It is only a matter of time until Ranulf goes back to England—for good. The longer he lives with us, the more it will hurt when he does leave. That is why I said it might be better if he stayed in Chester, better for my Rhodri and Eleri . . . and above all, for you, Rhiannon."

Rhiannon felt heat rising in her face. She wanted to demand that Enid explain herself, but she did not dare, for she was suddenly afraid of what Enid might answer. Was it possible that her stepmother could somehow have seen into her heart? "You are wrong, Enid," she said tautly. "Ranulf will come back. He promised."

DURING his six months in Gwynedd, Ranulf had been as secluded as any hermit, but Maud soon brought him up to date on the happenings in the world beyond Wales. Her most startling news was of the intensifying feud between Stephen and the Archbishop of Canterbury. Upon Theobald's return from the Council of Rheims, a furious Stephen had punished his defiance by expelling him from England. He had settled in Flanders, at Matilda's urgings, as she and an unlikely peacemaker, William de Ypres, sought in vain to reconcile this rift between Stephen and the Church. On September 12th, the archbishop's patience wore out and he placed England under Interdict. This was the Church's ultimate weapon, but this time it misfired. The Interdict was ignored throughout England, observed only in Theobald's own diocese of Canterbury. As to what would happen next, none could say. But it was a blessing, indeed, for the Angevin cause, Maud and Ranulf agreed, that Stephen should have estranged himself from the most powerful churchman in his realm.

Maud had other news, as well, for Ranulf. She confirmed that his sister was now living in Rouen with her sons. She informed him that Matilda had spent much of the year in Canterbury, supervising the building of Faversham, the abbey she and Stephen were founding; rumor had it that she was in poor health. She told him that the Bishop of Winchester had been suspended by the Pope for supporting Stephen over the archbishop. She shared another rumor, that William de Ypres's sight was clouding over. She had the latest stories from the Holy Land, where the French king was blundering badly, lurching from one mistake to another, nearly losing his life in a Turkish ambush. But the most shocking gossip concerned his queen. During their stay in Antioch, Eleanor had announced that she wanted to end their troubled marriage. Louis refused to let her go, and when they resumed their trek toward Jerusalem, Eleanor was taken by force from the city, compelled to accompany them.

This was high scandal, indeed. But Ranulf was even more astonished by what Maud revealed about Brien Fitz Count. Brien had turned Wallingford Castle over to his kinsman, William Boterel, and he and his wife had both taken holy vows, renouncing the world and their marriage and pledging the remainder of their lives to the service of Almighty God.

MAUD bent over her son's cradle, satisfying herself that he slept. "Are you still set upon leaving on the morrow, Ranulf? A fortnight is not a very long visit, not after vanishing into smoke for nigh on eight months."

"I promised my Welsh kin that I'd be back by the first frost," Ranulf explained, adding with a grin, "But I'll come to see that new babe of yours, lass. Believe it or not, your husband actually invited me back once the babe is born, and how could I resist such an unlikely invitation?"

Maud returned his grin with one of her own. "Who would have guessed," she said, "that hating Stephen would have such a beneficial effect upon Randolph's manners? It seems he'll go to any lengths to bring Stephen down, even if that means being polite to my kinfolk!"

Ranulf joined her at the cradle, gazing at her sleeping little son. "I think he looks like Robert," he said, and Maud agreed readily, for she wanted to believe that, too.

"Well, if you must go, at least take Nicholas and some of our men with you. They dare go no farther than the abbey at Basingwerk, though. Are you sure you and Padarn can get safely back on your own to your uncle's lands?"

When Ranulf nodded, Maud sighed, only half convinced. "Remember to talk to the abbot about the letters. If we are generous in our almsgiving, he ought to be willing to send one of his monks to Trefriw with letters for you. And they can also take letters of yours to me here at Chester. Even in these accursed times, monks are rarely attacked—if only because they have so little to steal."

"You have a very practical turn of mind, Maud," Ranulf said fondly. "Diolch yn fawr."

He'd taught her that was Welsh for "thank you." "Can you really speak Welsh all that well?" she asked curiously. "Randolph has not mastered a word of it, for all the time he has spent in Wales."

"I doubt that he tried very hard. Since I used to speak it as a lad, I had a head start."

"But your uncle knows French, does he not?"

"Yes . . . from what I gather, most of the men attending Owain Gwynedd's court speak some French. Whether a man knows any French depends upon how much contact he has with England. As for their women, most speak only Welsh."

"What of your cousins?"

"I've begun teaching them French . . . or trying to. Eleri loses interest too easily, but Rhiannon is a better pupil, most likely because her memory is honed sharper than my best blade. It has to be, for she must carry a mental map in her head in order to do the most simple task. Even crossing the hall can be fraught with peril if you cannot see where you are going."

"You think highly of her," Maud said, and he smiled.

"I always thought Maude was the bravest woman I'd ever known. Rhiannon has a quieter kind of courage, but in its way, it is even more impressive, for Rhiannon's war will last until her dying breath."

"Whenever I passed a blind beggar on the road," Maud confessed, "I would throw a coin and then hurry on by, averting my eyes. I did not know what life must be like for the blind, did not want to know."

"I asked Rhiannon once what it was like to be blind. She said, 'I do not know. I can only tell you what it is like to be me.'"

"She sounds," Maud said, "like a remarkable woman."

"I hope I have not made her seem too good to be true. A saint, she is not. She can be vexingly stubborn, and she has the same sort of prickly pride as Maude does."

"Why does that surprise you? For them both, pride is a defense, the only shield available to them. We all do what we can with what we have, Ranulf." Maud bent over and brushed a soft kiss against her son's dark hair. "Say something for me in Welsh," she asked. "Something poetic or profound."

Ranulf was quiet, considering. "Rhag pob clwyf eli amser," he said. "'For every wound, the ointment of time.'"

Their eyes met. "I thought you might quote me the Welsh equivalent of that Latin saying you always fancied, 'Carpe diem.'"

"'Seize the day'?" Shaking his head, he said softly, "I like this one better."

"Yes," she agreed, "so do I." Leaning over, she kissed him on the cheek, as gently as she'd kissed her son. "Wales has been good for you, Uncle. The next time you come, bring those Welsh cousins with you. I should like to meet them. Now . . . where are the letters you have for me?"

"They are over here, on the table. They are done, but not sealed yet." Reaching for the first on the pile, he held it up. "This goes to the priory in Bristol, where they are keeping Robert's bequest for me. I've instructed them to reimburse you for the money you've lent to me. The next two letters go to the stewards of my manors in Wiltshire. This one is for Hugh de Plucknet, and these two go to Cornwall . . . to Rainald and Luke. I've written, too, to Brien, and will be grateful if you'll see that he gets it."

He gazed down at Brien's letter, still marveling at his friend's decision to become a monk. How little, he thought, do we know of the hearts of others. He wondered if Brien's wife had truly wanted to be a nun, or if she'd sought to find in God what she'd lost in Brien. He wondered, too, what Maude's reaction had been. Above all, he wished Brien well, hoped fervently that Brien might find what he sought in the austere discipline and cloistered world of the Benedictines: inner peace and salvation.

Picking up another letter, he said, "This is for your mother in Bristol. Lastly, these are to be dispatched to Normandy, to Maude and young Harry. I also wrote down the names of the Jewish peddlers who came to my aid on the Chester Road. I hoped you might let your brother in Bristol know about them, that I owe them a great favor, indeed."

"I'll tell him, but I cannot see Will's bestirring himself on behalf of Jews, even ones who saved your life."

Ranulf did not disagree; he knew his nephew. Passing strange, that the best of Robert's manhood lived on in his daughter. Folding the letters, one by one, he reached then for the sealing wax. "Remind me to repay you for the cost of all this—you'll be sending out couriers to the four winds!"

She dismissed the expense with a wave of her hand. "You know I like nothing better than spending Randolph's money. But is that all? No other letters?"

Ranulf pressed his seal into the soft wax on the last of his letters. "What did you expect . . . that there would be one for Annora?"

"The thought did cross my mind."

He slowly shook his head, watching as she poured wine for them both. Holding out a cup, she said, "I heard from her . . . from Annora. She wrote to me this past spring. She had her baby, a girl, born last November. They named her Matilda, after the queen."

Ranulf drank in silence for several moments. "I am glad for her," he said resolutely. "She . . . she did seem happy, Maud?"

"Yes . . . for now." She wondered if she ought to warn him. Annora was still caught up in the newfound joy of motherhood, but in a year or two, the novelty of it might well begin to wane, and she might crave excitement again, once more yearn for risk and romance and Ranulf. It was not a good sign that she'd asked, so very casually, if Ranulf had returned to Normandy with the empress. Maud said nothing, though, for each man must find his own way. If Ranulf's way led back to Annora, she would be sorely grieved. But the choice was his.

"'For now,'" he echoed, sounding surprised. "You do not think her happiness will last?" She shrugged, and he leaned back in his chair, studying her pensively. "I thought you liked Annora?"

She shrugged again. "You loved the woman to distraction. What was I supposed to say—that I thought you could do better?"

He started to protest, then let it go. She saw the sadness shadowing his face, and she knew Annora was still in the room with them, the ghostly, unseen presence of a lost love, much in need of exorcism.

"Aunt Maude will want you to join her in Normandy," she said abruptly. "Uncle Rainald is sure to urge you to come to Cornwall. Your Welsh kindred want you to return to Gwynedd. But there is a voice missing from this debate—yours. What of you, Ranulf? What do you want to do?"

He was quiet for a few moments, and then gave her a crooked, rueful smile. "That is the trouble, Maud. I would to God that I knew!"

RANULF and Padarn had a blessedly uneventful journey and reached Trefriw safely in mid-October. Ranulf had spent lavishly in Chester, and their saddlebags were crammed full of gifts: a slender-bladed dagger for Rhodri, a polished metal mirror for Enid, an ivory comb for Eleri, a vial of Maud's favorite perfume for Rhiannon, bolts of fine linen and wool. They were all delighted with their presents and made much ado over his generosity and extravagance. But he had the comforting certainty that he would have been welcomed just as warmly as if he'd come back empty-handed.

He knew they were planning to celebrate his birthday, and so he had to stay at least through November. It seemed heartless, then, to leave so close to Christmas. And by then it would be foolhardy, indeed, to consider departing in the midst of a Welsh winter. And so the weeks passed into months, December into January, on into February, and then March of God's Year, 1149, the fourteenth of Stephen's reign, and Ranulf was still in Wales, continually telling himself he ought to go and always finding reasons to stay.

AS much as Ranulf had come to value his mother's homeland, he regretted its isolation. Cut off from England by mountains and miles—for it was well over two hundred miles from Trefriw to London—Wales seemed as remote at times as the island kingdom of Ireland. Stephen and the Archbishop of Canterbury had been coaxed by Stephen's queen into making their peace in November, but word did not reach Owain Gwynedd's court until December and it did not filter south to Trefriw for yet another month. It had begun to trouble Ranulf that he knew so little of what was occurring in the rest of Christendom, and he sensed that he would soon be ready to return to the other world, his father's world . . . and his own.

The seclusion that Ranulf found so vexing was a source of reassurance to Rhiannon. To her, Trefriw was a refuge, cloistered and sheltered by the cloud-kissed mountain peaks the Welsh called Eryri—"Haunt of Eagles." It was easy enough to forget there was another world beyond the River Conwy, and easy, too, to believe that because Ranulf seemed content with them, he would always be so. The only times she feared were when the letters came. Ranulf had told them of an ancient Greek legend, of mythical creatures, half woman and half bird, who lured sailors to their doom with their seductively sweet songs. It seemed to Rhiannon that these letters were siren songs, too, trying to beguile Ranulf back across the border, back to his former life.

There had been three of these letters so far, forwarded by the Countess of Chester to the White Monks at Basingwerk. The first had come from Ranulf's sister in Normandy, the next from his brother the Earl of Cornwall, and the third from the countess herself, just a fortnight ago, sharing with Ranulf her joy over the birth of her second son. Each time one of these letters came, Rhiannon had waited anxiously to find out if the siren songs would prevail. Each time her relief had been overwhelming when they did not. But on this rain-dark day in late March, her peace was threatened once again by the arrival of a Cistercian brother from Basingwerk.

The White Monk was welcomed heartily and offered a bed for the night; to the Welsh, hospitality was the Eleventh of the Lord's Commandments. They gathered around Ranulf then, as he read his letters. Rhiannon tensed when he announced that they were from his sister and nephew in Normandy, for she knew that the empress was her greatest foe. Ranulf read rapidly, exclaiming occasionally to himself in surprise. When he was done, he glanced up, saying, "My nephew Harry is returning to England, so that he may be knighted by the Scots king."

It was obvious to them that this was a pretext; if knighthood were all that Henry craved, his father could easily have knighted him in Normandy. "How old is the lad now? Sixteen?" Rhodri asked, and when Ranulf nodded, he said, "It might have been better if he'd waited another year or two. But was there ever a sixteen-year-old who was not eager to play a man's part?"

"Especially Harry," Ranulf said and smiled. "He was eager to do that at age nine! What amazes me is not his boldness, nor that Maude has reluctantly consented to this rash venture of his, for I daresay he gave her no choice. No . . . it is that the Earl of Chester has agreed to meet Harry at Carlisle and there make his peace with his old enemy, the Scots king. That is not only astounding, it is downright miraculous! I can only assume that as much as Chester loathes King David, he now hates Stephen even more."

Ranulf began then to tell them of Chester's bitter feud with the Scots king, but Rhiannon was no longer listening. Chester's feuding meant nothing to her. She waited mutely to hear all that did matter—whether or not Ranulf would be leaving them. She could not bring herself to ask outright, but her father soon did. "And will you be joining young Harry at Carlisle?"

"Yes," Ranulf said. "I must, Uncle. My sister entreats me to look after

Harry as best I can. If I stood aside and evil befell the lad, I'd never forgive myself."

Rhiannon caught her breath, then deliberately dug her nails into the palm of her hand until she could be sure she'd not cry aloud in protest or pleading. But her sister had less restraint. "You cannot go, Ranulf! We need you here as much as Harry does, for we're your family, too!"

Ranulf looked unhappily at his young cousin, not sure what to say. But his uncle said it for him. "You are not being fair, Eleri. Ranulf has to go, for it is a matter of duty and honour. What would you have him do, entrust his nephew's safety to a knave like Chester?"

Eleri was more than willing to let Henry fend for himself, but she eventually subsided, on the verge of tears. Only then did Rhiannon reach out and touch Ranulf's arm. "When," she asked uneasily, "will you be coming back?"

She had her answer in Ranulf's prolonged hesitation. "I do not know, Rhiannon," he admitted. "I just do not know."

RANULF found it more difficult than he'd expected to bid farewell to his Welsh family. They'd followed him to the gateway to see him off, and were doing their best to be cheerful and matter-of-fact about his departure. But only Padarn's enthusiasm was real, for he'd talked his father and Rhodri into letting him accompany Ranulf. For the others, Ranulf's leave-taking was a painful one, and he well knew it. For Rhodri, he'd been a substitute son, a bandage for the wound caused by Cadell's death. For Eleri, he'd been a big brother and a window to the world, able to give her intriguing glimpses of foreign lands and great cities. And for Rhiannon, he'd been what she needed most—a friend. When he rode away, he'd be leaving a jagged hole in their household, one that would not be easy to mend.

Spring had come to the Conwy Valley, and the hills were green with new growth and gold with wild gorse. The first butterflies of the season were fluttering about like flying flower petals, and high overhead, Ranulf heard the shrill cry of a kestrel, a soaring shadow against the halo cast by the sun. Never had Wales looked so beautiful, so deceptively peaceful, so hard to leave.

"I want to thank you all," he said, "for the best year of my life." He was embraced, then, by Rhodri, a vigorous, bone-bruising hug that squeezed the air out of his lungs. Enid gave him a languidly lovely smile, a decorous kiss on the cheek, and Eleri hurled herself into his arms, making a feeble joke about Englishmen and their bristly beards; it was, she complained tearfully, like nuzzling a hedgehog. From Rhiannon, he got a brief, heartfelt embrace, delicately scented with a fragrance of the Welsh meadows; it suited her better, he thought, than Maud's more exotic perfume.

"God keep you all safe," he said huskily, "until we are together again." Padarn was already mounted, impatiently eager to be off. Swinging up into the saddle, Ranulf sent his stallion cantering toward the gate. He waved once, but after that, he did not dare to look back again.

43

YORKSHIRE, ENGLAND

July 1149

ON Whitsunday, May 22nd, the King of Scotland knighted his nephew Henry and Roger Fitz Miles, the Earl of Hereford. David then made a public peace with his old enemy the Earl of Chester. Chester agreed to acknowledge David as Lord of Carlisle, and for that concession, he was given the Honour of Lancaster by David. They propped up their precarious alliance with a Sacrament, the proposed marriage of one of Chester's infant sons to one of David's young granddaughters. They were then ready to strike at Stephen. After some discussion, they decided to launch a surprise attack upon York, for they hoped the fall of England's second-largest city would deliver a crippling blow to Stephen's embattled kingship.

BY the end of the second week in July, they were within striking distance of York. It began to rain as they set up camp for the night, but the men didn't mind a summer soaking after a hot, dusty day on the road. By the time he'd made certain, though, that the sentries had been posted, Ranulf was drenched. He shared a tent with Henry and Roger Fitz Miles, but the Scots king, his son, and the Earl of Chester had their own tents, and it was toward the former that Ranulf headed. As he expected, he found them all in David's tent, discussing plans for the morrow's attack.

Ranulf had pessimistically predicted that Chester and David would soon be at each other's throats. Much to his surprise, the tenuous truce seemed to be holding, due in large measure to the youth who was David's grandnephew and Chester's first cousin by marriage. Henry showed a deft touch for defusing tension, a skill Ranulf suspected he'd learned in Normandy, caught in the crossfire of his parents' marital warfare.

No one noticed Ranulf's entrance, for they were gathered around the Earl of Chester as he drew for them a map of York's defenses. The city was protected by two rivers, the Ouse and the Fosse, and high earthen banks, erected over the ancient Roman walls. There were four main gates, all of stone, and two motte-and-bailey castles shielded behind timber palisades and deep ditches. Capturing York sounded like a formidable undertaking to Henry, and he kept interrupting with questions, all of which Chester answered with uncharacteristic patience.

Ranulf listened in amusement; who would have guessed that Chester, of all men, would have relished the role of tutor? But Henry had disarmed them all with his unabashed, eager curiosity. He'd so far shown none of the defensive bravado that infected so many sixteen-year-olds. He did not bluster; if he did not know something, he asked. He asked often, listened and learned, and he'd soon won over not only his Scots uncle and cousin but even the notoriously irascible Chester.

Ranulf, who'd always been extremely fond of Henry, now found himself feeling proud of his nephew, too, so much so that he'd begun to wonder if he'd judged Geoffrey too harshly. As far back as he could remember, he'd loathed his brother-in-law, detesting him for the misery he'd caused Maude. But during Henry's formative years, he'd been in Geoffrey's care, not Maude's. If Geoffrey could raise a son like Harry, Ranulf reasoned, he could not be such a worthless wretch, after all. Whatever grief the man had given Maude, he deserved credit for Harry, a fine young king in the making. God Willing, Ranulf added hastily, for he'd learned, at bitter cost, that only fools took victory for granted in a world so fraught with peril.

The talk had now shifted from York's defenses to its populace. When Chester and David both agreed that its citizens were almost as loyal to Stephen as the steadfast Londoners were, Henry wanted to know why.

Chester shrugged; he had no more interest in what motivated other people than he did in the history of the Druids. David was more politically astute, one of the reasons why his had been such a successful kingship for Scotland, and he said promptly, if somewhat pedantically, "Stephen has always had support in the towns, for they think he favors trade. He has been generous in granting them charters and he courts their guilds quite shamelessly. And then, too, York has prospered under Stephen's reign, for it has been spared the turmoil and lawlessness that have so troubled the southern parts. In contrast to shires like Oxford and Wiltshire and the god-forsaken Fens, Yorkshire has seen little bloodshed."

"Not since Cowton Moor, anyway," Chester muttered, unable to resist this snide mention of the Scots king's calamitous defeat by the English eleven years ago.

David gave him a cool glance of dismissal, more insulting in its way than outright anger would have been. "Moreover," he continued, "Stephen has made several visits to York and each time he was open-handed with royal boons. When the hospital of St Peter's burned down in the great fire of '37, Stephen and Matilda paid for its repairs, and then founded a leper hospital outside the city. These are the sort of goodwill gestures that people remember, lad."

Henry nodded thoughtfully. Ranulf teased him occasionally that he seemed to be storing away information like a squirrel hoarding acorns, and he always laughed, but it was more than a joke and they both knew it. This was a great adventure for him, but it was also an education. He was well aware that he lacked seasoning and he was even willing to admit it—to a select few—for he had no false pride. But it was a lack he was eager to remedy, and besieging York would make a good beginning.

There was a sudden commotion outside, and a few moments later, Bennet de Malpas was escorted into the tent. He was soaked to the skin, splattered with mud, and stumbling with fatigue as he hastened forward to greet his lord and the Scots king. But what riveted all eyes upon him was not his haggard, disheveled appearance; it was that he was supposed to be in York, spying for the earl. When he knelt before Chester, the earl said tensely, "You look like a man on the way to his own hanging. Go on, spit it out, Bennet. What do you have to tell us that we'll not want to hear?"

"There will be no surprise attack on York, my lord earl. They are expecting us. I do not know if we were betrayed or they just got lucky, but they somehow learned that we were marching on the city."

The men exchanged grim looks, and Bennet braced himself to reveal the rest, the worst. "My lords, there is more. The citizens sent an urgent plea to Stephen, seeking his aid. He's on his way to York with a large force of his Flemish mercenaries, and he moved with such speed that he's no more than a day away, two at most."

Afterward, slogging through the mud back to their tent, Henry was still stunned that their ambitious plans had come to such an abrupt end. The men had raged and cursed and fumed, but none of them, not even the volatile, fearless Chester, objected to David's morose conclusion—that their campaign was over even before it began. Henry was dismayed that they were letting Stephen chase them off, but he took his cues from his elders and held his peace. These men were all experienced soldiers, men of proven bravery. He would not insult them by questioning their courage. But his disappointment was too sharp to hide, at least from Ranulf.

"I know you are unhappy about this, Harry. We all are. But it would be foolhardy to continue on. We were relying upon surprise to carry the day. Now our foes are not only forewarned, but they'll outnumber us. Remember what I told you about Stephen—that he may not know how to rule, but he knows full well how to fight."

Henry nodded glumly. It seemed to him that there were three Stephens, so contradictory were the stories circulating about him. There was Stephen the man, good-hearted and well meaning and generous. There was Stephen the king, inept and easily led astray, with no political sense whatsoever. And there was Stephen the battle commander, tough-minded and fast-acting and dangerous. The men in Henry's world grudgingly liked the first Stephen and scorned the second, but they all respected the soldier.

"How did Stephen assemble an army so rapidly?" he asked, and Ranulf explained that by calling upon his Flemish mercenaries rather than his vassals, Stephen was able to respond with lethal speed, for he need not send out a summons to his barons and then wait for them to gather their own men. It was costly to keep an armed force always on hand, Ranulf conceded, but they were ready to march at the king's command. This was an interesting argument, that hired soldiers were a more effective way of fighting than the traditional reliance upon the king's vassals, and ordinarily Henry would have been intrigued, eager to explore it further. Now, though, he asked no more questions, trudging on in silence.

The rain was still pelting the camp, and so many men and horses had soon churned the soaked grassy ground into a muddy quagmire. Until the storm passed, fires could not be lit, and the soldiers were sheltering themselves as best they could. For supper, they'd had to content themselves with dried beef and bread; for beds, they had soggy blankets. The moors were often chilly after dark, even in high summer, and if the rain kept on, they faced a shivery night in wet, clammy clothes. And all for nothing, Henry thought, for on the morrow, they would turn tail and retreat, never having gotten within sight of York's walls.

"Uncle Ranulf, I've a question for you. I want to know if there is another reason for our retreat. Are you all seeking to protect me?"

"I'll not lie to you, Harry. That was a consideration," Ranulf admitted, and Henry came to a sudden stop.

"I knew it!" he accused. "I am not a child, Uncle Ranulf, and I will not abide being treated like one. I did not come to England to be coddled!"

"If your parents wanted to coddle you, lad, they'd have kept you in Normandy. Of course we care for your safety! You are England's future.

Should evil befall you, what hope would we have of overthrowing Stephen? Yes, you have brothers, but you are the one who has been groomed for the throne. You are the one whom men know. So we are not going to let you come to harm if we can help it. Plainly put, a king's life is worth more than the lives of other men."

Henry was quiet after that. "I just want to do my fair share," he said unhappily. "I am not afraid to take risks and I need to show men that, to prove to them that I would be a king worth fighting for."

"You will, lad. Your very presence here is sending a message, that you do not lack for courage. Show men that you have common sense, too, and they will rally to you as they never did to your mother. But there is one thing you must understand, Harry, for your life might well depend upon it."

"What is it?" Henry asked, impressed by his uncle's sudden gravity.

"Stephen did not take you seriously two years ago. But from now on, he will, lad. If you fall into his hands, this time he will not be paying for your return to Normandy."

THEY broke camp at dawn the next day. The Scots king and his son made for Carlisle, Chester for Cheshire, and Henry and Ranulf and Roger Fitz Miles for Bristol. Upon his arrival in York, Stephen was welcomed enthusiastically by its reprieved citizens. He was furious, though, to find the enemy gone, and sent men off in pursuit. But he realized they did not have much chance of overtaking their quarry, and a fast-riding courier was soon racing for Oxford with an urgent message for Stephen's nineteen-year-old son. Eustace was to stop Henry from reaching Bristol.

RANULF and Henry rode fast to outdistance pursuit, but once they reached Hereford in safety, they eased their pace and their vigilance. From Hereford, they continued on to Roger's stronghold in Gloucester. They were only two days now from Bristol, and Henry was irked when Roger insisted upon accompanying them south, for he was still sensitive about their overprotectiveness, especially now that he was sure the danger was past. His confidence was confirmed when they rode into Dursley Castle without incident the following afternoon.

Roger de Berkeley was Dursley's castellan, and he made them welcome, but without much enthusiasm. Ranulf did not take it personally, for he doubted that Roger de Berkeley would show enthusiasm even if he were being seduced by Eleanor of Aquitaine. He was the most melancholy man Ranulf had ever met; even when he smiled, no one could tell.

Anyone so doleful was not good company, and Henry, Roger, and

Hugh de Plucknet had soon found reasons to excuse themselves. Ranulf remained, for he felt sorry for Berkeley, who'd been ruined by a war not of his making. He'd not really cared who was king, but he'd had the bad luck to hold a very strategic stronghold, Berkeley Castle, which controlled the Gloucester-Bristol Road. A few years ago, he'd been lured into an ambush by Roger Fitz Miles's ruthless younger brother Walter, and threatened with hanging if he did not yield Berkeley Castle. Walter had gone so far as to string Berkeley up and cut him down just in time, but Berkeley had refused to turn over the castle, gambling on his kinship to the Fitz Miles family to save his life. In the end, it had. But he'd still lost Berkeley Castle, for he'd had to renounce his allegiance to Stephen to gain his freedom, and Stephen then seized the castle for himself.

Berkeley was miserly with words and left it for Ranulf to keep the conversation going. Ranulf soon ran out of topics to talk about and suggested a chess game until he could politely make his escape. But they'd just set up the board when the castle steward announced that a man was pleading to see Sir Roger straightaway. Berkeley seemed to be a man without normal curiosity, for he was inclining toward a refusal when the steward said, "I recognized him, my lord. It is Malcolm, from the Berkeley garrison."

The man was thin and balding and obviously agitated. Kneeling before Roger de Berkeley, he stammered, "It . . . it is me, Sir Roger . . . Malcolm. I had to warn you, for you were right good to me whilst you held the castle. We got word today from the king's son. Lord Eustace found out that the empress's son would be staying the night at Dursley, and he means to see that Lord Henry never reaches Bristol. He'll be here by dawn, mayhap sooner, and he wants our garrison to lay ambushes on the Bristol Road, just in case Lord Henry gets away from him at Dursley."

Roger Fitz Miles and Hugh de Plucknet had been drawn by the noise, returning in time to hear the last of Malcolm's warning. As Roger de Berkeley rewarded Malcolm, Ranulf and the other two men huddled together for a quick conference. They agreed with Ranulf's conclusion, that Dursley was not likely to withstand a siege, and Roger volunteered to fetch Henry, revealing his concern by the alacrity with which he started for the stairwell. Ranulf sent Hugh off to the stables to order their horses saddled. "I know this part of the country fairly well," he told Berkeley, "but not well enough. We need a man who knows every lane and byway and trail betwixt here and Bristol, for we'll have to avoid the main roads. Do you have a man like that, Sir Roger?"

Berkeley assured Ranulf that he did, with much more animation than he usually showed; Ranulf could well imagine his relief at not being caught up in a dangerous siege, one that would have imperiled the only castle he had left. He'd do whatever he could to make sure they were long gone by the time Eustace got here, and Ranulf couldn't blame him a bit. But it was then that Roger Fitz Miles came hastening back into the hall. "Harry is gone," he panted. "I cannot find him anywhere!"

When a search of the castle grounds turned up no traces of Henry, the men's anxiety rapidly gave way to outright alarm. At a loss, they regrouped in the great hall to decide what to do next. And it was then that Ranulf remembered how friendly his nephew had become with his squire. It had not surprised him that Henry should seek out seventeen-year-old Padarn's company, for he was rarely allowed the privilege of acting his age. Even in childhood, he'd been expected to show a maturity beyond his years, and he rarely disappointed. But Ranulf had come to realize that there must be times when his nephew just wanted to have fun. "Padarn," he said abruptly. "He may know where Harry has gone."

"That Welsh squire of yours?" Roger sounded as dubious as Hugh and Berkeley looked, but they were willing to grasp at any straw, and followed nervously after Ranulf as he went off in search of his squire.

They found Padarn in the stables. He was a wiry, lean youngster, very Welsh in appearance; it had taken Ranulf a while not to think of Ancel—and Annora—each time he glanced at Padarn's raven hair and black eyes. Padarn looked so guilty now that Ranulf knew his suspicions were correct. "Where is Harry?" he demanded, brushing aside the boy's unconvincing attempts at denial. "Padarn, we have no time for games. Harry's life could be forfeit if you do not speak up. Eustace is riding for Dursley, and if we do not get away soon, we'll not get away at all."

Padarn had a Welshman's innate suspicion of authority, but in the past year he'd learned to trust Ranulf's judgment. "Harry slipped out the postern gate at dusk and went into the town."

What to the Welsh youth was a "town" was to the men barely more than a hamlet, a church and a handful of cottages clustered in the protective shelter of the castle. "That makes no sense," Roger insisted. "There is not even an alehouse!"

Ranulf was remembering, though, what it was like to be sixteen. "A girl?"

Padarn nodded. "We saw her by the church as we rode in. She had hair the color of moonlight, and she gave Harry a 'come back' smile. You ought not to blame him, my lords," he added bravely. "Had he known about Eustace, he would not have gone." The Welsh were notorious for "not knowing their place," and at another time, Padarn was likely to have earned himself a reprimand for that familiar use of "Harry." But now the men had no time for breaches of protocol; they were hurrying to catch up with Ranulf as he headed back out into the bailey.

Once there, Ranulf snatched a lantern from a passing servant. "Let me try to find him first," he said. "Eustace could have men watching the village for all we know. If a crowd goes chasing out into the street, raising the hue and cry, that will be a sure sign that something is amiss." They agreed reluctantly, and Roger promised to have them mounted and ready to ride as soon as Ranulf and Henry returned. No one mentioned their secret, shared fear: that if Eustace did have spies about, Henry might well have been found already—by the wrong men.

The village was half hidden in the haze of a deepening turquoise twilight, but its inhabitants were still up and about, both apprehensive and excited by Henry's presence in their midst. Dogs were barking; somewhere a child was wailing. Aware of eyes following him as he moved down the dusty street, Ranulf was trying to think like a sixteen-year-old again. What would a youth most want after finding himself a lass with a "come back" smile? Privacy, of course. There was a small pond beyond the church, screened by yew trees and white willows. What better place for a tryst? Weaving his way between the moss-covered tombstones behind the church, he heard soft, smothered laughter as he approached the pond, merriment so quickly cut off that he knew they'd either heard him or spotted his lantern's glow. "Harry?" he said quietly into the silence. "You'd best come out, for I am not going away."

There was a rustling sound, the willow's cascading silvery camouflage parted, and his nephew emerged from the shadows. The girl stayed where she was; Ranulf caught only a fleeting glimpse of disheveled bright hair as Henry stepped forward into the light cast by Ranulf's lantern. "How did you know where to look for me?" He sounded both defiant and defensive. "I was not lost, Uncle Ranulf, am quite capable of finding my way back to the castle by myself."

Ranulf's relief found expression in anger. "You're lucky I did find you," he snapped, "instead of an irate father or a jealous husband!"

"You're my uncle, not my confessor," Henry snapped back, "though you are suddenly acting more like a gaoler than a kinsman . . . and I like it not. I do not need a wet nurse!"

"No," Ranulf agreed, "but you do need a bodyguard, lad. You're going to have to learn to live with that, Harry. Kings cannot wander off as they please. That is the price they pay for the power they wield. There is always a price. I just thank God and His Saints that you did not pay it tonight in blood."

Henry was still frowning, but he was more uneasy now than angry, for Ranulf was not given to hyperbole. "Is something wrong?" he asked warily, sensing that this was the question he should have asked first.

"Well, Eustace is about to attack Dursley, the Berkeley garrison is busy laying ambushes for us in the unlikely event we escape, whilst we pass the time playing hide-and-seek with you instead of riding for our lives."

Even in the flickering lantern light, Ranulf could see the color crimsoning across his nephew's cheekbones. "I am sorry," Henry said. "I did not know. It is not too late, is it?"

Henry's heartfelt apology only made Ranulf regret his sarcasm all the more. "No, lad, we still have time," he assured the boy quickly. "My nerves are on the raw, that's all. We feared, you see, that Eustace might have an assassin or two on the prowl."

Henry's eyes widened, for this had never occurred to him. "Stephen would not do that," he said, his tone nowhere near as certain as his words.

"Eustace would," Ranulf said flatly. "Never doubt that, Harry, not if you want to live to make old bones. Now . . . I suggest you bid your lass farewell, for we have a long, hard ride ahead of us."

The girl had ventured out from beneath the sheltering willow. Padarn had been right; her hair did have a silvery sheen. She would have been very pretty, indeed, if not for her pout. Arms akimbo, little chin jutting out, she was clearly losing patience fast. But then Henry came swiftly back to her side, took her in his arms, and kissed her with a boy's exuberance and a man's passion. When he finally released her, she looked dazed. Kissing her hand gallantly, he said, "Someday, sweetheart, you'll be able to tell your children that you once kissed a king!"

"Eustace and God Willing," Ranulf said dryly, amused in spite of himself, and Henry grinned.

"I hope you are not suggesting that the Almighty and Eustace are allies? I'd not presume to answer for Our Lord God, but I'm willing to wager that I can hold my own against Eustace."

His cockiness was contagious and Ranulf grinned, too. "I do believe, lad, that you will. Now . . . are you ready for the ride of your life?"

Henry nodded. "I say we race the Devil and Eustace to Bristol, winner take all!"

EUSTACE and his men arrived in Dursley before daybreak, but they were too late. Enraged that his prey had eluded him, Eustace set out in hell-bent pursuit. But Henry evaded the ambushes, outran Eustace, and managed to reach Bristol safely. Eustace chased him almost to the gates of Bristol. He did not have enough men, though, to besiege the city and reluctantly withdrew, laying waste to the countryside as he retreated back to Oxford.

STEPHEN had been forced to remain in Yorkshire that summer, for as long as the Scots king was at Carlisle, York was not safe. He put up several countercastles and did all he could to encourage his supporters and dishearten his foes, but it was not until September that he was able to return to London. He soon joined his son at Oxford, and Eustace set about convincing him that Henry had presented them with an opportunity that might not come again. Was it not better, he argued, to put an end to this accursed war once and for all? So persistent and persuasive was he that Stephen overcame his misgivings and reluctantly agreed to wage war with such ferocity that their enemies would be compelled to surrender—or starve.

EVEN the pro-Stephen chronicle, Gesta Stephani, was shocked by the campaign conducted that autumn by the English king and his son: "They took and plundered everything they came upon, set fire to houses and churches, and, what was a more cruel and brutal sight, fired the crops that had been reaped and stacked all over the fields, consumed and brought to nothing everything edible they found. They raged with this bestial cruelty especially round Marlborough, they showed it also very terribly round Devizes, and they had in mind to do the same to their adversaries all over England."

THE day had begun with trouble and it got steadily worse. In midmorning a messenger from John Marshal had reached Devizes with disturbing news. Marshal reported that he was being hard pressed by the king and Eustace. They had launched several lightning raids upon the town and castle, doing considerable damage before they were driven off. They'd laid waste to the nearby farms and manors, and when Marshal had attempted to bring in a supply convoy, they'd ambushed it and burned what they did not take away with them. John Marshal was the least likely man to panic, as Ranulf well knew. For him to admit that he did not know how he was going to feed his people through the winter, he had to be in dire straits, indeed.

Ranulf and Henry had gotten similar complaints from Marshal's brother-in-law Patrick Fitz Walter, Earl of Salisbury, and from the castellan of Trowbridge. Even Roger Fitz Miles had been harassed at Gloucester. Ghost villages were springing up all over Wiltshire and Gloucestershire, as terrified families fled to the towns for safety. Salisbury and Gloucester and even Bristol were flooded with refugees, people with nowhere to go and no money to buy food. Charred ruins were becoming commonplace throughout the desolated countryside, an acrid, burning smell was carried for miles on the October wind, and what had once been fertile farmlands were now scorched, blackened earth. Oddly enough, never had the roads been so free of bandits, though, for even the outlaws had fled from Stephen's marauding army.

Devizes had not been spared, either. Some of the royal army's worst depredations had taken place in and about Devizes. The town had been raided a fortnight ago and the castle subjected to several hit-and-run attacks. It was a rare day when Henry and Ranulf could not see smoke from the castle battlements, and their own provisions were dwindling dangerously. It reminded Ranulf of the sieges of Winchester and Oxford, only now England itself seemed under siege.

The day was coming to a dismal end when refugees arrived from Calne, a small village five miles to the north. They huddled together in the great hall, the most pitiful wretches Henry had ever seen, their clothes shredded and ripped in their flight through the woods, scratched and bruised and still shaking with fright. But they were the lucky ones, the ones who'd gotten away.

The tale they told was as deplorable as it was—by now—familiar. The Lord Eustace had raided Calne, they reported. His men had killed those few who'd dared to resist, setting fire to their church and then to their fields. They'd watched from hiding as their crops went up in flames, and they wept again as they spoke of it, for there would be no food to feed the village once winter came. Their houses could be rebuilt, but what could they eat? How would they survive until spring?

They asked Henry these questions, calling him "young lord" and pleading for his help. He wasn't sure if they knew who he was. They might have been told of his presence at Devizes. Or they might be assuming that he must be someone of importance since he was well dressed and well fed and lived in a castle. He was not even sure that his name would mean anything to them. This war had been ravaging England for ten years. Did these people truly care who ruled over them as long as they were left in peace? He did not know what to say to them. He did not know how to help them. He ordered them fed, and he yearned to assure them that the danger was past. But he feared that would have been a lie.

He stood it as long as he could. But his pity and anger finally got the best of him, and he bolted the hall, retreating up to the solar with a flagon of wine and a head full of unanswered questions.

He was not alone for long; Ranulf soon followed. He was relieved to see the flagon was untouched, for he'd known too many men who turned to wine when they needed a crutch, and sixteen was a vulnerable age for learning bad habits. Henry was straddling a chair, resting his chin on his arms as he stared into the fire. He didn't stir, not even after Ranulf pulled a chair up beside him. Ranulf was content to wait, and they sat in silence for a while, listening to the flames crackle in the hearth.

"I do not understand," Henry said at last, "why they do not just lay siege to Devizes? I am the one they want. Why do they not try to take me?"

"I've thought about that, too. First of all, they cannot be sure that you are at Devizes. What if they besiege Devizes and it turns out you were at Bristol or Gloucester or Marlborough all the while? None of those castles could be easily taken. Devizes or Marlborough could hold out for months, and Bristol till Judgment Day. And whilst they were laying siege, they'd be vulnerable to attack themselves. That is what happened to Stephen at Wilton. By striking fast and riding on, he avoids becoming a target. By surprise raids, he spreads fear over the entire countryside, for no one knows where he will attack next. And by burning the crops, he takes the food from our table, too, empties our larder."

"But the others will starve ere we do," Henry pointed out. "Castles always have food stored away. The villagers and villeins will go hungry first, and they'll die first, too. Are they willing to do that, Ranulf? To let so many die for no sin of their own?"

"I would have said no," Ranulf said, "had I not seen this suffering for myself."

"And yet you claim Stephen is a good man?" Henry sounded hostile, but Ranulf understood that he was not the real target of the boy's anger. He even welcomed this rage, as proof that his nephew no longer saw all this as a game. He remembered how it was to be that young, to feel invulnerable. Even their wild ride for Bristol had been as exciting as it was urgent, at least to Henry. But this was different. This was war at its ugliest, and no man could look upon it and be unchanged, not if he was of any worth. And so he was sorry for his nephew's pain, but glad of it, too, for this was a lesson Henry had to learn.

"That they would resort to such drastic measures tells me that they see you as a very real threat, Harry, so much so that they are willing to wade through blood to eliminate you now, whilst they still can. This savage campaign is an admission that they dare not let you reach full manhood. It also shows us that Eustace is the most dangerous sort of battle commander, the kind who cares not how many die as long as he has the victory."

Henry looked skeptical. "Why are you so sure this is Eustace's doing?"

"Because this campaign of theirs is both brilliant and brutal . . . far too brutal for Stephen to stomach on his own. One of Stephen's worst flaws is that he invariably listens to the wrong people. God help England if he is now listening to Eustace."

"If they keep on like this," Henry said somberly, "they'll end up ruling over a graveyard. Do they truly think they can starve us into submission?"

Ranulf nodded grimly. "Or else force us into doing battle."

"Hopelessly outnumbered? Thank you, no, Uncle. I like not those odds. I'd just as soon not starve either," Henry added, striving—with limited success—for flippancy. "Damn them," he cried suddenly, fiercely, "damn them for killing and not caring! My mother would never have permitted a slaughter like this, never . . ."

His hair, short and unruly, gleamed in the firelight like a bright, burnished cap, and his fair skin darkened now with a surge of hot blood. He looked angry and shaken, young and resolute, all at the same time. "What can we do to stop this, Uncle Ranulf?"

"Nothing," Ranulf admitted reluctantly. "We can only wait, see what happens. We are going to have to depend upon the Almighty and our allies for our deliverance, lad, for this is one trap we cannot escape on our own."

"'Our allies'?" Henry echoed, and the same thought was in both their minds. John Marshal and the Earl of Salisbury and Roger Fitz Miles and Robert's son Will were all in the same sorry plight. Rainald was still in Cornwall, Baldwin de Redvers was said to be ailing, and Henry's parents were in Normandy, unaware of their son's peril. Robert and Miles were dead, Brien living as a monk. That narrowed the field to two. But by the time the Scots king could muster an army and march into England to their rescue, it would be too late. So "allies" came down to one powerful, self-serving, unpredictable man: Randolph de Gernons, Earl of Chester.

After a few moments of heavy silence, Henry laughed softly. At Ranulf's look of surprise, he said with a wry smile, "I was just thinking . . . When my mother got herself into a tight corner, she could always rely upon Uncle Robert to rescue her. And who do I get—the Earl of Chester!"

He laughed again, and this time, so did Ranulf. When put that way, what else was there to do but laugh?

44

CHESTER CASTLE, ENGLAND

October 1149

THE letter came at noon, and Chester and his brother retired to his bedchamber to read it. Maud was standing by that door now, unable to wait any longer. She knew Chester would not like her intrusion, but she pushed the door open and entered anyway. William de Roumare and Bennet de Malpas and Ivo de Coventry all glanced up in surprise; her husband was nowhere in sight. The letter lay open upon the table, and she moved forward, picked it up and read rapidly. Her brother-in-law frowned; his own wife would not have dared to meddle like that. He left it to Chester to reprimand her, however; he would not have admitted it, even to himself, but he was never fully at ease with Chester's high-spirited, strong-willed wife.

Maud put the letter down, glancing toward the corner privy chamber and then back at her husband's men. "The rumors are true then," she said. "My cousin Harry is in grave peril." When they nodded, she cried impatiently, "And what are you going to do about it? You do mean to go to his aid, do you not?"

Bennet de Malpas and Ivo de Coventry were more than willing to defer to Chester's brother. William de Roumare was irked by this abrupt female interrogation, but he found himself answering as if she'd willed it. "Of course we want to help him, Maud. And indeed we will, if only we can find a way. We cannot meet Stephen on the field, though, for we lack enough men for a pitched battle."

"Then stir up trouble for Stephen elsewhere and take the pressure off Harry and Marshal and the others under attack. You must draw Stephen away from Wiltshire ere it is too late!"

"I assure you we've already thought of that," William de Roumare said stiffly. "But it will not work."

"Of course it will! Remember how Baldwin de Redvers attacked

Corfe to lure Stephen west whilst my aunt and my father landed at Arundel? And then there was—"

"You are forgetting Oxford. When Stephen had Maude trapped in the castle there, not even the Lord Christ could have drawn him away, for nothing was more important than capturing his enemy, the empress. You may be sure that he wants her son no less badly, and he'll let England go up in flames ere he lets the lad get away."

Maud stared at him in dismay. He was as cautious as Chester was reckless, the anchor to Chester's sails, but his argument held the ring of truth. At that moment, her husband emerged from the privy chamber. "I thought I heard your voice," he said. "Let me guess . . . you want me to swear a blood oath that I'll rescue your cousin and uncle, preferably by nightfall."

"I cannot jest about this, Randolph, not when the danger is so great. Will says nothing can be done, but surely you can come up with a plan if you keep on trying."

"I already have."

That got the men's attention, too. "What mean you to do, Randolph?" his brother asked, sounding perplexed. "If we cannot chase Stephen away and cannot lure him away, what in God's Name is left?"

"But we *can* lure him away," Chester insisted. "It is just a matter of finding the right bait."

He seemed so pleased with himself that Maud knew this was no empty boast. What was he up to? Whatever it was, she did not doubt he'd benefit by it, too, for that was ever his way. And after a moment's reflection, she knew what he had in mind, a stratagem at once ruthless and vengeful and sure to succeed. The look she gave him then was one she'd rarely bestowed upon any man but her father and never before upon her husband—one of awed admiration. "Lincoln," she breathed, and Chester grinned raffishly.

"Just so," he said. "Lincoln."

MEN were gathering outside Stephen's command tent, eavesdropping upon the quarrel raging within. A newcomer jostled the man next to him, wanting to know what was going on. "That hellspawn Chester has attacked Lincoln, and the townspeople are pleading with the king to come and save them ere the city falls. The king wants to set out straightaway and the Lord Eustace is trying to talk him out of it. If you come closer and keep still, you can hear for yourself."

Stephen hated to argue, and Eustace was often able to use that to his advantage. But not this time. His father remained adamant, determined to come to the aid of the besieged Lincolners, and nothing Eustace could say would sway him.

"Those people suffered dreadfully after the Battle of Lincoln, Eustace. Hundreds drowned when they tried to flee the city and their boats overturned in the flooded river, and countless others were slaughtered by that whoreson, Chester. Through it all, they stayed loyal to me. How can you expect me to ignore their plea for help?"

"Catching Henry is more important, Papa! If we can get rid of Maude's whelp, we've won our war, and we can deal then with Chester. Why can you not see that?"

"Because by then it would be too late for the people of Lincoln!"

"So what?" Eustace was being deliberately, brutally blunt; he prided himself upon his candor, upon daring to say what other men would not, and he hoped that a dose of unsparing honesty might bring his father back to his senses. "So what?" he repeated. "People die all the time, Papa. Why are the Lincolners more important than the Wiltshire villagers who'll starve this winter? We agreed to do whatever we must to end this war, even if it meant innocent people would die. For England's greater good, we agreed; for a peaceful land. If that was true yesterday, it is still true today. Let the men of Lincoln fend for themselves."

Stephen slowly shook his head. "I cannot do that, Eustace. They trusted me once before and I let them down. I could not help them then, but I can now. I'll not turn away from them in their hour of need."

Eustace's frustration served now as fuel for his anger, blazing beyond his control. "It is your pride you want to save, not the Lincolners! Ever since your defeat there, you and Chester have been snarling over that wretched city like two dogs over a bone. Go ahead then, abandon our campaign and race north to their rescue. But it will avail you naught. Men will still remember how badly you were beaten at Lincoln!"

Eustace had meant to wound, and yet he felt an odd pang of remorse when he saw the hurt on his father's face. He did not know how to make it right, though, for an apology would be an admission of weakness.

Stephen looked at his son, saying nothing. Eustace could feel his face getting warm. Just when he thought he could endure it no longer, his father brushed past him and lifted the tent flap. "Make ready to depart at first light," he commanded someone beyond the range of Eustace's vision. "I will be riding for Lincoln on the morrow."

THE citizens of Lincoln put up such a desperate defense that they were able to stave off Chester's attack until Stephen came to the rescue. Chester withdrew his forces, but he did not go far, and the battle shifted from the city to the shire. Lincolnshire became a bloody ground, as the king and his mightiest subject fought a series of inconclusive skirmishes, ambushes, and raids. In the words of the chronicler of the Gesta Stephani, "They alternated betwen success and disaster, never without the greatest injury to the county, never without loss and harm to its people."

Stephen's failure to subdue the rebel earl was observed in other quarters, and the erratic Hugh Bigod was emboldened enough to stir up trouble again in East Anglia. This was his third uprising, but this time he got more than he bargained for. Chester was keeping Stephen busy in Lincolnshire and the task of dealing with Bigod fell to Eustace. He raced north and soon had Bigod in full retreat.

Henry and his allies were quick enough to take advantage of all this chaos and unrest. He and Ranulf joined the Earls of Hereford and Gloucester and raided deep into Devon and Dorset. They set about making life as miserable as possible for Henry de Tracy, Stephen's chief supporter in the West Country, with some success. Tracy prudently refused to do battle, though, withdrawing behind the fortified defenses of his castle at Barnstaple. But Henry then bloodied his sword for the first time in the capture of the town and castle at Bridgport.

NATURE showed the southwest of England more mercy that year than Man did, and November, usually the least welcome of visitors, was blessedly mild-mannered. But the reprieve was brief for the homeless and the hungry, and by mid-December, winter was stalking the war-ravaged shires in earnest. In the mornings, the ground was glazed with a killing black frost, the winds soon stripped the trees bare, and ponds and lakes began to ice over.

The more weather-wise of Henry's men were keeping a wary eye upon the gathering clouds, for a mottled mackerel sky was a harbinger of rain or snow. They were riding fast, heading back toward Devizes, having gotten word that Eustace was once again on the prowl in Wiltshire. A second warning from John Marshal had alarmed Henry enough to send an advance guard ahead to reinforce the castle garrison. Roger and Will had thought he was being overly cautious. But Henry had insisted, and Ranulf had backed him up, reminding them that Robert had always been one for taking extra precautions, too.

In supporting one nephew, Ranulf inadvertently offended the other, for Will had become very thin-skinned since his father's death, twisting any praise of Robert into an implied criticism of himself. Roger ought to have understood Will's insecurities if any man could, for Miles had also cast a smothering shadow, but he'd so far shown little patience with Will's defensive outbursts. And Henry was too young and too confident to comprehend such crippling self-doubts. So it fell to Ranulf to act as peacemaker. He did not mind, for he truly did feel sorry for Will; he knew that men were indeed thinking what Will feared: that the son would never measure up to the sire.

The wind had picked up as the day wore on, gusting from the northeast, another sign of unsettled weather on the way. They'd halted to give their horses a rest, but it was too cold for the men to enjoy the respite themselves. Ranulf joined Henry in the shelter of a massive gnarled oak. "Are you still uneasy about Devizes, lad? You could not have picked a better man to leave in command than Hugh de Plucknet. He was utterly fearless during our escape through the snow at Oxford. I've told you about that, have I not?"

"Repeatedly," Henry said, then ducked, laughing, out of range when Ranulf tried to elbow him in the ribs. "You read me all too well, Uncle Ranulf. I was thinking of Devizes . . . and of war and why some men are so much better at it than others. What makes a good battle commander? Courage alone is not enough. Roger is so reckless that it is downright scary at times, but he does not seem to have a grasp of strategy. So what is it, then? If he'd not been born an earl's son, Chester would likely have been hanged as a bandit, but men say he is a right able battle commander. And my uncle David is very good, indeed, at governing, but not as good at fighting. Is it not possible to be good at both?"

Ranulf nodded. "Your uncle Robert was such a man, lad. He was a brilliant battle commander, but he would also have made an excellent king."

"But with one flaw." Henry glanced around to make sure his cousin was not within earshot. "Will would have been his heir!"

That had never occurred to Ranulf. "God save England," he said, with feeling, and they both laughed. But then Ranulf stiffened, moving away from the tree with a startled oath, for the sky to the north was streaking with smoke.

DUSK came early in December, and the fading light slowed them down. They forged ahead, though, sure that the smoke was coming from Devizes, and soon had confirmation of their fears. A lone rider was galloping south at a reckless speed. He shouted at sight of them, yanking his lathered stallion to a shuddering halt scant feet from Henry.

"Devizes is under attack, my lord! Eustace burned the town and then laid siege to the castle. By the time we got there, they'd breached the outer defenses and had driven the garrison into the keep. When we rode in, Sir Hugh and his men sallied forth on the attack again. I suppose they thought the whole of your army had arrived. Of course we then went to their aid, but we're outnumbered, my lord. You must get there fast or you'll lose the men, the town, and the castle, too!"

RIDING into Devizes was like riding into Hell. Orange flames were shooting up into the darkening sky, black, suffocating smoke was everywhere, and bodies were stacked like firewood in the narrow streets. But the bloody fighting was done. Eustace and his men were in retreat, having broken off the battle once they heard the sounds of an approaching army.

Hugh de Plucknet was limping toward them. Blood was running down his leg, his face was begrimed with smoke, and one eye was squinting, half closed by a rapidly swelling bruise. But he was grinning broadly. "Your timing was well-nigh perfect, my lord," he told Henry gleefully. "We were being hammered right bad. But they turned tail once they realized you were coming up upon them. Say what you will of Eustace, he's got brains as well as ballocks, for he knew when he was beaten. And to give the Devil his due, he can fight with the best of them!"

Hugh sounded almost admiring. That would have perplexed Henry at one time, but he was learning that for some men, courage was the true coin of the realm, and as long as a man had it to spend, he could earn himself unlimited credit, whatever his political debts. But while Henry was coming to understand this point of view, he did not share it, and he found it hard to muster up any respect for Eustace, whose only demonstrable talent seemed to be for killing.

Roger was all for pursuing the enemy, but Ranulf and Will thought it a waste of time, and Henry agreed; the men would just scatter in the darkness. For now, it was enough that he'd driven Eustace off and saved Devizes. From all he'd heard of his rival, this would fester with Eustace like a running sore, that he'd been put to flight by the whelp, the stripling, the foe he'd so openly scorned.

Henry felt triumphant, tired, and angry by turns. Dismounting hastily, he set men to fighting the fires. People had begun to creep out of hiding, and cries and lamenting soon filled the air as the survivors discovered the bodies of loved ones. Embers lit the night like winter fireflies, and when snow began to fall, the scene took on an air of eerie unreality to Henry, a weird juxtaposition of fire and ice, heat and cold, grief and joy.

He watched as a church was given up to the flames, as slate-roofed cottages were saved and thatched ones doomed, as horses were blindfolded and led to safety from the blazing stables. All around him, men were shivering and sweating, slipping in the snow only to be singed in the smoldering ruins. People were celebrating their deliverance and mourning their dead, even as the fires continued to burn and the snow to drift down into their midst, and as he walked through the wreckage of this prosperous market town, he heard himself proclaimed as its saviour.

Ranulf eventually found Henry in a churchyard, watching somberly as a weeping man and woman crouched over the body of their four-year-old son, trampled by the horses of Eustace's fleeing soldiers. "The fires are almost out. Come on back to the castle, Harry. You must be half frozen by now."

Henry nodded, then flinched when the woman began a high, keening wail. "I am thankful that we got here in time," he said. "I am beholden to God, and to Hugh de Plucknet for not giving up. I know we won a victory here this night. But I am beginning to see, Uncle, that victories in this war are not what they seem. For what have we truly won? The chance to do it all again on the morrow."

Ranulf could not argue, for he'd come to realize that, too, a bitter lesson learned at grievous cost in the past two years. He did not know whether to be sorry or glad that his nephew was learning it so young.

THE winter weather put a temporary halt to campaigning. Henry paid a prudent courtesy call upon the Bishop of Salisbury, who was still pressing the Church's claim to Devizes. He visited John Marshal, who was just fourteen miles away, at Marlborough. And he and Ranulf passed a quiet Christmas at Devizes Castle.

January was cold and blustery, and Ranulf and Henry were surprised in midmonth by the unexpected arrival of John Marshal and the Earls of Hereford, Gloucester, and Salisbury. After a hearty meal of roast goose and pork pie, they withdrew to the solar, where the men soon revealed why they were at Devizes—to convince Henry that he ought to go back to Normandy.

Although they phrased it as tactfully as possible, the gist of their message was unmistakable: Henry had become a liability. He stiffened in shock, but did not interrupt, hearing them out in silence. Only then did he say coolly, "It sounds as if you want to get rid of me."

Roger and Will and the Earl of Salisbury at once made vociferous denials. John Marshal sat back in his seat, arms folded across his chest, looking like a bored pirate chieftain. When Henry glanced his way, he drained his wine cup, set it down with a thud, and then said candidly, "You are right. We do want you out of England, at least for a while."

The other men protested even more vehemently, but Henry paid them no heed. "Go on," he told Marshal. "Explain yourself."

"It is a matter of survival, ours and yours. You do not have enough of an army to force another Battle of Lincoln upon Stephen, not yet. But as long as you remain on English soil, you'll be a target for Stephen and Eustace. You saw what they did to these shires last autumn. Well, it will happen all over again come spring, and it will keep on happening until you get safely beyond their reach . . . back to Normandy."

"What are you saying, that I should just give up?"

The older man shook his head impatiently. "Good Christ, no! We want the crown for you almost as much as you want it yourself. But this is not the way to win your war. You've acquitted yourself well this past year," he said, and Henry flushed with pleasure, for he knew Marshal was not a man to pay polite compliments. "What we need now, though, is some time to heal our wounds and plant our crops and strengthen our defenses. You can give us that time—but not if you stay in England."

They all watched Henry intently once Marshal was done speaking. But he gave them no clue as to what he meant to do. "I shall think upon what you've told me," he said, and they had to be content with that, for they'd learned that, like his mother, he'd balk if pushed.

RANULF thought Marshal's argument made sense. But he was not sure if Henry had been ready to hear it. It was only natural that he'd long for a decisive victory to end his first campaign. Ranulf did not want his nephew's pride to put him at needless risk. But neither did he want the youth to return to Normandy thinking that he'd failed. An uncle-nephew talk was in order, he decided.

He was groping his way up the spiral stairwell toward Henry's bedchamber when he collided with someone coming down. His initial contact was enough to tell him he'd bumped into a female, and his first guess was that she was a maidservant, for she was carrying a tray and wine flagon. But then he caught a whiff of jasmine perfume, too expensive for a serving-girl, and realized that this was Henry's bedmate.

"Lora?" There was a wall sconce several feet above them, casting a feeble light upon the stairs, and before she ducked her head, he saw the tear tracks on her cheek. "What is wrong, lass?" he asked, wondering why she should be weeping alone out in the stairwell. This could be no lovers' quarrel, for her tryst with Henry was a business transaction. He'd met Lora upon his visit to Salisbury, and had taken a fancy to the young prostitute, coaxing her into coming back with him to Devizes. Ranulf had approved of his nephew's taste, for she was fair of face and lush of body and seemed quite worldly for her years, just eighteen or thereabouts. "What is it, lass?" he asked again, gently. "Why do you weep?"

She startled him, then, with a flare of temper, for until now, she'd always appeared cheerful and accommodating. "Did you think whores had no tears?" she snapped. "If we do not often weep, it is only because we learn early on that it avails us naught."

Beneath the sarcasm was a genuine hurt, and he took no offense. "Can I help?" he asked, and she shook her head, swiping at her wet cheek with the back of her hand, a gesture he found plaintively childlike.

"I did not mean to bite your head off," she said. "You've always been right good to me, Lord Ranulf, and deserve better than that. I was crying because Lord Harry told me he is leaving."

"I see," Ranulf said, for he did. Her tears made perfect sense now. Of course she would be sorry to see their liaison end, for she'd achieved the pinnacle of success for one in her precarious profession: she'd found herself a highborn protector, one who was young and personable in the bargain. Little wonder, he thought, that the lass dreaded going back to her old life in Salisbury.

Lora could not read books, but she'd learned, of necessity, to read men. "I'll not deny," she said, "that I shall miss the comforts of a castle. Servants and a feather bed and a roof that does not leak and no lack of candles or firewood—who would willingly give up such ease? But whether you believe me or not, it is Lord Harry I shall miss the most. He never made me feel like a whore. Not once!" she added defiantly, as if to fend off his disbelief.

"Is that so uncommon, Lora?" he asked, and she nodded, marveling that a lord like Ranulf could ask so innocent a question; she did not doubt that Henry, even at sixteen, already understood more than his uncle about mankind's propensity for careless cruelties.

"Very uncommon, my lord," she said bleakly. "But Lord Harry has a good heart. Moreover, he truly likes women."

"Most men do, lass," Ranulf pointed out in amusement, and was surprised when she shook her head again.

"No, my lord." She contradicted him with an odd smile, one that was both cynical and sad. "Most men like to lay with women."

Ranulf felt pity stirring, and he hoped it did not show upon his face. "Harry truly has no choice, Lora. He must return to Normandy . . . but not for good. He'll be back."

The smile she gave him now was polite and practiced and far too knowing for her years. "Yes," she said, "but not for me."

"I RAN into Lora in the stairwell. She said you've decided to go. For what it is worth, Harry, I think you made a wise choice."

Henry shrugged. "Well . . . my father always said that if you want to get invited back, you'd best know when to go home."

Ranulf was not fooled by the levity. "It sounds to me," he said, "as if you're uneasy in your own mind about this."

Henry shrugged again. "It is just that if I go now, Ranulf, all my efforts will have been so . . . so damned inconclusive."

"You're going home alive, Harry. What is inconclusive about that? For nigh on a year, Stephen and Eustace did their accursed best to hunt you down, but to no avail. You think that went unnoticed? All over England, there are men thinking to themselves: If they could not bring the empress's son to ruination at sixteen, how are they going to fare against him once he reaches nineteen or twenty? No, lad, this campaign of yours was a rousing success, for you opened the door wide for your next foray. And you've got a powerful ally on your side—time."

"I've a better ally than that. I've got Eustace, too," Henry said, and smiled at Ranulf's surprise. "Fortune's Wheel has turned with a vengeance, Uncle. Why was it so easy for Stephen to steal my mother's crown? The country was not full of men afire to put Stephen on the throne. They just did not want the empress, Geoffrey of Anjou's wife. And now . . . now none of them can be utterly sure that I'll make a good king." His smile flashed again, sudden and sardonic. "But there's hardly a soul in England," he said, "who doubts that Eustace would make a bad one!"

RANULF accompanied Henry to Wareham, and promised to join him and Maude in Normandy after he paid a farewell visit to his Welsh kin. He and Padarn then started off on their long journey back to Gwynedd. Henry sailed with the tide for Barfleur.

Henry received a joyous welcome from his parents and partisans in Normandy. Geoffrey was pleased enough with his firstborn's prowess to declare Henry legally of age. He then did something which greatly gratified his wife, horrified Stephen, alarmed the French king—newly back from the Holy Land—and astonished most of Christendom. He'd always contended that he was holding Normandy for Henry. But he'd won the duchy by his own efforts, and in their world, men rarely yielded up power of their own free will. That was what Geoffrey now did, though, relinquishing his rights to Normandy in his son's favor. While still a month shy of his seventeenth birthday, Henry became Duke of Normandy.

45

TREFRIW, NORTH WALES

February 1150

It was a typical February afternoon—raw and grey. Selwyn, one of the youths honing his skills of manhood in Rhodri's service, had built a fire in the open hearth, burying a log in wood ash so it would burn slowly and steadily. Bechan, the serving-maid, was dipping candles in sheep's tallow, for only the very wealthy and the very extravagant burned wax candles for everyday use. Olwen, who attended Rhiannon and Eleri, had positioned a spindle close to the hearth so she could spin flax in comparative comfort. And Rhiannon had brought a mortar and pestle to the table, where she set about crushing wood betony. The cook had been ailing, she explained to the curious Selwyn, and when mixed with honey, powdered betony leaves eased coughing and shortness of breath.

Selwyn was never satisfied with a simple answer and he wanted to know all about the other uses of betony. Rhiannon answered patiently as he flung question after question her way, for she liked the boy, but she was glad, nonetheless, when he fetched a whetstone and began to sharpen his sword. He was touchingly proud of the weapon—his first—for he was only fourteen, and he was soon so intent upon his task that Rhiannon and herbal remedies were forgotten.

Rhiannon welcomed the silence, for she'd awakened that morning with a headache that was so far resisting both sage and pennyroyal. She'd been able, though, to use the headache to escape accompanying Enid and Eleri on a courtesy call to a neighbor who'd recently given birth to her first child. Enid and Eleri had not objected, for the woman invariably fluttered around Rhiannon like a deranged moth, so acutely uncomfortable with Rhiannon's blindness that she made everyone else equally uncomfortable with her.

Rhiannon had another—secret—reason for not wanting to visit Blodwen. She agreed heartily with Eleri's caustic assessment of Blodwen as a woman "who has feathers where her brains ought to be." She could bear Blodwen's twittering and fidgety hospitality—if she had to. What she could not endure was that the Almighty had seen fit to give foolish, shallow Blodwen what Rhiannon would never have herself: a newborn son.

Snatching up his mantle, Selwyn muttered something about an "errand." Rhiannon suspected he was off to the kitchen, for he seemed to spend half of his time there, trying to inveigle cider and honeyed wafers from the cook. He'd been gone only a few moments when the door opened again and a familiar voice bellowed out an unnecessary proclamation of his arrival.

Rhiannon was delighted; her father had been at Aber for the past week, attending his king, Owain Gwynedd. "Papa, you're back early!" Pushing her chair away from the table, she started toward the sound of his voice.

The warning was not in time. Her father cried out her name, but by then she'd already stumbled over something out in the middle of the floor, something hard and heavy, something that should not have been there. As she fell, she felt a sudden surge of heat and she twisted desperately away from it. She avoided the open hearth, but hit the ground hard enough to drive all the air out of her lungs. Momentarily stunned, she lay still until her father reached her, with Olwen just a step behind.

"I am not hurt, Papa," she insisted, and after she'd repeated it for the fourth time, he finally believed her. He was assisting her to her feet when Selwyn came back into the hall. Rhodri glanced from the boy to the offending whetstone, and then erupted. Ranulf had once told Rhiannon and Eleri about a legendary mountain called Vesuvius, said to belch forth fire and smoke. Rhiannon thought her father's temper was like that volcano, usually so inert and sluggish that his rare explosions were terrifying. There was no doubt that Selwyn was thoroughly cowed, reduced to incoherent stammerings as Rhodri berated him furiously for his carelessness.

"The day I took you into my household, I warned you that you were never to leave things strewn about or to move furniture, did I not? You swore upon your very soul that you would be heedful . . . and so what happens? My daughter nearly fell into the fire because you did not put your whetstone away!"

Rhiannon eventually managed to reassure her father, assuage his anger, and spare Selwyn the worst of his wrath. By then she was exhausted, for she'd been more shaken by her fall than she was willing to admit. As soon as she could, she withdrew to the bedchamber she shared with Eleri, and lay down, fully clothed, upon the bed.

Her cheek was stinging and would likely bruise. But the bruises that troubled her were the ones on her memory. It would be a while before she could forget her terror as she felt the flames. What frightened her just as much was the reminder of how fragile the defenses of her world were. All it took was one misplaced whetstone to reveal how vulnerable she truly was.

When she finally fell asleep, it wasn't peaceful. She was dreaming of Ranulf, but there was no joy in it, just unease and shadows and an ominous sense of foreboding, for they'd not gotten a letter from him in months, and Rhiannon had no proof that he was even still alive. She tossed and turned restlessly, and was glad to be awakened by the opening door.

It was a man's footstep, too light for Rhodri, too heavy for Selwyn. Rhiannon sat up, puzzled, and listened again. Who else could it be but Papa or the lad? And then she caught her breath. "Ranulf?" she whispered, half afraid to let herself hope, and was rewarded with a sound sweeter to her than the heavenly harps of the Almighty's own angels—Ranulf's laughter.

"You are truly amazing, lass! How is it that you can remember the sound of my step after so many months?"

She could have told him it was because she'd heard those footsteps echoing through her dreams almost every night since he'd gone away, but of course nothing short of torture would have gotten that out of her. "I am so glad you've come back, Ranulf," she said instead, and added a silent prayer that this time he would stay.

THE fortnight that followed was the happiest of Rhiannon's life. She knew it couldn't last, that sooner or later Ranulf would ride off again; he'd said as much, that he'd agreed to join Henry in Normandy. But she resolutely refused to think about that. He could always change his mind. For the moment, it was enough that he was safe and well and home.

Ranulf had returned in high spirits, bringing gifts and gossip from the world that lay beyond the mountains of Eryri. He enthralled them with dramatic accounts of the escape from Dursely and the triumph at Devizes. He horrified them with stories of the suffering Stephen had loosed upon his own subjects. And he fascinated them with reports of the scandal that had trailed the French monarchs all the way from Palestine.

Rhiannon and Eleri did not find Eleanor's thwarted attempt to escape her marital bonds as surprising as Ranulf had; Welsh women enjoyed liberties unheard-of in the rest of Christendom, one of them being the right to walk away from a miserable marriage. They sympathized instinctively with the spirited French queen, were indignant that she should have been forced to accompany her husband from Antioch, and listened spellbound when Ranulf revealed the unexpected twist to this sad tale.

On their way home from the Holy Land, he related, they'd passed some days in Italy, as guests of the Pope, and the elderly pontiff had set himself a herculean task: mending the rift between these utterly mismatched souls. He had even gone so far, Ranulf divulged, as to escort them to bed and urge them to make their peace between the sheets. The Pope's blessing seemed to have paid off, for Eleanor was now pregnant, for only the third time in thirteen years. The child was due that summer, and the French king's subjects were waiting anxiously to see if, after a miscarriage and a daughter, she would at last bear him a son.

Each morning, Rhiannon awakened with the same subversive thought, one she quickly disavowed: Would this be the day that Ranulf announced he'd soon be leaving? But it was not Ranulf who brought this interlude to an abrupt end; it was her father.

A damp darkness had fallen by the time Rhiannon started out to the stables with a jug of milk, meant for the stable cat and her kittens. Cats were rarely kept as pets, except in nunneries, but Rhiannon was enchanted by them, for she did not need sight to appreciate their sleek lines and soft fur and lulling purr. She had just reached their well when Rhodri rode in. Hastily dismounting, he sent his horse off to the stables with Selwyn, and hurried toward his daughter.

"Is Ranulf within? I must talk to him straightaway, lass. I've come up with a way to keep him in Wales, here with us where he belongs!"

Rhiannon's heartbeat picked up a quicker rhythm. "Truly, Papa? How?"

Rhodri reached out and gripped her by the elbows; she could tell by the tone of his voice that he was smiling. "I am going to name him as my heir and convince him to take Eleri as his wife." He heard her gasp and enveloped her in an expansive hug; she found her face pressed against the wet wool of his mantle, the feel scratchy and smothering. "It is the ideal solution, Rhiannon. Where could I hope to find a better brother-in-law for you? And Ranulf and Eleri will have a good marriage, whilst making their home and raising their children on our land. I tell you, lambkin, it is well-nigh perfect!"

Rhiannon was too stunned to respond, but Rhodri was too jubilant to notice. "You'd best go feed those flea-bitten cats ere I decide to drown the sorry lot," he teased. "But do not tarry longer than need be with the mangy beasts, for we'll have much to celebrate this night!"

Rhiannon caught the edge of the well enclosure, held on so tightly that the stones left imprints in the palms of her hands. She needed the physical contact, a way of reassuring herself that there was still something in her world that was familiar, safe. She'd sometimes wondered what it must be like to be drunk, to have all her senses blurred by mead. Now . . .

she knew. Reality as she'd known it had fled forever as soon as her father had begun speaking.

Gradually some of the shock faded, and her numbed brain started to function again. She could not let this happen. She must stop her father ere it was too late. She'd dropped the milk jug, tripped over it now as she moved away from the well, but managed to keep her footing. She'd gotten herself turned around, though, and when she started for the house, she was actually going in the opposite direction. It was not until she caught the smell of hay and horses that she realized her mistake. Spinning away from the stable, she began to retrace her steps, nearly weeping with frustration and fear that she'd not be in time. When she heard her name called behind her, she grabbed Selwyn's arm as he came up beside her. "Take me to the hall," she demanded, "quickly!"

Selwyn was surprised, for Rhiannon could be as prickly as a hedgehog when her independence was concerned. But he did as she bade, and led her back across the bailey, doing his best to avoid the worst patches of mud. Rhiannon would not have noticed had he steered her into a swamp, and she forgot to thank him when they at last reached the hall. "Papa," she cried, "Papa, where are you?"

"Whatever is the man up to, Rhiannon? Never have I seen Rhodri look so full of himself, like a lad who'd discovered where his birthday present was hidden away!" The voice was Enid's, amused and fondly indulgent. "He said nary a word, did not even shed his mantle ere he dragged Ranulf off to our bedchamber! Do you know what—"

Rhiannon heard no more. Turning away, she plunged through the doorway, back out into the blackness of the bailey. It was all she could think to do, for she could not go to her bedchamber; Eleri was there and would need one look at her face to know something was dreadfully wrong. She could not deal with Eleri or Enid now. She had to have some time alone, time to decide what to do. The afternoon drizzle had stopped and the air was dry but very cold. She stepped unheedingly into the puddles, getting her feet wet and her skirts muddied. She was shivering, and when she tasted salt on her tongue, she realized she was crying, too, but for the moment, all that mattered was reaching the stables, the only sanctuary she had left.

Stumbling into the stables, she called out repeatedly until she was sure she was alone, and then sank down upon a bale of hay. She heard nickering and snorting as horses craned their necks over their stall doors, hoping she'd brought treats again, and once the cats discovered her, the kittens began to pounce on her ankles and climb up her skirts. She felt leaden with fatigue, not moving even when they dug their needle-sharp little claws into her leg. She could not let this marriage come to pass. Blessed Lady Mary, hear your servant Rhiannon's plea. It must not happen.

She would have to tell her father. She'd fought so hard to keep her secret. Mayhap Enid suspected, but no one else did. She'd made sure of that. All for naught now. And once she spoke up . . . what then? She'd break her father's heart by thwarting this marriage. And what of Eleri? What if she truly wanted to marry Ranulf? Ranulf. He'd have to be told, too, and nothing would ever be the same between them after that. Their friendship—all she'd dared hope to have from him—would be spoiled, poisoned by his pity. And then he'd go away again, and this time he would not be back.

She shivered again, as much from the anticipated humiliation as from the cold. How could she bear to do this? Casting aside her pride would be worse than being stripped naked. But how could she keep silent? How could she live under the same roof with Ranulf and Eleri once they were wed? Bidding them goodnight at the door of their bedchamber. Hearing the new intimacy in their laughter. Lying awake at night, unwillingly imagining their lovemaking. Awaiting Eleri's announcement that she was with child. How could she ever endure it? How could she not give herself away a hundred times a day?

What then, was she to do? Papa's house was her only refuge. She had nowhere else to go. No other kin. Even if she'd wanted to pledge the rest of her life to God, no convent would accept a blind nun. She could feel the stirrings of an old enemy, one she'd thought she'd long ago vanquished. But panic could never truly be defeated; the best she could hope for was to keep it caged, under control. Now, though, she could hear it rattling the latch, seeking a way out.

She forced herself to draw several deep, bracing breaths, willing the cage bars to hold. Why had she been so quick to conclude that her father would prevail? Ranulf might well refuse. For an instant, hope flickered. But what man would not want to wed Eleri? She was pretty, lively, clever . . . whole.

In the years since her sight faded, many of Rhiannon's visual images had faded, too. But she'd loved the sea, and she could still summon up vivid memories of foaming waves churning shoreward, breaking upon the beach and then retreating, leaving a trail of white spume across the wet sand. The jealousy that engulfed her now was like one of those powerful, surging waves, crashing down upon her without warning and receding just as quickly, leaving her shaken by the impact and horrified by the realization that she could feel such intense resentment toward Eleri, who'd done nothing to deserve it. It was not fair to blame Eleri for not being blind. But neither was it fair that she should be punished for a love that she'd have taken quietly to her grave. How could the Almighty ask so much more of her? Was it not enough that she must live out her days in darkness? Shocked that she could harbor such a blasphemous rage against God, she hastily crossed herself and then began to weep, muffling her sobs in her mantle so that no one passing by could hear.

"WELL?" Ranulf asked, leaning back in his seat with a curious smile. "What would you say to me, Uncle?"

"It is much too important to discuss sober, lad. Help yourself to some mead whilst I decide how best to begin."

Ranulf obligingly took several swallows, although he'd not yet developed a taste for the Welsh beverage. "This gets to me faster than wine," he warned. "Two flagons and I'm likely to start telling you secrets not even my confessor ought to hear!"

Rhodri laughed, then reached across the table and gripped his nephew's arm. "I've never been one for tact or diplomacy, so I'm just going to blurt it out. Ere I do, though, there is something you need to know. Were you aware that under Welsh law, women cannot inherit land?"

Ranulf was startled. "No, I was not. That surprises me very much, for it was my understanding that Welsh law was uncommonly kind to women."

"The restriction was not meant to punish our womenfolk. It is a matter of practicality. You see, lad, land is a sacred trust to us, passed down from father to son. A man cannot sell his son's birthright; he but holds the land for his heirs. And because we know mankind is by nature as predatory as the wolf, no one can inherit who is not able to defend his lands from attack. Our laws exclude men crippled or deaf or blind or stricken with leprosy, as well as women."

"What happens if a man has no male heirs?"

"When he dies, his lands escheat to the king."

Ranulf sipped his mead slowly, grappling with the implications of what he'd just been told. "Jesú, but you're in the same plight as my father was after the White Ship sank! When you lost your last son, Cadell, you lost your lands, too, then?"

Rhodri nodded. "Or so I thought . . . until God sent you back to us, Ranulf."

"Me? I'm only half Welsh!"

"Half is enough. Our law allows the sons of Welsh women to inherit, even if the father is an alltud, a foreigner."

"But . . . but I am illegitimate! Surely you've not forgotten that?"

"A son need not be born in wedlock to claim his birthright, not in

Wales. It is enough if he is recognized by his father . . . or in your case, by your closest male kin—me!"

Ranulf gaped at the older man, dumbfounded. "Are you saying that you want to name me as your heir?"

"I want to do more than that, Ranulf. I want you as my heir . . . and son-in-law. I know I've taken you by surprise," he added hastily, "but just wait, lad, hear me out. Eleri will be sixteen next month, old enough to be wed. She'd make you a good wife, I've no doubt of it. She is pretty and spirited and I know you're right fond of her—"

"Of course I am! But we are first cousins. We'd have to seek a dispensation from the Church ere we could wed, and it is not likely we'd get one."

Rhodri grinned triumphantly. "You'd not need one, not in Wales. We wed our cousins all the time. 'Marry in the kin,' we say, and 'fight the feud with the stranger.'"

"I . . . I do not know what to say, Uncle. In truth, I never thought of Eleri as a wife."

"I know I've caught you off balance, lad. Suppose we back up, give you a chance to catch your breath. Let's start with Wales. Could you be happy living here?"

Ranulf was silent for some moments. "Yes," he said at last, sounding surprised, "I believe I could . . ."

Rhodri nodded emphatically. "Of course you could! It was meant to be, Ranulf. You think it was mere chance that brought you into Wales? Indeed not! I prayed to the Almighty for aid and He heard my plea. If only Angharad could have known that her son would be restored to us! And once you wed Eleri—"

Ranulf gave an abrupt, overwhelmed laugh. "Whoa! You're going too fast for me, Uncle. You're offering me so much—your lands and your daughter. It does not seem like a fair bargain. What do you get in return?"

"You'd be giving me a gift beyond price: peace of mind. This land was my father's and his father's before him. I do not want our family to lose it, and if you stay in Wales, we will not. And of equal importance to me, I know you'd do right by my daughters. I'd not want to count all the nights I've lain awake, fearing what might happen to Rhiannon after I died. She will be dependent upon the goodwill of Eleri's husband once I am gone, so in choosing a husband for Eleri, I must choose for them both. With you, I could be sure that my Rhiannon would always have a home, that she would want for nothing."

"Rhiannon," Ranulf said thoughtfully. "Yes, I am beginning to see . . ."

Rhodri started to speak, but then stopped. He'd said enough. Now it was up to his nephew. He must not push. Ranulf had to want this for it to work. But forbearance did not come easily to him; he'd always been one for acting, even if it was ill advised, and he was soon squirming impatiently. "I do not mean to rush you, Ranulf. Take as much time as you need," he offered, with an utter lack of conviction.

Ranulf reached for his mead cup, regarding his uncle with affectionate understanding. "You'd not be able to wait for your own salvation, Uncle! I was tempted to tell you I'd need a week to make up my mind, but you'd be sore crazed by midnight. Fortunately for your nerves, I can give you my answer now. I cannot marry Eleri. But I will marry Rhiannon . . . if she'll have me."

Ranulf got the reaction he'd expected; his uncle's jaw dropped and his eyes opened wide. But he'd thought that surprise would give way to elation. Instead, Rhodri looked wary.

"Rhiannon holds my heart in the palm of her hand," Rhodri said, choosing his words with conspicuous care. "After she lost her sight, I swore by our own St Davydd that she'd lose nothing else, not as long as I drew breath. When she reached womanhood, I tried mightily to find her a husband, for I wanted her to have all that other women did. She may not be as fair to look upon as Eleri, but she is still a handsome lass, and kind and quick-witted in the bargain. But she could have been as beautiful as this French queen I hear so much talk about, and as saintly as the Blessed Virgin Mary, and it would still have availed her naught. I could find no man willing to take a blind wife. Why, then, would you be willing, Ranulf?"

"I am not asking for a 'blind wife.' I am asking for Rhiannon. But it is a fair question, Uncle. Two years ago, I would not have been willing, either. But I lived under the same roof with Rhiannon for nigh on a year. I've seen her light candles and mend tablecloths and do any number of chores that I would not have believed a blind person could do. She taught me that 'blind' was not another word for 'helpless,' and I came to admire her courage and value her integrity. Your daughter is a remarkable woman. The men who were so quick to reject Rhiannon just never got a chance to find that out."

"That is an honest answer. I can see the sense in what you say. But tell me this, Ranulf. Why Rhiannon and not Eleri? Why choose the harder road?"

"If you were to start hunting a husband for Eleri, you'd have no trouble finding a hundred men willing—nay, eager—to take her to wife. Eleri does not need me. Rhiannon does. I can give her what no one else will, what other women take for granted—a home and children."

"Are you sure, lad . . . truly sure this is what you want?" When Ranulf nodded, Rhodri bounded out of his chair, raced around the table, and grabbed his nephew in a loving choke-hold. "You've won me over," he chortled. "Now go win my Rhiannon!"

RANULF eventually found Rhiannon in the stables, seated on a bale of hay, a sleeping kitten in her lap. "There you are, lass! Why are you sitting out here in the dark?" Hearing his own words, he laughed ruefully. "Hellfire, I'm still doing it!"

"Well . . . at least you've stopped flinching every time you use the word *see* in my hearing." Try as Rhiannon might to keep her voice level, it sounded suspiciously husky and strained to her ear; most sighted people were not as sensitive to tones, though, and she hoped he'd not notice. She'd known that sooner or later someone would come looking for her. But she'd not expected it to be Ranulf, and she stiffened as he moved toward her across the straw. She was not ready for this, nowhere near ready.

Ranulf hung his lantern on an overhead hook and sat down beside her on the bale. "I had the most astounding talk tonight with your father. It is as if my whole life was turned upside down in a matter of moments—just like an hourglass!"

He laughed again and Rhiannon discovered that she couldn't swallow; there was an excited edge to his laughter that she'd never heard before. He did not sound to her like a man who'd just rejected a marriage proposal. She could think of nothing to say that would not betray her and listened in growing despair as he said, "I'd not realized until tonight how much I wanted to stay in Wales. When I came back, it was like coming home. Passing strange that I could not see that for myself, that I needed to have it pointed out to me."

"I know," Rhiannon said faintly, "about . . . your talk. Papa confided in me beforehand." Her words seemed to come of their own volition, and she felt a sudden dizziness, as if she were teetering on the edge of an abyss. But she was less afraid of falling then of prolonging this torment. "Then . . . you accepted Papa's offer?"

"No . . . I could not."

Rhiannon sat very still, as if one false move could send her plummeting off into space. "Why?"

"Because he offered me the wrong daughter, Rhiannon."

She'd not dared to move. Now she dared not speak, either. Had she misunderstood? If only God would restore her sight, if just for a moment, long enough for her to see his face and judge for herself if she'd heard him right.

"Rhiannon . . . you did hear what I said? I am making a botch of this, I know. Mayhap I'd best say it straight out. I want to marry you."

Her heart was pounding so loudly that she was sure he could hear. At the touch of his fingers on her cheek, her pulse jumped. "Why?" she whispered. "Why me and not Eleri?"

"That is what your father asked, too. I could tell you that it's because Eleri is not yet sixteen and I'm thirty-one and I want to marry a wife, not raise one. Or I could tell you that whilst I am very fond of Eleri, my feelings for you run much deeper. And it would all be true, Rhiannon. But what matters more than any of that is the way I felt when Rhodri offered me Eleri. There was no need to choose. I just knew. You were the one I wanted."

He'd taken her hand as he spoke, and now he pressed a kiss into her palm. "Do you need time to think about it, Rhiannon? I realize this took you as much by surprise as it did me, but—"

"No . . . I do not need time. My answer is yes. I would be honoured to be your wife."

Even then it did not seem real to her, though, not until he tilted her face up and kissed her gently, first on her cheek and then on her mouth.

RHIANNON awoke the next morning with an irrational fear that she might have dreamed it all. "Eleri? Olwen?" Getting no response, she slid out of bed. But for the first time in years, she'd forgotten to lay out her clothes for the next day. Retrieving her chemise, she pulled it over her head and moved to their washing laver, shivering as she splashed cold water onto her face. She'd begun to brush her hair by the time Eleri returned.

"I fetched you some buttermilk, Rhiannon. I'm putting it on the table, in the right corner."

"Thank you. Eleri . . . did anything out of the ordinary happen yesterday?"

"Nothing that comes to mind. It was a day like any other, as far as I recall. One of the goats strayed off, Selwyn's tooth was hurting him, Ranulf asked you to marry him, and we had that wretched salted herring again for dinner." Turning, she saw that Rhiannon had sat down abruptly on the edge of the bed. "You are not going to tell me, girl, that you forgot!"

"Of course not!" Rhiannon bit her lip. "I was just so afraid," she confessed, "that it had all been a dream."

When Eleri sat down on the bed, too, Rhiannon gave her a quick hug. Eleri knew that Ranulf had chosen Rhiannon over her, for in his exhilaration, Rhodri had not thought to keep that to himself. She'd seemed genuinely joyful about the marriage, but Rhiannon could not bear for her sister's pride to have gotten even the slightest scratch, and she needed to be sure that no shadows lurked in the corners of Eleri's certainty. "Eleri . . . are you truly content with this?"

"'Content'? That is such a tame, bland word to describe what I'm feeling! Unless . . . you did not really think I would ever have married Ranulf, do you? By Corpus, you did!" She sounded suddenly and highly indignant. "How could you have believed that of me, Rhiannon? I would never have betrayed you like that, never!"

"You . . . you knew?"

"That you were utterly daft about the man? Of course I did!" Eleri snatched up a pillow and smacked her sister with it. "That is for being such a prideful fool and this is for not confiding in me!" Another whack with the pillow. "Not that I needed to hear you admit it, for you melted every time you said his name. Of course I knew! Did you forget which of us is the blind one?" she needled, and Rhiannon grabbed for the pillow. They engaged briefly in a tug-of-war, but then Eleri let go unexpectedly and Rhiannon went over backwards onto the floor rushes. Eleri tried to catch her, only to lose her own balance and go tumbling off the bed, too.

It had been a long while since they'd had a pillow fight, and sprawled now in the floor rushes, her mouth full of feathers. Rhiannon remembered why she'd given it up. "I'm too old for this sort of tomfoolery," she complained good-naturedly. "I landed right on my tailbone, you brat! And where are all these feathers coming from?"

"Usually from ducks," Eleri drawled, getting up on her knees to retrieve the torn pillow and loosing another flurry of escaping feathers. Rhiannon inhaled a few, sputtered, and then began to laugh. So did Eleri, and they clung together, laughing until their cheeks were streaked with tears and the air was so feather-filled that it seemed to be snowing and Enid was standing in the doorway, gazing down at them in consternation.

"What in Heaven's Name is going on here? Look at you, rolling about on the floor like a couple of puppies and . . . and the room is full of feathers!"

"I guess the duck died," Eleri quipped, and that nonsensical answer set the sisters off again, while Enid looked on in disapproving bafflement. Rhiannon was still giggling when Eleri called out cheerfully, "Come on in, Ranulf. You're missing all the fun!"

Rhiannon didn't really believe Ranulf was in the doorway; that was the sort of prank Eleri loved to pull. But then Enid gave a dismayed cry. "Ranulf, do not look! It is not fitting that you should see Rhiannon in her chemise!"

"Why ever not?" Eleri held out her hand so her stepmother could help her up. "Once they're wed, he'll see her in her skin, will he not?" She managed to get Enid out by the simple expedient of refusing to let go of the older woman's arm. By then Rhiannon had been able to scramble to her feet and was brushing ineffectually at the feathers clinging to her chemise. It was not until she heard Ranulf say her name that she was sure he was still in the room.

Rhiannon was slightly embarrassed; Ranulf was the last person she'd have wanted to catch her playing the fool. But she had a far more pressing concern than her dignity, and the only way she knew to dispel it was to confront it head on. "Good morrow," she said, although she thought such formality sounded silly, coming from a woman with feathers in her hair. "There is something I must ask you, Ranulf. Now that it is the morning after, have you had any second thoughts?"

It was an awkward question for Ranulf, and one that showed him just how well she knew him, for upon awakening that morning, his first thought had indeed been, What have I done? It was not so much that he regretted his marriage proposal as that in the cold light of day, he fully comprehended the magnitude of what he'd be undertaking. His earlier joke about an upended hourglass no longer seemed funny, for that was exactly what he'd done—turned his life upside down. Marriage was one of God's Sacraments, a lifelong commitment, and marriage to Rhiannon would have its own unique pitfalls. Because her vulnerability was so much greater, so much greater, too, would be his sense of obligation to her. She deserved all that he had to give. But what if it was not enough? He still felt that what he'd done was right, but it could not have hurt if he'd taken a little more time to think it through. If God let him reach his biblical three score years and ten, would he still be jumping off cliffs without ever looking to see where he'd land?

His hesitation stirred up Rhiannon's anxiety into outright alarm. "You must tell me if it is so," she entreated. "If you have misgivings, better that we talk about them now . . . ere it is too late."

"No, it is nothing like that, lass." Stepping toward her, he reached for her hand. "I am not sure how best to explain this. Until I walked through that door and saw you thrashing about in the floor rushes, I admit I was feeling some unease, fear that I would let you down or cause you hurt. I was thinking of our marriage in sobering terms—responsibility and commitment and duty. What I should have remembered, though, is that I am still getting to know you . . . and you are constantly surprising me."

Rhiannon tilted her head, listening as much to his intonation as to his words. He did not sound as if he were weighed down with regrets, but mayhap she was hearing only what she wanted to hear. "I am not following you."

"There seem to be so many Rhiannons. First there was the nurse, striving to save my life. Then my cousin, who soon became my companion and confidante. Even my confessor," he said, and for a moment, they both remembered that summer afternoon by the rushing waters of Rhaeadr Ewynnol. "But now . . . well, now I am seeing you in an altogether different light."

He could not help smiling then, for he saw she still did not understand. But she did not realize how she looked—barefoot in her chemise, russet hair in beguiling dishevelment down her back, wispy white feathers kissing her cheek, her throat, the curve of her bosom. Half waif, he thought, and half wanton, a woman to cleave unto, as Scriptures said.

"What I mean," he said, "is that I am of a sudden seeing you as a bedmate, Rhiannon."

He could see a blush tinting the whiteness of her throat and cheeks, but there was nothing shy in the smile she gave him. "Well, then," she said happily, "we'd best be married as soon as possible."

THEY were, much to Enid's chagrin. She argued in vain that such a hasty wedding would be sure to give rise to scandal, but her protests fell upon deaf ears. Rhodri did not believe that anyone could think ill of his Rhiannon. Eleri took the opposite tack, pointing out with cynical but accurate insight that the marriage was bound to cause gossip in any event. And Rhiannon and Ranulf cared only about getting married before the start of Lent, when marriages were prohibited. They settled upon Shrove Tuesday, beating the Lenten deadline by one day, placating the indignant Enid by agreeing to have a lavish celebration after Easter, then upsetting her anew by not bothering to post the banns.

They were wed in a simple ceremony at Llanrhychwyn, a small stone chapel in the hills above Trefriw. It was nothing like the great cathedrals where Ranulf had witnessed the weddings of his Norman-French kin, but it was newly whitewashed with lime, aglow with candles, fragrant with scented floor rushes, and in the secluded stillness, they could hear the rustling of yew trees in the wind, the clarion cry of a soaring hawk, even the distant howling of a Welsh wolf.

Afterward, they had a quiet wedding dinner back at Rhodri's manor, attended only by the members of his household, a meal of roast goose and baked trout and mead and harp music. Instead of the usual raucous bedding-down revelries, Rhiannon's sister and stepmother then accompanied her up to the wedding chamber, where they made her ready for Ranulf, while he enjoyed a final flagon with the man who was now both his uncle and father-in-law.

As a king's son, Ranulf had witnessed more than his share of weddings, and he knew from experience how bawdy and boisterous the bedding-down revelries could get, the humor both explicit and uninhibited, a carnal and often crude celebration of life and lust and the anticipated pleasures of the marriage bed. But Ranulf felt sure that their bedding-down revelries would have been dreadfully different. They would have been subdued and decorous and seemly enough to have satisfied the most pious of priests, for the wedding guests would not have known how to deal with a blind bride. They'd have been painfully polite, offering Rhiannon their pity instead of their lewd mockery, and Ranulf was very glad she'd been spared that. She already knew full well that others viewed her as an oddity. Tonight he hoped to show her that she was a desirable woman to the only man who mattered, the one she'd married.

That proved to be very easy to do, for once they were lying together in their marriage bed, she soon discovered incontrovertible proof of his passion, and he discovered in his turn that her other senses were functioning perfectly. She was eager to touch what she could not see, eager to please him, and afterward, he felt confident that her deflowering had been as satisfying for her as it had been for him. "I did not hurt you too much, did I?" he asked drowsily, surprised to realize how much that mattered to him.

She shook her head, tickling his chest with a long strand of her hair, and then trailing it still lower, across his belly. "Ranulf . . . do we have to wait till morning ere we can do it again?"

"Shameless wanton," he murmured, and there was such tenderness in his voice that she found herself blinking back tears.

"Ranulf . . . I want you to know that I understand divided loyalties. You chose me and Wales, but that does not mean you repudiated your past life. England will always exert a powerful pull upon you, and whenever you feel the need, you must follow it. You may return to England as often as you wish and I'll not object . . . just as long as you keep coming back."

"I do have other loyalties," he admitted. "But from now on, my first loyalty will be to you. That I promise you, Rhiannon."

She wondered if that was an oblique reference to the woman he'd loved so deeply and disastrously. But she dared not ask, dared not summon up Annora's restless spirit to haunt their marriage bed. Instead, she settled back in his arms, shifting so she could hear his heart beating against her cheek until she fell asleep.

46

ROUEN, NORMANDY

August 1151

MAUDE could have lodged in Rouen's great castle, as Geoffrey did whenever he was in the city. Or she could have moved into the royal residence adjacent to the priory of Notre-Dame-du-Pré. Instead she chose to live among the monks, dwelling in the guest quarters of the priory, an austere and surprisingly stark milieu for a woman who'd once reigned over an imperial court.

ON the first Sunday in August, Ranulf and his niece the Countess of Chester arrived at the priory. They were both a long way from home, but they were bringing Maude wounding news, not the sort of grief to be delivered in a letter.

Maud had gone to the church, ostensibly to light a candle and offer up prayers, actually to give her aunt the only solace she could—some private time to grieve. Blinking in the glare of shimmering white sunlight, Maud paused in the doorway, waiting for Minna to catch up with her; the German widow was showing her age, moving stiffly and slowly even on warm summer afternoons.

Out in the garth, Ranulf was carrying on an animated conversation with a new arrival. The man was a stranger to Maud, and yet there was something vaguely familiar about him, enough to kindle her curiosity. He looked to be in his early twenties, with very vivid coloring—curly copper-gold hair, fair ruddy skin dusted with freckles, silver-grey eyes. Like Ranulf, he was a little above average height, but he seemed taller, for he was powerfully built, with a deep chest and broad shoulders that she was eyeing appreciatively when Minna's startled "Mein Gott!" echoed behind her. "It is Lord Harry!"

"Harry?" Maud was astonished. "My cousin Harry?" Not having

seen Henry on either of his last two trips to England, her memories were of a precocious ten-year-old. But what surprised her more than his maturity was how unlike his parents he was. He might have been a foundling, she marveled, so little did he resemble her aunt or Geoffrey. He did have Geoffrey's coloring, but the freckles were all his own, and so was the brawn. He had none of his father's flash, none of his mother's aloof elegance. And when she went to greet him, she discovered that his personality was—like his appearance—very much his own, too.

For Maude's son, he showed a remarkable indifference to protocol and ceremony, and his humor held none of Geoffrey's darker undertones. He charmed Maud at once, for he was playful and irreverent and quite sure of himself. The rapport was mutual, like recognizing like, and with a fine feel for teamwork, they soon pounced on Ranulf, for his impulsive and hasty and unforeseen marriage was too tempting a target to resist.

"And so there I was," Henry grumbled, "haunting all the ports in Normandy, waiting for reliable Uncle Ranulf to arrive as he'd promised. I spent so much time hanging around Barfleur that two of the fishing boats offered to take me on as a crew member. And just where was Ranulf whilst I was turning down a chance to catch cod? Off in the Welsh wilderness, taking advantage of a trusting damsel in distress."

"One who was unable to see what she was getting," Maud chimed in. "Although I know many wives who would count that as a blessing!"

Minna went hot with embarrassment. That Ranulf should have chosen a handicapped wife was a mystery she could not begin to fathom; the only thing more incomprehensible to her was that others would joke about it. She frowned at Henry and Maud, baffled and indignant that they could salt Ranulf's wounds like this.

"There is a lot to be said for having a blind wife," Ranulf protested. "She is sure to overlook my flaws, is she not? Nor will she care when I get grey and wrinkled. But even if she had keener sight than an eagle, Rhiannon would still turn a blind eye to my failings. I only hope you can find a wife as merciful, Harry, for from what I've heard, you'll need all the forgiveness you can get!"

"Jesú, it is worse than we feared, Maud." Henry was grinning. "Damn me if else, but the man has gone and fallen in love with his own wife!"

That got a laugh from all but the thoroughly mystified Minna. Ranulf had the last word, though. "Keep it up," he warned, "and I'll name the pair of you as godparents, which would necessitate a long and arduous winter journey into Wales for the christening."

Maud was slow on the uptake for once, and yielded with a feigned gasp of horror. Henry was quicker. "Are we talking about a theoretical child," he queried, "one likely to come in God's own time? Or a flesh-and-blood babe, with a definite due date?"

"November," Ranulf said nonchalantly, and then gave himself away with a radiant smile. "Rhiannon is vowing to deliver on my birthday and—"

At that point, he found himself fending off his niece, who was scolding him for not telling her while smearing his face with haphazard kisses. Henry offered his congratulations, too, plus a tongue-in-cheek suggestion that the baby be named after him. Ranulf agreed gravely that he would, provided it was a girl, and Minna gave up any pretense of understanding male humor. "Why are you here, Lord Harry?" she asked, as soon as she could get a word in. "We thought you and Lord Geoffrey were guarding the border against the French."

"We have a truce in effect, for the French king has taken to his sickbed. What of you, Ranulf? What brought you and Cousin Maud to Rouen?"

"Bad news, I fear. A friend of your mother's has died."

"It has been a sad season for Mama," Henry said regretfully. "In April, Adeliza died at a nunnery in Flanders; I suppose you heard? What of this latest death? Is it anyone I know?"

"Yes, it is. The lord of Wallingford Castle, Brien Fitz Count."

Henry was quiet for a moment, thinking of his Christmas reunion with his mother at Wallingford. "She took shelter with Brien," he said, "after her escape from Oxford. He was a man worth mourning."

Brien's shadow seemed to follow them back across the garth to Maude's chambers. At sight of her son, Maude's face lit up. Henry could not remember ever having seen his mother cry, but he noticed now that her eyes were suspiciously red-rimmed, the lids swollen and tender. "I know about Brien Fitz Count's death. I am sorry, Mama. He was a good friend to us, a good man."

Maude swallowed. "Yes," she said softly, "he was."

"It does not seem fair. Uncle Robert and Brien sacrificed so much for us. Of all men, they ought to have lived to see us triumph."

Maude nodded somberly. Although she was gazing into his face, Henry had the odd feeling that she was not really seeing him. "The greatest regrets," she said, "are always for what might have been."

ALTHOUGH the French king had grudgingly recognized Geoffrey as Duke of Normandy, relations between the two men had always been strained, and deteriorated rapidly when they clashed over the fate of Giraud Berlai. Berlai was the seneschal of Poitou, a man who stood high in the French king's favor. But if he was a loyal vassal to Louis, to Geoffrey he was merely a rebel, one of the ringleaders of an abortive rising of Angevin barons. Geoffrey had quelled the rebellion without difficulty, but Berlai had retreated to his castle at Montreuil-Bellay and begun to harass the countryside. After he'd harried monks from St Aubin's, Geoffrey lost all patience and vowed to bring the man down, no matter how long it took. When he lay siege to Montreuil, Berlai was defiant, contemptuously confident that the castle could withstand any assault. He'd underestimated Geoffrey's resolve, though. The siege had lasted three full years, but the fortress was now in ruins and Berlai in an Angers prison.

The French king was enraged by Geoffrey's harsh treatment of his vassal, and dismayed by Geoffrey's unforeseen decision to turn Normandy over to Henry. It was in France's interests to make sure that Normandy and England were not united again, and Louis was not willing, therefore, to see Normandy ruled by a man with such a strong claim to the English crown. He'd refused to recognize Henry's title, revitalized his alliance with Stephen, and invited Eustace to join his campaign.

The past year had been one of sporadic and inconclusive warfare. Henry had been besieging a rebellious lord at Torigny when he'd learned that the French king and Eustace were advancing upon Arques. He swiftly gathered a mixed force of Normans, Angevins, and Bretons and confronted the French. But Louis chose to withdraw and battle was averted. Geoffrey then seized a castle at La Nue belonging to Louis's brother, and the French retaliated by burning the town of Séez. There were a few months of relative peace after that, but then, in midsummer, the French began massing troops along the River Seine between Meulan and Mantes, and Geoffrey and Henry hastened to protect their borders from this new threat.

War seemed to be inevitable—until the French king was stricken with a fever, necessitating his return to Paris. It was possible that he would now heed the advice of France's premier churchman, the venerable Abbot Bernard of Clairvaux, who'd long been urging peace. But it was just as likely that he'd resume hostilities once he recovered. Henry and Geoffrey could only wait and see.

HENRY dominated the conversation at supper that night, thanking his mother for her continuing efforts to make the French king see reason, giving Ranulf and Maud an insider's account of the political and military maneuvering that had occupied so much of his time this past year, telling them of the skirmishes and raids and Geoffrey's prolonged siege of Montreuil-Bellay.

"Berlai bragged that the castle could never be taken, with a keep high enough to scrape the sky and double walls, encircled by a deep, natural chasm called the 'Judas Valley.' It kept my father from getting close enough to use his siege engines. So do you know what he did? He moved the yearly fair from Saumur to Montreuil, and paid the fairgoers to assist his soldiers in filling up the ditch!"

Henry laughed and pushed his chair back. Ranulf glanced toward Maude, for it could not be easy for her to hear Henry speak so glowingly of Geoffrey. But she showed no overt displeasure; he supposed she'd had to accept it, that her son and his father would always be close. He'd noticed, though, that she no longer spoke of Geoffrey with such searing bitterness. Mayhap what he'd heard was true, that they'd finally made their peace. A pity they could not have done so twenty years ago. Why was it, he wondered, that whatever came to his sister, always came too late?

"Was that how Geoffrey took the castle?"

Henry shook his head. "No, Cousin Maud. Even though his mangonels were then able to do considerable damage, Berlai still held out. Whenever breaches were made in the walls, they repaired the damage with oaken beams, and Berlai boasted from the battlements that he'd never surrender. But he'd reckoned without Vegetius, a Roman sage who'd written a classic treatise on siege warfare. Papa got an idea from his writings, and he filled an iron vessel with Greek fire, then used a mangonel to hurl it at the castle walls. It ignited on impact and the wooden beams caught fire. Greek fire is very hard to put out and they could not keep the flames from spreading."

"Greek fire," Ranulf echoed thoughtfully. "Crusaders brought back tales from the Holy Land of Greek fire. But I'd not heard of it's being used in the West ere this."

"Papa was the first," Henry said proudly. "When his father went off to wed the Queen of Jerusalem, he learned the ingredients and shared the secret in a letter to Papa. I'm not sure what he mixed—naphtha and lime and tar and sulphur—but whatever, it worked. In no time at all, Berlai and his men came—as Papa put it—slithering out like snakes!"

"Is it true that the French king got Abbot Bernard to excommunicate Geoffrey for refusing to set Berlai free?"

Henry looked over at his uncle and nodded. "It seems the Church has a third category of sin; in addition to mortal and venal, there is also political." His mouth quirked at the corners, in just the suggestion of a smile. "Fortunately," he said, "Papa appears to be bearing up rather well."

"I expect he would," Maude said dryly, for the counts of Anjou had always taken excommunication in stride; one of Geoffrey's more infamous forebears had sinned on such a grand scale that he'd made no less than three pilgrimages of atonement to the Holy Land. "How long do you think this truce will last, Henry?"

As always, he smiled at her use of "Henry." She'd made a good-faith attempt to switch over to "Harry" in order to please him, but she was so obviously uncomfortable with the informality that he'd soon taken pity and urged her to revert back to his given name. Now she alone called him Henry and she'd come to relish the exclusivity of it. He was still as restless as he'd been as a boy, never able to sit still for long, and he'd begun pacing as he considered her question. She felt a great surge of pride as she watched him, and an empty, hurtful ache, a bittersweet regret that this son she so loved could not have been Brien's.

"It is hard to say, Mama. It all depends upon who has the French king's ear. If it is Abbot Bernard and the Bishop of Lisieux, they may well persuade him to talk peace. If he is fool enough to keep listening to Eustace, we'll all be the losers for it."

Ranulf was intrigued by his nephew's candor, for it was his experience that young men invariably proclaimed their eagerness to go to war, and with many, that eagerness was even genuine. But Harry had an uncommonly pragmatic view of warfare for one in only his nineteenth year; he'd proved himself willing to do what must be done to win, but it was clear he took no pleasure in it. To test his theory, Ranulf said, "So you hope your differences with Louis can be settled by negotiation?"

"Of course. I'd choose bargaining over bleeding any day, as would all men of sense. So it goes without saying, then, that Eustace is lusting after a bloodletting. The more I learn about this rival of mine, Uncle Ranulf, the more I realize that Eustace is the most convincing argument possible against hereditary kingship."

Ranulf and Maud laughed, but Henry's mother did not, for that sounded like blasphemy to her, even in jest. "How could anyone argue against hereditary kingship?" she protested, and Henry grinned.

"I can assure you, Mama, that I'd be the last one to make such an argument," he said and was leaning over to give her a hug when one of Maude's servants entered with an urgent message. Once such a message would have been for Maude; now it was for Henry, for "the lord duke."

"It is from Papa," Henry said, gazing down at the familiar seal. Moving toward the nearest lamp, he read rapidly. "That contest over the French king's ear? Well, it seems that Eustace lost. Louis has agreed to enter into negotiations and Papa wants me to return straightaway, for we are expected in Paris in a week's time."

"Thank Heaven," Maude said fervently. "Now we can concentrate upon the real enemy—Stephen and his wretched son."

"Easy, Mama," Henry cautioned. "We've not made peace yet. These talks might well come to naught. But we have nothing to lose and possibly much to gain. So . . . it looks like I'm off to Paris." He glanced at the letter again and then over at Ranulf. "At the very least," he laughed, "I'll finally get to meet Eleanor of Aquitaine!"

THEY had just passed the abbey of Saint-Denis, so Henry knew Paris was only seven miles away, and he spurred his stallion to catch up with Geoffrey. "Tell me," he said, "about the French king. What sort of man is he?"

"One of meagre importance if not for a hungry sow." Seeing his son's bafflement, Geoffrey grinned. "You never heard that story, then? Louis was the second son, pledged to the Church. But when he was ten, he was snatched from the cloisters and thrust back into the world, courtesy of that aforesaid pig. It was foraging for food along the River Seine just as Louis's elder brother, Philippe, happened to ride by. When the sow spooked his horse, Philippe was thrown and killed. So little Louis was suddenly the heir apparent, and it is a great pity, for he would have made a far better monk than he has a king."

"Tell me more, Papa," Henry urged. "What are his virtues and his vices?"

"His greatest vice is that he has none." Geoffrey laughed at his own joke, and then gave his son a serious answer. "He is very devout, has good manners and a good heart. Nor does he lack for courage. But he is cursed with the worst sort of stubbornness, the stiff-necked, inflexible obstinacy of the weak. And because he is so troubled by self-doubts, he tends to be too easily influenced—invariably by the wrong people. He is melancholy by nature and suffers periodic pangs of guilt over his disastrous attack upon Vitry—that the town where more than a thousand villagers took refuge in the church and died when it caught fire. And he is burdened with a paralyzing sense of sin, a truly pitiful affliction for a man wed to one of the most desirable women in Christendom!"

"He shuns her bed?" Henry was incredulous. "Jesú, the man must be mad!"

"You'll get no argument from me, Harry. But monks are not supposed to indulge in carnal lust, and Louis remains a monk at heart, a monk married to Eve. They sound even more mismatched, by Corpus, than your mother and me!"

"They do, indeed," Henry agreed cheerfully; he had no illusions whatsoever about his parents' marriage. "Tell me more about Eve. Is she that, in truth?"

"Well . . . she is indeed willful, much more than any woman has a right to be. She is worldly for certes and high spirited and too clever by half. Is she a wanton, too? Mayhap yes, mayhap no. I never had the opportunity to find out for myself. But then, I never thought wantonness to be a female character flaw, at least not in another man's wife!"

Off to their right, a village came into view, which Geoffrey identified as Clignancourt. In the distance the wooded hill of Montmartre rose up against the hazy August sky. Geoffrey said there were the ruins of an ancient Roman temple on the summit, which offered an impressive view of Paris. Henry was sorry they did not have time to stop and see. He'd never paid much mind to gossip himself, but his father was a reliable source for humor and scandal. "I've heard such unlikely tales about their crusade, Papa. Just what did happen in Antioch?"

"Louis made an ass of himself, refused to go to the rescue of Edessa, and doomed the crusade, the Prince of Antioch, and his marriage—all in one fell swoop."

That made no sense to Henry. "I thought it was the fall of Edessa that stirred men to take the cross. So why did Louis balk?"

"That is what Prince Raymond wanted to know, too. Ever since Edessa's capture by the Turks, he'd feared that Antioch would be next, and he was relying upon the French king's crusaders to stave off disaster. When Louis insisted that he could do nothing until he'd fulfilled his vow to reach Jerusalem, Raymond took it badly. Eleanor agreed with Raymond, but she had no luck in changing Louis's mind, and by all accounts, the quarreling got very hot, indeed."

"Raymond was her kinsman, was he not?"

"Her uncle. Like many a younger son, he'd gone off to seek his fortune in the Holy Land, and by luck and guile and a fair measure of charm, he'd won himself a great heiress and the principality of Antioch. But when Eleanor sided openly with Raymond, Louis's advisors claimed that proved she was not to be trusted."

"I'd say it proved she had more common sense than Louis. If Antioch fell, Jerusalem's fall would be a foregone conclusion. Was this when Eleanor declared her intent to end the marriage?"

Geoffrey nodded. "And she was shrewd enough to pick the one argument likely to shake Louis to the depths of his pious soul—that their marriage was a sin. Raymond had revealed to her, she contended, that she and Louis were fourth cousins and thus forbidden to wed without a papal dispensation. She then reminded Louis that after eleven years of this 'sinful' marriage, he still lacked a male heir. What greater proof could there be of God's displeasure? Louis was distraught, for in his innocent, odd way, he truly loved his wife. He could not bear to lose her—and Aquitaine—but neither could he abide the fear that he'd offended the Almighty. As I said, Eleanor knew her man; her thrust had gone right to the heart."

"What provoked him then, into dragging her away from Antioch by force?"

"He sought counsel and comfort from his chaplain and a Templar named Thierry Galeran, a eunuch who'd long chafed under Eleanor's barbs. He seized his chance to repay her in kind, and he and Odo, the chaplain, convinced Louis that Eleanor's real reason for seeking a divorce was arrantly sinful—because she'd taken Raymond as her lover."

Henry was not easily startled, but now he almost dropped the reins, so hastily did he swing around in the saddle to stare at his father. "They accused her of bedding her own uncle? Jesus wept! Was it true?"

"I seriously doubt it," Geoffrey conceded, with a trace of regret. "Sins are no more equal than men, and incest is a grievous transgression, indeed, far more damning than mere adultery. It is clear from his subsequent conduct that Louis did not really believe it, either, else he'd never have been able to reconcile with her and share her bed again. Be that as it may, he was hurt and jealous and angry, and he heeded his counselors, compelled Eleanor to accompany him to Jerusalem.

"What happened after that, lad, you doubtless know. Louis made a halfhearted assault upon Damascus, retreated after four days, and the glorious Second Crusade was over."

"I'd say your decision not to take the cross was a wise one, Papa. And their troubles did not end in the Holy Land, did they? I heard they had a harrowing journey home."

"That they did. Eleanor's ship was captured by the Greeks, rescued in the nick of time by the King of Sicily's fleet, then blown far off course toward the Barbary Coast, finally coming ashore at Palermo, where Eleanor was gravely ill for weeks, and where she got word of her uncle Raymond's death, slain in a courageous, foolhardy clash with the Turks, his head cut off and sent as a gift to the Caliph of Baghdad."

"And she blamed Louis for that, I daresay?"

"Wouldn't you? But by then they'd reached Tusculum, where the Pope did his best to mend the rifts in their marriage, assuring them they had God's Blessing upon their union and tucking them into bed together to make sure poor dim Louis got the point! When she became pregnant, Louis could not contain his joy, never doubting that the Almighty would at last reward him with a son."

"It must have been a nasty shock when Eleanor gave birth to a second daughter. But I'd wager," Henry added wryly, "that Louis blamed Eleanor and not God."

"His counselors did, for certes. The talk in Paris is that a divorce is inevitable. Louis is still resisting—so far. But the marriage is being crushed under a double burden: his conscience and his need for a son. I'd not offer odds on its survival."

Ahead lay the wooden stockade that protected the right bank of the River Seine. To Henry's right, he could see a small chapel, surrounded by weathered tombstones; this open, marshy field was the Cemetery of the

Holy Innocents, burial ground for Paris. He instinctively made the sign of the cross, but his thoughts were still focused upon the hapless French king and his beautiful, wayward queen.

"So Louis is well meaning and out of his depth—shades of Stephen—whilst Eleanor is willful and mayhap wanton. What else need I know?"

"That she is dangerous," Geoffrey said and laughed. "Consider yourself warned, lad!"

Henry laughed, too. "You need not worry. I plan to be on my best behavior in Paris. I shall have to be, since you're intent upon stirring up trouble enough for the both of us!"

THE heart of Paris was a walled island in the middle of the River Seine, the Île de la Cité. Its eastern half was given over to God, to the archbishop's church and lodgings. The western half held the royal palace. In between lay a maze of narrow, crooked streets, by turns mud-clogged or dust-choked, for the ancient Roman paving stones had survived only in patches. These streets were deep in shadow even at midday, for the houses had overhanging upper stories that effectively blotted out the sun, and they were noisy from dawn till dusk, echoing with the strident cries of peddlers, the pleas of beggars, the boisterous tomfoolery of students, the arguments of tradesmen, the barking of dogs, and always, always the chiming of church bells, pealing out over the city in deafening waves of shimmering sound.

This was Henry's first glimpse of Paris, and it would be a memory that time would not fade. For the rest of his life, he was to remember the August heat and the clamor and the foul smell of the river, the clouds of white doves circling above the steep tiled roofs as he and his father rode across the bridge known as the Grand Pont, toward the palace where the French king and his queen awaited them.

The Grand Pont was the finest stone bridge Henry had ever seen, almost twenty feet wide, lined on each side with cramped wooden stalls and booths, most occupied by money changers and goldsmiths. It was crowded with pilgrims and merchants and students, exchanging their coins for the French silver deniers. They moved aside for the Angevins and their entourage, and Henry heard his name and Geoffrey's bandied behind them. It seemed all of Paris knew they were meeting with Louis. He just hoped that some good would come of it.

They were on the island now, passing through the gateway into the Cité Palace. A flight of broad stone stairs led up to the great hall. As they reined in, Geoffrey said that he'd heard of knights riding their horses up the steps and into the hall, and for a moment, their eyes met in a glance of mutual mischief. But the temptation was fleeting. Dismounting, they made a decorous entrance into the hall, not without a shared twinge of regret.

Once stilted greetings had been offered and introductions made on Henry's behalf, he stepped aside, deferring to his father, for this was Geoffrey's moment, and he was content to have it so. He welcomed this opportunity to study their adversaries, most of whom he was meeting for the first time.

Louis Capet, the Most Christian King of France, was in his thirty-first year, but he looked younger, tall and slender, with mild blue eyes and bright blond hair. Henry had heard he often wore a hair shirt, and he could not help speculating whether Louis was wearing one now, under his royal robes. He could think of far better uses for the flesh than mortifying it.

Louis's disgruntled brother Robert, Count of Dreux, stood close at hand, glowering at Geoffrey. Rumor had it that he'd returned from the crusade so disgusted with his elder brother's military leadership that he'd had it in mind to relieve Louis of the burden of kingship. But even if the rumors were true, nothing had come of his seditious ambitions. Mayhap incompetence was in their blood, Henry thought uncharitably, and turned his attention to a more interesting member of the royal family, Raoul de Péronne, Count of Vermandois, seneschal of France, Louis's cousin and brother-in-law, for the Church had finally agreed to recognize his adulterous marriage to Eleanor's sister.

Raoul was much older than Henry had expected, well past fifty. His silvered hair was still abundant, he covered the loss of an eye with a jaunty leather patch, and he had an easy self-confidence that many a younger man might have envied. But Henry could not get past the fact that Raoul must be nigh on thirty years older than Petronilla. He'd long thought their reckless affair was foolhardy. Now that he'd met Raoul, it seemed even more incomprehensible to him. A young heiress with a sister on the French throne, rich lands in Burgundy, and her own considerable charms did not need to settle for scandal and a married, aging lover—and yet she had.

Geoffrey liked to say that if marrying for lust was foolish, marrying for love was madness. For his age, Henry had a fair amount of experience with lust, none yet with love, but he saw no reason to doubt his father's jaded assessment of matrimony. He wondered if the impetuous, passionate Petronilla was in the hall, for he was looking forward to meeting her. And he wondered, too, if she and Raoul still thought it had all been worth it.

Standing at the rear of the dais, trying to be as inconspicuous as possible, was a man Henry had met at his father's court, the Count of Meulan,

Waleran Beaumont. Waleran's luck had yet to change for the better. After being forced to choose between Stephen and Maude, he was now caught again between two feuding overlords, Geoffrey and Louis. His presence here at Paris showed that he'd cast his lot—however reluctantly—with the French king. He'd come to regret it, though. Henry meant to see to that.

The stocky, balding man in the white surcoat and blood-red cross of the Knights Templars must be Thierry Galeran, the embittered eunuch whose enmity had done Eleanor such damage. Henry felt an involuntary flicker of pity, for his youthful imaginings could envision no greater loss than the one the Templar had suffered. Thierry Galeran was flanked by the Bishop of Lisieux and Odo de Deuil, formerly Louis's chaplain, now the new abbot of Saint-Denis. But all of the men upon the dais, even the king, were overshadowed by an aged, gaunt figure clad in the unbleached white habit of the Cistercians, the most celebrated monk of their age, Bernard of Clairvaux.

Bernard was sixty-one, but if Henry had not known that, he'd have added another decade to his age. His hair was snow-white, although his beard still held glints of auburn. Tall and stoop-shouldered, he was so thin that he seemed skeletal, for he'd ruined his health with the harsh privations he'd imposed upon himself in his continuing struggle to humble the body and elevate the soul. But illness had not weakened his intellect or diminished the power of his personality. His smoldering, deep-set eyes burned with combative zeal, with the mesmerizing force of one who knew with absolute certainty that he did God's Work.

It was Bernard and not Louis who seized the initiative, demanding to know if Geoffrey had brought Giraud Berlai to Paris, as agreed upon. Henry thought it ironic that the saintly abbot would be so concerned over the fate of a lawless baron like Berlai, for the man was no better than a brigand. He understood why, of course. It was all about power. Even princes of the Church were protective of their prerogatives. Especially princes of the Church, he amended, and then braced himself for what was to come.

"Indeed, I did," Geoffrey said blandly, with a smile that should have warned them, but didn't. Turning, he ordered one of his men to fetch Giraud Berlai into the hall, and then he winked at Henry, who camouflaged a smile. He did not fully understand why his father took such pleasure in baiting his enemies; he preferred a straight-as-an-arrow path to the target himself and thought feuding was a waste of time. But he tended to be tolerant of other men's amusements and he made ready to watch Geoffrey's sport.

A collective gasp swept the chamber at sight of Berlai, for the man was weighed down with heavy shackles, filthy, and obviously frightened. He had been gagged, and when he was thrust to his knees before the dais, his eyes pleaded mutely for mercy. Berlai's bravado was utterly gone, stripped away like his fine clothes, for it had taken only a few months in one of Geoffrey's dungeons to break his spirit.

Henry could see from the shocked faces that they'd not expected this, and yet they should have. His father made an unforgiving enemy, as his uncle Hélie had learned. Five years in a Tours prison, his health so impaired by the captivity that he'd died soon after his release. Henry felt scant sympathy for Hélie, though; he'd asked for what he'd gotten. He had even less pity for Berlai, who'd terrorized the Angevin borderlands with impunity, sure that the French king's favor and his own formidable stronghold would keep him safe from retribution.

As a provocation, Geoffrey's action could hardly have been improved upon. Louis was infuriated to see his seneschal treated like a common felon, a man of low birth. Bernard was even more outraged, for he'd excommunicated Geoffrey for holding Berlai prisoner, and he saw Geoffrey's deliberate defiance as an affront to the Almighty. There was a moment of utter silence, and then pandemonium. Voices rose furiously, accusing, threatening, demanding. And in the midst of the maelstrom, being indignantly assailed from all sides, Geoffrey glanced over at his son and grinned.

Henry felt more like a witness than a participant, watching the turmoil with benign detachment, for this was his father's hunt. Louis had begun to shout, his fair skin blotching with hot color. The white-maned Bernard was stabbing the air with a gnarled forefinger, looking for all the world like one of the Old Testament prophets, poised to hurl celestial thunderbolts. But if Geoffrey was impressed, he gave no indication of it. Henry took a step toward the dais, and it was then that he saw her.

She'd come in unobtrusively through a side door, but she was wearing a spectacular shade of emerald silk, and the color caught his eye. He half turned, and then stopped, transfixed. She was a beautiful woman, slender and graceful, with chiseled cheekbones and fair, flawless skin, a sensual mouth, eyes as green as her gown. But he'd seen beautiful women before. He'd never seen one so vibrant, though, or so vividly compelling. She was watching the uproar as if it were a play put on for her benefit, those glowing green eyes sparkling with sunlight and curiosity and silent laughter, and when she glanced in Henry's direction, she held his gaze, a look that was both challenging and enigmatic.

Henry drew a deep, dazzled breath. He was utterly certain that this was Eleanor of Aquitaine, and no less sure that the French king must be one of God's greatest fools.

47

PARIS, FRANCE

August 1151

THE French king was glaring at Geoffrey. "Giraud Berlai is my seneschal. How dare you drag him before me in chains?"

Geoffrey's response was one of injured innocence. "I think I've showed admirable restraint," he protested. "I did not hang him, did I?"

Geoffrey's audience was not amused, Abbot Bernard least of all. "Your mockery is offensive to the Almighty."

"No, my lord abbot, it is offensive to you. Despite your insistence to the contrary, you are not the sole interpreter of the Almighty's Will."

It had been many years since anyone had dared to challenge Bernard's moral authority; most of his countrymen had long since elevated him to living sainthood. He seemed stunned by Geoffrey's audacity, and Henry spoke up quickly before he could recover and retaliate.

"My lord father has a legitimate grievance against Berlai. We're here to talk about it. That is why you invited us to Paris, is it not, my lord abbot—to talk?"

The abbot's struggle to achieve true humility was an ongoing one; he battled his pride daily and, all too often, lost. He did not appreciate being reminded that his obligation was to act as peacemaker, and it was particularly galling that the reminder should have come from Henry, for he was convinced that these Angevins sprang from a depraved stock, doomed and damned. He did not lack for discipline, though. Stifling his resentment, he said coldly:

"You are right, my lord duke. The purpose of this conference is to discuss our differences openly and freely, then seek a way to resolve them without further bloodshed." Giving Henry a nod of austere approval, he turned the power of his accusing eyes back upon Henry's father.

"When you refused to release Giraud Berlai from your prison, I was then compelled to lay upon you the dread anathema of excommunication.

I did this with the greatest reluctance, for I would not see any man denied God's Grace. If you release Berlai now, I will at once absolve you of this sin of disobedience and restore you to the Church."

"I have no intention of releasing Berlai, my lord abbot. The man is a rebel and brigand, and I see it as no sin to punish him as he deserves. But if it is a sin, then I have no wish to be absolved of it. Since you claim to have God's Ear day and night, you may tell Him that for me, that I seek no absolution for an act of simple justice."

When Geoffrey began to speak, Bernard stiffened, righteously indignant that his olive branch should not only have been spurned, but snapped in half. By the time Geoffrey was done, though, he was speechless with horror. So were the French king and most of the onlookers, for Geoffrey's defiance sounded to them like the worst sort of blasphemy.

Even Henry winced, wishing that his father could have been more judicious, less reckless in his refusal. He understood Geoffrey's hostility toward Berlai, and felt that after a three-year siege, it was not unjustified. He understood, too, Geoffrey's resentment at the posturing of the French king and Abbot Bernard, but posturing still seemed a poor reason for going to war. He'd fight the French king if he had to, but he'd rather be fighting Stephen, and he could only hope that his father would remember that—ere it was too late.

If Geoffrey had an innate sense of the dramatic, so, too, did Bernard. Drawing himself up to his full and formidable height, he thrust out his arm as if he meant to impale Geoffrey upon it. "Be not deceived, for God is not mocked, and whatsoever a man soweth, that shall he also reap. You have prayed for damnation and the Lord God has heard you. Repent now, you impious, wicked man, whilst you still can. Heed me well, for I see your death if you do not, and within a month's time."

Bernard's prophetic trances were known throughout France, and this one sent a frisson of uneasy excitement shuddering across the hall. The French king paled noticeably, some of Geoffrey's own men began to edge away from him, while others moved in for a better view, just in case the Lord chose to take His Vengeance here and now. Henry could not help admiring the abbot's theatrical flair, but he was suspicious of the prophecy itself, for the timing was too convenient to be credible. Geoffrey looked even more skeptical; one of his eyebrows had shot upward in a familiar gesture of disbelief.

"A month, you say? Could you be more specific, my lord abbot? If you can give me the exact date, that would make it easier for me to plan Berlai's public hanging in the time I have left."

The abbot stared at the younger man and then slowly and deliberately made the sign of the cross. "It is true what men say, that the counts of Anjou come from the Devil's seed. You blaspheme as easily as you breathe, mock all that is holy, you have no shame—"

"And I am doomed, too; let's not forget that. How good of you to speak up for the Lord like this. Whatever would He do without you?" The abbot sucked in an outraged breath, but Geoffrey gave him no chance to respond. "Well, then, if I have so little time left, I see no reason to waste any more of it here." And without a warning, without another word, Geoffrey turned on his heel and stalked from the hall.

Geoffrey's abrupt exit created almost as much of a sensation as Abbot Bernard's portentous prophecy. Henry was taken aback, too, for this hadn't been in the script. Geoffrey's nonplussed men were scrambling to follow, dragging out the wretched Berlai, while Henry's own attendants looked to him for their cue. Feeling left in the lurch, he wasn't sure if he should stalk out, too, stay and attempt to salvage the talks, or make a measured, dignified withdrawal. But as he observed the chaos that Geoffrey had set loose in the hall, he made an interesting discovery. The French king and his counselors were enraged and appalled, but they were also dismayed. So . . . they did want peace.

That was useful to know. Assuming, of course, that his father was not already leaving Paris behind in the dust of this hellishly hot summer day. How much of his dramatic departure had been fueled by genuine anger . . . and how much for effect? But he had managed to get the last word in his clash with the sainted Bernard, and Henry thought even the Almighty would not have found that an easy feat.

He was not surprised to find himself the focus of all eyes. The entire hall was waiting to see what he would do. By now he'd made up his mind, and he moved without haste toward the dais, where he bade farewell to the French king and the venerable Abbot of Clairvaux. He was courteous and composed and gave away nothing, not until his gaze fell again upon the woman in green silk. For just a moment, he hesitated, and then thought, Hellfire and furies, why not? Beckoning to his men, he turned and crossed the hall toward her.

Up close, she was even more stunning, those magnificent cheekbones highlighted with subtle, sun-kissed warmth, emerald eyes enhanced by the longest lashes he'd ever seen. "Madame," he said gravely, and kissed her hand with a courtly flourish. But then he added, for her ears alone, "If you are not the Queen of France, by God, you ought to be."

Her mouth put Henry in mind of ripe peaches. It curved at the corners, not quite a smile, but enough to free a flashing dimple. "My lord duke." Her voice was as arresting as her appearance, low-pitched and sultry. "And if you are not yet the King of England," she murmured, "by God, you will be."

There was a glint of gentle mockery in those shimmering sea-green eyes, but there was something else, too, something elusive and intriguing. This exchange of theirs could not have been more public, under the full scrutiny of the French court, and yet it was also a moment of odd intimacy; it was almost as if, Henry decided, they were sharing a joke no one else got.

IT had been arranged for the Angevins to stay at the Benedictine abbey of Saint-Germain-des-Pres, on the Left Bank of the Seine, and it was there that Henry found his father. Nor did he need to coax Geoffrey into resuming the peace talks; that was always Geoffrey's intent. He confessed readily that his walkout had been a calculated ploy, meant to checkmate Abbot Bernard and unsettle the French. Henry was not surprised, for only Maude had been able to send Geoffrey's temper up in flames. With the rest of his foes, he was always coldly in control, as Abbot Bernard and Louis would soon discover.

The talks began anew on the morrow, in an atmosphere of strained and pessimistic civility. In the days that followed, Henry was formally introduced to Queen Eleanor, met her notorious younger sister, Petronilla, and had several opportunities to take the measure of the French king and his barons. But that seemed all he'd be taking away from his Paris visit, for the negotiations were soon deadlocked. Geoffrey was not willing to free Berlai, while Henry was loath to make further territorial concessions to the French Crown. Geoffrey had already ceded half of the county of the Vexin in order to induce Louis to recognize him as Duke of Normandy, and the French king was now demanding the remainder of the Vexin as his price for extending recognition to Henry, a price he found too high. With neither side willing to yield, this peace conference seemed likely to be but a prelude to war.

IN midweek, the French king gave a lavish feast and entertainment for his obstinate vassals, but if he'd harbored any hopes of wining and dining the Angevins into a more obliging frame of mind, he was to be disappointed. Geoffrey and Henry were agreeable guests; they exchanged pleasantries with the French king, flirted with Eleanor, tactfully avoided any mention of Eustace, and even treated Abbot Bernard with polite deference. But that was just good manners; the negotiations remained bogged down in a quagmire of mutual suspicions and shared intransigence.

The following morning saw an early visitor to the queen's chambers, for the Countess of Vermandois was becoming uneasy on her sister's behalf and had decided a candid talk was in order. Petronilla had no illusions about the troubled state of Eleanor's marriage. She envisioned it as a sun-scorched, arid field, parched and barren and dangerously dry . . . and if there was ever a man with a knack for striking sparks, it was Count Geoffrey of Anjou. The more time that Eleanor spent with Geoffrey and his son, the more smoke Petronilla smelled.

Petronilla's disapproval was practical, not moral, for her conscience was an elastic one, able to stretch enough to accommodate a multitude of sins. Nor could she fault Eleanor's taste, for Geoffrey was undeniably one of the handsomest men she'd ever laid eyes upon. But her sister's timing was deplorable. Geoffrey might be gorgeous, but Petronilla did not think he could be trusted to bed Louis's queen without boasting about it afterward, and infidelity was a lethal weapon to give an aggrieved husband on the brink of divorce.

She didn't worry about finding Louis in Eleanor's bed, despite the earliness of the hour. Since the tragedy at Vitry, Louis's marital ardor had been effectively quenched by his numbing sense of guilt, and that flame had never burned very hot even in the first years of the marriage. Louis's love for his wife had always been struggling against the lessons he'd learned too well during his boyhood at the abbey of Saint-Denis: that carnal lust was sinful, women were the Devil's lures, and celibacy the chosen path to salvation.

Thinking now of the barrenness of her sister's marriage bed stirred an old memory. One of Eleanor's ladies-in-waiting had eavesdropped upon a confidential conversation between the two sisters and overheard the queen say, "I thought I'd married a king and found I'd married a monk." The young woman could not resist sharing so sensational a bit of gossip, and had been dismissed in disgrace once Eleanor discovered her betrayal. It was a much-quoted remark, but only Petronilla knew it was a counterfeit coin. The girl had gotten the words right, the intonation wrong. People repeated it as mockery; it had been said, though, in frustration and sadness.

Eleanor looked up in comical disbelief as Petronilla was ushered in, for the younger woman had been known to sleep till noon. "I'd wager you've not been to bed at all!" But she agreed to dismiss her attendants when Petronilla asked, watching her sister with quizzical curiosity as she continued to brush her hair. "So . . . what has gotten you up at such an ungodly hour? Did you have another quarrel with Raoul?"

"Eleanor, surely you've noticed by now that Raoul and I like to quarrel? That is how we liven up our lovemaking." Petronilla settled herself on the edge of the bed and began to pet her sister's brindle greyhound. "I am here to talk about Geoffrey of Anjou. Let me say at the outset that I do not blame you for being tempted. That man could start a lust-crazed riot in a convent full of nuns."

"Mayhap Benedictines, but surely not Cistercians? Your tribute to

Geoffrey's manhood definitely conjures up some intriguing images, and I daresay he'd be the first to agree with you. But all those lustful nuns notwithstanding, I have no intention of taking Geoffrey as my lover."

"Truly?" Petronilla was relieved, yet puzzled. "I must have misread the signs. But I ought to warn you—I think Louis did, too. I watched him watching you and Geoffrey last night, and he looked very disgruntled."

"I surely hope so."

"Eleanor . . . what is going on? What are you up to?"

Eleanor looked at her thoughtfully, then put her finger to her lips, and moved swiftly and soundlessly across the chamber. Petronilla watched in astonishment as she jerked the door open. "Is it as bad as that? You really think Louis's men would spy on you?"

Eleanor's lip curled. "Thierry Galeran would hide under my bed—if only he could fit. Yes, I am quite sure I am being watched. The death vigil for my marriage has begun, and with the venerable Abbot Bernard himself standing ready to give the Last Rites."

Petronilla should not have felt any surprise. Abbot Suger of Saint-Denis had been the French king's chief adviser, utterly insistent that his marriage was valid in God's Eyes. But he'd died that past January, and the French king was now heeding Abbot Bernard—Abbot Bernard who believed that if all women were suspect, daughters of Eve, Eleanor was one of Lucifer's own.

But even though the news was expected, it still came as a shock, for the ramifications would be earthshaking. Divorce was usually disastrous for a woman; she would invariably lose custody of her children, her dower rights, and often her good name as well. Eleanor would also lose a crown. For a woman who'd been Queen of France, the rest of her life was likely to be anticlimactic. Petronilla thought it was the true measure of her sister's desperation that she'd wanted a divorce, even knowing what it might cost her.

"Eleanor . . . there is still time to resurrect your marriage. Louis does love you, and if you could only get pregnant again—"

"No. The marriage has been dead for years, Petra. I would not try to breathe life back into a corpse. Better we finally bury it. It is not the divorce that is stealing my sleep at night, it is what happens afterward. It would indeed be ironic, Sister, if the peace should prove more perilous than the war!"

Petronilla nodded somberly. Eleanor was the greatest heiress in Christendom, for she held Aquitaine in her own right, a vast and rich province, stretching from the River Loire to the Pyrenees, comparable in size and wealth to France itself. Once Eleanor was free, she'd be a tempting prize, indeed, and she'd be fair game for any baron with more ambitions than scruples. All too often, heiresses were abducted and forced into marriage, as both women well knew. The year before his death, their father had become betrothed to the daughter of the Viscount of Limoges, only to have her stolen away and wed against her will to the Count of Angoulême. So the danger was a real one, and would remain so until Eleanor was safely wed again.

But as Eleanor's liege lord, Louis would be the one to choose another husband for her, and Petronilla did not think he'd choose a husband to her liking. Whatever Louis's failings as a husband, he was still King of France. It seemed to Petronilla that whomever Eleanor married next, it was bound to be a comedown. She could not help thinking that Eleanor's wretched marriage to Louis was still the lesser of evils, but she knew better than to say so. Eleanor took no more kindly to unsolicited advice than she did; she would only be leaving herself open to a pointed reminder of her own stubborn insistence upon having Raoul, even if that meant they'd be together in Hell.

No matter what angle she viewed it from, her sister's future looked precarious at best. But one thing she never doubted—that Eleanor would not sit placidly by whilst her destiny was decided by others. "What mean you to do?"

Eleanor sat down beside her on the bed. "Well, this much I know for certes—that the only fate worse than being yoked to Louis for the rest of my life would be marriage to a man handpicked by that sanctimonious, self-proclaimed saint, Bernard."

Eleanor's greyhound reached up suddenly, swiping her cheek in a wet kiss and making her laugh. Almost at once, though, she sobered. "And so," she continued coolly, "I mean to do my own husband-hunting."

Petronilla rolled her eyes. "And you dare to call me reckless!"

"Why is it reckless to want a say in my own life? You can well imagine the sort of pathetic French puppet they'd choose for me, a lackey who'd look to Paris for guidance the way infidels look toward Mecca. Do you think I'd entrust Aquitaine to such a weak-willed wretch? I need a husband who'd not be afraid to defy the French Crown or even the Church, a man who could command respect from my duchy's unruly, quarrelsome barons." She paused, and then added dryly, "A man I could respect, too, would be a pleasant change."

"You are not asking much, are you?"

Eleanor reclined back against the pillows and smiled impishly at her sister. "Oh, but I want much more than that, Petra. Those were Aquitaine's needs, but I have my own, too. I want a man who knows his own mind, who sees nothing odd about reading for the fun of it. A man who likes to laugh, even at himself. A man who is not so intent upon the glories of the next world that it blinds him to the pleasures of this one." Eleanor was no longer smiling. "Above all, I want a man I do not have to coax to my bed."

"And where do you expect to find this paragon of manhood? I can think of only one man who measures up to those exacting standards, and Raoul is already spoken for!" Picking up the brush, Petronilla combed out her sister's long hair, then began to braid it with nimble fingers. "What of Geoffrey? Why then were you flirting with him? Merely to vex Louis?"

"I had a twofold purpose. I wanted to remind Louis how mismatched we are, just in case he'd begun to have second thoughts about the divorce. The only voice he heeds these days is that of our saint in residence, who divides all of womankind into three categories: nuns, sluts, and potential sluts. So I knew he'd look upon flirtation as only slightly less heinous a sin than sacrilege, and I was right. You see, Petra, those famed mystical trances of Bernard's are only part of his sleight-of-hand. When Louis opens his mouth, lo and behold—Bernard's words come out."

It was not often that Eleanor let her bitterness show so nakedly, and Petronilla felt a surge of immediate and indignant sympathy. Her loyalties burned too hot and too deep ever to allow for detachment or objectivity; she supposed that Louis had his side, too, but she had no interest whatsoever in hearing it. Eleanor was right to look for a way out, she decided. The marriage was indeed dead and decomposing, and keeping up the pretense would be like living in a charnel house, trying all the while to ignore the stench.

"Forget what I said earlier about attempting to mend the rift. I'd not urge you to run back into a burning building just because you had nowhere else to go. But I am still curious about that 'twofold' remark of yours. Why else were you seeking Geoffrey out? I know you claim you have no interest in a dalliance, but you must have been tempted, at least a little . . . ?"

"I am beginning to think Raoul had best keep an eye on you till Geoffrey departs Paris! Must I assure you again that I am not as susceptible as you to a handsome face? Geoffrey of Anjou was my red herring, no more than that."

Petronilla's frown was one of bafflement. She had hunted enough to understand Eleanor's allusion; drawing a herring across a trail was said to throw pursuing dogs off the scent. But she did not see its application, not at first. When it finally came to her, she gasped aloud and inadvertently jerked on Eleanor's braid. "Holy Mother Mary! It is not Geoffrey at all, is it? Not the sire—the son!"

Eleanor laughed. "Glory be, at last! Are we such an unlikely pairing, that you never once thought of Henry?"

"It is a brilliant match, Eleanor," Petronilla enthused. "When I was ransacking my brain for a suitable husband, I did not even think of him, I admit it . . . mayhap because of the age difference. And yet he is the ideal choice! Of course he is rather young, but he is no green lad, for certes. No son of Maude and Geoffrey could lack for boldness, so you'd be getting a husband willing to challenge the French Crown. One with prospects enough to unsettle even the most complacent of former husbands—Duke of Normandy, heir to Anjou and Maine, not to forget that very intriguing claim across the Channel. Jesú, Eleanor, he might be King of England one day!"

"I'd say that is a foregone conclusion, Petra. Henry strikes me as a bowman who rarely misses the target. I'd wager he gets whatever he aims for."

Petronilla looked closely into her sister's face, and then grinned. "So, that is the way the wind blows, does it? I think you fancy the lad!"

Eleanor grinned, too. "Let's just say I think he has . . . potential."

Petronilla burst out laughing, leaning over to give her sister an exuberantly affectionate embrace. Eleanor's greyhound took that as an invitation and jumped onto the bed. "Felice, down!" Eleanor fended off the dog with a pillow, laughing, too, and for a few moments, they managed to forget about the high stakes, the all-or-nothing gamble that Eleanor was about to make.

It did not even occur to Petronilla to wonder if Henry would be receptive to Eleanor's overtures. No man in his right mind would turn down Eleanor and Aquitaine; that she never doubted. Nor did she see a need to speak of Eleanor's daughters, six-year-old Marie and one-year-old Alix. They were lost to Eleanor, whether she married Henry or not, for the French king would never give them up. There'd already been discussions about finding them suitable highborn husbands, forging marital alliances that would further French interests, and as likely as not, they'd grow to girlhood in far-off foreign courts, just as the eight-year-old Maude had once set sail for Germany, child bride of the Imperial Emperor Heinrich V.

"You have not yet had a heart-to-heart talk with Henry?"

Eleanor shook her head. "I have been observing him closely all week, and I like what I've seen so far. He is quick-witted, deliberate, and rather cocky—but I need to know if he is also discreet. If Louis had even a suspicion of what I was planning, I'd find myself convent-caged for the remainder of my days, and I do not think I'd make a good nun."

Eleanor had spoken lightly, but there was too much truth in what she'd said for humor. Petronilla was suddenly and uncharacteristically pensive. Eleanor was right. Louis would do almost anything to keep her from marrying Henry and uniting Aquitaine with Normandy and mayhap even England. She could not have chosen anyone better calculated to appall the king and desolate the man.

"Eleanor, are you sure you want to do this? Have you thought about all you'd be risking?"

"Of course I have," Eleanor said impatiently. After a moment, though, she smiled. "But then I think about all I'd be gaining!"

PARIS had been sweltering in a high-summer heat wave, but the weather changed abruptly by week's end. The city awoke to a steady downpour and dropping temperatures. It was a dismal day outside, and no less gloomy within the Cité Palace, where the peace negotiations had broken down in recriminations and acrimony. Geoffrey had a hangover and a throbbing headache, and he'd walked out in midmorning, once again declaring he'd had enough and would be departing for Anjou on the morrow. This time Henry believed him.

Henry remained a while longer, in a final attempt to come to terms with the French king. It was another exercise in futility, for neither one was willing to compromise. The rain was still falling by the time Henry and William de Vere, his chancellor, emerged out onto the wide stone steps of the Cité Palace. Henry was just starting down them when he was accosted by a woman in a red mantle.

"May I have a few moments of your time, my lord Henry?" Her face was half-hidden by her hood, but Henry readily agreed, for he'd recognized the voice and was curious to find out what the Lady Petronilla wanted from him.

Sending his men back into the hall, Henry fell into step beside Petronilla, hiding his surprise when she led him out into the deserted, rain-drenched royal gardens. If not for the weather, it would have been an idyllic setting, with bordered walkways, raised flower beds abloom with poppies, Madonna lilies, and spectacular scarlet peonies, a grassy mead spangled with snow-white daisies, and an abundance of fragrant red roses. Today, though, it was wet and wind-raked, the turf seats soaked, the paths pockmarked with puddles; even the River Seine looked different, flat and leaden-grey under a lowering slate sky.

Petronilla kept up a comfortable flow of chatter, the sort of soothing small talk that put people at their ease and yet revealed nothing of importance. She tactfully made no mention of the flagging peace negotiations, instead told Henry an amusing story about her young son's latest misdeed, asked politely about his mother, the empress, and reminded him playfully that they'd nearly been kin, for several years ago, Geoffrey had suggested a marriage between Henry and Marie, Louis and Eleanor's baby daughter. Henry had almost forgotten that, and he was glad now that nothing had come of it, for he had no wish to be so closely bound to the French king. After a moment, he laughed aloud, unable to envision the exotic Eleanor of Aquitaine as his mother-in-law.

The rain had eased up, but not for long; the clouds were thick and foreboding. By now they'd reached the far end of the island, jutting out into the Seine like the prow of a ship. A trellised garden arbour lay just ahead, sheltered by climbing roses and tangled honeysuckle. It was so well shielded that Henry did not at first see the woman seated within, not until he and Petronilla were almost upon her. She was clad in a hooded mantle of a glistening silver grey, and looked elegant and somehow ethereal, too, a maid of the mist that was rising off the river. When Henry glanced her way, she reached up and drew back her hood. He came to an abrupt halt, staring at the French queen, and then moved swiftly toward her.

As he kissed her hand, Eleanor gave him a vivid smile. "I apologize for the deception, and for dragging you out into the rain, but I needed to speak with you—in private."

"I'm willing to brave some rain for your sake." When she gestured toward the bench, he did not need to be asked twice, and seated himself beside her in the trellised hideaway. Only then did he remember Petronilla, but she was already retreating back up the walkway to keep watch. The dreary day had suddenly taken a dramatic upswing for the better. Henry could not imagine a more pleasant pastime than an intrigue with Eleanor; that he did not yet know the nature of this intrigue troubled him not at all. "This is very clandestine and mysterious," he acknowledged, "and I am eager to find out why you'd want to talk in such secrecy. Not that I am complaining, just curious."

"After being lured out into a secluded garden, many men would leap to the simplest, most obvious conclusion, that the woman had dalliance in mind."

"I doubt that there is anything obvious about you, Lady Eleanor," Henry parried. She did not have sea-green eyes, after all; he was close enough now to see gold flecks in the green. Hazel suited her better, he decided, for it was an uncommon color, subtle and ever-changing. She was watching him with an odd intensity, as if a great deal depended upon his answer. "A rain-soaked garden is a good place for privacy," he said, "but not for a tryst. It would be too damnably wet."

His candor seemed to amuse her; like a shooting star, that dimple came and went. "Moreover," he continued, "infidelity has more serious consequences for a woman than for a man, and for a queen, most of all. No, whatever your reasons for this rendezvous, it is not because you yearned for an hour of high-risk sinning with a stranger."

She said nothing, but her sudden smile was blinding. "Why do I get the feeling," he joked, "that I've just passed some sort of test?"

Eleanor laughed, marveling at his intuitiveness, and sure now that her instincts had been right. He was looking at her with alert interest, slight wariness, and undisguised desire. As their eyes met, he grinned.

"But if you ever did decide to throw yourself at me, I'd be right pleased to catch you."

"How gallant of you, Henry."

"My friends call me Harry."

His nonchalance was just a little too studied to be utterly convincing; she suspected that he was not as confident as he'd have her believe. But she was not put off by this hint of youthful insecurity. She found it rather endearing, for she was untroubled by the ten-year gap in their ages. In some ways, he seemed more mature to her than her husband, who at thirty was still dithering indecisively at every royal crossroads.

"Harry?" she echoed. "I like that. Tell me . . . what do your bedmates call you?"

He blinked. "Unforgettable." But he could not quite carry it off, and burst out laughing. So did Eleanor, for she was more and more charmed by this engaging youth; bravado and self-deprecating humor and unabashed lust were an appealing brew to a woman whose marriage had been sober and chaste and desert-dry more often than not.

Henry still did not know what she wanted from him, but he was willing to wait—with rare patience—until she was ready to reveal her intent. He was also very willing to carry on this fascinating flirtation, and he was disappointed when she then steered the conversation into a more innocuous channel, one with no erotic depths.

The rain had stopped, and he jerked his hood back, running his hand absently through his damp, unruly hair, all the while trying not to stare too openly at the soft hollow of her throat or the solitary raindrop that had splashed onto her cheek and trickled like a wayward tear toward her mouth. She was the most desirable woman he'd ever seen, and when he found himself thinking that a man could get drunk just by breathing in her perfume, he realized how prescient his father had been to call her "dangerous."

Eleanor was well aware of the effect she was having upon him. For fully half of her life, men had been looking upon her with hot hunger and carnal lust; only the man she'd married had never been singed by her heat. Here in this trellised grotto that was scented with honeysuckle and glimmering with crystal droplets of rain, she was seducing Henry merely by inflaming his imagination.

The conversation was deceptively casual; for the moment, they were both pretending to be oblivious of the undercurrents swirling between them. The questions were mainly Eleanor's, the answers Henry's. He explained that his father had gotten the informal surname Plantagenet because of his habit of wearing a sprig of broom or planta genesta in his cap. He confirmed that he called himself Henry Fitz Empress rather than Fitz Count or Fitz Geoffrey. While he did not elaborate upon his reasons for this break with tradition, Eleanor understood the realism of it and approved. After fourteen years of marriage to a man without a shred of practicality in his soul, she could appreciate Henry's pragmatism as much as she did his ambition.

Petronilla had lamented the fact that Henry did not resemble his father more closely. While she'd agreed that he was attractive, he was too rough-hewn for her taste, utterly lacking Geoffrey's flamboyant good looks and dashing sense of style. Eleanor conceded that no one would ever call Henry suave, as they did Geoffrey. Geoffrey always looked as if he'd just been visited by his tailor, whereas Henry's clothes were of good quality but carelessly worn, as if he'd flung on the first garment at hand. Geoffrey had hair any woman might envy, bright gold and gleaming, rarely mussed. Henry's hair was redder, unfashionably short, and usually tousled. Petronilla had remarked that he looked more like a huntsman than a highborn lord, and Eleanor tended to agree with her sister. She thought it a fine joke that the son of the Empress Maude and Geoffrey le Bel should be so down-to-earth, so indifferent to the trappings of power.

But Henry was not indifferent to the power itself, that she never doubted. As she studied him now, she was struck again by his presence. She had to keep reminding herself that he was not yet nineteen, for already he had it, that indefinable quality that would give him the mastery of other men.

He'd been in motion constantly as he talked, gesturing expressively with his hands, stretching out his legs. He wore high leather boots, not shoes, as if he'd dressed for a day's hunting, and with sudden insight, she realized that this was indeed how he seemed to her—as a man always on the verge of action. His energy was awesome, like a fire at full blaze, and she found herself wondering what it would be like to feel all that energy between her thighs. The erotic image of the two of them entwined together in a rumpled bed startled her somewhat, for she'd not expected to be drawn so strongly to him.

"I think," she said, "that it is time I told you why I contrived to meet you out in these rain-sodden gardens. You were right when you said it was an unlikely place for a tryst. But it is a good place to avoid eavesdroppers or onlookers, whilst not compromising me beyond repair if we are discovered together." Her dimple flashed again, almost too quick to catch. "Rumors to the contrary, I am more careful of my reputation than certain churchmen claim."

Henry saw no reason not to name her enemy straight out. "If we are choosing up sides, Lady Eleanor, I would rather be on yours than on Abbot Bernard's," he said, and this time her dimple lingered.

"It is passing strange," she said, "the odd turns that fate takes. No sensible man would set out upon a long journey without knowing the roads to follow, and yet we all blunder through life without any maps whatsoever. I've puzzled you, I can see. I was remembering that long-ago suggestion of your father's, that we consider marriage for you and my daughter Marie. Who would ever have imagined then what lay ahead? Do not ever doubt, Harry, that the Almighty has a sense of humor!"

This was the first time she'd called him Harry, and he was young enough to take pleasure in that. But he also felt a distinct letdown. Was this why she'd wanted to see him alone—to revive those scuttled marriage plans? That was such a prosaic and mundane solution to a marvelous mystery. No intrigue, merely a marital alliance. Hiding his disappointment, he said, "I am not sure I understand, Lady Eleanor. Are you offering me your daughter again?"

"No, Harry, I am offering myself."

Henry had been shifting in his seat. But he stopped in midmotion and stared at her. So, she thought, he can sit still, after all. He scarcely seemed to be breathing, his eyes intently searching her face. She knew without being told that he was seeking to make sure she was serious, for it was becoming evident to her that there was a cool, calculating brain behind the heat of those smoke-grey eyes.

"I accept."

"Do not be too quick to commit yourself, Harry. Do you not want me to specify what I am offering ere you say yes?"

"I assumed you were talking of divorce. But if I misread you and you are offering a liaison, the answer is still the same. I would take you," he said huskily, "any way I could get you, even barefoot and in rags."

"Yes," she murmured, "but you would not *marry* me without Aquitaine," and Henry began to laugh, recognizing in this worldly older woman a true kindred spirit.

"You are right," he admitted. "I would not marry you without Aquitaine. No more than you would marry me without Normandy. Since we are being so candid, what of England? Is this marriage of ours contingent upon my first becoming king of the English?"

"No," she said, "I'll take you as you are, my lord duke. Your capture of the English crown is not a contingency. But I think I can safely say that it is an inevitability."

Henry exhaled an uneven, admiring breath. "What a Queen of England you will make!" To Eleanor's amusement, he'd already slid over on the bench so that their bodies were now touching. How quick men were to claim possession, to plant their flags! This lad would need no prompting, for certes. He'd made a very promising beginning, kissing her fingertips, her palm, and then the pulse at her wrist. Laying her hand flat against his chest, over his heart, she said reluctantly:

"I dare not take you to my bed, Harry. No one can have even a glimmering of suspicion about us, for if they do, Louis will never set me free."

He knew she was right. He was warmed, too, by the note of genuine regret in her voice. But that still did not make it any easier to agree. "How long do you think it will take to have your marriage annulled?"

"Most likely about six months or so," she said, and smiled when he winced and muttered an obscenity under his breath. His eagerness was sweet balm for an old wound.

When Henry had seen her in the hall, she'd always been wearing the newly fashionable wimple, a delicate white scarf which framed her face while covering her neck and hair. Today she'd reverted to the older style and wore only a gossamer veil, which left her slender throat bare and gave him his first glimpse of her long, glossy braids, adorned with gold-thread ribbons.

He should have been surprised that her hair was not blonde, for fairness was the defining measure of beauty in their world. But he was not, for he was learning that Eleanor of Aquitaine was a law unto herself in all things. At first, he thought the braids were black, but when he reached for one and entwined it around his hand, he saw it was actually a very dark brown, burnished with auburn glints. He wondered how long it would be ere he'd get to see her hair spilling across his pillow, and his fingers twitched with the urge to untie those ribbons.

"One kiss," he said. "Surely we can risk that. We do have a plight troth to celebrate, after all."

Even as he spoke, he was already leaning toward her, and Eleanor decided that a kiss was not an unreasonable request. She tilted her face up and he caressed her cheek with his fingers before claiming her mouth with his own. The kiss was unhurried, gentle at first, but with enough passion to make it interesting. When they drew apart, Eleanor was smiling, very pleased with herself and this youth who would soon share her dreams and her bed. They would rule an empire together, she and Harry, and she would give him all the sons a man could want, confounding Louis and Bernard and those who'd dared to judge her so harshly, to scorn her so unfairly as that greatest of all failures, a barren queen.

She was still congratulating herself on how well her plans had gone when Henry began kissing her again. Her brain warned her this was too reckless, but her body was more receptive to the message it was getting from Henry. His mouth was hot, his hands sliding up her back, under her mantle, pulling her in tight against him. She started to tell him this was dangerous, but by then he was fondling her breasts, kissing her throat, and instead of protesting, she sought a closer embrace, followed him heedlessly into the flames.

"Christ on the Cross!"

The cry was strident, sharp enough to rip them apart. Flushed and dazed, they spun around to confront a highly indignant Petronilla. "Have you both gone stark mad?" she demanded. "If you mean to put on a public display, by all means, let's invite the entire court so everyone can watch!"

By now, Eleanor had recovered her breath and her senses. "The rain has stopped, so people will be coming out into the garden. Harry . . . you must go."

Henry was shaken, too, belatedly realizing how foolish they'd been. "You are right," he agreed hoarsely, and managed a crooked grin. "I do not trust myself around you!"

But still he lingered, until Petronilla turned and gave him a slight push. "Hurry," she urged, "for I do not trust either one of you!"

Henry insisted upon kissing Eleanor's hand one last time before turning away, adjusting his clothing as he strode along the pathway. He paused once, looking back at Eleanor, as she'd known he would, and she watched until he'd vanished from view.

Stepping into the trellised arbour, Petronilla sat beside her sister and reached over to pull Eleanor's hood up. "I hope to God he does not look at you like that out in the hall. Apart from the danger of starting a fire, it would be a signed confession of adultery!"

"You need not worry, Petra. Harry will be discreet."

"For your sake, he'd better be!" Petronilla gave Eleanor a sidelong, appraising glance, and then, a sly smile. "So," she said, "how did your hunt go? Did you get your quarry?"

Eleanor nodded, only half listening to her sister's banter. She was still gazing out across the wet, empty garden. "In truth," she said softly, "I think Harry and I may be getting more than we bargained for."

UPON his return to the abbey guest quarters, Geoffrey had instructed his men to prepare for departure in the morning, and then took his hangover and his headache off to bed. He awoke long before he was ready, to find his head still hurting, the rain still coming down, and his son carrying on like a lunatic, banging around the darkened chamber in search of a lamp and making enough racket to be heard back in Anjou. Rolling over, Geoffrey groaned and called Henry a foul name just as a light flared, half blinding him.

"Go away, Harry, ere I get my strength back and kill you," he mumbled, trying to blot out the glare and noise with his pillow. But his son seemed to have developed a death wish, for he snatched the pillow away and insisted that Geoffrey sit up, utterly unfazed by the steady string of curses being hurled at his head.

"Here, Papa, have some wine. It'll make you feel much better," he said, sounding so odiously cheerful that Geoffrey began to suspect that Maude was an even worse wife than he'd realized, for how could this be a son of his loins?

He protested in vain, soon found himself propped up with pillows, scowling at Henry as the young man sloshed a wine cup into his hand and then settled himself cross-legged on the foot of the bed. "Maude put you up to this. I know she did, so you might as well admit it."

Henry laughed. "Stop grumbling, Papa, and listen. I have a great favor to ask of you."

"Quit whilst you're ahead, Harry, whilst you're still in my will." Geoffrey took a tentative swallow of the wine and grimaced. "Where did you get this? It tastes like goat piss."

"You were certainly guzzling it down last night without complaint. I am serious, Papa. I want you to set Giraud Berlai free."

Geoffrey's wine cup froze in midair. "Are you drunk?"

"I am as sober as the sainted Bernard, and very much in earnest, Papa. On the morrow I am going to tell Louis that I've decided to cede the Vexin to him. I want peace with the French king, and I want you to help me get it."

"This morning you were determined to hold on to the Vexin. What has changed since then?"

"Everything!" Henry leaned forward, splashing wine onto the bed, but not even noticing. His eyes were shining, his color high. Geoffrey had rarely seen him so excited, not off the hunting field.

"I think you'd better tell me what this is all about, lad," he said, and grabbed for Henry's wine cup, just in time to keep it from being dumped in his lap. "Why are you suddenly willing to give up the Vexin?"

"For Aquitaine," Henry said, and grinned. "For Eleanor and Aquitaine. I'd say that is a fair trade, Papa, more than fair."

"You . . . and Eleanor?" Geoffrey was stunned, but not disbelieving; his son was too euphoric to doubt. "Are you saying what I think you are, lad?"

Henry nodded vigorously. "As of this afternoon, I have a wife . . . or I will have as soon as she gets shed of Louis. Once she does, we shall wed. So you see why I need to make peace with Louis. I want nothing to distract him from the urgent matter of getting his marriage annulled."

"Holy Mother of God . . ." Geoffrey shook his head slowly. "I thought I'd taken your measure, Harry, but clearly I've been undervaluing you!"

"No, Papa. As much as I'd like to claim credit for this, the idea was Eleanor's. She is a remarkable woman, and if she were mine, I would never let her go. But Louis will, and once he does, the English crown will be ours for the taking. Can you imagine how Stephen will react when he hears?"

Henry laughed again, swung off the bed, and went to get another flagon from the table. "So . . . what say you, Papa? Will you set Berlai free for me?"

"Of course I will. Although you'll owe me for this, lad, and you may be sure I'll remind you frequently of that. Now pour me some more of this swill and let's talk. I agree that Stephen will likely have a seizure when word of this gets out, for the day you wed Eleanor, you'll cast a shadow across half of Europe . . . and all of France. That is why you must think about how Louis will react, too. He is your liege lord as well as Eleanor's, and if you marry the woman without his consent—which he'd never give—you'll be making a mortal enemy."

"He'll not like it any," Henry admitted, "but he'll get over it."

"No, Harry, I think not. He does love her, you see. And if she divorces him because they are fourth cousins or whatever, and then marries you, also a fourth cousin . . . well, believe me when I say a wound like that will never heal. Trust me on this, for I know more about hating than you. He'll be cursing you both with his dying breath."

"Mayhap you are right," Henry agreed, "but what of it? Surely you are not suggesting that I do not marry her?"

Geoffrey's smile was wry. "No, I am not—and you'd not heed me even if I did. You cannot turn down an opportunity like this, for marriage to Eleanor could make you master of Europe one day. Normandy and Aquitaine and England and Anjou and Maine—Christ Jesus, Harry, Caesar might well envy you! And if you were mad enough to spurn Eleanor's offer, you'd have to worry then about the man she might marry in your stead. I just want you to understand that she'll be bringing you the undying enmity of the French king as her marriage portion. It is still, as you said, a fair trade, but you need to bear that clearly in mind, for this marriage will turn Christendom upside down and that is no lie."

"I understand that, Papa, truly I do. But can I not have one day just to be happy about it?"

Henry's smile was coaxing, and so contagious that Geoffrey had to smile back. "Fair enough, lad." Reaching out, he clinked his wine cup against Henry's in a mock salute. "To you and your bride-to-be. I think I can safely predict that your life together will never be dull. What of your mother? Do you plan to tell Maude?"

He'd caught Henry off balance. "I'd rather not," he confessed, "for the fewer people who know, the better. But I suppose I should, for Mama would not soon forgive me if I did not."

"No, she would not. But you need not worry about her keeping your secret. Whatever she may say to you about this marriage in private, she'd never breathe a word to the world at large."

Henry lowered his wine cup. "You think she will not approve?"

Geoffrey's mouth twitched. "The empress will counsel you to wed Eleanor as soon as she is free to do so. But I suspect that the mother will find it deplorable that her beloved son must settle for damaged goods."

He saw Henry's head come up at that, and held up a hand to stave off his protest. "You do not like that, do you? Well, you'd best get used to hearing it, Harry, for you will be marrying a woman whose honour is frayed around the edges, or so men think."

"Spiteful gossip and slander," Henry said scornfully, and Geoffrey shrugged.

"Gossip is still something we all have to live with, lad. If you can ignore it, more power to you. Look, Harry, I am not saying I believe the stories. I told you honestly on the road to Paris that I do not know if the rumors about Eleanor are true. Nor will I lie to you now just because it would be what you want to hear. Eleanor might well be as pure and chaste as the Blessed Lady Mary. Or she may indeed have strayed. But—"

"If she did, Louis gave her cause!"

"I am not arguing with you, lad. You need not defend her to me. But I will give you some advice, and I hope you heed me. Let it lie. Decide now that whatever may or may not have happened in her past is between Eleanor and her confessor, and do not pry. Can you do that?"

"Yes," Henry said, after a long pause. "But I still say rumors prove nothing. Accusing a woman of wantonness is the easiest way to discredit her, for some of the mud is always sure to stick."

"You are right. But God help you, for you are also sounding like a man smitten," Geoffrey joked. "There is another matter we ought to talk about, though. You were eighteen last March, and if memory serves me, Eleanor turned twenty-nine this summer. Are you comfortable with so great an age difference?"

Henry shrugged. "Ten years, five months—not so vast a gap. If my memory serves, Mama is eleven and a half years older than you!"

"Yes, and we've had twenty-three years of wedded bliss and marital joy," Geoffrey said, with a tight smile, too much rancor for humor.

Henry was quiet for a moment, not wanting to hurt his father by pointing out the obvious, that Maude had never wanted to marry Geoffrey, whereas he was very sure, indeed, that Eleanor wanted to marry him. "It does not trouble me, Papa, truly not," he assured his father. "She is still young enough to bear children and that is what counts. I have no doubt that she'll give me sons. She has been unfairly blamed for failing to bear Louis an heir, for you said yourself that he shied away from their marriage bed. Believe me, that is not a problem she'll ever have with me!"

"No, with you, I'd say the problem will be getting you out of her bed, not into it!"

"Papa . . . I am sensing some misgivings on your part. Are you just playing the Devil's advocate or do you truly have qualms about this marriage?"

Geoffrey did not respond as Henry hoped, with a hearty denial. Staring down into the dregs of his wine cup, he said, "Not qualms, lad, not exactly. I want you to be King of England, and your prospects will be greatly enhanced by marriage to Eleanor. I am pleased for you, God's Truth. I just wish you were not so taken with the woman herself."

"Why ever not? I think it is my great, good fortune that I shall have a wife I find so desirable. Not only is she beautiful, but she is clever and witty and educated, bred to be a queen. How lucky can I get?"

"I am going to give you some more advice, Harry, that I do not expect you to take. Save your passion for your concubines, your respect for your wife. The best marriages are those based upon detached goodwill or benign indifference. But unfortunately for you, the one emotion you will never feel for Eleanor of Aquitaine is indifference."

"Jesú, I would hope not! Papa, I know you mean well. But miserable marriages are not passed down from father to son like hair color or height. It is no secret that you and Mama made mistakes. But why should I not learn from them rather than repeat them?"

"Why not, indeed?" Geoffrey conceded. "I hope you do, lad. God knows, I hope you do."

This was not a conversation Henry had expected to have with his father; he'd thought Maude would be the one to harbor doubts. He was both amused and irked that Geoffrey should be so protective, for his wariness reflected poorly upon Eleanor.

"Papa, you need not worry about this marriage. I have always known that one day I would rule over England. I have never doubted that. And I am just as sure now that Eleanor is the woman meant to rule with me. I know in my heart that it is so, I swear I do."

"I'd say the body part you're heeding at the moment is not your heart," Geoffrey drawled and then laughed abruptly. "Do not mind me, Harry. I am right proud of you, and who knows, mayhap even a little envious! Congratulations, lad, you've captured a queen."

And in that moment, the full wonder of it hit Henry, too. "Yes," he said jubilantly, "I did!" Laughing, he raised his wine cup high. "To Eleanor, Duchess of Aquitaine, Queen of France, and—one day—Queen of England."

48

LE MANS, FRANCE

September 1151

THE sudden concessions by the Angevins astonished the French court. Such a dramatic volte-face was bound to stir up speculation, but the French king accepted it as Divine Intervention. So did Abbot Bernard, who felt grimly gratified that he'd been able to instill the Fear of God in so great a sinner as the arrogant Count of Anjou. Giraud Berlai did not care what had motivated Geoffrey's change of heart; he was just hysterically happy not to be going back to the Angers dungeon. And so the contentious peace talks came to an unexpected and gainful end. Geoffrey was restored to the Church once Berlai was set free. Henry did homage to the French king for his duchy, while Eustace's spies looked on glumly, and Eleanor watched with a secret smile.

Henry and Geoffrey then rode west into Maine. Upon reaching Le Mans, they parted company, Henry remaining in the city while Geoffrey pushed on for Tours and then Angers. They had much to do and less than a fortnight in which to get it done, for a summons must be sent out to the barons of Anjou and Maine and Normandy, bidding them to appear at Lisieux on September 14th. Henry could now direct all his energies and efforts toward recovering his mother's stolen crown. The time was ripe to plan a full-scale invasion of England.

HENRY was a light sleeper and awakened as footsteps approached his bed. The chamber was still filled with night-shadows, but the figure bending over him was holding a candle, revealing a face that was youthful, troubled, and familiar. "Ivo?"

The squire jumped and splashed hot wax onto Henry's pillow. "I am so sorry, my lord! I thought you still slept."

"I was—until you woke me up." With an effort, Henry stifled his irritation; Ivo's tongue-tied shyness could be a trial, but he was a good lad. "You must have a reason for hovering by my bed in the middle of the night," he prompted. "So . . . what is it?"

"It is nigh on toward dawn," Ivo mumbled, and Henry's patience started to unravel. Ivo fidgeted, splattering some wax upon himself this time, and Henry began to realize that there was more to the boy's reticence than his usual bashful diffidence.

"Ivo, what are you so loath to tell me? What is wrong?"

The boy continued to squirm. When he finally met Henry's eyes, Henry was chilled by what he saw in them—anguished pity. "My lord, it is your father. He . . . has been taken sick."

Henry felt a rush of relief. Youth and optimism usually went hand in hand, but Ivo was an exception, so anxiety-ridden that he not only expected the worst, he actively courted it, invariably turning a cough into consumption, a scratch into a festering wound, a growling dog into a rabid wolf. "I saw my father just three days ago, Ivo, and he was fine. Now what is this all about?"

"A man has ridden in, my lord, insisting that we let him speak to you straightaway. He says you must come back with him to Château-du-Loir, that Lord Geoffrey wants to see you ere. . ." The boy faltered, gulped, and fell miserably silent.

"This is crazy! Why is my father at Château-du-Loir? That is barely twenty miles from here and he left Le Mans on Tuesday—"

"He got no farther than Château-du-Loir, for he fell ill that same night." The voice came from the doorway, and as the man stepped forward, Henry recognized one of his father's household knights. "The lad is telling you true, my lord Henry. The count is in a bad way, and asking for you."

"This makes no sense. How could he fall sick so fast?" Swinging out of bed, Henry grabbed for whatever clothes he could find. "Tell me," he demanded, his voice muffled within the folds of his tunic. "Tell me what happened."

"We reached the castle in late afternoon, and it was so hot that he decided to take a swim in the river. But that night he was stricken with chills and fever, and he did not feel well enough the next morning to continue on to Tours. None of us thought his ailment was serious, my lord, he least of all. But he got worse yesterday, bad enough to send for a doctor, and then, to fetch you." His eyes were hollow, his fatigue showing plainly, and something far more frightening to Henry—despair. "I rode all night . . ."

By now Henry was half dressed, reaching for the boots Ivo was holding out. "What does the doctor say?"

The man looked away. "He is dying, my lord."

Henry stared at him. "I do not believe you," he said roughly. "I do not believe you!"

AS they galloped south, Henry was oblivious to the dust and late-summer heat, equally unmindful of the curious stares of other travelers and the commiserating glances of his companions. His thoughts were racing ahead, toward the man lying at Château-du-Loir. Geoffrey had just celebrated his thirty-eighth birthday during their stay in Paris. He was in robust health. How could he be dying?

Henry set such a breakneck pace that his escort was hard pressed to keep up, and by the time Château-du-Loir came into view, their horses were well lathered and the men soaked in sweat. There was no challenge; the drawbridge was already lowering to admit them. As they rode into the inner bailey, two men hastened out to intercept them. Henry knew them both: Thomas de Loches, his father's chaplain and chancellor, and Jocelyn de Tours, his seneschal and longtime friend. Familiar faces, but contorted and ravaged now by grief.

Henry's stallion shied away as they approached, pawing at the dry, cracked earth, but Henry made no effort to rein the animal in. He sat frozen in the saddle, his hand clenched on the leather pommel, for as long as he did not dismount, they could not tell him that he was too late and his father was dead.

SHOCK hits men in different ways. It muted the gregarious Jocelyn de Tours, but the normally taciturn Thomas de Loches was suddenly voluble, compelled to give Henry every detail of his father's last three days, assuring him repeatedly that the doctor had done all he could. His words swirled about Henry like drifting leaves; every now and then he was able to catch one, but most floated down out of reach. His father had died within the hour. That was all he could think about as they entered the stairwell that led up to Geoffrey's bedchamber—that he was just an hour too late.

His steps flagged as they drew near the door. But the priest forged ahead, and he had no choice but to follow. The chamber was shuttered against the September sunlight; candles flickered wanly upon the table. Henry had yet to look toward his bed. "Was . . . was he shriven?"

The priest seemed to take that as a personal reproach. "Of course he was! I heard his confession myself, absolved him of his earthly sins, and put the Body and Blood of Christ upon his tongue. He went to His Maker in a state of grace, you may be sure."

"Was he in his senses?"

The chaplain nodded. "He knew he was dying, and his thoughts were for you. He made us all swear that we would acknowledge you as his lawful heir. To you, he bequeathed Anjou and Maine, and to his son Geoffrey, the castles of Chinon, Loudun, and Mirebeau. He urged you not to rule one province by the customs of another; each domain must be allowed its own identity, be it Normandy, Anjou, or England. When my lord Jocelyn praised him for bringing peace to Anjou and winning Normandy, he said . . . he said that you were his greatest success and his only regret was that he'd not live to see you crowned as King of England."

Jocelyn de Tours smiled sadly. "Actually, he called it 'that godforsaken isle,' for he never did have much regard for England or the English, did he? But that was only one of his regrets. He also said—"

"Nothing of importance," the priest cut in hastily. "My lord Henry . . . have you any questions?"

Henry shook his head, his mouth too dry for speech. But when they would have withdrawn, he reached out and caught Jocelyn's sleeve. Neither spoke for several moments, the Angevin baron offering Henry what he most needed just then: silent sympathy. Jocelyn watched Henry glance toward the bed and then away, the muscles in his throat tightening convulsively. "What else, Jocelyn? What did the chaplain not want me to hear?"

"Thomas speaks fluent French and Latin and Provençal, but bless him, humor remains an alien tongue. He was not trying to keep anything from you, Harry. He just thought it unseemly that Geoffrey should be joking on his deathbed. But that is what I'd rather remember, and I suspect you will, too, lad. What vexed him the most about dying, he said, was the wretched timing of it, that the sainted Bernard should now get to claim the credit!"

Jocelyn was smiling through tears. When he looked into Henry's face, he clasped the youth's shoulder in a gesture of wordless and futile comfort, then retreated quickly.

Henry did not move until the door closed. Approaching the bed with a leaden step, he stood staring down at his father's body. The doctor had done his work well, and Geoffrey's features were composed, his hands folded peacefully on his chest, a rosary loosely entwined around his fingers. His skin had a waxen cast, and his lips were pale, but his body had not yet begun to stiffen, and it was possible for Henry to imagine that he was merely asleep, that at any moment, he'd open an eye and wink.

But it was no practical joke and only the Abbot Bernard would be laughing. Henry reached out tentatively, his fingers brushing back the hair falling across Geoffrey's forehead. The skin still felt warm to the touch and he backed away. After a moment, he sank to his knees beside the bed. He did not pray, though. He wept.

GEOFFREY LE BEL was buried, at his request, in the cathedral church of St Julien in his mother's city of Le Mans, where he'd long ago wed the Empress Maude and where his eldest son had been born. After the funeral, Henry had no time to mourn. Riding for Angers, he claimed his legacy, accepting the homage of his Angevin vassals as the new Count of Anjou and Maine.

A BRISK October wind was sweeping through the priory of Notre-Dame-du-Pré, sending clouds scudding across the twilit sky and stripping the trees bare in a foretaste of winter. Heedless of the chill, Maude was standing in the doorway, wrapping her arms around herself to stop from shivering as she watched her sons dismounting in the priory garth.

It took a while for them to get their men settled, their horses led off to the priory stables. Eventually, though, Maude was able to usher them inside, toward the hearth.

"Are you hungry? I can send to the kitchen for food . . ." Her offer was met with shrugs and silence. They looked exhausted, numbed and overwhelmed by the magnitude of their loss, all the more devastating because it had been as sudden as an amputation. The sight of their grieving tore at Maude's heart. She would have given anything to be able to stanch their bleeding, but she did not know how. The ground she'd gained in these past three years was strewn again with pitfalls and snares, and Maude, the bravest of the brave, now found herself so afraid of making a misstep that she dared not move at all.

"Tell me about the funeral," she said at last. "Did it go as planned?"

Henry nodded, slumping down in a chair close to the hearth. She'd rarely seen him look so listless, drained of his usual exuberance and energy. Maude knew he'd been accustomed since early youth to shouldering a man's responsibilities. But she felt that burying his father was one burden too many. She'd have spared him that if she could, but she'd not been consulted. He'd taken it all upon himself, and she could see the cost now in the distance reflected in his eyes.

Will's eyes were red-rimmed, and he was blinking so rapidly that he felt the need for a mumbled complaint about the smoky hearth. "It was a fine funeral, Mama," he said and flushed when his voice cracked; he was fifteen now and had hoped that he'd outgrown that particular indignity. "We buried Papa in front of the High Altar, and Harry ordered a splendid tomb. Papa's chancellor chose the epitaph, though. 'By your sword, O Prince, the crowd of robbers is put to flight, peace flourishes, and churches enjoy tranquillity.'"

Will cast an oblique glance toward his eldest brother, then confided. "Harry says that if the fever had not killed Papa, he'd have died laughing at that epitaph. But I like it. What about you, Mama? What do you think?"

Maude hesitated, groping for a tactful response. But Geoff forestalled her. He'd yet to take off his mantle, and had been stalking about the chamber, giving off almost as much heat as the hearth. "Why ask her, Will?" he jeered. "The only epitaph she'd have favored would have been one that said, 'Hallelujah—dead at last!'"

Maude gasped, for this resentful seventeen-year-old youth had the power to wound her as none of her enemies ever could. Will looked stricken, and Henry dangerously dispassionate, a sure sign that his temper was about to erupt. Their disapproval only made Geoff all the more defiant. "I am just saying what the whole world knows," he insisted. "You hated Papa, and never made any secret of it. You can pretend now that you were not glad to hear he'd died, but what fool would believe—"

"Shut your mouth, Geoff!"

"You keep out of this, Harry! You may be Mama's pet, but I take no orders from you!"

"Yes," Henry said icily, "you do," and Geoff discovered that running headlong into reality hurt far worse than any of the bruises and scrapes of boyhood mishaps. He could not remember a time when he'd not been jealous of his elder brother. It had gnawed away at him, that Harry was the heir, the firstborn, the favored one, that someday he would inherit it all—the lands, the titles, the power. Someday. Far in the future. Not now. Harry was not supposed to have it so soon. It was not fair. None of it was fair. Papa was dead, and he'd not even gotten to say farewell. Mama would now play the grieving widow. And Harry . . . his vexing, insufferable, boastful brother Harry was now his liege lord. It had happened in Angers. He'd gone from rival to vassal as he'd watched Harry being invested as Count of Anjou and Maine. But it was not until tonight that he had fully understood all the implications of that ceremony, and the realization was more bitter than he could bear.

"I've a right to speak my mind, Harry!"

"If your mind was a well, it would be bone-dry," Henry said scathingly, and to Geoff's secret shame, he was the first to look away. He did not lack for reasons to detest his brother, but this was the most compelling reason of all—that his will was always the weaker of the two, the first to break.

Saving face as best he could, he muttered that he was going off to bed.

As much as he wanted to storm out in high dudgeon, he lost his nerve at the last moment, too shaken and miserable to dare to defy mother and brother both, and bade them goodnight with a poor pretense of civility. When they did not object, he felt as if he'd made his escape from enemy territory, and yet he was perversely aggrieved, too, that they'd been willing to let him go.

"Mama . . ." Will had far more freckles than either of his older brothers, scattered profusely across an open, appealing face, one that was not structured for secrets or scowls. He was the most equable of her sons, good-natured and accommodating, neither as moody as Henry nor as high-strung as Geoff. Henry and Geoff had inherited their fair share of Geoffrey's sardonic humor, and a goodly portion, too, of the infamous Angevin temper. But not Will. He was an anomaly, an innocent in a domain in which innocence did not often thrive, and while Maude's deepest love was reserved for Henry, her strongest protective urges were for Will. He was regarding her now with anxious blue eyes, slouching down further and further in his seat, like a turtle withdrawing into its shell. "Mama . . . Geoff was not right, was he? You were not glad when Papa died . . . ?"

"No!" Maude's protest was involuntary, indignant. She stepped toward her youngest, meaning to reassure him, when she happened to glance over at Henry. He, too, was watching her intently, even warily, and as their eyes met, she suddenly understood about the funeral.

It had been done very fast, allowing enough time for Henry's brothers to ride from Angers to Le Mans, but not for her to travel the much greater distance from Rouen. She'd not comprehended the reason for the rush, as Henry's claim to Anjou was uncontested; there were no rival claimants racing him to Angers. But now she knew, and she was sorry she did. Henry had been afraid to give her a chance to attend Geoffrey's funeral, afraid that she'd have refused.

"No, Will, I was not gladdened by your father's death. I will not lie to you, lad. There was a time—early in our marriage—when I might have been. But that was so long ago, Will, a lifetime ago. I was truly shocked by Geoffrey's death . . . and pained by it." If the pain had been more for her sons than for Geoffrey, she saw no reason to confess it. Will did not reply, but his shy half-smile told her that she'd found the right words, said what he needed to hear.

Turning then toward her firstborn, she reached out, letting her hand rest lightly on his shoulder. "I would have come, Henry," she said softly. "I swear to you that I would have come." He nodded and ducked his head, but not before she saw the tears shining behind his lashes.

"YOU look weary, my lady." Minna's fingers were not as nimble as they'd once been, but it never occurred to her to let one of Maude's younger attendants tend to her needs; nor had it occurred to Maude. She tilted her head back so Minna could finish unfastening her braids, just as she'd done every night for more years than either woman could remember.

"I am tired," Maude acknowledged, "too tired to sleep. I am afraid, Minna, that Geoff is slipping out of reach again. He is so angry, needing to blame someone for his father's death, and I suppose it is either me or the Almighty."

"You often despaired of ever breaking through all his walls," Minna pointed out, "but he was slowly letting some of his defenses down, and he will again. Every freeze is followed by a thaw, madame."

"I hope so, Minna, how I hope so. But I am not as confident as you, not about Geoff. You see, he could never forgive me for not loving Geoffrey. And now . . . now he cannot forgive me for loving Henry."

As candid as they usually were with each other, Minna had learned to weigh her words when discussing Maude's sons. She was very fond of Maude's youngest, for Will had a singular sweetness, a naïf-like charm that was uniquely his own. Henry, she adored. Even at his wayward worst, he was still "Madame's true son," whose destined kingship would redress all of her lady's struggles, all of her suffering.

But she viewed Geoff with a jaundiced German eye, seeing a spoiled young lordling with an overabundance of grievances and no sense of obligation or duty, only a sense of entitlement. That was an opinion, however, that she could never share with Geoff's mother, and she concentrated, instead, upon brushing out Maude's hair, still a deep, rich black, although her next birthday would be her fiftieth.

"They were afraid that I'd welcomed Geoffrey's death," Maude confided. "I swore to them that I had not, and that was the truth, Minna. I'd be the last one to doubt Henry's abilities, but he is still so young. Geoffrey could have done what I cannot—keep the peace in Normandy whilst Henry seeks to overthrow Stephen. I can fight for my son, but not on the battlefield. It always comes back to that. Henry had need of his father. There was a time when I was not willing to admit that, but—"

The knock was so soft that Maude was not sure at first what she'd heard. When it came again, Minna hastened over and opened the door. Henry paused on the threshold at sight of his mother's unbound hair. "You're getting ready for bed. I'd not realized it was so late."

Before he could back out, Maude beckoned him in. "I always have time to talk with you." Minna had already disappeared, conveniently remembering a sudden need for night wine. Reclaiming her seat, Maude watched her firstborn prowl restlessly about the chamber. "Is Will abed?"

Henry nodded. "It upset Will that Papa left Chinon and the other castles to Geoff, nothing to him. I explained that these castles had long been regarded as the rightful appanage of the House of Anjou's younger son, that Papa was merely following family tradition, and it in no way meant that he'd favored Geoff. I did my best to assure Will of this, and I also assured him that he'd not be left to beg his bread. But I think it would help, Mama, to hear it from you, too."

"I'll speak to him tomorrow," Maude promised. "I'll remind him that once he is of age, we'll find him an heiress to wed."

"There is something else I want to discuss with you, Mama. It is about what happened in Paris."

"I was wondering about that," Maude admitted. "Why did you change your mind about relinquishing the Vexin?"

"I daresay you've heard the rumors about the French king's troubled marriage. Well, the rumors are true. Louis has decided to divorce his wife. And once he does, I mean to marry Eleanor myself."

"Good God!" Maude sat back in her chair, openmouthed. "You've always been one for surprises, Henry, but this time you've truly outdone yourself!"

"Thank you," he said dryly, "assuming that was meant as a compliment?"

"You sound very sure that this will come to pass. I gather, then, that you and Eleanor have reached some sort of understanding?"

The corner of Henry's mouth twitched. "I think you can safely say that."

"No wonder you were willing to give up the Vexin! You do realize, though, what a hornet's nest you'll be stirring up? You could have no better stepping-stone to the English throne than Aquitaine. But the French king will view this marriage as unforgivable treachery."

"So Papa said, too," Henry conceded.

"You and Eleanor—who would ever have guessed?"

"Let's hope no one does, Mama, not until we're safely wed."

She nodded. "Henry . . . you know how much I want you to be King of England. But I also want you to be happy. For the highborn, marriage is a practical matter, indeed, with no allowance made for sentiment. A political union. A means of gaining territory. A way to forge an alliance. No one ever asks if the couple is mismatched, if they are likely to be compatible. But believe me, those are not frivolous questions. You may be seeking a consort and wedding a duchess, but you'll be living with a woman, and now is the time to consider her. I know you want Aquitaine. Do you also want Eleanor?"

He regarded her impassively, for he'd inherited Geoffrey's irritating knack of being able to mask his thoughts when he chose. "Yes," he said, "I want her."

"Well . . . then I can give you more than my approval. I can give you my blessings, too."

"Truly?" Henry's smile offered her a sudden glimpse of sunlight breaking through the clouds, dispelling the oppressive mourning gloom. "Credit where due, Mama, you can surprise, too. Papa was so sure you'd have misgivings about the marriage!"

A tart rejoinder hovered on her lips, that Geoffrey had not known her nearly as well as he'd imagined. It went unsaid. Instead, she reminded herself that their marital war was over at last. No more uneasy truces, just the eternal peace of the grave. As she embraced Henry, she could not help thinking, though, that the final victory had been Geoffrey's. She knew that her sons loved and respected her; at least Henry and Will did. But she doubted that they'd have grieved as much for her as they now grieved for Geoffrey.

THE storm caught North Wales by surprise, for it was only November. The snow started during the night, and the Welsh awoke to find that winter had arrived with a vengeance. By midday the wind had intensified; soon even the silhouetted peaks of Eryri were no longer visible. Ranulf had not seen so much snow since he'd been trapped in the siege of Oxford. As the storm increased in severity, it began to seem as if Trefriw were under siege, too, but by a more formidable foe than Stephen. Fortunately, this was an enemy that could be safely waited out, and the only weapon the besieged needed was patience. But that evening Rhiannon went into labor.

She was not due for another fortnight, and they hoped at first that these were false labor pains. It soon became apparent, however, that the baby was coming—in the midst of a blizzard, with no midwife. Ranulf had been desperate enough to try to fetch the woman; he got no farther than the stable, barely made it back to the hall.

That night seemed endless. Neither Ranulf nor Rhodri slept at all, huddled by the fire, waiting for word. Above-stairs in the birthing chamber, Rhiannon struggled to deliver her child, attended by the willing but inexperienced hands of Enid, Eleri, Olwen, and Heledd, their elderly cook. Downstairs, Ranulf struggled, too, seeking to convince himself that all would go as it ought. But Enid was barren, Eleri and Olwen were virgins, and Heledd's own childbearing more than thirty years distant.

Men were barred from the birthing chamber, but from time to time, Enid or Eleri would emerge with forced smiles and assurances that grew less and less convincing with repetition. Bechan, the serving-maid, crept about like a stray cat, shrinking into corners and daubing at her eyes with the corner of her apron. It was obvious that she was already mourning her mistress, and Ranulf could not trust himself to glance in her direction, lest he banish her from the hall. But how could he blame the wench for lacking faith when he had so little of it himself?

With the coming of dawn, the blizzard at last showed signs of abating. White waves no longer swept across the bailey, obscuring all traces of land; for the first time in many hours, Ranulf could make out the sloping contours of the stable roof. Pulling up the hood of his mantle, he plunged out into the bailey. The cold seared his lungs, brought tears to his eyes. Wading through drifts deep enough to drown in, he slogged toward the stable. It was slow, hazardous going, but he battled on until he reeled into the stable, sinking down on a bale of hay. The horses peered over their stall doors, grateful for the human company, hungry for their breakfast of fodder and hay. Ranulf was still trying to get his breath back when the door banged again and two more hooded figures staggered in.

He'd not realized that he was being followed, for their cries had been carried away by the gusting snow. Like him, they headed toward the bales of hay and collapsed against the wall. Padarn recovered first, his the resilience of youth, and volunteered to tend to the horses. Panting and wheezing, Rhodri blew on his chapped hands, stamped his feet to warm them, and brushed snow off his eyebrows, mustache, and even his lashes. "Have you lost your wits altogether?" he accused. "How far did you think you'd get?"

"The storm seemed to be easing up. Since the midwife lives only a few miles from here, I thought I could make it—"

"Christ Jesus, Ranulf, where is your common sense? This was a fool's gamble if ever I saw one!"

Ranulf could not argue the point. "I did not realize how bad it still was, not until I was out in it. But I had to try, Uncle. It has been more than twelve hours. I know the women say that is not unusual, but would they tell us if it were? So much can go wrong in a birthing, and without a midwife . . ." His shoulders sagged and he said, very low and fast, "My mother died in childbed, and the babe with her."

"I know, lad, I know. It is never easy for the woman, nor for the man, either. I remember all too well what the waiting was like, each time my Nesta was brought to bed of one of our bairns. I could not help noticing how raw your nerves became as Rhiannon's time drew nigh. None of us reckoned upon this accursed storm, but you were already sorely afeared. You would not even choose names for the baby, lest you tempt fate. This is not like you, Ranulf. Why are you so loath of a sudden to let yourself hope for the best?"

Ranulf's smile was bleak. "For most of my life, I not only hoped for the best, I expected it, as if it were my god-given birthright. That was the worst sort of arrogance, Uncle, and it brought nothing but grief—not just to me, but to the innocent, too. I truly thought the rest of my life would be penance for these sins; I deserved no less . . ."

"But you do not deserve Rhiannon and your babe . . . is that what you fear? That God means to punish you for daring to be happy?" Rhodri slid over on the bale until he was close enough to grasp the younger man's arm. "Why is it that the Almighty forgives us more readily than we forgive ourselves? Listen to me, lad. I cannot tell you there is no danger in childbirth. But I can tell you how good you've been for my daughter, how much—"

"Come quick!" Padarn had been keeping vigil at the door. Spinning around, he gestured urgently. "They are shouting for us!"

Lurching to their feet, Ranulf and Rhodri hastily followed Padarn out into the snow. Linking arms, they ploughed through the drifts, for they now had the wind at their backs. As they stumbled toward the hall, Eleri appeared in the doorway. Her hair was in disarray, her color ashen, her eyes swollen with fatigue, her gown splattered with blood. But her smile was incandescent.

THE entire household had crowded into Rhiannon's chamber to admire her newborn son, everyone from the timid Bechan to the burly stable grooms. She accepted their congratulations and good wishes with exhausted aplomb, but was grateful when Eleri eventually took charge and insisted that they all withdraw so she could rest. She groped quickly for Ranulf's hand, letting him know she wanted him to stay, needlessly so, as nothing short of force could have dislodged him from her bedside. A reluctant Rhodri was the last to leave, pushed out by his wife and daughter as he craned to get one more loving look at his grandson. Once they were finally alone, Ranulf leaned over and kissed his wife, then his son.

Rhiannon smiled tiredly. The baby had begun to whimper, and she drew back the bed covers, guiding his little mouth toward her breast. He needed no further urging, was soon sucking contentedly upon her nipple. She'd refused from the outset to consider a wet nurse, and Ranulf now understood why; nursing was an especially intimate act for a mother unable to see her child.

"What color is his hair?" she asked, and he reached over to stroke the infant's head; the silky, scant hair was as soft as the downy plumage of a baby chick.

"It is hard to say," he teased, "for he is well-nigh bald. If I had to guess, I'd say a flaxen shade. It's like to change anyway. Which is fine with me; I'd not mind if it turned green."

"I think I'd prefer a more conventional color." Rhiannon's smile ended as a yawn. "I want you to name him, Ranulf."

"Are you sure, love? It would not be a Welsh name."

She squeezed his hand in reply. "You wish to call him Robert, after your brother?"

Ranulf gently wiped away the milk dribbling down his son's chin. "No," he said, "I want to name him Gilbert."

49

BEAUGENCY, FRANCE

March 1152

In late September, Louis and Eleanor had begun a royal progress through her domains. They were welcomed with enthusiasm, for Eleanor had always been extremely popular with her people, and they were heartened by rumors of an impending split with her "foreign" French husband. These rumors gained credence as the weeks passed, for in the course of the progress, French garrisons and Crown officials were replaced with men of Eleanor's choosing, men of Aquitaine. The French sovereigns celebrated their Christmas court at Limoges; it was to be their last one as man and wife. In February, they parted, Eleanor returning to Poitiers, Louis to Paris. By now all knew a divorce was both imminent and inevitable.

On the Friday before Palm Sunday, the Archbishop of Sens convened a Church Council at the royal castle of Beaugency, not far from Orléans. Evidence was presented that the French king and his queen were related within the prohibited degree, for her great-grandmother had been a granddaughter of his great-grandfather. The clerics were not long in delivering their solemn verdict—that the marriage must be annulled on grounds of consanguinity. The young princesses, Marie and Alix, were declared to be legitimate and their custody was granted to the French king. Eleanor relinquished her queenship, and resumed those titles that were hers by birthright: Duchess of Aquitaine and Countess of Poitou. The French king was now free to wed again, to seek a wife able to give him a son and heir. At the prodding of Eleanor's advocate, the Archbishop of Bordeaux, the Council agreed that she was free to wed, too, but of course not without Louis's consent, for her former husband was still her king and liege lord.

THE following morning was a mild, sunlit Saturday, a good day for travel. But the Count of Vermandois did not doubt that his sister-in-law would have ridden out in the teeth of a raging gale, so eager did she seem to leave Beaugency and her former life behind. He would be sorry to see her go, and he said so now, telling her that the royal court would be a dull place without her, that her going would break male hearts and quench candles all over Paris.

Eleanor smiled, for she liked Raoul. His gallantry might be a bit heavy-handed at times, but she'd take that any day over the sort of somber piety she'd been living with for the past fourteen years. Gathering her into his arms, Raoul winked over her shoulder at his wife. "You do not mind if I run off with Eleanor for a few weeks, do you, Petra?"

"Of course not," Petronilla said absently, not hearing a word he'd said. She was finding this harder than she'd expected—saying farewell to her sister, knowing how drastically their lives were about to change. "I shall miss you, Eleanor," she said, summoning up a game but forlorn smile. "Who will I have to quarrel with once you're gone?"

"That is what husbands are for." As the sisters embraced, Eleanor found her eyes misting, too. "You must visit me at Poitiers later in the spring," she said, adding significantly, "I will tell you when to come."

Petronilla nodded, and Raoul cheerfully promised to accompany her. The two women said nothing, for it was understood that Petronilla would find a way to come alone. Raoul was Louis's cousin and liegeman and seneschal of France; they could not compromise his honour by allowing him to attend Eleanor's wedding to Henry Fitz Empress. Eleanor had no illusions about what was to come. There was a time when she'd been careless of consequences, but no longer. Louis would see her marriage as a grievous betrayal, both of the man and of the monarch. What would he do? She knew him so well, and yet she was still not sure how he'd react. She felt confident that she and Harry would be a match for him. But she was determined to shield any others from Louis's wrath, and so Raoul must be kept in ignorance, for his own protection.

The great hall was thronged with clergy and curious onlookers, eager to watch this historic parting between the French king and his notorious queen. As soon as Eleanor appeared, heads turned and necks craned. The men who'd command her escort were waiting by the door: Saldebreuil de Sanzay, her constable, and Geoffrey de Rancon, Lord of Taillebourg. She smiled at sight of them, for they were more than loyal vassals; they were friends, men who would willingly lay down their lives to keep her safe. Louis was nearby, engaged in conversation with the Archbishops of Rouen and Reims, not yet aware of her presence. She was about to start toward him when she saw the tall, white-haired figure by the hearth, his simple monk's habit contrasting dramatically with the colorfully clad nobles and the ornately garbed princes of the Church. The holy man of France, the venerated and honoured Abbot of Clairvaux. Her sainted enemy.

Abbot Bernard greeted her with frigid formality. He so resembled one of the patriarchs of old—pale and haggard, burning dark eyes and flowing long hair—that Eleanor wondered cynically if he'd deliberately cultivated the image. "I understand," she said, "that you convinced Louis not to bring my daughters to Beaugency to bid me farewell. He told me that he would have done so—if not for you, my lord abbot."

He was quite untroubled by the accusation. "That is true," he said calmly. "I thought it was for the best. Such a meeting was bound to be painful."

"Am I to believe, then, that you were acting out of Christian kindness?"

"I care for all of God's lost lambs, madame, even the foolish ones who keep straying into the hills where wolves prowl and dangers lurk. The Lord forgives much, provided that there is true repentance. It is always possible to come back into the fold, back into grace."

"With you as my guide? I'd rather take my chances with the wolves."

"Take care, madame, lest you imperil your immortal soul. You do but prove I had good reason to keep your daughters away from your baneful influence." As wrathful as he was, the abbot still remembered to keep his voice down, for this was not a conversation for others to hear. "Your lack of gratitude should not surprise me, though, given your lamentable lack of decorum and discretion—"

"Gratitude? My apologies, my lord abbot. It seems I've been maligning you unfairly, for you do have a sense of humor, after all!"

"It is foolhardy to court danger, madame, but it is lunacy to court damnation. You do indeed owe me a debt of gratitude. If not for my forbearance, you might have been cast aside for adultery rather than consanguinity."

"It is also foolhardy, my lord abbot, to hold your foes too cheaply. Your convictions to the contrary, most women are not idiots. I could not have been accused of adultery, for you have no proof, and well you know it. And even if you'd found men willing to swear falsely that it was so, a verdict of adultery would have prohibited Louis from marrying again . . . as you well know, too."

"I see no point in continuing this conversation. If you would spit upon salvation, so be it, then. I leave your sins to God. Fortunately for the king and for France, he is now free of your unholy spell, free to choose a wife devout and docile and virtuous, a wife who will give him the heir you could not."

Eleanor's eyes shone with a greenish glitter. "What a pity," she said, "that the Blessed Virgin Mary is not available, for she would have suited his needs admirably."

Bernard drew in his breath with a sibilant hiss. "You are an evil woman, wanton and truly wicked, and you will indeed suffer for—"

"No—no, she is not!" Neither Eleanor nor the abbot had heard Louis's approach, and they both spun around at the sudden sound of his voice. "You are wrong, Abbot Bernard," he said, with a firmness Eleanor had seen him show all too rarely. "I know her far better than you, and there is no evil in her soul, only a misguided sense of . . . of levity."

Eleanor was tempted to retort that to a man like the abbot, levity might well be the greatest sin of all, but she did not, for Louis's sake. The abbot was regarding the king with the pained patience of a tutor for a likable but slow student. "You are sometimes too tolerant, my liege," he said, "too forgiving for your own good."

That, Eleanor couldn't resist. "Did not Our Lord Christ preach that forgiveness was a virtue?" she murmured, earning herself a toxic look from the abbot, a reproachful one from the king. Seizing her elbow, Louis steered her away from Bernard, toward a recessed window seat. He did not suggest that they sit; the time was past for that.

"Why is it that turmoil and commotion always follow after you as faithfully as that dog of yours?" Louis asked, pointing to the greyhound that had trailed them into the window alcove. But he sounded more plaintive than protesting, even mustering up a sad smile as their eyes met. His was an easy face to read; it took one glance to reassure Eleanor that he'd not overheard her Blessed Virgin gibe. She was glad, for it was Bernard she'd wanted to wound, not Louis.

That was not always so. There'd been times when she'd yearned for words sharp enough to draw blood, to leave ugly scars. She'd blamed Louis for much that had gone wrong in their marriage, for not being bolder or able to laugh at life's perversities, for not being more like the swaggering, spirited, roguish men of her House, for no longer heeding her advice as he'd done in their first years together, for loving God far more than he could ever love her, and for the reluctant desire and sense of shame that he'd brought to their marriage bed.

But she'd not hated him for these failings—anger and frustration and occasional contempt, but not hatred. That had come only after Antioch, after Louis had accused her of harboring an incestuous passion for her uncle and threatened to have her bound and gagged and dragged away by force if need be. Ever a realist, she'd yielded, far too proud to fight a war she could not hope to win; she was learning that women must pick their battles with care, that strategy mattered more than strength. Eventually Louis had apologized and swore upon the True Cross that he knew her to be innocent. But by then it was too late. By then her uncle had been slain by the Turks, his impaled head rotting above the caliph's palace in the hot Baghdad sun, and Eleanor could not look upon her husband without Raymond's doomed and bloodied spectre coming between them.

But now that she'd regained her freedom, she found herself remembering how it had been at first for them, a fifteen-year-old bride and her sixteen-year-old groom, shyly appealing, awed by her beauty and eager to please her. Before he'd begun to yearn for the peace of the cloister, before those poor souls had died in the flames of a Vitry church, before the miscarriage and daughters instead of sons, before his hair shirt and her disgrace, before the crusade and Antioch and Raymond's needless death, before Abbot Bernard. For a poignant moment, she could see that long-lost youth reflected in the depths of translucent blue eyes. And then the memory faded and she was looking at a man decent and ineffectual and despairing, a man she could pity but not respect and never love.

"I promise you," he said earnestly, "that I will not speak ill of you to our daughters."

She knew better. His intentions were good; they always were. But he would never be able to forgive her for Henry Fitz Empress, no more than she'd been able to forgive him for her uncle Raymond.

"I ought to have brought them," he said, striving to be fair. "You can see them whenever you come to Paris, that I promise you, too. I would ask, though, that . . . you not come for a while, Eleanor."

"No," she agreed, "not for a while." Knowing that she'd never be welcome in Paris. She had to believe she'd see her daughters again, for she would never give up what was hers. But as Louis leaned over and kissed her circumspectly on the cheek, she realized—as he did not—that it was not likely they'd ever meet again. A door was slamming shut, and there'd be no going back.

There was nothing more to be said. Louis seemed to grasp that, too, for he stepped aside and wished her "Godspeed," which struck her as an odd epitaph for a marriage. "I wish you well, Louis," she said, and discovered that she meant it. "I wish you happiness, a wife with no 'misguided sense of levity,' and the son you so crave." And that, too, she meant—almost.

Raoul and Petronilla followed Eleanor from the hall, out into the bailey, where her armed escort waited. Uncomfortably aware of Abbot Bernard's disapproving gaze, Louis did not. Instead, he retreated from the hall with what dignity he could. Once he'd reached the privacy of his bedchamber, he unlatched the shutters, leaned out in time to see Eleanor riding across the bailey, out of the castle and out of his life. He watched from the window, mourning what they'd lost and what they'd never had. He kept vigil until she'd disappeared into the distance, until even the dust had settled again onto the grooved, pitted road. But she'd never looked back.

AN early spring had begun to repair the damage done by winter. The trees were budding and the wild daffodils known as Lent lilies were gilding the river meadows with splashes of gold; the Loire shimmered like liquid silver, reflecting the sky and clouds and the soaring spirits of the Aquitanians. Most of the men in Eleanor's escort detail were Southerners, never happy in the less hospitable domains of the French king. They were a different breed, these sons and daughters of Aquitaine, for theirs was a warmer, more indolent clime, a land of rich harvests and fertile vineyards and lush emerald valleys. They understood that life was short and unpredictable and therefore it behooved a prudent man to taste as many of its pleasures as he could. If their exuberant joie de vivre conflicted with the Church's stringent teachings about the mortification of the flesh, that never seemed to trouble them much. They were glad to be escaping the rigors of northern winters, even gladder to be leaving behind the French king's austere, staid court. The jokes flew by faster than the miles as they galloped south, so delighted were they to be bringing their beautiful duchess home.

Not all of the members of Eleanor's household were born and bred in Aquitaine. One of her ladies-in-waiting came from a wilder region, the fog-drifted seacoast of Brittany. Yolande had been with Eleanor only a few months; it had been her misfortune to join the French queen's retinue just as Eleanor's queenship was breathing its last. But if she minded trading Paris for Poitiers, she showed no sign of it. Riding alongside the Lady Colette, Eleanor's longtime attendant, she kept up a running commentary of cheerful observations and ingenuous questions.

They would be back at Poitiers for Easter, would they not? Was it true that the famed troubadour and poet Bernard de Ventadour would be joining the duchess's court? Did Colette think the duchess was in true danger from would-be suitors? Would they still be stopping for the night at Blois?

Why had the duchess been so loath to accept the invitation they'd gotten from its young count? He'd sounded quite charming, judging from his letter. And very highborn, for was he not the English king's brother?

Yolande was almost as much in awe of the black-eyed, elegant Colette as she was of the duchess herself. Colette's moods were as changeable as the weather; she could go from sun to frost and back to sun fast enough to set Yolande's head to spinning. Today, though, the forecast seemed favorable. Colette listened to Yolande's chatter with good-humored indulgence, answering her queries and making wry asides of her own.

They'd soon be back in Poitiers, she assured the Breton teenager, within four days if all went well. She'd not be at all surprised if Bernard de Ventadour sought the duchess's patronage; poets and troubadours would be flocking to Aquitaine like migrating swallows in the spring. Indeed, there was a very real danger now that the duchess was free to wed again; why did Yolande think they had so large an escort?

One of Eleanor's household knights dropped back beside them, presenting Colette with a fragrant sprig he'd just plucked from a flowering blackthorn bush. She thanked him with a coquettish flutter of her lashes, a hinted smile, but after he'd spurred his stallion on, she dropped the blossoms down into the dust, and the softhearted Yolande winced, hoping the knight hadn't seen.

As if they'd not been interrupted, Colette resumed the conversation. Yes, she confirmed, they'd still be passing the night at Blois, but in St Lomer's Abbey, not the castle. Count Theobald had been too importunate for the duchess's liking. Lady Eleanor thought he'd seemed much too eager for her to accept his hospitality. As for his charm, that was no recommendation. Speaking from her own experience, she'd learned that most charming men were about as trustworthy as Barbary pirates. And no, Count Theobald was the English king's nephew, not his brother. Yolande had confused the son with the father, Count Theobald of Champagne and Blois, King Stephen's elder brother, who'd died in January. The eldest son, Henry, had inherited Champagne, and the second son, Theobald, got Blois. Surely Yolande had not forgotten about the plight troth?

Yolande blushed, for while she did have difficulty keeping track of the various barons and lords and peers of the realm, she ought never to have gotten so muddled about Theobald of Blois. It was less than two months since Theobald's brother, Henry, the new Count of Champagne, had pledged to wed the little Princess Marie. The plight troth had provoked a sharp quarrel between the French king and Eleanor, for she had not been consulted, and was angry that she'd been given no say in a decision that would shape the entire course of her daughter's life.

Yolande's elder sisters had been married off in that same summary way; her father had conferred with neither her mother nor the prospective brides beforehand. Nor was it likely that she'd be consulted, in her turn. But that was the way of the only world she knew, and it had not occurred to Yolande to object.

It had occurred to Eleanor, although the French king and his counselors had gone ahead with the plight troth, nonetheless, and six-year-old Marie was now the Count of Champagne's betrothed. How soon she would become his wife would depend upon her father and husband-to-be, for in that, too, her mother would not be consulted.

Just as Yolande knew Eleanor would not be heeded when the time came to choose another husband for her. The man would have to meet the French king's approval, and mayhap the Abbot Bernard's, too, to be judged as a loyal vassal, one worthy enough to be entrusted with Aquitaine. As to what Eleanor might want, that would not matter much in the councils of power. Yolande had been bedazzled from the first by her glamorous, audacious mistress, and she thought it would break her heart to see her lady snared and earthbound for the rest of her days, wings clipped so she could no longer fly.

Nudging her mare closer to Colette's sleek white mule, she said diffidently, "Colette . . . what does the future hold for our lady?"

"You need not fret on her behalf, child. This I can tell you for true, that the duchess could teach a cat about landing on its feet." Colette was frowning into the distance. The sun had set and they were losing the light; they'd soon have to bring out the lanterns. "Look," she said, "something is afoot."

Yolande peered into the gathering dusk, and saw that Colette was right. As a horseman emerged from a grove of trees beside the road, her pulse sped up. Colette was urging her mule forward and she followed hastily. But by now it was evident that the rider was alone and some of her alarm eased. Whatever this was about, at least it was not an ambush.

Eleanor had reined in her mare. Protectively flanked by Saldebreuil de Sanzay and Geoffrey de Rancon, she watched with wary curiosity as the stranger was led forward. He was young, not much more than twenty, dark as a Spaniard, with bold, admiring eyes and courtly manners that did not jibe with the plain homespun of his garb. His cap was off with a sweep, and the movement gave her a brief glimpse of a sword hilt as his mantle parted. "Madame," he said, "I've been watching for your approach."

Eleanor beckoned him closer. "Why?"

He did not mince words. "To warn you away from Blois," he said bluntly.

Eleanor's eyes narrowed. "Count Theobald?"

He nodded. "If you enter the city tonight, you'll not find it easy to leave on the morrow. The count was sorely aggrieved, my lady, when you declined to stay at his castle. He means to remedy that, by force if need be. He has it in mind to insist that you lodge with him rather than the monks, and I daresay he has a biddable priest ready and willing to perform a hasty marriage ceremony once you've . . . accepted the inevitable."

Eleanor's mouth tightened. "Accepted the inevitable." A discreet description, indeed, of abduction and rape. Beside her, Geoffrey de Rancon was swearing under his breath, revealing a command of obscenity that any sailor might have envied. Saldebreuil de Sanzay was more controlled, but no less enraged. They'd known they might run into trouble. They'd not expected, though, that they'd encounter it so soon, within a day of the divorce.

"So the hunt has already begun, has it?" she said grimly.

Rancon was still fuming. "We would never have let that whelp take you, my lady—never!"

"I know that, Geoffrey. But it would have been an ugly clash and likely a bloody one. Men ought not to die because of a boastful lordling's lust—not my men, by God. They deserve better than that." Eleanor wasted no more time fulminating upon Count Theobald's treachery. "Tell the others," she said, her eyes resting speculatively upon their Good Samaritan. "You've done me a service I will not soon forget. I was very fortunate that you somehow became privy to Theobald's plans, a remarkable stroke of luck . . . if that is indeed what it was?"

Even in the fading light, she could see a flash of white as he grinned. "You are quick, my lady, as well as fair. As you guessed, luck had nothing to do with it. As soon as word got out that the Church synod would be convened at Beaugency, we knew you'd have to take this road back to Poitiers. I was sent into Blois a week ago, charged to see to your safety whilst you were in the city. Sometimes a lone man can do more good than an army."

"If it is the right man," Eleanor agreed, and he grinned again.

"It was not that difficult to root out the count's acorns. He was careless and one for bragging." A disdainful shrug. "The Almighty might not look upon clumsiness as a sin, but I do, and it gladdens me greatly that the count will have so much to repent upon the morrow."

"I value a man who knows his own worth. I could easily find a place for you in my household if you were interested. But you are not . . . are you?"

They smiled at each other in perfect understanding. "No, my lady. I am quite content as I am, serving my lord Duke of Normandy."

Rancon and Sanzay exchanged startled glances, even more perplexed when Eleanor showed no surprise at all. "You must thank your lord for me," she said. "Who knows, mayhap one day I may have the opportunity to thank him myself."

He laughed softly, the triumphant laugh of a man who'd acquitted himself well and who would soon be reaping the rewards of it, and then offered to show them a little-used lane that would allow them to detour safely around the city, so they'd be miles away by the time Theobald began to suspect that his scheme had gone awry.

But as Eleanor started to turn her mare, Sanzay drew her aside for a roadside colloquy, switching from French to their native Provençal. "My lady, I confess to some unease about all this. How can we be sure the Duke of Normandy is acting in good faith? He might well want to thwart Theobald in order to claim you for himself. We'll be entering his territory once we draw near to Tours. What if this man of his is luring you into a trap?"

"He can be trusted. You need not fear."

Sanzay was puzzled by her certainty, rather than reassured. "How can you be so confident of that?"

"Because a man need not take by force what is to be given to him freely, Saldebreuil."

It was so dark now that she could no longer see his face, but she could hear the changed rhythm of his breathing. "Are you saying what I think you are?" he asked at last, and Eleanor laughed.

"Yes, I am . . . and now you know just how much I trust you, dear friend. Hold your questions, though, until after we've left Blois—and its hungry young count—far behind in the dust!"

BY riding all night, Eleanor and her entourage reached safety at Tours, the capital of Henry Fitz Empress's province of Touraine. They arrived at the abbey of St Martin's in time to attend Palm Sunday Mass, and then collapsed gratefully upon the beds provided for them in the monastery's guest quarters.

The next morning, they were on the road again, sending out scouts to reconnoiter the terrain ahead. They'd left the fine weather of Passion Week behind at Tours; the sky was lowering and they were caught in a brief, drenching shower before noon. They were just a few miles from Port-de-Piles, intending to ford the River Creuse there, when one of their scouts came into view, traveling at such a fast gallop that they were alerted even before he'd gotten within shouting range.

Geoffrey de Rancon and Saldebreuil de Sanzay spurred their horses out to meet him. So did Eleanor, who was never one for waiting. "Bad news, my lady," Sanzay declared as she drew up alongside them. "There are men lying in wait at Port-de-Piles, and I think we can safely assume that they're up to no good."

Eleanor mouthed an unladylike oath. "They have most peculiar courting customs in these parts." But her irony was outward camouflage; inwardly, she seethed, outraged that her divorce had of a sudden made her fair game, that there were so many men willing to chase her down like a prize doe. "Do you have any idea who this latest suitor might be?"

To her surprise, Rancon nodded. "The lad here says it is as maladroit an ambush as he's ever seen. So sure are they of taking you unaware at the ford that they did not bother to post any guards themselves. He had no trouble getting close enough to look them over, and recognized their leader straightaway. Another young lordling on the prowl, and to add insult to injury, this cub's but a second son! Passing strange, that the Duke of Normandy should have done you such a good turn at Blois, for his brother now seeks to do you an ill one at Port-de-Piles."

"God and His good angels!" Geoffrey Fitz Empress was all of what ... seventeen? No, nigh on eighteen. She'd made it a point to learn as much as she could about Henry's background, and that included his brothers, but she'd certainly not anticipated meeting one of them in an ambush by the River Creuse. She shook her head, marveling at life's odd twists and turns. "This gives a whole new meaning to the saying, 'keeping it in the family.'"

Rancon looked mystified, but Sanzay gave a startled snort of laughter. "You have a wicked tongue, my lady," he said with a grin, "damn me if you do not!"

"Someone else said that, too. Abbot Bernard, I believe." It was drizzling again, and Eleanor pulled up her hood as the raindrops began to splatter about them in earnest. "We'll have to find another crossing. Does anyone know of one?"

Rancon did. "There is another ford downstream, not far from where the Creuse and the Vienne flow together." He laughed suddenly. "With luck, the Fitz Empress stripling will be waiting out in the rain for the rest of the day. I'd love to see his face when he realizes he's been outwitted. What a surprise the lad is in for!"

Eleanor winked at Sanzay. "Indeed, he is," she said blandly, "but you do not know the half of it!"

SAFE in her own domains, Eleanor lingered for two days at her uncle's castle at Châtellerault, and on Thursday of Holy Week, she was at last approaching the city she most loved, perched on a bluff overlooking the River Clain, the ancient capital of Poitou—Poitiers.

The city walls shone in the spring sunlight, graceful church spires reaching up toward the heavens, and as ever, Eleanor's heart rose at the sight. Of all the loves of her life, her first and last and greatest would always be for this land of her birth. Aquitaine was in her blood; even its air seemed sweeter to her. She could see the turrets of her palace now, rising up into the sky, crowned with clouds, and the joy of her homecoming was tempered somewhat by regret, for marriage to Henry Fitz Empress might well lead to a throne, but it would also lead away from Aquitaine.

Coming from the north, they crossed the Clain at the bridge called Pont de Rochereuil. It was then that they heard the bells, pealing out across the city, filling the valley with silvery, celestial sound. Eleanor was baffled, for by tradition, church bells were muted during the final three days before Easter, when they would ring in the Resurrection. So why were they chiming now?

Saldebreuil de Sanzay was the first to comprehend. Turning in the saddle, he smiled at Eleanor. "The bells are for you, my lady," he said. "They are welcoming you home."

50

BURY ST EDMUNDS, ENGLAND

April 1152

THE Black Monks of St Edmund's Abbey had gathered for their daily chapter meeting. They opened with a prayer to the Blessed St Edmund, whose holy shrine attracted such large and profitable crowds of pilgrims to their monastery. After reading aloud a chapter of their Benedictine Rule, they moved on to more secular concerns: a discussion of finances, the need to find a new tenant for one of the abbey's manors, the allocation of weekly duties among the monks. When Abbot Ording stepped up to the lectern, his audience expected to hear the familiar words "Let us now speak of matters of discipline," freeing the brothers to come forward and accuse themselves—or one another—of mistakes, misdeeds, and occasional sins. Instead, Abbot Ording said somberly, "I have news to impart. The king and his son, the Count of Boulogne, will be arriving on the morrow, and they will, of course, expect us to offer them the hospitality of our abbey."

A royal visit was never an unmixed blessing, for the cost of entertaining a king's entourage could strip an abbey's larders bare, especially if the king chose to linger in their midst. But the dismay that greeted Abbot Ording's announcement went well beyond economic anxieties. The sad fact was that in this, the seventeenth year of Stephen's reign, the English king found himself at war with his own Church.

This latest clash had been the most serious one yet. Stephen had become convinced that the only way to safeguard the throne for his son was to have Eustace crowned in his own lifetime, in accordance with Continental custom. But the Archbishop of Canterbury refused to cooperate and Stephen had at last lost all patience. Early in the year, he'd summoned a Church Council to London and demanded that they agree to anoint Eustace then and there. The archbishop had again balked, but this time his refusal rocked Stephen's throne to its very foundations, for he claimed to be acting under direct orders from the Pope, who would not recognize Eustace's right to an ill-gotten crown, one obtained by perjury.

Never before had the papacy spoken out so boldly against Stephen's kingship. So great was Stephen's outrage that he'd taken a very imprudent action, ordering the clerics arrested until Archbishop Theobald agreed to perform the ceremony. But in the confusion, the archbishop managed to slip away and once again fled England, seeking refuge in Flanders. Stephen soon came to his senses, released the clerics, and permitted the archbishop to return. But the rift had not been mended, and as long as Stephen remained at loggerheads with his chief primate, he would find no warm welcome in the abbeys and priories of his realm.

The monks of Bury St Edmunds did their best, though, to put their grievances aside for the length of the king's stay. The guest hall was made immaculate, Abbot Ording turned over his own quarters for Stephen's comfort, and the abbey cook served up a dinner that would have done any king proud: baked lamprey eels, stewed mutton, stuffed capon, custard, applesauce, a spiced chicken broth, and hot bread. The abbot was grateful that the fare was so appetizing, for he took his obligations as a host seriously. He could only hope that the pleasures of the meal would compensate for the stilted and desultory nature of the dinner conversation.

So much was not suitable table talk. Above all, no mention could be made of the nineteen-year-old youth who not only held Normandy, Anjou, Maine, and Touraine, but who now had the blessings of the Pope as he cast his eyes toward England.

Abbot Ording sighed, for so many names would sink like stones in the conversational waters. The Earl of Chester, who'd dared to defy the Crown and gotten away with it . . . so far. Hugh Bigod, who was the reason why Stephen had gone north in a show of force, hoping—not very realistically, in the abbot's opinion—to intimidate Bigod into obedience. Robert Beaumont, who was ostensibly loyal but rarely at Stephen's court. Rainald Fitz Roy, who was rumored to be in Normandy at the behest of his fellow barons, urging his nephew to invade England as soon as possible. Roger Fitz Miles, who'd recently duped Stephen into believing he was contemplating a switch in loyalties, when in reality, he'd merely been trying to lure Stephen away from his siege of Wallingford Castle.

No, the list of safe topics was a short one, indeed. Political talk led invariably to Henry Fitz Empress, and discussion of Church matters would only remind them all of Stephen's feud with the archbishop. Abbot Ording sighed again, not yet desperate enough to comment upon the mercurial spring weather, and then brightened. "Is the Bishop of Winchester still in Rome, my liege?" Although even that was a sensitive subject, for all knew Stephen's brother had made the arduous journey to the papal court in a foredoomed attempt to regain some of his dwindling influence with the Vatican.

Stephen sopped up gravy with a bread finger, smiling at his uncomfortable host. "No, he has departed Rome. But I do not expect him to be back in England until the autumn, for he intends to return by way of Spain. He has always wanted to see the holy shrine at Santiago de Compostela."

That drew a quick response from Stephen's second son. "I'd rather see Paris myself, or mayhap Poitiers."

The abbot had never met the young Earl of Surrey before. Will was, like all of Stephen's children, quite good-looking, flaxen-haired and blue-eyed. He was also one of the wealthiest eighteen-year-olds in Christendom, for three years ago his father had secured for him a great child-heiress, Isabella de Warenne, who'd inherited the earldom of Surrey after her father died on crusade. He had a winning smile, the untested confidence of youth, and the brash cockiness so common to the sons of kings, laughing immoderately at all his own jokes and interrupting his elders much too freely for the abbot's liking. But he still made a favorable impression, especially among those familiar with Eustace's barbed defenses and sudden sarcasms.

"Poitiers?" Stephen was smiling quizzically at his son. He was, as the abbot and much of England well knew, the most indulgent of fathers, denying his children nothing. Not only had he bestowed the prestigious abbacy of Westminster upon his illegitimate and unqualified son Gervais—an appalling appointment in Abbot Ording's judgment—but he'd even founded a Benedictine nunnery in Kent so that he could name his young daughter, Mary, as its prioress. It occurred to the abbot that his failings as a king had not served him well in fatherhood, either, for with his sons as with his barons, he could not bring himself to disappoint, to discipline, or to demand the respect due him. "Why Poitiers, lad?" he asked curiously, and Will grinned impishly.

"Because of the Lady Eleanor, of course! Poitiers will be attracting more pilgrims than any shrine in Christendom now that she is in the marriage market again."

Stephen laughed, but Eustace did not. "If you're looking for a whore," he said impatiently, "you can find any number of sluts right here in Bury St Edmunds, Little Brother. There is no need to go all the way to Aquitaine for one."

The silence that followed was stifling. Will flushed, but he was not as cocky as the abbot first thought, for although he glared at his elder brother, he held his tongue. The abbot was offended, as were most of those who'd overheard Eustace, for he'd just broken one of their society's unwritten rules: Whatever men might say among themselves in private, a highborn lady's honour was not besmirched in a public setting.

Stephen was no less dismayed than the monks. "Have you forgotten that we're dining at God's Table?" he asked testily. His first inclination was to insist that Eustace apologize to the abbot and his brethren, but his son was no errant schoolboy. At twenty-two, he was a man grown, a man who must accept responsibility for his own acts, his own words, no matter how ill-considered. Signaling for more wine, he regarded his eldest with baffled anger. Whatever had possessed Eustace to defame a woman who'd been his own brother-in-law's queen? And within hearing of Bury St Edmunds's abbot, of all men!

The abbot was watching Eustace, too, with more objective, and therefore more discerning, eyes than Stephen. He was not long in concluding that Eustace's affront had been a deliberate provocation, well calculated to embarrass his father, the most chivalrous of men, before an audience of monks. But Eustace's triumph did not seem to have given him much pleasure. His smile was at once defiant, brittle, and defensive, almost as if he'd been the one wronged, and somewhat to the abbot's surprise, he found himself feeling a twinge of pity for them both. Fathers and sons. Always a Gordian knot, for certes, but how much more troubling when there was a crown caught up in its tangled coils.

No one seemed to know what to say. It was the abbey's hospitaller who finally came to the rescue. "It is my duty and privilege, Your Grace, to meet all the needs of the guests staying within the walls of our abbey. May I ask how long you plan to remain with us?"

With an effort, Stephen forced his eyes away from his son. "We'll be staying just one night, departing on the morrow." Adding politely, "As much as we would enjoy your hospitality, my queen and the Lady Constance are awaiting us at Cantebrigge."

The monks tried to conceal their relief that his visit would be so brief, with mixed success. But one of the other abbey guests, a prosperous wool merchant, was looking perplexed. After some hesitation, he said, "Begging your pardon, my liege, but I live in Cantebrigge. I arrived at the abbey last night, for I always stay with the good monks on my trips to Ipswich and—" Catching himself, he gave an abashed smile. "But that is of no earthly interest to you. What I wanted to tell you was that the queen is not in Cantebrigge. Not unless she arrived after I rode out yesterday morn . . ."

Now the perplexity was Stephen's. "No, she ought to have reached Cantebrigge days ago. This makes no sense . . ." Frowning, he pushed his food around on his trencher, his appetite gone. After a few moments, he beckoned to a knight at the end of the table. "Everard, I want you to ride to Cantebrigge as soon as the meal is done and find out if the queen and the Countess Constance are there or not."

Everard was one of Stephen's household knights, in his service long enough to gauge the urgency of his king's need. "I'll be off as soon as I get my horse saddled," he said, shoving away from the table. With that, Stephen gave up all pretense of unconcern. His eyes raking the hall, he found another face he could trust, and dispatched the man south to the Earl of Oxford's castle at Hedingham, for that was Matilda's last known stopping place. After that, the meal broke up, the monks and abbey guests scattering to their various pursuits, leaving the abbot to do his best to allay the unease of his king. But less than an hour had passed in this awkward manner before they heard shouting out in the garth.

Stephen came swiftly to his feet at sight of the man striding into the hall, for he should have been miles away by now, riding hard for Hedingham. "What in blazes are you doing back so soon, Guy? Hedingham is a good twenty miles away and if you expect to reach it by dark—"

Sir Guy now committed a serious breach of protocol; he interrupted his king. "My liege, hear me out. I encountered a messenger on the road, one of the Earl of Oxford's men. He was on his way here, seeking you."

A second man had followed Sir Guy into the hall. Coming forward, he knelt before Stephen. "My lord king, I am Sir Robert Fitz Henry. I serve the Earl of Oxford, am here at his bidding. A few days after her arrival at Hedingham, your lady queen took sick. She refused to let us send for you, insisting she'd not have you worried for naught. But she took a turn for the worse, and last night she asked for you and for—" He bit back the words so hastily that he seemed to have swallowed them, only making his omission all the more conspicuous.

Stephen frowned. "Who else did she want? Our daughter Mary?"

"Yes, my liege. But she also asked us to send to Holy Trinity Priory for . . ." Again his words trailed off, for he could see that Stephen still did not understand. He paused, then looked away so he'd not have to watch as Stephen finally realized what he was so reluctant to say. "She asked," he said, "for her confessor."

MATILDA had always envisioned time as a river, flowing forward inexorably into the future, forcing people to keep up with the current as best they could. No more, though. Time had become tidal. Lying in the shuttered dark of an unfamiliar bedchamber, she could feel it receding toward the horizon, leaving her stranded upon the shore. As a little girl in Boulogne, she'd often walked along the beach, throwing back the starfish trapped by the ebbing tide. Now, forty years later, when it was her turn to be marooned by the retreating waves, there was no one to save her as she'd saved the starfish, but she did not mourn for herself. Dying was not so terrible, for all that people feared it so. She was in God's hands, a feather floating on the wind, waiting to see if He would call her home.

If only Stephen understood that, if only he would not grieve so. He'd not left her bedside for days, pleading with her to hold on to hope, to fight off Death, not comprehending that Death was not always the enemy. She was so tired, so very tired. For too long, she'd been ailing, in body and spirit, struggling to keep her malaise secret from Stephen. So much bloodshed, so many graves, so many widows and orphans, and all for what? A tarnished crown that had brought them both more pain than pleasure. But he could not relinquish it, must keep on fighting to hold on to it—for Eustace. For the son she loved, who ought never to be entrusted with a king's sovereign powers.

The chamber was dimmed, for the candles had begun to hurt her eyes. Stephen was clutching her hand, lacing her limp fingers through his, his grip so tight that her wedding ring was pinching her flesh. Constance was weeping again, crumpled in the window seat. Matilda ached for her, the daughter by marriage who'd become as dear as her daughters by birth. Will was swiping at his face with his sleeve, her fledgling, her secret favorite. And Eustace . . . half hidden in the shadows, ashamed to let anyone—even his stricken family—see his tears.

At sound of a woman's step, her lashes fluttered, but it was Cecily again. Stephen kept insisting that Mary was on her way, likely to arrive at any moment, and she'd clung to his assurances with all the forgiveness and faith of the love she'd so long ago pledged to him. But this was to be one promise he could not keep. Mary would be too late.

"Stephen . . ." Not even a whisper in her own ears, but he somehow heard her and leaned over, vivid blue eyes of their lost youth, awash now in tears. "Look after Constance . . ." But who would look after him? Surely the Almighty would, for even his worst mistakes were well intentioned.

Did this too-clever son of Maude's have such a good heart? No . . . God would judge what mattered most.

Stephen was kissing her hand, pressing it against his wet cheek. His beard was grizzled with silver, like an early frost. How old he seemed of a sudden. She wanted to tell him one last time that she loved him, to promise that she'd be waiting for him at Heaven's Gate. But she could not catch her breath. She closed her eyes and when she opened them again, the room was filling with light. She could hear sobbing, but it seemed to be coming from a great distance. It grew more and more faint, until at last she could not hear it at all.

MATILDA died on Saturday, May 3rd, 1152, in her forty-seventh year. Her body was taken with royal ceremony to Faversham, Kent, and buried before the High Altar in the church of St Saviour's, the Cluniac abbey she and Stephen had founded four brief years before.

THE church was very quiet. Cupping his candle, the young monk slipped around the roodscreen, into the choir. The white marble of the queen's sepulchre glimmered in the shadows. As he drew near, he saw that someone had laid a yellow primrose upon the tomb. He was not surprised by the floral offering, for all at St Saviour's were in mourning for their queen. She'd spent as much time as she could spare at the abbey, finding within its cloistered walls the peace that was so elusive in the rest of her husband's realm. She'd been extremely generous with the monks, and they in turn had given her their wholehearted devotion. Brother Leonard knew that he was not the only one of his brethren who'd loved the queen.

The funeral had been over for hours, but there had been too much pain in this church for it to have faded away so soon. It seemed to echo in the stillness, the way the smell of smoke lingered even after a fire had been doused. Brother Leonard knew he was being fanciful, but he could not help himself. The faces of the queen's loved ones still haunted him, for never had he seen a family so desolated, so overwhelmed by their loss.

The king had done all that was expected of him, accepting condolences, keeping watch over his daughter-in-law and stunned daughter, but his eyes were glazed, his shoulders bowed. He'd buried his heart with his wife, and all who looked upon him knew it. The queen's younger son had wept openly throughout the service, as had his Warenne child-wife and most of the mourners. The Lady Constance had almost fainted as they first entered the church, and although she'd insisted upon remaining, there were times when Stephen's encircling arm seemed all that was keeping her on her feet.

Brother Leonard gently fingered the stem of the primrose, wishing he'd thought to bring flowers, too. He'd remedy that on the morrow. The primrose was freshly plucked, for it had not yet begun to wilt. Despite his best intentions, he found himself thinking of another flower, the Lady Mary. Never had he seen a prioress who looked remotely like Mary. She was just shy of sixteen, and under other circumstances, the dramatic Benedictine black of her habit would have set off her fairness to perfection. But on the day of her mother's funeral, she was a lost waif, berating herself to anyone who'd listen for not getting to Hedingham Castle in time to bid her mother farewell. It shamed Brother Leonard that he'd been most affected by Mary's grieving, for he feared that his sympathy was suspect, unduly influenced by her youth and beauty.

The queen had often teased him that his conscience was too tender. Remembering that now, his eyes blurred with sudden tears. What would she say if she'd known he'd cast admiring glances at her nun daughter? Most likely she'd have understood, for he'd never known anyone as forgiving . . . as good. How could she and the king have ever bred a son like the Count of Boulogne?

And yet . . . and yet he'd found himself pitying Eustace, too, at the funeral. Standing apart from the others, keeping his face averted so none could notice his swollen, red-rimmed eyes, he'd looked so reclusive in his grief, so utterly alone that Brother Leonard could not help hurting for him. He was all too familiar with the queen's temperamental son, for twice Eustace had come to Faversham at his mother's behest, but never before had he noticed how solitary Eustace seemed. He could recognize loneliness easier than most. For much of his life, he'd been an outsider, never having a sense of belonging until fate and the queen had brought him to Faversham. At first it seemed foolish, indeed, to compare himself—an outcast orphan of low birth—with the King of England's son and heir, and Eustace had soon forfeited his sympathy by turning upon his weeping wife, rebuking her for making a spectacle of her grief. But when he thought about the funeral later, it was Eustace's isolation that the monk would remember, his inability to end his self-imposed exile even on the day of his mother's funeral.

Letting the flower drop back onto the tomb, Brother Leonard said softly, "Ah, my lady, how will we ever learn to abide your loss?" Crossing to the High Altar, he knelt and began to pray for Matilda's soul, although he was confident that if ever there was one judged worthy of passing straight through Purgatory into Heaven, it would be the queen. He was still on his knees when he heard the voices in the nave.

"Do you wish me to go with you, my lord?"

"No, I'd have you await me out here."

Brother Leonard scrambled to his feet, for he'd recognized the second voice, a low guttural growl that still evoked distinctive echoes of his native Flanders. He heard the tapping now of a cane against the tiles, and was tempted to duck out before William de Ypres became aware of his presence. But he hesitated too long. The cane halted its sweep, and the Fleming said challengingly, "Who is there?"

"It is me, my lord . . . one of the monks." Although Ypres had always treated him with a gruff, offhand courtesy, Brother Leonard was never fully at ease in his company. The Fleming had been the queen's closest ally; between them, they'd managed to keep Stephen and the Archbishop of Canterbury from a final and irrevocable split, patching up one peace after another as the need arose. But Brother Leonard was not ignorant of Ypres's lurid past. Monks liked to gossip, too, and he'd heard all the stories, knew that until Ypres had begun to lose his sight, he'd been one of the king's most brilliant and brutal mercenary captains. Reason told him that the man was no longer dangerous, for he was in his sixties, an age as vast as Methuselah's to the twenty-year-old monk, and he was utterly blind in one eye, going blind in the other. But whenever he gazed into those oddly opaque eyes, Brother Leonard felt as if he were looking at an aged wolf, fangs worn down, but by no means harmless.

"Brother . . . Leonard, is it not?"

"Yes, my lord, it is." Surprised and rather flattered that the Fleming remembered him so readily, he gestured toward the queen's tomb. "I was saying a prayer for my lady. I . . . I owed her so much. I was hired to help out in the infirmary, and when the queen learned of my desire to serve God, she persuaded Abbot Clarembald to accept me as a novice, even though I was of humble birth and without two coins to rub together. And when it was time for me to take my vows, she came down from London to bear witness. She did all that for me," he said wonderingly, "and got nothing in return. But as long as I have breath, she'll have my prayers."

"You're wrong, lad. It gave her great pleasure that she'd been able to guide you 'onto the road to Heaven,' as she liked to say." Ypres's smile was both wry and weary. "She talked of you often, you and all her other lost lambs."

Without warning, tears flooded the young monk's eyes. "I know it is not for a poor wretch like me to question the Ways of Almighty God, but . . . but why did He have to take her now, when we still needed her so much?"

The Fleming reached out, resting the palm of his hand against the cold, unyielding marble of Matilda's tomb. "If you truly loved her, lad," he said, "be grateful that He did take her now."

51

POITIERS, POITOU

May 1152

PETRONILLA found Eleanor up on the battlements of the palace keep. The sky was streaking and the Rivers Clain and Boivre curved around the city like flowing ribbons of gold, but the light had yet to fade. Following Eleanor's gaze toward the north, Petronilla saw what had drawn her eyes: a small band of fast-riding horsemen, leaving a trail of dust in their wake as they approached the Pont de Rochereuil. "Eleanor . . . you think that is Harry?"

Eleanor nodded. "He said he'd be arriving on Whitsunday Eve, late in the day, between Vespers and Compline."

"Yes, but surely he'd have a more impressive escort than that?"

"Jesú forfend," Eleanor said emphatically. "The last thing we want is to attract attention ere we're safely wed. He said he'd bring just enough men to fend off robbers, traveling as inconspicuously as possible." She kept her eyes intently upon those distant riders, who were now passing the abbey of St Jean de Montierneuf. "Although I doubt that he'd have brought a large retinue in any event. He does not seem to care much for pomp and ceremony."

"A son of the Empress Maude? If that is so, he must be a changeling!" When Eleanor failed even to acknowledge the jest, Petronilla subjected her sister to a closer scrutiny. "Eleanor . . . are you having misgivings?"

"Not about the man, Petra. But the marriage . . . yes, a few misgivings."

Petronilla was not taken totally by surprise, for she'd noticed that Eleanor had become more and more preoccupied and pensive as her wedding day drew near. "Why?"

Eleanor was quiet for a few moments. "I suppose," she said, "because of the past two months, two months in which I was accountable to no man for what I did or what I wanted. I've never had freedom like that before, and I found it a sweet taste, indeed . . ."

"But what good is freedom without security, Eleanor? You need a man to protect Aquitaine from the French Crown and to protect you from those hordes of would-be husbands, eager to share your domains with you, whether you willed it or not."

"You need not fret, Petra. I am not about to leave Harry at the altar. You are right—I do need a man for the very practical reasons you've just argued. And for reasons you did not mention. I want more children. I want a man in my bed again, one who has more in mind than prayer. And I want a crown, I'll not deny it. All of which I've a good chance of getting from Harry."

Sure now that it was indeed her future husband who was entering her city, Eleanor moved away from the battlements, for she wanted to be below in the great hall to greet him upon his arrival. "I just wish," she said, with a skepticism that held an oddly wistful note, too, "that the balance of power in a marriage was not tilted so much in the man's favor."

HENRY could not seem to get comfortable in the bed. For the tenth time, he repositioned his pillow. When he flung the sheets back, he soon felt chilled, but when he drew the covers up, he was too hot. By his increasingly exasperated reckoning, it was well past midnight. This sleepless night before his wedding was shaping up to be the longest one of his entire life.

In less than twelve hours, he and Eleanor were to be wed in the cathedral of St Pierre. She'd made all the arrangements, leaving him nothing to do but show up. He could see the sense in it, for Poitiers was her capital city. He just wasn't accustomed to being a bystander, marching to a drumbeat not his own.

Their wedding was to be a simple affair, not at all the sort of lavish royal spectacle that would normally have attended the marriage of a Duke of Normandy and a Duchess of Aquitaine, a onetime queen and a would-be king. Henry remembered hearing that when Eleanor and the French king wed, the revelries had lasted for three full days. But for them, there would be nothing so extravagant or elaborate, just a wedding supper after the church ceremony, for had they invited all their vassals to celebrate their wedding, as would be customary, they'd have risked having their nuptials interrupted by an invading French army.

Henry hoped that Eleanor did not feel cheated. Mayhap one royal wedding in a woman's lifetime was enough for her. For himself, he did not care. He'd always been more interested in where he was going than in how he got there. And even if he'd been one to enjoy such prolonged and high-flown festivities, not here, not now, not in this company for certes.

Eleanor had summoned a few of her most eminent vassals to bear witness to her wedding, those men too devoted or too proud to learn of her marriage after-the-fact. Geoffrey de Rancon, Lord of Taillebourg. Saldebreuil de Sanzay, formerly Eleanor's constable, newly named as her seneschal. The lords of Lusignan and Thourars. The Count of Angoulême. They'd not liked Eleanor's first marriage to the French king, and it soon became obvious to Henry that they were not enthusiastic about her second match, either. Their courtesy was cold enough to threaten frostbite, and they watched him as warily as sheepdogs protecting their flocks from a marauding Angevin wolf.

Henry was surprised neither by their suspicions nor by their audacity, for these southern barons were known for their recalcitrance and prickly independence. While they were celebrated for their generosity and humor and joyful zest for life, their conviction that Aquitaine was Eden and they God's Chosen People had given them a sense of moral superiority that their neighbors often found intolerable.

It had been Geoffrey's acerbic opinion that the Aquitanians were an ungovernable lot, ready to rebel at any pretext, not in the least awed by authority, as quick to quarrel as they were to laugh. How much of his father's caustic appraisal was true, Henry had yet to judge. He did not doubt, though, that Eleanor's vassals would gladly give him as much grief as they'd given Louis—if he let them.

But if he'd anticipated some initial resistance from Eleanor's barons, he'd not expected trouble from her family. In addition to her sister, she'd invited her maternal uncles, Hugh de Châtellerault and Raoul de Faye, and her illegitimate half-brothers, William and Joscelin, and from them he'd gotten something he'd never encountered before and was utterly unprepared for—condescension.

Shoving his pillow back against the headboard, Henry found himself remembering a story Ranulf had once told, of a man supposedly shot by his own arrow when it ricocheted off a tree. He hadn't believed it then—or now—but he did feel as if his surprise for Eleanor had somehow rebounded upon him, too. Thinking that his bride would surely be pleased to discover on her wedding night that he could speak her native tongue, he'd made an effort to learn the dialect of the South known as langue d'oc, or Provençal. As he'd always had a good ear for languages, he'd soon picked up enough to impress Eleanor—and also to understand the smug conversational currents flowing around him.

Unlike her barons, Eleanor's kin had welcomed him with expansive goodwill—to his face. But behind his back, they laughed and jested in their own tongue, always at his expense. They joked about his inferior bloodlines, debating which was worse, having an Angevin sire or a Norman-Scots dam. They boasted to Henry that Eleanor was descended from Charlemagne, and then snickered to one another about the Demon Countess of Anjou, the Devil's daughter. They lavished compliments upon Henry and then mocked his short hair, calling him a shorn sheep, for all men of fashion wore theirs shoulder-length.

Henry was able to shrug off their supercilious comments about his heritage, reasoning that if they'd not thought the King of France good enough for Eleanor, it was only to be expected that he'd fall short, too. And as he cared nothing for fashion, he could not be wounded by disapproval of that sort. But it stung his pride to be treated like a raw, green lad. It had never occurred to him that Eleanor's family might see their clandestine courtship as a hunt, their wedding as the kill, and Eleanor as the hunter, he the quarry. Did these dolts truly think that nineteen was so young, that their age difference gave Eleanor such an advantage? Did Eleanor?

And that was the real reason why he lay awake and restless hours after going to bed. Eleanor. Not her unruly barons, not even her vexing relatives. Eleanor.

She'd welcomed him as if he were the most honoured of guests, gracious and obliging, concerned for his comfort. He'd caught her in no indiscretions, no lapses in langue d'oc. She'd been the ideal hostess, poised and polished, as regal in bearing as if that lovely dark head were still adorned with a crown. But as much as he admired her social graces, he looked in vain for the woman he would wed. The teasing temptress in that rain-drenched Paris garden was gone, eclipsed by the Duchess of Aquitaine, worldly and desirable and distant.

He supposed he could not blame her if she was suffering a few eleventh-hour qualms. Watching her entertain him with such impersonal perfection, he'd found himself thinking of an old adage: A burnt child dreads the fire. After fourteen years with St Louis, most of them miserable, was it any wonder that she might be skittish of marriage? Who would understand that better than he? For much of his life, he'd been an unwilling eyewitness to the carnage-strewn battlefield that was his parents' marriage, hostage to their embittered and irreconcilable demands.

He'd found it easy enough to reassure himself that if Eleanor was indeed having some doubts, it was only to be expected. But if he was so sure of that, why was he unable to sleep? He refused to believe he might be nervous. The one and only time he'd ever experienced anxiety over bedsport was before his first sexual encounter, at age fourteen. He'd never expected to feel such unease again. But he'd never lain with a woman as seductive and highborn and daunting as Eleanor. His bedmates had been numerous, for he rarely slept alone. But they were usually bedazzled village girls or high-paid harlots. Never a queen, one of the greatest beauties in Christendom.

He'd sometimes felt sorry for women, as they seemed to have a much harder row to hoe than men. What man could be more strong-willed or daring than his mother? A king's daughter, an empress, a would-be queen in her own right, she'd still been expected to obey his father, and had lost every major battle of their marital wars. It was not that Henry thought women should be given an equal say in the matters of men; he could not imagine anyone making an argument that preposterous. He could not help sympathizing with their plight, nonetheless, for he could envision few fates worse than to be utterly powerless. But as he tossed and turned in one of Eleanor's guest bedchambers, he discovered that women were not as powerless as he'd often thought. Eleanor's weapon might be a smile instead of a sword, but she could wreak her own sort of havoc, for certes. How else explain why he was still lying awake in the early hours of this, his wedding day?

HENRY and Eleanor were married that Whitsunday afternoon, out in the spring sunlight by the door of the cathedral church of St Pierre. The churchyard was thronged with excited, jostling spectators, for word had soon spread through the city and people turned out in large numbers to watch their lady wed.

Standing before the Bishop of Poitiers, Henry had eyes only for his bride. Eleanor's wedding gown was form-fitting to the hips, with a swirling full skirt and train, sleeves tight to the elbow and then billowing out in graceful hanging cuffs. The material was a richly woven silk brocade, a deep, dusky shade of gold. Her hair was plaited into two long braids, entwined with gold-thread ribbons, her veil as light as sunlight and almost as transparent, held in place by a gleaming coronet. She wore his bride-gift on her right hand, an emerald ring of beaten gold. The jewel had reminded him of her eyes, but today her hazel irises reflected the color of her gown, taking on a tawny, amber glow.

Cat's eyes, he thought, giving away no secrets, and slipped the wedding band onto each of her fingers in turn before sliding it down onto the third finger of her left hand, the one judged closest to the heart. Having promised before man and God to cleave unto this beautiful stranger from this day forth, till "death us do part," he said, "With this ring, I thee wed," and as a loud burst of cheering rocked the churchyard, he could only hope that this was indeed well done.

UPON their return to Eleanor's palace, Henry was not pleased to find that the trestle tables had not yet been set up in the great hall. It seemed there was to be dancing before the meal began. Since there would also be entertainment afterward, this meant that the festivities would last till well past dark. He wanted nothing so much as to be alone with Eleanor, to discover again the woman who'd bewitched him in the royal gardens of the Cité Palace, but that would be hours away. Till then, he would have to curb his impatience, politely put up with her barons and family as best he could.

He did try. He would later—much later—insist to Eleanor that he'd acted in good faith, striving to play the part expected of him, that of the eager, joyful bridegroom. Eager he was, without doubt. Joyful . . . no. He was too tense, too irritated by his new in-laws for genuine joy. But he would have been able to give a reasonably convincing performance—if only he'd not understood langue d'oc.

In his boyhood, one of his favorite stories was of a young man who found a magical cloak, one that rendered him invisible whenever he wore it. Henry had been fascinated by the folktale, but he'd never realized that such a power might be a two-edged sword. Hearing what was not meant for his ears was not a pleasurable experience. The jokes were ribald and forthright in French, but far more offensive in Provençal. Normally he'd have taken the teasing in stride, for that was every bridegroom's lot. But his sense of humor seemed to have decamped in the night. He could deflect the bawdy jokes aimed at him; he was not easily embarrassed. But the private jesting by Eleanor's brothers and uncles could not be laughed off, for their mockery was premised upon a highly insulting assumption—that Eleanor would soon have him jumping through hoops and begging for favors like a lady's spaniel lapdog.

He danced several carols with Eleanor, chatted amiably with Petronilla, the only member of his wife's family he could abide, and listened with feigned enthusiasm to a song by the troubadour and poet Bernard de Ventadour, one too lavish in praise of Eleanor's beauty for his liking. Bored and tired and increasingly restive, he found it helped to fortify himself with the free-flowing wine, although he was usually a very sparing drinker. Accepting his third cup of spiced hippocras, he traded thinly veiled barbs with Geoffrey de Rancon. He'd not met Rancon before Poitiers, but the man was known to him; he'd heard the sorry saga of Rancon's deadly blunder on the march toward Jerusalem, one that had caused the deaths of countless crusaders.

Rancon had been ordered by the French king to halt at the summit of Mount Cadmos, but he'd chosen to disregard Louis's instructions and led the vanguard onward in search of a better campsite. The king, riding in the rear, was unaware of this, and allowed the rearward to lag behind, thinking they would soon be upon Rancon's encampment. When the watching Turks swooped down upon them, the French panicked and the rugged mountain terrain was soon soaked in Christian blood. The king himself had narrowly escaped death, and although Eleanor remained steadfastly loyal to her beleaguered vassal, Geoffrey de Rancon had been sent home in disgrace.

Henry was not well disposed toward any man so cavalier about disobeying a royal command, convinced that inevitably led to anarchy, to Stephen's England. Excusing himself as soon as he could, he was turning to look for Eleanor when he heard her brothers laughing behind him.

"There he goes, on her scent again. I'd wager that in no time at all, she'll have the lad heeling and going down on command, without even needing a leash!"

"Well, early training works wonders with greyhound pups, fledgling hawks, and yearling colts, Will, so why not with young husbands? It is just a matter of using the right bait!"

Under other circumstances, Henry might have reacted with indifference or annoyance, depending upon his mood. Now he swung around with an oath, his temper flaring up so fast that he had no chance at all of quenching it. Anger long-smoldering took only seconds to become a conflagration.

ELEANOR had been slow to realize that something was troubling her new husband, distracted in part by her obligations as hostess and in part by her own edginess about the marriage. Nor did she find it easy to read Henry. He was not like Louis, whose face was a faithful mirror for his every thought. No . . . Harry was going to be more of a challenge. She was sure he'd give away clues; all men did. But it might take her a while to learn to recognize them.

It was not until their return from the church that she'd begun to sense something was amiss. She'd noticed at breakfast that Henry looked as if he'd slept poorly, but she'd taken his wakefulness as a compliment. Watching him as they danced, though, she'd concluded that he was not enjoying himself. She would have to make sure that the festivities did not drag on too long. She did not know yet how she'd manage that, but she'd find a way. This marriage had to succeed; there was too much at stake.

Declining an offer to join in the circle forming for the next carol, she beckoned to her sister. "Have you seen Harry?"

"Over there, with Will and Joscelin."

One glance was enough to alert Eleanor to trouble. Henry's back was to her, but her brothers looked as if they'd been caught bloody-handed over a dead body. She headed toward them, but Henry was already stalking away. "Wait," she cried out before her brothers could bolt. "The pair of you look guiltier than horse thieves. What happened?"

They exchanged uncomfortable looks. Will shook his head, almost imperceptibly, but Joscelin refused to take the hint. "We have to tell her, Will," he insisted. "Better she hears it from us."

Eleanor did not like the sound of that at all. "For the love of God, Jos! Just say it straight out."

"Eleanor . . . he understands langue d'oc!"

"Oh, no . . ." Eleanor stared at them in dismay. If Harry had heard even half of the jokes floating around the hall . . . "What did you say, Jos? Will?"

Will shrugged, refusing to meet her eyes. Looking shamefaced, Joscelin mumbled, "We were jesting. He ought to have let us know he spoke our tongue." Squirming under his sister's accusing eyes, he glanced toward Will for help, got none, and sighed. "We . . . well, we joked that he'd soon be following you about like one of your greyhounds, or words to that effect . . ."

Eleanor was not mollified, realizing she'd just been given a cleaned-up version of what Henry had overheard. "I've never had a taste for watered-down wine, Jos," she warned. "How can I make amends unless I know just how grievously you offended him? Try the truth this time."

But at that moment, there was a stir throughout the hall. The musicians had stopped in the midst of the carol. The dancers halted in puzzlement, the musicians looking apologetically in Eleanor's direction. She knew they would not have ceased playing so abruptly unless ordered to do so, and there were just two people present with the authority to give such a command. Gathering up her skirts, she started hastily toward her husband. But she was too late; Henry was already mounting the steps of the dais.

Standing alone upon the dais, Henry soon attracted attention. He waited, though, until all eyes were upon him. "The dancing will resume in a few moments," he said, and startled murmurs rippled across the hall, for he'd spoken in their tongue. Having made his point, he switched then to French, for he understood Provençal better than he spoke it. "My lady duchess and I would like to thank you for celebrating our wedding with us. We hope that you enjoy yourselves during the dancing and the feasting to follow. But I prefer to have a private wedding supper with my beautiful wife. Judging from what I've been hearing in this hall, I am quite sure that you will understand."

Never had Henry seen a crowd fall silent so fast. It was suddenly and utterly still. From his vantage point upon the dais, he could see shocked faces, abashed and uneasy looks as people tried to recall whether they'd compromised themselves in his hearing. He was depriving the guests of the favorite part of any wedding celebration, the boisterous bedding-down revelries. But there were no protests, no objections. His last statement had been a threat, sheathed but with a sharp blade, withal. As he had said, they understood perfectly.

By now he'd located Eleanor, standing a few feet away. She was looking up at him in astonishment, eyes wide, lips parted, at a rare loss for words. Before she could recover from her surprise, he came swiftly down the dais steps, holding out his hand. She took it and the guests moved aside to let them pass. The spell held; not until they'd exited the hall did bedlam break out behind them.

Henry's anger had been too hot not to have soon burned itself out. It was already cooling by the time he stepped from the dais, and now he found himself surrounded by charred embers and ashes, wondering how such a brief fire could have done so much damage. Eleanor was walking sedately at his side, her fingers still linked in his, deceptively docile. But she was no more submissive a wife than his mother had been, and while he was grateful for her public compliance, he was not deceived by it. He'd dragged her away from her own wedding feast, and even if he'd not said so plain out, not a soul in the hall doubted his intent—that he was not willing to wait any longer to take his wife to bed. If Geoffrey had done that to his mother, Maude would have been mortified—and she'd never have forgiven him, not in this life or the next. That Henry knew with a chilling certainty. What sort of a start had he gotten their marriage off to?

By the time they'd reached the stairwell leading up to their wedding chamber in the Maubergeon Tower, he'd faced a hard truth. At the very least, he owed her an apology. And if that was not enough for her, he'd have to abase himself if need be, no matter how painful that was to his pride, for her grievance was a just one.

A smoking rushlight in an overhead wall sconce dispersed some of the darkness in the stairwell. Eleanor stumbled over her trailing skirts, and when Henry reached out to steady her, she said suddenly, "I still cannot believe you truly did that!"

He stiffened, then turned to face her. "I know you must be angry, Eleanor, but—"

He got no further. With a rustle of silk and an elusive scent of unnamed, exotic flowers, she was beside him on the stair, her arms going up around his neck. "Why ever should I be angry? You did enliven the festivities for certes, gave our guests enough to talk about for days to come, and showed my barons that you're a man who knows what he wants—and when he wants it, by God!" Her laugh was low, her amusement too genuine to doubt. But Henry could not quite believe his luck.

"You truly are not wroth with me? Whilst I had good cause for my anger, I never meant to shame you, that I swear upon the surety of my soul."

"Harry . . . it does not shame a woman that her husband wants her. It only shames her if he does not."

"I do want you," he said, with a shaken laugh. "You have no idea how much!"

When she smiled, he kissed her. This was not the chaste Kiss of Peace they'd exchanged in the cathedral. It was one to fire the blood and bring men to ruin. No matter how close he held her, it was not close enough. Her breath was hot against his ear, her fingers entwined in his hair. She tasted of wine and temptation, her kisses as hungry as his own, and he forgot time and place and the world beyond her embrace, aware only of this moment and the woman in his arms and the need to make her his.

It was the sound of rending silk that brought Eleanor back to reality. "Harry . . . Harry, wait," she gasped. "Let me catch my breath . . ."

His own breath was coming in short, uneven bursts, too. As he drew back, his shoe struck something metallic. Bending down, he retrieved her coronet, and they both laughed, for neither one could remember when it had been discarded. "Whenever I thought about our wedding night," he said, "I never saw myself ravishing you in a stairwell . . ."

"Well, then," she said, "let's find ourselves a bed."

They continued climbing the stairs, pausing every few steps to kiss again. When they finally reached the door, Henry said, "Wait. Let's do this right." And before she realized what he was about, he caught her up into his arms, carried her over the threshold, and across the chamber to their marriage bed. Given the urgency he'd shown in the stairwell, Eleanor expected him to join her at once in the bed. To her surprise, he moved away.

"You are not going to quench the candles, are you?" she asked, hoping he was not. Louis had always insisted upon making love in the dark.

"Jesú, no!" He gave her a startled smile over his shoulder. "Who wants to fumble around in the dark? I suppose that works well enough for bats, but not for me."

Fortunately, Eleanor's servants had already made the chamber ready for them. Wood was stacked in the hearth, to be fired if need be. The floor was strewn with fresh rushes, intermingled with fragrant herbs like sweet woodruff and costmary. Knowing how she loved flowers, Colette and Yolande had filled the room with bouquets of periwinkle and violets and even a few early-blooming white roses. A flagon of wine and two gem-encrusted goblets had been set out upon the table, and after he slid the door's bolt into place, Henry poured wine into one of the goblets and carried it back to the bed.

"To our union," he said, holding out the cup. She saluted his wordplay with a smile, took a sip and passed the cup back. He sat beside her upon the bed, and they took turns drinking, watching each other avidly all the while. Eleanor was pleased that he no longer seemed in such a hurry, reassured that he could exercise this sort of self-control. Would he be as good a lover as his passion promised? So much she did not know about him, so much they both had to discover. But what she'd learned so far, she liked—very much, indeed. Handing Henry the goblet, she began to unbraid her hair.

Once her hair was free, she shook her head until it drifted about her shoulders in a dark, glossy cloud, making her look even more desirable and wanton than in Henry's most erotic dreams. "The first time I saw you, there in your husband's hall ere half the French court, I'd have bartered my soul to have you here like this, in my bed."

"You can keep your soul," she assured him, reclining back against the pillows in a pose that was both playful and provocative. "I'll settle for your body, my lord husband."

Henry laughed, and when she started to unlace her gown, he caught her hand in his. "No," he said, "let me." Eleanor lifted her hair up out of the way and he soon had the laces loosened, so deftly done that she knew he'd had some practice at this. Her gown had gotten a small tear in that frenzied embrace out in the stairwell, and it tore still further as he drew it over her head, but he offered no apology, for he was learning what mattered to her and what did not. Her chemise was of silk, too, ivory-white and as soft as her skin. Her shoes were a patterned Spanish leather, slit over her instep and fastened with an ankle thong, her stockings gartered above the knee with beribboned scarlet ties. Watching him through her lashes as he slid a stocking down her leg, she murmured, "Now I know what a birthday present feels like as it is being unwrapped."

"Some gifts are worth taking time and trouble with." Leaning forward, he kissed her again, and then slowly and deliberately removed her last garment. As the chemise fluttered down to the floor, his breath quickened. "Helen of Troy must have looked like you," he said, and she laughed softly.

"That is a pretty compliment," she said, "and I like it well. I like even better what I see in your eyes. We've waited a long time for this night, Harry, but there is no need to wait any longer." He was in full agreement with her, already jerking at his belt. As he started to strip off his tunic, she reached over to help him, saying, "My turn."

"Next time, love. I can do it much faster!" This he proceeded to prove, as tunic and shirt went sailing across the room. His chausses were short, reaching to the knee, and quickly disposed of. That left only the linen braies, and as he slid them down over his hips, he grinned, saying, "This you can help with, love!" Marveling at how very different were the men she'd married, Eleanor did.

Eleanor was realistic enough to be aware that their first lovemaking might be less than perfect. They might well need time for their bodies to become attuned, to discover what pleased each other, to trust enough to let down their defenses. As drawn as she was to Henry, she had no way of knowing what sort of lover he would be, not until they were in bed together on their wedding night. And if she'd misjudged him, by then it would be too late. She was sure he'd need no coaxing, for he was young and hot-blooded. But he might still prove to be a selfish lover, one intent only upon his own pleasures. Or too quick, too eager, spilling his seed too soon. Because she found that such a troubling prospect, she'd labored to rein in her expectations, reminding herself that a wedding-night disappointment did not mean marital disaster. They could adapt, they could learn. He was not like Louis.

She soon discovered that she need not have worried. Making love with her new husband was as natural and easy as breathing, as satisfying and sensual an experience as she could ever have hoped for. There was not much tenderness in this initial coupling; they were both too aroused for that. What happened between them was impassioned, intense, and white-hot, like falling into a fire and somehow emerging unscathed. That was Eleanor's first coherent thought afterward. She lay very still, loath to let Henry go even though he was no longer supporting his weight with his elbows, having collapsed on top of her as he reached his climax. She could hear the hammering of his heart, feel sweat trickling down between their bodies. It was not particularly comfortable, but she would have been content to stay like that for some time to come. When he finally lifted himself up, she felt bereft as he withdrew, and protested, "No, not yet . . ."

"I must be squashing you," he insisted, rolling over onto his back. His voice was normally hoarse and low-pitched, but now it had taken on a husky rasp, his words coming out slow and scratchy. Turning his head on the pillow so he could look at her, he said, "Good God, woman . . ." Eleanor smiled without opening her eyes.

"Well put," she agreed, and after a few more moments, he groped for her hand, kissing her palm.

"Forget what I told you in Paris," he said. "I would have married you without Aquitaine . . ."

"You are a gallant liar," she said, and he laughed. He seemed to be reviving faster than she was. Leaning over, he kissed the corner of her mouth, then reached down to recover their wine cup from the floor rushes. Finding it empty, he swung off the bed for a refill, pausing to snatch up a towel along the way. Back in bed, he shared both with Eleanor, trading sips as he patted her dry and then rubbed himself, far more vigorously.

Eleanor stretched lithely, propping their pillows behind her back. "It seems ungracious to complain after you just gave me the most memorable wedding night any woman ever had," she said. "But you also abducted me from our wedding supper ere I could get even a crust of bread."

"I've never yet let a hostage of mine starve." Rising from the bed again, he strode over to ring for a servant. Eleanor enjoyed watching him, for he was so comfortable in his nakedness, so utterly unself-conscious, so unlike Louis. She wondered how long it would be ere she stopped comparing them, how long ere Louis's spectre faded into insignificance. She did not think Harry would leave room in his marriage for any other man, even a memory.

A servant soon came in response to the summons, and Henry opened the door just wide enough to order supper. The chamber was strewn with their discarded clothing, and as he started back to the bed, she asked, "Do you think we ought to pick up our clothes ere they bring in the food?"

He glanced about at the telltale disarray, then shrugged. "Why? This is our wedding night. I doubt that anyone thinks we're playing chess up here to pass the time." But he was still pondering her query, and as he got back into bed with her, he gave her a curious, speculative look. "Was Louis one for setting up the chessboard?"

"In a manner of speaking," she conceded. "It is only natural that people should have been so interested in what happened—or not—in our marriage bed. He was the king, after all. But that scrutiny always made him uncomfortable. He would never have allowed servants to enter our room had it looked like this one does, as if we'd undressed in a mad race for the bed."

"That sounds like a race well worth running," he joked, "given what is waiting at the finish line." He had an exceptional memory, as Eleanor now discovered. "And always in the dark, too?"

She nodded, somewhat reluctantly, for she did not really want to discuss her first husband with her second. Not only did it seem a gratuitous cruelty to Louis, but she could not abide the thought that Harry might pity her, a Queen of France who'd been forced to live almost as chastely as a nun. "I cannot believe you remembered my query about the candles! I think you may be too quick for my own good."

"Not when it truly counts," he promised, and Eleanor rolled over into his arms, relishing another pleasure that had been scarce in her first marriage—the sweet sin of laughing together in bed.

ELEANOR had never had a meal like this one, eaten in bed, a table pulled within reach so they could help themselves, for neither she nor Henry wanted servants hovering about. Henry preferred to do the honours himself, lifting the chafing dishes to offer her a spiced meatball, a taste of savory rice, a few spoonfulls of pea soup. "Your cooks must think I have a harem hidden away up here," he said, "for they've sent enough to feed a dozen hungry souls. Do you want some more of the roast pheasant?"

"No . . . what are those dishes off to your right?"

Henry lifted the lids. "This looks like lamprey eels, in some sort of sauce, and this one has beef-marrow tarts." When she selected the latter, he passed it to her on a napkin. "So . . . where were we? Ah, yes, you were telling me that your father once clashed with Abbot Bernard, too?"

Eleanor nodded. "He was not as stalwart as Geoffrey, though," she said regretfully, "for when Abbot Bernard confronted him with the Host, he went pale as death and toppled over like a felled tree."

"A pity," Henry said succinctly, and Eleanor smiled fondly at him, for she found his skepticism a pleasant contrast, indeed, to Louis's absolute certainty that Bernard was a living saint.

"I think it bodes well for our marriage," she teased, "that we seem to dislike all the same people." Leaning over, she fed him the last of her marrow tart. "When shall I get to meet your mother, Harry?"

"I'd not be in such a hurry if I were you," he said wryly. "Most people find my mother to be a very formidable lady, indeed. It will be fascinating—in a scary sort of way—to watch the two of you take each other's measure. But that is not likely to come about in the near future. Remember what I told you last night . . . that my English allies are growing impatient? They insist they need me in England, and cannot comprehend why I've kept finding excuses to put off the invasion. I just hope they understand why I could not risk telling them about our marriage plans. But I promised my uncle Rainald that I'd be at Barfleur in a fortnight and we'd start gathering a fleet."

Eleanor was momentarily taken aback, for she'd expected that they'd have more than a fortnight together. But she could hardly complain, for it was not as if he were going off on a pleasure jaunt. "Do you want me to go with you to Barfleur?"

Henry was delighted with her matter-of-fact response. How many men were lucky enough to have a wife with such political acumen, and as seductive as Eve in the bargain? "I would love to have you with me at Barfleur," he said, "but I need you more here, in Poitiers. I can rely upon my mother to keep watch over Normandy whilst I am in England. I want you to make sure that Aquitaine stays calm, too, Eleanor, or as calm as it ever gets."

"I will," she said, and he kissed her gratefully, then selected a ginger-filled wafer for them to share.

"What about your mother? Do you remember her, Eleanor?"

"Truthfully, not a lot. Aenor, she was called. Did you know that is what my name means? 'The other Aenor.' I was eight when she died, but I have few vivid memories of her, for she was not like your mother, Harry, not a woman to be reckoned with. She was soft-spoken, not one for drawing attention to herself. I do not think she was ever happy with my father, nor he with her. They were coerced into the marriage by my grandfather and her mother, and I can understand why they were loath to wed. It had created enough of a scandal when my grandfather carried off the wife of one of his own vassals. But then to marry his son to that woman's daughter—you can well imagine the gossip that stirred up!"

Henry sat up so abruptly that he almost spilled his wine. "Did I hear you right? Your grandfather was having a tryst with Aenor's mother?"

"Not just a tryst, Harry. A notorious dalliance. The lady, who had the remarkably apt name of Dangereuse, was wed to a neighboring lord, the Viscount of Châtellerault. My grandfather always did have a roving eye, and he never seemed to see marriage as much of a hindrance—his or anyone else's."

"I assume he already had a wife when he stole the viscount's?"

"By then he was working on his second marriage. His first wife was a kinswoman of yours, Harry, Ermengarde, your father's great-aunt. Fortunately for us, that marriage fell apart ere they had any children. My grandfather took as his next wife the long-suffering Lady Philippa, heiress to Toulouse. She gave him two sons and five daughters, but their marriage was no happier than his first. As he put it, he loved women too much to confine himself to just one."

"But Dangereuse was different, not a passing fancy?"

"More like a grand passion. Philippa had put up with his straying as best she could, but his infatuation with Dangereuse could not be ignored, for after he wooed her away from her husband, he brought her right under his roof, settled her here in the Maubergeon Tower. That was too much for Philippa, and who can blame her? When my grandfather refused to send Dangereuse away, Philippa left him. She retired to Fontevrault Abbey, where—as unlikely as it seems—she became good friends with Grandpa Will's first wife, Ermengarde, who dwelt at the nunnery whenever the whim took her. Imagine the conversations they must have had on those long winter nights!"

"I'm still mulling over the fact that your grandfather was having an affair with his son's mother-in-law!" Henry said with a grin. "It is not as if I come from a line of monks myself. My own grandfather could have populated England with all his by-blows. But I have to admit that this grandfather of yours seems to have had a truly spectacular talent for sinning. What did the Church say about these scandalous goings-on?"

"Oh, he was often at odds with the Church, but it never bothered him unduly. In truth, Harry, nothing did. He liked to scandalize and shock people, but there was no real malice in him. As you may have guessed, I adored him. Most people did, for he had more charm than the law should allow. He did treat my grandmother rather badly—one of them, anyway! But I was too young to understand that, and by the time I did, he was long dead. What I remember most is his laughter, and I suspect that is what truly vexed his enemies, that he got so much fun out of life. He could find a joke in the most dire circumstances, as his songs attest. That shocked people, too, that a man so highborn would write troubadour poetry, but he enjoyed it and so what else mattered?"

Henry brushed back her hair. "Tell me more," he urged, and she shivered with pleasure as he kissed the hollow of her throat.

"Well . . . Grandpapa Will painted an image of Dangereuse on his shield, saying he wanted to bear her in battle, just as she'd so often borne him in bed. He liked to joke that one day he'd establish his own nunnery—and fill it with ladies of easy virtue. And when he was rebuked for not praying as often as he ought, he composed a poem: 'O Lord, let me live long enough to get my hands under her cloak.'"

Henry gave a sputter of laughter. "Between the two of us, we've got a family tree rooted in Hell! Once Abbot Bernard learns of our marriage, he'll have nary a doubt that our children will have horns and cloven hooves."

"The first one born with a tail, we'll name after the good abbot." Eleanor reached for a dish of strawberries in sugared syrup, popping one neatly into his mouth. He fed her the next one, and when she licked the sugar from his fingers, as daintily as a cat, his body was suddenly suffused in heat. Dipping his finger in the syrup, he coated one of her nipples. She looked startled, but intrigued, and when he lowered his mouth to her breast, she exhaled her breath in a drawn-out sigh. "Abbot Bernard preaches that sin is all around us," she said throatily, "but I doubt that even he ever thought to warn against strawberries!"

"He'd likely have an apoplectic seizure if he only knew what can be done with honey," Henry predicted, and Eleanor began to laugh.

"I think," she said, "that you and I are going to have a very interesting marriage."

Henry thought so, too. "I want you, Eleanor."

Her eyes reflected the candle flame, but brighter and hotter, making promises that would have provided Abbot Bernard with a full year of new sermons. "My lord duke," she said, "tonight all of Aquitaine is yours for the taking."

THEY were both exhausted, but neither was ready yet to let the night go. Staving off sleep, they lay in each other's arms, watching as the hearth flames wavered and danced and sent up white-gold sparks. Henry could not remember ever feeling so content. God truly did reward those willing to gamble. Breathing in the scent of his wife's perfume, he nuzzled her neck and she nestled closer.

He was not at all surprised that she could fire his passion as no other woman had. But he'd not expected to feel so intensely protective. She was quite capable of taking care of herself. He'd never thought to meet a woman more self-sufficient than his mother, but here she was, her thigh resting on his, her hair tickling his chest. It was not that she needed him to take care of her; it was that he wanted to, and this was a novel sensation for him. Lust took on a new taste altogether when tenderness was added to the brew.

How had she gotten to him like this? Mayhap it was just the afterglow. It was only natural that he'd feel close to her after lovemaking like theirs. Any more heat and they'd have set the bed on fire. Or was it that any last lingering doubts about her honour had gone up in smoke? However much he'd insisted to his father that he did not believe the gossip and innuendoes and rumors, there'd been a small, dark corner of uncertainty, one he'd not acknowledged even to himself . . . until now.

But no more. No matter what men said of her, he knew now that she was not a wanton. She was passionate and blessedly uninhibited and ardent. But she knew none of a courtesan's erotic tricks, those special, seductive ways of pleasuring a man that most wives never mastered. He'd lain with enough harlots to recognize practiced passion, and from harlots, that was indeed what he wanted. But not from Eleanor. He'd not wanted her to be too knowing, too artful in her caresses, for she could never have learned such skills from monkish, fettered Louis. If she had ever been unfaithful, he was sure now it had been a brief tryst, no more than that.

It was passing strange, for he ought not to care what she'd done whilst wed to another man. But he did. If tenderness was an unfamiliar emotion for him, so was this urge, too. He'd never been jealous of a bedmate before, never felt possessive of one, either. Was it because she was his wife? Was that what made it so different, so much more complicated?

"Harry . . . what are you thinking about?"

"Papal politics, the price of corn, whether I ought to get my stallion shoed, the usual . . ." he joked, while tightening his arm around her shoulders. She had the most luxuriant hair he'd ever encountered in a bedmate; he could not keep his hands away from it, running its silkiness through his fingers, wondering why men found blonde hair so alluring. It reached well past her hips, ebony in the night shadows, a deep rich brown whenever the firelight played upon it. Separating a long, gleaming strand, he entwined it around his fingers, looping it about his wrist.

Her lashes flickered. "Are you worried that I might run off whilst you sleep?"

"I just want to keep you close," he said, and she smiled drowsily.

"You need not worry, Harry," she said. "I'll not stray . . ."

EUSTACE had moved to the open window, watching the river traffic on the Seine. Behind his back, the French king exchanged puzzled looks with his brother Robert and his cousin Raoul. Louis was as surprised as anyone by Eustace's unexpected arrival in Paris. He must have left England within a few days of his mother's funeral, which bespoke an unseemly haste to Louis. Moreover, his presence was something of an embarrassment now that Louis had made peace with his rival the Duke of Normandy. The other men in the chamber were regarding Eustace with no favor, for he had few friends at court. But he had to be made welcome. They could hardly turn away the Count of Boulogne, the French king's brother-in-law.

Eustace was well aware that these men liked him not. But he harbored no goodwill toward most of them, either. While he'd always been on civil terms with the French king, he could not respect a man so weak-willed. Louis's blustery brother the Count of Dreux he disliked heartily, an antagonism Robert returned in full measure. Nor did he think much of Louis's dissolute kinsman Raoul de Péronne. Raoul's courtesy too often held a hidden sting, a hinted smugness that Eustace found infuriating, coming as it did from a man who'd made a fool of himself over a slut young enough to be his daughter. He had no reason to think badly of the Templar, Thierry Galeran, and he did not know Hugh de Champfleury, Louis's new chancellor. As for Waleran Beaumont, the less said of him, the better; Eustace would never forgive him for going over to Maude. And these were the men whose voices Louis most heeded? If so, no wonder his brother-in-law seemed to lurch from one blunder to another, like a ship with no rudder.

"Did you bring Constance with you?" Louis queried politely as Eustace turned away from the window. Eustace shook his head, started to say that Constance had remained behind to tend to his father, whose grieving was still raw. He caught himself in time, for that would only stir up another flurry of commiserations. He'd already accepted their condolences, wanted no more. If he would rather mourn his mother in private, that was betwixt him and God and no concern of theirs.

What he really wanted to discuss with Louis was the calamitous mistake he'd made in coming to terms with Maude's whelp. Henry Fitz Empress could not be trusted; what Angevin could? Not for nothing did men call Anjou the Devil's birthplace. Sooner or later Louis would realize how badly he'd erred. Eustace hoped to make it sooner. But he preferred to wait for a more opportune moment. He had a better chance of convincing Louis if they were alone.

Since Eustace seemed to feel no obligation to stoke the conversational fires, it fell to the ever-courteous king to perform that task for him. It was not easy going, for so many subjects held pitfalls. Fortunately, Louis got some help from the affable Raoul, who was a past master at social discourse, the sort of talk that was lively and smooth-flowing and said nothing of any consequence. But Louis was not enjoying himself and it was a relief to be summoned away by Adam Brulart, his secretary, hovering anxiously in the doorway.

"Well, what shall we talk about now?" Raoul asked Eustace. "I can always tell you the story of my life. I daresay you've been awaiting that with bated breath."

Eustace stared suspiciously at the older man, sure that Raoul was mocking him, but not sure what to do about it. Humor was the weapon he most mistrusted, for it was one he'd never learned to handle with any skill. But he was spared the need to reply. Glancing about the chamber, Raoul frowned, then rose from his seat. "Cousin? Is something amiss?"

By now other heads were turning toward Louis, too. He did look sickly, Eustace conceded, for he had no more color than a corpse candle and an odd, glazed stare, as if he were not seeing any of them. Filled with foreboding, Eustace started toward him. Raoul and Robert were already there, asking questions that Louis did not seem to hear.

It fell to Adam Brulart to tell them. After a troubled look at his king's ashen face, the clerk said reluctantly, "The King's Grace has just learned that the Lady Eleanor and the Duke of Normandy were wed in Poitiers on Whitsunday."

As the unhappy clerk had known it would, his news created a furor. Voices rose as men struggled to make themselves heard. Eustace finally prevailed, for he'd had much practice in shouting others down. "Is it true?" he demanded of Louis. "Just tell me if it is true!"

Louis swallowed. "A mistake," he said. "It must be a mistake. Eleanor would not do that to me. I know she would not . . ."

He was a minority of one in that belief. Several of the men had begun to curse. Raoul had paled; clutching his royal cousin's arm, he said urgently, "I did not know, Louis. I swear by the Holy Cross that I did not know!" Louis said nothing, for he was not listening. Neither was Eustace. Turning away, he rested his palms flat against the wall, standing motionless, arms outstretched, head down. Normandy, Anjou, Maine, Touraine, and now Aquitaine, too—Blood of Christ! Without warning, he balled his fist, hammered it into the wall repeatedly, leaving a smear of blood behind. In the confusion, no one noticed.

The French king continued to insist plaintively that it must be a mistake. He was Eleanor's liege lord. She had no right to wed without his consent. And never would she have wed Henry Fitz Empress. Had she not wanted to annul their marriage because their kinship was an affront to the Almighty? It had gnawed away at her peace. She'd told him so—often. But she was even more closely akin to Henry than she was to him. So such a marriage could never be. She would not mock God's Law like that. She would not mock him. But his protests carried less and less conviction and at last he slumped down in a chair, too stricken to keep up the pretense any further.

Gradually the other men quieted and a discomfited silence filled the chamber. Watching Louis bleed was painful for them, too, but none knew how to treat a heart wound. After much shuffling of feet and clearing of throats, they seemed to have reached an unspoken consensus that the greatest kindness they could do their king would be to leave him alone. They began to mumble regrets, to murmur vaguely of duties elsewhere, putting Eustace in mind of the hushed, unnatural voices of the mourners at his mother's funeral. Crossing the chamber swiftly, he planted himself directly in front of his brother-in-law's hunched figure, arms folded across his chest, legs spread, impossible to ignore.

"What mean you to do about this?"

Louis looked up blankly, a man roused from his own private hell, blinking as if surprised to find the men still here. "What can I do? They are already wed."

"But you are not going to let them get away with it, are you? They had no right to wed and well they knew it. If it is too late to prevent the marriage, it is not too late to punish them for it. If you do not, others will think that they, too, can defy you with impunity." Eustace's mouth twisted and for a moment, he thought of his father. "You have no choice," he said, "but to make an example of them, one that others will not soon forget."

He'd struck a common chord. For once, he did not lack for allies, and they all agreed that Eleanor and Henry must be held to account for their treachery. There must be a reckoning. If Thierry Galeran was spurred on by his known hatred for Louis's queen, that could not be said of Louis's chancellor, and Hugh de Champfleury argued somberly, too, for retribution. When at last eyes turned toward Raoul, he did not hesitate for long. His fondness for Eleanor was genuine, but his position was precarious enough as it was. No, in this case, she was on her own. "A man does what he must," he said carefully. "You must think of the Crown, my liege."

Such unanimity was rare in Louis's royal councils. He knew they were right. So great a betrayal could not be ignored. It must be avenged. She'd lied to him from the first, with her talk of conscience and God's Will. Mayhap this had even been planned from the onset, as far back as last summer's peace conference with the Angevins. Mayhap that was why Count Geoffrey and his spawn had become so reasonable of a sudden? That suspicion twisted the knife almost beyond bearing. How she must be laughing at him, lying in bed with the Angevin stripling, congratulating themselves for having made such an utter fool of the King of France. Well, let her beloved Aquitaine be overrun by French troops, let her watch as Poitiers burned, let her see then if she still felt like laughing.

"I shall summon them both to my court," he said abruptly, "to answer a charge of treason."

They approved, nodding grimly. Raoul glanced around at their faces, wondering if he was the only one who thought it unlikely that the guilty pair would obey the summons. He knew his sister-in-law better than any of them, and he could not see her submitting meekly to a judgment of the French court. Ah, Eleanor, he thought bleakly, what have you done? For such a clever lass, how had she gotten herself into such a predicament? What had possessed her to put her world at risk like this, with nothing between her and disaster but luck and a cocky nineteen-year-old?

As satisfied as Eustace was with this outcome, he still harbored a few qualms. Louis sounded steadfast enough now, but how long would that last? "What happens," he said, "if they dare to defy the summons?"

Louis raised his head. His eyes held a blue-ice glitter that Eustace had never seen before, that he found very heartening. "Then," Louis said, "it will be war."

52

FONTEVRAULT ABBEY, ANJOU

June 1152

THE sun was high overhead, filling the cloisters with brilliant white-gold light. Eleanor and the Abbess Mathilde were sauntering along the walkway, in such animated conversation that they did not notice when Yolande lagged behind, tugging at Colette's sleeve to attract her attention. "Did you hear that? The abbess called our lady's new husband 'Harry.' How does a nun know the duke so well?"

Colette's black eyes held an amused glint. "That is a scandalous suggestion," she chided, and Yolande blushed brightly.

"I did not mean there was anything improper betwixt them!"

Colette sighed. "I was but teasing you, child. The abbess is Lord Henry's aunt, his father's elder sister, so it is hardly surprising that she calls him 'Harry.' You do not know of her history, then? If not for a drunken helmsman and a hidden reef in Barfleur Harbor, she would have been Queen of England, for she'd been wed as a child to the English king's only lawfully begotten son, the one who drowned in the wreck of the White Ship."

Although it had been more than thirty years since the sinking of the White Ship, its tragic fate continued to haunt the imagination, its story to find new audiences. Yolande might be ignorant of English politics, but she knew every one of the legends that had sprung up around the White Ship, and she stared after the abbess with avid curiosity. "Truly? How unlucky she was!"

"Oh, I'd say she was very lucky, indeed, for she could have been on the White Ship, too. But fortunately for her, she'd sailed with the old king. Far better to be widowed than drowned, Yolande, even if it does mean forfeiting a crown!"

They'd not been as discreet as they'd believed; their voices carried across the garth. Eleanor gave her new kinswoman an apologetic smile, but the abbess shrugged, unperturbed. "I fully expect," she said dryly, "that as I lie on my deathbed, I'll still hear whispers about the White Ship. Who knows, even the Almighty's angels may have a question or two to put to me!"

Eleanor laughed. She'd expected to encounter one of God's holy lambs, for Mathilde had lived most of her life within Fontevrault's sheltering walls. Instead she'd found a handsome woman of forty or so, one who ruled her cloistered domains with competence, pragmatic piety, and wry good humor. Eleanor thought those were admirable qualities for abbess and queen alike. "I remember," she said, "a childhood riddle that my sister fancied: What can never be outrun? The answer was supposed to be my shadow, but it could as well have been gossip and rumor, too."

"We've both been the quarry in that hunt," Mathilde said candidly, but Eleanor took no offense, for she knew none was intended. She should have realized that Geoffrey's sister would have her share of Angevin spice; whatever might be said of her husband's family, no one could ever accuse them of being bland. Smiling, she followed the abbess down the shallow steps into the church.

Almost at once, Eleanor stopped in surprise. She'd often wondered why churches were invariably filled with shadows and solemnity instead of ablaze with God's light and joy. Here in this Benedictine nunnery of the Blessed Lady Mary, she'd finally found a church to gladden her heart and dazzle her eyes. Sun spilled into the chancel from ten soaring windows, the frescoed walls of the nave glowed with vibrant color, and the floor, a gleaming white marble, shimmered like glazed ice.

Eleanor had always been intrigued by Fontevrault, for it had been founded upon the precept of the Lord Christ to St John, "Son, behold thy mother." At Fontevrault, women reigned supreme; even the adjoining community of monks was subject to the authority of the abbess. That alone would have endeared Fontevrault to Eleanor. The fact that it had once given sanctuary to her grandmother and was now ruled by her husband's aunt made it all the more appealing, and she'd been pleased to grant the abbey a charter confirming their existing privileges. She'd also made a generous donation of five hundred sous to the convent's coffers. But as she gazed admiringly now upon the sunlit splendor of the Great Minster, she wished she'd given more.

Dipping her fingers into the font of holy water, Eleanor dutifully made the sign of the cross. "Did you see much of Harry as he was growing up?"

"Not as much as I would have liked. He's always been my favorite nephew, although I suppose I ought not to admit that? Tell me, is it true that the French king ordered you both to his court to defend yourselves against a charge of treason?"

Eleanor nodded. "We got the summons just as Harry was about to depart for Barfleur. He told Louis's messenger that it was not convenient for him to visit Paris this summer, but he'd let Louis know when he had some free time."

Mathilde joined in her laughter. "That sounds like Harry. Bless him, it sounds like Geoffrey, too. But might it not have been wiser to seek to placate Louis?"

"Possibly," Eleanor conceded, "but it would not have been as much fun," and the abbess concluded that her nephew and his beautiful, controversial bride were a well-matched pair, indeed.

When Eleanor began to ask about Henry's childhood, Mathilde was pleased, seeing Eleanor's curiosity as a promising proof that their marriage would prosper, for only a contented wife would be interested in her husband's boyhood misdeeds. Since Henry had never lacked for imagination, she did not lack for stories, and she was quite willing to acquaint Eleanor with some of Henry's more memorable escapades: the time he found a fox cub and smuggled it into the castle, hoping to tame it, only to have it eat his mother's pet magpie; the time he tried to climb from his bedchamber, using sheets knotted together, and fell into the moat; the time he sneaked blue woad dye into his brother Geoff's bath.

They were still laughing over that last prank when they heard the footsteps out in the nave. Turning, they saw an elderly nun hastening toward the chancel, at a pace rapid enough to compromise her dignity.

"Holy Mother," she panted, "there are men come to see the duchess. We wanted to escort them to the guest hall, explaining that males may not roam about in a nunnery at will, but they refused to wait, insisting upon seeking out the duchess for themselves."

"Did they, indeed?" the abbess said, sounding to Eleanor more like Geoffrey facing down Abbot Bernard than one of Christ's Brides. "Just who are these ill-bred intruders, Sister Pauline?"

"The duchess's kinsman, the Viscount of Châtellerault, and her seneschal, Reverend Mother. They were most rude—" The banging of the church door cut off the remainder of her complaint, and she spun around with an indignant cry. "There they are!"

Eleanor's uncle Hugh de Châtellerault had always been volatile, given to emotional outbursts and dramatic posturing. She saw nothing significant or sinister in his discourtesy, for he was quite capable of forcing his way into a nunnery on a whim. But Saldebreuil de Sanzay was another sort of man altogether, rarely riled, the most levelheaded of all her counselors. And Eleanor had never seen him look as he did now—thoroughly alarmed.

Neither man responded to the abbess's sharp challenge, not even hearing her. At sight of his niece, the viscount quickened his stride. "Christ Jesus, Eleanor," he erupted, hoarsely accusing, "what have you brought upon us?"

Eleanor's eyes narrowed, moving dismissively from her uncle to Sanzay. "Saldebreuil? What has happened?"

"War, my lady," he said grimly. "A French army has gathered on the Norman border, poised to strike."

Eleanor caught her breath. Could she have so misread Louis? She'd expected him to rant and rave and even to bluster and threaten, but not to back up those threats with force. His nature was pacific and passive, not at all martial. He was never belligerent or combative, not unless goaded to it—as at Antioch. She should have guessed there would be those to goad him at Paris, too.

"Louis is not being a gracious loser, is he?" she said, with more coolness than she felt. "And as always, his sense of timing is deplorable. If he'd just waited another fortnight, Harry would have been in England when he attacked."

The viscount gave a snort of disbelief. "You truly think your young lordling will be our salvation?"

Her coolness was no longer feigned. "That is not the first time you've spoken of my husband with disdain. Let it be the last, Uncle. Harry is more than a match for Louis, as he'll soon prove."

Her seneschal slowly shook his head. "You do not know all of it, my lady, nor the worst of it. The French king has assembled a formidable coalition, allying himself with his brother, the Count of Dreux, Count Eustace of Boulogne, the Counts of Champagne and Blois . . . and Lord Henry's younger brother, Geoffrey Fitz Empress."

Eleanor paled. Beside her, the Abbess Mathilde gasped; Fontevrault was close enough to the border of Poitou for her to have picked up sufficient langue d'oc to understand the gist of what Sanzay had just said, that her nephew had been betrayed by his own brother. There was a moment or two of stricken silence as Eleanor admitted to herself just how badly she and Henry had erred, utterly underestimating the furor their marriage would create. But then she rallied and smiled scornfully. "Harry is a match for any of them, too."

Her uncle started to scoff, but daunted by her warning, he thought better of it just in time. Sanzay looked at her in somber sympathy. "Mayhap he would be a match for any of them," he agreed politely, "but for all of them?"

"Yes!" Eleanor glared at them defiantly. "You do not know Harry. I do. He will prevail against them, that I can assure you."

Neither man looked convinced, but neither dared to contradict her. "I hope your faith in the duke is not misplaced, my lady," Sanzay said bleakly, "for this will not be a war you can afford to lose. You see, the French king has promised his allies that your domains will be carved up between them like a Michaelmas goose."

"The French king," Eleanor echoed acidly, "can promise them half of Heaven for all the good it will do him. Louis was ever one for promising more than he could deliver, and his greedy accomplices will learn that soon enough. We'll see no blood spilled on our soil, for they'll never get that far. Nonetheless, it behooves us to take all sensible precautions. We'd best return to Poitiers straightaway, for there is much to be done."

The men were in full agreement with that, if with nothing else she'd said. Her vassals must be warned, men summoned for military duty, castles made ready to withstand sieges, patrols sent out to guard their borders. These were familiar activities, and for that reason, reassuring to Eleanor's uncle and seneschal, much more so than her conviction that the Angevin youth she'd wed would be able to defeat a vengeful king, his most implacable enemy, his own brother, and three highborn and land-hungry lords, all eager to turn Normandy and then Aquitaine into a smoldering wasteland of razed castles and plundered towns.

Reaching out, Eleanor took Mathilde's hands in hers, bade her farewell, and promised to return to Fontevrault once the war had been won. The abbess kissed the younger woman lightly and approvingly on both cheeks. "Bear in mind," she said, "what Scriptures tell us, that David prevailed over the Philistine with but a sling and a stone. I think we can safely say that Harry will be far better armed."

Eleanor smiled and they embraced briefly. It was only then that the abbess realized how much of Eleanor's impressive aplomb was sheer bravado, for she whispered, softly and urgently, in Mathilde's ear, "Pray for us."

IN July, the French king invaded Normandy and laid siege to the castle Neufmarché. On the 16th, Henry led an armed force from Barfleur, riding hard for Neufmarché. But he was too late. By the time he got there, the castle had already fallen to the French. At Henry's approach, Louis pulled back, and a battle was averted. When Louis withdrew toward Chaumont, Henry followed and the skies over the Vexin were soon smoke-blackened. Then in August, Louis suddenly crossed the Seine again. Henry broke off his harrying campaign in the Vexin and raced for Verneuil, Louis's likely target. But on a sweltering-hot Monday, the French army appeared before William de Breteuil's castle at Pacy.

FROM the battlements at Pacy, William de Breteuil looked out upon a scene that fulfilled all his expectations of the netherworld. Darkness was falling and torches had begun to flare in the enemy encampment. Bodies still lay sprawled beneath the castle walls, for it was too risky to come within arrow range merely to retrieve the dead. The assault had been a bloody one, fiercely fought on both sides. The defenders had been able to repel the first attack, although at a high cost. They'd lost more men than they could spare, and when the onslaught resumed on the morrow, William doubted that they could hold out for very long.

Moving stiffly, for he'd suffered a leg wound in the assault, William clambered down a rope ladder and limped across the bailey. A few of their dead still lay unclaimed, where they'd fallen from the battlements, but most had been dragged into the great hall, which was doing double duty as charnel house and hospital. As he sent men to relieve their comrades up on the walls, William found himself wondering how many of them would be among the wounded and dead at this time tomorrow.

He fully expected to be one of them, for he would never yield. He'd fought too long and too hard to gain Pacy ever to relinquish it, not if he still had breath in his body. He knew the odds were against him, but that had been true all his life. He ought never to have gotten Pacy for his own; it was also claimed by the powerful Beaumont family. But the strife over the English crown had offered opportunities for men wise enough or lucky enough to choose the winning side, and in 1141, Count Geoffrey of Anjou had granted him all he'd ever wanted, the honour and castle of Pacy sur Eure. He would rather die defending it than surrender and have to watch as the French king turned it over to Waleran Beaumont.

He found his wife in the great hall, tending to the wounded. Bending over a youth who'd been burned when a fire arrow ignited his clothing, she was applying goose grease and fennel to his raw, blistered arm, so intent upon her task that she did not notice her husband's approach, not until he said, "Emma," very low.

She looked exhausted, her skin sallow in the smoky rushlight, her eyes shining with blinked-back tears. There were bloodstains on her skirt and her hair had been pulled back severely, caught up in an untidy knot at the nape of her neck, her veil long gone. He'd never seen her so disheveled or so indifferent to her appearance. Moving away from the moaning man at her feet, she let William lead her toward a window seat.

"It is so ungodly hot," she said, but she did not suggest that the window be unshuttered. She knew better; while night attacks were rare, they were not unheard-of. Her husband had slumped into the seat beside her, his chin sunk down on his chest. She could see dried blood in his beard and hoped it was not his. She knew, though, that he'd been in the midst of the hand-to-hand fighting up on the wall. Just as she knew he'd be there on the morrow, swinging a sword as long as he had the strength to wield it. After a while, he bestirred himself and began lying to her again, saying what he thought she needed to hear, assuring her that they'd be able to stave off the next assault, that they'd be able to hold out until the duke arrived.

Emma wanted desperately to believe him. But the duke had been heading for Verneuil, and they could not be sure that their man had reached him with their urgent plea for aid. And even if he had, even if the duke at once swung about and rode for Pacy, it was nigh on forty miles between the two strongholds. Pacy would suffer the same fate as Neufmarché, and by the time the duke got there, it would be too late.

"Will . . ." She got no further. It would do no good to urge him to surrender. She'd never known a man so stubborn, so prideful, for there was no pride as fierce as that of an outsider, one whose birthright was tainted by the Bar Sinister. William's father had been a Fitz Osborn, an only son, but born out of wedlock. He'd spent his life in an embittered struggle to claim the honours of Breteuil and Pacy, and her William had then taken up the quest, too. No . . . God help him, but he would never yield, not with his father's vengeful ghost dogging his every footstep. "Come abovestairs," she said wearily, "and let me put some fresh plantain leaves on your wound, Will."

They were just entering the stairwell when they heard the shouting. William spun around so hastily that he tripped. Emma grabbed his arm to help him regain his balance, and held tight, for they shared the same fear—that the French king had decided not to wait until the morrow, was attacking now.

As they hurried back into the hall, one of William's knights came bursting through the door. "My lord, come quick! Something strange is happening in the French camp!" Laboring for breath, he leaned upon a chair for support and startled them then with a sudden smile. "It is going to sound mad, I know, but it looks like they are pulling out!"

William did not believe it, not until he stood on the battlements and saw for himself the confusion and turmoil in the French camp. "Jesú," he breathed, awed beyond words at God's Goodness, for the French army was indeed in retreat, breaking camp with such urgency that he knew there could be but one explanation. They'd gotten warning of another army's approach. "Tell my wife," he directed joyfully, "to go to the chapel, thank the Almighty and the duke for our deliverance!"

As the Pacy garrison watched and cheered and hooted from the battlements, the French army made a hasty retreat, leaving behind bodies and tents and smoking campfires. Soon afterward, riders came into view. The horses were caked with lather, and the men looked as though they'd been bathing in dust. But their smiles shone triumphantly on begrimed, drawn faces, and when the drawbridge was lowered to admit them into the castle, they were mobbed by the grateful garrison. The youth on a raw-boned grey stallion was just as fatigued and filthy as the others, but the word soon spread among them that this was their duke, and Henry rode into the most heartfelt and heartening welcome of his life.

Shoving his way toward Henry, William de Breteuil had a protective arm around his wife's shoulders and was brandishing a wineskin in jubilant celebration. "Drink, my lord," he urged, sloshing the wineskin upward. "All that I have is yours for the asking." And to the men crowding to get closer, "For the love of God, give the duke some room! How can he dismount with you coming at him from all sides?"

"I cannot stay," Henry interjected, reaching gratefully for the wineskin. "We have not a hope in Hell of overtaking them, not after the way we've had to use our horses. But we ought to make sure that they are in full retreat. We'll be back, though, so start breaking out your wine casks!"

"Your men can drain every last one," William promised, "and with my blessings. If I had all the wine in Christendom at my disposal, I'd pour it out like a river for your troops and never count the cost. You saved us from certain defeat, my lord, and I still do not know how you did it. You could not have gotten here faster if your horses were winged. In all honesty, I never expected you to reach us in time."

Henry took another deep swallow from the wineskin, and then grinned down at his beaming vassal. "Neither," he said, "did Louis!"

MAUDE was a woman with a keen sense of injustice, one who neither forgave nor forgot her grievances. She'd not thought there was anything more she could learn about betrayal, for she'd been wronged so often. Her father had betrayed her by naming her as his heir and then failing to safeguard the succession for her. Stephen had betrayed her trust and stolen her crown. The English had betrayed her by refusing to accept her as queen, despite Stephen's decisive defeat at Lincoln. Geoffrey's betrayals were beyond counting. By her stringent standards, even Robert had betrayed her at first, by acquiescing in Stephen's illicit kingship. But nothing had prepared her for the pain of her son's betrayal.

She was both infuriated and horrified that her second son could have played into their enemy's hands like this. What had ever possessed Geoff to behave so treacherously? Was he truly so jealous of Henry that he could rejoice in his brother's downfall? Or was he so foolish that he did not even realize they meant Henry's ruin? She'd never had any doubts about how to deal with disloyalty, nor had she ever had any mercy to spare for those who knowingly sinned against God and man. But this sinner was her son, flesh of her flesh. As angry as she was with Geoff, she could not help fearing for him, too.

But her greatest fear was for Henry. She'd never have thought she could regret Geoffrey's death so deeply. If only he were still alive to come to Henry's aid! Why had the Almighty chosen to take Robert and Brien, too, when her son had such need of them now? Night after night, she paced the floor of her bedchamber, for when she slept, her dreams were dreadful. She'd never feared to risk her own life. But Henry's life was far more precious to her, his death the one loss she could not have survived.

Maude was preparing for bed when her son arrived at the priory. With Minna's help, she hastily rebraided her hair, made herself as presentable as she could in the brief span before he was ushered into her chamber. Until he entered, she was not sure which son to expect. Hoping against hope that it might be a contrite Geoff, come to his senses, she felt a surge of relief, nonetheless, at sight of her youngest.

"Will, where have you been? Did you not realize how worried I would be when I did not hear from you?"

He looked surprised and then sheepish. "No," he admitted, "I did not. I am sorry, Mama, but you need not have fretted. At sixteen, I'm old enough to take care of myself. I've been with Harry, of course. Where else would I be?"

"That had occurred to me," she conceded, "for I know you've always gotten along better with Henry than with Geoff. But I needed to know for certes, Will!"

"No one gets along with Geoff." Will almost added, "except the whores who're paid to put up with him," remembering in the nick of time that he was speaking to his mother. "Harry or Geoff—that was an easy choice, Mama." He startled her then, though, by saying matter-of-factly, "After all, Harry is going to be King of England one day."

She studied his sunburned, freckled face, the guileless blue eyes. Who would have guessed that her last fledgling, so cheerful and forthright, had such a practical core? "Are you so sure then, that Henry will win this war?"

He seemed puzzled by the question, that it need even be asked. "Mama, he is already winning! Did you not hear about Pacy?" When she nodded, he straddled a chair, leaning forward eagerly. "A pity you could not have been there to see it; you'd have been so proud of Harry. We half killed ourselves racing for Pacy, and we did lose some of our horses. But we got there in time to save the castle and scare off the French. This is the second time, too, that the French king has refused to do battle with Harry. How does he expect to win this war if he keeps skulking away whenever Harry gets within a mile of the French army?"

"I daresay quite a few men are asking themselves that same question. What happened after you rescued the lord of Pacy? I heard that Henry then invaded Dreux. Is that true?"

Will nodded vigorously. "That is why I am here, Mama, to let you know what has been occurring. Harry thought you ought to hear it from me," he explained and grinned. "He probably reckoned that a brother would boast of his exploits more than a courier would. But he has earned the right to do a bit of bragging, Mama, and I'm happy to do it in his stead. After the French retreated, Harry said it was time to teach Louis's allies that this war was going to be a costly one for them, too. We crossed into the Count of Dreux's lands, burned Brezolles and Marcouville, and Harry demanded hostages from the count's vassal, Richer de l'Aigle. After that, we took and burned his castle at Bonmoulins. The local people were right glad to see it burn, saying it was a brigand's castle, a veritable den of thieves."

Minna approached then with a brimming wine cup, and Will interrupted himself long enough to accept it with a beatific smile. It was becoming obvious to Maude that her youngest son saw this dangerous and needless war as a grand adventure. "Where is Henry now? Where did he go after destroying the castle at Bonmoulins?"

"He is garrisoning all his castles along the Norman border, and once he is sure that Normandy is no longer threatened, he said he'll be able to quell the rebellion in Anjou." Will stifled a huge yawn. "I have much more to tell you, Mama, but I think I'd best save the rest for the morrow. My men are bedding down in the priory guest hall, and with your permission, I'll join them, for it's been a long ride, a long day."

"Of course." Maude bade her son goodnight, kissed him on a smooth, beardless cheek, and agreed to meet him for Morrow Mass the following morning. But once he departed, all her energy seemed to have gone with him, and she sat down wearily upon a coffer chest. After a time, she felt Minna's hand on her shoulder. For Minna understood, too, why Henry had sent Will to Rouen. He'd done it for her, Maude knew. So that her youngest would not be present when Henry dealt with his faithless brother.

ELEANOR awakened with a start. The chamber was dark, save for a single night candle. Colette, a sound sleeper, lay motionless on her pallet by the bed, but Eleanor's greyhound had begun to whine, and Yolande was fumbling with her bed-robe as she stumbled sleepily toward the door. The knocking continued, louder now. When Yolande opened the door, Eleanor recognized the voice seeking entry: Jordan, her clerk. Why would he be awakening her in the night unless the news was dire? She was grabbing for her bed-robe when Yolande spun around, eyes wide with shock. "My lady, it is your husband!"

Eleanor went cold. "He is not dead?"

"No, my lady, no! Jordan says he is here!" Opening the door wider, Yolande cried, "Jordan, tell her!"

"It is true, madame. The duke has just ridden into the bailey." As if realizing how unlikely this sounded, Jordan insisted, "I saw him dismounting with my own eyes, my lady, I swear I did!"

"Has he been wounded?"

"No, my lady, not judging by what I saw."

While Jordan's assurance dispelled Eleanor's fears about Henry's safety, her unease persisted. She was optimistic by nature, as all gamblers are, but it was difficult to be sanguine about her husband's midnight arrival. Why would Harry break off his campaign and return without warning to Poitiers? She could think of only one reason: the war's tide had turned against him, so badly that Aquitaine itself was now threatened with invasion. By all accounts, he'd been more than holding his own. But she knew fortune was never so fickle as on the battlefield. What else could it be?

By now, Colette was up, too, hastily pulling on her chemise as Yolande shooed Jordan back outside while they dressed. Slipping into her bed-robe, Eleanor was searching in the floor rushes for her shoes when they heard the voices out on the stairwell. Eleanor forgot about her shoes, started for the door as it burst open again, and a moment later, she was in her husband's arms.

"I am so glad to see you," she said once he'd stopped kissing her, somewhat surprised herself by just how glad she was. "But I do not understand why you are here. Is the war about to spill over into Aquitaine?"

Henry smiled and shook his head. "No, love," he said. "The war is over."

BELOW in the great hall, it was chaos. Henry's men were tired and hungry and triumphant, in need of food and wine and well-deserved accolades, all of which the palace inhabitants were more than willing to provide. For once, the cooks did not mind being roused from their beds to prepare a late-night meal. As word spread that their duchess's young husband had routed their enemies and protected Aquitaine from invasion, people began to crowd into the hall, eager to share in the excitement, and a boisterous celebration was soon in progress.

Up in the Maubergeon Tower, a private celebration was already under way. Eleanor and her ladies could not do enough for Henry, and despite his exhaustion, he found himself enjoying all the attention, joking that this was every man's dream come true, to be waited upon by three fair women. Was he thirsty? Yolande flew downstairs to fetch a flagon of spiced hippocras. Was he hungry? Colette was happy to send to the kitchen for venison stew and hot bread and honeyed wafers. When he expressed a need for a bath, one was swiftly arranged. Eleanor unbuckled his scabbard, assisted him in removing his muddied boots, and insisted that he settle himself comfortably upon the bed while he awaited the arrival of his food and bath. Propped up by pillows, basking in female admiration, Henry told them about the war.

"Louis has offered a truce and gone back to Paris to nurse a fever and his bruised pride," he related, with a sardonic smile that could not hide his jubilation. "His stouthearted accomplices had already made themselves scarce, for this war did not turn out to be as much fun as they'd expected. After I raided into Dreux, Stephen's nephews decided they were urgently needed at home, lest I pay a visit to Champagne or Blois next. They were always more keen on the spoils of war than the war itself. All save Eustace, who's like to be sore crazed with rage at such spineless allies."

Henry paused then, as Yolande came rushing back into the chamber with several precariously balanced wine flagons. Pouring a cup of hippocras, Eleanor carried it over to the bed and sat beside him as he drank. "What of your brother, Harry? What happened in Anjou?"

"Geoff's rebellion sputtered out like a dying candle. The malcontent lords he'd lured to his banner scattered to the winds as soon as I crossed into Anjou. I had no trouble convincing Geoff's castellans at Mirebeau, Loudun, and Chinon that it was in their interest to yield the castles to me. Geoff and those of his followers not already in hiding holed up in Montsoreau. I laid siege to it and captured it easily enough to embarrass Geoff, who had no choice then, but to seek my forgiveness."

"I see." Eleanor did not expect him to cast his brother into a dungeon and let him rot. But she feared that if he was too lenient with Geoff, other would-be rebels might learn the wrong lesson from his forbearance. "And did you? Did you forgive him?"

"Yes," Henry said, "I did." He drank, watching her all the while. "But first I took away his castles."

Eleanor's smile was dazzling. "Men will be talking about this war for years to come," she predicted. "You humbled the French king, put the fear of God into his lackeys, thwarted your chief rival for the English throne, chastened your brat of a brother—and you did all that in less than two months." Leaning toward him, she murmured, "After such a remarkable campaign, the least I can do is give you an equally memorable welcome home."

Her breath was warm on his skin, her eyes a luminous cat-gold, and Henry wondered if he'd ever learn to take her beauty for granted, if he'd ever look at her without feeling his pulse jump. "That is a most intriguing offer, Eleanor. Could you be more specific?"

Eleanor laughed softly. "All in good time." Colette was beckoning from the doorway and she slipped off the bed to confer. Colette reported that the food was almost ready, and the bathwater was being heated, would be brought up after the meal.

"Yolande and I will sleep elsewhere tonight," she said, smiling, and without waiting to be asked, she began to unfasten Eleanor's night plait; Colette knew enough of men to be sure that Henry would want his wife's hair loose and free-flowing for their lovemaking. With deft strokes, she brushed Eleanor's hair until it felt like silk and looked like fire-lit sable. "How perfect it would be," she whispered, "if tonight you conceived a son."

Eleanor's throat tightened, so great was her desire to bear Henry an heir. He had proved himself, and in spectacular fashion, to her and to the world. But her battlefield would be the birthing chamber, and if she could give him the son God had denied to Louis, that would be her joy, her triumph, and her vindication.

"God Willing, Colette," she said, and turned back toward Henry, only to come to a surprised stop. When Colette started to speak, she shook her head, putting her finger to her lips as Colette joined her beside the bed.

Colette thought Henry looked very appealing and unguarded in sleep; she'd never noticed before that he had such long golden lashes. "Do you want me to send the food up later?"

"No . . . let him sleep. Lord knows, he has earned a night's rest." Eleanor eased herself onto the bed, but Henry didn't stir. Gesturing for Colette to hand her a blanket, she gently tucked it around him, then slid under the covers. Blowing out all the candles but one, Colette quietly withdrew. At the door, she paused. Eleanor was propped up on her elbow, gazing down at her sleeping husband. Colette would have expected to find indulgent amusement in her face, and did. But as she watched, the amusement gave way to a different sort of smile, one like a caress, surprising and revealing. Smiling, too, Colette closed the door.

HENRY did not at once remember where he was; it had been weeks since he'd slept in such a soft bed. Half asleep, he wondered why he was still dressed, especially since there seemed to be a female form beside him in the bed. Yawning, he leaned over to get a look at his bedmate, admiring the bare shoulder emerging from the sheets. As he did, he caught a beguiling, familiar fragrance. Eleanor's perfume? Jesus God! Wide awake now, he sat bolt upright as it all came back to him. How could he ever have fallen asleep in Eleanor's bed?

His movement had shaken the mattress, and her lashes were beginning to flutter. Hoping she wasn't too vexed with him, he was framing an apology as she opened her eyes and smiled up at him. Captivated by the sudden appearance of her dimple, he had a powerful urge to kiss it, and from there, it seemed only natural to move to her mouth. He would later swear to Eleanor that he'd not meant to make love to her yet, not until he'd washed off the dust of the road, but she kissed him back with enough ardor to blur his good intentions. And so what happened next was not only predictable, it was inevitable.

RAISING up on his elbow, Henry grinned, for his discarded tunic had been flung across the room and landed atop Felice, Eleanor's greyhound. It seemed to have snagged on her collar, for it was draped over her like a tent as she sniffed about in the floor rushes. Shifting so he could slide his arm around Eleanor's shoulders, he smoothed her hair back from her face. Her throat was reddened, chafed by his beard, and he stroked the soft skin with his fingers, saying ruefully, "I really did plan to take a bath first. But you're too tempting for your own good, love."

Eleanor yawned, then gave him a smile of drowsy contentment. "I'm not complaining . . ."

"No," he conceded, "you've been very good-natured about all of this. Are you always going to be such an obliging wife?"

"Not likely," she said and laughed. "At the moment, I'm inclined to deny you very little. But that mood is sure to pass, so you'd best take advantage of it whilst you can."

Henry laughed, too, and pulled her still closer. She traced the freckles on his throat with the tip of her tongue, her fingers playing pleasurably with the hair on his chest, gently scraping his skin with her nails. "I just noticed something. Your hair and beard are sort of a copper color, and your chest hair is golden. But down here," she said, trailing her fingers across his belly, toward his groin, "the hair is bright red!"

He wouldn't have thought she could arouse him again so soon, but his body was telling him otherwise. "Flames are always reddest where the fire burns hottest. Did you not know that?"

"If your fire burned any hotter," she teased, "all of Poitiers would have gone up in flames." Leaning over, she kissed him gently. No longer playful, she looked intently into his face. "Ah, Harry," she said, softly and quite seriously, "I am so proud of you."

What surprised Henry was not her words, it was his response to them. He already knew that he'd waged an extraordinary campaign, one that men would not soon forget, not in France nor England. While he was pleased by all the plaudits he'd reaped, he did not need this acclaim to understand the full magnitude of what he'd accomplished. Never had the English crown been so close, and his one regret was that his father had not lived to see his triumph. He'd not expected Eleanor's praise to mean so much to him, for he'd not realized until now just how much her opinion had begun to matter. Instead of jesting, he said simply, "I'm glad."

"I want to give a great feast for you," she said, "one so lavish and bountiful that people will talk of it in awe. I know you do not care much for such revelries, but trust me—this one you will enjoy, Harry. You and I will sit at the high table, eating porpoise and swan, whilst we watch my male kinfolk eating humble pie!"

"You are right," Henry said, laughing. "I daresay I would enjoy that!"

"I suppose I ought to summon a servant, for you must be starved." But Eleanor could not bring herself to move. A pity she and Harry could not spend the entire day in bed, the door bolted, the world shut out. "Passing strange," she said, "for we're into our fourth month of marriage and we've had only a fortnight together so far. I suppose England is already beckoning, too. How long can you stay this time?"

"As long as you want."

She sat up, staring at him. "Are you serious?"

"I've been thinking about it. If England has survived for nigh on seventeen years under Stephen, it can muddle through for another few months. And so . . . I have decided to put off my invasion for a while. I thought I'd let you show me Aquitaine instead?" Despite himself, his voice rose questioningly, for they were still, in so many ways, intimate strangers, and he could not be sure that she'd not be disappointed by the delay, craving the English crown more than his company. He saw at once, though, that he need not have worried. Kneeling naked before him on the bed, her eyes sparkling and her hair in wanton disarray, she looked of a sudden very young, giving him a glimpse of the girl who'd gone off with such high hopes to wed the French king.

"You and Aquitaine? Harry, nothing would please me more!"

53

NEWBURY, ENGLAND

October 1152

THE town of Newbury was an ancient one, strategically situated on the road that ran north to Oxford and south to Winchester. The site had once been settled by the Romans, then the Anglo-Saxons, and it was here that John Marshal had chosen to erect a castle. On this blustery October Thursday, Eustace was approaching Newbury from the east, along the Reading Road. The siege works were already in sight, encircling the castle and occupied town, when an armed force rode out to challenge him.

Eustace recognized the Earl of Northampton, the most steadfast of his father's allies. It took him a moment, however, to identify the man riding beside Northampton, for William de Mohun had not often come to Stephen's court. Lord of Dunster, Mohun had been granted the earldom of Somerset by Maude, a title Stephen refused to acknowledge. He was a strikingly handsome man, with a reputation as foul as his appearance was fair. He'd deserted Maude after the siege of Winchester and gone over to Stephen's side, yet his main interest was in feathering his own nest. The war had spawned so many men like Mohun, brigand barons who'd taken advantage of the conflict to rob and extort with impunity. But not after he was king, by God. Eustace knew how he'd rule. Like the old king. Not like his father. Never like his father.

Mohun's presence at the Newbury siege was disheartening, for it showed Eustace just how badly his father's circle of supporters was shrinking if he had to rely upon such untrustworthy self-seekers. Ypres was blind, Warenne dead on crusade, Robert Beaumont well-nigh invisible, Hugh Bigod and the Earl of Chester in the enemy camp. And how many more would be turning traitor once they heard about that Angevin whoreson's triumph over the French king? Eustace was not a fool. He knew that his father's kingship was wounded and bleeding. Not hemorrhaging, but even a steady trickle of blood could prove fatal if not stanched. How was he to do that, though? Holy Christ on the Cross, how?

Halting his men, Eustace rode out to meet Northampton and Mohun. He brushed aside their surprised queries, ignored their curiosity. He knew he'd have to talk about the disastrous Normandy campaign, but the longer he could put it off, the better. Instead, he asked brusquely about the siege.

John Marshal, they informed him indignantly, was as treacherous as a serpent and as false as Judas himself, may God smite him as he deserved. This was less than illuminating to Eustace, but with some prodding, he got them to begin with the facts. At the start of the siege, Newbury's castellan had sought a brief truce so that he might warn his lord, John Marshal, of the castle's peril. Eustace nodded; that was only to be expected. Marshal had then asked for a longer truce, one that would enable him to confer with the empress and her son, for he held Newbury in their names. Again, this was in accordance with the laws of war, and Eustace was hard put to hide his impatience.

"I assume my father agreed?" His mouth twisted; as if Stephen, the soul of chivalry, would have refused! "But he did demand hostages?"

"Indeed he did, my lord. Marshal agreed quite readily, yielding up his youngest son, a lad of about four or five. But then he betrayed us—and the boy. He took advantage of the truce to sneak supplies and men into Newbury, enabling them to withstand a long siege."

Eustace knew that his youth put him at a disadvantage with his father's supporters, and to compensate for that, he'd cultivated the world-weary, jaded air of a man who'd seen too much ever to be truly surprised. The pose slipped now, though, and he whistled soundlessly, almost admiringly, for few men would have had the ice-blooded audacity to gamble with such high stakes.

"Sounds like Marshal has sons to spare," he joked grimly. "Did my father warn him that the boy's life would be forfeit?" That was not a question he should have had to ask—not of any king but his father. He was relieved when Northampton nodded somberly.

"Of course he did, my lord Eustace. He sent a warning yesterday to Marlborough, telling Marshal that the lad will be hanged unless Marshal agrees to yield Newbury."

"Marlborough is how far? Twenty miles? So we'll hear today then," Eustace said, and smiled. "It seems I shall be just in time for Newbury's surrender."

DINNER was normally served in the morning, but it had been delayed by Eustace's arrival, and the trestle tables were not set up in Stephen's tent until noon. The meal was surprisingly good for camp fare—a savory capon stew—and conversation flagged as men concentrated upon their trenchers.

The faces were all familiar to Eustace. In addition to Northampton and Mohun, their dinner guests included Stephen's loyal seneschal, William Martel, and a handful of highborn lords. William d'Aubigny, Earl of Arundel, had begun to play a more active role on Stephen's behalf since losing Adeliza to a Flemish convent and an untimely death. Aubrey de Vere, Earl of Oxford, was Stephen's chamberlain, but like so many in this war, his past was chequered, for at one time, he'd been allied with Maude. The same was true of Roger Beaumont, Earl of Warwick, a cousin of the Beaumont twins and a former partisan of the empress. Eustace was glad they were eating with such gusto, for it put off their inevitable and intrusive questions about the Normandy debacle.

Stephen alone had no appetite for the stew; it was growing cold on his trencher as he toyed with a piece of bread. Eustace had not seen him since the spring, and he was taken aback by how much Stephen seemed to have aged. He did think Stephen was old; to twenty-two, fifty-six was tottering on the edge of an open grave. But his father had never looked his age before. Eustace studied Stephen as he ate, not liking what he saw. Mama's death was a wound that ought to be healing by now. It had been five months, after all. He missed her, too. But Papa could not afford to give in to his grieving. There was too much at stake for that.

The meal was almost over when the talk turned to the topic Eustace had wanted to avoid, yet knowing all the while that it would come up, that it must be dealt with, for Henry Fitz Empress's triumph would affect them all. It was the affable, tactless William d'Aubigny who breached the tacit conspiracy of silence. Sopping up gravy with a thick chunk of bread, he looked inquiringly down the table at Eustace. "Now that you're here, lad, you can tell us what truly happened in Normandy this summer. What with the rumors and gossip, who knew what to believe? Did the French king really get chased all the way back to Paris with his tail between his legs?"

Stephen glanced up swiftly, frowning. His sympathy stung Eustace as much as Aubigny's clumsy curiosity, and he said roughly, before Stephen could intercede on his behalf, "If you heard that the French king's milksop allies fled like rabbits, that is true enough, and may God forgive them, for I never shall. As for my brother by marriage, Louis hardly covered himself in glory, either. He, of all men, had reason to avenge himself upon Maude's whelp, but he had no stomach for fighting, for—"

Stephen leaned over. "Eustace . . ."

Eustace shook off his father's hand. He knew he was being dangerously indiscreet, but he no longer cared. "You wanted the truth, did you not? Well, I am giving it to you. Henry Fitz Empress did not win the war; Louis lost it. Twice he balked at doing battle with Henry—twice! No wonder he was not man enough for that wanton wife of his, for I've seen snakes with more backbone."

There were some involuntary laughs at that, quickly smothered. Eustace ignored them, unable to stop himself now even if he'd wanted to; his rage had been too long pent up. "Once it became clear that this would be no quick and easy war of conquest, Louis's resolve began to waver like a broken water reed. Instead of confronting Henry at Pacy, he showed his heels. I'd stayed behind to garrison Neufmarché, and by the time I got to Louis, it was too late; all the fight had gone out of him."

Pausing to gulp down the last of his wine, Eustace shook his head in angry bafflement. "Louis sees ill omens if he so much as stubs his toe. The botched attack on Pacy was bad enough, but then his cousin died suddenly and after that, he was well-nigh useless, convinced that all these setbacks must be proof of God's disfavor. His brother and my craven cousins had already flown the coop for Dreux, Blois, and Champagne, and so this wretched war ended with the King of France stricken with a convenient fever, skulking back to Paris in shame."

Stephen agreed with his son's scornful assessment of the French king's inept campaign, but he wished Eustace had waited until they were alone to express it, for he knew every embittered word would eventually get back to Louis; the men in this tent could never resist repeating such choice gossip. "When you spoke of Louis's mourning his cousin, I assume you mean the Count of Vermandois? We heard that he'd died during the campaign."

Eustace nodded. "The one besotted with Eleanor's sister. Louis was right fond of the man, God knows why. In truth, I think he was just looking for an excuse to end the war, and I suppose Raoul's death was as good a reason as any. Better than that sudden fever, for certes!" He laughed harshly. "So . . . now you know what 'truly happened in Normandy this summer,' my lord of Arundel. It was great fun; a pity you missed it."

No one knew what to say. Stephen yearned to console his son, but he realized that any comfort he'd offer would ring false to Eustace. Even if Almighty God were to send an archangel into their midst to absolve Eustace of any blame, it would change nothing. All over England, men would still be talking of Henry Fitz Empress, bedazzled by the apparent ease of his victory over the King of France. When he returned to England, this time he would come as a man of proven prowess on the battlefield, a man dangerous to defy. Already a far greater threat than ever his mother had posed. And who knew that better than Eustace?

A servant was moving around the table, refilling their wine cups. Stephen took a swallow; it tasted bitter. "I was surprised," he said, "when Henry did not start gathering another fleet at Barfleur. Do you know why, Eustace?"

The younger man shrugged. "I heard that he was loath to leave his bride. Judging by his haste in getting back to her bed, all those lurid stories told about her must be true. But no woman can compete with a crown, not for long. Once he gets his fill, he'll start casting his eyes toward England again. That I do not doubt."

Neither did Stephen. "Did you hear any talk about how long he means to stay in Aquitaine? Now that winter is nigh, mayhap he'll tarry there till the spring?"

"I expect he will, although I heard nothing about his plans ere I sailed for England. The only gossip coming out of Aquitaine concerned the incident at Limoges."

Glancing about the table, Eustace saw no comprehension on the watching faces, only puzzlement and curiosity. "I see you have not heard yet about that. After Henry hurried back to Eleanor, they set off on a progress through her domains. Almost at once, they ran into trouble—at Limoges, where the citizens balked at offering them hospitality. When Henry demanded an explanation, the abbot of St Martial's pointed out that he and Eleanor were camped on the edge of town and claimed that the Limousins had a duty to provide food for their liege lord only when he actually lodged within the city walls."

"This is preposterous!" the Earl of Northampton exclaimed, and the others chimed in, too, equally indignant, for in that moment every man there felt a fleeting sense of solidarity with Henry, briefly seeing him not as an enemy but as one of their own, a highborn lord denied his just due by those who owed him deference and respect. Even Eustace's voice had a grudging note of approval as he described now the retaliation taken by his hated nemesis upon the recalcitrant citizens of Limoges.

"That reasoning did not satisfy Henry, either. The accounts I heard say that he treated the Limousins to a display of Angevin rage that they'll not soon forget. He then ordered the city's walls razed, so there'd be no such disputes on future visits."

This time the murmurs were both appreciative and amused. Stephen alone was dubious. "Surely it was not necessary to take such a drastic measure as that," he protested, "when a warning would have sufficed." Reaching for his wine cup, he was bringing it up to his mouth when he realized they were all staring at him in astonishment. "What is it?" he said defensively, for this was not an uncommon occurrence. He'd make an observation that seemed eminently reasonable, only to have his barons react as though he'd suddenly begun to speak a tongue utterly incomprehensible to them.

"Christ Jesus, Papa, that was an unforgivable insult!"

"Lord Eustace is right, my liege. Such a deliberate provocation must never go unpunished, for men would see that as weakness, as—"

"I know that," Stephen interrupted impatiently. "But in destroying the city walls, that punishment fell upon the innocent as well as the guilty, upon those citizens of Limoges who'd had no say in it, who likely did not even know why Henry was so wroth with them."

Stephen stopped then, for it was obvious he was wasting his time and his breath. They did not understand his point of view any more than he understood theirs. A familiar and frustrating sense of isolation swept over him. Did all kings feel so solitary, so alone? What did youths like his son and Maude's son know about the loneliness of kingship? What did they know about the conflicting claims of justice and mercy? Only one person had ever understood how hard the choices could be. Only Tilda, may God assoil her sweet soul. Only Tilda.

SERVANTS had cleared away the dishes and were dismantling the trestle tables when the messenger arrived from John Marshal. Ushered into Stephen's tent, he knelt awkwardly in the cramped space, and held out a sealed parchment. As Stephen broke the seal and began to read, the others watched, glad that this troublesome siege was finally over.

"Holy Christ . . ." Stephen's hoarse whisper was almost inaudible, but they all saw the color drain from his face. "The man is mad," he said, sounding stunned. "He must be . . ."

When they crowded around, clamoring for answers, Stephen handed Marshal's letter to his son. Eustace scanned it rapidly, his eyes widening. "Marshal says he'll not surrender the castle. As for our threat to hang his son, he said go ahead, hang him, that he has the hammer and anvil to forge other and better sons."

These were men not easily shocked, but John Marshal had managed to do just that. There was silence and then uproar, with all talking at once. Stephen had reclaimed Marshal's letter; he kept rereading it as if expecting to find there'd been some mistake, for he simply could not believe any man capable of saying of his five-year-old son, "Hang him."

"I never thought I'd see such evil as Geoffrey de Mandeville loosed on the Fenlands," he said, "but even he murdered other men's children, not his own . . ."

"I always heard that Marshal had no nerves at all. Look at the way he held out up in that burning church at Wherwell, willing to risk being broiled alive rather than surrender. But this . . . Jesú!" Eustace elbowed around the encircling men to reach his father. "Papa . . . I am truly sorry. I know how hard this will be for you."

Stephen had never heard his son sound so solicitous. Raising his eyes from the letter, he saw Eustace was watching him intently. So were the other men. He did not at first understand. When he did, he expelled his breath in an audible rush, as if he'd just taken a blow to the pit of his stomach. "You cannot think," he said incredulously, "that I am going to do it?"

"Papa, you have no choice."

"Lord Eustace is right, my liege." Northampton heaved a sound much like a sigh. "I hate this," he said heavily. "What man would not? But it must be done. You cannot let Marshal defy you like this. You threatened to hang his son if he did not yield Newbury. Now you have to follow through with your threat. You cannot back down, God help you, but you cannot!"

"No! I will not kill a child just to save face!"

But when Stephen looked to the other men for support, he found none. One by one, they began to voice their agreement with Eustace and Northampton. Mohun was chillingly composed, contending that the age of the hostage was immaterial. Aubrey de Vere mumbled his assent, as if hoping God would not hear. William d'Aubigny wanted no part in it, but when forced to declare himself, he condemned the child with tears in his eyes. Shaken by their unexpected unanimity, Stephen turned to his seneschal, for he knew William Martel to be a decent, God-fearing man, one whose judgment he trusted. But Martel, too, argued for the hanging, all the more convincing for his obvious distress.

Stephen would later look back upon that afternoon as one of the worst of his life. Reeling under their assault, he continued to insist that he'd not execute a child, no matter what the provocation. But they continued to insist that he must, and they had logic and history and political necessity on their side, whereas he had only instinct, an aversion rooted in emotion, heartfelt but not easy to articulate.

He could not rebut their arguments. All they said was true. Hostages lost their value if there was no risk. Why would a man ever keep faith if he could be sure his hostages would come to no harm? A king's word must be good. Whether he promised or threatened, he must do what he said he would. If Marshal was allowed to get away with this, other would-be rebels would take heart. Respect was but one side of the royal coin; the other was fear. For unless men feared to cross him, why would they stay loyal? He had a tenuous grip at best upon the allegiance of his subjects, war-weary and yearning for peace. And now he was no longer facing a haughty, irksome woman as his rival for the throne. With Henry Fitz Empress breathing down his neck, he had no margin for error. He could afford to make no more mistakes, to do anything that might cause men to doubt his will, to see him as weak or indecisive.

They were accustomed to speaking their minds freely with Stephen, and they did not hold back now. They reminded him that his uncle, the old king of blessed memory, had agreed to mutilate his own granddaughters, so important was it that the king's word could be trusted. They reminded him, too, how he'd gallantly allowed Maude to ride away safe from Arundel, whereas had he taken her captive, the war would have ended then and there. They'd staked their futures upon his kingship. And what of his son? How could he risk Eustace's birthright upon an impulse of misguided mercy?

"I am not saying it is right, my liege," William Martel said softly, "only that it is necessary. Sometimes an innocent must be sacrificed so that other innocents may live. Is it not better that one child should die if his death would hasten the end of this accursed war?"

"I suppose it would depend upon whether the child was yours." But Stephen was beaten and he knew it. He could not fight them all, for much of what they'd said had hit its target dead on. How many had died in the thirteen years since he'd let Maude go free at Arundel? Whenever he'd heeded his own inner voice, it was invariably wrong.

The men read surrender in his silence, and were relieved that they had prevailed. But this would not be a victory to celebrate; it would be one to forget—if they could. Now that the crisis was over, the toll it had taken showed clearly on their faces. William de Mohun alone seemed to have emerged unscathed in this battle between conscience and kingship, and the others suspected that was because his own conscience had been stillborn. He proved that by volunteering for a task any rational man would have shunned, offering to take charge of the execution of John Marshal's son. They were more than willing to put the onus off onto him, and Eustace nodded assent, all the while thinking that Mohun was a fool if he believed this would gain him any royal favor. Who wanted to dine with a hangman, to break bread with a gravedigger?

When Mohun reentered the tent, the men hoped he'd come to report that it was done. But instead, he announced with odious indifference that the arrangements had all been made. "Do you want to witness the hanging, my liege, or shall I just inform you once it is over?"

Stephen raised his head, regarding Mohun with revulsion. But it was nothing compared to his own self-loathing. "If a child is to die by my command, I owe it to him to watch." Turning hollowed, accusing eyes upon his accomplices—for that was how he saw them—he said bitterly, "We all owe him that much."

EXECUTIONS were usually a grisly form of entertainment, drawing large crowds in cities and towns. Rarely had a hanging been as poorly attended as this one, but as word spread through the camp, few of the men wanted to watch. Only the calloused and morbidly curious were gathered by the tree chosen as a gallows. Most found reasons to keep away.

Stephen's barons were there, but by command, not choice. They shifted uneasily, for few men could contemplate a child's death with William de Mohun's sangfroid. He might not know it yet, but Mohun had gained himself several new enemies this day, cursing him under their breaths for putting Stephen—and them—through this needless ordeal. Why had the fool just not gone off and done it?

Eustace felt honour-bound to stand shoulder to shoulder with his father, although he would rather have been anywhere else in Christendom. He'd not thought he would hate anyone more than Henry Fitz Empress, but John Marshal now ran Henry a close second. No matter how long it took, he would make Marshal pay for springing this diabolic trap upon them; the death of the boy was only a down payment on the debt. He knew full well that his father would never forgive himself for what they were forced to do here. As much as he hated to admit it, he was feeling a certain queasy tension, too, as the time drew nigh. He could only hope that the lad would not weep and sob.

But when William Marshal appeared, Eustace discovered that there was more to be feared than tears. A lively, handsome child, brown-haired and sturdy, William was utterly at ease, for he'd been well treated during his weeks in the royal encampment. He was too young to understand what being a hostage meant; he knew only that the king had been unfailingly kind to him, and he smiled at sight of Stephen, with an appalling and heartrending innocence.

They'd set up a barrel under the tree, so that the lad would break his neck when it was kicked away, instead of slowly strangling, William de Mohun explained, oblivious, as the men shrank back as if he were a leper.

Stephen's throat had closed up, and it hurt to breathe, but he forced himself to watch as William Marshal was led toward the barrel.

The boy paused to gaze admiringly at William d'Aubigny's lance, which the man had been shifting nervously from hand to hand, wondering why the earl looked so odd when he asked if he could hold it later. Aubigny's face twisted in anguish, and he muttered an obscenity that made William giggle, for he'd heard enough cursing from his father to recognize it for what it was.

The soldier chosen as hangman was being well paid for his labors, but brought face to face with his young victim, he wanted only to get it over with as soon as possible, and he reached out suddenly, scooped William up, and deposited him on the barrel. The child looked startled, but not alarmed. He rather liked being the center of attention, for as the youngest of four sons, he wasn't paid much mind in the Marshal household. Curious and trusting, he entered willingly into the spirit of this strange new game, and did not object as the noose was fastened around his neck.

An unnatural hush fell over the camp. The hangman made ready to kick the barrel away, looking to William de Mohun for his signal. Shamed by his weakness, Eustace averted his eyes. But Stephen was already in motion. Striding forward, he waved the hangman back. "Enough! I will not do this. Do you all hear me? By God, I will not!"

The hangman hastily moved aside, torn between relief and fear that he'd be cheated of his fee. Reaching up, Stephen took the rope from the bewildered child's neck, and set him back on his feet. By then, Eustace was beside him. "Papa, what are you doing?"

"What I should have done at the outset. God forgive me for letting it go this far."

"You're making a fool of yourself—again. You do realize that? Once word gets out how Marshal duped you and then defied you, you'll be a laughingstock!"

"Look at the lad, Eustace. Damn you, look at him! We came within a hairbreadth of hanging this child, and for what? No crown is worth this!"

"It is my crown, too! And I'll not stand idly by whilst you lose it, that I swear!"

William Martel and the Earl of Northampton were hovering about them, pleading that they stop, to no avail. William Marshal had begun to fidget, troubled by the anger in their voices. Moving closer to Stephen, he tugged at the king's sleeve, saying plaintively, "I do not want to play this game anymore."

Stephen looked down at the boy. "You do not have to, lad. It is over." Bending, he lifted William into his arms, and carried him toward the tent as the others watched, wordlessly.

54

WALLINGFORD, ENGLAND

December 1152

A SWIRLING, wet snow had been falling since dawn. By the time the Bishop of Winchester arrived at his brother's siege, he was chilled to the bone and grateful for even the meagre warmth of the brazier in Stephen's command tent. Stephen seemed genuinely glad to see him, for in the two months since his return from Rome, they'd begun to mend the rifts in their relationship. Just as their estrangement had been mainly the bishop's doing, so, too, was their reconciliation. His papal disgrace and thwarted ambitions had given the bishop a greater appreciation for familial bonds, a belated realization that he'd served neither Stephen nor God with wholehearted devotion. In his youth, he'd craved power and glory, the Holy See of Canterbury, possibly even a cardinal's hat. He knew now that some dreams were dust; he would rise no higher in the Church.

But all was not lost. His brother still needed him, and so did England. It had been a year of mourning, first their brother Theobald and then Stephen's Matilda. And Stephen would soon be facing the gravest threat yet to his embattled kingship. Stephen might be clinging to the shreds of a lifetime's optimism, but the bishop was too realistic to underrate the danger. They dared not hold Maude's son too cheaply. The French king had already learned that, to his cost.

"I hear your men finally captured Newbury?"

Stephen nodded, watching his brother warily. But the bishop continued to sip his mulled wine; if he, too, was critical of Stephen's handling of the Newbury siege, he was keeping it to himself. Stephen was grateful for that; too many others had faulted him for sparing John Marshal's son. "I sent the little lad to Constance in London," he said, waiting for a negative response. Again, he was reprieved; the bishop merely nodded.

"Is it true that Eustace has crossed the Channel again?"

"Yes. He wants to hire more mercenaries, whilst keeping a hawk's eye on Maude's son. And he heard that the French king was threatening to break the truce, so I suspect he also hopes to prod Louis into another war, if he can."

Stephen did not sound as if he expected Eustace to succeed. Neither did the bishop. The French king could not be eager to take on Henry Fitz Empress again. And even if Eustace did talk him into another campaign, Louis had proved he was no match for Henry on the field. It was their accursed luck, the bishop thought morosely, that Maude's son would be one of those blessed few born with a flair for command.

Stephen seemed to have read his brother's sour musings, for he said suddenly, "Normandy is lost to us. If we are to defeat Maude's lad, it must be here—on English soil. That is why the fall of Wallingford matters so much. It has become a symbol of Angevin defiance, the castle the king could not win. Twice I tried to take it by force, twice I failed. And because that is so, its surrender will daunt our foes and hearten our supporters beyond measure."

The bishop forgot his aching back, his frozen feet, and chilblained hands, for this was news of consequence, indeed. "Wallingford is going to yield to you?"

"They have no choice," Stephen said, "for they are running out of food. The castellan asked to be allowed to send an urgent message to Henry Fitz Empress, advising him that unless he can come to their aid, they will be forced to yield."

While to the uninitiated that might have sounded suspiciously like John Marshal's ruse at Newbury, the bishop knew that was strictly in accordance with the laws of war, for such an appeal allowed a besieged garrison to surrender with honour if help was not forthcoming. And for Wallingford, it would not be. Not only was it the dead of winter, but Henry was not even in the country, still dallying with his new wife in far-off Aquitaine. Rejuvenated and revitalized, the bishop gave Stephen the rarest sort of smile, one of unqualified approval. "Well done, Stephen! The fall of Wallingford could be a turning point in your kingship."

"God grant it so," Stephen said fervently, "for I cannot lose this war. I cannot let my son down."

HENRY and Eleanor's return to Poitiers was a hectic one, with vassals awaiting them in the great hall, petitioners seeking audiences, and a vast pile of letters accumulated in their absence, for not all of their correspondents had been able to track them on their progress through Aquitaine. After two days of continuous chaos, Eleanor decided they both could use some quiet time together, and surprised Henry with a candle-lit supper for two up in their bedchamber. Henry joked that he'd never heard of a man's having a secret tryst with his own wife, but he was pleased, for privacy was a scarce commodity in their lives.

Over an Advent meal of herring and pike, they enjoyed a rare luxury—a conversation overheard by no others. Eleanor was able to confide her concern about her widowed sister. Petronilla had recently suffered another blow, for the French king had awarded the wardship of Petronilla and Raoul's young son to Waleran Beaumont. Henry in turn complained about his vexing brother Geoff, having just found out that Geoff had been pestering their aunt, the Abbess Mathilde, entreating her to intercede with Henry on his behalf to get his forfeited castles back.

"Why Mathilde?" Eleanor asked. "Surely your mother would be the natural choice to mediate betwixt you?"

"Geoff would not dare approach our mother," Henry said, with a scornful smile. "He has yet to face her, according to her last letter. My aunt said she blistered his ears, but that is nothing to what Mama would have done!"

He told her, then, of the other news in his mother's letter: Stephen's clash of wills with John Marshal at Newbury.

Eleanor was riveted by the tale. "How could any man be so indifferent to his own child?"

"Marshal is a gambler, willing to take great risks even if the odds are not in his favor. He proved that when he was trapped in a burning bell tower at Wherwell Abbey; I told you that story, love, remember? I'm guessing that he was gambling again at Newbury, this time upon how well he knew Stephen."

"A diabolic wager, for certes," Eleanor said, shaking her head incredulously, "with his son's life as the stakes . . ."

"He judged Stephen rightly, though," Henry pointed out, "but at what a cost if he had not!"

"I cannot help wondering," Eleanor said, "how the boy's mother felt about it. Henry . . . you would not have hanged the child?"

"No," Henry said, leaning over to pour them both more wine, "I would not. But neither would I have threatened to hang him, as Stephen did. That was his great mistake. No man ought to make a threat he is not willing to carry out, especially a king—"

They were interrupted then by the arrival of a courier from England, bearing an urgent message for Henry. Excusing himself, he hastened down to the great hall. He was gone longer than Eleanor had expected; the servants had cleared away the dishes and brought up a bowl of costly imported oranges before he returned. Eleanor had been peeling an orange for him, but she set the fruit aside at sight of her husband's face. "The news was not good?"

He shook his head. "A desperate appeal from William Boterel, the castellan of Wallingford Castle. They have been under siege for months, and they doubt that they can hold out much longer. Stephen has seized the bridge, so they no longer have a way of getting supplies into the castle and their larders are well-nigh empty."

"This Wallingford . . . is it an important castle, Henry?"

"Yes, for it controls the Upper Thames Valley. But it has more than tactical significance. The man who held it, Brien Fitz Count, was the most steadfast of my mother's supporters. It was to Wallingford that she fled when she made that miraculous escape from Oxford. Wallingford . . . well, it came to signify resistance, our hope for victory . . ." He'd begun to pace. Halting before the hearth, he stood for several moments, gazing into the flames.

Watching him, Eleanor already knew what he would do. "You are going to Wallingford's rescue," she said. "You are going to brave a January crossing of the Channel and launch a winter campaign. You do realize, Harry, how mad that sounds?"

"Of course I do," he said, and smiled wryly. "That is why I'll take Stephen utterly by surprise."

THE hearth had burned low, and embers glowed in the shadows, visible from the bed. Henry leaned over and kissed his wife's throat, just below her ear. "Why are you not asleep yet?"

"I've a lot to think about," she said, "much of it troubling. I intend to invite my sister to stay with me once you've gone. She still mourns for Raoul, and now her son has been taken away from her . . . Where is the justice in that?"

"Well . . . in fairness to Louis, he probably meant to reward Beaumont, not to punish Petronilla. After all, how often are women given wardships?"

"Precisely my point," she retorted. "Women are the ones who must bear children, suffering the travails of the birthing chamber, and indeed, often dying to give life. And yet we have no say about what happens to the child afterward. It would never even have occurred to John Marshal to consult his wife ere he dared Stephen to hang their son. No more than Louis cared how he grieved Petra by putting her children's future into the hands of a self-seeking lout like Waleran Beaumont. It is so unfair, Harry, so outrageously unfair."

Henry had honestly never given the matter of wardships much thought. His views about women were conflicted, as the son of a strong-willed, defiantly independent woman in a world that taught him females were inferior, meant to be ruled by men. Following neither the well-traveled road of tradition nor the rocky, lonely trail Maude had blazed, he'd found his own path, not challenging their society's concept of male dominance, but acknowledging individual accomplishments in women like his mother—or his wife.

"There is some truth to what you say," he conceded, made cautious because they were venturing into unmapped territory; until now, they'd rarely discussed her daughters. "You are talking, too, about Marie and Alix . . . are you not?"

"Yes," she admitted, "I suppose I am . . ."

Henry propped himself up on his elbow, but it was too dark to see her face. "I'm sorry," he said. "If I could get them back for you, Eleanor, I would. But it is beyond my power, and not even a crown will change that."

"I know," she said. "Why do you think I mention them so seldom? Because they are lost to me. Louis will never allow me to see them, and there is nothing I can do about it." She turned toward him in the dark, seeking his embrace. "He'll teach them to hate me, Harry, and there is nothing I can do about that, either."

Henry tightened his arms around her. "It is not as easy as people think to poison a child's mind. During my mother's years in England, there were few at my father's court to speak well of her. God knows he did not. Your Marie is older than I was when my mother left us, old enough to hold fast to her own memories—as I did."

"Yes, but you knew your mother had not abandoned you. Abandonment will be the least of my maternal sins."

"I'll not deny that they'll hear slanderous stories about you. But your notoriety might well work to your benefit, for you'll not be like other discarded wives, Eleanor, to be cast aside and forgotten. Your daughters will grow up knowing that you are the Duchess of Aquitaine and Normandy and, God Willing, Queen of England. How can your girls not be curious about you? And once they are old enough, I think they'll want to find out for themselves what sort of woman you are."

"Jesú, Harry, what comfort can I take in that? The chance of a reunion twenty years from now?" But almost at once, Eleanor regretted her sharpness. "I am not being fair, am I? Had you offered me empty promises, vowed to win them back, then I'd have blamed you for lying to me. My nerves are on the raw tonight, more so than I realized."

Henry kissed her gently. He could not ease her yearning for her daughters. But he did have a parting gift for her. "When you write to your sister, ask her to join you at Angers, not Poitiers."

"Why?"

"I shall ask my mother to watch over Normandy in my absence. And of course you will continue to govern Aquitaine. But I would also have you act on my behalf in Anjou."

As he'd guessed, that pleased her immensely. "Do you trust me as much as that, then?"

"Why not? You have sound political sense and good judgment, too . . . for a woman," he teased, and pretended to wince when she nipped his neck. How he was going to miss sharing her bed in the months to come. "With you and my mother keeping vigil for me, I'll not have to worry about my fool brother stirring up another revolt. Without Geoff to distract me, I'll have a better chance of avoiding a heroic, martyr's death on some godforsaken English field."

"Do not jest about that," she chided, with a gravity that he found quite flattering. She quickly lapsed back, though, into the bantering levity that was the coin of their marital realm. "I do not want you to take any needless risks, Harry. I would hate to have to start husband-hunting all over again."

"I doubt that you'd have to hunt very hard," he said dryly. "Most likely you'd find yourself fending off suitors at my wake." Yawning, he drew her into an even closer embrace, and soon after, fell asleep. When he awoke, it was almost dawn. The fire had gone out and the chamber was cold and damp. But Eleanor's body was warm against his, her skin soft to his touch, and fragrant with her favorite perfume, one that she said put her in mind of summer roses and moonlight and honey-sweet sins.

Why was it sinful, though, to lay with his wife? Henry could not understand the Church's reasoning. Why was celibacy so holy, carnal lust so sinister? Even in wedlock, it remained suspect, for he'd heard priests claim that a man sinned if he loved his wife with too much passion. If that was true, he was putting his immortal soul in peril about twice a night. Laughing softly to himself, Henry reached for Eleanor.

Eleanor awoke with reluctance, for she'd been dreaming that she and Henry were making love, alone in a secluded meadow, with scented clover for their bed and a sapphire-blue sky for their ceiling. She'd never done that, never made love out in the open under a hot summer sun, and her first thought upon awakening was a drowsy regret for all she'd missed. And then she smiled, understanding why her dream had veered off into that meadow.

"Now you're seducing me in my dreams, too," she murmured, and laughed when he said that was passing strange, for in his dreams, she was always the temptress. She knew that their honeymoon harmony was not likely to last. They were both too self-willed not to clash occasionally, and she did not doubt that they would sail into rough seas at times. But she felt quite confident that their marriage bed would always be a safe harbor.

Whether they called it lust or passion or even love, what they found together in bed was rare and real and had nothing to do with crowns or kingships. She understood how lucky they'd been, hoped that he did, too.

He'd begun to stroke her thighs, and wherever his fingers touched, her skin seemed to burn. The frigid December dawn receded, and she was back in her dream, their bodies entwined, aware only of each other, the urgency of their need, and then, the shared intensity of their release.

Lying, slaked and spent, in a tangle of sheets, they soon discovered that sexual heat did not linger, and they dived, shivering, under the coverlets, where they got into a playful tussle when Henry tried to warm his cold feet against her legs. That led to the first pillow fight of their marriage, which ended abruptly when Eleanor's greyhound decided to join in the fun.

After evicting the dog, they settled back against the pillows, and Eleanor told Henry about her erotic dream. He promised that he'd find them a private meadow, provided that she was willing to wait for the spring thaw. But then they looked at each other, their laughter stilled, remembering that he would be in England in the spring, fighting a war.

Eleanor was quiet for a time after that. Once he rode away from Poitiers, who could say how long they'd be apart? She dared not wait, would have to tell him now. "Harry . . . do you think there is any chance that you might be back by August?"

"I do not know," he admitted. Shifting so he could see her face, he gave her a quizzical look. His birthday was in March, hers in June, their anniversary in May. What significance did August have in their lives? True, they'd met for the first time in August, but he knew his wife was not sentimental. "Why August?" he asked, and then caught his breath. "Eleanor?"

Eleanor had known he'd guess the truth; he was nothing if not quick. "Yes," she said, "I think I am with child."

INDIFFERENT to gossip, they remained abed for most of the morning. Henry was as solicitous as he was jubilant, summoning servants to light the hearth and fetch cider and honeyed bread for their breakfast, promising Eleanor that he'd not be gone a day longer than necessary, promising, too, to bring back a crown for their babe to play with. He was so delighted by the prospect of fatherhood that he was quite unfazed when she confessed that she could not be utterly certain yet, having missed only one flux so far. He blithely insisted that she was right to tell him now, that this was news to be shared in bed, not to be imparted in a letter. He even did his best to assure her that he'd not be disappointed if their first child was a girl, with such conviction that she almost believed him.

"Did you never doubt that I would give you a son?"

"No," he said emphatically, "never," and this time she did believe him.

Reaching for his hand, she laced their fingers together. "Harry . . . do you not think it is time we owned up to it?"

As cryptic as that might have sounded to others, he understood. She saw comprehension in his eyes, and a certain wariness as he considered his response. Not surprisingly, he settled upon humor. "You first."

Eleanor was never one to resist a dare. "All right," she agreed, "I will. When I began to confide in my sister about you, Petra listened and then exclaimed, 'You fancy him!' She was right, I did. I did not realize how much, though, until we were alone in the garden. You do remember what happened when we kissed?"

Henry's mouth quirked. "Till my dying day."

"I was caught by surprise, for fires usually have to be stoked ere they flame up like that. I remember telling Petra that you and I might be getting more than we'd bargained for. And the same can be said for our marriage." She flashed a sudden smile, at once mischievous and tender, too. "I discovered on our wedding night that setting a fire in a rainy garden was child's play, compared to the conflagration you could kindle in bed. But even then, I did not expect to fall in love with you . . . certainly not so quickly and completely. You were supposed to be satisfied with my body, not lay claim to my heart, too!"

Henry leaned over swiftly, seeking her mouth. She returned the kiss with enthusiasm, but when it ended, she said, "Your turn."

"You already know," he protested. "You would not have been so candid were you not sure of me."

That was a shrewd thrust, and she acknowledged it as such. "Pride is a shield as well as a sin. You're right, I would not have been so quick to put it down had I not been convinced I'd not need it. I know that you care, Harry. You prove that, in bed and out. But I would like the words, too."

So commanding was his self-assurance that she rarely remembered his youth. But now she found herself being reminded that he was not yet twenty, for he'd begun to look distinctly uncomfortable. She was not offended by his reluctance, for she could understand why he might be leery of letting down his own defenses, caught too often in the crossfire of his parents' war. But she'd spoken no less than the truth. She did need the words, especially now that she faced months of separation and anxiety, a lonely pregnancy under the constant threat of widowhood. "Louis was not so tongue-tied," she gibed sweetly, and Henry grimaced.

"That was a low blow," he complained. "I am utterly besotted with you, woman, as anyone with eyes to see could tell. Is that not enough for you?" She said nothing, greenish-gold eyes never leaving his face, and he capitulated with a smothered oath. "I do love you, Eleanor." Pulling her into his arms, he kissed her again. "God help me, but I do . . ."

Generous in victory, she forbore to tease, although the temptation was considerable, for his declaration of love had sounded almost like a confession. It might not be polished or even voluntary, but it was heartfelt, that she did not doubt. She'd known from the first that he would never be a man for romantic gestures or pretty speeches. So be it, then. What he could give her mattered far more than the superficial and studied gallantries of courtly love.

Sliding his hand between their bodies, he rested it upon her belly, so flat and taut that he could not easily envision it swollen with new life. "I would that I could promise to be back for the birth," he said regretfully, "but I cannot."

"I know," she reassured him, "I do. I ask only that you promise to take care, Harry, to remember that your life belongs to me now, too."

AFTER a hurried trip to Rouen to bid his mother farewell and to borrow the vast sum of seven thousand pounds from moneylenders, Henry set sail from Barfleur on Epiphany Eve. By dawn, his ships were within sight of the Dorset coast. Entering the River Frome, Henry's fleet anchored at Wareham, after a crossing so rough that the men would have gladly kissed the ground—had a raw, sleet-laden wind not been blasting across the harbor.

Unloading soldiers and horses was never easy, and in weather like this, it became a logistical nightmare. By the time the first of Henry's army came ashore, men from the castle were hastening down onto the docks. Turning at sound of his name, Henry found himself enveloped in a hearty avuncular embrace.

"Holy Rood, but you feel like a block of ice, lad!" Stepping back, Rainald beamed at his nephew. "We could not believe it when we first spotted sails on the horizon. This must have been the voyage to Hell and back!"

"Close enough," Henry admitted. "I am right glad to see you here, Uncle, but surprised, too, since you had to come all the way from Cornwall. How were you able to get to Wareham so fast?"

"My usual good luck. I happened to be at Bristol with Will when he got his summons." As Rainald glanced back, Henry saw that his cousin Will was coming toward him, with another familiar figure at his side: Roger Fitz Miles. Henry greeted them both warmly, but he could not help feeling a regretful twinge, too, for although Will was his kinsman and Roger his friend, he knew neither one of them could hold a candle to their deceased fathers. What he would not have given to be waging this campaign with his uncle Robert!

Henry remained on the docks for a while, supervising the landing. The others kept close by, hunched deep in their mantles and cursing the cold as they gave him their news. They expected the Earls of Chester and Salisbury and Ranulf and John Marshal to be awaiting him at Devizes Castle. Ranulf might be delayed, since getting word into Wales had been no easy feat; why he'd chosen to live in the back of beyond, Rainald would never understand. Baldwin de Redvers would be answering the summons, too, his health permitting, and Chester's brother, William de Roumare, was likely to appear as well.

That was heartening news to Henry, for his thirty-six ships held only one hundred forty knights and three thousand foot soldiers, not a large force to overthrow a king. He made a mental note to find out how many men had sailed with his great-grandfather when William the Bastard had invaded England in God's Year 1066, and then strode down to the water's edge to shout a warning, for a young soldier was attempting to unload a horse without blindfolding it first.

The sleet was giving way to hail, and Henry finally allowed his kinsmen to escort him up to the castle. As loath as he was to admit it, he was exhausted, very much in need of a blazing fire and a few hours' sleep. But as they approached the castle, pealing church bells began to echo on the stinging sea air, calling Christ's faithful to hear Mass on this, the holy feast of the Epiphany.

The Earl of Gloucester at once drew rein. "We ought to give thanks to God for guiding you safely through that storm, Harry." While Henry was in agreement that the Almighty deserved his gratitude, he'd have preferred to tender it after he'd been fed and thawed out. But he could think of no graceful way of refusing, for what sort of impious wretch did not have time for God? And so he did not object as his cousin led them into the small Benedictine priory east of the castle. Dismounting in the garth, they slipped in a side door of the nave, left open for latecomers.

The church was crowded, monks kneeling in the choir, townspeople in the nave. A few heads turned at their entrance, but most kept their eyes upon the priest as he solemnly intoned the introit for the Mass. "Behold, the Lord the ruler cometh, and the kingdom is in his hand."

Henry's head came up sharply. The response of his companions was far more dramatic. They looked at one another in astonishment, and then, at Henry, with something approaching awe.

"God's Word on High," Will said softly, crossing himself.

"What . . . divine prophecy?" But Henry's skepticism merely glanced off Will's certainty, and he nodded earnestly.

"Most men will think so." Rainald grinned jubilantly, for if his one nephew interpreted the priest's words as holy writ and the other as fortuitous happenchance, he saw them as a political windfall. "Maude must have told you about Stephen's ominous mishap ere the Battle of Lincoln, Harry. When his candle broke in his hand during the Mass, a shiver of foreboding swept through the entire congregation, so sure were they that this was an evil omen for a man about to go forth and do battle. But that was a puny portent, indeed, when compared to this!"

So intent were they upon the amazing aptness of God's Word that they had forgotten for the moment that they were in God's House. As their voices rose, people were turning to stare in their direction, with disapproving frowns and puzzled mutterings. Wareham's castle had long been an Angevin stronghold, though, and the three earls were known on sight to some of the parishioners. Those who'd recognized the earls soon guessed Henry's identity, too, and once they did, their priest's words took on a new and fateful significance. As they enlightened their neighbors, the church was soon in a state of excitement and disquiet.

Henry watched the turmoil in fascination. His uncle had been right! Leaning over, he murmured to Roger, "This is a tale to grow with each telling, and by the time it reaches Stephen's ears, people will be swearing that an Angel of the Lord appeared to me in the midst of a burning bush!"

55

SIEGE OF WALLINGFORD

January 1153

STEADY rain had turned Stephen's siege encampment into a morass. Knowing how wretched the roads were, Stephen was amazed to see William de Ypres ride into the camp, for after his sight had begun to fail, the Fleming rarely traveled beyond his own estates. But whatever had motivated Ypres to venture so far from Kent, Stephen was delighted that he had, for the gaunt, grizzled old soldier brought back memories of a happier time, memories of Matilda.

Horse litters were used only by the aged and the infirm and, sometimes, women. Most people would have agreed that a blind man could travel in a horse litter without shame. But pride was the only crutch William de Ypres would permit himself, and he'd continued to ride, as always, although his vision had now deteriorated to such an extent that he'd reluctantly agreed to let his mount be led. Theirs was an age in which the blind were too often condemned to a beggar's fate, but Ypres was a very wealthy man, able to hire men to act as his eyes, and to judge by the conscientious way they watched over him, he paid them handsomely. The ground was treacherous, glazed and pitted, and even with their assistance, Ypres stumbled several times and once almost lost his footing altogether. But by then Stephen was there, guiding him into the shelter of his command tent.

"You remember my son?" Stephen said, beckoning his youngest forward to greet the Fleming. "Eustace is here, too, and will be right glad to see you. He always did think you walked on water, Will!"

Ypres was trying in vain to warm his hands over the brazier. "Eustace is in England?" he asked, surprised. "I heard he'd crossed over to France again."

"He did, but he came back as soon as he got word that Henry Fitz Empress had sailed from Barfleur."

"So it is true then? Maude's son has come in answer to the Wallingford garrison's plea? I was not sure if the rumors could be trusted."

"It has been my experience," Stephen said wryly, "that rumors and falsehoods are kin more often than not. But this time they speak true, Will."

"Well," Ypres said after a brief silence, "the lad does not lack for backbone, does he?"

"He comes by it honestly," Stephen said generously, "for I've known few men who could match Maude's grit. But grit alone is not enough, as her son is about to learn. All his strongholds are in the west, which means he'll have to make a long and dangerous march clear across England, in the midst of winter, through shires hostile to him, whilst lugging along food for his army, since he'll not be able to live off the land. And if and when he does reach Wallingford, I'll be waiting for him. God Willing, I'll be able to end this accursed war at last."

There'd been a time when Stephen would have sounded jubilant in predicting victory. Now, he just sounded tired. "God Willing," Ypres echoed, knowing that they were both thinking of Matilda, cheated of what she'd most wanted—to see peace finally come to her husband's realm.

Stephen tilted his head, listening, and then rose. "I'll be back," he announced, and ducked under the tent flap. Riders were dismounting, stumbling toward the closest fire. "I thought I heard your voice," Stephen said, moving toward his eldest son. "You found nothing out of the ordinary?"

"Nothing. We circled the entire camp, spoke with all the sentries. They're as edgy as bridal-night virgins, flinching at shadows, as if they expect Fitz Empress to come charging over the hill at any moment."

"It'll get worse ere it gets better. Come back with me to the tent. You'll not believe who rode into camp this afternoon—none other than Will de Ypres!"

Stephen was startled by the look that crossed his son's face, one of dismay. "Eustace? I thought you'd be pleased. You always seemed so fond of him?"

Eustace shrugged. How could he explain that he was loath to see Ypres for that very reason, because the man had once loomed so large in his life? It was painful to see what he'd been reduced to, this man who'd once been feared by so many. It was like looking upon a lamed stallion, able only to hobble about when once it could race the wind. He glanced at his father's puzzled face, then away, fumbling for an excuse to avoid the Fleming. But then he heard the shouting.

Stephen heard it, too, and felt a sudden unease. A lone rider was coming in, much too fast.

WITHIN the tent, Ypres found himself alone with Stephen's younger son. The Fleming had never had any dealings with Will, whose childhood had coincided with Ypres's tenure as the king's mainstay, the queen's confidant. Doing some mental math, he concluded that Will was nigh on nineteen, although he seemed younger, untested. Ypres had heard it said that he'd inherited a goodly measure of Stephen's affability. He hoped the lad had gotten some of Matilda's mettle, too.

"May I ask you something?" Will spoke up suddenly, his curiosity getting the better of him. "Can you see anything at all?"

The question was oddly childlike, direct and without artifice, and Ypres answered in kind. "In one eye, nothing. In the other, I can still distinguish light and shadow . . . for now."

Will nodded solemnly. But then he stiffened. "Did you hear that yelling? I'd best find out what it's about."

Straining to hear, Ypres could make out only a babble of rising voices. Once he would have been in the midst of the action. Now he must wait until someone remembered to return and tell him what was happening. It felt at times as if the very center of his world had become hollow, and try as he might to fill it with faith, the emptiness lingered. He was not sure why his faith was not enough, although he suspected that it was because it had come to him so late in life. If he were God, he'd look askance, too, at deathbed conversions. No matter what the priests might tell him, piety must lose some of its lustre when it was not altogether voluntary.

It was Will who eventually brought Ypres the news that had set the camp in such an uproar. "Malmesbury Castle is under siege," he reported breathlessly. "The castellan sent my father an urgent plea for aid, saying the town has fallen to Henry Fitz Empress, and the castle is like to fall, too, unless the king comes to their rescue."

Ypres showed no surprise; he'd been half expecting something like this. "I see," he said laconically, and Will looked at him in bemusement.

"Well, I do not," the youth admitted. "It sounds to me like Papa and the others are going to abandon the siege, and I do not understand why. I thought Wallingford mattered!"

"It does. Its fall would be a severe blow to the Angevins. The trouble is, lad, that Malmesbury's fall would be a great setback, too—for us. It is the only royal stronghold of note left to Stephen in the west. Losing it would hurt us fully as much as Wallingford's loss would hurt Henry Fitz Empress."

Will frowned. "Well . . . would not the loss of the one offset the other? We take Wallingford, let them take Malmesbury . . . check and mate."

"Unfortunately, it is not that simple. You see, the king cannot afford to ignore a challenge to his authority, lest others see that as weakness. If he did, he'd risk losing more than Malmesbury."

"But that is not fair! If Henry makes Papa come to him, we'll forfeit all the advantages we would have had at Wallingford." When Ypres nodded, Will edged closer.

"My lord Ypres . . . do you think my father is a good battle commander?"

"Indeed he is," Ypres agreed, reassuring Will by how readily he answered. "He is one of the best I've seen." Leaving unsaid his private conviction that if Stephen were not, his kingship would never have survived this long, given how inept he'd proved to be at statecraft.

Will hesitated. "What of Henry Fitz Empress? Is he a good battle commander, too?"

"Yes, lad," Ypres said grimly. "It is beginning to look as if he is."

DESPITE the wet, frigid weather and the washed-out roads, Stephen responded to Malmesbury's peril with commendable speed. Accompanied by those barons still loyal to him, he approached Malmesbury from the north, along the Cirencester Road. His scouts had warned Stephen that the River Avon was running high, but by the time his army made camp, darkness had fallen over the frozen Wiltshire countryside, and it was not until the morning that he discovered the full extent of the flooding.

The February dawn was storm-darkened, sleet and gusting winds assailing the king's men with unrelenting ferocity as Stephen rode out to inspect the River Avon.

The Tetbury branch of the Avon narrowed as it flowed around Malmesbury, and was usually as easily forded as any stream. Despite the warning by his scouts, Stephen was unprepared for the sight that now met his eyes. The heavy rains had transformed the placid Avon into a churning cauldron, wide and deep and dangerous. Spilling over its banks, it swallowed up adjoining fields, sweeping uprooted trees along on its current as if they were twigs. Occasionally the men glimpsed a half-submerged body: drowned rabbits and badgers, an exhausted, foundering deer, a dog's bloated corpse.

Stephen reined in his stallion, gazing out upon the floodwaters with consternation. Beside him, he heard men cursing. The wind was stinging, iced with sleet, and they soon turned back toward their camp.

FORTUNATELY, the wind muffled the sounds of altercation coming from Stephen's tent, for he would not have wanted this dissension to be overheard by his soldiers. He was stunned by the resistance he was encountering; it had never occurred to him that he might have to battle Henry Fitz Empress, Nature's fury, and his own barons, too.

But that was proving to be the case. Led by Robert Beaumont, Earl of Leicester, they were arguing against launching an attack upon Malmesbury. The Earls of Derby and Arundel were most vocal in Beaumont's support, but the Earls of Oxford and Warwick were murmuring muted agreement, too. Only Eustace and the Earl of Northampton showed any zeal for the upcoming battle. William de Martel and Stephen's younger son took no active part in the discussion; they would do whatever Stephen willed. And in the shadows, William de Ypres listened in silence to the discord swirling about him.

"It would be folly to attempt an assault upon Malmesbury under these circumstances," Robert Beaumont insisted calmly. He had none of his twin's flamboyance, had always been overshadowed by Waleran, and had seemed content that it was so. But in the years since Waleran's self-imposed exile from England, Robert had come into his own, and his sober, reasoned argument was falling on receptive ears.

Sensing that, Eustace focused his energies and his anger upon Beaumont, saying scornfully, "Just why do you think we marched on Malmesbury, my lord? To admire the winter countryside?"

That would have provoked a heated retort from Waleran. But Robert retained his composure, even his manners. "We had no way of knowing that the river would be impassable," he pointed out coolly. "Now that we do, it behooves us to reconsider. I do not see how it will advance the king's cause to lose half our army in the Avon."

"If Robert Fitz Roy had been so leery of getting his feet wet in the Fossedyke," Eustace riposted, "there'd have been no Battle of Lincoln, now would there?"

"Would that not have been for the best?" his brother asked, not meaning to be sarcastic, blushing when several of the men snickered and Eustace glared at him.

William d'Aubigny interceded before Eustace could turn upon his discomfited brother. "I do not believe this is a battle we can win," he confessed, glancing apologetically toward Stephen. "Even if we get across the Avon, the wind is coming from the south. They'd have it at their backs, whilst we'd be getting hit in the face with sleet and icy rain. It is asking a lot of men to fight under conditions like that. Would it not be wiser to wait for—"

"Wait for what—the spring thaw?" Eustace raged. "Or for some of you to find your misplaced manhood? That much time we cannot spare!"

Robert Beaumont remained coldly impassive, but the hot-tempered Earl of Derby took immediate offense, and Stephen was forced to intervene. "It is obvious that we'll do no fighting this day. If we must wait upon the weather, so be it."

The squabbling subsided, but the ill will remained. And nothing had been resolved. Stephen was shaken by what he'd witnessed. Eustace's gibes to the contrary, these men were not craven. But neither were they eager to do battle on his behalf. Was it truly just the vile weather that daunted them?

"My liege." William de Ypres had risen to his feet, groping for his cane. "These old bones stiffen up in cold like this. May I ask you to summon my attendants, so they can escort me back to my own tent?"

Stephen was astonished, unable to believe he'd just heard William de Ypres, of all men, complaining of his infirmities and asking for help. After a moment's reflection, he realized what the Fleming was up to. "It'll be easier," he said, "to take you myself," brushing aside other offers, for he knew that Ypres wanted an opportunity to confer with him alone.

Sleet was bombarding the camp, the wind tearing at the tents, making life miserable for men and horses alike. Stephen gripped the Fleming's arm tightly, steering him around the worst of the muddy sloughs. But Ypres stopped just before they reached his tent. "My men are within," he said, "and what I have to tell you cannot be overheard."

"We've braved worse perils together than winter weather," Stephen said. "What is it, Will?"

"I can no longer wield a sword for you. But I can still be your ears, my liege. That is the real reason I asked to accompany you on this march, so that my men might listen and watch and learn. They're quite good at it, as well they ought to be, for that was what I hired them for. And what they have told me is that you dare not fight on the morrow. You have more to fear than a flooded river."

"What are you saying, Will? That I ought to fear treachery?"

"No, I'd not go that far. Your camp is rife with rumors, though. Supposedly, some of your barons have been in secret communication with Henry Fitz Empress. There is no proof to speak of, but I'd not dismiss these stories out of hand."

"Who?" Stephen demanded, and Ypres shrugged.

"I would that I had evidence to offer, but I do not. Should you mistrust Beaumont because he keeps aloof from your court? Or because he wed his daughter to the Earl of Gloucester? Was he seeking a wealthy husband for his girl? Or a link to the Angevin camp for himself? Or both? And what of that private peace made between the Earls of Derby and Chester? Is that cause for suspicion? I wish I knew, but it would take a soothsayer to sort it all out. What I can say for a certainty is that these men have no stomach for this particular battle . . . whatever their reasons. If you force them into it, they'll follow you. But I do not trust them to hold fast if the battle turns against you."

Stephen sucked in his breath. "Lincoln," he said hoarsely, and for an unsettling moment, it was almost as if he were reliving that nadir of his kingship, abandoned on the field by the men he had most reason to trust.

Ypres nodded. "Just so, my liege. I think they'd bolt at the first hint of trouble."

A sudden blast of wind blew back Stephen's hood, and he grasped at it with frozen fingers. "But what would you have me do, Will? How can I retreat without doing battle? How can I lose face like that?"

"Would you rather lose your crown?" Ypres asked bluntly. "You cannot risk it. How many Lincolns can you hope to survive, Stephen?"

It was the first time that he'd ever called Stephen by his given name. Stephen looked at him, realizing with relief just how much he trusted this aging, unscrupulous mercenary. Before he could respond, though, another voice cut into their conversation, as sharply as any sword thrust.

"I cannot believe it!" The wind had covered the sound of Eustace's approach. His hood had fallen back and the rain had plastered his hair to his skull, running in rivulets down his face. His skin was reddened and chapped by the cold, but he seemed oblivious to the storm, staring first at his father and then, accusingly, at Ypres. "That you would betray us like this! When I was a lad, I . . . I thought you were a godsend, my father's champion—" His voice choked. "More fool I, for forgetting what you really were—a man selling his soul to the highest bidder! How much is Henry paying you this time?"

"Eustace, you are wrong!" But Stephen's protest went unheeded; his son had already spun on his heel. "Will . . . Will, I am sorry. I'll make him understand . . ." Even in his agitation, Stephen did not forget Ypres's need, and he hastily led the other man the few remaining steps toward his tent before plunging after his son.

Ypres caught hold of the tent moorings and stood motionless for several moments, shivering, in the freezing rain. He could do nothing for Matilda's son. His kingship was already lost. The best they could hope for now was to try to save Stephen's tottering throne. The Fleming was sure Matilda would have understood. He was just as sure Stephen did not, at least not yet. But Eustace did. The fear in his voice told Ypres that he understood all too well.

A WAN February sun flitted between clouds, providing little warmth, but still a welcome sight to the winter-weary residents of Wiltshire. Ranulf and his Welshmen were pleased to see it, too, for as inured as the Welsh were to wet weather, their journey from Wales had tested even their proverbial hardihood. But they were young, eager for excitement and plunder, and their spirits rose as soon as the road started to dry out. Ranulf's mood was less festive; if ever he'd viewed war as an adventure, those days were long gone. As they rode south, he was preoccupied and tense, spurred on by concern for his wife and child back in Wales and increasingly anxious for his nephew, as his hopes faltered that he'd reach Malmesbury in time.

Ranulf approached Malmesbury, therefore, with some degree of trepidation, not knowing what they'd find, sure only that he'd never forgive himself if evil had befallen Henry in his absence. As they'd ploughed their way along the waterlogged roads of Wales and western England, he'd done his best to reassure himself that Henry would be a match for Stephen. Stories of Henry's spectacular summer campaign against the French king had penetrated even into the mountain fastness of Eryri, and he'd eventually gotten glowing reports from Maude, Rainald, and his niece in Chester, as well as a firsthand account from Henry himself. But as proud as he was of his nephew's growing fame, he could not banish a nagging unease, for he knew what a capable commander Stephen was.

Much to Ranulf's amazement, by the time he reached Malmesbury, it was all over. Stephen and Henry had agreed to a truce, and Stephen had then pulled back his army without ever taking the field. North of the Avon, Stephen's camp was deserted, nothing remaining but the charred ashes of quenched fires and mounds of rubbish strewn about. Within

Malmesbury itself, the mood was mixed: for Henry's soldiers, jubilation, and for most of the citizens, relief, at least for those not mourning loved ones slain in the capture of the town.

The truce was all that people were talking about, and Ranulf had no trouble learning the terms—terms as favorable to Henry as they were detrimental to Stephen. It had been agreed that Stephen would retreat, a battle would be avoided, and Henry would halt his siege of Malmesbury Castle. Stephen's castellan would then raze the castle to the ground, thus denying the stronghold to both sides. And Stephen, in turn, had agreed to end the continuing siege of Wallingford, nor to assault it again for six months.

Ranulf was astounded by what his nephew had accomplished—a reprieve for Wallingford and a humiliating setback for Stephen—all without a battle's being fought. Once he finally located Henry, walking in the cloisters with the abbot of Malmesbury's great Benedictine abbey of St Mary and St Aldhelm, he wasted no time congratulating his nephew upon his brilliant and bloodless victory. He knew at once that he'd trod amiss, for the stately abbot stiffened, then excused himself so abruptly that Ranulf realized he'd somehow offended.

Ranulf was not left alone with Henry for long. As Abbot Peter stalked away, Rainald came barreling up the walkway toward them. But Ranulf had not forgotten the abbot's odd reaction, and once boisterous greetings had been exchanged with his brother, he asked Henry why the abbot had seemed so irate.

"Because my victory was not bloodless for the townspeople or the monks. Malmesbury has long been a royal stronghold for Stephen, and when we attacked, some of the citizens joined the castle garrison in the town's defense. We were able, though, to get over the walls with scaling ladders. Most of the garrison managed to reach safety within the castle, but some of them fled into the abbey. Our men followed, and blood was spilled in the church itself."

Ranulf crossed himself. "No wonder the abbot was wroth."

"It was even worse than you think, Uncle. Not only were some of the men seeking refuge in the church slain, but so were a few monks who'd tried to intervene." Henry shook his head, in remembered anger. "Breton mercenaries . . . all they know is killing."

"Ah, but you'd have been so proud of our nephew, Ranulf," Rainald interjected. "Harry acted at once to reassure the monks and townspeople, whilst also showing our men what would happen to those who dared shed blood in God's House."

"What did you do, Harry?" Ranulf was relieved that Henry had taken action, and curious to know what he'd done, for one of the most vexing challenges facing a battle commander was how to keep his army under control. Some did not try very hard; Geoffrey had been one of those. Others deliberately encouraged their soldiers to commit cruelties, as one more weapon of war, the way the Earl of Chester had turned his men loose on Lincoln. Even commanders like Robert Fitz Roy, who did attempt to rein in their troops, were not always successful.

"I got rid of them," Henry said. "I do not expect soldiers to act like holy monks, but I'd warned them that I'd not abide sacrilege or wanton killing. If the Bretons are not yet out of England, they soon will be. I sent them under guard to Bristol, to be put on the first available ship back to Normandy. The only thing worse than keeping them bloody-handed in my hire would have been for them to turn up next in Eustace's service!"

As they talked, they'd been walking briskly back toward the abbey guest hall. Ranulf explained that he'd been delayed first by family illness—the night before he was to depart, his young son had been stricken with a high fever—and then by the sorry state of the roads. Henry and Rainald gave him a more detailed account of their assault, and revealed their immediate plans: to remain at Malmesbury just long enough to make sure that Stephen's castellan would follow through with the order to destroy the castle, and then head for Bristol. For with Wallingford no longer in immediate danger, they could take their time in deciding where they should strike next.

Henry paused just as they reached the hall. "It could not have been easy for you, Uncle Ranulf, riding away from your wife and son, not knowing how long you'd be gone. I'll not forget that, you may be sure."

"Introduce me to Eleanor and we'll call it even," Ranulf said, and Henry pushed him, laughing, into the hall. Within, it was full of familiar faces, and Ranulf spent the next quarter hour greeting friends and kinfolk. He was heartened to see how many of England's barons had responded to Henry's summons, and as he glanced about the noisy, crowded hall, it seemed to him that he could almost see the benevolent ghosts of his brother Robert, Miles, and Brien, watching in satisfaction from the shadows.

Laughing at his own sentimentality, he elbowed his way back to his nephew's side. "Why do you think Stephen balked at doing battle with you, Harry? The talk I heard in the town was that he was thwarted by the winter storm and flooding, but there has to be more to it than that."

"You'd be loath to fight, too," Rainald said smugly, "if you had to keep looking over your shoulder."

Ranulf's eyes narrowed. "Was that it, Harry? Did Stephen distrust his own barons?" he asked, and Henry shrugged.

"You'd have to ask Stephen," he said, but then he grinned. "It would not surprise me, though."

It was clear to Ranulf that his nephew knew more than he was willing to admit, at least in public. He asked no more questions, content to wait until Henry was ready to confide in him, and followed his nephew as they started toward the high table being set up on the dais.

Trestle tables had already been brought in, and men began to wander over, claiming their seats for dinner. But before Henry reached the dais, Jordan de Foxley, Malmesbury's castellan, was ushered into the hall. Henry greeted him amiably, for he had no personal animosity toward the man, who'd only been doing his duty as a soldier. "You're welcome to join us for dinner, Sir Jordan. Afterward, we can discuss your plans for razing the castle."

Kneeling before Henry, the castellan said, low and urgent, "Thank you, my lord duke. But I have need to speak with you now. If you spare me a few moments, I can assure you that you'll not regret it."

It was deftly done, and many in the hall did not even notice Henry's discreet departure, although they did wonder why dinner was being delayed. They were not kept long in suspense. Less than half an hour had elapsed before Henry returned to the hall, strode up onto the dais, and called for silence.

"I have just met with the castellan of Malmesbury Castle," he announced, "and I am pleased to inform you that he has offered to turn the castle over to me, intact and whole—"

Henry got no further; whatever else he'd been about to say was drowned out by a burst of cheering. Dinner was forgotten. For some time afterward, the hall was in tumult, a scene of triumphant and raucous celebration.

Ranulf watched from the dais as the castellan was escorted back into the hall, this time to be greeted as a hero by Henry's elated barons. In the course of this war, there had been many defections; some men had switched sides more than once. Ranulf sensed that this defection was different, though, that the Malmesbury castellan's action was a straw in the wind. He dearly loved his nephew and wanted very much to see Henry as England's king. But he could not help the words that came unbidden now to his lips, too softly to be overheard. "Poor Stephen . . ."

HENRY celebrated his twentieth birthday at Bristol, planning the next stage of his campaign. Soon after Easter, he was joined by Robert Beaumont. The earl's holdings included more than thirty fortified castles scattered throughout the Midlands, strongholds now put at Henry's disposal as this powerful and cautious lord publicly allied himself with the Angevin cause, formally acknowledging Maude's son as the rightful heir to the English throne.

56

SIEGE OF WALLINGFORD

July 1153

HENRY resumed his campaign after the spring thaw. He suffered a loss in May—the death of an ally and kinsman, the Scots king—but he experienced no setbacks upon the field. He captured Berkeley Castle, then laid siege to the Earl of Derby's stronghold at Tutbury, and once that castle fell, the earl renounced his allegiance to Stephen. Henry then gained control of Warwick Castle, having reached an understanding with the countess, a half-sister of Henry's new ally, Robert Beaumont. The Earl of Warwick was so distressed by his wife's action that when he died soon afterward, it was commonly believed that his sudden demise was due to "shame and grief." After occupying Coventry and visiting Leicester and sacking Bedford, Henry then headed toward Wallingford—and a final reckoning with Stephen.

Stephen had built a countercastle across the river from Wallingford at Crowmarsh. Henry's first assault upon Crowmarsh won the outer bailey, but the garrison rallied and drove his men back. Henry and his army then settled down to lay siege to the castle, waiting for Stephen.

ONCE again two enemy armies were confronting each other across a river; this time it was the Thames. At Stephen's approach, Henry issued a challenge to do battle, one Stephen had every intention of accepting. With his eldest son at his side, he rode out to inspect his troops. His was the larger army, and although he knew that was no guarantee of victory, he felt a reassuring surge of optimism as he looked upon his men. "We'll fight at dawn," he told Eustace, "and you'll command the vanguard."

That was an honour Eustace felt he deserved, but it pleased him that his father thought so, too. "All I've ever wanted," he said earnestly, "is to meet Maude's whelp on the field, and teach him a lethal lesson in what manhood is all about. By this time tomorrow—Papa!"

It happened without warning, seemingly without reason. Stephen's horse reared up suddenly, forelegs flailing at the sky, and then began to buck wildly. Caught off balance, Stephen was pitched over the stallion's head.

WHEN the Bishop of Winchester and the Earl of Arundel were ushered into William de Ypres's tent, he dismissed his attendants so they could confer in private. Not that there were any secrets left to guard; there was not a man in the camp still unaware of what had happened that afternoon. Stephen had been thrown from his horse, not just once, but three times in succession. As Stephen was known to be a skilled rider and his mount was a well-trained and battle-seasoned stallion, those who'd witnessed the king's mishap were at a loss to explain it—except as an ominous portent of disaster.

What the bishop and the earl had come to tell Ypres, he already knew, for his men had been canvassing the camp for hours, seeking to gauge the level of unease. And so when the bishop said that Stephen's odd accident had spooked his soldiers fully as much as the stallion, Ypres interrupted impatiently.

"Let's get to the heart of the matter. That skittish horse is not the reason why our men are balking. It is merely an excuse. The king's men were already loath to fight for him."

He'd half expected the bishop to argue with him, but Stephen's brother surprised him, showed that he could hear the truth without flinching. "What you mean," he said, "is that they are loath to fight against Henry Fitz Empress, against the man they want as their next king."

And there it was, out in the open at last. His shoulders slumping, the bishop sat down wearily on Ypres's coffer. The Earl of Arundel hovered by the tent's entrance, fidgeting with the hilt of his sword. Ypres did not need to see his face to envision his discomfort, for he knew William d'Aubigny to be an essentially decent man, but one without imagination or initiative, caught up, like so many others, in a civil war not of his making. A war that had bled England white for far too many years. It was time to put an end to it. Ypres knew that was what Matilda would have wanted. But would she have understood that peace could not come without sacrificing her son?

The bishop roused himself at last, glancing first at the edgy Arundel, and then at the impassive Fleming. "How are we going to convince Stephen?"

STEPHEN had retired to his tent to nurse his bruises, puzzled and embarrassed by his stallion's erratic behavior, but not alarmed, for it had not occurred to him that men might find dire significance in his triple fall. He was utterly unprepared, therefore, for the message his brother and William de Ypres were attempting to deliver—that there could be no battle on the morrow.

"I dare not fight because a horse threw me?" he said incredulously. "You cannot be serious!"

"I am hardly noted for my humor, now am I?" Bishop Henry said irritably. "Stephen, I assure you that never have I been more serious. I am going to be brutally blunt about this, for I know no other way to do it. You've always liked your truth and your wine sweetened, but all the sugar in Christendom could not make this easier for you to swallow. Your barons do not want to fight Henry Fitz Empress, and if you force them to follow you into the field, I very much fear you'll have reason to regret it."

Stephen stared at his brother, stunned by what he was hearing. "They think I have been such a bad king?"

For all of the bishop's bold talk of "brutal bluntness," he could not bring himself to give Stephen an honest answer to that question. He chose to dodge the blow, deferring to Ypres. The Fleming displayed a soldier's skill at deflection, for he did not answer Stephen's plaintive query, either. Instead, he said, "My liege, do you not see? You won your war against Maude. The fight is now over the succession. In the past, your barons have fought and bled and died to keep you on the throne. But they are not willing to risk death for Eustace. They fear the sort of king he would be . . . and in truth, so do I."

That was a truth, though, that Stephen could not accept. He immediately launched into an impassioned defense of his son, with such vehemence that they suspected he was attempting to quell his own inner doubts about Eustace's fitness to rule.

But neither the bishop nor the Fleming would relent, not with so much at stake. They took turns pointing out to Stephen just how precarious his position was. Henry enjoyed the support of the Church; the Archbishop of Canterbury was even now in his siege encampment. Unlike Stephen, he had the wholehearted support of his barons and vassals, including the Earls of Chester, Leicester, Gloucester, Hereford, Salisbury, and Cornwall. And more and more, public opinion was shifting in his favor. People had heard about the Epiphany Day prophecy. Men claimed that at Malmesbury, even the wind had been Henry's ally. Was it surprising, then, that soldiers would react with superstitious dread when Stephen was unhorsed three times before doing battle with his rival? Need they remind him that men who expected to be defeated usually were? Need they remind him of Lincoln?

When they'd exhausted all their other arguments, Ypres and the bishop were forced to make the most painful one of all. Men did not yet know Henry Fitz Empress all that well, but what they'd so far seen of him, they liked. They did know Eustace, and liked him not. Throughout England, he'd earned himself a reputation for courage, but also for cruelty and arrogance and vengefulness. Men might have accepted him as king had they been given no choice. But they would not fight to make him king.

Eventually, Stephen stopped arguing with them. No matter what they said, though, he kept repeating stubbornly, "I will not betray my son." And nothing seemed likely to break the impasse, for Stephen's paternal instincts were stronger than those for self-preservation.

Surprisingly, it was the Earl of Arundel who found a solution. He and the Earl of Northampton had entered the tent in answer to the bishop's summons; he'd hoped that Stephen would be swayed by the realization that even the steadfast Northampton would rather negotiate than fight. But Northampton's gruff plea had fallen on deaf ears. It was Arundel who saw what these men more clever than he had not, that Stephen would grasp at any alternative which avoided an outright repudiation of his son.

"We are not asking you to make peace with Henry Fitz Empress, my liege. We seek only a truce, no more than that. So many lives have already been lost. Would it not be better to talk rather than bleed—just this once? If the talks come to naught, what have we lost?"

It was a disingenuous argument, for to seek a truce would be a damaging admission of weakness on Stephen's part. But it offered Stephen what he so desperately needed—a reprieve, however brief, time in which to try to find a way to save his son's kingship.

"So be it," he said dully. "But what makes you think Henry will agree to a truce?"

His brother was not about to give Stephen a chance to change his mind. "Let's find out."

ALTHOUGH some moments had passed since Henry had stalked out in a fury, the impact of his anger still smoldered. It was the first time that most of the men had seen Henry's temper at full blaze, and they'd found it to be a sobering sight. Only the Earl of Chester was impervious to the heat, for he'd been on the safe side of the fire; like Henry, he'd wanted to scorn the offer of a truce and seek a battlefield resolution. But the others had all counseled caution, urging Henry to agree to the truce and enter into negotiations, arguing that there'd been enough killing. Unable to make any inroads or win any converts, Henry finally lost patience and departed, leaving behind dismay and disquiet.

When Henry's cousin Will suggested tentatively that one of them must follow after Henry and make him see reason, there were murmurings of agreement, but no volunteers. "I will talk to him," the Archbishop of Canterbury said resolutely, feeling it was only fair, for no one had pressed Henry harder to make peace than he.

"Nay, my lord archbishop, let my brother go." Rainald nudged Ranulf with his elbow, then winked. "We can spare him easier than you!"

Ranulf jabbed back, but he did not object to being offered up as a sacrificial lamb, for he knew his nephew better than that. "I'll go," he agreed, "but not yet. It'll be better if he comes around on his own to our way of thinking."

The archbishop looked suddenly hopeful. "Are you so sure that he will?"

"Yes," Ranulf said, "I am. You see, our future king has a hot temper but a cool head!"

When he did seek Henry out later, he found his confidence had not been misplaced. Henry was inspecting a partially constructed belfry tower, intended to be used in the assault upon Crowmarsh's outer walls; work upon it had been suspended at the approach of Stephen's army. From the way Henry was bantering with the soldiers, it was clear to Ranulf that the crisis was past. "Do I need a white flag?"

Henry shook his head. "Did you all draw lots to see which one got to soothe my ruffled feathers?"

"I insisted upon the honour. You know I've always been a glutton for punishment," Ranulf said, and fell in step beside his nephew, following Henry away from the belfry, out of earshot of the soldiers.

"Can you understand, Uncle Ranulf, why I wanted to fight?"

"Of course I can. If you defeat Stephen on the field of battle, the crown is yours for the taking—here and now. No concessions, no compromises, no waiting. But a lot more blood."

"You're supposed to twist my arm," Henry objected, "not break it. I know we must accept their offer of a truce. I am not convinced that I can bargain for the crown instead of fighting for it, but at least we have to try."

"I was sure that you'd agree," Ranulf admitted, "but I am right glad to hear you say so, lad!"

"With the Church and common sense on your side, what else could I do?" Henry smiled tightly, without much humor. "Uncle . . . you know Stephen as well as any man alive. Do you truly think he will agree to disinherit his son?"

"Not willingly, no. But he cannot fight you and his brother and barons, too. It may take a while, but I think he'll eventually be forced to it."

"I would never agree," Henry said, thinking of his unborn child. In less than a fortnight, Eleanor's lying-in would begin. But not only could he not be with her, he'd have to wait weeks to find out if she'd borne him a son, if she and the babe were well. More women died in childbed than men did on the battlefield. Eleanor was strong and healthy, but so was his mother, and she'd almost died giving birth to Geoff. Frustrated and thwarted, compelled to do what he most hated in all the word—wait—he swore suddenly, with feeling.

"I tell you this, Uncle, that I'd pawn my soul to the Devil for a chance to shed blood on the morrow, provided that it was Eustace's. Nor would I be loath to see some of Stephen's spilled, too. But it seems it is not to be . . . not yet."

Ranulf sympathized, for he knew that his sister and nephew saw this bloody and ruinous civil war in stark and simple terms—as evil that had sprouted from one poisonous seed, the usurpation of their crown. To others, it might matter that Stephen had been consecrated as England's king, anointed with the sacred chrism that forever set a king apart from other men. That alone was enough to make some reluctant to see him deposed. But to Henry, it counted for nothing, as a fraud born of a theft. The urge to avenge his mother's wrongs raced in tandem with his own mettlesome ambitions, and it could not be easy to rein in either of them. Ranulf felt enormously proud of his nephew now, that he was willing to try.

"No more talk about pawning souls, though," he joked, "not in the archbishop's hearing, anyway. You do not want to remind him that the Devil's daughter roosts in a branch of your family tree, do you?" That got a grin from Henry, and Ranulf reached out, clouting the man fondly on the shoulder. "You are twenty and Stephen fifty-seven. Time is your ally, Harry, not his. And as unhappy as you are with this truce, just think how Eustace must feel!"

"EUSTACE, wait! Stay and hear me out. It is true that I agreed to ask for a truce, but only because they gave me no choice. I have no intention, though, of bargaining with Maude's son, that I swear to you, lad, upon your sweet mother's soul!"

"Do not besmirch Mama's memory with your lies!" Eustace was drunk on despair; the very ground seemed to be shifting under his feet and all he had to hold on to was his rage. "You betrayed me, admit it! I know you mean to make a deal with that Angevin hellspawn! But what sort of man would disown his own son?"

"Will you listen to me? I agreed to a truce, nothing more! I would never betray you. Our men have lost heart for further fighting, but we can remedy that. Together, we can find a way, Eustace, to restore their faith in you. But you must trust me, for I cannot do it alone—"

"Trust you? What a sour joke that is! You'd give your last coin to a beggar by the roadside, even if it meant your own would starve! By the time Maude's accursed son is done with you, you'll be plucked clean and thanking him for leaving you a chamber pot to piss in, old man! But you'll not barter away my birthright, by all that's holy, you will not! I'll see you both in Hell first!"

Stephen caught his arm as he swung away, but Eustace jerked free, and within moments, he'd disappeared into the darkness beyond Stephen's tent. Badly shaken, Stephen deemed it best not to follow; they both needed time to calm down before their healing could begin. It was a sensible decision, but one he would soon come to lament. For in the morning, he discovered that Eustace was gone. He had ridden off in the night, leaving Stephen with an anguished regret, that his son's last words to him had been a curse.

THE Archbishop of Canterbury and the Bishop of Winchester negotiated a fortnight's truce, under terms beneficial to Henry. Stephen and Henry agreed to lift the sieges of Wallingford and Crowmarsh. Stephen also consented to raze his castle at Crowmarsh, and Henry permitted its eighty-man garrison to march out, unharmed. But the preliminary efforts to end the war by mediation did not progress well. Eustace cast a long shadow.

Eustace soon made his presence felt in a far more ominous way. Gathering a large band of mercenaries, he rode north into Cambridgeshire, and began to pillage and rob. Whether he was simply venting his own fury and frustration or seeking to bait Henry into coming after him, no one knew for certain, possibly not even Eustace himself. But the skies over Cambridgeshire were once again darkening with smoke, as in the wretched days when Geoffrey de Mandeville had rampaged through that unhappy shire.

THE monks of Bury St Edmunds knew that Eustace's army was on the prowl and getting closer, for panicked refugees had been streaming into the monastery for days. Abbot Ording continued to hope, though, that his abbey would be spared, for St Edmund's tomb was England's most sacred shrine. Surely the king's son would not allow his brutal hirelings to desecrate such holy ground? He'd held to that hope right up to the moment that a terrified lay brother stumbled into the Chapter House, crying out that Eustace's men had been sighted on the Cantebrigge Road, heading for their abbey.

When Eustace rode into the abbey precincts, he found Abbot Ording waiting for him. Flanked by his prior and hospitaller, with the other brothers huddled a few steps behind, the abbot sought to ward off disaster with a wan welcoming smile. They were indeed honoured, he said, to have the

Count of Boulogne as their guest again, and he'd already given orders to prepare his own quarters for the count's comfort, just as he'd done at the count's visit last year with his lord father, the king. Their cook was busy making a dinner sure to be to the count's liking: fresh pike from their fish pond and a special delicacy, rabbit stew.

Eustace seemed taken aback, and the abbot prayed that their feeble defense—hospitality—would hold. Was it too much to hope for, that if Eustace was treated as a guest, he'd act like one? But this Eustace bore little resemblance to the privileged, unhappy youth the abbot remembered. Unkempt and almost gaunt, blue eyes bloodshot and suspicious, this was no pampered king's son. The abbot had seen men like this before, men haunted and hunted, some of them brigands and bandits, others merely victims of bad luck, but all of them with nothing left to lose.

"Thank you, my lord abbot. I would be pleased to dine with you and your brethren." But if Eustace had been surprised into civility, he had not been dissuaded from his purpose. "But first we have a matter of money to discuss. I am running short of funds to pay my troops. I am sure, though, that I can rely upon the generosity of your abbey." He named a sum, then, that caused the monks to gasp.

The abbot had gone ashen. "My lord, that . . . that is a vast amount of money!"

Eustace smiled, chillingly. "You are too modest, my lord abbot. So prosperous an abbey could easily spare that much. In fact, I'd say it was a bargain, indeed, in view of what you'd be gaining—the favor of a future king."

"My lord count, I swear that you've been misled. Even if our revenues were twice what they are, we would not be able to raise such a sum!"

A muscle twitched in Eustace's cheek and his smile became a grimace. "Think you that I am some green, callow stripling, to be put off with soft words and honeyed lies? All know that you Black Monks have even more money than the Jews!"

"I entreat you—" the abbot began hoarsely, but his prior could no longer keep silent. Well past sixty, too old to be intimidated, he glowered at this intruder in their midst, his high, reedy voice cracking with indignation, not fear.

"There can be no greater crime than to steal from Almighty God. Look to your immortal soul, son of Stephen, ere it is too late!"

The prior might have lacked the majestic presence of an Abbot Bernard, but he did make an impressive sight, tonsured silver hair streaming down onto the somber black cowl of the Benedictine order, cobalt-blue eyes aiming at Eustace like arrows, a clenched fist upraised as if to invoke the Almighty's intercession.

For a brief moment, Eustace looked at the aged monk, and then he turned in the saddle, saying to his men, "Take whatever we need, whatever you want."

At first, the monks offered no resistance, watching in appalled silence as Eustace's soldiers plundered and despoiled their abbey. The stables were hit first, and then the storehouses. Abbot Ording's lodgings, too, were stripped bare. The guest hall, the monks' dorters, the kitchen and bakehouse and buttery, even the infirmary—all were ransacked.

The looting soon spilled over into the town, and smoke began to stain the cloudless August sky. Somewhere a woman was screaming; Abbot Ording flinched away from the sound, groping for his rosary. This was his domain; the townspeople, too, were under his protection. And yet he could do nothing for them. His eyes blurred with tears and he sank to his knees in the dust, praying to St Edmund to protect his own.

When some of the soldiers emerged from the church, laden with chalices and expensive altar cloths and St Edmund's special silver candlesticks, there were gasps of outrage from the monks. At sight of the pyx, holy receptacle for the Host, now tucked under a brigand's arm, several of the younger monks could not contain their fury and rushed at the offender, only to be beaten down into the dirt by his comrades, for mercenaries rarely held monks in much esteem.

"Do not resist them!" the abbot cried. Crouching over one of his bruised and dazed monks, he pillowed a bleeding head in his lap, staring up at the king's son, white-faced and accusing. "St Edmund will punish you for the evil you have done. You have sinned against him and against the Almighty, and for that, there can be no forgiveness."

There was a time when Eustace would have been dismayed and alarmed by the abbot's words. Now he did not care. What did God's Curse matter when compared to the loss of a crown? "Tell your St Edmund to do his worst," he said mockingly. His men laughed, impressed by his bravado, but the monks shuddered and Abbot Ording made the sign of the cross.

STEPHEN had easily captured the North Sea port town of Ipswich, and for the past ten days, he'd been besieging Hugh Bigod's castle. The siege was faring well, but he was not. He sought to fill all his waking hours with enough activity to keep from thinking of his renegade son and crippled kingship, only to lie wakeful and wretched, night after endless night.

The Bishop of Winchester was no longer with him, having gone off to consult again with his erstwhile adversary the Archbishop of Canterbury. Stephen might have admired his brother's newfound zeal for peacemaking, had he not known that any proposed peace plan must, of necessity, involve a repudiation of Eustace. But the others in his dwindling inner circle were here at Ipswich: the Earls of Arundel and Oxford; William Martel; his younger son, Will; and even William de Ypres, again exposing himself to the rigors of the road and the pity of others for Stephen's sake. And yet never had Stephen felt so isolated, so utterly alone.

The blows had been coming in swift succession, giving him no time to recover his bearings. Eustace's rebellious flight had been followed by the sudden death of one of the few men Stephen truly trusted, Simon de Senlis, Earl of Northampton. And as he mourned his old comrade-in-arms, word began to filter into Suffolk of Eustace's outlaw raids, tales of crops burned in the fields and villages torched, culminating in last week's outrage at Bury St Edmunds. Horrified and heartsick, Stephen refused to discuss his son's marauding with any of his men, forcing them to join him in a conspiracy of silence, in which it was tacitly understood that as long as Eustace's banditry was not acknowledged, nothing need be done about it. Before the others, Stephen stubbornly held his peace; alone in the night, he prayed for his son to come to his senses, and he grieved.

After occupying the town, Stephen had found lodgings at Holy Trinity, a small priory of Augustinian canons. He'd returned this Monday at dusk, after another long, tiring day at the siege site. Although he knew the others were waiting for him in the guest hall, he slumped down in a chair by the window; at times he found it hard to remember why it mattered whether he took this castle or not. He'd been told that Henry had gone north, that he was now laying siege to William Peverel's castle at Stanford, apparently as a favor to the Earl of Chester. He wondered if it ever occurred to Henry that they were playing a peculiar form of chess. A castle taken here, another lost there, and the game went on.

He was turning away when several men raced past the window, running flat-out on a hot August evening, when even a brisk walk would work up a sweat. He leaned out, saw nothing in the gathering dusk, but the oddness of it lingered and when William Martel entered a few moments later, he commented upon it, half humorously, to the seneschal. "I just saw two of the Black Canons sprinting across the garth. They're usually so protective of their dignity, but these lads were kicking up so much dust you'd swear Satan had come calling!"

William Martel did not return his smile. "It is Eustace."

Stephen froze. "What of him?"

"He is here, my liege. He just rode into the priory."

THEIR shouting had carried beyond the chamber, out into the garth where men gathered to listen. When Stephen and Eustace finally emerged, their covert audience scattered in haste, but neither man noticed, so caught up were they in their private war. Stephen kept staring at this stranger who was his son, unable to admit that there was nothing left to be said. He'd raged and cursed and then pleaded, but he'd gotten no answers from Eustace, only angry abuse. Eustace had offered neither explanations nor apology for what he'd done. He'd come back, he said defiantly, because if he were not here to defend his rights, no one else would. And for Stephen, that was the most painful of his wounds, that Eustace had been so quick to believe in his betrayal.

Eustace stumbled as they entered the hall, jostling his father, and only then did Stephen realize how much his son had been drinking. But he found a small measure of comfort in that; if Eustace had not dared to face him sober, how could he be as unrepentant as he claimed?

Their entrance killed all conversation. Several of the Augustinian canons were present, but not for long, for as soon as Eustace came through the door, they made a hasty exit. Stephen's men seemed no less hostile than the canons, although they at least attempted—however poorly—to hide their antipathy. Eustace raked the hall with a bold, challenging stare, as if defying anyone to speak out. None did, yet there was no thaw in the air, no easing of the tension.

"Come, take a seat," Stephen insisted. Eustace's arm was rigid under his hand, but Stephen's grip was too tight to shake off, and he reluctantly allowed his father to steer him toward the high table. Familiar faces were all about him. Arundel. That Judas Fleming. His milksop of a little brother. To his fury, none of them seemed willing to meet his eyes. Did they think they could make him disappear by pretending not to see him? If they hoped he'd slink away in the night, they would be sorely disappointed. He'd never make it easy for them. They'd have to confront him openly from now on, if they dared.

It enraged him, though, to be shunned like this, as if he were a foul, stinking leper instead of the rightful heir to the English throne. Draining his wine cup, much too fast, he signaled for a refill. The food on his trencher was a favorite dish of his, a lamprey-eel pie, but he was too angry to savor it and ate quickly, without tasting what he swallowed, brooding upon the injustice of it all, silently cursing Henry Fitz Empress and his weak-willed father with every bite.

It was proving to be a miserable meal for Stephen, too; the food on his trencher went untouched, even unnoticed. What was he going to do? If he punished his son as he deserved, he'd risk pushing Eustace into open rebellion. But the monks of St Edmunds had been grievously wronged, and how could he ignore that? Eustace could not have served Henry better than he had at Bury St Edmunds; why could he not see that? If only Tilda were here to counsel the lad; mayhap she could have made him see reason. Each time Stephen glanced up, he saw men warily watching Eustace.

How long would they remain loyal if he continued to force Eustace upon them? And yet how could he ever abandon his own son?

So unnaturally quiet was it that the sound of an overturning chair was shockingly loud, startling them all. Seeing his son on his feet, Stephen felt a throb of despair. What sort of mischief was Eustace up to now? Could he not even get through a single meal without shaming them both?

But once he got his first clear look at his son's face, he cried out sharply. Something was wrong. Eustace was clutching at his throat, his eyes cutting frantically toward Stephen. When he lurched into the table, knocking a wine flagon over onto the other diners, there were curses and even a few audible mutterings about "drunken sots."

Stephen knew better. "Eustace, what is wrong? Tell me!"

Eustace seemed to be trying to do just that. His mouth was working, but no words were emerging. By now they'd all realized that he was having some sort of seizure. Chairs were shoved aside and men scrambled away from the table, away from Eustace, for the same thought was in most of their minds: a plundered abbey and a saint's curse.

Eustace's face was suffused with blood. He sank to his knees, one hand still clawing at his throat, the other reaching out toward his father.

"He is choking!" Time seemed to have slowed, even to have stopped, as Stephen struggled to get to his son. Eustace was convulsing; there was spittle and blood on his lips and his skin had taken on a bluish hue. Stephen began to pound him desperately upon the back and shoulders. Someone was shouting for a doctor. There were a few cries, too, for a priest. But most of the men just stood there, watching. Eustace's eyes were rolling back. His body jerked in several uncontrollable spasms and then went limp. Those who'd ventured closer now caught the smell of urine. Death was no stranger to any of them. But few had ever witnessed a death like this one, so sudden and swift and divinely ordained. For surely it could not be mere happenchance that Eustace would be struck down in all his youthful arrogance just days after defiling a holy shrine?

As Stephen cradled his son and wept, men glanced at one another, and then crossed themselves. Vengeance is mine, saith the Lord, and St Edmund was not to be mocked, for he tended to his own. And as the shock began to subside, more than a few of the witnesses gave silent thanks to this vengeful saint, even as they looked with pity upon their stricken king.

Stephen's younger son still stood, rooted, at the end of the table. He did not seem capable of movement, so chalky-white that he appeared likely to keel over himself at any moment. When someone shoved a wine cup into his hand, though, he drank obediently. As color slowly came back into the boy's face, William de Ypres said, "Go to your father, lad. He has need of you."

The youth blinked, then did as he was bade, moving as if in a daze.

He did not have it in him to take charge, but fortunately there would be others to do what must be done. William Martel was already at Stephen's side, gently seeking to coax him away from his son's body.

Ypres was more than willing to let others shoulder the burdens for a change. Surprised by how tired he suddenly felt, he fumbled for a chair, sat down wearily midst the wreckage of Eustace's last meal. He'd choked on a mouthful of lamprey eel, the same dish that had supposedly caused the old king's death, too. Ypres's mouth twitched in a grim and private smile, for the eerie aptness of it appealed to his sense of irony. If Henry Fitz Empress were prudent, he'd ban eels from the royal table in future. Why tempt Providence, after all?

IT had been a hot summer for England, an even hotter one for Aquitaine. By midmorning, Eleanor's lying-in chamber was already sweltering and the windows were opened as wide as they could get. Insects soon invaded the room, and as her ladies fanned Eleanor and wiped the sweat from her face, they also had to swat away flies. In late afternoon, thunder rumbled in the distance, a promise of relief that never came. The air remained utterly still, stifling. Eleanor refused to cry out, too proud to lay bare her pain for the world, listening under those unshuttered windows. She held on to her sister's hand, so tightly that her nails left scratches on Petronilla's wrist, but the other woman did not complain. Theirs was a sisterhood not just of blood, but of the birthing chamber, too, for Petronilla knew firsthand—as Colette and Yolande did not—what Eleanor was enduring.

Childbirth was the Curse of Eve, but Eleanor's curses were directed at her absent husband, at a world in which women must reap what men had sown. The midwife was shocked, but Petronilla grinned and confided that during the most difficult of her three deliveries, she'd vowed to live as chastely as a nun from then on, whether Raoul liked it or not. "But fortunately for the future of mankind," she quipped, "God has given women flawed memories!"

Eleanor laughed, to the midwife's amazement. But then she groaned, biting down on her fist. When the contraction passed, she muttered that if the folklore was true that sons were birthed more easily than daughters, it must be because girls knew what awaited them outside the womb. And again the midwife marveled, for it had been her experience that the birthing chamber was a setting for hope and fear and joy and, too often, peril, but rarely for humor.

Not until dark did the heat begin to abate. From her bed, Eleanor could see a starlit, ebony sky. When Yolande tilted a cup to her swollen, bitten lips, she swallowed thirstily, too tired even to identify what she was drinking. Deep shadows lurked under her eyes, hollowed her cheekbones, and for the first time, she looked her age to Yolande, a woman of thirty-one, a woman past her first flush of youth, all the glamor and glitter stripped away by her twelve-hour ordeal. But as Eleanor smiled down at the infant in her arms, Yolande felt tears sting her eyes, so great was her regret that her lady's husband would never see that smile.

"Ah, madame, if only you could be there when Lord Harry hears!"

"I wish so, too, Yolande," Eleanor admitted, "but it was not to be." Fighting her fatigue, she looked again at her baby, and then up at the women hovering by the bed. "Nor would I have minded being there when Louis and Abbot Bernard hear," she murmured, and this time her smile was irrepressible, wickedly triumphant.

RANULF had been to the Lincolnshire market town of Stanford once before, on his odyssey with the Fenland orphans; he'd had to seek out a barber in St Peter's Street to yank Simon's infected tooth. The barber was still there, older and grayer and understandably alarmed by the siege under way up the road, barely a stone's throw from his small, cramped shop.

The castle of William Peverel boasted a newly constructed circular stone keep, rising above the meadows of the River Weland. It had held out for the past fortnight under heavy bombardment, the local quarries providing ample ammunition for Henry's mangonels. But September got off to a promising start; the garrison was offering to talk.

The Benedictine priory of St Leonard's, just east of the town, had become Henry's headquarters, and the Black Monks were making heroic efforts to accommodate not only the Duke of Normandy and his entourage, but a handful of demanding lords, including the notorious Earl of Chester, long the bane of Lincolnshire. On this ominously overcast morning, Ranulf had lingered at the priory to tend to a personal matter; he was sending one of his Welshmen home with a letter for Rhiannon. He'd thought that their separation would get easier with time; the opposite seemed to be occurring. Without even realizing what was happening, he'd given his heart away, and England was now the alien land.

Padarn was waiting out in the priory garth with their horses, and they headed into the town. By the time they reached the siege, rain had begun to fall. The marketplace adjoined the castle, and would normally have been crowded with stalls and booths, had the siege not utterly disrupted town life. Instead of customers, it was occupied by soldiers, and it was here that Ranulf found his nephew, conferring bareheaded in the rain with Rainald and a visibly irate Earl of Chester.

Catching sight of Ranulf, Henry beckoned to him, just as the clouds split asunder and a torrent engulfed the marketplace. Men scattered for cover, Ranulf following Henry toward the closest shelter, the alcove of All Saints' Church. As they waited for the rain to subside, Henry revealed why Chester was so disgruntled, even though the garrison had agreed to surrender.

"We discovered that William Peverel was never in the castle. It seems he is holed up at Nottingham, so of course that is where Chester wants us to go next. I told him that I'd have to think about it. Helping Chester settle scores with all his enemies could well turn into a lifetime's occupation!" Henry said and laughed.

Ranulf laughed, too, pleased to see his nephew in such high spirits. August had not been a good month for Henry, not at first, for he was waiting impatiently for word from his wife, finding it hard to focus all his energies upon the Stanford siege, still vexed that he'd been cheated of a battlefield confrontation with Stephen and Eustace at Wallingford.

But that had all changed dramatically once they learned of the events at Ipswich on August 17th. Most people seemed convinced that Eustace's death was divine retribution for his sins, and even more impressive proof that the Almighty favored the Angevin cause. Naturally, Henry did nothing to contradict this view, remarking privately to Ranulf that God could hardly be improved upon as an ally. But whether he owed a debt of gratitude to an unforgiving saint or a lamprey eel, the result was the same: the removal of the last obstacle in his march to the throne.

Roger Fitz Miles was holding forth on that very subject a few feet away, assuring all within hearing that peace was at hand, it was just a matter now of working out the details.

"One of which is the Earl of Surrey," Henry interjected. "You do remember him, Roger—Stephen's other son? How can you be sure that Stephen will not want him to step into Eustace's shoes?"

"No one can see Will as England's next king, not even Will himself," Ranulf commented, and then added, sotto voce, for Henry's ear alone, "You know that, too, Harry. You might as well face it, lad. You're not going to be able to fight for the crown. You'll just have to grit your teeth and let us hand it over to you at the bargaining table."

But Henry always gave as good as he got. "I think you mean at Stephen's grave, do you not, Uncle? That is the fly in the ointment, after all. Unless you want me to start sending the man eel pies?"

"Only as a last resort!" But no sooner were the words out of Ranulf's mouth than he regretted them, for he had too complicated a history with Stephen to joke comfortably about his demise. Before he could say more, a voice carried across the marketplace, calling out for Henry. A rider was cantering toward the church, close enough now to be recognized as one of Rainald's household knights.

Dismounting, he swore lustily as he stepped down into a widening puddle; the churchyard was fast becoming a sea of mud. "My lord duke, I have a message for you. One of the monks was coming to find you, and I told him I'd pass the word on. A courier has ridden into the priory with a letter for your eyes only."

"From Aquitaine?"

While many of Henry's men knew how anxiously he was awaiting word from his wife, this particular one did not even know Eleanor was pregnant. Surprised by the urgency in Henry's voice, he nodded, and then stood, gaping, as Henry snatched the reins from his hand, vaulted up into the saddle, and galloped off on his horse.

By the time Ranulf and Roger got to their own horses and followed, Henry was out of sight. They spurred their mounts along High Street, on toward the priory, arriving onto a scene of jubilation. Henry was standing in the guest hall, surrounded by Abbot Thorald's smiling monks. As soon as he saw Ranulf, he broke away from his well-wishers, strode across the hall, and gave his uncle a wet, joyful hug. "Eleanor has borne me a son!"

It took a while for a semblance of calm to return to the hall, and Ranulf had to wait to learn that Eleanor was in good health, that the baby had his father's bright hair, and that she'd christened him William.

"She claims she named him after my great-grandfather, William the Bastard," Henry chortled, "but I know damned well she really had her father and her beloved 'Grandpapa Will' in mind. I guess I can count myself lucky she did not name the lad after another one of her illustrious ancestors—Charlemagne!"

"I am gladdened for you, Harry," Ranulf said, experiencing a sudden longing for his own small son, Gilbert. "Eleanor has given you a great gift, indeed."

Roger agreed, although he could not keep from pointing out the political benefits of this birth. "Stephen lost a son, you gained one. The contrast will not escape people, that your fortunes are rising as Stephen's are plummeting."

"Especially once they learn that my son was born on a Monday eve, two days after the Assumption," Henry said, and nodded as they stared at him in amazement. He was no longer smiling, for that was so uncanny a juxtaposition of life and death, hope and doom, that there could be no joking about it. "On the same day that Eustace was dying at Ipswich, Eleanor was giving birth to William."

IT took another two months of negotiations to end the war, but an end did come, due in great measure to the patient and persistent mediation of the Church. The eventual agreement was a compromise in the truest sense of the word, in that no one was fully satisfied. Stephen acknowledged Henry's hereditary right to the English crown, and agreed to accept Henry as his "son and heir." Henry, in his turn, conceded that Stephen should continue as king for the remainder of his life. Stephen's surviving son, William, was to receive all those lands and titles that Stephen had held prior to his kingship, and Henry agreed to recognize him as Count of Boulogne and Mortain and Earl of Surrey; as his young Warenne wife was a great heiress in her own right, William would emerge from the peace conference as the richest lord in England, his wealth eclipsed only by that of the king.

The other provisions of the agreement were aimed at implementing it. The Tower of London and the castles of Windsor, Oxford, Lincoln, and Winchester were to be entrusted to castellans acceptable to both sides. Solemn oaths were to be exchanged to uphold the pact, Henry was to do homage to Stephen, and their barons would then do homage to him as England's future king. The men disinherited by the war were to have their lands restored. Foreign mercenaries were to be expelled, and castles constructed since the death of the old king were to be razed. Lastly, Stephen agreed to consult with Henry in the governance of the realm, although it was deliberately left vague as to how that would work out in practice, for no one truly knew; they were breaking new ground.

On November 6th, 1153, almost eighteen years after Stephen had claimed Maude's crown, he met with her son at Winchester, the city that had suffered more than any other during those desolate, blighted years when it was believed that Christ and all his saints slept. They agreed to the terms hammered out by their go-betweens, the Archbishop of Canterbury and the Bishop of Winchester. Although a formal treaty still had to be concluded in December, the people of England at last dared to hope that peace was within reach.

RANULF found it unsettling at first to be back at Winchester. More than twelve years had passed since their catastrophic rout, and while much of the city had been rebuilt, there were still scars of the siege and fire to be found, most of them on the souls of its citizens. His return stirred up memories Ranulf would rather not have relived, yet upon reflection, it seemed appropriate to him that the healing should begin here.

The gathering in the great hall of the castle was an odd experience, too, for him: fraternizing with men he'd have been crossing swords with had they met on the battlefield. As he watched the awkward interaction, it was obvious that he was not the only one unsure of his footing. There were a few satisfied faces to be found. The Archbishop of Canterbury and

Stephen's brother were basking in their success as peacemakers. But most of those present looked more wary than joyful. It would be a slippery road ahead, for certes, but God Willing, not a bloody one.

Across the hall, Stephen was mingling with men who'd done their utmost to dethrone him. He was making a gallant attempt to be cordial, with better success than most. But then, he'd never been one for collecting grudges; Ranulf would wager that there were few, indeed, whom Stephen would not be able to forgive. John Marshal. Chester. The latter's absence was both a puzzle and a blessing. Ranulf could not imagine what might have kept Chester away from Winchester and a chance to gloat, but thank God for whatever it was; even on his best behavior, he'd have muddied the waters enough to splatter them all.

As Stephen moved toward the hearth, his son trailed after him. He'd not let Stephen out of his sight all day, so plainly in over his depth that Ranulf felt pity flickering. Was Will wounded at being bypassed? It was true that he'd not been raised with the expectation of kingship, as Eustace had. Stephen had consoled himself with that; he'd confided as much to Ranulf earlier in the day. Ranulf wondered if Will had ever indulged in secret dreams of crowns and sceptres. Even if so, no one else seemed to have ever thought of him in regal terms. He was not like Harry.

Glancing around then in search of his nephew, Ranulf finally located him standing alone in the shadows on the dais. This was the first time all day he'd not been mobbed, for suddenly his world was overpopulated with men eager to ingratiate themselves. Ranulf supposed it was only to be expected, for people always prized tomorrow more than yesterday. Stephen might now be guaranteed that he'd die as a king, but Henry's favor would be courted more ardently, for he was England's future. Whether Stephen knew it yet or not, the remainder of his reign had become a death vigil.

Taking advantage of this rare chance to catch his nephew alone, Ranulf moved swiftly across the hall, up onto the dais. Henry was watching the activity below him with what appeared to be alert interest. But Ranulf recognized that look for what it was, a mask. "What is the matter, Harry? I know you've never been one for waiting . . ." He stopped, for Henry was shaking his head..

"It is not that. As you said, Uncle, time is on my side, not Stephen's."

"What is it, then?"

"I do think this settlement was best for England. As you also pointed out, there has been far too much bloodshed. I know it will not be easy to make this pact work, but I can rely upon the Church to stave off any double-dealing down the road. Oddly enough, I think I can rely upon Stephen's good faith, too." His smile came and went, almost too quick to catch. "Do not tell my mother I ever said that, though!"

"You still have not told me what is troubling you?"

"It just seems so . . . so incomplete, Uncle Ranulf, to have it end like this. This is not the resolution I'd sought, and Stephen is not the enemy I'd thought I'd find. We talked alone for the first time last night, just the two of us. I do not know what I'd expected, but . . ." Henry frowned impatiently, for he was not accustomed to having such trouble expressing himself. "There was nothing to be said. I could not even hate him as I ought. You know that he has promised to treat me as his son? Well, as crazy as it sounds, it is almost as if he is starting to think of me that way, Ranulf!"

"Not so crazy if you know Stephen," Ranulf said. "There is an . . . an innocence about him, lad, and despite his blundering and the grief he's brought upon himself and others, it still survives, like a candle that is never quite quenched. I suspect that he'd not find it hard at all to treat you as a son, Harry, for that is the world as he'd like it to be, a world where men are honourable and women comforting, where good deeds are always rewarded and debts paid and Christian kindness prevails—"

"But his debt is not paid!" Henry interrupted, with sudden intensity. "Not to my mother!" He caught Ranulf's arm, grey eyes flashing, as the words came rushing out, no longer measured or even voluntary. "He did her a great wrong. Not all men think so, but you must, Ranulf, for you know what he took from her, more than a crown. I've been fighting for the throne, but I was fighting for her, too, to make Stephen pay for all he'd stolen from her. I feel cheated now, if you want the truth. The kingship is mine, or it will be. But I could not redress her grievances, and it was not supposed to be like that!"

"I know. Nothing on God's earth will give Maude more pride and pleasure than seeing you as England's king. But you are right; it is not enough. What she lost, no one could get back for her, not even you, lad. But you are wrong if you think Stephen has somehow escaped payment. He buried his wife. His son died in his arms. He could not secure the throne for his other son. And he will live out his days knowing that men judged his kingship as an abysmal failure."

"And one day, he may even die," Henry said dryly, but he'd begun to sound amused. "Now that you have convinced me, Uncle, it is only fair that you get to come back with me to Rouen and convince my mother!"

"Sorry," Ranulf said, grinning, "but as soon as this war is finally pronounced dead and ready for burial, I'm off to Wales, so fast you will not even see my dust. And for at least a year thereafter, I am instructing my niece not to send on any messages or letters. Every time I get a letter from you, lad, I end up packing my saddlebags, sharpening my sword, and sleeping around campfires instead of snug in my wife's bed!"

Instead of smiling, Henry gave him a thoughtful look. "There is something I ought to tell you, for I know how fond you are of my cousin

Maud. We thought it best to say nothing until this council was over. A few of us know besides me: the archbishop and Stephen and his brother and the Earl of Derby, who found out on his own, being wed to Peverel's daughter. Everyone has been asking after Chester's whereabouts. He is at Gresley Castle up in Derbyshire, and not likely ever to rise from his sickbed, if the accounts I've heard are true."

Ranulf whistled softly. Chester was such an elemental force that he'd seemed well-nigh invincible, if not downright immortal. "After I saw him survive a blow to the helmet that broke Stephen's axe but left him with no more than a headache, I'd have wagered on him against Death itself," he admitted. "As the joke goes, God would not want him and the Devil would not take him. Maud will cope; we need not fret about that. But why the secrecy? Let's be honest; we'd have to hunt far and wide to find any mourners for Chester's funeral. And what does Peverel have to do with this? Given how much he hates Chester, he'd like nothing better than to spit into Randolph's open coffin, but so would half of Christendom!"

"Spitting would not have satisfied Peverel. He had murder in mind, a poisoned wine that claimed three other lives and so sickened Chester that he is not expected to live."

As Ranulf stared at Henry in astonishment, another voice delivered a harsh judgment. Neither one had heard Stephen approach, and they both spun around as he said, "It would be better for England, better for us all that he does not recover. You can be sure, Cousin, that he would give you fully as much trouble as he gave me. A scorpion must sting, for that is its nature."

Henry had at last found some common ground with Stephen. "I daresay you are right. I gave him a very ample grant this spring, but it would not have kept him content for long. If he does indeed die, his epitaph should be that his hand, like Ishmael's, was against every man."

Stephen nodded, all the while studying Henry so intently that he finally felt compelled to say coolly, "Cousin? Is there something wrong?"

Stephen caught himself, and smiled ruefully. "I was staring at you, was I not? Do not take this amiss, but I found myself thinking how very young you are. Not in judgment or maturity, in years. Should God grant you as many winters as I have seen, twenty will seem heartrendingly young to you, too, Cousin," he explained, and Henry could only look at him in bemusement, sure now that it had not been his imagination; Stephen was regarding him with a benevolence that was indeed paternal. He dared not meet Ranulf's knowing eyes, lest he laugh at the absurdity of it all, that this war which had lasted for almost all of his life should end, not in bloodshed, but adoption.

THE day was to conclude with a Mass of Reconciliation at St Swithun's Cathedral. As Henry and Stephen emerged from the shadows of the castle barbican, they drew rein, startled, for High Street was thronged with spectators, men and women and youngsters who'd been waiting patiently in the winter cold for hours, all in hope that peace would be made. At sight of Stephen and Henry riding side by side, a vast roar went up from the crowd, so loud it could almost have been heard in Heaven.

Henry felt his throat tighten as he looked out upon their faces, some beaming, others streaked with thankful tears. Although this was his first visit to Winchester, he felt a close kinship with its citizens, for he'd grown up on tales of their suffering and their steadfast loyalty to the Angevin cause. Their joy was as contagious as it was rapturous, and he wished passionately that his mother could have been here to witness it.

As Henry urged his stallion forward, the noise intensified. Hats and caps were tossed into the icy air, parents lifted children so they could see, and Henry heard his name taken up as a chant by the crowd. It was only then that he glanced over his shoulder and saw that Stephen had halted for the moment, a generous gesture but also a realistic recognition that the cheers belonged to Henry.

57

DOVER-CANTERBURY ROAD, KENT, ENGLAND

March 1154

EARLY in Lent, Henry accompanied Stephen to Dover to meet the Count of Flanders and his wife, Henry's paternal aunt. On this rain-sodden March Friday, they departed Dover Castle in mid-morning, bound for Canterbury. They were still about five miles from the city when the archbishop's saddle girth began to slip. A hasty examination revealed that the girth buckle was giving way and the royal cavalcade halted while the problem was corrected.

As the delay lengthened, Henry found it increasingly difficult to hide his impatience. Stephen's son, Will, and a few of his companions were amusing themselves by galloping their horses across a nearby meadow. Henry was half tempted to join in, but although the rain had stopped, the ground was still muddy and slick, and he was not willing to endanger his stallion just to keep boredom at bay.

As he fidgeted by the side of the road, watching the races, he was joined by one of the archbishop's clerks, who reported that the saddle girth was taking longer than expected to repair. When the clerk lingered after delivering his message, Henry was pleased, for he'd found Thomas Becket to be good company.

At first glance, they seemed too unlike for friendship; Becket was more than twelve years Henry's senior, having been born a month after the sinking of the White Ship, and they did not share the same affinity for the religious life. But what they had in common mattered more than what they did not: a keen intelligence, a love of learning, unfettered ambition, and an ironic eye for life's incongruities. Henry thought he could find use for a man of Becket's talents, looking ahead to that day when England's government would be his for the shaping. But whether Becket ever became a royal councilor or not, at the moment, he was a welcome diversion, and Henry was in need of one; had he been asked to describe Purgatory, he'd have said it was a place of infernal and endless waiting.

The past few months had been busy ones for Henry and Stephen: formalizing the agreement they'd struck at Winchester, getting the barons of the realm to do homage to Henry as their future king, issuing orders to demolish those castles judged illegal, preparing to expel foreign mercenaries. Becket knew they'd not been pleasant months for Henry, filled with dawn-to-dusk activity, but not much satisfaction. It was with a touch of sympathy, therefore, that he asked, "Is it true that your uncle has gone back to Wales?"

Henry nodded. "I tried to talk him out of it, but he reminded me that he'd not seen his wife and son for more than a year. I reminded him in turn that I'd not seen my wife for more than a year, either, and had yet to lay eyes upon my son. But he then pointed out that it was my crown, not his, and that left me with nothing to say except 'Godspeed.'"

"How much longer ere you can go back to Normandy?"

"I would that I knew. Soon, I hope. Others might see me as the heir apparent, the next king. But just between you and me, Thomas, I feel more like the chief mourner at a funeral, waiting around for the 'deceased' to take sick. Surely I can put my time to better use than that?"

"Some men might be content to keep a death watch," Becket agreed, sounding amused, "but for certes, not you."

Henry glanced curiously at the older man. Becket stood high in the archbishop's favor, and with so illustrious a patron, he could have a promising career in the Church, if he wanted it. But did he? "I know you've been in the archbishop's service for the past eight years. He told me that when the next opening for an archdeacon comes up, he means to appoint you. You'd have to take holy orders, first, of course. And you have not . . . have you?"

"Not yet."

Henry considered that answer, trying to understand how a man could choose of his own free will to give up so much, even for God. "I do not think I'd have made a good priest myself," he said at last.

"I suspect you'd have had particular trouble with the vow of chastity," Becket said dryly, and Henry grinned.

"I probably would not have done so well with the obedience vow, either," he conceded. "Fortunately, the qualifications are less stringent for kings."

Becket grinned, too. "I understand it helps," he said slyly, "if a king does not fall off his horse."

Henry had heard, of course, of Stephen's balky stallion. "At least not three times in a row," he laughed, and then grabbed for Becket, pulling the other man aside just as several of the racers galloped past, spraying mud in all directions.

Henry's quick action had saved Becket from a thorough dousing, but the hem of his mantle had still gotten splattered. He frowned at the splotched wool, then gazed after the riders, shaking his head in disapproval. "What a pity," he said, "that some men make such poor use of the wits God gave them." And then, "Jesú!" for as they watched, one of the horses slipped in the mud, scrabbled futilely to retain its footing, and went down.

Henry had not seen the rider. It was not until he heard Stephen's anguished cry that he realized it was Will. With Becket a stride or two behind, he hastened toward the fallen stallion. But Stephen got there first, made fleet by his fear. Will was pinned under the horse, and it took several men to pull him free. The hapless stallion was beyond help, doomed by a shattered foreleg, thrashing about in terror until a soldier mercifully put an end to its suffering.

At first sight, the king's son did not seem likely to survive his stallion. Will's face was blanched under a coating of mud, his flaxen hair darkening with blood. His mouth was contorted, blue eyes clouded with fear and pain, and he plucked frantically at Stephen's sleeve as his father bent over him. "It hurts so . . . ," he moaned, and Stephen found himself thrust back in time to an August night, hot and humid, watching in horror as Eustace choked to death. Merciful God, not again!

"Papa . . ." Will clung to Stephen's hand as if his father alone could save him. "Do not let me die . . ."

"You are not dying, Will," Stephen promised recklessly. "I swear you are not!"

But Will did not believe him. "I've sinned," he sobbed, "but I am sorry. Do not let me be damned . . ."

Shouting hoarsely for a doctor, Stephen blotted blood away as it trickled down into Will's eyes. "Lie easy, lad," he pleaded. "You make it worse for yourself when you move."

"I ought to have told you . . ." Will's eyes were riveted upon his father's face. "I did not truly think they'd do it, though. I swear I did not . . ."

"I know, lad," Stephen said soothingly, "I know. Try not to talk."

"I must," the youth insisted weakly, "lest I die ere I am shriven of my sin." Sweat beaded his forehead, his upper lip. "Murder," he whispered. "The Flemings . . . they mean to kill him . . ."

"Kill him?" Stephen repeated numbly. "What are you talking about?"

"The Flemings . . ." Will's voice faltered. "They spoke of killing Maude's son . . ."

"Christ Jesus . . ." Stephen raised his head, appalled by what he'd just heard, only to see Henry standing behind him, so close that he must have heard, too.

STEPHEN had been searching all over Christ Church Priory for Henry, finally finding him in the cloisters with Thomas Becket. They fell silent as he approached, Henry's face giving away nothing of his thoughts—or his intentions. "How is Will?" he asked politely, noncommittally.

"God is indeed good, for the doctor says he'll live." Stephen told them then, about Will's injuries: a gashed forehead, cracked ribs, and the most serious, a broken thigh bone. His convalescence would be a lengthy one, but he would heal in time. Henry and Becket wished Will a quick recovery, a response dictated by courtesy, not telling Stephen what he needed to know. He'd considered saying nothing, gambling on the off chance that Henry might have missed Will's mumbled confession. But as his eyes met Henry's, Stephen realized how foolish that would have been; Maude's son was not one to be bluffed.

"Once I was sure that Will's life was not in danger, I asked him about the Flemings. One of his men speaks Flemish, and he'd overheard some of the Flemish hirelings talking in a Dover alehouse. They were sorely vexed about the peace terms, angry at being cast out of England, and blaming you for their plight, Harry. Will's servant told him that they were saying it would be for the best if you had a 'mishap' of some sort. But Will swears he did not take it seriously. He dismissed it as drunken maunderings, and that is why he said nothing. If he'd believed you to be in real danger, he'd have spoken up straightaway."

Stephen sounded earnest, yet uneasy, too. Henry did not doubt his sincerity; he believed in his son. And it could have happened just as Will claimed, for he'd struck Henry as an amiable mediocrity. But even a capon might envy the cock; who was to say?

"I daresay you are right, Cousin. The foolish babbling of men in their cups. It is not surprising that Will acted as he did."

Stephen's relief was palpable. "I am gladdened that you understand, Harry. It would have been a great pity had Will's name been tarnished by alehouse gossip. You have no reason to doubt my son's good faith, that I swear to you."

"You need not fret, Cousin, for I've taken Will's measure."

Stephen smiled. "Well, I'd best get back. The doctor gave Will a potion for his pain, but I want to be there when he awakens. Archbishop Theobald was kind enough to put Will up in his own lodgings. If you could find time to stop by later, I know it would mean much to Will . . . ?"

Henry promised that he would, and Stephen was soon striding off buoyantly, intent upon thanking the Almighty for sparing his youngest son. Henry and Becket waited until he'd disappeared into a side door of the cathedral. Only then did they turn away, continuing along the cloister path.

"I hope you plan to watch your back," Becket said quietly. "I've been told that few knives are sharper than a Fleming's blade."

"So I've heard, too." Henry's smile held an edge of its own. "You asked," he said, "when I'd be returning to Normandy. I think the time has come. I would not want to overstay my welcome, after all."

ON the morning after Henry's return to Angers, Eleanor awoke with a languorous sense of well-being, which lasted until she realized that she was alone. Sitting up, she brushed her hair out of her eyes. Could Harry not have lingered in bed just this once? No wonder his enemies claimed his energy was demonic. Her clothing lay strewn about the chamber, and the sight brought a soft smile to her lips as she remembered their urgency to reach the bed. Her husband's scabbard had been hung over a chair and was still there, so at least he was somewhere in the castle. With a sigh, she reached for her bed-robe.

Opening the shutters, Eleanor stood at the window, breathing in the mild April air. She'd selected one of her favorite gowns, a rich wine-red, and she was about to summon Yolande to help her dress when she heard an odd thumping sound out in the stairwell. She opened the door just in time to admit Henry. He had their son slung over his shoulder and was guiding two servants up the stairs as they struggled with a large, unwieldy burden: a carved oaken cradle.

"I thought the tadpole might like to swim in our pond for a while." Henry gestured toward the hearth as the men dragged the cradle across the threshold. "Put it over there."

"Harry, you're holding that child like a sack of flour."

"He does not mind," Henry insisted, and as he turned, Eleanor saw that Will did seem content. Now in his eighth month, he was such a placid, cheerful baby that Eleanor sometimes joked he must be a changeling, and he appeared to have taken in stride being awakened and carried off by a man who was a stranger to him.

After the servants had departed, Henry settled his son in the cradle, rocking it back and forth as Will yawned and then began to suck contentedly upon a rattle. When Eleanor joined them, the little boy gurgled happily at sight of her and reached up to snatch at the long tresses tumbling over her shoulder. Evading his grasp, she kissed the crown of his head. "I still find myself marveling at those golden curls of his," she confided, "for Marie and Alix both have dark hair like mine."

"Ought he to be putting that rattle into his mouth?"

"He is teething, Harry. When his discomfort gets too bad, we rub honey on his gums or give him a liquorice root to suck on." Retrieving her brush, Eleanor retreated to the bed. "Do you intend to keep Will in here with us? I doubt that will work out very well."

"Why not? The lad and I have a lot of catching up to do." Henry was continuing to rock the cradle and Eleanor had to restrain herself from warning that he'd make Will seasick if he did not ease up. His first efforts at fatherhood might be heavy-handed, but she did not want to discourage him. She was pleased that he was so taken with their son, for too many men treated the nursery as alien territory.

Henry was laughing, for Will was now trying energetically to capture his feet. "Trust me, Will, even if you somehow got those into your mouth, toes do not taste good. He squirms about like an eel, Eleanor. Is he always this lively?"

"Ever since we took off the swaddling."

"I've seen babies swaddled. They look like little caterpillar cocoons. Surely they do not enjoy being wrapped up that way?"

"I never thought about it," Eleanor admitted. "But it is for their own good, for it keeps them warm and safe." Henry was leaning over the cradle again, tickling Will and making him squeal with glee. Eleanor watched, smiling. "I hope you'll be such an attentive father for our other children," she teased. "A soothsayer told me that we'd have a baker's dozen ere we're done, so you'd best gird your loins!"

"For you, anytime." But his smile was fleeting. He looked down at Will, then back at Eleanor, grey eyes guarded. "There is something you need to know. I have another son."

Her brush halted in mid-stroke. "Do you, indeed? Do not keep me in suspense, Harry. The 'why' is rather obvious. But what of the 'when' and 'where' of it?"

"He was born last December, in London. I named him Geoffrey." Henry was annoyed to hear himself adding needlessly, "After my father." But he was not as confident as he sought to appear, for he was not sure how Eleanor would react. She was the most unpredictable woman he'd ever met, and while that was a great part of her charm, there were times—like now—when he'd have welcomed a fire that gave off a little less heat.

"You intend to recognize him as your own?"

"He is mine, Eleanor. How could I turn away from him?"

"And the mother?"

"She meant nothing to me. If she'd not gotten with child, I'd have long since forgotten her name."

It was an unchivalrous answer, but the one Eleanor wanted to hear. "Well, then," she said, "I suppose I should offer my congratulations."

He did not respond at once, searching her face for sarcasm. "You truly mean that, Eleanor?"

"Why not? I do not begrudge you your joy in this child, and I would not attempt to talk you into shirking your obligations to him. It is all too easy for men to walk away afterward. I find it rather refreshing, Harry, that you did not."

He was quiet for a moment, marveling. "You never fail to surprise me. It does not vex you that I bedded another woman?"

"More than one, I'd wager," she said, with a sardonic smile. "It is not as if this comes as any surprise. You were gone nigh on sixteen months, after all. I'd not have expected you to refrain from eating until you could get home to dine with me, so why would I expect you to abstain from other hungers?" She shrugged significantly, then reclined back against the pillows, letting her bed-robe slip open enough to reveal a glimpse of thigh. "It goes without saying, though, that your dining out had best be done at a distance, Harry."

Henry grinned. "You need not worry about that, love. Given a choice, I'd eat all my meals at home!" As he moved away from the cradle, Will whimpered in protest, but he didn't notice; at the moment, his wife was claiming all of his attention. "You are the most amazing woman, Eleanor. I have to admit that I was not expecting you to be so understanding."

"I've always understood men," she said blandly, "and I've always tried to be tolerant of their failings. I'd like to think that you'd be as tolerant, too, Harry . . . should the need ever arise."

He stopped abruptly, halfway to the bed. "If you're suggesting . . ."

"You sound upset. Why is that?"

"Infidelity is not the same sin for men and women," he said tautly, "for it puts a child's paternity into question. You're clever enough to realize that, Eleanor, to know—"

He cut himself off in midsentence, and she said encouragingly, "Know what? Do go on, Harry."

By now, though, he'd caught on. But mixed in with his relief was a genuine anger, for he was not accustomed to being laughed at. "Damn you," he said softly, and her eyebrows arched upward in feigned surprise.

"Why, Harry," she murmured, "are you trying to seduce me again?"

The corner of his mouth twitched in involuntary amusement. "What would you have me say, Eleanor? That I am sorry?"

She shook her head impatiently. "I do not care if you tumbled an English harlot, Harry. I am not about to get jealous because you scratched an itch—as long as that is all it was."

He thought he saw now where he'd erred. Crossing to the bed, he threw the covers back, seating himself beside her. "If I said I'd never stray, I'd be lying, and we both know it. But you have my heart, not to mention my crown. Surely that matters more than an occasional trespass?"

"A crown, you say?" She pretended to ponder it, and then reached out, inviting his embrace. As her arms slid up around his neck, she kissed him with incendiary effect. Finally getting his breath back, he murmured against her throat,

"That kiss was hot enough to leave a brand. If that is indeed what you intend, you might want to aim somewhat lower."

She laughed and drew him deeper into the bed. But as he started to strip off her robe, she caught his hand in hers. "Promise me that you'll remember what I am about to tell you, Harry. Whenever you're tempted to 'trespass' in the future, just bear in mind that I am willing to be reasonable—but not saintly."

"I'll promise anything on earth, love, if it'll keep you from ever getting saintly." After that, they did not talk, concentrating upon ridding him of his clothes. They were making progress when an indignant wailing blared from the cradle. His face red, mouth puckered, and eyes tearing, their small son was venting his outrage at being ignored, loudly and persistently.

Henry shot up in the bed. "Christ Almighty, is all that noise coming from him?"

"I did warn you," Eleanor said, beginning to laugh, "that having Will sleep with us might not be one of your better ideas. Welcome to fatherhood, Harry!"

SOON after his return from England, Henry found himself forced to deal with some of Eleanor's rebellious barons. This he did with such dispatch that by the end of June, he was able to take his wife and son to Rouen for their first meeting with his mother.

HENRY was unable to sit still; he kept getting up and prowling aimlessly about the chamber, all the while keeping a wary eye upon the women in his life. They were making polite conversation, seemingly at ease, but he could not enjoy the lull, constantly scanning the skies for approaching clouds. The only one more obviously uncomfortable than Henry was his brother Geoff; he was slouched down in his seat, twitching nervously every time his mother glanced his way. Will at last took pity upon them both and suggested that they adjourn to the stables to see his new roan stallion. His brothers accepted his offer with alacrity, and retreated in unseemly haste.

Watching them go, Eleanor shook her head. "Men are not usually so squeamish about bloodshed."

Maude blinked, looking at Eleanor so blankly that she wondered if she'd made a mistake. But then the older woman smiled. "Men do not know nearly as much about women as they think. Geoffrey was sure that I'd not approve of you, but I'd hoped that Henry would have more sense."

Eleanor had decided beforehand that honesty was the only weapon likely to penetrate her mother-in-law's defenses. "It just matters so much to Harry that we get along. I'll admit that I was somewhat uneasy myself about this meeting. If you believed even half of what's been said of me, you'd have good reason to fear for Harry's immortal soul!"

"Gossip," Maude said dismissively. "The world is full of mud, and unfortunately there is no shortage of people eager to splatter it about, with women the targets of choice. You need not have fretted about your reception, Eleanor. I can think of at least three compelling reasons why I should want to welcome you into my family. The first and foremost one is sitting on your lap," she said, gesturing toward Will, balancing on Eleanor's knee.

"Would you like to hold him?" Eleanor suggested, and Will switched laps with aplomb. "And the other reasons?"

"You make my son happy. And then of course," Maude said with a faint smile, "there is Aquitaine."

Eleanor returned the smile. "I appreciate your candor. As it happens, there is a fourth reason, too. We were not going to say anything until I could be certain, but I'd like you to know. I may be pregnant again."

"So soon? That is indeed blessed news!" Maude detached her grandson's clutching fingers from the rosary at her belt. "No, Will, not the Pater Noster. You said that you are not sure yet, Eleanor?"

"I've missed just one flux so far. But yes . . . yes, I am sure. Sometime in Lent, by my calculations, I hope to give Harry another son."

"Two pregnancies in two years of marriage, possibly two sons." After a moment, Maude smiled, saying with satisfaction but some pity, too, "Poor Louis."

OCTOBER that year was an idyllic month, mild and dry, with clarion blue skies and mellowed golden sunlight. Londoners were determined to make the most of this respite before the winter freeze, and the Friday horse fair at West Smithfield had drawn a large, boisterous crowd. A race was in progress across the meadow, and most of the bargaining had been suspended so people could watch. Although neither Ranulf nor Padarn had wagered on the outcome, they found themselves cheering as loudly as the other spectators, caught up in the excitement. The winner, a rangy bay, edged out a lathered chestnut in a rousing finish that satisfied all but the chestnut's backers. Ranulf was turning toward a piebald filly that had taken his eye when he heard his name called out behind him.

Bearing down upon him was a ghost from his past: Fulk de Bernay, Annora and Ancel's elder brother. Once greetings had been exchanged, Fulk clapped Ranulf heartily on the shoulder. "What are you doing in London? We'd heard that you'd gone off to live on top of a Welsh mountain."

Ranulf was accustomed by now to jokes about his adopted Welsh homeland, and had learned to shrug them off. "Since the peace seems to be holding, I decided this would be a good time to show England to my wife and son. We went to Chester first, collecting my niece Maud, her sons, and her mother, who happened to be visiting. We've been to Coventry, Woodstock, Oxford, and my father's tomb at Reading, and for the past week, we've been enjoying the sights of London. From here we go on to Canterbury and then Dover to meet the king, and on our way back to Wales, we hope to stop at Bury St Edmunds to see St Edmund's shrine."

Ranulf was not normally so loquacious, but the words just kept cascading out, as if of their own will. This unexpected encounter had unnerved him somewhat, stirring up memories he'd as soon forget. Fulk looked eerily like Ancel and his gleaming dark eyes could have been Annora's. But it was reassuring that he was being so friendly, for there could be no better proof that Ancel had not shared his secret; at least Annora's family had been spared that ultimate rupture.

Fulk was regarding Ranulf with evident puzzlement. "It just goes to show," he said, "how outlandish rumors can get. Do you know what we heard, Ranulf? As crazy as it sounds, that this Welsh wife of yours was blind!"

He laughed; Ranulf did not. "Rhiannon *is* blind," he said evenly, and embarrassed color flooded into Fulk's face.

"I . . . I am sorry," he stammered. "But you said you were showing her the sights and I . . . I just assumed . . . How could she . . . That is . . ."

Ranulf let him flounder on like that for a few moments more. He wanted to ask Fulk why he thought the blind were bereft of their other senses, too. Rhiannon was enthralled by the pealing chimes of St Paul's Cathedral. She could hear her footsteps echoing across the marble tiles as she approached its High Altar, she who'd never known any church but the small, secluded chapel at Llanrhychwyn where they'd been wed. When he'd led her out onto London Bridge, she'd felt the life-force of the Thames, surging against the wooden pilings. And when he walked with her on the beach below Dover's white cliffs, she would experience the sea, hearing the waves break upon the wet sand, the gulls shrieking overhead, feeling the salt spray on her face, sensing the vastness that she could not see. But he knew Fulk would never understand, and so he said only, "No offense meant, so none taken."

Fulk was fumbling his way out of the pit he'd dug for himself. "You said you have a son?"

"Yes . . . Gilbert will be three next month."

Fulk smiled in surprise. "Passing strange, for Ancel named his first-born Gilbert, too. I expect to see him at Martinmas. Shall I give him a message from you?"

"Tell him . . . tell him I wish him well." Ranulf hesitated. "How is Annora?"

"She seems content enough. She has a little lass of her own, and Gervase still dotes upon her every whim—" Fulk caught himself, with a self-conscious laugh. "It does not bother you to hear me say that? I know you two were plight-trothed, but that was such a long time ago . . . ?"

"You are right," Ranulf agreed politely. "It was a long time ago." He started to excuse himself then, with a polite smile. "I promised my niece that I'd buy her a mare this afternoon, so I'd best get to it—"

"Ranulf, wait. I've a question to put to you. I heard that Henry Fitz Empress has been taken gravely ill. Can that be true? The word in the ale-houses is that he might not live. But surely that is just idle tavern talk?"

"There is some truth in it, Fulk. My nephew was stricken with a high fever last month and was ill enough to give us all a scare. But he recovered fully and the last I heard, he was dealing with a troublesome vassal in the Vexin."

"Thank God," Fulk said, with such fervor that Ranulf stared at him, for Fulk had been one of Stephen's most steadfast supporters. It was heartening to realize that even Harry's former foes now saw him as England's only hope for a lasting peace.

WHEN she awoke, Rhiannon could not at once remember where she was. "Ranulf?" She called out again, quietly, in case the others were still sleeping, for they'd been sharing their chamber for most of this trip with Olwen, Gilbert, and Gwen, his young nurse. She heard nothing, though, not even the soft sounds of breathing. By now her memory was awakening, too. They were at Canterbury, in a guest chamber of the royal castle. But where was Ranulf?

He entered as she was fumbling for her bed-robe. "So you're finally awake, love. You were so tired yesterday that I thought it would do you good to sleep in this morning. I've got breakfast here for two, and whilst we linger over it, Maud is taking Gilbert and her lads to the marketplace. With luck, we might actually have an entire hour or two all to ourselves."

"Bless her," Rhiannon said happily, making room for Ranulf in the bed. Between sips of cider and bites of honeyed bread, they exchanged sticky kisses. "Did you remember to give Gwen money in case Gilbert sees something he wants to buy at the market?"

"I did," he said, "and told Gwen that he could have whatever he wanted, provided it was not alive. I asked him this morning what part of the trip he'd enjoyed most, thinking he'd pick the royal menagerie at Woodstock or mayhap the ferry ride across to Southwark. But do you know what he said? What he liked best was when Maud bought him a pasty at the cookshop by the river!"

Rhiannon laughed. "Does that surprise you? This is the child, after all, whose first complete sentence was 'Feed me!'" Ranulf shared the last of the bread with her and she settled back into his arms. "I truly like Maud, even more than you predicted I would. It will be a year in December since she was widowed, so she'll soon be able to consider marrying again. Do you think she will?"

"She says no . . . though she puts it more colorfully than that. I'm very fond of Maud, too, Rhiannon, but I'd rather not be discussing her marriage prospects right now. I'm sure we can put this time to better use," he suggested and set about proving it.

But within moments, there was a loud, insistent knocking on the door. "Ranulf? Let me in!"

Ranulf swore softly; so did Rhiannon. When the pounding persisted, they reluctantly drew apart and he swung off the bed, opening the door to his niece. "Maud? What are you doing back so soon? You promised you'd keep the children away at least until—"

"I am sorry," Maud panted, "but as soon as we got to the marketplace, we heard . . . People were talking of nothing else. Last night an urgent message arrived for the Archbishop of Canterbury, summoning him to Dover. Stephen has been stricken with the bloody flux, and the doctors fear the ailment is mortal. Ranulf . . . he is said to be dying."

THE royal castle of Dover was unnaturally still. At midday the bailey would normally have been bustling with activity. Now it was all but deserted. The few men to be seen moved hurriedly about their tasks, hasty, almost furtive in their movements, as if fearful of calling attention to themselves. As soon as he rode through the gateway, Ranulf felt a chill of familiar foreboding. Bristol Castle had looked like this, too, as Robert lay dying.

"You take our horses to the stables," he told Padarn. "Then meet me in the hall."

Padarn nodded. "Will you be able to see him?"

"I do not know," Ranulf admitted, relieved when Padarn asked no further questions. Nor had Rhiannon. He was grateful for that, as he could not have explained even to himself why he felt such an urgent need to see Stephen before he died. For Rhiannon, though, no explanation was necessary. She'd sent him off with a quiet "Godspeed."

The great hall was crowded, and Ranulf's entrance went unnoticed. Almost at once, he spied a familiar face, one of the archbishop's clerks, and as soon as he could, he caught Thomas Becket's eye.

Becket had risen in the world since they'd last met; he'd been appointed that past June as the new archdeacon of Canterbury. Now he greeted Ranulf with the somber courtesy befitting the occasion, but with just enough warmth to indicate his pleasure at seeing Ranulf again. It was adroitly done, and confirmed Ranulf's earlier impression of Becket as a man who had the makings of a superior diplomat, skilled at conveying nuances and shadings, while keeping his own secrets safe. Taking Ranulf aside, he quietly confided the worst, that Stephen was not expected to see another sunrise.

BECKET had gone to arrange Ranulf's admission into the royal sickroom. Waiting by the hearth, Ranulf happened to notice William de Ypres, sitting alone in a window seat. On impulse, he walked over. "Do you remember me? I'm Ranulf Fitz Roy."

Squinting up at him, the Fleming said, "Well, well, if it is not the empress's brother. Although I suppose you'll soon be known as the king's uncle."

"Why are you all so sure that Stephen is dying?"

"He has begun to pass clotted blood. I'd say that's as good a sign as any to send for the priest."

Ranulf winced. "Is he in much pain?"

"More than he'll admit." After a moment, Ypres said, "Do you know why he was in Dover? He was meeting the Count of Flanders again, discussing their plans to go on crusade. God love him, a crusade!"

Ranulf's throat constricted. "He'd have made a fine crusader," he said softly, and the Fleming nodded.

"A better crusader than a king, for certes."

"I know," Ranulf agreed. "So why did we both race to his deathbed, then?"

Ypres shrugged. "Your guess is as good as mine," he said flippantly, but Ranulf knew better. The Fleming would never admit it, but they'd come to Dover for the same reason—to mourn.

KINGS were not accorded privacy; even dying was done in public. Stephen's chamber was thronged with people: the Archbishop of Canterbury, several doctors, a few priests, William Martel, Abbot Clarembald of Faversham, the Earl of Arundel, Stephen's grieving son, just recovering from his March accident, now about to be dealt another crippling blow. Will was the only family member present, for Stephen's brother was coming from Winchester and was not likely to arrive in time. Nor was his daughter, Mary, for she had departed the nunnery in Kent for Romsey Abbey in Hampshire, and seemed destined once again to miss saying her final farewell to a dying parent.

Becket ushered Ranulf toward the bed and then stepped back so that he might have some small measure of privacy. Ranulf was shocked at sight of Stephen. Until then he'd believed Stephen might still rally, for the bloody flux was not always fatal. But as he looked down into Stephen's face, he saw there was no hope. Death was not only on the way, it was already in the chamber.

Stephen's eyes were sunken back in his head, fever-glazed and bloodshot, but still lucid. As Ranulf bent over the bed, he saw recognition in their depths, and genuine joy that he'd come. Stephen was too weak to talk much, but when Ranulf took his hand, he managed a feeble squeeze, even a shadowy flicker of a smile.

"Look after Maude's lad . . ." Ranulf nodded mutely. Stephen's mouth was moving again. "Tell Maude . . ." But he got no further. Ranulf wondered if his strength had given out or he'd just realized there was nothing to be said.

Stephen's eyes had closed. His breathing had an audible rasp, and Ranulf was glad he'd been shriven already, for it sounded as if each faltering breath could be his last. Ranulf found himself thinking of his nephew, just a few heartbeats away from becoming England's king . . . at twenty-one. Stephen was fifty-eight and could easily have lived another ten or fifteen years. Instead he was dying less than a twelvemonth after they'd come to terms at Winchester. It occurred to Ranulf that mayhap Harry truly did have an ally in the Almighty.

Stephen's lashes quivered. "Cousin . . ." Ranulf leaned closer to catch the whispered words. "I hope the lad gets more joy from his kingship than I did from mine . . ."

58

ROUEN, NORMANDY

October 1154

A SQUALL had blown in from the west soon after Petronilla's arrival in Rouen. Within the castle, fires were kindled in every hearth and shutters hastily latched, but the solar continued to echo with the sounds of the storm's fury. The wind's howling put Eleanor in mind of hungry wolves, and the rain beat a steady tattoo against the slated roof, loud enough at times to intrude upon their conversation.

Petronilla moved her chair closer to the hearth. "So . . . how do you like sharing a city with your mother-in-law? I know it did not take you long to vanquish Louis's mother, but she lacked the Lady Maude's imperial will. If the empress is even half as formidable as her foes claim, she'd be a match for Barbary pirates, infidels, and Abbot Bernard, too!"

"Why is it," Eleanor wondered, "that no one wants to believe Maude and I are on good terms? She is not a meddlesome mother-in-law, for she has far too much dignity for that. As for her 'imperial will,' I thanked God for it when Harry was taken so ill last month. When his fever would not break, the doctors began to despair, but not Maude. She fought Death the way she did Stephen—no quarter given—and she won. We took turns nursing him, and kept Death at bay long enough for Harry to rally. And once he was up and about, what did he do? Just as soon as he had the strength to climb into the saddle, he was off to Torigny to besiege the castle of a rebel baron, God save us all!"

Eleanor shook her head, sounding both amused and exasperated, and then shifted uncomfortably in her chair. Yolande emerged from the shadows, offering a cushion, and Petronilla gave her a sympathetic look. "Is the babe getting restless again?"

Eleanor grimaced. "Much of the time, I feel as if I've swallowed a frog," she confided, "and February seems so far away . . ."

"Men do not know what joys they are missing, do they? I remember complaining to Raoul about one of my pregnancies, for it was hellishly hot and sweltering that summer and I felt like a beached whale. His response? To tell me I should be thankful a woman's pregnancy lasted only nine months, as he'd read in a bestiary that an elephant carried her calf for nigh on two years!"

For most of the past year, Petronilla could not talk of Raoul without tears. That she could now jest about her late husband showed Eleanor that even heart wounds could heal, if given enough time. Positioning the cushion behind her aching back, Eleanor smiled at her sister. "Did you hear about Louis?"

"That he went off on pilgrimage?"

"Louis has always yearned to visit the holy shrine at Santiago de Compostela, and now he is doing just that. But for once he has more in mind than the salvation of his immortal soul. You see, Petra, the King of Castile has a marriageable daughter, and if she finds favor with Louis—that is, if she is unlike me in all particulars—he will probably return to France with a bride. By a very roundabout route, though," Eleanor said and grinned. "Rather than ask me for a safe-conduct through Aquitaine, Louis traveled to Castile by way of Toulouse!"

Petronilla grinned, too. "Louis will have to perform an exorcism to rid his marriage bed of your ghost," she predicted, "and even then—"

"My lady!" Yolande had departed the solar only moments before. Now she was back, flushed and breathless. "The empress . . . she is here! I just saw her ride into the bailey!"

Eleanor and Petronilla exchanged alarmed looks. What would have brought Maude out in such a storm—except news of dire urgency? Nor were they reassured when Maude was ushered into the solar, for she was soaked to the skin, her mantle muddied and her hair windblown, the first time that Eleanor had ever seen her elegant mother-in-law in such disarray.

"Good Lord, Maude, you look like a drowned cat! What possessed you to leave the priory in such vile weather? Unless . . . nothing has happened to Harry?"

"No," Maude cried, "oh, no! My news is from England, Eleanor, from the Archbishop of Canterbury." She paused for breath, and then she smiled, a smile of triumph and joy and vindication, a smile nineteen years overdue.

"Stephen is dead," she said, "and England's crown now belongs to my son. Henry is to be king."

STEPHEN died on October 25th in the year of Our Lord 1154, and was buried with his wife and son Eustace at the abbey he and Matilda had founded at Faversham. It was a quiet end to such a bloody war, and an ironic one, that after almost two decades of a disputed succession, Henry's accession should be so peaceful and uncontested. So confident was the young king that he even delayed his departure long enough to bring his siege at Torigny to a victorious conclusion.

Once Henry did take action, he moved with characteristic dispatch. By November 7th, he was at Barfleur, assembling a large fleet. But for all that Henry ruled Anjou, Maine, Touraine, and Aquitaine, and was now to rule the kingdom of England, he had no dominion over the weather. That November saw storm after storm raking the Channel, battering the seaports, churning up towering waves, and making it too hazardous to attempt a crossing. Barfleur's inns and taverns overflowed with Henry's entourage, brawls broke out among his bored soldiers, tempers frayed, and anxious eyes scanned the evening skies, searching in vain for signs of clearing. After four weeks of waiting, Henry lost all patience. They would sail on the morrow, he announced, and let the storms be damned.

A HIGH wind was whipping through the streets of Barfleur, tearing ale poles from their hangings, banging shutters, and discouraging all but the hardiest souls from gathering to watch as the royal fleet got under way. No rain had fallen since dawn, but the sky looked angry, splotched with ominous, leaden clouds, and patches of pale fog hid the horizon. Out in the harbor, the ships were pitching, masts bobbing up and down, queasy passengers huddled at the gunwales for one last glimpse of shore. Anchors were being winched up, sails unfurled, but the king's ship was still moored at the quay, waiting for Henry to board.

The quay was almost deserted. "Watch your step," Henry cautioned. "The footing is slippery in spots." Maude nodded, tightening her hand on his arm. He stopped, then, for they'd reached the gangplank. "So . . . this is farewell, Mama. Unless you change your mind and come with us?"

She smiled, shaking her head. "We've already discussed this, Henry. It is best that I remain here, keeping an eye on Normandy in your absence."

"I wish you'd reconsider. Will and my uncles and cousins will be there to witness my coronation, as will Eleanor's brothers and Petronilla. Even Geoff," he added dryly, glancing over his shoulder toward the ship, but failing to find his disgruntled brother midst the passengers milling about on the deck. "You ought to be there, too, Mama—you above all others." He saw, though, that she would not relent, and yielded reluctantly. "As you wish, then. I do not understand your decision, but I will accept it."

"Just as I've accepted your decision to sail on such a foul day," she pointed out, "although I like it not."

"I could wait no longer, Mama. But you need not fear, for we will outrun the storm. I am just sorry the seas were so rough on St Catherine's Day. What could have been more fitting than to sail on the same day as the White Ship?"

She suspected he was joking, yet the very suggestion gave Maude a superstitious chill. "Jesú forfend! That would have been tempting Providence for certes, and had you been foolhardy enough to do so, I very much doubt that anyone would have dared to sail with you!"

"No?" Henry said and laughed. "I'd wager Eleanor would have!"

Maude looked across at the ship, soon spotted her daughter-in-law, warmly wrapped in a fur-trimmed red mantle, and nearby, a nurse, holding Maude's small grandson. "Yes," Maude conceded, "Eleanor probably would." For better or worse, her son and his wife were well matched, hawk mating hawk and flying high.

And then it was time. Stepping forward, she gave him a hasty farewell hug. "God keep you safe, Henry."

"He will," he assured her, "and when next I see you, Mama, I'll bring back a crown . . . and another grandson for you." A quick kiss, haphazardly aimed at her cheek, and he was gone, crossing the gangplank with a swift, confident step, eager to depart, to claim his kingdom.

Alone on the quay, Maude watched as her son's ship headed out into the harbor. The sails were billowing, the mast lantern swaying wildly, and she said a brief, silent prayer for her sons, for all those crossing the Channel on this raw December morning, and then, for the souls of the doomed passengers who'd drowned in the wreck of the White Ship.

Braving the wind, Minna ventured out onto the quay. Maude did not seem aware of her approach, keeping her eyes upon the fleet. But then she said softly, "Henry does not understand why I'd not come. But how could

I tell him, Minna? He'd think that I begrudged him his kingship, and nothing could be more untrue than that. I am so proud that he is to be king. It is just that I could not watch as the crown was placed upon his head, for that would have stirred up too many hurtful memories, too many regrets. England is Henry's kingdom, but it was never mine . . ."

Minna said nothing, for between them, there was no need of words. The wind was knifing across the quay, and freezing rain had begun to splatter onto the wet wooden planks. Beyond the harbor, Henry's fleet was disappearing into the fog.

HENRY'S fleet had scattered in the fog, but all eventually came ashore safely. Henry and Eleanor's ship dropped anchor in a cove near the New Forest, after fighting raging seas for twenty-four turbulent hours. Without waiting for a royal escort, they rode for Winchester, and within days, were welcomed into London. Coronation plans were rushed forward, and on the 19th of December, Henry and Eleanor were crowned in a splendid ceremony at Westminster's great abbey. What would become known as the Plantagenet dynasty had begun.

WESTMINSTER PALACE was not habitable, for it had been despoiled after Stephen's death, and Henry and Eleanor were forced to lodge across the river at Bermondsey, in a once-royal manor now owned by the Cluniac priory of St Saviour. Ranulf and Rhiannon had found lodgings at Bermondsey, too, in one of the priory guesthouses. They had very comfortable quarters, for the monks had been lavish with their hospitality. Rhiannon had been puzzled at first by such solicitude, for she'd been slow to comprehend how important her husband now was, as kinsman and close confidant of the young king. And once she did understand, she was frightened, for never had England's siren songs sounded so tempting, so seductive. How long could Ranulf resist their blandishments?

She no longer feared losing Ranulf to Annora, or even to England. After nearly five years of marriage, she did not doubt that he loved her. Her fear was of losing Wales. Lying awake on this cold December night, waiting for Ranulf to return from a private meeting with his nephew, she made herself face a troubling truth: that her husband might well want her and Gilbert to live in England now that Harry was king.

Ranulf did not know how unhappy she was in this alien land, for she'd confided only in the Almighty. How could she complain? His family had tried to make her welcome. Harry and Eleanor, Maud, Amabel, even Rainald, in his bluff, hearty way—they'd all been kind. But there was no acceptance beyond their small, select circle. She knew that to most people, she would always be an oddity, an object of curiosity, pity, and suspicion. Ranulf Fitz Roy's blind, Welsh wife.

Across the room, Gilbert mumbled in his sleep, and Rhiannon sat up, listening intently until she was sure he was dreaming. He was not happy in England, either, as homesick as she was. She'd been assuring him that they'd be going home soon, but no longer, for there was no comfort in a lie. Tonight when he'd complained of "missing Grandpapa and Aunt Eleri," she'd said only, "Me, too, Gilbert, me, too . . ."

Tossing and turning in the bed, she tried to imagine what her father and sister would be doing now. Sleeping, most likely. Eleri might still be awake, though, for she'd gotten pregnant within two months of her summer wedding. Where would she be when Eleri's time was nigh? How could she not be there for her little sister in the birthing chamber?

Pummeling her pillow, she wondered if Ranulf understood about hiraeth. It translated as "longing," but meant so much more, the love of the Welsh for their homeland, a sense of belonging, pride in their past, why they did not thrive when uprooted, like plants set down in foreign soil. If Ranulf wanted them to live in England, she would offer no protest, for she would have followed him to Hell if need be. But it would be a life in exile.

Rhiannon was sure she'd be awake till dawn, but sometime before midnight, she fell into an uneasy doze. Her dream was not a pleasant one, and she awoke with relief, to find her husband in bed beside her. As soon as she moved, he drew her into his arms. "Harry and Eleanor asked after you, Rhiannon. How is your headache?"

"Much better," she lied. "How was your evening?"

"Interesting." Ranulf tightened his arms around her, breathing in her fragrance, familiar and flower-sweet. "It's begun to snow," he murmured, "just in time for Christmas."

"Gilbert will be right glad," she said softly. Their first Christmas away from Wales. How much snow could make up for that?

"Harry is a whirlwind on two feet, lass. King only four days and already with plans enough to keep him busy for years. He means to name Thomas Becket as his chancellor and Robert Beaumont as a justiciar. To punish William Peverel for poisoning the Earl of Chester, to expel the last of the foreign mercenaries, and reclaim those crown castles which Stephen lost and appoint new sheriffs and make the King's Peace more than just a hope and a prayer. And all that is just for a start!"

"I hope he plans to rest on the seventh day."

Ranulf laughed. "That is what Eleanor said, too!" Leaning over, he kissed the corner of her mouth. "Harry offered me an earldom tonight," he said, and Rhiannon went rigid in his arms, for a moment able to hear nothing but the beating of her own heart.

"I . . . I thought he would," she managed to whisper at last.

"I knew he would, too. He takes pleasure in giving, and who can give more than a king? It was no easy task, convincing him that I did not want it—"

"You turned down an earldom?"

"You sound like Harry did, love—like you swallowed your tongue! Yes, I did. I told Harry I'd be right pleased to accept as many manors as he can spare, preferably in the Marches, but I'll be wanting no English earldom. That is why I was late getting back. It took me nigh on two hours to persuade him that I was not drunk!"

"But . . . but why?"

"I think you know, Rhiannon. Our son is three quarters Welsh. I want him to grow up in Wales, to know where he belongs. An English earldom would yoke him to England, whether he willed it or not. When he is of an age to know his own mind, mayhap he might choose that golden yoke. But the choice ought to be his. Until he can make it, though, I must choose for him—and I choose Wales."

"Ranulf . . . are you sure?"

"Very sure. I just hope our lad finds half the happiness in Wales that I did." He kissed her again, and tasted tears. "Rhiannon? Have I let you down? Mayhap I ought to have talked it over with you first, but I thought we were in accord on this. You do want us to go back to Wales?"

"Yes," she said, "dear God, yes!"

"Well, then," he said, "after Christmas, we'll go home."

THE January sky was a glazed, boundless blue, and Bermondsey was adrift in a sea of snow, glistening like crystal as the sun rose overhead. The air was cold and clear, the wind stilled. "You've a good day for travel," Henry said. "Take care of my uncle, Rhiannon. Any man who'd turn down an earldom needs looking after!"

Rhiannon heard laughter, caught an elusive hint of summer roses, and was then enveloped in a brief, perfumed embrace by England's queen. "Godspeed," Eleanor said warmly. "Yn iach, Rhiannon."

Rhiannon flashed a startled smile. "Yn iach," she echoed, touched that Eleanor should have taken the trouble to learn how to bid her a Welsh farewell. Ranulf was now back beside her, and after he'd assured her that Gilbert and Gwen were settled into the horse litter, she let him assist her up into the saddle.

Ranulf was bantering again with Henry, who was about to depart in a day or so for Oxford, telling Eleanor that if Harry did not get back in time for the birth of their babe, she ought to have sole say in picking the name. Eleanor agreed, and warned her husband that she might be tempted to name the child Stephen, or mayhap even Louis.

Rhiannon politely joined in the laughter, but she marveled at Eleanor's sangfroid. Had Ranulf not been there for Gilbert's birth, it would have been a far greater ordeal. No, as much as she liked Harry and Eleanor, they were a breed apart, this king of twenty-one and his celebrated queen, surely the only woman who would ever wear the crowns of both England and France. She wished them well, but she was so very glad to be going home with Ranulf, who did not yearn to soar up into the heavens, who felt no need to see how close he could get to the sun without being scorched.

"Are we ready?" she asked, and Ranulf made one last joke, wished Eleanor a safe and easy lying-in, and promised to be back ere the new babe could learn to walk. Swinging up into the saddle then, he reached for the lead attached to Rhiannon's mare, and they started off on their long journey back to Wales.

Ranulf had no regrets about what he was leaving behind. After nineteen years of fighting over the English throne, he had no doubts whatsoever that the most dangerous quarry was neither wild boar nor wolf. No hunt was so hazardous as the pursuit of power. Fortunately, his nephew Harry was a skilled huntsman, one of the best he'd ever seen.

He glanced back once. Henry and Eleanor were still out in the snow-blanketed bailey. They waved as Ranulf turned, and that was to be the memory he would carry into Wales: the two of them, standing together in the bright winter sunlight, smiling, sure that the world, like the English crown, was theirs for the taking.

Afterword

HENRY II was one of England's greatest kings, a man whose successes and failures were all on a grand scale. Even readers untutored in British history are familiar with the story of Henry and Eleanor's turbulent, passionate, and—ultimately—disastrous marriage. Their firstborn son, William, died in 1156, at age three. But they were far luckier than most medieval parents, for Eleanor bore Henry eight children and all but William survived the perils of a twelfth-century childhood. Two of their sons, Richard Lionheart and John, succeeded to the English throne, and the dynasty they began would rule England for more than three hundred years. Henry died in 1189, betrayed by his own sons and murmuring, "Shame, shame upon a conquered king." Eleanor survived him by nigh on fifteen years, dying in 1204 at the remarkable age of eighty-two. At a later time, I hope to continue with Henry and Eleanor's unique saga.

Maude was one of the few people whom her son truly trusted, and he relied upon her judgment and advice until she sickened and died on September 10, 1167, in her sixty-sixth year. She was buried in the abbey church of Bec, although her body was reinterred at Rouen's great cathedral in the nineteenth century. Chroniclers report that her epitaph read, "Great by birth, greater by marriage, greatest in her offspring, here lies the daughter, wife, and mother of Henry."

Henry's troublesome brother Geoffrey was made Count of Nantes but died unexpectedly on July 25, 1158, at age twenty-four. Henry's brother William fared better, holding the vicomté of Dieppe and rich estates in fifteen English shires, but he, too, died young, on January 30, 1164, at age twenty-seven.

Maude's half-brother Rainald prospered under his nephew's reign.

One of Henry's most steadfast supporters and advisers, he died on July 1, 1175. Robert's widow, Amabel, did not remarry and died in 1157. Their daughter, Maud, does not seem to have remarried either, after Chester's death; she died in July of 1189. Her grandson Ranulf de Blundevill was the Earl of Chester who figured so prominently in my second novel, *Here Be Dragons*.

Stephen's brother the Bishop of Winchester had a falling-out with Henry in 1155 and spent several years in French exile. He eventually returned to England, and in 1168, he gave away virtually all of his considerable wealth to charity. He died on August 8, 1171, "full of days."

Stephen's son William died childless in 1160. His sister, Mary, had lived most of her life in the cloistered quiet of the nunnery, becoming abbess of the convent at Romsey. Suddenly she found herself a great heiress, the Countess of Boulogne. Coerced by Henry into leaving the nunnery, she was wed to the son of the Count of Flanders. This marriage created a firestorm of controversy, and the outraged Pope excommunicated Mary's new husband. Mary bore him two daughters and eventually gained his permission to return to the convent. In 1169, she took the veil again at the French nunnery at Austrebert, and died there in 1182 at age forty-five.

William de Ypres returned to his native Flanders at Easter, 1157. He spent his last years at the monastery of St Peter at Loo, dying there in January of 1165, at age seventy-five.

Waleran Beaumont's influence waned drastically after Henry's coronation. He died in April 1166. His twin brother's star continued to rise, and until Robert's death in April 1168, he stood high in Henry's favor. John Marshal died circa 1164. His son William, spared the hangman's noose by Stephen at Newbury, played a major role in the reigns of Henry's sons, becoming Earl of Pembroke and a celebrated soldier-statesman, even serving as a regent of England at one point.

The French king wed twice more after divorcing Eleanor. He and his second wife had a daughter, who—improbably enough—was wed as a child to Henry and Eleanor's eldest surviving son. His third wife bore him the son he so craved. Louis died in 1180.

After Eustace's death, Constance returned to France, and the following year the French king married her to the Count of Toulouse. Regrettably, her second marriage was no happier than her first, and in 1165 she returned to her brother's court.

Bernard, the Abbot of Clairvaux, died on August 20, 1153, and probably never knew that Eleanor had given Henry a son just three days earlier. The Catholic Church canonized Bernard as a saint in January 1174.

I was unable to find a death date for Eleanor's sister, Petronilla. Abbot Bernard had placed a curse upon her adulterous union with Raoul de

Péronne, and when her son contracted leprosy and both her daughters had troubled, childless marriages, there were those to say that Bernard's dire prophecy had been borne out. It is not likely, though, that Eleanor agreed.

Owain Gwynedd ruled North Wales for more than thirty years, until his death in November 1170. His actual name was Owain ap Grufydd, but he became better known to his countrymen as Owain Gwynedd, and eventually as Owain Fawr—Owain the Great. Readers of *Here Be Dragons* may be interested to learn that he was the grandfather of Llewelyn Fawr.

Author's Note

I ORIGINALLY began including an author's note in my books because "my" people led such extraordinary lives, filled with enough drama, tragedy, and eerie coincidence to put a Hollywood scriptwriter to shame, and I felt the need to verify the historical accuracy of the more improbable events. Well, this is my fifth book, but nothing has changed.

Maude truly did escape from the siege of Oxford Castle by donning a white cloak, climbing down a rope, and walking right through Stephen's army in the midst of a blizzard. What writer would dare to invent an episode like that?

The account of John Marshal trapped in the burning bell tower at Wherwell nunnery comes from the epic medieval poem *Histoire de Guillaume le Mareschal* and is confirmed by other contemporary sources. The only liberty I took was in making Gilbert Fitz John the unnamed knight who took refuge with Marshal in the tower. The near hanging of Marshal's small son at Newbury also comes from the *Histoire,* which provides an appealing glimpse of Stephen, playing a game on the floor of his tent with the child he'd spared, using plantain leaves for swords.

Robert Fitz Roy did manage to march an army halfway across England in the dead of winter, catching Stephen by surprise and forcing the Battle of Lincoln, a feat that still has military historians marveling. His nephew Henry later duplicated this exploit on a lesser scale by racing to the rescue of besieged Pacy, the first time that Henry displayed his remarkable talent for speed beyond the reach of mortal men. Throughout Henry's eventful reign, he was constantly baffling his foes with his uncanny ability to appear without warning at any trouble spot in his far-flung empire. The French king was once heard to complain that he could almost believe Henry had learned to fly.

Stephen had indeed planned to sail on the White Ship, but changed his mind at the last moment. Eustace's bizarre death did occur as I describe, and on the very day that Eleanor bore Henry their first son. All of the odd omens I mention were reported by the chroniclers of the time. Were some of them conveniently remembered "after the fact"? Possibly. But theirs was a superstitious age. Ours is, too, of course. Times and beliefs change; people don't.

This was the most challenging and difficult of all my books, in part because the sources were so often muddled or contradictory. Before I venture into that unmapped territory, though, I would like to anticipate some reader queries: Maude's half-brother Ranulf Fitz Roy is fictional. Since Henry I is known to have sired at least twenty illegitimate children, I decided one more wouldn't hurt! This was the first time that I'd allowed a fictional character to share center stage with historical figures, and I wasn't sure I'd feel comfortable with Ranulf. Somewhat to my surprise, I discovered that I enjoyed playing God with him, having the sole say in determining his destiny. I've been told by readers that they approach my afterwords with some trepidation, knowing how rare "happy endings" are in real life, especially in the twelfth century. I am pleased to report, therefore, that it is safe to envision Ranulf and Rhiannon living out their days together in the beautiful Conwy Valley, in the protective shadow of Eryri.

I've chosen the medieval names for towns, just as I've preferred to use Welsh spellings for Welsh place names. Cantebrigge is known today as Cambridge, Stanford is now Stamford, Blancminster has become Oswestry, and Le Strete soon gave way to Stockbridge. I made a few minor changes with proper names, for clarity's sake. The Earl of Chester's Christian name is given as both Ranulf and Randolph; I chose the latter to avoid confusion with Maude's half-brother. For the same reason, I sought to keep the number of Maudes and Matildas in the book to a minimum. For Henry I's natural daughter who drowned in the wreck of the White Ship, I used an earlier variation of the name Maude: Mahault. Stephen's doomed sister was reported by the chroniclers as Maude, but also as Lucia, and so Lucia she became.

This is probably a good time to explain that Maude and Matilda are essentially the same name. Matilda is the Latinized version, Maude the vernacular. The empress would have signed her charters as Matilda, but she'd have called herself Maude. Faced with two major female characters who bore the same name, I naturally decided to make use of both Matilda and Maude.

Readers of my earlier novels may have been puzzled to find Owain Gwynedd referred to as a Welsh king. Owain was the last Welsh ruler to use this title.

And for those familiar with the story that Geoffrey wanted Henry to cede Anjou to his brother once he'd become England's king, I believe this myth was convincingly rebutted by W. L. Warren in his masterly biography, *Henry II*.

I've long wanted to refute a popularly held belief that the sidesaddle was introduced into England by Richard II's queen in the fourteenth century. Although this legend has been disproved by historians, it still crops up occasionally in history books. But when Maude fled Winchester, the hostile Worcester Chronicle took gleeful note of the fact that she was forced to ride astride, like a man.

What Rhiannon called her "inner vision" was actually a reflection of sound waves off the facial muscles, hence its more common name, "facial vision." Her total blindness was the result of sympathetic ophthalmia; the loss of sight in one eye put the other eye at risk, too. And Ranulf's Norwegian dyrehund is known today as the Norwegian elkhound. For plot purposes, I needed an ancient breed, distinctive in appearance, not commonly known in England. The fact that I have a Norwegian elkhound myself may have influenced me, too—just a little!

If I seem to be slighting Henry and Eleanor in this author's note, that is because they speak very well for themselves. I enjoyed writing about Eleanor's twilight years in *Dragons*, and like many of my readers, I visualize the aged Eleanor as the *Lion in Winter*'s Katharine Hepburn. It was more challenging to write about the young Eleanor, colliding with Henry in Paris like two runaway comets, changing the history of Christendom with their passion and their ambition. Readers often ask me to "cast" my books for the screen. I've always thought that Timothy Dalton was born to play Llewelyn, either the grandsire or the grandson, but after that, I usually draw a blank. I have to admit, though, that I think Kenneth Branagh and Emma Thompson would make a splendid Henry and Eleanor.

I would like to end this note by focusing one last time upon Maude and Stephen. The legend that Maude and Stephen were lovers and Henry their son has been thoroughly discredited by historians. As the British scholar Marjorie Chibnall points out in her recent biography of Maude, *The Empress Matilda*, this myth did not surface until the thirteenth century and may be traced to confusion over Stephen's adoption of Henry as his heir once peace was finally made between them. What of Maude's relationship with Brien Fitz Count? One of her biographers suggests that they may have been lovers, a suggestion Ms. Chibnall firmly rejects. That they were devoted to each other, none can deny, and it is hard not to conclude that Brien's devotion was personal rather than political, for he ruined himself on Maude's behalf, resolutely refused to accept any rewards for his steadfast and dangerous loyalty, and took holy vows upon her departure from England. I doubt, though, that they ever became lovers in the physical sense. K. S. B. Keats-Rohan, in his insightful and well-researched article "The Devolution of the Honour of Wallingford, 1066–1148," describes Brien as Maude's "courtly lover," and I suspect that is as close to the truth as we are likely to get.

I broke with conventional wisdom in this book, for it has been an accepted belief that Maude had no children before Henry. But in her biography, Ms. Chibnall reports that a German chronicler claimed that Maude bore a child to her first husband, a child who died soon afterward. According to Ms. Chibnall, this chronicler, Hermann of Tournai, was a near contemporary of Maude's but not always a reliable source. She does not dismiss his story out of hand, though, for the same reason that I tend to believe it. I do not think Maude's father would have risked naming her as his heir unless he knew she could conceive a child. The emperor had an illegitimate daughter; moreover, the woman was almost always blamed for a childless marriage in the Middle Ages. Why would Henry have staked his dynastic hopes upon a woman who might be barren? To me that is a persuasive argument for the veracity of Hermann of Tournai's account.

Stephen is my third weak king. But unlike the pathetic Henry VI or the petty Henry III, Stephen had some very attractive qualities. He was courageous, generous, optimistic, and good-natured. Unfortunately for England, he was also impractical, impulsive, an appallingly bad judge of character, blind to consequences, insecure, and easily influenced. After reading my manuscript, a friend said "Poor Stephen. He lost so much when he gained a crown." I think she is right. But the English people lost far more.

It might be said that both Stephen and Maude were victims of their age, for the twelfth century was not friendly terrain for a too-forgiving king or a sovereign queen. History has not been kind to either of them. In Maude's case, I think the judgment might be overly harsh, for if you study her past, you find three Maudes. There was the young woman who made a successful marriage to a manic depressive and so endeared herself to her German subjects that they were loath to see her return to England. There was the aging matriarch who passed her last years in Normandy, on excellent terms with the Church and her royal son, respected for the sage counsel she gave Henry. In between, there was the harpy, the termagant so reviled by the English chroniclers, whose mistakes were exaggerated and magnified by the hostile male monks writing her history.

Maude could be infuriating and exasperating, but she had great courage, and she never lost a certain prickly integrity. As for Stephen, I think the truest verdict was one passed by a contemporary chronicler: "He was a mild man, gentle and good, and did no justice."

S.K.P.
July 1994

Acknowledgments

I WAS very fortunate; while researching and writing *Saints*, I never lacked for support and encouragement. A number of people have been helpful, but I would like to single out the following ones for special thanks. My parents, for always being there for me. Valerie Ptak LaMont, for her writer's insight and honesty. Scott Ian Barry, for letting me draw upon his expertise as an animal behaviorist in the attack scene with Loth, Ranulf's Norwegian dyrehund. Jill and John Davies, for a special afternoon in Lincoln, tracking the Fossedyke to find where Robert Fitz Roy was likely to have crossed with his army. The best editors and agents that any writer could hope to have: Marian Wood and John Jusino of Henry Holt and Company, Susan Watt of Michael Joseph Ltd., Molly Friedrich of the Aaron M. Priest Literary Agency, and Mic Cheetham. As well, the staffs of the University of Pennsylvania, the British Library, and the research libraries of Shrewsbury, Oxford, Winchester, and Lincoln.

Acknowledgments

I was very fortunate, while researching and writing this book. I never lacked for support and encouragement. A number of people have been helpful, but I would like to single out the following ones for special thanks: My parents, for always being there; [illegible] Lawton, for her editor's insight and honesty; Scott [illegible] Barry for letting me draw upon his expertise as an animal behaviorist in the attack [illegible] with [illegible], Norwegian elkhound; Jill and John Davies, for their [illegible] wonderful recall, [illegible] where Robert Fitz Roy was likely to have crossed with his army; the best editors and agents that any author could hope to have—Marian Wood and [illegible] of Henry Holt and Company, Susan [illegible] of Michael Joseph Ltd, Molly Friedrich of the Aaron M. Priest Literary Agency and Mic Cheetham. As [illegible] the staffs of the University of Pennsylvania, the British Library and the research libraries of Shrewsbury, Oxford, Worcester and Lincoln.

Dave O'Shea

About the Author

SHARON KAY PENMAN is the author of four previous novels: *The Sunne in Splendour*, and the trilogy *Here Be Dragons*, *Falls the Shadow*, and *The Reckoning*.